Author of the National Bestseller *The Reality Dysfunction*

PETER F. HAMILTON

THE NEUTRONIUM ALCHEMIST

PART 2: CONFLICT

ASPECT

WARNER BOOKS

THE INTERNATIONAL SENSATION
THE SCIENCE FICTION EVENT OF THE DECADE

PETER F. HAMILTON

THE REALITY DYSFUNCTION, Part 1: *EMERGENCE*

THE REALITY DYSFUNCTION, Part 2: *EXPANSION*

THE NEUTRONIUM ALCHEMIST, Part 1: *CONSOLIDATION*

THE NEUTRONIUM ALCHEMIST, Part 2: *CONFLICT*

and coming soon

THE NAKED GOD

ISBN 0-446-60546-8

$6.50 US / $8.50 CAN.

EAN

more . . .

THE NEUTRONIUM ALCHEMIST

PART 2: CONFLICT

PETER F. HAMILTON

THE NEUTRONIUM ALCHEMIST

PART 2: CONFLICT

ASPECT®

WARNER BOOKS

A Time Warner Company

WARNER BOOKS EDITION

Cover design by Don Puckey and Carol Russo
Cover illustration by Jim Burns

Warner Books, Inc.
1271 Avenue of the Americas
New York, NY 10020

Visit our Web site at
http://warnerbooks.com

 A Time Warner Company

Printed in the United States of America

First Warner Books Printing: May, 1998

10 9 8 7 6 5 4 3 2 1

CAST OF CHARACTERS

SHIPS

LADY MACBETH

Joshua Calvert	Captain
Melvyn Ducharme	Fusion specialist
Ashly Hanson	Pilot
Sarha Mitcham	Systems specialist
Dahybi Yadev	Node specialist
Beaulieu	Cosmonik

OENONE

Syrinx	Captain
Ruben	Fusion systems
Oxley	Pilot
Cacus	Life support
Edwin	Toroid systems
Serina	Toroid systems
Tyla	Cargo officer

VILLENEUVE'S REVENGE

André Duchamp	Captain
Desmond Lafoe	Fusion specialist
Madeleine Collum	Node specialist
Erick Thakrar	Systems specialist/CNIS undercover agent

UDAT

Meyer	Captain
Cherri Barnes	Cargo officer

FAR REALM

Layia	Captain
Furay	Pilot

| Endron | Systems specialist |
| Tilia | Node specialist |

ARIKARA

Meredith Saldana	Rear-Admiral, squadron commander
Grese	Lieutenant, squadron intelligence officer
Rhoecus	Lieutenant, voidhawk liaison
Kroeber	Commander

BEEZLING

| Kyle Prager | Captain |
| Peter Adul | Alchemist team physicist |

HABITATS

TRANQUILLITY

Ione Saldana	Lord of Ruin
Dr Alkad Mzu	Inventor of the Alchemist
Parker Higgens	Director Laymil project
Oski Katsura	Laymil project electronics division chief
Kempster Getchell	Laymil project astronomer
Monica Foulkes	ESA agent
Lady Tessa	ESA head of station
Samuel	Edenist intelligence agent
Pauline Webb	CNIS agent
Father Horst Elwes	Priest, refugee
Jay Hilton	Refugee
Kelly Tirrel	Rover reporter
Lieria	Kiint
Haile	Juvenile Kiint

VALISK

Rubra	Habitat personality
Dariat	Horgan's possessor
Kiera Salter	Marie Skibbow's possessor
Stanyon	Council member
Rocio Condra	Possessor blackhawk Mindor

Bonney Lewin	Hunter
Tolton	Fugitive
Tatiana	Fugitive

ASTEROIDS

TRAFALGAR

Samual Aleksandrovich	First Admiral Confederation Navy
Lalwani	Admiral, CNIS chief
Maynard Khanna	Captain, First Admiral staff officer
Motela Kolhammer	Admiral, 1st Fleet commander
Dr Gilmore	CNIS research division director
Jacqueline Couteur	Possessor
Murphy Hewlett	Confederation Marine lieutenant

KOBLAT

Jed Hinton	Deadnight
Beth	Deadnight
Gari Hinton	Jed's sister
Navar	Jed's half-sister

AYACUCHO

Ikela	Owner of T'Opingtu company, partizan leader
Liol	Owner of Quantum Serendipity
Voi	Ikela's daughter
Prince Lambert	Captain starship *Tekas*
Dan Malindi	Partizan leader
Kaliua Lamu	Partizan leader
Feira Ile	Ayacucho SD commander, partizan leader
Cabral	Media magnate, partizan leader
Mrs Nateghi	Lawyer
Lodi Shalasha	Garissan radical
Eriba	Garissan radical
Kole	Socialite
Shea	Prince Lambert's girlfriend

JESUP

| Quinn Dexter | Messiah of the Light Bringer sect |

Lawrence Dillon   Disciple
Twelve-T   Gang lord
Bonham   Disciple
Shemilt   Disciple, SD commander
Dwyer   Disciple, systems specialist

PLANETS

NORFOLK

Louise Kavanagh   Refugee
Genevieve Kavanagh   Refugee
Luca Comar   Grant Kavanagh's possessor
Marjorie Kavanagh   Louise's mother
Mrs Charlsworth   Kavanagh sisters' nanny
Carmitha   Romany
Titreano   Possessor
Celina Hewson   Louise's aunt
Roberto Hewson   Louise's cousin

OMBEY

Ralph Hiltch   ESA head of station, Lalonde
Cathal Fitzgerald   Ralph's deputy
Dean Folan   ESA G66 division
Will Danza   ESA G66 division
Kirsten Saldana   Princess of Ombey
Roche Skark   ESA director
Jannike Dermot   ISA director
Landon McCullock   Police commissioner
Diana Tiernan   Police technology division chief
Admiral Farquar   Royal Navy, Ombey commander
Nelson Akroid   Armed Tactical Squad captain
Finnuala O'Meara   Rover reporter
Hugh Rosler   DataAxis technician
Neville Latham   Exnall's chief inspector
Janne Palmer   Royal Marine colonel
Annette Ekelund   Possessor
Gerald Skibbow   Refugee
Dr Riley Dobbs   Royal Navy personality debrief
                           psychology expert

Jansen Kovak	Royal Navy medical institute nurse
Moyo	Possessor
Stephanie Ash	Possessor
Cochrane	Possessor
Rana	Possessor
Tina Sudol	Possessor

NEW CALIFORNIA

Jezzibella	Mood Fantasy artist
Leroy Octavius	Jezzibella's manager
Libby	Jezzibella's dermal technology expert
Al	Brad Lovegrove's possessor
Avram Harwood III	Mayor of San Angeles
Emmet Mordden	Organization lieutenant
Silvano Richmann	Organization lieutenant
Mickey Pileggi	Organization lieutenant
Patricia Mangano	Organization lieutenant
Gus Remar	Rover reporter
Kingsley Pryor	Lieutenant commander, Confederation Navy
Luigi Balsmao	Commander Organization fleet
Cameron Leung	Possessor blackhawk *Zahan*
Oscar Kearn	Captain Organization frigate *Urschel*

KULU

Alastair II	The King
Simon, Duke of Salion	Chairman security commission
Lord Kelman Mountjoy	Foreign Office minister
Lady Phillipa Oshin	Prime minister
Admiral Lavaquar	Defence chief
Prince Howard	Kulu Corporation president
Prince Noton	Ex-president Kulu Corporation

NYVAN

Gelai	Possessor, Garissa genocide victim
Ngong	Possessor, Garissa genocide victim
Omain	Possessor, Garissa genocide victim
Richard Keaton	Data security expert

Baranovich	Organization lieutenant
Adrian Redway	ESA head of station

OTHERS

CONFEDERATION

Olton Haaker	Assembly President
Jeeta Anwar	Chief presidential aide
Mae Ortlieb	Presidential science aide
Cayeaux	Edenist ambassador
Sir Maurice Hall	Kulu Kingdom ambassador

EDENISTS

Wing-Tsit Chong	Edenism's founder
Athene	Syrinx's mother
Astor	Ambassador to the Kulu Kingdom
Sinon	Syrinx's father

Lady Macbeth slipped slowly into place above the docking cradle, her equatorial verniers sparkling briefly as Joshua compensated for drift. Optical-band sensors gave a poor return here; Tunja's ruby glow was insipid even in clear space, and down where Ayacucho lurked among the disk particles it was an abiding roseate gloom. Laser radar guided the starship in until the cradle latches clamped home.

The bay's rim lights sprang up to full intensity, highlighting the hull, their reflected beams twisting about at irregular angles as the thermo-dump panels folded back into the fuselage. Then the cradle started to descend.

In the bridge not a word was spoken. It was the mood which had haunted them all the way from Narok, an infection passed down from captain to crew.

Sarha looked over the bridge at Joshua for some sign of . . . humanity, she supposed. He had flown them here, making excellent time as always. And apart from the kind of instructions necessary to keep the ship humming smoothly, he hadn't put ten words together. He'd even taken his meals alone in his cabin.

Beaulieu and Dahybi had told the rest of the crew of the Norfolk possession, and how concerned Joshua had been for Louise. So at least Sarha knew the reason for his blues, even though she found it slightly hard to believe. This was the Joshua with whom she'd had an affair for over six months last year. He was so easy about the relationship that when they did finally stop sleeping together she'd stayed on as part of the crew without any awkwardness on either side.

Which was why she found it difficult that Joshua could be so affected by what had happened to Louise, by all accounts a fairly simple country girl. He *never* became that entangled. Commitment wasn't a concept which nested in his skull. Part of the fascination was his easygoing nature. There was never any deceit with Joshua, you knew just where you stood.

Perhaps Louise wasn't so simple after all. Perhaps I'm just jealous.

"Going to tell us now, Captain?" she asked.

"Huh?" Joshua turned his head in her general direction.

"Why we're here? We're not chasing Meyer anymore. So who is this Dr Mzu?"

"Best you don't ask."

A circuit of the bridge showed her how irritated everyone was getting with his attitude. "Absolutely, Joshua; I mean, you can't be sure if we're trustworthy, can you? Not after all this time."

Joshua stared at her. Fortunately, belaboured intuition finally managed to struggle through his moping thoughts to reveal the crew's bottled-up exasperation. "Bugger," he winced. Sarha was right, after all they'd been through together these people deserved a better style of captaincy than this. Jesus, I'm picking up Ione's paranoia. Thank God I didn't have to make any real command decisions. "Sorry, I just got hit by Norfolk. I wasn't expecting it."

"Nobody expected any of this, Joshua," Sarha said sympathetically.

"Yeah, right. Okay, Dr Mzu is a physicist, who once worked for the Garissan navy—"

They didn't say much while he told them what the flight was about. Which was probably a good thing, he guessed. It was one hell of a deal he'd accepted on their behalf. How would I feel if they'd dragged me along without knowing why?

When he finished he could see a mild smile on Ashly's face, but then the old pilot always did claim to chase after excitement. The others took it all reasonably stoically;

though Sarha was looking at him with a kind of bemused pique.

Joshua hitched his face up into one of his old come-on grins. "Told you, you were better off not knowing."

She hissed at him, then relented. "Bloody hell, wasn't there anybody else the Lord of Ruin could use?"

"Who would you trust?"

Sarha tried to come up with an answer, and failed hopelessly.

"If anyone wants to bail out, let me know," Joshua said. "This wasn't exactly covered in my job description when you signed on."

"Neither was Lalonde," Melvyn said dryly.

"Beaulieu?" Joshua asked.

"I have always served my captain to the best of my ability," the shiny cosmonik said. "I see no reason to stop now."

"Thanks. All of you. Okay, let's get *Lady Mac* powered down. Then we'll have a quick scout around for the doctor."

The Dorados Customs and Immigration Service took seventy-five minutes to process the *Lady Mac*'s crew. Given the quarantine, Joshua had been expecting some hassle, but these officers seemed intent on analysing every molecule in the starship. Their documentation was reviewed four separate times. Joshua wound up paying a five-thousand-fuseodollar administration fee to the chief inspector before they were confirmed to be non-possessed, had the appropriate Tranquillity government authorization to be flying, and declared suitable citizens to enter Ayacucho.

The lawyers were waiting for him at the end of the docking bay airlock tube. Three of them, two men and a woman, their unfussy blue suits cloned from some conservative chain-store design program.

"Captain Calvert?" the woman asked. She gave him a narrow frown, as if uncertain he could be the person she wanted.

Joshua rotated slightly so his silver star on his epaulette was prominent. "You got me."

"You are the captain of the *Lady Macbeth*?" Again the uncertainty.

"Yep."

"I am Mrs Nateghi from Tayari, Usoro and Wang, we represent the Zaman Service and Equipment Company which operates here in the spaceport."

"Sorry, guys, I don't need a maintenance contract. We just got refitted."

She held out a flek with a gold scale of justice symbol embossed on one side. "Marcus Calvert, this is a summons for fees owing to our client since August 2586. You are required to appear before the Ayacucho civil claims court at a date to be set in order to resolve this debt."

The flek was pressed into Joshua's palm. "Whaa—" he managed to grunt.

Sarha started giggling, which drew a cool glare from Mrs Nateghi. "We have also filed a court impounding order on the *Lady Macbeth*," she said frostily. "Please do not try and leave as you did last time."

Joshua kissed the flek flamboyantly and beamed at the woman. "I'm Joshua Calvert. I think you should be talking to my father. He's Marcus Calvert."

If the statement threw her, there was no visible sign. "Are you the *Lady Macbeth*'s current owner?"

"Sure."

"Then you remain liable for the debt. I will have the summons revised to reflect this. The impounding order remains unaffected."

Joshua kept his smile in place. He datavised the flight computer for a review of all 2586 log entries. There weren't any. "Jesus, Dad, thanks a bunch," he muttered under his breath. No way—absolutely not—would he show the three vultures how fazed he was. "Look, this is obviously an oversight, a computer glitch, something on those lines. I have no intention of contesting the debt. And I shall be very happy to pay off any money owing on *Lady Mac*'s account. I'm sure nobody wants this regrettable misunderstanding to come to court." He jabbed a toe at Sarha whose giggles had turned to outright laughter.

Mrs Nateghi gave a brisk nod. "It is within my brief to accept payment in full."

"Fine." Joshua took his Jovian Bank credit disk out of his ship-suit's top pocket.

"The cost in 2586 to the Zaman Company for services rendered comes to seventy-two thousand fuseodollars. I have an invoice."

"I'm sure you do." Joshua held out the credit disk, anxious to be finished.

The lawyer consulted her processor block, a show of formality. "The interest accrued on your debt over twenty-five years comes to two hundred and eighty-nine thousand fuseodollars, as approved by the court."

Sarha's laughter ended in a choke. Joshua had to use a neural nanonics nerve impulse override to stop himself from snarling at the lawyer. He was sure she was doing the same to stop her equally blank face from sneering. Bitch! "Of course," he said faintly.

"And our firm's fee for dealing with the case is twenty-three thousand fuseodollars."

"Yes, I thought you were cheap."

This time, she scowled.

Joshua shunted the money over. The lawyers hauled themselves away down the corridor.

"Can we afford that?" Sarha asked.

"Yes," Joshua said. "I have an unlimited expense account for this trip. Ione's paying." He didn't want to dwell on what she'd say when she saw the bill.

I wonder why Dad left in such a hurry?

Ashly patted Joshua's shoulder. "Real chip off the old block, your dad, eh?"

"I hope he hurries up and possesses someone soon," Joshua said through gritted teeth. "There's a few things I'd like to talk to him about." Then he thought about what he'd just said. Maybe not as funny and cuttingly sarcastic as he'd intended. Because Dad was there in the beyond. Suf-

fering in the beyond. That's if he wasn't already . . . "Come
on, let's make a start."

The club he wanted, according to the spaceport personnel,
was the Bar KF-T; that's where the action was. Along with
the dealers, pushers, and pimps, and all the rest of the people in the know.

The trouble was, Joshua found after a straight two-hour
stint of surfing the tables, they didn't know the one piece of
information he needed. The name of Alkad Mzu had not left
a heavy impression on the citizens of Ayacucho.

At the end he gave up and went to sit with Ashly and
Melvyn at a raised corner table. It gave him a good view
over the dance floor, where some nice girls were moving in
trim movements. He rolled his beer bottle between his
palms, not much interested in the contents.

"It was only a long shot, Captain," Melvyn said. "We
ought to start sniffing around the astroengineering companies. Right now they're so desperate for business that even
the legitimate ones would happily consider selling her a
frigate."

"If she wants to disappear, she has to do it at the bottom
of the heap," Joshua said. "You'd think the dealers would
have heard something."

"Maybe not," Ashly said. "There's definitely some kind
of underground league here. It can't be the same as the
usual asteroid independence movements; the Dorados are
already sovereign. I got a few hints when they thought I
was offering *Lady Mac*'s services, plenty of talk about revenge against Omuta. Mzu could have turned to them, after
all they're her people. Unfortunately, the likes of you and I
can hardly pass ourselves off as long-lost cousins of the
cause." He held up his hand, studying it dispassionately.

Joshua looked at his own skin. "Yeah, you've got a point.
We're not exactly obvious Kenyan-ethnic stock are we?"

"Dahybi might make the grade."

"I doubt it." His eyes narrowed. "Jesus, will you look at
how many of those kids are wearing red handkerchiefs

around their ankles." Six or seven times that evening while he'd been scouting around teenagers had asked him to take them to Valisk.

"We could do worse than the Deadnights," Melvyn said broodingly. "At least there aren't any possessed here."

"Don't count on it." Ashly leaned over the table, lowering his voice. "My neural nanonics suffered a couple of program load errors this evening. Not full glitches, but the diagnostics couldn't pinpoint the cause."

"Humm." Joshua looked at Melvyn. "You?"

"My communications block had a five-second dropout."

"Some of my memory cells went off-line earlier, too. I should have paid more attention. Shit. We've been here barely three hours, and we've each been close enough to one to be affected. What does that come to in percentages of the population?"

"Paranoia can be worse than real dangers," Melvyn said.

"Sure. If they are here, they're obviously not strong enough to mount an all-out takeover campaign. Yet. That gives us a little time."

"So what's out next move?" Melvyn asked.

"Other end of the spectrum, I suppose," Joshua said. "Contact someone in government who can run discreet checks for us. Or maybe it wouldn't be a bad idea to let slip the *Lady Mac* is for hire. If Mzu is here to get help, the only place it'll come from is the nationalist community. They might even wind up trying to charter us to deploy the damn thing."

"Too late now," Ashly said. "We're officially here to buy defence components for Tranquillity. And we've been asking too many questions."

"Yeah. Jesus, I'm not used to thinking along these lines. I wonder if any of my fellow captains have been approached for a combat charter?"

"Only if she's actually in this asteroid," Ashly said. "Nothing to stop the *Samaku* docking at one of the others when it arrived. That's even if she came here in the first place. We ought to be checking that."

"I'm not an idiot," Joshua moaned. "Sarha's working on it."

Sarha's smile appeared a little frayed after the third time Mabaki bumped against her. The crowd in the Bar KF-T weren't that excitable. She could certainly thread her way through without jostling anyone.

Mabaki waggled his eyebrows when she glanced back. "Sorry." He grinned.

It wasn't so much that he bumped her, as where. And how the touch tarried. She told herself a pathetic middle-aged letch was probably going to be one of the smaller tribulations they would encounter on this crazy course Joshua had set.

Just before she gave in and tried a datavise, she located Joshua standing over by the bar (where else, she asked herself). "That's him," she told Mabaki.

Sarha tapped Joshua on the shoulder as he was accepting a beer bottle from the barmaid. "Joshua, I found someone I think can . . ." She trailed off in confusion. It wasn't Joshua. That she of all people could be mistaken was astonishing. But he did look remarkably similar, especially in the treacherously shimmering light thrown out by the dance floor's holographic spray. Same broad chest to accommodate a metabolism geneered for free fall, identical prominent jaw folding back into flat cheeks. But this man's skin was darker, though nothing like the ebony of most Dorado Kenyan-ethnics, and his glossy hair was jet-black rather than Joshua's nondescript brown.

"I'm sorry," she stammered.

"I'm not." He could certainly manage the Joshua charm-grin, too. Possibly even better than Joshua.

"I was looking for someone else."

"I hate him already."

"Goodbye."

"Oh, please, I'm too young for my life to end. And it will when you leave. At least have a drink with me first. He can wait."

"No he can't." She began to move away. Some erratic impulse made her look back in perplexity. Damn, the likeness was extraordinary.

His smile widened. "That's it. You're making the right choice."

"No. No, I'm not."

"At least let me give you my eddress."

"Thank you, but we're not staying." Sarha forced her legs to work. She just knew her face would be red. How stupidly embarrassing.

"I'm Liol," he called out after her. "Just ask for Liol. Everybody knows me."

I'll bet they do, she thought, especially the girls. The crowd closed around her again, Mabaki tagging along faithfully.

Second time lucky. Joshua was sitting at a table in a shadowy corner, and he was with Ashly and Melvyn, so there was no mistake this time.

"Officer Mabaki works for the Dorados Immigration Service," Sarha explained as she pulled up a chair.

"Excellent," Joshua said. "I'd like to purchase some of your files."

It cost him fifteen thousand fuseodollars to learn that the *Samaku* had definitely docked at Ayacucho. One passenger had disembarked.

"That's her," Mabaki confirmed after Joshua datavised a visual file to him. "Daphine Kigano. You don't forget women like that."

"Daphine Kigano, really? Bit of a viper was she?"

"You're telling me." Mabaki savoured another sip of the Tennessee Malt Joshua had bought him. "She was some friend or other of Ikela's. You don't mess with those sort of connections."

Joshua datavised the club's net processor for a civil information core, and accessed a file on Ikela. It was mostly public relations spin released by T'Opingtu, but it gave him an idea of what he was dealing with. "So I see," he muttered. "Can you tell us what starships have left since Daphine Kigano arrived?"

"That's simple. None. Well, not unless you count the Edenist delegation, but they're from this system's gas giant anyway. There are still some inter-orbit ships flying, but no Adamist starships. The *Lady Macbeth* is the first starship to arrive since the *Samaku* departed."

After Mabaki left a grin spread over Joshua's face. It was the first in a long time which didn't have to be printed there by neural nanonics. "She's still here," he said to the others. "We've got her."

"We've got a lead on her," Melvyn cautioned. "That's all."

"Optimist. Now we know who to ask for, we can start focusing our efforts. I think this Ikela character would be a good place to start. Hell, we can even get a legitimate appointment. T'Opingtu is the kind of company we ought to approach for Tranquillity's SD spares, anyway." He drained his beer bottle and put it back on the table. A flash of movement caught his eye, and he slapped his hand down on the spider which was scuttling clear of the soggy mat.

"Oh, well," Samuel said. "At least we know why he's here. I suppose Ione Saldana must have commissioned him to track Mzu."

"That stupid little cow," Monica complained. "Doesn't she have any idea what kind of issues she's fooling with? And sending some bloody mercenary on the chase!"

"Lagrange Calvert," Samuel mused. "I suppose she could have done worse. He's certainly got the balls for a mission like this."

"But not the style. God, if he starts blundering around asking questions everyone in the Dorados is going to know Mzu is running loose. Here of all places! I ought to terminate him; it'd save us a nasty headache in the long term."

"I do wish you wouldn't keep on about how much easier life would be if we killed everyone who poses the slightest inconvenience. Calvert is an amateur, he's not going to bother us. Besides, he won't be the one who stirs up the public." Samuel indicated the row of AV pillars set up along one side of the rented office. Edenist agents were busy monitoring the output of every Ayacucho-based media company.

News of Ikela's death was already breaking, tying it in with reports of a "disturbance" at the offices of Laxa and Ahmad. Police were treating the death as suspicious, refusing to comment to the rovers gathered outside the doors of the legal firm. Although they'd already let slip that they would like to question Kaliua Lamu about the death.

Monica winced at that. She shouldn't have blown him, but they had been desperate for the information. The financier had demanded that Monica protect him from his erstwhile comrades: a request she could hardly refuse. He and his family were already on board one of the Edenist delegation's voidhawks, waiting to be spirited away to safety. "Don't I know it. That Cabral is going to make our life hell," she grumbled. "I don't know why you let him and the other two go."

"You know perfectly well why. What else could we do? For goodness' sake, Feira Ile is Ayacucho's SD chief; and Malindi is president of the Merchant's Association; and both of them sit on the Dorados governing council. I could hardly authorize their abduction."

"I suppose not," she sighed.

"It's not as if they can tell people what they were doing, or even that they were there."

"Don't count on it. They're certainly above the law here; and if any word of Mzu does leak out it'll inflame the nationalist sympathy."

"I think we had better assume it will do. Cabral will make sure of it. After all, he voted to help her retrieve the Alchemist."

"Yes." She let out an exasperated groan. "God, we walked right past her!"

"Ran past," Samuel corrected.

Monica glared at him. "Any sightings?"

"None at all. However we are losing an unusual number of spiders."

"Oh?"

"Children are going around killing them. It's some kind of organized game. Several day clubs are running competitions to see who can find the most. There are cash prizes. Clever," he acknowledged.

"Somebody's well organized."

"Yes and no. Children are a most peculiar method of attack, the numbers they can eliminate will inconvenience us rather than block us. If it was another agency that discovered we were infiltrating the asteroid, they would release a tailored virus to kill the spiders." He cast an inquiring glance. "No?"

She puckered her lips in an ironic smile. "I would imagine that could well be standard operating procedure for some people."

"So . . . it isn't an agency, but it is someone who has connections that reach down into local day clubs. And quickly."

"Not the partizans. They were never that well organized, and their membership is mostly aging reticents. The group that has Mzu?"

"By process of elimination, it must be."

"Yes, but so far we only know one member, this Voi girl. If there is an inner core of partizans I find it hard to believe the ESA didn't know about them."

"And us." He looked over to the agents monitoring the news, his face flickering through a range of expressions as he exchanged a barrage of questions and answers across the general affinity band. "Interesting."

"What?" she asked patiently.

"Given Ikela's mysterious death and his wealth, there's been no mention of his daughter by any media company. That's normally the first thing reporters focus on: who's going to inherit."

"Cabral's shielding her."

"Looks like it."

"Do you think he could be involved with this new group?"

"Very unlikely. From what we know about him, his partizan involvement was minimal, he was part of it for form's sake."

"So what the hell group is Voi mixed up with?"

Much later, when he had the time to sit down and think about it, Liol gave Lalonde as the reason for being so slow off the mark. He would never have been so sluggish under normal circumstances. But after accessing Kelly Tirrel's report he hit Ayacucho's clubs and bars, drinking and stimming out with methodical determination. A lot of people were doing exactly the same thing, but for a different reason. They merely feared the possessed, while Liol had watched his life's dream crumple in less than a second.

It had always been a dangerous dream. A single hope which has lasted from the earliest days of childhood is not a sound foundation on which to build a life. But Liol had done it. His mother had always told him his father would come back one day; an assurance she kept on repeating through another three husbands and countless boyfriends. He will return, and he'll take us away with him; somewhere where the sun shines dazzling white and the land is flat and endless. A universe away from the Dorados, worldlets haunted by the momentous horror and tragedy of the past.

The dream—the sure knowledge—of his destiny gave Liol attitude, setting him apart from his peers. His was among the first generation of Garissans born after the genocide. While others suffered from their parents' nightmares, a young Liol flourished in the expanding caverns and corridors of Mapire. He was the champion of his day club; idolized as reckless by his teeny friends, the first of all of them to get drunk, the first to have sex, the first to try soft drugs, and then not so soft, the first to run a black stimulant program through newly implanted neural nanonics. A genuine been-there-done-that kid, as much as you could go and do within the limited scope for experience permitted in orbit around Tunja.

His zest even carried over into his early twenties, when the years of his father's non-return were beginning to pile up in an alarming quantity. He still clung to his mother's promise.

A goodly number of his contemporaries emigrated from the Dorados when they reached their majority, a migration worrying to the council. Everyone assumed Liol would be among them, surely the first who would want to seek new opportunities. But he stayed, joining in the effort to build the Dorados into a prime industrial state.

Garissa's refugees had been awarded the settlement rights to the Dorados by the Confederation Assembly as part of their restitutions against Omuta for the genocide. Every multistellar company mining the ore had to pay a licence fee to the council, part of which was used to invest in the asteroids' infrastructure, while the remainder was paid directly to the survivors, and their descendants, by now scattered across the Confederation.

By 2606 this dividend had grown to a respectable twenty-eight thousand fuseodollars per annum. With such a guaranteed income as collateral, Liol had little trouble collecting loans and grants from the bank and the Dorados Development Agency to start his own business. In keeping with his now somewhat unhealthy obsession with spaceflight, he formed a company, Quantum Serendipity, specializing in servicing starship electronics. It was a good choice; the number of starship movements in the Tunja system was growing each year. He was awarded subcontracts by the larger service and maintenance companies, working his way up the list of approved suppliers. After two years of steady growth, he leased a docking bay in the spaceport, and made his first bid for a complete starship maintenance service. Year three saw Quantum Serendipity buy a majority share in a small electronics station; by producing the processors in-house he could undercut his competitors and still make a profit.

He now had the majority shares in two electronics stations, owned seven docking bays, and employed seventy people. And six months ago, Quantum Serendipity had landed a service contract for the communications network linking Ayacucho's SD platforms; a rock-solid income which was on the verge of pushing him into a whole new level of operations.

Then news of the possession arrived from the Confederation Assembly, swiftly followed by Kelly Tirrel's report. The first didn't bother Liol half as much as his competitors, with his SD contract he could keep his company afloat throughout the crisis. But the second item, with its hero-of-the-day, super-pilot Lagrange Calvert rescuing little kiddies in his starship. That came close to breaking Liol. It was the end of his world.

None of his friends understood the reason behind his sudden ferocious depression, the worrying benders he launched himself into. But then they had never been told of his dream, and how much it meant to him, that was private. So after a couple of abortive attempts to "cheer him up" had failed dismally amid his tirades of calculatingly vicious abuse, they had left him alone.

Which was why he'd been surprised when the girl in the Bar KF-T had spoken to him. Surprised, and not a little bit blasted. The come-on routine he gave her was automatic, he didn't have to think. It was only when she'd gone that a frown crossed his flattish, handsome face. "Joshua," he said in a drink-fuddled voice. "She called me Joshua. Why did she do that?"

The barmaid, who by now had given up on the idea of lugging him home for the night, shrugged gamely and moved on.

Liol drained his whisky chaser in one swift toss, then datavised a search request into the spaceport registration computer. The answer seemed to trojan a wickedly effective sober-up program into his neural nanonics.

*   *   *

Alkad had seen worse rooms when she was on the move thirty years ago. The hotel charged by the hour, catering for starship crews on fast stopovers, and citizens who wanted somewhere quiet and private to indulge any of a variety of vices which modern technology could provide. There was no window, the hotel was cut into rock some distance behind the cliff at the end of the biosphere cavern. It was cheaper that way. The customers never even noticed.

Big holograms covered two of the walls, showing pictures of some planetary city at dusk, its jewelscape of twinkling lights retreating into a horizon of salmon-pink sky. The bed filled half of the floor space, leaving just enough room for people to shuffle around it. There was no other furniture. The bathroom was a utilitarian cubicle fitted with a shower and a toilet. Soaps and gels were available from a pay dispenser.

"This is Lodi Shalasha," Voi said when they arrived. "Our electronics supremo, he's made sure the room's clean. I hope. For his sake."

The young man rolled off the bed and smiled nervously at Alkad. He was dressed in a flamboyant orange suit with eye-twisting green spirals. Not quite as tall as Voi, and several kilos overweight.

Student type, Alkad categorized instantly, burning with the outrage that came from a head stuffed full of fresh knowledge. She'd seen it a thousand times before when she was a lecturer; kids from an easy background expanding their minds in all the wrong directions at the first taste of intellectual freedom.

His smile was strained when he looked at Voi. "Have you heard?"

"Heard what?" the tall girl was immediately suspicious.

"I'm sorry, Voi. Really."

"*What?*"

"Your father. There was some kind of trouble at the Laxa and Ahmad offices. He's dead. It's all over the news."

Every muscle in the girl's body hardened, she stared right through Lodi. "How?"

"The police say he was shot. They want to question Kaliua Lamu."

"That's stupid, why would Kaliua shoot my father?"

Lodi shrugged hopelessly.

"It must have been those people running to the offices. Foreign agents, they did it," Voi said. "We must not let this distract us." She paused for a moment, then burst into tears.

Alkad had guessed it was coming, the girl was far too rigid. She sat Voi down on the bed and put her arm around the girl's shoulders. "It's all right," she soothed. "Just let it happen."

"No." Voi was rocking back and forth. "I must not. Nothing must interfere with the cause. I've got a suppressor program I can use. Give me a moment."

"Don't," Alkad warned. "That's the worst thing you can do. Believe me, I've had enough experience of grief to know what works."

"I didn't like my father," Voi wailed. "I told him I hated him. I hated what he did. He was weak."

"No, Ikela was never weak. Don't think that of your father. He was one of the best navy captains we had."

Voi wiped a hand across her face, simply broadening the tear trails. "A navy captain?"

"That's right. He commanded a frigate during the war. That's how I knew him."

"Daddy fought in the war?"

"Yes. And after."

"I don't understand. He never said."

"He wasn't supposed to. He was under orders, and he obeyed them right up to his death. An officer to the last. I'm proud of him. All Garissans can be proud of him." Alkad hoped the hypocrisy wouldn't taint her voice. She was alarmingly aware how much she needed Voi's people now, whoever they were. And Ikela had almost kept the faith, it was only a white lie.

"What did he do in the navy?" Voi was suddenly desperate for details.

"Later, I promise," Mzu said. "Right now I want you to

activate a somnolence program. Believe me, it's the best thing. We were having a hard enough day before this."

"I don't want to sleep."

"I know. But you need it. And I'm not going anywhere. I'll be here when you wake up."

Voi glanced uncertainly at Lodi, who nodded encouragingly. "All right." She lay back on the bed, shuffled herself comfortable, and closed her eyes. The program took hold.

Alkad stood up and deactivated the chameleon suit. It was painful peeling the hood off her face, the thin fabric stuck possessively to her skin. But the room's cool air was a tonic; she'd sweated heavily underneath it.

She split the seal on her blouse and began to wriggle her arms out of the suit.

Lodi coughed frantically.

"Never seen a naked woman before?"

"Er, yes. But . . . I. That is—"

"Are you just playing at this, Lodi?"

"Playing at what?"

"Being a good-guy radical, a revolutionary on the run?"

"No!"

"Good. Because you're going to see a lot worse than a bare-arsed woman my age before we're done."

His skittish attitude calmed. "I understand. I really do. Er—"

Alkad started on the trousers, they were tighter than the hood. "Yes?"

"Who are you, exactly?"

"Voi didn't explain?"

"No. She just told me to alert the group for possible action. She said we must be careful because the asteroid was probably under covert surveillance."

"She was right."

"Yeah, I know," he said proudly. "I was the one who worked out the Edenists were spreading those spiders."

"Clever of you."

"Thanks. Our junior cadres are cleaning them from critical areas, corridor junctions and places. But I made sure they skimp around this hotel; I didn't want to draw attention to it."

"A smart precaution. So do these cadres of yours know we're here?"

"No, absolutely not; nobody else knows. I swear. Voi said she wanted a safe room; I even paid cash."

Maybe I can still salvage this after all, Alkad thought. "Tell you what, Lodi; I'm going to have a shower first, then afterwards you can tell me all about this little group of yours."

As with most crews when they were docked, Joshua liked to book in at a hotel even if it was only for a single night. It wasn't necessarily more convenient than staying in the *Lady Mac*, it just made a change. This time, though, the crew returned to the starship; and Joshua depressurized the airlock tube once they were all back on board. It would hardly stop anyone in an SII suit, but *Lady Mac* had her fair share of internal defence systems. And besides . . . at the back of his mind was the notion that a possessed would be hard-pressed to wear and operate a spacesuit; if Kelly was right, their rampant energistic ability would completely screw up the suit's processors. He sealed himself up in his sleep cocoon with his paranoia reduced to its lowest level in days.

It was a sombre breakfast as they began to drift into the galley cabin and collect their food five hours later. Everyone had accessed the local news companies. Ikela's murder was the premier item.

Ashly glanced at the galley's AV pillar as he plugged his cereal packet into the milk nozzle.

"Got to be a cover-up," the pilot grunted. "Too much smoke, too little fire. The police should have made an arrest by now. Where's someone as prominent as this Lamu character going to hide in an asteroid?"

Joshua glanced up from his carton of grapefruit. "You think Mzu did it?"

"No." Ashly retrieved the now-chilly packet and gulped

down a mouthful of the mushy wheat paste. "I think someone trying to get Mzu did it; Ikela just got in their way. The
police must know that. They simply can't blurt it out in
public."

"So did they get her?" Melvyn asked.

"Am I psychic?"

"Such questions are irrelevant," Beaulieu said. "We don't
have enough information to speculate in this fashion."

"We can certainly speculate on who else is trying to nab
her," Melvyn said. "For my money, it's got to be the bloody
intelligence agencies. If we can confirm she made it here,
so can they. And that's serious trouble, Captain. If they can
kill someone like Ikela with impunity, they're not going to
worry much about riding over us."

Joshua switched his empty carton of grapefruit for a can
of tea and a croissant. He stared around at his crew as he
chewed on the bland pastry (another reason he liked hotels,
free-fall food was always soft and tacky to avoid crumbs).
Melvyn's words were unsettling, none of them were really
used to personal, one-on-one danger; starship combat was
so very different. Then there was the possibility of encoun-
tering the possessed as well. "Beaulieu's right, we don't
have enough data yet. We'll spend the morning rectifying
that. Melvyn and Ashly, you team up; I want you to concentrate on industrial defence contracts, see if you can find
traces of the kind of things Mzu would require for retrieving and deploying the Alchemist. Principally, that'll be a
starship, but it'll still need fitting out; if we're really lucky
she could have ordered some kind of customized equipment. Dahybi, Beaulieu; try and find out what happened to
the Daphine Kigano alias, where she was last seen, her
credit disk number, that kind of thing. I'm going to find out
what I can about Ikela and his associates."

"What about me?" Sarha asked indignantly.

"You're on duty in here, and you don't let anyone apart
from us on board. From now on, there will always be one
of us on the bridge. I don't know that there are any possessed in Ayacucho, but I'm not risking it. There's also the

intelligence agencies to consider, along with local security forces, and whoever Mzu is lined up with. I think now might also be an appropriate time to take the serjeants out of zero-tau just in case events turn sour. We can pass them off as cosmoniks easily enough."

Ione was finding the whole sensation of independence most peculiar, both individually and in unison with the mirror fragment minds in the other serjeants. Her thoughts were fluttering across the affinity band like birds fleeing a hurricane.

We must try and separate more, she said.

To which her own thoughts replied: **Absolutely.**

She felt like giggling; the kind of giggle that came from being tickled by a merciless lover: unwelcome yet inevitable.

The affinity contact with the other three serjeants reduced, paring down to essential information: location, threat status, environment interpretation. She couldn't help the little frisson of eagerness at the experience; this was the first time she had ever been anywhere outside Tranquillity. Ayacucho might not be much, but she was determined to soak in as much of it as she could.

She was following Joshua out of the transit capsule which had delivered them from the spaceport. The axial chamber was just a low-gee bubble of rock, but at the same time it was a bubble of rock which she hadn't seen before. Her first foreign world.

Joshua got into a waiting tube lift and sat down. She chose the seat opposite him, the composite creaking as it adjusted to her weight.

"This is all so strange," she said as the lift moved off. "Part of me wants to be next to you."

His face became immobile. "Jesus, Ione, why the fuck did you shove your personality into the serjeants? Tranquillity's would've been just fine."

"Why, Joshua Calvert, I do believe you're embarrassed."

"Who me? Oh, no, I'm quite used to sexless two metre monstrosities making a pass at me."

"Don't be so grumpy. It's unbecoming. Besides, you should be grateful. My instinct is very protective towards you. That might give me an edge."

Joshua's retort was lost somewhere in his throat.

The lift's doors opened on a public hall in the asteroid's commercial district where several late office workers scurried to work while a pair of mechanoids cleaned the walls and floor. It was less spartan than the axial chamber, with a high, arched roof and troughs of plants spaced at regular intervals. But it was still only a tunnel through rock, nothing exuberant. Unfortunately the serjeant didn't have lips that could easily be compressed into a pout, otherwise she would have done it. She really wanted to see the biosphere cavern.

Joshua started off down the hall.

"What do you hope to accomplish here?" she asked.

"T'Opingtu is a big company; someone will have been appointed to run it straightaway. And Ikela would make sure his replacement is someone he can trust, someone from his immediate circle. It's not much, but it's the best lead we've got."

"I really don't think you'll be able to get an appointment today."

"Don't be such a downer, Ione. Your trouble is Tranquillity is incorruptible and logical, that's all you're used to. Asteroids like Ayacucho are neither. The size of the contract I'm going to dangle in their faces will get me straight into the top office. There's an etiquette to this kind of business."

"Very well, you get in. Then what?"

"I won't know until I get there. Remember this is strictly a data acquisition mission, everything is helpful even if it is only negative. So keep your senses open and your memory on full record."

"Aye, Captain."

"Okay, now we're primarily interested in anything we

can learn about Ikela's life. We know he was an Garissan refugee, so who did he move with from the past, was he a strong nationalist? Names, contacts, that kind of stuff."

"My personality didn't suffer any damage during the replication process, I can think for myself."

"Wonderful. A bodyguard with an attitude."

"Joshua, darling, this isn't attitude."

He stopped and jabbed a finger at the husky construct. "Now look—"

"That's Pauline Webb," Ione said.

"What? Who?"

Three people were marching down the public hall towards Joshua. Two African-ethnic men flanking a white woman. He didn't like the look of the men at all; they were wearing civilian suits, but combat armour would have been more appropriate. Boosted, and no doubt containing a wide variety of extremely lethal implants.

Pauline Webb stopped a couple of metres short of Joshua and gave the serjeant a curious glance. "Your appointment is cancelled, Calvert. Collect your crew, get back in your starship, and go home. Today."

Joshua produced his most nonchalant grin. "Pauline Webb. Fancy seeing you here."

Her narrowed eyes gave the serjeant another suspicious glance. "This situation is not your concern anymore."

"It is everybody's concern," Ione said. "Especially mine."

"I didn't know you things could operate independently."

"Now you do," Joshua said politely. "So if you'll just step aside . . ."

The man directly in front of Joshua folded his arms and planted his feet slightly apart, a true immovable object. He smiled carnivorously down at Joshua.

"Er, perhaps we could come to an arrangement?"

"The arrangement is simple," Webb said. "If you leave, you get to live."

"Come on, Joshua," Ione said. The serjeant's all-too-human hand closed on his shoulder, forcing him to turn.

"But—"

"Come on."

"That's smart advice," Webb said. "Listen to it."

Ione let go of his shoulder after a few paces. A fuming Joshua allowed her to escort him back down the hall towards the lift. When he glanced over his shoulder Webb and her two troopers were standing watching him.

"This isn't her turf," he hissed at the serjeant. "We could have caused a scene, made trouble for her. The police would have sorted her out as well as us."

"Any incident with the authorities here would have been resolved in her favour. She's a CNIS officer assigned to Mzu; the local Navy Bureau would have backed her, and you and I would be in deep shit, not to mention jail."

"How the hell did Webb know where I was going?"

"I imagine *Lady Mac*'s crew is under clandestine surveillance right now."

"Jesus!"

"Quite. We will have to withdraw and come up with a new strategy."

They reached the lift doors, and Joshua datavised for a ride back to the axial chamber. He cast another glance over his shoulder to check on Webb, a sly smile germinating on his face. "You know what this means, don't you?"

"What?"

"The agencies don't have her yet. We're still in with a chance."

"That's logical."

"Of course it's logical. We may even be able to turn this to our advantage."

"How?"

"I'll tell you when we're back in *Lady Mac*. Everyone's going to have to undergo decontamination first. Christ knows what sort of covert nanonics they've stung us with. We'll be broadcasting our own thoughts back to them if we're not careful."

The lift doors opened and he stepped inside. Someone had slapped half a dozen twenty-centimetre circular holomorph stickers at random over the walls, with a couple more on the ceiling. One was at head height; it started its cycle, a tight bud of lavender photons swelling out from the centre into the form of a scantily clad teenage cheerleader. She shook her silver baton enthusiastically. "Run, Alkad, run!" she yelled. "You're our last hope; don't let them catch you. Run, Alkad, run!"

Joshua stared at it in stupefaction. "Jesus wept."

The cheerleader winked saucily, and syphoned back down below the sticker's surface. Three more began their cycle.

2

Arnstadt fell to the Organization fleet after a ninety-minute battle above the planet. The Strategic Defence network was hammered into oblivion by Capone's antimatter-powered combat wasps. There had been some advance warning from the Edenists, giving the local navy time to redeploy their ships. Three squadrons of voidhawks had arrived from the habitats orbiting one of the system's gas giants, reinforcing the Adamist vessels.

None of the preparations altered the final outcome. Forty-seven Arnstadt navy ships were destroyed, along with fifteen voidhawks. The remaining voidhawks swallowed away, withdrawing back to the gas giant.

The Organization fleet's transport starships moved unopposed into low orbit, and spaceplanes began to ferry a small army of possessed down to the surface. Like all modern Confederation planets, Arnstadt had few soldiers. There were several marine brigades, which were mainly trained in space warfare techniques and covert mission procedures. Wars in this era were fought between starships. The days of foreign invasion forces marching across enemy territory had vanished before the end of the twenty-first century.

With its SD network reduced to radioactive meteorites flaring through bruised skies, Arnstadt was incapable of offering the slightest resistance to the possessed marching down out of their spaceplanes. Small towns were infiltrated first, increasing the numbers of possessed available to move on to larger towns. The area of captured ground began to increase exponentially.

Luigi Balsmao set up his headquarters in one of the orbiting asteroid settlements. Information on the people captured by the advancing possessed was datavised up to the asteroid where the structure coordination programs written by Emmet Mordden decided if they should be possessed or not. Organization lieutenants were appointed, their authority backed up by the firepower of fleet starships in low orbit.

With the subjugation of the planet confidently under way, Luigi split half of the fleet into squadrons and deployed them against the system's asteroid settlements. Only the Edenist habitats were left alone; after Yosemite, Capone wasn't about to risk a second defeat on such a scale.

Starships were dispatched back to New California, and fresh cargo ships began to arrive soon, bringing with them the basic components for a new SD network along with other equipment to help consolidate the Organization's advance. Rover reporters were allowed to see carefully selected sections of the planet under its new masters: children left non-possessed to run around freely, possessed and non-possessed working side by side to restart the economy, Luigi stamping down hard on any possessed who didn't acknowledge the Organization's leadership.

News of the successful invasion swept across the Confederation, backed up by sensevise recordings from the reporters. Surprise was total. One star system's government —no matter what its nature—taking over another was a concept always considered totally impossible. Capone had proved it wasn't. In doing so he set off a chain reaction of panic. Commentators began to talk about planetary level exponential curves, the most extreme showing the entire Confederation falling to the Organization within six months as the industrial resources of more and more systems were absorbed by Capone's empire.

On the Assembly floor, demands that the Confederation Navy should intervene and destroy the Organization fleet became almost continuous. First Admiral Aleksandrovich had to make several appearances to explain how impractical the notion was. The best the navy could do, he said, was to seek out the source of Capone's antimatter and prevent a third system from being taken over. Arnstadt was already lost. Capone had secured a victory which couldn't be reversed without a great loss of life. At this stage, such casualties were wholly unacceptable. He also pointed out that, sadly, a great many non-possessed crews were cooperating with the Organization to operate their starships. Without them, the invasion of Arnstadt could never have happened. Perhaps, he suggested, the Assembly should consider introducing an emergency act to deal with any such traitors. Such legislation might, in future, discourage captains seeking to sign up with Capone for short term gain.

• • •

"Escort duties?" André Duchamp asked wearily. "I thought we were here to help defend New California itself. What exactly does this escort duty entail?"

"Monterey hasn't given me a detailed briefing," Iain Girardi said. "But you will simply be protecting cargo ships from attack by the Confederation Navy. Which is exactly what your contract stipulated."

"Hardly," Madeleine growled. "Nor does it say anywhere that we help a deranged dictator who wiped out an entire fucking planet. I say jump out, Captain. Power up the patterning nodes right now and get the fuck out of here while we still can."

"I would have thought this was a more appealing task for you," Iain Girardi said. His acceleration couch webbing peeled back, and he drifted off the cushioning. "The majority of the crews in the cargo ships are non-possessed, and you won't be permanently in range of the Organization's SD platforms. If anything, we're giving you an easier job with less risk for the same money."

"Where would we be going?" André asked.

"Arnstadt. The Organization is shipping industrial equipment there to help restart the planetary economy."

"If they hadn't blown it all to shit in the first place they wouldn't need to *restart* it," Madeleine said.

André shushed her impatiently. "It seems fine to me," he told Iain Girardi. "However, the ship will require some maintenance work before we can undertake such an assignment. An escort flight is very different from supplementing planetary defences."

Iain Girardi's humour appeared strained for the first time. "Yes. I'll have to discuss the nature of the repairs with Monterey." He datavised the flight computer for a communications channel.

André waited with a neutral smile.

"The Organization will bring the *Villeneuve's Revenge* up to full combat-capable status," Iain Girardi announced. "Your hull and sensor suite will be repaired by us, but you must meet the cost of secondary systems."

André shrugged. "Take it out of our fee."

"Very well. Please dock at Monterey's spaceport, bay VB757. I shall disembark there; you'll be assigned a liaison officer for the mission."

"Non-possessed," Desmond Lafoe said sharply.

"Of course. I believe they want you to take some reporters with you, as well. They'll require access to your sensors during the flight."

"*Merde.* Those filth. What for?"

"Mr Capone is highly focused on the need for accurate publicity. He wants the Confederation to see that he is not a real threat."

"Unlike Arnstadt," Madeleine said swiftly.

André piloted the starship down from its emergence zone to the large asteroid. Spaceflight traffic above New California was heavy: starships raced between the orbital asteroids and the emergence zones, spaceplanes and ion field flyers flew a constant shuttle service from the planet. Although the starship only had sixty-five per cent of its sensor clusters remaining, André kept them fully extended to gather what information he could.

When the flight computer told her Girardi was talking to Monterey again, Madeleine opened an encrypted channel to André: "I don't think we should dock," she datavised.

The captain extended the datavise to include Erick and Desmond. "Why not?"

"Look at those ships out there, if anything there's more activity than before the planet was possessed. I didn't realize how damn professional this Capone Organization is. We're not going to get out of this, André, we're in too deep. The second we dock they'll swarm on board and possess us."

"Then who will crew the ship for them? *Non*, they need us."

"She has a point about the Organization's size and motivation, though," Erick datavised. "The possessed are dependent on us flying the warships, but what happens when there are no more worlds left to invade? Capone took Arnstadt in less than a day, and almost doubled his military resources doing so. He's not going to stop now. If he and the rest of the possessed keep on winning at that rate, there will be no place left for non-possessed anywhere in the Confederation. That's what we'll be helping bring about."

"I know this." André cast a guilty glance at Girardi to make sure he wasn't aware of the conversation. "That is why I agreed to the escort duty."

"I don't get it," Madeleine said.

"Simple, *ma chérie*. The Organization repairs the *Villeneuve's Revenge* for me, fills up our cryogenic fuel tanks, equips us with combat wasps, and sends us off on a flight. Then while we're en route, we vanish. What is to stop us?"

"Their liaison officer, for a start," Desmond said.

"Ha, one man. We can overcome him. Capone has made his greatest mistake in trying to dishonour André Duchamp. It is I who is using them now, for the benefit of my fellow man, *comme il faut*. I am no quisling. And I think we should make sure the reporters know of this savage blow we will strike against Capone."

"You really intend to leave?" Madeleine asked.

"Naturally."

Erick grinned, as best as his new skin would allow him. For once Duchamp's devious nature could actually work for the best. He opened a new file in his neural nanonics memory cell and started recording the sensor images. CNIS would want to know about the Organization's disposition; though he suspected the New California system would already be under full covert surveillance.

"What about Shane Brandes?" Desmond asked.

André's face darkened. "What about him?"

"How long were you planning to leave him in zero-tau?"

"I could hardly drop him off at Chaumort, it was too small. We want a backwards planet where we can dump him in the middle of a desert or a jungle."

"Lalonde would do," Madeleine said under her breath.

"Well, if you're looking for somewhere he won't come back from," Desmond offered maliciously.

"No," Erick datavised.

"Why not?" André asked. "Give him to the Organization when we dock. It is an excellent idea. Shows them how loyal we are."

"We kill him, or dump him. But not that. You didn't see what they did to Bev."

André flinched. "Very well. But I'm not hanging on to that bastard forever, his zero-tau is costing me power."

Villeneuve's Revenge docked in its designated bay, its crew alert for any treachery from the Organization. There was none to see. As Iain Girardi promised, maintenance teams immediately started to work on the starship's battered hull and defunct sensors. It took eleven hours to withdraw the damaged sections and install new replacements. Integration and diagnostic checks took another two hours to complete.

Once André agreed that they were ready for escort duties, the Organization started loading combat wasps into the launch tubes. An airlock tube slid out from the docking bay wall to connect with the *Villeneuve's Revenge*.

It was Desmond, armed with a machine pistol bought on Chaumort, who went down to the lower deck with Girardi. He made sure the tube was completely empty before opening the hatch and letting the Organization man out. Only when Girardi had swum down the length of the tube, and closed the far hatch behind him, did he give André the all-clear.

"Send your liaison officer through," André datavised to the spaceport.

As arranged, the man wore nothing, towing his clothes in a small bag behind him as he came along the tube. Desmond made every test they could think of, requesting complex datavises from the liaison officer's neural nanonics, exposing him to different processor blocks.

"I think he's clean," Desmond datavised.

Madeleine unlocked the manual latches on the hatch to the lower deck.

The liaison officer introduced himself as Kingsley Pryor. To Erick, his subdued behaviour and quiet, stumbling voice indicated someone emerging from shock.

"There will be a convoy of twelve cargo ships departing for Arnstadt in three hours," Kingsley Pryor told them. "The *Villeneuve's Revenge* will be one of five combat-capable ships escorting them. Your job is to defend them from any sneak attacks from Confederation Navy ships. If it does happen, they'll probably use voidhawks against us." He gave the bridge a thoughtful look. "I wasn't told there would only be four of you. Is that enough to operate at full combat efficiency?"

"Of course it is," André responded hotly. "We have survived much worse than a voidhawk attack."

"Very well. There is one other thing you should know. The Organization is held together by fear and respect, obedience must be total. You have accepted our money and signed on with the fleet, we will not tolerate any disloyalty."

"You come on my ship, and tell me—" André blustered loudly.

Kingsley Pryor held up a hand. Weak though the gesture was, it silenced Duchamp immediately. Something in the liaison officer's manner put a great deal of weight behind his authority. "You signed a pact with the devil, Captain. Now I'm explaining the small print. You don't trust us, fair enough; we don't really trust you either. I'm sure that now you've seen New California firsthand you've realized just how powerful and dedicated the Organization is, and you're having second thoughts about supporting us. Perfectly natural. After all, it would be very easy for a starship to disappear in the direction of the Confederation. Let me try and dissuade you. While your ship was being repaired, a nuclear explosive was included inside one of the new components. It has a seven-hour timer which must be reset by a code. I do not have that code, so you cannot use debrief nanonics to extract it from me. A liaison officer in one of the other escort ships will transmit that code at us every three hours, resetting the timer. In turn I will transmit the code I have been given at the other ships, which have been similarly modified. If all of us stay together, there will be no problem. If one ship leaves, they will be killing themselves and the crew of another ship."

"Remove it now!" André shouted furiously. "I will not fly under such a blackmail threat."

"It is not blackmail, Captain, it is enforcement, making sure you abide by the terms of your contract. I believe the argument goes along the lines of: If you intended to keep the agreement you made with us you have nothing to worry about."

"I will not fly with a bomb on board. That is final!"

"Then they will come on board, and possess you. And another crew will be found. It is the ship and its capability they want, Captain, not you as an individual."

"This is intolerable!"

For a moment a real anger shone in Kingsley Pryor's eyes. He sneered at André. "So is a free man agreeing to help Capone, Captain." Then the emotion was gone, leaving only the meek expression in its wake. "Shall we get the reporters on board now? We haven't got too much time before we have to be at the jump coordinate."

Jed Hinton was still a hundred metres from the pub when he knelt down and took the red handkerchief off his ankle. Koblat's adults were starting to get nettled by Deadnight; kids that followed the cause were being hassled. Nothing serious, some jostling in public places, arguments at home. The usual crap.

Digger, of course, despised the recording; descending into a rage whenever it was mentioned. For once Jed enjoyed a guilty delight at the way he intimidated Miri and Navar, forbidding them to have anything to do with it. Without realizing, he'd altered the political structure of the family. Now it was Jed and Gari who were the favoured ones, the ones who could access Kiera Salter, and talk about her ideas with their friends, and know the taste of freedom.

Jed walked into the Blue Fountain, making out like it was cool for him to be there. Normally he'd be anywhere else, it was Digger's pub. But Digger was busy these days; not working the tunnelling units, but out at the spaceport doing maintenance on the machinery in the docking bays. There were three shifts a day now, supporting the increasing number of flights. Yet although everyone knew perfectly well starships were arriving and departing several times a day, there was no official log. Three times he'd accessed the net and asked the spaceport register for a list of ships docked only to be told there were none.

Fascinated, the Deadnight kids had asked around, and together they'd pieced together the basics of the quarantine-busting operation. They had all been excited that day, starships arriving illegally was *perfect* for them. Beth had smiled at him and said: "Bloody hell, we might just make it to Valisk, after all." Then she'd hugged him. She'd never done that before, not in that way.

He asked the barman for a beer, slowly scanning the pub. A room where the images within the ten-year-old landscape holograms covering the walls were diminishing to blurred smears, their colours fading. The naked rock they covered would be less depressing. Most of the scuffed composite and aluminum tables were occupied. Groups of men sat hunched over their drinks and talked in low tones. Nearly a quarter of the customers were wearing ship-suits, bright and exotic compared to the clothes favoured by Koblat's residents.

Jed located the crew from the *Rameses X*, the starship's name stencilled neatly on their breast pockets. Their captain was with them, a middle-aged woman with the silver star on her epaulette. He went over.

"I wonder if I could talk to you, ma'am?"

She glanced up at him, faintly suspicious at the respectful tone.

"What is it?"

"I have a friend who would like to go to Valisk."

The captain burst out laughing. Jed flushed as the rest of the crew groaned, trading infuriatingly superior expressions.

"Well, son, I can certainly understand how come your friend is so interested in young Kiera." She winked broadly.

Jed's embarrassment deepened, which must have been obvious to all of them. True, he had spent hours on his processor block with a graphics program, altering the image from the recording. Now the block's small AV pillar could project her lying beside him on the bed at night, or looming over him smiling. At first he'd worried he was being disrespectful, but she would understand the need he had for her. The love. She knew all about love, in its many forms. It was all she spoke of.

"It's what she offers," he stammered helplessly. "That's what we're interested in."

That just brought another round of hearty laughter from the group.

"Please," he said. "Can you take us there?"

The humour sank from her face. "Listen, son, take the advice of an older woman. That recording: it's just a big bullshit con. They want you there so they can possess you, that's all. There's no paradise waiting at the end of the rainbow."

"Have you been there?" he asked stiffly.

"No. No, I haven't. So you're right, I can't say for certain. Let's just put it down to a healthy dose of cynicism; everybody catches it when they get older." She turned back to her drink.

"Will you take me?"

"No. Look, son, even if I was crazy enough to fly to Valisk, do you have any idea how much it would cost you to charter a starship to take you?"

He shook his head mutely.

"From here, about a quarter of a million fuseodollars. Do you have that kind of money?"

"No."

"Well, there you are then. Now stop wasting my time."

"Do you know anyone who would take us, someone who believes in Kiera?"

"Goddamnit!" She screwed around in her chair to glare at him. "Can't you inbred morons pick up a simple hint when it's smacked you in the face?"

"Kiera said you'd hate us for listening to her."

The captain let out an astonished snort of breath. "I don't believe this. Don't you see how gullible you are? I'm doing you a favour."

"I didn't ask you to. And why are you so blind to what she says?"

"*Blind*? Fuck you, you teeny shit."

"Because you are. You're scared it's true, that she's right."

She stared at him for a long moment, the rest of the crew fixing him with hostile stares. They'd probably beat him up in a minute. Jed didn't care anymore. He hated her as much as he did Digger and all the others with closed minds and dead hearts.

"All right," the captain whispered. "In your case I'll make an exception."

"No," one of the crew said, his hand going out to hold her arm. "You can't, he's only a kid with a hard-on for the girl."

She shook off the restraining hand and brought out a processor block. "I was going to hand this over to the Confederation Navy, even though it would be difficult to explain away given our current flight schedule. But I think you can have it instead, now." She took a flek from its slot in the block and slapped it into an astonished Jed's hand. "Say hello to Kiera for me. If you aren't too busy screaming while they possess you."

Chairs were pushed back noisily. The crew of the *Rameses X* left their unfinished drinks on the table and marched out.

Jed stood at the centre of a now-silent pub, every eye locked on him. He didn't even notice, he was staring raptly at the little black flek resting in his palm as if it were the key to the fountain of youth. Which in a way, he supposed, it was.

•   •   •

The *Levêque* was orbiting fifteen thousand kilometres above Norfolk, its complete sensor suite extended to sweep the planet. Despite the Confederation Navy's hunger for information, little data was returning. Slow cyclonic swirls of red cloud had mushroomed from the islands, mating then smoothing out into a placid sheet, sealing the world behind a uniform twilight nimbus. Small ivory tufts of cirrocumulus swam above the polar zones for a few hours, the last defiant speckling of alien colour; but in time even they fell to melt into the veil.

The consolidation was five hours old when the change began. *Levêque*'s officers noticed the cloud's light emission level was increasing. The frigate's captain decided to play safe and ordered them to raise their orbit by another twenty thousand kilometres. By the time their main fusion drive ignited, the crimson canopy was blazing brighter than any firestorm. They ascended at five gees, badly worried by the glare expanding rapidly across the stars behind them. Gravitonic sensors reported discordant ripples within the planetary mass below. If the readings were truthful, then the world should be breaking apart. Heavily filtered optical-band sensors revealed the planet's geometry remained unchanged.

Seven gees, and the cloud's surface was kindling to the intensity of a nuclear furnace.

Luca Comar looked upwards in a dreamy daze. The red cloud guarding the sky above Cricklade manor's steep roof was writhing violently, its gold and crimson underbelly caught by potent microburst vortices. Huge churning strips were being torn open, allowing a fierce white light to slam down. He flung his arms wide, howling a rapturous welcome.

Energy stormed through him at an almost painful rate, bursting from some non-point within to vanish into the raging sky. The woman beside him was performing the same act, her features straining with effort and incredulity. In his mind he could feel the possessed all across Norfolk uniting in this final supreme sacrament.

Boiling fragments of cloud plunged through the air at giddy velocities; corkscrew lightning bolts snapping between them. Their red tint was fading, sinking behind the flamboyant dawn irradiating the universe beyond the atmosphere.

A thick, heavy light poured over Luca. It penetrated straight through his body. Through the mossy grass. Through the soil. The whole world surrendered to it. Luca's thoughts were trapped by the invasion, unable to think of anything but sustaining the moment. He hung suspended from reality as the last surge of energy unwound through his cells.

Silence.

Luca slowly let out his breath. He opened his eyes cautiously. The clouds had calmed, reverting to rumpled white smears. Warm mellow light was shining over the wolds. There was no sun, no single source point, it came from the boundary of the enclosed universe itself. Shining equally, everywhere.

And they'd gone. He could no longer hear the souls in the beyond. Those piercing pleas and promises had vanished. There was no way back, no treacherous chink in the folds of this fresh continuum. He was free inside his new body.

He looked at the woman, who was glancing around in stupefaction.

"We've done it," he whispered. "We escaped."

She smiled tentatively.

He held out his arms, and concentrated. Not the smoke-snorting knight again; the moment required something more dignified. Soft golden cloth settled around his skin, an imperial toga, befitting his mood.

"Oh, yes. Yes!"

The energistic ability was still there, the imposition of will upon matter. But now the cloth had a stronger, firmer texture to the artefacts he'd created before.

Before . . . Luca Comar laughed. In another universe. Another life.

This time it would be different. They could establish their nirvana here. And it would last forever.

The cluster of five survey satellites from the *Levêque* gradually spread apart as they glided through the section of space where Norfolk should be. Communications links beamed a huge flow of information back to the frigate. Every sensor they had was switched to maximum sensitivity. Two distinct spectrums of sunlight fell on them. Tremulous waves of solar ions dusted their receptors. Cosmic radiation bombardment was standard.

There was nothing else. No gravity field. No magnetosphere. No atmospheric gas. Space-time's quantum signature was perfectly normal.

All that remained of Norfolk was the memory.

• • •

When it was discovered in 2125, Nyvan was immediately incorporated into the celebration of hope which was sweeping Earth in the wake of Felicity's discovery. The second terracompatible planet to be found, a beautiful verdant virgin land, proof the first hadn't been a fluke. Everybody on

Earth wanted to escape out to the stars. And they wanted to go there now. That, ultimately, proved its downfall.

By then, people had finally realized the arcologies weren't going to be a temporary shelter from the ruined climate, somewhere to stay while Govcentral cooled the atmosphere, cleaned up the pollution, and put the weather patterns back to rights. The tainted clouds and armada storms were here to stay. Anyone who wanted to live under an open sky would have to leave and find a new one.

In the interests of fairness and maintaining its own shaky command over individual state administrations, Govcentral agreed that everyone had the right to leave, without favouritism. It was that last worthy clause, included to pacify several vocal minorities, which in practice meant that colonists would have to be a multi-cultural, multi-racial mix fully representative of the planet's population. No limits were placed on the numbers buying starship tickets, they just had to be balanced. For those states too poor to fill up their quota, Govcentral provided assisted placement schemes so the richer states couldn't complain they were being unfairly limited. A typical political compromise.

By and large, it worked for Nyvan and the other terra-compatible planets being sought out by the new ZTT drive ships. The first decades of interstellar colonization were heady times, when common achievement easily outweighed the old ethnic enmities. Nyvan and its early siblings played host to a unity of purpose rarely seen before.

It didn't last. After the frontier had been tamed and the pioneering spirit flickered into extinction the ancient rivalries lumbered to the fore once again. Earth's colonial governance gave way to local administrations on a dozen planets, and politicians began to adopt the worst jingoistic aspects of late twentieth-century nationalism, leading the mob behind them with absurd ease. This time there were no safeguards of seas and geographical borders between the diverse populations. Religions, cultures, skins, ideologies, and languages were all squeezed up tight in the pinch chamber of urban conglomeration. Civil unrest was the inevitable result, ruining lives and crippling economies.

Overall, the problem was solved in 2156 by the Govcentral state of California, who sponsored New California, the first ethnic-streaming colony, open only to native Californians. Although initially controversial, the trend was swiftly taken up by the other states. This second wave of colonies suffered none of the strife so prevalent among the first, clearing the way for the mass immigration of the Great Dispersal.

While the new ethnic-streaming worlds successfully absorbed Earth's surplus population and flourished accordingly, the earlier colonies slowly lost ground both culturally and economically: a false dawn shading to a perpetual twilight.

"What happened to the asteroids?" Lawrence Dillon asked.

Quinn was gazing thoughtfully at the images which the *Tantu's* sensors were throwing onto the hemisphere of holoscreens at the foot of his acceleration couch. In total, eleven asteroids had been manoeuvred into orbit around Nyvan, their ores mined to provide raw material for the planet's industries. Ordinarily, they would develop into healthy mercantile settlements with a flotilla of industrial stations.

The frigate's sensors showed that eight of them were more-or-less standard knots of electromagnetic activity, giving off a strong infrared emission. The remaining three were cold and dark. *Tantu's* high-resolution optical sensors focused on the closest of the defunct rocks, revealing wrecked machinery clinging to the crumpled grey surface. One of them even had a counter-rotating spaceport disk, though it no longer revolved; the spindle was bent, and the gloomy structure punctured with holes.

"They had a lot of national wars here," Quinn said.

Lawrence frowned at him, thoughts cloudy with incomprehension.

"There's a lot of different people live here," Quinn explained. "They don't get on too good, so they fight a lot."

"If they hate each other, why don't they all leave?"

"I don't know. Ask them."

"Who?"

"Shut the fuck up, Lawrence, I'm trying to think. Dwyer, has anyone seen us yet?"

"Yes, the detector satellites picked us up straightaway. We've had three separate transponder interrogations so far; they were from different defence network command centres. Everyone seemed satisfied with our identification code this time."

"Good. Graper, I want you to be our communications officer."

"Yes, Quinn." Graper let the eagerness show in his voice, anxious to prove his worth.

"Stick with the cover we decided. Call each of those military centres and tell the bastards we've been assigned a monitor mission in this system by the Confederation Navy. We'll be staying in high orbit until further notice, and if any of them want fire support against possessed targets we'll be happy to provide it."

"I'm on it, Quinn." He began issuing orders to the flight computer.

"Dwyer," Quinn said. "Get me a channel into Nyvan's communications net." He floated away from his velvet acceleration couch and used a stikpad to steady himself in front of his big command console.

"Er, Quinn, this is weird, the sensors are showing me like fifty communications platforms in geosync," Dwyer said nervously. He was using grab hoops to hold himself in front of his flight station, his face centimetres from a glowing holoscreen, as though the closer he could get the more understanding of its data he would have. "The computer says they've got nineteen separate nets on this world, some of them don't even hook together."

"Yeah, so? I told you, dickbrain, they got a shitload of different nations here."

"Which one do you want?"

Quinn thought back, picturing the man, his mannerisms, voice, accent. "Is there a North American-ethnic nation?"

Dwyer consulted the information on the holoscreen. "I got five. There's Tonala, New Dominica, New Georgia, Quebec, and the Islamic Texas Republic."

"Gimmie the New Georgia one." Information began to scroll up on his own holoscreen. He studied it for a minute, then requested a directory function and loaded in a search program.

"Who is this guy, Quinn?" Lawrence asked.

"Name's Twelve-T. He's one mean fucker, a gang lord, runs a big operation down there. Any badass shit you want, you go to him for it."

The search program finished its run. Quinn loaded the eddress it had found for him.

"Yeah?" a voice asked.

"I want to talk to Twelve-T."

"Crazy ass mother, ain't no fucker got that handle living here."

"Listen, shitbrain, this is his public eddress. He's there."

"Yeah, so you know him, datavise him."

"Not possible."

"Yeah? Then he don't know you. Any mother he need to rap with knows his private code."

"Okay, the magic word is Banneth. And if you don't think that's magic, trace where this call is coming from. Now tell the man, because if I come calling, you're going out hurting."

Dwyer gave another myopic squint at his displays. "He's tracing the call. Back to the satellite already. Hot program."

"I expect they use it a lot," Quinn muttered.

"You got a problem up there, motherfucker?" a new voice asked. It was almost as Quinn remembered it, a low purr, too damaged to be smooth. Quinn had seen the throat scar which made it that way.

"No problem at all. What I got up here is a proposition."

"Where you at, man? What is this monk shit? You ain't Banneth."

"No." Quinn swayed forwards slowly towards the camera lens in the centre of the console and pulled his hood right back. "Run your visual file search program."

"Oh, yeah. You used to be Banneth's little rat runner; her whore, too. I remember. So what you want here, ratty?"

"A deal."

"What you got to trade?"

"You know what I'm riding in?"

"Sure. Lucky Vin ran a trace, he's pissin' liquid nitrogen right now."

"It could be yours."

"No shit?"

"That's right."

"What've I gotta do for it, hump you?"

"No, I just want to trade it in. That's all."

The whisper lost its cool. "You want to trade in a fucking Confederation Navy frigate? What the fuck for?"

"I need to talk to you about that. But there's some good quality hardware on board. You'll come out ahead."

"Talk, motherfucker? If your hardware's so shit-hot, how come you wanna dump it?"

"God's Brother doesn't always ride to war. There are other ways to bring His word to the faithless."

"Cut that voodoo shit, man. Damn, I hate that sect shit you arcology freaks use. Ain't no God, so he sure as shit can't have no Brother."

"Try telling that to the possessed."

"Motherfuck! Smartass motherfucker! That's what you are, that's all you are."

"Do you want to deal or not?" Quinn knew he would; what gang lord could resist a frigate?

"I ain't promising shit up front."

"That's cool. Now I need to know which asteroid to dock with. And it's going to have to be one which doesn't ask too many questions. Have you got any weight in orbit?"

"You know it, man, that's why you come to me. You might talk like you the King of Kulu's brother, but here it's me who's got the juice. And stink this, I don't trust you, rat runner."

"With this much firepower behind me, think how much I care. Start fixing things."

"Fuck you. A strike like this is gonna take a few days to set up, man."

"You have forty-eight hours; then I want a docking bay number flashing in front of me. If not, I will smite you from the face of the world."

"Will you cut that freaky crap—"

Quinn cancelled the circuit and threw his head back laughing.

* * * * *

It had only taken a few hours for the screen of red cloud to engulf the sky above Exnall. The tenuous beginnings of the early morning had been supplanted by billowing masses of solid vapour sweeping up from the south. Thunder arrived in accompaniment, bass grumbles which seemed to circle and swoop around the town like jittery birds. There was no telling where the sun was now, but its light still seemed to slip through the covering to illuminate the streets in natural tones.

Moyo marched down Maingreen on his mission to find some kind of transport for Stephanie's children. The more he thought about the prospect, the happier it made him. She was right, as always, it did give him something positive to do. And no, he didn't want to spend eternity in Exnall.

He passed the doughnut café and the baseball game in the park, oblivious to either. If he searched with his mind, he could perceive the buildings around him like foggy shadows; all space was dark, while matter was amended to a translucent white gauze. Individual objects were hard to distinguish, and small ones almost impossible; but he thought he stood a good chance of recognizing something like a bus.

The street sweeper was busy again. A man in a grey jacket and cloth cap, pushing his broom in front of him as he made his way slowly along the pavement. Every day he had appeared. He never did anything else but sweep the pavements, never talked to anybody, never responded to any attempts at conversation.

Moyo was slowly coming to learn that not all of Exnall's possessed were adapting readily to their new circumstances. Some, like the sports nuts and café owners were obsessively filling every moment of their day with activity no matter how spurious, while others would amble around in a listless mockery of their earlier existence. That assessment put his own labours perilously close to the apathetic ones.

A dense collection of shadows at the rear of one of the larger stores caught his attention. When he walked around the building there was a long van parked in the loading bay. It had suffered some damage in the riot; struck by white fire the front two tyres had melted into puddles of sticky plastic, the navy-blue bodywork was blackened, and in some places cracked open, the windshield was smashed. But it was certainly big enough.

He stared at the first tyre, visualizing it whole and functional. Not an illusion, but how the solid matter should actually be structured. The hardened plastic puddle started to flow, amoebic buds swelling up to engulf the naked hub.

"Yo there, man. Having some fun?"

Moyo had been so involved with the tyre he hadn't noticed the man approaching. At first sight the man looked as if he'd grown a dark brown mane; his beard came down to his waist as did the corkscrew locks of his luxuriant hair. A pair of tiny amber hexagonal glasses which were almost curtained by tresses seemed perversely prominent. The flares of his purple velvet trousers were embellished with tiny silver bells which chimed with each step, not in tune, but certainly in keeping.

"Not exactly. Is this your van?"

"Hey, property is theft, man."

"Property is what?"

"Theft. You're like stealing from what rightfully belongs to all people. That van is an inanimate object. Unless you're into a metallic version of Gaia—which personally I'm not. However, just because it's inert that doesn't mean we can abuse its intrinsic value which is the ability to carry cats where they want to go."

"Cats? I just want it to ferry some children out of here."

"Yeah well okay that's cool, too. But what I like mean is that it's like community property. It was built by people, so all people should share it equally."

"It was built by cybersystems."

"Oh, no, that's real heavy-duty corporate shit. Man, they've got into your skull big-time. Here, take a toot, Mr Suit, take yourself out of yourself." He held out a fat reefer which was already alight and sending out a pungent sweetness.

"No thanks."

"Takes your mind to other realms."

"I've just got back from one, thank you. I have no intention of returning."

"Yeah, right, dig your point. The baddest trip of them all."

Moyo couldn't quite make out what he was confronting. The man didn't seem like one of the apathetic ones. On the other hand, he obviously hadn't managed to adapt very well. Perhaps he came from a pre-technology age, where education was minimal and superstition ruled everyone's life.

"What era do you come from?"

"Ho! The greatest one there ever was. I dug the era of peace, when we were busy fighting the establishment for all the freedom you cats just take for granted. Heck, I was at Woodstock, man. Can you dig that?"

"Um, I'm very happy for you. So you don't mind if I rebuild the van, then?"

"Rebuild? What are you, some kind of anti-anarchist?"

"I'm someone who's got children to look after. Unless you'd rather they were tortured by Ekelund's people."

The man's body bucked as if he'd been struck a physical blow; his arms wove in strange jerky motions in front of him. Moyo didn't think it was a dance.

"I hate your hostility groove, but I dig your motivation.

That's cool. A square cat like you is probably having a lot of trouble adjusting to this situation."

Moyo's jaw dropped open. "*I'm* having trouble?"

"Thought so. So like what kind of magical mystery tour are you planning here?"

"We're taking the children out of Exnall. Stephanie wants to drive up to the border."

"Oh, man!" A wide smile prised apart layers of hair. "That is so beautiful. The border again. We're gonna roll this old bus out and set the draft dodgers free in the land of Mounties and maple leaves. What a trip! Thank you, man, thank you." He walked over to the battered van and stroked its front wing lovingly. A small wavy rainbow appeared on the bodywork where his hand had touched it.

"What do you mean, we?"

"Come on, man, lighten up. You don't think you can handle that kind of scene alone, do you? The military mind is full of low cunning; you wouldn't get a mile out of town without them throwing up roadblocks across the freeway. Maybe a few of us would fall down some stairs while we're being arrested, too. It happens, man, all of the frigging time. The federal pigs don't give a shit about our rights. But I've been here before, I know how to go sneaky on them."

"You think she'd try and stop us?"

"Who, man?"

"Ekelund."

"Hell, who knows. Chicks like that have got it real hard up their asses. Between you and me, I think they're maybe like aliens. You know, UFO people from Venus. But I can see you're sceptical right now, I won't press it. So how many kids are you planning on squirrelling away in here?"

"About seven or eight, so far."

Without quite understanding how it happened, Moyo found a friendly arm around his shoulder, guiding him to the van's cab.

"That's worthy. I can dig that. Now you just ease yourself up in the driver's seat, or whatever the hell they call it these days, and dream up some controls we can all handle. Once you've done that and I've given us a cool disguise we can hit the road."

Twinkles of light were shooting all over the van's body-work, sketching glowing lines of colour in the damaged composite. It was as if a flock of acidhead fairies had been let loose with spray cans. Moyo wanted to complain at this ideological hijack, but couldn't manage to think up the correct words. He took the easy option, and sat in the driver's seat like he'd been told.

*   *   *

There was a gap between the deuterium tank's cryostat ducts and the power feed sub-module which routed superconductor cables to nearby patterning nodes, a narrow crevice amid the boxy, nultherm foam-coated machinery. In the schematics which the flight computer provided, it was listed as a crawlway.

For pigmy acrobats, maybe, Erick thought irascibly. He certainly couldn't wear any protective gear over the SII suit. Sharp corners and bloated tubes jabbed and squeezed against him every time he moved. It couldn't be doing the medical nanonic packages around his arm and torso any good. Thankfully the black silicon covering his skin was an effective insulator, otherwise he would have been either roasted, frozen, or electrocuted long ago.

Along with Madeleine he'd been burrowing through the innards of the *Villeneuve's Revenge* for nine hours now. It was nasty, tiring, stressful work. With his body in the state it was he had to keep a constant check on his physiological status. He was also running a mild relaxant program in primary mode; claustrophobia was a problem prowling wolfishly around the fringes of conscious thought.

The crawlway ended a metre short of the hull, opening out into a hexagonal metallic cave bordered with stress structure girders, themselves spiralled by cables. Erick squirmed out into this cramped space and drew a sharp breath of relief, more psychological than practical given he was breathing through a respirator tube. He switched his collar sensors to scan around, seeing the fuselage plate behind his head. It appeared perfectly normal, a smooth, slightly curving silicon surface, dark grey with red code strips printed around the edges.

With his legs still jammed in the crawlway, Erick pulled the sensor block from the straps securing it to his side. It contained six separate scanner pads which he slipped out and started fixing to the hull plate and girders.

"Plate 3-25-D is clean," he datavised to André eight minutes later. "No electromagnetic activity; and it's solid, too, no density anomalies."

"Very good, Erick. 5-12-D is next."

"How is Madeleine doing?"

"She is methodical. Between you, eighteen per cent of the possible locations have now been eliminated."

Erick cursed. The four of them had carefully gone over the starship's schematics, working out every possible section of the hull were the device could have been hidden by Monterey's maintenance crews. With Pryor on board observing the bridge, they were limited to two crew searching at any one time, the two supposed to be asleep. It was going to take a long time to cover all the possible areas.

"I still say it's probably a combat wasp. That would be the easiest method."

"*Oui,* but we won't know for sure until you have eliminated all the other options. Who can tell with such treacherous bastards?"

"Great. How long to Arnstadt?"

"We have another five jumps to go. Two of the other escort ships are manoeuvring sluggishly, which gives us additional time. They are probably searching as we are. You have perhaps another fifteen hours, twenty at the outside."

Not enough, Erick knew, not nearly enough. They were going to have to go to Arnstadt. After that he didn't like to think what the Organization would require from them. Nothing as simple as escort duties, that was for certain.

"All right, Captain, I'm on my way to 5-12-D."

• • •

The chamber which the Saldanas used for their Privy Council meetings was called the Fountain Room, a white marble octagon with a gold and opal mosaic ceiling. Imposing three-metre statues stood around the walls, sculpted from a dark rock which had been cut out of Nova Kong, depicting a toga-clad orator in various inspirational poses. The Fountain Room wasn't as grandiose as some of the state function rooms added to the Apollo Palace in later centuries, but it had been built by Gerald Saldana soon after his coronation for use as his cabinet room. The continuity of power was unbroken since then; the Saldanas were nothing if not respectful for the traditions of their own history.

There were forty-five members of the current Privy Council, including the Princes and Princesses who ruled the Principalities; which meant a full meeting was held only every eighteen months. Normally the King summoned twenty to twenty-five people to advise him, over half of which were nearly always family. Today there were just six sitting around the Fountain Room's triangular mahogany table with its inlaid crowned phoenix. It was the war cabinet, chaired by Alastair II himself, with the Duke of Salion on his left, followed by Lord Kelman Mountjoy, the Foreign Office Minister; on the King's right-hand side was the Prime Minister, Lady Phillipa Oshin; Admiral Lavaquar, the defence chief; and Prince Howard, president of Kulu Corporation. No aides or equerries were present.

Alastair II picked up a small gavel and tapped the much-battered silver bell on the table in front of him. "The fifth meeting of this cabinet committee is now in order. I trust everyone has accessed the latest reports concerning Arnstadt?"

There was a subdued round of acknowledgement from the cabinet.

"Very well. Admiral, your assessment?"

"Bloody worrying, Your Majesty. As you know interstellar conquest has always been regarded as completely impractical. Today's navies exist to protect civil starships from piracy and deter potential aggressors from committing random or sneak assaults. If anyone strikes at us for political or economic reasons they damn well know we will strike back harder. But actually subduing an entire system's population was not a concept any of our strategy groups even considered until today. Ethnically streamed populations are too diverse, you simply cannot impose a different culture on a defeated indigenous people, it will never be accepted, and you lose the peace trying to enforce it. QED, conquests are impractical. Possession has changed that. All Confederation worlds are vulnerable to it, even Kulu. Though had the Capone Organization fleet jumped into orbit here, they would have lost."

"Even armed with antimatter?" Prince Howard inquired.

"Oh, yes. We would have taken a pounding, no doubt about it. But we would have won; in terms of firepower our SD network is second only to Earth's. The thing which concerns our strategists most is the Organization's theoretical expansion rate. They have effectively doubled their fleet size by taking Arnstadt. If another five or six star systems were to fall into Capone's hands, we would be facing parity at the very least."

"We have distance on our side," Lady Phillipa said. "Kulu is nearly three hundred light-years from New California. Deploying any kind of fleet over such a distance would be inordinately difficult. And Capone is having trouble resupplying his conquests with He_3, he simply isn't getting any from the Edenists."

"Your pardon, Prime Minister," the admiral said. "But you are taking a too literal interpretation of these events. Yes it would be physically difficult for Capone to subdue Kulu, but the *trend* he is starting would be a different matter indeed. Others returning from the beyond are equally capable, and some have considerably more experience in empire building than he does. Unless planetary governments remain exceptionally vigilant in searching for outbreaks of possession, what happened to New California could easily be repeated. If Capone was all we had to worry about, I would frankly be very relieved. As to the Organization's He_3 shortage: deuterium can and will be used as a monofuel for starship drives. It's less efficient and its radiation output has a progressively detrimental effect on the drive tube equipment, but do not imagine for a moment that will prevent them from using it. The Royal Navy has contingency plans to continue high-level operations in the event that Kulu loses every single He_3 cloudscoop in the Kingdom. We can fly for years, conceivably decades, using deuterium alone should the need arise."

"So lack of He_3 isn't going to stop him?" the King asked.

"No, sir. Our analysts believe that given the internal nature of Capone's Organization he will have to continue his expansion efforts in order to survive. The Organization has no other purpose, growth through conquest is all it is geared up for. As a strategy for maintaining control over his own people it is excellent, but sooner or later he will run into size management problems. Even if he realizes this and tries to stop, his lieutenants will stage a coup. If they didn't they'd lose their status along with him."

"He seems to be running New California efficiently enough," Lord Mountjoy said.

"That's a propaganda illusion," the Duke of Salion said. "The agencies have come up with a similar interpretation as the navy. Capone boasts he has established a working government, but essentially it's a dictatorship backed by the threat of ultimate force. It survives principally because the planetary economy is on a war footing which always distorts financial reality for a while. This idea of a currency based on magic tokens is badly flawed. The energistic ability of the possessed is essentially unlimited, you cannot package it up and redistribute it to the have-nots as if it were some kind of tangible commodity.

"And so far no one has challenged Capone, he's moved too swiftly for that. But the Organization's internal political situation won't last. As soon as any kind of routine is established, people can start to look at how they are being made to live and consider it objectively. We estimate that serious underground opposition groups are going to start forming within another fortnight among both communities. From what we've actually seen and what we can filter through the propaganda, it would be very tough for possessed and non-possessed to live peacefully side by side. The society Capone has built is extremely artificial. That makes it easy to destroy, especially from within."

Lord Mountjoy smiled faintly. "You mean, we don't have to do anything but wait? The possessed will wipe themselves out for us?"

"No. I'm not saying that. Our psychologists believe that they cannot form societies as large or as complex as ours. We have system-wide industrial civilizations because that is what it takes to maintain our socioeconomic index. But when you can live in a palace grander than this one simply by wishing it to be, what is the point of having states whose populations run into hundreds of millions? That's what will eventually neuter Capone; but it doesn't get rid of the general problem which the possessed present. Not for us."

"I never thought a military solution was the right one, anyway," Alastair said with a contrite nod at the admiral. "Not in the long term. So what kind of threat are we facing from the possessed infiltrating us? Have we really caught all of them who were at liberty in the Kingdom? Simon?"

"Ninety-nine point nine per cent, Your Majesty, certainly here on Kulu itself. Unfortunately, I can't give you absolutes. Sheer probability dictates that several have eluded us. But the AIs are becoming increasingly proficient in tracking them down through the net. And of course, if they begin to build up in any numbers they become easy for us to spot and eradicate."

"Hardly good for morale, though," Lady Phillipa said. "Government can't guarantee you won't get possessed, but if it does happen don't worry, we'll see it."

"Admittedly inconvenient for individual subjects," Prince Howard observed. "But it doesn't affect our overall ability to respond to the threat. And the Kulu Corporation has already built a prototype personal monitor to safeguard against possession."

"You have?"

"Yes. It's a simple bracelet stuffed with various sensors which is linked permanently into the communications net. It'll stretch our bandwidth capacity, but two AIs can keep real-time tabs on every person on the planet. If you take it off, or if you are possessed, we'll know about it straightaway and where it happened."

"The civil rights groups will love that," she muttered.

"The possessed will not," Prince Howard said levelly. "And it is their opinion which matters the most."

"Quite," Alastair II said. "I shall publicly put on the first bracelet. It ought to help ease public attitude to the notion. This is for their own good, after all."

"Yes, Your Majesty," Lady Phillipa conceded with reasonable grace.

"Very well, we cannot guarantee absolute safety for the population, but as my brother says, we can still conduct broad policy. For the moment, I have to be satisfied with that. As to the principal thrust of that broad policy, we must make a decision about Mortonridge. Admiral?"

"My staff tactical officers have been running battle simulations along the lines young Hiltch suggested. His experience has been a lot of help, but for my mind there are an awful lot of variables and unknowns."

"Do we win any of these simulations?" the Duke of Salion asked.

"Yes. Almost all of them, providing we devote sufficient resources. That seems to be the clinching factor every time." He gave the King a worried look. "It's going to be risky, Your Majesty. And it is also going to be extremely costly. We must maintain our current defence status throughout the Kingdom simultaneously with running this campaign. It will take every military reserve we have, not to mention stretching our industrial capacity."

"That should keep the baronies happy," Lady Phillipa said.

Alastair II pretended he hadn't heard. "But it can be done?" he pressed the admiral.

"We believe so, Your Majesty. But it will require the full support of the Edenists. Ideally, I'd also like some material cooperation from the Confederation Navy and our allies. The more we have, the greater chance of victory."

"Very well. Kelman, this is your field. How did your audience with the Edenist ambassador go?"

The foreign minister attempted not to smile at the memory; he still wasn't sure which of them had been the more surprised. "Actually, Ambassador Astor was extremely receptive to the notion. As we know, the old boy doesn't exactly have the easiest of jobs here. However, once I asked, he immediately put the whole embassy over to working on the practical aspects. Their military and technology attachés agree that the Jovian habitats have the capacity to produce Tranquillity serjeants in the kind of quantities we envisage."

"What about commitment?" Prince Howard asked.

"Such a request would have to be put before their Consensus, but he was sure that given the circumstances Jupiter would consider it favourably. He actually offered to accompany whatever delegation we send and help present the argument for us. It might not sound like much, but I consider such an offer to be significant."

"Why exactly?" the King asked.

"Because of the nature of their culture. Edenists very rarely enact a Consensus, normally there is no need. They share so much in terms of ethics and motivation that their decisions on most subjects are identical. Consensus is only required when they confront something new and radical, or they are threatened and need to select a level of response. The fact that the ambassador himself is in agreement with our request and that he is willing to argue our case for us is a very positive factor. More than anyone, he understands what it has cost us to ask for their help in the first place, the pride we have swallowed. He can convey that for us."

"In other words, he can swing it," Prince Howard said.

"I consider it a high probability."

The King paused for a moment, weighing up the troubled faces confronting him. "Very well, I think we should proceed to the next stage. Admiral, start to prepare what forces you need to support the liberation of Mortonridge."

"Yes, Your Majesty."

"Kelman, the immediate burden rests upon your ministry. The admiral says he requires support from the Confederation Navy and our allies, it will be up to the diplomatic service to secure it. Whatever interests we have, I want them realized. I suggest you confer with the ESA to see what pressure can be applied to anyone displaying less than wholehearted enthusiasm."

"What level of assets do you want activated?" the Duke of Salion asked cautiously.

"All of them, Simon. We either do this properly or not at all. I am not prepared to commit our full military potential against such a powerful enemy unless we have total superiority. It would be morally unacceptable, as well as politically unsound."

"Yes, sir, I understand."

"Excellent, that's settled then."

"Um, what about Ione?" Lady Phillipa asked.

Alastair almost laughed openly at the Prime Minister's meekness. Not like her at all. Everyone did so tiptoe around the subject of Tranquillity in his presence. "Good point. I think it might be best if we employ family here to complement Kelman's people. We'll send Prince Noton."

"Yes, Your Majesty," Lord Mountjoy said guardedly.

"Any other topics?" the King asked.

"I think we've achieved all our aims, sir," Lady Phillipa said. "I'd like to announce that plans to liberate Mortonridge are under way. A positive step to regain the initiative will be just what people need to hear."

"But no mention of the Edenists," Lord Mountjoy interjected quickly. "Not yet, that still needs to be handled with care."

"Of course," she said.

"Whatever you think appropriate," Alastair told them. "I wish all of you good luck on your respective tasks. Let us hope Our Lord smiles on us, the sunlight seems to be decidedly lacking of late."

•   •   •

It was only the third time Parker Higgens had been invited into Ione's apartment, and the first time he'd been in alone. He found himself disturbed by the big window in the split-level entrance lounge which looked out into the circumfluous sea; the antics of the shoals of small fish flashing their harlequin colours as they sped about did not amuse him. Strange, he thought, that the threat of pressure which all that water represented should be so much more intimidating than the vacuum outside the starscraper windows.

Ione welcomed him with a smile and a delicate handshake. She was wearing a yellow robe over a glittering purple bikini, her hair still damp from her swim. Once again, as he had been right from the first moment he saw her, Parker Higgens was captivated by those enchanting blue eyes. His only comfort was that he wasn't alone in the Confederation, millions suffered as he did.

"Are you all right, Parker?" she inquired lightly.

"Yes, thank you, ma'am."

Ione gave the window a suspicious look, and it turned opaque. "Let's sit down."

She selected a small circular table made from a wood so darkened with age it was impossible to identify. A pair of silent housechimps began to serve tea from a bone china set.

"You seem to have made a lot of new friends in Trafalgar, Parker. An escort of four voidhawks, no less."

Parker winced. Did she have any idea how penetrating that irony of hers could be? "Yes, ma'am. The navy science analysts are here to assist with our interpretation of the Laymil recordings. The First Admiral's staff suggested the procedure, and I had to agree with their reasoning. Possession is a terrible occurrence, if the Laymil had a solution we should not stint in our efforts to locate it."

"Please relax, Parker, I wasn't criticising. You did the right thing. I find it most gratifying that the Laymil project has suddenly acquired so much importance. Grandfather Michael was right after all; a fact he must be enjoying. Wherever he is."

"You have no objection to the navy people scrutinizing the recordings, then?"

"None at all. It would be a rather spectacular feather in our cap if we did produce the answer. Although I have my doubts on that score."

"So do I, ma'am. I don't believe there is a single answer to this problem. We are up against the intrinsic nature of the universe itself, only God can alter that."

"Humm." She sipped her tea, lost in contemplation. "Yet the Kiint seem to have found a way. Death and possession doesn't bother them." For the first time ever she saw real anger on the old director's gentle face.

"They're not still working here are they, ma'am?"

"Yes, Parker, they're still here. Why?"

"I fail to see the reason. They knew all along what had happened to the Laymil. Their whole presence here is some absurd charade. They never had any intention of helping us."

"The Kiint are not hostile to the human race, Parker. Whatever their reasons are, I'm sure they are good ones. Perhaps they were gently trying to nudge us in the right direction. Who knows? Their intellects are superior to ours, their bodies too, in most respects. You know, I've just realized we don't even know how long they live. Maybe they don't die, maybe that's how they've beaten the problem."

"In which case they can hardly help us."

She stared at him coolly over the rim of her cup. "Is this a problem for you, Parker?"

"No." His jaw muscles rippled as he fought his indignation. "No, ma'am, if you value their input to the project I will be happy to set aside my personal objection."

"Glad to hear it. Now, there are still four thousand hours of sensorium records in the Laymil electronics stack which we haven't accessed yet. Even with the new teams you brought it's going to take a while to review them all. We'll have to accelerate the process."

"Oski Katsura can construct additional reformatting equipment, that ought to speed things along. The only area of conflict I can see is weapons technology. You did say you wished to retain the right of embargo, ma'am."

"So I did." He has a point. Do I really want to hand Laymil weapons over to the Confederation, no matter how noble the cause?

It is no longer a relevant question, Tranquillity said. We know why the spaceholms committed suicide. Our earlier assumption that it was inflicted by an external force is demonstrably incorrect. Therefore your worry that the data for some type of superweapon exists is no longer applicable. No superweapon was designed or built.

You hope! What if the spaceholms built one to try and stop the approach of the possessed Laymil ships?

Given the level of their knowledge base at the time of their destruction, any weapons built in defence of the spaceholms would not be noticeably different to our own. They did not think in terms of weapons; whereas there is a case to be made for plotting human history in terms of weapons development. It may well be that anything the Laymil came up with would be inferior.

You can't guarantee that. Their biotechnology was considerably more advanced than Edenist bitek.

It was impressive because of its scale. However, their actual development was not much different to the Edenists. There is little risk of you worsening the situation by allowing unlimited access to the recordings.

But not zero?

Of course not. You know this, Ione.

I know it. "I think we'd better rescind that proscription for the time being," she told Parker Higgens.

"Yes, ma'am."

"Is there anything else we can do to assist the Confederation Navy? Our unique position here ought to count for something."

"Their senior investigator came up with two suggestions. Apparently Joshua Calvert said he found the original electronics stack in some kind of fortress. If he were to supply us with the coordinate of this structure we could explore it to see what other electronics remain. If one stack can survive undamaged, then there must be others, or even parts of others. The data in those crystals is priceless to us."

Oh, dear, Tranquillity said.

Don't you dare go all sarcastic on me, not after Joshua agreed to find the Alchemist. We both agreed he's grown up a lot since that time.

Unfortunately his earlier legacy remains.

Just in time she guarded herself against a scowl. "Captain Calvert isn't here at the moment. But, Parker, I'd advise against too much optimism. Scavengers are notorious braggarts, I'd be very surprised if this fortress he spoke of exists in quite the same condition he claimed."

Neeves and Sipika may have the coordinate, Tranquillity said. They might cooperate. If not, we are in an official state of emergency; debrief nanonics could be used.

Well done. Send a serjeant in there now to interview them. Make it clear that if they don't tell us voluntarily it'll be extracted anyway. "I'll see what can be done," she said in the hope of countering his disappointed expression. "What was the other suggestion?"

"A thorough scan of Unimeron's orbital track. If the planet was taken into another dimension by Laymil possessed there may be some kind of trace."

"Surely not a physical one? I thought we had this argument before."

"No, not a physical one, ma'am. We thought, instead, there may be some residual energy overspill in the same way the possessed betray their presence. It may be there is a detectable distortion zone."

"I see. Very well, look into it. I'll authorize any reasonable expenditure for sensor probes. The astroengineering companies should welcome the work now I've stopped ordering weapons for the SD network. We might even get some competitive prices."

Parker finished his tea, not quite certain he should ask what he wanted to. The responsibilities of the project directorship were sharply defined, but then he was only human. "Are we well defended, ma'am? I heard about Arnstadt."

Ione smiled, and bent down to scoop Augustine from the floor. He'd been trying to climb the table leg. "Yes, Parker, our defences are more than adequate." She ignored the old director's astonishment at the sight of the little xenoc, and stroked Augustine's head. "Take it from me, the Capone Organization will never get into Tranquillity."

3

Hull plate 8-92-K: lustreless grey, a few scratches where tools and careless gauntlets had caught it, red stripe codes designating its manufacturing batch and CAB permitted usage, reactive indicator tabs to measure radiation and vacuum ablation still a healthy green; exactly the same as all the other hexagonal plates protecting the delicate systems of the *Villeneuve's Revenge* from direct exposure to space. Except it was leaking a minute level of electromagnetic activity. That was what the first scanner pad indicated. Erick hurriedly applied the second over the centre of the source. The sensor block confirmed a radiation emission point. Density analysis detailed the size of the entombed unit, and a rough outline of its larger components.

"I got it, Captain," Erick datavised. "They incorporated it in a hull plate. It's small, electron compressed deuterium tritium core, I think; maybe point two of a kiloton blast."

"You're sure?"

Erick was too tired to be angry. This was his ninth search, and they were all imposing far too much stress on his convalescent body. When he finished each ten-hour session spent snaking through the starship's innards he had to go straight on bridge duty to maintain the illusion of normal shipboard routine for Kingsley Pryor and the eight rover reporters they were carrying. On top of that the Organization had played dirty. Just as he knew they would.

"I'm sure."

"Thank the blessed saints. Finally! Now we can escape these devils. You can deactivate it, can't you, *mon enfant?*"

"I think the best idea would be to detach the plate and use the X-ray lasers to vaporise it as soon as it's clear."

"Bravo. How long will it take?"

"As long as it does. I'm not about to rush."

"Of course."

"Are there any reasonable jump coordinates in this orbit?"

"Some. I will begin plotting them."

Erick slowly swept the rest of the little cavity for any further incongruous processors. Opposite the hull plate was a spiral of ribbed piping, resembling a tightly coiled dragon's tail, which led to a heat exchange pump. He had emerged at its rim, wedged between the curving titanium and a cluster of football-sized cryogenic nitrogen tanks which pressurized the vernier rockets. A small, cramped space, but one providing a hundred crannies and half-hidden curves. It took him half an hour to sweep it properly, forcing himself to be methodical. Not easy with an armed mini-nuke eighty centimetres from his skull, its timer counting down.

When he was satisfied there were no booby triggers or alarms secreted in the cavity, he squirmed around to face the hull and eased himself further out of the crawlway like paste from a tube.

Normally, a starship's hull plates were detached from the outside, with the seam rivets and load pins easily accessible. This was a lot more difficult. The arcane procedure for an internal jettison ran through Erick's neural nanonics, an operation which must surely have been dreamed up by committees of civil servant lawyers on permanent lunch breaks and with no knowledge of astroengineering. It was highly tempting just to shove a fission blade into the silicon and saw around the mini-nuke in a wide circle. Instead he datavised the flight computer to switch off the sector's molecular binding force generator, then applied the anti-torque screwdriver to the first feed coupling. It might have been imagination, but he thought his new AT arm was slower than the other. The nutrient reserves were almost depleted. His thoughts were too cluttered to really bother about it.

Eighty minutes later, the plate was ready. The little cavity swarmed with discarded rivets, load pins, flakes of silicon, and several tool heads he'd lost. His suit sensors were having trouble supplying him with a decent image through all the junk. He slotted the last tools back in his harness and wriggled even further out of the crawlway, feeling around with his toes for a solid foothold to brace himself against. When he was in position he was bent almost double with his back pressing against the plate. He started to shove, his leg muscles straining hard. Physiological monitor programs began signalling caution warnings almost immediately. Erick ignored them, using a tranquillizer program to damp down the swelling worry about the further damage he was causing himself.

The plate moved—neural nanonics recording a minute shift in his posture. Then he was rising in millimetre increments. He waited until the neural nanonics reported the plate had shifted five centimetres, then stopped pressing. Inertia would complete the work now. Cramp persecuted his abdomen.

A wide sliver of silver-blue light shone into the cavity as he retreated back down into the crawlway. One edge of the plate was loose, rising up out of alignment. His suit collar sensors hurriedly reduced their receptivity as the beam animated the rivet fragments into a glittering storm.

The plate lumbered upwards. Erick checked the edges one last time to see if they were all clear, then datavised: "Okay, Captain, it's free. Fire the verniers. Let's separate."

He could actually see the silent eruptions of the tiny chemical rocket nozzles ringing the starship's equator, quick luminous yellow fountains. The hull plate appeared to be moving faster now, receding from the cavity.

Kursk was visible outside. The *Villeneuve's Revenge* was in low orbit, soaking in the wellspring of lambent light shimmering off the planet's cloud-daubed oceans.

It was the Capone Organization's second conquest: a stage three world, six light-years from Arnstadt. With a population of just over fifty million, it was evolving from its purely planetary-based economic phase to develop a small space industry. Consequently, it was an easy target. There was no SD network, yet it had valuable modern astroengineering stations and a reasonable population. The squadron of twenty-five starships which Luigi Balsmao dispatched to subdue the planet had encountered almost no opposition. Five independent trader starships docked at Kursk's single orbiting asteroid settlement had been armed with combat wasps; but the weapons were third-rate, and the captains less than enthusiastic about flying out to die bravely against the Organization's superior firepower.

Along with the other escort ships, the *Villeneuve's Revenge* had been assigned to the new Organization squadron within eight hours of arriving at Arnstadt. A subdued but furious André was unable to refuse. They had even seen action, firing half a dozen combat wasps against the two defenders who had responded to their arrival.

With their depleted crew numbers, everyone had to be on the bridge during the last stage of the mission, which meant they couldn't continue their search for the bomb. Which in turn meant they couldn't duck out of the final engagement.

With the small battle won, and the planet open to Capone's landing forces, the *Villeneuve's Revenge* had been given orbital clearance duties by the squadron commander. Tens of thousands of tiny fragments thrown out by detonating combat wasps now contaminated space around the planet, each one presenting a serious potential impact hazard to approaching starships. Combat sensor clusters on the *Villeneuve's Revenge* were powerful enough to track anything larger than a snowflake that came within a hundred kilometres of the fuselage. And André was using the X-ray laser cannons to vaporise any such fragment they located.

Erick watched hull plate 8-92-K shrink, a small perfect black hexagon against the glittery deep turquoise ocean. It turned brilliant orange in an eyeblink, then burst apart.

"I think it is time we had a small discussion with Monsieur Pryor," André Duchamp datavised to his crew.

*   *   *

It was almost as if the Organization's liaison man was expecting them when André datavised his command code to open the cabin door. It was Kingsley Pryor's designated sleep period, but he was fully dressed, floating in lotus position above the decking. His eyes were open, showing no surprise at the two laser pistols levelled at him.

Nor fear, Erick thought.

"We have eliminated the bomb," André said triumphantly. "Which means you have just become surplus to requirements."

"So you're going to slaughter the other crews, are you?" Kingsley said quietly.

"Pardon?"

"I have to transmit a code every three hours—seven at the most, remember? If that doesn't happen one of the other starships will explode. Then they won't be in any position to transmit their code, and another will go. You'll start a chain reaction."

André maintained his poise. "Obviously, we will warn them we are leaving before we jump outsystem. Do you take me for a barbarian? They will have time to evacuate. And Capone will have five ships less." There was a glint in his eye. "I will make sure the rover reporters understand that. My ship and crew are striking right at the heart of the Organization."

"I expect Capone will be devastated at the news. Deprived of a warrior like you."

André glared furiously; he could never manage sarcasm, however crude, and he hated being on the receiving end. "You may inform him yourself. We will return you to him via the beyond." His grip on the laser pistol tightened.

Kingsley Pryor switched his glacial eyes to Erick, and datavised: "You have to stop them murdering me."

The message was encrypted with a Confederation Navy code.

"Knowing the nature of the possessed, I expect that code was compromised a long time ago," Erick datavised back.

"Very likely. But do your shipmates know you are a CNIS

officer? You'd join me in the beyond if they did. And I'll tell them. I have absolutely nothing to lose, now. I haven't for some time."

"Who the fuck are you?"

"I served a duty tour in the CNIS weapons division as a technical evaluation officer. That's why I know who you are, Captain Thakrar."

"As far as I'm concerned that makes you a double traitor, to humanity and the navy. And Duchamp won't believe a word you say."

"You need to keep me alive, Thakrar, very badly. I know which star system the Organization is planning to invade next. Right now, there is no more important piece of information in this whole galaxy. If Aleksandrovich and Lalwani know the target, they can intercept and destroy the Organization fleet. You now have no other duty but to get that information to them. Correct?"

"Filth like you would say anything."

"You can't risk the possibility that I'm lying. I obviously have access to the Organization's command echelons, I wouldn't be in this position if I didn't. Therefore I could quite easily know their overall strategic planning. At the very least, procedure says I should be debriefed."

The decision seemed more enervating than all that time spent in the cavity working on the hull plate. Erick was repelled by the notion that a piece of shit like Pryor could manipulate him. "Captain?" he said wearily.

"Oui?"

"How much do you think he's worth if we turn him over to the Confederation authorities?"

André gave his crewman a surprised look. "You have changed since you came on board, *mon enfant.*"

Since Tina . . . who wouldn't? "We're going to be in the shit with the Confederation when we return. We did sign up with Capone, remember, and we helped with this invasion. But if we bring them a prize like this, especially if we do it in full view of the rovers, we'll be heroes; it'll wipe the slate clean."

As always, avarice won with Duchamp. His gentle face's natural smile expanded with admiration. "Good thinking, Erick. Madeleine, help Erick stuff this pig into zero-tau."

"Yes, Captain." She pushed off the hatch rim and grabbed hold of Pryor's shoulder. On the way she couldn't resist giving Erick a troubled look.

He couldn't even raise a regretful grin in response. *I thought it was over, that getting rid of the bomb would finish it. We would dock at some civilized spaceport, and I could turn them all over to the local Navy Bureau. Now all I've done is swapped one problem for another. Great God Almighty, when is this all going to end?*

• • • •

The beyond was different, not changed, but the rents which tore open into the real universe fired in flashes of sensation. They enraged and exhilarated the souls which dwelt there; a pathetic taster, a reminder of what used to be. Proof that corporeal life could be theirs again.

There was no pattern to the rents. The beyond did not have a structured topology. They occurred. They ended. And each time a soul would wriggle through to possess. Luck, chance, dictated their appearance.

The souls screamed for more, scrabbling at the residual traces of their more fortunate comrades who had made it though. Pleading, praying, promising, cursing. The tirade was one-way. Almost.

The possessed had the power to look back, to listen harder.

One of them said: We want somebody.

The gibbering souls shrieked their lies in return. I know where they are. I know how to help. Take me. Me! I will tell you.

The chant of a billion tormented entities is not one to be ignored.

Another rent appeared, loud sunlight piercing an ebony cloud. There was a barrier at the top, preventing any soul

from surging through into the glory. Its extended existence
igniting an agonized desire within those who flocked around
it.

See? A body awaits you, a reward for the information we
need.

What? What information?

Mzu. Dr Alkad Mzu, where is she?

The question rippled through the beyond, a virus rumour,
passed—ripped—from one soul to another. Until, finally,
the woman came forth, rising from the degradations of perpetual mind-rape to embrace and adore the pain which saturated her new body. Feelings rushed in to inflate
consciousness: warmth, wetness, cool air. Eyes blinked
open, half laughing, half-weeping at the agony of her
scalded, skinless limbs. "Ayacucho," Cherri Barnes coughed
to the gangsters standing over her. "Mzu went to Ayacucho."

• • • •

The top secret file contained a report which the First Admiral found even more worrying than any naval defeat. It had
been written by an economist on President Haaker's staff,
detailing the strain which possession was placing on the
Confederation economy. The major problem was that modern conflicts tended to be resolved by fifteen-minute engagements between opposing squadrons of starships; fast,
and usually pretty decisive. It was an exceptional dispute
which led to more than three navy engagements.

Possession, though, was shutting down the interstellar
economy. Tax revenue was falling, and with it the government's ability to support its forces on month-long deployment missions. And the Confederation Navy placed the
primary drain on everyone's finances. Enforcing the quarantine was good strategic policy, but it wasn't going to solve
the problem. A new strategy, one which had to include a
final solution, had to be found within six months. After that,
the Confederation would start to fragment.

Samual Aleksandrovich exited the file as Maynard

Khanna ushered the two visitors into his office. Admiral Lalwani and Mullein, the captain of the voidhawk *Tsuga*, both saluted.

"Good news?" Samual Aleksandrovich asked Lalwani. It had become a standing joke at the start of their daily situation meetings.

"Not entirely negative," she said.

"You amaze me. Sit down."

"Mullein has just arrived from Arnstadt; *Tsuga* has been on intelligence gathering duties in that sector."

"Oh?" Samual cocked a thick eyebrow at the youngish Edenist.

"Capone has invaded another star system," Mullein said.

Samual Aleksandrovich swore bitterly. "That's not negative?"

"It's Kursk," Lalwani said. "Which is interesting."

"Interesting!" he grunted. His neural nanonics supplied him with the planet's file. Not *knowing* the world he was supposed to protect kindled obscure feelings of guilt. Its image appeared on one of the office's long holoscreens, just a perfectly ordinary terracompatible world, dominated by large oceans.

"Population fifty million plus," Samual Aleksandrovich recited from the file. "Hell. The Assembly will combust, Lalwani."

"They've no right," she said. "Your original confinement strategy is working very effectively."

"Apart from Kursk."

She ducked her head in acknowledgement. "Apart from Kursk. But then that isn't due to the quarantine order failing. The quarantine was intended to prevent stealthy infiltration, not armed invasions."

Samual's mind went back to the classified report. "Let's hope the noble ambassadors see it that way. Why did you say it was interesting?"

"Because Kursk is a stage three world: no naval forces, no SD network. A pushover for the Organization. However, all they earned themselves was a few orbital industrial stations and a big struggle to quash the planetary population, the majority of whom live in the countryside, they're still very agrarian. In other words, the possessed are up against small, solid communities of well-armed farmers who have had plenty of advance warning."

"But possessed forces backed up by starships, nonetheless," Samual observed.

"Yes, but why bother possessing fifty million people who can make no positive contribution to the Organization?"

"Possession makes no sense generally."

"No, but Capone's Organization needs sound economic support, certainly his fleet does. It won't operate without a functioning industrial capacity behind it."

"All right, you've convinced me. So what analysis has your staff come up with?"

"We believe it was principally a propaganda move. A stunt, if you like. Kursk wasn't a challenge to him, and it isn't an asset. Its sole benefit comes from the psychology. Capone has conquered another world. He's a force to be reckoned with, the king of the possessed. That kind of garbage. People aren't going to look at how strategically insignificant Kursk is, all they'll think about is that damn exponential expansion curve. It's going to place a lot of political pressure on us."

"The President's office has requested a briefing on the new development in two hours, sir," Maynard Khanna said. "It will be reasonable to assume the Assembly will follow that up with a request for some kind of large-scale high-visibility military deployment. And a victory. It will be expedient for the politicians to demonstrate the Confederation can strike at the enemy, that they're not sitting back doing nothing."

"Wonderfully precise thinking," Samual Aleksandrovich grumbled. "National navies have only released seventy per cent of the forces pledged to us; we are barely managing to enforce the quarantine; we can't track down where the hell Capone's antimatter is coming from. Now they expect me to ransack what forces I have to build some kind of interdiction flotilla. I wonder if they'll give me a target, too, because I certainly can't see one. When will people learn that if we kill the possessed bodies all we're doing is simply adding to the numbers of souls in the beyond; and I doubt the families of those we kill will thank us."

"If I can offer a suggestion, sir," Mullein said.

"By all means."

"As Lalwani said, *Tsuga* has been collecting intelligence from Arnstadt. It's our contention that Capone isn't having it all his own way, not down on the planet itself. The SD platforms are having to fire on almost an hourly basis to support the Organization lieutenants on the surface. There is a lot of resistance down there. The Yosemite Consensus believes that if we were to start harassing the ships and industrial stations Capone has in orbit, it would make life very difficult for him. Constant reinforcement over interstellar distances is going to place a considerable strain on his resources."

"Maynard?" the First Admiral asked.

"Possible, sir. The general staff already has appropriate contingency plans."

"When don't they?"

"Primarily, it would mean the observation voidhawks seeding Arnstadt's orbital space with stealthed fusion mines; a decent percentage should manage to trickle past the SD sensors. Equip them with mass-proximity fuses and any ships down there would be in deep trouble. No one would know when an attack was coming; it would rattle the crews once they realized we were blitzing them. Fast-strike missions could also be mounted against the asteroid settlements; jump a ship in, fire off a random salvo of combat wasps, and jump out again. Something similar to the Edenist attack against Valisk. It would have the advantage that we were mainly destroying hardware rather than people."

"I want the feasibility studies run today," the First Admiral said. "Include Kursk as well as Arnstadt. That'll give me something concrete when I'm called to explain this latest fiasco to the Assembly." He gave the young voidhawk captain a speculative gaze. "What exactly is Capone's fleet doing right now?"

"Most of it is spread through the Arnstadt system, keeping the asteroid settlements in line until their populations are fully possessed. A lot of captured ships are being flown back to New California, we assume to be armed ready for his next invasion. But it's a slow job; he's probably short of crews."

"For once," Lalwani said sorely. "I can't get over how many of those independent trader bastards went to work for him."

"Recruitment is slowing considerably now the quarantine is in place," Maynard Khanna said. "Even the independent traders are reluctant to take Capone's money now they've heard about Arnstadt, and the Assembly's proclamation must have had some effect."

"That or they're too busy raking it in by breaking the quarantine, I expect." She shrugged. "We've been getting reports; some of the smaller asteroids are still open to flights."

"There are times when I wonder why we bother," Samual Aleksandrovich marvelled. "Thank you for the briefing, Mullein, and my gratitude to *Tsuga* for a swift flight."

"Has Gilmore made any progress?" Lalwani asked when the captain had left.

"He won't admit it, but the science teams are stumped," Samual Aleksandrovich said. "All they can come up with is a string of negatives. We're learning a lot about the capabilities of this energistic ability, but nothing about how it is generated. Nor have Gilmore's people acquired any hard data on the beyond. I think that worries me the most. It obviously exists, therefore it must have some physical parameters, a set of governing laws; but they simply cannot detect or define them. We know so much about the physical universe and how to manipulate its fabric, yet this has defeated our most capable theorists."

"They'll keep at it. The research teams at Jupiter have done no better. I know that Govcentral have established a similar project; and no doubt the Kulu Kingdom will be equally industrious."

"I think in this instance they might all even be persuaded to cooperate," Samual Aleksandrovich mused. "I'll mention it during my presidential briefing, it'll give Olton something to concentrate on."

Lalwani shifted around in her chair, leaning forwards slightly as if she was discomforted. "The one piece of genuinely good news is that we believe Alkad Mzu has been sighted."

"Praise the Lord. Where?"

"The Dorados. Which lends a considerable degree of weight to the report. That's where seventy per cent of the Garissan refugees finished up. There is a small underground movement there. She'll probably try to contact them. We infiltrated them decades ago, so there shouldn't be any problem."

Samual Aleksandrovich gave his intelligence chief a pensive stare. He had always been able to rely on her utterly. The height of the stakes these days, though, were breaking apart all the old allegiances. Damn Mzu's device, he thought, the alleged potency of the thing even gnaws at trust. "Which 'we' is that, Lalwani?" he asked quietly.

"Both. Most intelligence agencies have assets in the underground."

"That's not quite what I meant."

"I know. It's going to be down to the agents on the ground, and who reaches her first. For me personally, Edenist acquisition would not be an unwelcome outcome. I know we won't abuse the position. If CNIS obtains her, then as admiral of the service I will follow whatever orders the Assembly's Security Commission delivers concerning her disposal. Kulu and the others could give us a problem, though."

"Yes. What do the Edenists propose to do if you get her?"

"Our Consensus recommends zero-tau storage. That way she will be available should the Confederation ever face an external threat which needs something as powerful as the Alchemist to defend it."

"That seems a logical course. I wonder if the Alchemist could help us against the possessed?"

"Supposedly, it's a weapon of enormous destructive power. If that's true, then like every weapon we have in our arsenal today, it will be utterly ineffective against the possessed."

"You're right of course. Unfortunately. So I suppose we are going to have to depend on Dr Gilmore and his ilk for a solution." And I wish I had the confidence I should have in him. Saviour-to-be is a terrible burden for anyone to carry around.

•   •   •

It was the one sight Lord Kelman Mountjoy had never expected to see. His job had taken him to countless star systems; he had stood on a beach to watch a binary dawn over the sea, admired Earth's astonishing O'Neill Halo from a million kilometres above the north pole, enjoyed lavish hospitality in the most exotic locations. But as Kulu's foreign minister, Jupiter was always destined to be *verboten*.

Now, though, he accessed the battle cruiser's sensor suite throughout the entire approach phase. The starship was accelerating at one and a half gees, carrying them down towards the five-hundred-and-fifty-thousand-kilometre orbital band occupied by the Jovian habitats. Two armed voidhawks from the Jovian defence fleet were escorting the warship in. Just a precaution, Astor had assured them. Kelman had accepted gracefully, though most of the Royal Navy officers were less charitable.

The habitat Azara was looming large ahead of them, a circular spaceport disk extending out of its northern endcap. Although Edenism didn't have a capital, Azara played host to all of the foreign diplomatic missions. Even the Kingdom maintained an embassy at Jupiter.

"I still can't get used to the scale here," Kelman confessed as the acceleration began to fluctuate. Their approach was in its final stages, the battle cruiser flowing through the thick traffic lanes of inter-orbit ships towards the spaceport. "Whenever we build anything large it always seems so ugly. Of course, technically the Kingdom does own one bitek habitat."

"I thought Tranquillity was independent," Ralph Hiltch said.

"Great-grandfather Lukas granted its title to Michael as an independent duchy," Prince Collis said affably. "So, strictly speaking, in Kulu law, my father is still its sovereign. But I'd hate to try and argue the case in court."

"I didn't know," Ralph said.

"Oh, yes. I'm quite the amateur expert on the situation," Prince Collis said. "I'm afraid we do all harbour a rather baroque interest in Cousin Ione and her fiefdom. All of my siblings access the official file on Tranquillity at some time while we're growing up. It's fascinating." Alastair II's youngest child smiled whimsically. "I almost wish I'd been sent with that delegation instead of Prince Noton. No offence," he added for Astor's benefit.

"Your Highness," the Edenist ambassador murmured. "This would seem to be the time for breaking taboos."

"Indeed. And I shall do my best to throw off my childhood prejudices. But it will be hard. I'm not accustomed to the notion of the Kingdom being dependent on anyone."

Ralph looked across the small lounge. All of the acceleration couches had tilted down from the horizontal, transforming into oversized armchairs. Ambassador Astor lay back bonelessly in his, a politely courteous expression on his face, as always. Ralph had no idea how he maintained it without the benefit of neural nanonics.

"Attempting to remedy a situation not of your making is hardly dishonourable, Your Highness."

"Oh, Ralph, do stop blaming yourself for Ombey," Kelman Mountjoy protested. "Everyone thinks you've done a superb job so far. Even the King, which makes it official. Right, Collis?"

"Father thinks very highly of you, Mr Hiltch," the Prince confirmed. "I dare say you'll be lumbered with a title once this is over."

"In any case, I don't believe this proposed alliance could be said to make the Kingdom dependent on us," Astor said. "Liberating the possessed of Mortonridge is both necessary and advantageous to everyone. And if, afterwards, we understand each other a little better, then surely that's for the best, too."

Kelman exchanged an amused glance with Astor as Ralph Hiltch shuffled around in discomfort. For all that they came from totally different cultures, he and the Edenist shared remarkably similar rationalities. Communication and understanding came swiftly between them. It was a cause of growing dismay to Kelman that the freedom he'd enjoyed all his life, allowing him to develop his intellect, was maintained by guardians such as Ralph and the navy, who could never share his more liberal outlook. Small wonder, he thought, that history showed empires always rotted from the core outwards.

There were checks as soon as they docked. Brief almost-formalities; the inevitable test for static, confirmation that processors worked in their presence; verifications which everybody had to comply with. Including the Prince. Ambassador Astor made sure his own examination was a very public one. And Collis was charm personified to the two Edenists running sensors over him.

Azara's administrator was waiting with a small official reception committee at the spaceport's tube station. In most Edenist habitats, the post of administrator was largely ceremonial; though in Azara's case it had evolved into something approaching Edenism's foreign minister.

Quite a considerable crowd had assembled to see the delegation; mostly young, curious Edenists, and staff from the foreign embassies.

A smiling Collis listened to the administrator's short speech, replied with a few appropriate words, and said he was eager to see the inside of a habitat. The whole group ignored the waiting tube carriage and walked out of the station.

Ralph had never been inside a habitat either. He stood on the lawn outside the tube station and stared along the cylindrical landscape, mesmerized by the beauty of the sight. This was a lush, dynamic nature at its most majestic.

"Makes you wonder why we ever rejected bitek, doesn't it?" Kelman said quietly.

"Yes, sir."

The Prince was mingling among the crowd, smiling and shaking hands. Walkabouts were hardly a novelty for him, but this was unplanned, and he didn't have his usual retinue of ISA bodyguards, just a couple of dour-faced Royal Marines that everyone ignored. He was clearly enjoying himself.

Kelman watched a couple of the girls kiss him, and grinned. "Well, he is a real live prince, after all. I don't suppose they get to meet very many of them around here." He glanced up at the radiant axial light tube and the verdant arch of land overhead. There was something distinctly unnerving about knowing the vast structure was alive, and looking right back at him, its huge thoughts contemplating him. "I think I'm glad to be here, Ralph. And I think you had the right idea to ask for an alliance. This society really has a frightening potential, I never actually appreciated that before. I always thought it would be they who were the losers as a result of our foreign policy. I was wrong: no matter all the barriers and distance we throw up, they won't make the slightest difference to these people."

"It's too late to alter that now, sir. We're free of their energy monopoly. And I'm not sorry about that."

"No, Ralph, I don't suppose you are. But there are more aspects to life than the purely materialistic. I think both our cultures would benefit from stronger ties."

"You could say the same about every star system in the Confederation, sir."

"So you could, Ralph, so you could."

*   *   *

The second general Consensus within a month, and probably not the last within this year, it acknowledged wryly amid itself as it formed.

The most unfortunate aspect of Lord Kelman Mountjoy's request, Consensus decided, is its innate logic. Examination of the war simulations presented to us by Ralph Hiltch show a very real possibility that the liberation of Mortonridge will succeed. We acknowledge those among us who point out that this success is dependent on no further external factors being applied in the favour of the possessed. So already we see the risk rising.

Our major problem derives from the projected victory being almost totally illusory. We have already concluded that physical confrontation is not the answer to possession. Mortonridge simply confirms this. If it takes the combined strength of the two most powerful cultures in the Confederation to liberate a mere two million people on a single small peninsula, then freeing an entire planet by such a method clearly verges on the impossible.

Hopes across the Confederation would be raised to unreasonable heights by success at Mortonridge. Such hopes would be dangerous, for they would unleash demands local politicians will be unable to refuse and equally unable to satisfy. However, for us to refuse the Kingdom's request would cast us in the role of villain. Lord Kelman Mountjoy has been ingenious in placing us in this position.

"I would disagree," Astor told the Consensus. "The Saldanas know as well as us that military intervention is not the final answer. They too are presented with an enormously difficult dilemma by Mortonridge. As they are more susceptible to political pressures, they are responding in the only way possible.

"I would also say this: By sending the King's natural son with their delegation they are signalling the importance they attach to our decision, and an acknowledgement of what must inevitably come to be should our answer favour them. If both of us commit ourselves to the liberation there can be no return to the policies of yesterday. We will have established a strong bond of trust with one of the most powerful cultures in the Confederation currently contrary to us. That is a factor we cannot afford to ignore."

Thank you Astor, Consensus replied, as always you speak well. In tribute of this, we acknowledge that the future must be safeguarded in conjunction with the present. We are presented with an opportunity to engender a more peaceful and tolerant universe when the present crisis is terminated.

Such a raison d'être is not a wholly logical one to place ourselves on a war footing. Nor is the kindling of false hope which will be the inevitable outcome.

However, there are times when people do need such a hope.

And to err is human. We embrace our humanity, complete with all those flaws. We will tell the Saldana Prince that until such time that we can provide a permanent solution to possession he may have our support for this foolhardy venture.

• • •

After a five-day voyage, *Oenone* slipped out of its wormhole terminus seventy thousand kilometres above Jobis, the Kiint homeworld. As soon as they had identified themselves to the local traffic control (a franchise run by humans) and received permission to orbit, Syrinx and the voidhawk immediately started to examine the triad moons.

The three moons orbited the planet's Lagrange One point, four million kilometres in towards the F2 star. Equally sized at just under eighteen hundred kilometres in diameter, they were also equally spaced seventy thousand kilometres apart, taking a hundred and fifty hours to rotate about their common centre.

They were the anomaly which had attracted the attention of the first scoutship in 2356. The triad was an impossible formation, too regular for nature to produce. Worse, the three moons massed exactly the same (give or take half a billion tonnes—a discrepancy probably due to asteroid impacts). In other words, someone had built them.

It was to the scoutship captain's credit she didn't flee. But then fleeing was probably a null term when dealing with a race powerful enough to construct artefacts on such a scale. Instead, she beamed a signal at the planet, asking permission to approach. The Kiint said yes.

It was about the most forthcoming thing they ever did say. The Kiint had perfected reticence to an art form. They never discussed their history, their language, or their culture.

As to the triad moons, they were an "old experiment," whose nature was unspecified. No human ship had ever been permitted to land on them, or even launch probes.

Voidhawks, however, with their mass perception ability, had added to the sparse data over the centuries. Using Oenone's senses, Syrinx could feel the moons' uniformity; globes of a solid aluminum silicon ore right down to the core, free of any blemishes or incongruities. Their gravity fields pressed into space time, causing a uniquely smooth three-dimensional stretch within the local fabric of reality. Again, all three fields were precisely the same, and perfectly balanced, ensuring the triad's orbital alignment would hold true for billions of years.

A pale silver-grey in colour, they each had a small scattering of craters. There were no other features; perhaps the strongest indicator to their artificial origin. Nor could centuries of discreet probing by the voidhawks find any mechanical structures or instruments left anywhere. The triad moons were totally inert. Presumably, whatever the "experiment" was, it had finished long ago.

Syrinx couldn't help but wonder if the triad had something to do with the beyond and the Kiint's understanding of their own nature. No human astrophysicist had ever come up with any halfway convincing explanation as to what the experiment could be.

Maybe the Kiint just wanted to see what the shadows would look like from Jobis's surface, Ruben said. **The penumbra cones do reach back that far.**

It seems a trifle extravagant for a work of art, she countered.

Not really. If your society is advanced enough to build something like the triads in the first place, then logic dictates that such a project would only represent a fraction of your total ability. In which case it might well be nothing other than a chunk of performance art.

Some chunk. She felt his hand tighten around hers, offering comfort in return for the brief hint of intimidation she had leaked into the affinity band.

Remember, he said, we really know very little about the Kiint. Only what they choose to tell us.

Yes. Well I hope they choose to let slip a little more today.

The question over the true extent of the Kiint's abilities nagged at her as *Oenone* swept into a six-hundred-kilometre parking orbit. From space Jobis resembled an ordinary terracompatible world; although at fifteen thousand kilometres in diameter it was appreciably larger, with a gravity of one point two Earth standard. It had seven continents, and four principal oceans; axial tilt was less than one per cent, which when coupled with a suspiciously circular orbit around the star produced only mild climate variations, no real seasons.

For a world housing a race which could build the triads there was astonishingly little in the way of a technological civilization visible. Conventional wisdom had it that as Kiint technology was so advanced it could never resemble anything like human machinery and industrial stations, so nobody knew what to look for; either that or it was all neatly folded away in hyperspace. Even so, they must have gone through a stage of conventional engineering, an industrial age with hydrocarbon combustion and factory farming, pollution and exploitation of natural planetary resources. If so, there was no sign of it ever existing. No old motorways crumbling under the grasslands, no commercial concrete cities abandoned to be swallowed by avaricious jungles. Either the Kiint had done a magnificent job of restoration, or they had achieved their technological maturity a frighteningly long time ago.

Today, Jobis supported a society comprised of villages and small towns, municipalities perched in the centre of land only marginally less wild than the rest of the countryside. Population was impossible to judge, though the best guesstimate put it at slightly less than a billion. Their domes, which were the only kinds of buildings, varied in size too much for anyone to produce a reliable figure.

Syrinx and Ruben took the flyer down, landing at Jobis's only spaceport. It was situated beside a coastal town whose buildings were all human-built. White stone apartment blocks and a web of small narrow streets branching out from a central marina made it resemble a holiday destination rather than the sole Confederation outpost on this placid, yet most eerily alien of worlds.

The residents were employed either by embassies or companies. The Kiint did not encourage casual visits. Quite why they participated in the Confederation at all was something of a mystery, though one of the lesser ones. Their only interest and commercial activity was in trading information. They bought data on almost any subject from anyone who wanted to sell, with xenobiology research papers and scoutship logs fetching the highest prices. In exchange, they sold technological data. Never anything new or revolutionary, you couldn't ask for anti-gravity machines or a supralight radio; but if a company wanted its product improving, the Kiint would deliver a design showing a better material to use in construction or a way of reconfiguring the components so they used less power. Again, a huge hint to their technological heritage. Somewhere on Jobis there must be a colossal memory bank full of templates for all the old machines they'd developed and then discarded God-alone-knew how long ago.

Syrinx never got a chance to explore the town. She had contacted the Edenist embassy (the largest diplomatic mission on Jobis), explaining her mission, while *Oenone* flew into parking orbit. The embassy staff had immediately requested a meeting with a Kiint called Malva, who had agreed.

She's our most cooperative contact, Ambassador Pyrus explained as they walked down the flyer's airstairs. Which I concede isn't saying much, but if any of them will answer you, she will. Have you had much experience dealing with the Kiint?

I've never even met one before, Syrinx admitted. The landing field reminded her of Norfolk, just a patch of grass designated to accommodate inconvenient visitors. Although it was warmer, subtropical, it had the same temporary feel. Few formalities, and fewer facilities. Barely twenty flyers and spaceplanes were parked outside the one service hangar. The difference to Norfolk came from the other craft sharing the field, lined up opposite the ground-to-orbit machines. Kiint-fabricated, they resembled smaller versions of human ion field flyers, ovoid but less streamlined.

Then why were you sent? Pyrus asked, diffusing a polite puzzlement into the thought.

Wing-Tsit Chong thought it was a good idea.

Did he now? Well I can hardly contradict him, can I?

Is there anything I should know before I meet her?

Not really. They'll either deal with you or not.

Did you explain the nature of the questions I have?

Pyrus waved an empty hand around at the scenery. You told me when you contacted the embassy. We don't know if they can intercept singular-engagement mode, but I expect they can if they want. Next question of course is would they bother. You might like to ask Malva exactly how important we are to them. We've never worked that out either.

Thank you. Syrinx patted the top pocket of her shiptunic, feeling the outline of her credit disk. Eden had loaded it with five billion fuseodollars before she left, just in case. Will I have to pay for the information, do you think?

Pyrus gestured at the Kiint transport craft, and a hatch opened, the fuselage material flowing apart. It was close enough to the ground not to need airstairs. Syrinx couldn't quite judge if its belly was resting on the ground, or if it was actually floating.

Malva will tell you, Pyrus said. **I advise total openness.**

Syrinx stepped into the craft. The interior was a lounge, with four fat chairs as the only fittings. She and Ruben sat down gingerly, and the hatch flowed shut.

Are you all right? an anxious *Oenone* asked straight-away.

Of course I am. Why?

You started accelerating at roughly seventy gees and are currently travelling at Mach thirty-five.

You're kidding! Even as she thought it, she was sharing *Oenone*'s mind, perceiving herself streaking across a tall mountain range eight hundred kilometres inland from the town at an awesome velocity for atmospheric travel. **They must be very tolerant of sonic booms on this planet.**

I suspect your vehicle isn't producing one. My current orbital position doesn't allow optimum observation, but I can't locate any turbulence in your wake.

According to *Oenone*, the craft decelerated at seventy gees as well, landing some six thousand kilometres from the spaceport field. When she and Ruben stepped out a balmy breeze plucked at her silky ship-tunic. The craft had come to rest in a broad valley, just short of a long lake with a shingle beach. Cooler air was breathing down from the snowcapped peaks guarding the skyline, ruffling the surface of the water. Avocado-green grass-analogue threw thin coiling blades up to her knees. Trees with startlingly blue bark grew in the shape of melting lollipops, colonizing the valley all the way up to the top of the foothills. Birds were circling in the distance; they looked too fat to be flying in the heavy gravity.

A Kiint dome was situated at the head of the lake, just above the beach. Despite the fresh mountain air, Syrinx was perspiring inside her ship-tunic by the time they had walked over to it.

It must have been very old; it was made from huge blocks of a yellow-white stone that had almost blurred together. The weathering had given it a grainy surface texture, which local ivy-analogues put to good use. Broad clusters of tiny flowers dripped out of the dark leaves, raising their pink and violet petals to the sun.

The entrance was a wide arch, its border blocks carved with worn crestlike symbols. A pair of the blue-bark trees stood outside, gnarled from extreme age, half of their branches dead, but nonetheless casting a respectable shadow over the dome. Malva stood just inside, a tractamorphic arm extended, its tip formshifting to the shape of a human hand. Breathing vents issued a mildly spicy breath as Syrinx touched her palm to impossibly white fingers.

I extend my greetings to you and your mind sibling, Syrinx, the Kiint broadcast warmly. **Please enter my home.**

Thank you. Syrinx and Ruben followed the Kiint along the passage inside, down to what must have been the dome's central chamber. The floor was a sheet of wood with a grain close to red and white marble, dipping down to a pool in the middle which steamed and bubbled gently. She was sure the floor was alive, in fact the whole chamber's decor was organic-based. Benches big enough to hold an adult Kiint were like topiary bushes without leaves. Smaller ones had been grown to accommodate the human form. Interlocked patches of amber and jade moss with crystalline stems matted the curving walls, threaded with naked veins of what looked to be mercury. Syrinx was sure she could see them pulsing, the silver liquid oozing slowly upwards. An aura of soft iridescent light bounced and ricocheted off the glittery surface in playfully soothing patterns.

Above her, the dome's blocks capped the chamber. Except from inside they were transparent; she could see the geometric reticulation quite plainly.

All in all, Malva's home was interesting rather than revelational. Nothing here human technology and bitek couldn't reproduce with a bit of effort and plenty of money. Presumably it had been selected to put Confederation visitors at ease, or damp down their greed for high-technology gadgets.

Malva eased herself down on one of the benches. **Please be seated. I anticipate you will require physical comfort for this session.**

Syrinx selected a seat opposite her host. It allowed her to see some small grey patches on Malva's snowy hide, so pale they could have been a trick of the light. Did grey indicate aging in all creatures? **You are very gracious. Did Ambassador Pyrus indicate the information I would ask for?**

No. But given the trouble which now afflicts your race, I expect it is of some portent.

Yes. I was sent by the founder of our culture, Wing-Tsit Chong. We both appreciate you cannot tell me how we can rid ourselves of the possessed. However, he is curious about many aspects of the phenomenon.

This ancestor of yours is an entity of some vision. It is my regret I never encountered him.

You would be most welcome to visit Jupiter and talk to him.

There would be little point; to us a memory construct is not the entity, no matter how sophisticated the simulacrum.

Ah. That was my first question: Have the souls of Edenists transferred into the neural strata of our habitats along with their memories?

Is this not obvious to you yet? There is a difference between life and memory. Memory is only one component which comprises a corporeal life. Life begets souls, they are the pattern which sentience and self-awareness exerts on the energy within the biological body. Very literally: you think, therefore you are.

Life and memory, then, are separate but still one?

While the entity remains corporeal, yes.

So a habitat would have its own soul?

Of course.

So voidhawks have as well.

They are closer to you than your habitats.

How wonderful, *Oenone* said. **Death will not part us, Syrinx. It has never parted captains and ships.**

A smile rose to her face, buoyed by the euphoria of the voidhawk's thoughts. **I never expected it to, my love. You were always a part of me.**

And you I, it replied adoringly.

Thank you, Syrinx told Malva. **Do you require payment for this information?**

Information is payment. Your questions are informative.

You are studying us, aren't you?

All of life is an opportunity to study.

I thought so. But why? You gave up star travel. That must be the ultimate way to experience, to satisfy a curious mind. Why show an interest in an alien race now?

Because you are here, Syrinx.

I don't understand.

Explain the human urge to gamble, to place your earned wealth on the random tumble of a dice. Explain the human urge to constantly drink a chemical which degrades your thought processes.

I'm sorry, she said, contrite at the gentle chide.

Much we share. Much we do not.

That's what puzzles myself and Wing-Tsit Chong. You are not that different from us; ownership of knowledge doesn't alter the way the universe ultimately works. Why then should this prevent you from telling us how to combat the possessed?

The same facts do not bring about the same understanding. This is so even between humans. Who can speak of the gulf between races?

You faced this knowledge, and you survived.

Logic becomes you.

Is that why you gave up starflight? Do you just wait to die knowing it isn't the end?

Laton spoke only the truth when he told you that death remains difficult. No sentient entity welcomes this event. Instinct repels you, and for good reason.

What reason?

Do you embrace the prospect of waiting in the beyond for the universe to end?

No. Is that what happens to Klint souls, too?

The beyond awaits all of us.

And you've always known that. How can you stand such knowledge? It is driving humans to despair.

Fear is often the companion of truth. This too is something you must face in your own way.

Laton also called death the start of the great journey. Was he being truthful then as well?

It is a description which could well apply.

Syrinx glanced over to Ruben for help, not daring to use the singular engagement mode. She felt she was making progress, of sorts, even if she wasn't sure where it was leading—though some small traitor part of her mind resented learning that Laton hadn't lied.

Do you know of other races which have discovered the beyond? Ruben asked.

Most do. There was a tinge of sadness in Malva's thoughts.

How? Why does this breakthrough occur?

There can be many reasons.

Do you know what caused this one?

No. Though we do not believe it to be entirely spontaneous. It may have been an accident. If so, it would not be the first time.

You mean it wasn't supposed to happen?

The universe is not that ordered. What happens, happens.

Did these other races who found the beyond all triumph like the Klint?

Triumph is not the object of such an encounter.

What is?

Have you learned nothing? I cannot speak for you, Ruben.

You deal with many humans, Malva, Syrinx said. You know us well. Do you believe we can resolve this crisis?

How much faith do you have in yourself, Syrinx?

I'm not sure, not anymore.

Then I am not sure of the resolution.

But it is possible for us.

Of course. Every race resolves this moment in its history.

Successfully?

Please, Syrinx. There are only differing degrees of resolution. Surely you have realized this of all subjects cannot be a realm of absolutes.

Why won't you tell us how to begin resolving the crisis? I know we are not so different. Couldn't we adapt your solution? Surely your philosophy must allow you some leeway, or would helping us negate the solution entirely?

It is not that we cannot tell you how we dealt with the knowledge, Syrinx. If it would help, then of course we would; to do otherwise would be the infliction of cruelty. No rational sentient would condone that. We cannot advise you because the answer to the nature of the universe is different for each sentient race. This answer lies within yourselves, therefore you alone can search for it.

Surely a small hint—

You persist in referring to the answer as a solution. This is incorrect. Your thoughts are confined within the arena of your psychosocial development. Your racial youth and technological dependence blinds you. As a result, you look for a quick-fix in everything, even this.

Very well. What should we be looking for?

Your destiny.

• • •

The hold-down latches locked the *Tantu* into the docking cradle, producing a mechanical grinding. Quinn didn't like the sound, it was too final, metal fingers grasping at the base of the starship, preventing it from leaving unless the spaceport crew granted permission.

Which, he told himself, they would. Eventually.

It had taken Twelve-T almost a week to organize his side of the deal. After several broken deadlines and threats and high-velocity abuse, the necessary details had finally been datavised to the *Tantu*, and they'd flown down to Jesup, an asteroid owned by the government of New Georgia. The flight plan they'd filed with Nyvan's traffic control was for a cryogenic resupply, endorsed and confirmed by the Iowell Service & Engineering Company who had won the contract. As the fuel transfer didn't require the *Tantu*'s crew to disembark, there was no requirement for local security forces to check for signs of possession. The whole routine operation could be handled by Iowell's personnel.

When the docking cradle had lowered the frigate into the bay, an airlock tube wormed its way out of the dull metal wall to engage the starship's hatch. Quinn and Graper waited in the lower deck for the environmental circuit to be established.

The next five minutes, Quinn knew, were going to be crucial. He was going to have to use the encounter to establish his control over Twelve-T, while the gang lord would undoubtedly be seeking to assert his superiority at the same time. And although he didn't know it, Twelve-T had a numerical advantage. Quinn guessed there would be a troop of gang soldiers on the other side of the hatch, congested with weapons and hyped-on attitude. It's what he would have done.

What I need, he thought, is the kind of speed which boosting gives the military types. He felt the energistic power shifting inside his body, churning through his muscles to comply with his wishes. Light panels in the airlock chamber began to flicker uncertainly as his robe shrank around his body, eradicating any fabric which could catch against obstructions.

A cold joy of anticipation seeped up within his mind as he prepared to unleash his serpent beast on the waiting foe. For so long now he had been forced to restrain himself. It would be good to advance the work of God's Brother again, to watch pride shatter beneath cruelty.

Twelve-T waited nervously in the docking bay's reception chamber as the airlock pressurized. His people were spread around the dilapidated chamber, wedged behind tarnished support ribs, sheltered by bulky, broken-down cubes of equipment. All of them covered the ash-grey circular carbotanium hatch with their weapons, sensors focused and fire-control programs switched to millisecond response triggers.

That shit Quinn might have raged about the delays, but Twelve-T knew he'd put together a slick operation. This whole deal needed the master's touch. A fucking frigate, for shit's sake! He'd busted his balls arranging for the starship to dock without the cops realizing what was going down. But then the gang had interests all over New Georgia, half their money came from legitimate businesses. Companies like Iowell—a small operation established decades ago—were easy to muscle in on. The spaceport crew did as the union told them, managers could be persuaded to take their cut.

Getting his soldiers up to Jesup had been a bitch, too. Like him, they all had the gang's distinctive silver skull, skin from their eyebrows back to the nape of the neck had been replaced by a smooth cap of chrome flexalloy. Metal and composite body parts were worn like medals, showing how much damage you'd taken for the gang.

Try slipping twenty of them into Jesup without the administration cops taking an interest.

But he'd done it. And now he was going to find out just what the fuck was really going on. Because sure as turds floated to the top, Quinn Dexter wasn't on the level.

The instrument panel beside the hatch let out a weak bleep.

"It's ready," Lucky Vin datavised. "Shit, Twelve-T, I can't get anything from the sensors in the tube. They've crashed."

"Quinn do that, man?"

"I ain't too sure. This place . . . it ain't the maintenance hotspot of the galaxy, you know."

"Okay. Pop the hatch." He opened the datavise to include the rest of his soldiers. "Sharpen up, people, this is it."

The hatch seal disengaged, allowing the actuators to hinge it back. Absolute blackness filled the airlock tube.

Twelve-T craned his neck forwards, scar tissue stretching tightly. Even with his retinal implants switched to infrared there was nothing to see in the tube. "Screw this—"

The blackness at the centre of the tube bulged out, a bulbous cone devouring the chamber's photons. Five maser carbines and a TIP pistol fired, skewering the anti-light chimera from every direction. It broke open, petals of night peeling apart from the centre to splash against the chamber walls.

Twelve-T's neural nanonics began to crash. Blocks clipped to his belt chased them into electronic oblivion. The last datavise he received was from his maser carbine, telling him the power cells were dropping out. He tried to grasp the ten-millimetre machine gun velcroed to his hip, only to find his arm shuddering; the pistonlike actuators he'd replaced the forearm muscles with were seizing up.

A missile composed of tightly whorled shadow swelled up out of the centre of the flowering blackness. Too fast for the eye to follow in real-time—certainly as far as Twelve-T's faltering retinal implants were concerned—it shot across the chamber and bounced.

The first scream clogged the chamber's air. One of the soldiers was crumpling up, his body imploding in a series of rapid strikes. He seemed to be dimming, as if he were caught at the middle of a murky nebula. Then his head caved in, and it was blood not the sounds of agony that went spraying across the chamber.

A second soldier convulsed, as if she were trying to jam her head down towards her buttocks. She managed a single bewildered grunt before her spine snapped.

The third victim darkened, his clothes starting to smoulder. Both of his titanium hands turned cherry-red, glowing brightly. When he opened his mouth to scream a column of pink steam puffed out.

Twelve-T had it worked out by then. There was always a translucent cloud around the soldiers as they were slaughtered, a grey shadow that flickered at subliminal speed. His disabled arm levered the machine gun off the velcro, and he turned desperately towards the source of the latest screams. His soldiers were losing it, flinging themselves at the exit hatch, wrestling with each other in their struggle to escape.

The light panels were turning a dark tangerine and beginning to sputter; black iron grids had materialized across them, growing thicker. Oily smoke began to pour forth. The fractured buzzing sound of the conditioning fans was dying away. Globules of blood oscillated through the air, fringes rippling like restive jellyfish. Twelve-T knew then he'd been fucked. It wasn't Quinn Dexter, rat boy from the arcologies. This was the worst it could possibly get.

He'd never liked Nyvan. But what the fuck, it was his home planet. Now the possessed were going to violate it, subdue every living body. And he was the total fucking asshole who'd let them in.

Another of his soldiers was being chopped apart, haloed in quivering dusk. Pure fury powered Twelve-T's malfunctioning body into a final act of obedience. He swung the machine gun around on the macerated soldier and squeezed back on the trigger. It was only a short burst. A blue flame spat out of the muzzle to the accompaniment of a thunderous roar. Without a neural nanonics operational procedure program to help him, the recoil was far more powerful than he expected. His shoes were ripped free of the stikpad, and he was somersaulting backwards through the air, hollering in surprise.

The universe paused.

"Shatter!" a furious voice bellowed.

The machine gun obeyed, its cool silicolithium fragmenting like a shrapnel grenade. Needle slivers sliced deep into Twelve-T's flesh, some ricochetting off the metal casings of his replacement parts. He was flailing wildly now, trailing fantails of blood from his shredded hand.

"Hold him," someone instructed curtly.

Quinn slowed himself back from the speedstate, energistic currents sinking down to quiescent levels. As they did, the rest of the world began to accelerate. It had been awesome, moving through an airlock chamber populated by statues, time solidified to a single heartbeat. Their time, not his. God's Brother had granted him impunity from the actions of any non-possessed. What greater sign that he was indeed the chosen one?

"Thank you, my Lord," he whispered, humbled. Planets would truly bow before him now; just as Lawrence had prophesied.

Most of the blood had impacted on a surface, splattering wide into big smears and sticking tenaciously. Grotesque corpses drifted peacefully in the warm air streams. The remnants of the gang were in a sorry state. With four possessed in the airlock chamber and pulsing with malevolent power, their artificial body parts had either frozen or were running out of control. And they were all combat vets, heavily dependent on replacements, almost up to cosmonik level. Lawrence and Graper were plucking weapons from unresisting hands, claws, and wrist sockets.

Quinn kicked off towards Twelve-T. His robe resumed its usual extravagant cut as he glided across the compartment.

Twelve-T was sweating heavily. One of the soldiers whose arms were mostly the original organic was bandaging the gang lord's ruined hands with strips torn from his own T-shirt.

"I admire your strength," Quinn said. "It can be harnessed to serve God's Brother."

"Ain't no God, can't have no fucking—" Pain gripped his left arm, forcing him to cry out. His skin hissed as it rose in huge blisters.

"You wanted to irritate me," Quinn said mildly.

Twelve-T glowered helplessly. He wasn't used to so much pain, none of them were. Neural nanonics always protected them. That meant it was going to get bad, he realized, real bad. Unless . . .

"And I won't allow you to suicide," Quinn said. "I know

that's what you were thinking. Everybody does when they grab what's gonna happen."

The strips of cloth bandaging Twelve-T's hands hardened into shiny nylon. Their ends flexed up like blind snakes, then slowly knotted together.

"You're so close to me, Twelve-T," Quinn said earnestly. "Your serpent beast is almost free. You would never have become what you are without realizing what your true nature is. Don't hold back, embrace God's Brother. Live in the Night with us."

"You'll make a mistake, asshole. And I'll be around waiting for it."

"I don't make mistakes. I am the chosen one."

"Holy fuck."

"Follow me, Twelve-T. Submit to your true self and know the glory of His word. Betray your people for greed and profit. That way you will never know defeat again. My disciples fuck who they want when they want. They see their enemies burn in torment. Enjoy rewards you have never dared take before. Help me, Twelve-T. Tell me where the asteroid cops are. Shunt your gang's money into my credit disk. Show me where the spaceplanes are that can take my disciples down to the surface. Do it, Twelve-T."

"You won't get down to the planet," Twelve-T grunted. "People are too frightened of the possessed landing. There's all kinds of weird checks going on down there. You might have beaten my troops, big deal; but you dead freaks ain't going to turn my planet into holiday hellpark."

"You understand nothing," Quinn said. "I don't give a fuck about the souls in the beyond. I'm not here to save anyone, least of all them. God's Brother has chosen me to help Him bring down the Night."

"Oh, sweet shit," Twelve-T whimpered. Quinn was a loon. A motherfucking twenty-four-karat loon.

"I want two things from this planet," Quinn continued. "A starship I can use to take me home to Earth; because that's where I can hurt the Confederation most. It'll have to be a cargo ship of some kind, one which Govcentral's defences will accept is harmless. I'm sure there are plenty docked here right now, right?"

A small jaw muscle twitched on Twelve-T's face.

"Good," said Quinn. The gang lord's thoughts had betrayed him, bitter defeat mingling with the dregs of resentment and anger. "You want to know what the other thing is, don't you? It's simple, I intend Nyvan to be the first planet the Light Brother can bring into His kingdom. I'm going to bring the Night to this planet, Twelve-T. Endless Night. Night without hope. Until He comes from the other side of the beyond to grant you salvation."

Making sure every word was perfectly clear, Twelve-T said: "Go fuck yourself." He braced himself for the retribution.

Quinn laughed softly. "Not that easy, shithead. I told you, I want your help. I need a local smartarse to straighten out crap like a ship and how to sneak my possessed disciples past the pigs guarding the planet. Someone who knows all the access codes around here. And that's you, Twelve-T. As He chose me, so I have chosen you." He glanced around at the gang's remaining soldiers. "We'll open the rest of this worthless trash for possession; then convert all of Jesup. After that, nobody down below will be able to resist us."

"Oh, Jesus, help us," Twelve-T begged. "Please."

"Ain't no God," Quinn mimicked savagely. "So he ain't got no son, has he?" Laughing, he pushed Twelve-T down towards the decking. The gang lord's knees bent, allowing the stikpad to fasten to his trousers. Quinn stood in front of the supplicant and beckoned Lawrence over. "I know you're a tough mother, Twelve-T. If you're possessed you'll only try to fool your new owner, jazz me about as best you can. You and your dumb pride. I can't afford that kind of shit anymore. That means I'm gonna have to squeeze what I want to know out of you myself, so I know you're being honest."

Kneeling before the monster, head bowed, Twelve-T said: "I will never help you."

"You will. I have many ways of binding my disciples to

me. For most it is love or fear. For you, I choose dependence." He placed his hands on either side of Twelve-T's silver head. The feat was the converse of a coronation. Quinn lifted the silver cap from the gang lord's skull with an almost gentle reverence. It came loose with a soft sucking sound. The bone underneath was covered in a sticky red mucus. Ichor dribbled over Twelve-T's face, mingling with sticky tears.

Lawrence took the cap from Quinn, acting as jester to the king. A little mad giggle escaped from the boy's lips as he held it in front of the stricken gang lord, its mirror surface ensuring he witnessed his own reduction to impotent vassal.

Quinn's hands descended again. This time the noise was louder as the bone creaked and split. He lifted the top of the skull high, smiling at the bloody trophy. Twelve-T's naked brain glistened below him, wrapped in delicate membranes, small beads of fluid weeping up from the tightly packed ribbons of tissue.

"Now I can keep a real close eye on what you're thinking," Quinn said.

4

"So your group has no organized structure, as such?" Alkad asked.

"We're organized, all right," Lodi Shalasha insisted. "But nothing formal. We're just like-minded people who keep in touch and help each other out."

Alkad pushed her legs down into the chameleon suit trousers. There was still a residue of cold sweat smearing the fabric from when she'd worn the suit last night. Her nose wrinkled up in distaste, but she kept on working the trousers up her shins. "You said you had junior cadres, the ones clearing the spiders away. That sounds like a regular underground movement hierarchy to me."

"Not really. Some of us work in day clubs, that way we help to keep the memory of the genocide alive for the children. Nobody should be allowed to forget what was done to us."

"I approve."

"You do?" He sounded surprised.

"Yes. The original refugees seem to have forgotten. That's why I'm in this mess right now."

"Don't worry, Doctor; Voi will get you off Ayacucho."

"Perhaps." Alkad prided herself that the somnolence program had been for the best. When the girl had woken this morning she'd been subdued, but still functional. The grief for her father was still there, as it should be, but it hadn't debilitated her.

Over breakfast, Alkad had explained what her priorities were: to get away from the Dorados as fast as possible now her location was blown to the intelligence agencies, and the remaining principal requirement for a combat-capable starship (she still couldn't bring herself to mention the Alchemist). It would be too much to hope for the ship to be crewed by Garissan patriot types; a mercenary crew would just have to do now. The three of them had discussed possible options, and Voi and Lodi had started arguing over names, who to contact for what.

Voi had left by herself to secure a starship. It would be inviting disaster for Alkad to be seen with her again. As a pair they were too distinctive, however adroit the chameleon suits were at hiding their peripheral features.

"Hey, you've made the news." Lodi waved his communications block enthusiastically. He'd entered a reference search program to monitor the media output. "Access the Cabral NewsGalactic studio."

Alkad struggled the suit on over her shoulders, then datavised the room's net processor for a channel to the studio.

Cabral NewsGalactic was showing a recording of a holomorph sticker which had a young cheerleader shouting: "Run, Alkad, run!"

"Mother Mary," Alkad muttered. "Is this the work of your people?"

"No. I swear. I've never seen one before. Besides, only Voi and I know your name. None of the others even know you exist."

Alkad went back to the studio. A rover reporter was walking down one of Ayacucho's main public halls. The stickers were everywhere. A cleaner mechanoid was trying to spray one off the wall, but its solvent wasn't strong enough. Smears of black semi-dissolved plastic dribbled down the metallic wall panel.

"It is as if a plague has visited Ayacucho," the rover reporter said cheerfully. "The first of these stickers appeared about six hours ago. And if I didn't know better I'd say they've been breeding like bacteria. Police say that the stickers are being handed out to children; and detectives are currently correlating security monitor recordings to see if they can identify the main distributors. Though sources inside the public prosecutor's office tell me they're not sure exactly what charges could be brought.

"The question everyone is asking is: Exactly who is Alkad, and what is she running from?"

The image went back to the studio anchorman. "Our company's investigations have uncovered one possible answer to the mystery," he said in a sombre bass voice. "At the time of the genocide, the Garissan navy employed a Dr Alkad Mzu to work on advanced defence projects. Mzu is said to have survived the genocide and spent the last thirty years under an assumed name teaching physics at the Dorados university. But now foreign intelligence agencies, acting in response to Omutan propaganda, have started hunting her under the pretext of illegal technology violations. A senior member of the Dorados governing council, who asked not to be named, said today: 'Such an action by these foreign agents is a gross violation of our sovereignty. I find it obscene that the Omutans can lay these unfounded allegations against one of our citizens who has dedicated her life to educating our brightest youngsters. If this is their behaviour after thirty years of sanctions, then we must ask why the Confederation ever lifted those sanctions in the first place. They certainly do not seem to have had the desired effect in remedying the aggressive nature of the Omutan government. Their current cabinet is just a new collar on the same dog.'

"The council member went on to say that if Alkad Mzu turned up at his apartment he would certainly offer her sanctuary, and that every true Dorados citizen would do the same. He said he would not rest until all suspected foreign agents had been expelled from the asteroids."

"Holy Mother Mary," Alkad groaned.

She cancelled the channel and slumped down onto the bed, the suit's hood hanging flaccidly over her shoulder. "I don't believe this is happening. Mother Mary, they're turning me into a media celebrity."

"That's my uncle for you," Lodi said. "Did you check out

the positive bias in those reports? Mary, you'd be elected president tomorrow if we were ever allowed to vote around here."

"Your *uncle*?"

He flinched. "Yeah, sure. Cabral's my uncle. He's made a mint out of exploiting the little-Garissan attitude. I mean, just look at the kind of people living here, they lap it up."

"He's insane. What does he think he's doing giving me this kind of public profile?"

"Whipping up public support in your favour. This kind of propaganda is going to make life ten times harder for the agencies chasing you. Anyone tries to take you out of Ayacucho against your will today, they'll wind up getting lynched."

She stared at him. That eager face which permitted so much inner anger to show without ever dimming the natural innocence. Child of the failed revolutionaries. "You're probably right. But this isn't happening the way I ever expected it to."

"I'm sorry, Doctor." He pulled a worn shoulder bag out of the cupboard. "Do you want to try some of these clothes now?"

He was proffering some long sports shorts and an Ayacucho Junior Curveball Team sweatshirt. With a short cut wig and the chameleon suit reprogrammed, they intended her to walk out of the room as an average sports-mad teenager. A male one.

"Why not?"

"Voi will call soon. We ought to be ready."

"You really believe she can get us off this asteroid in a starship, don't you?"

"Yes."

"Lodi, do you have any idea how difficult that is to arrange, now of all times? Underground movements need to have contacts infiltrated right through the local administrative structure; dedicated, devoted people who will risk everything for the cause. What have you got? You're rich kids who've found a new way to rebel against their parents."

"Yes, and we can use that money to help you, if you'd just let us. Voi taught us that. If we need something, we buy it. That way there's no network for the agencies to discover and penetrate. We've never been compromised. That's why you stayed in this room all night without anyone storming the door with an assault mechanoid."

"You may have a point there. I have to admit the old partizans didn't do too well, did they." She gave the chameleon suit hood a reluctant grimace, then started to smooth back her hair ready to slip it on.

Joshua held the petri dish up to the cabin's light panel, squinting at the clear glass. It looked completely empty; his enhanced retinas couldn't even find dust motes. But lurking inside the optically pure dish were thirteen nanonic monitor bugs which the medical packages had extracted from *Lady Mac*'s crew and the serjeants. They were subcutaneous implants, agents stinging them by casually brushing up against an unsuspecting victim.

"How come I rated three?" Ashly complained.

"Obvious subversive type," Sarha said. "Bound to be up to no good."

"Thanks."

"You're all in the clear," she said. "The medical analysis program can't spot any unusual infections or viruses. Looks like they weren't playing nasty."

"This time," Joshua said. As soon as the scanners in the starship's surgery had located the first of the monitor bugs he'd ordered Sarha to run a full biochemical analysis on everyone. Microbes and viruses were far easier to introduce in a target than nanonics.

Fortunately, the agencies had been curious rather than hostile. But this was the sharpest reminder to date of the stakes involved. They'd been lucky thus far. It wouldn't last, he thought. And he wasn't the only one who realized that. The cabin had a kind of after-game locker-room atmosphere, with a team that was very relieved to have scraped a draw.

"Let's start from the beginning," he said. "Sarha, are we secure now?"

"Yes. These bugs can't datavise through *Lady Mac*'s screening. They're only a problem outside."

"But you don't know when we got stung?"

"There's no way of knowing, sorry."

"Your friend Mrs Nateghi," Melvyn suggested. "It was rather odd."

"You're probably right," Joshua said reluctantly. "Okay, assume everything we've done up until now has been compromised. First off, is there any point in continuing? Jesus, it's not as if we don't know she's here. The bloody news studios have been broadcasting nothing else. Our problem is how difficult it's going to be to contact her without anyone else tagging along. They're bound to try and sting us again. Sarha, will our electronic warfare blocks work against these monitor bugs?"

"They should be able to scramble them; we picked up top-of-the-range systems before we left Tranquillity."

"Fine. From now on, nobody goes into Ayacucho without one. We also take a serjeant each when we venture out. Ionc, I want you to carry those chemical projectile guns we brought."

"Certainly, Joshua," said one of the four serjeants in the cabin.

He couldn't tell if it was the one who'd accompanied him earlier. "Right, what kind of data have we pulled in so far? Melvyn?"

"Ashly and I got around to the five major defence contractors, Captain. The only orders coming in are for upgrades to the asteroid's SD platforms, and there's precious few of them. We got offered some magnificent discounts when we asked about supplying *Lady Mac* with new systems. They're absolutely desperate for work. Mzu hasn't ordered any equipment from anybody. And nobody is refitting starships."

"Okay. Beaulieu?"

"Nothing, Captain. Daphine Kigano disappeared within

fifteen minutes of arriving here. There's no eddress for her, no credit records, no hotel booking, no citizenship register, no public record file."

"All right. That just leaves us with Ikela."

"He's dead, Joshua," Dahybi said. "Hardly the best lead."

"Pauline Webb was very keen to stop me having any contact with T'Opingtu's management. Which means that's the direction to take. I've been reviewing every byte I can find on Ikela and T'Opingtu. He came to the Dorados with a lot of money to start up that company. There's no mention of where it came from; according to his biography he used to work for a Garissan engineering company as a junior manager. Which doesn't add up.

"Now if you were Alkad Mzu, on the run and in need of a starship that can deploy the Alchemist, who are you going to go to when you get here? Ikela fits the search program perfectly: the owner of a company which manufactures specialist astroengineering components. Remember she fooled the intelligence agencies for close on thirty years. Whatever plan she formatted with her colleagues after the genocide, it was well thought out."

"Not perfect, though," Ashly said. "If it was, Omuta's star would be turning nova right now."

"The possessed glitched it for them, that's all," Sarha said. "Who could anticipate this quarantine?"

"Whatever," Joshua said. "The point is, T'Opingtu was probably set up to provide Mzu with the means to deploy the Alchemist. Ikela would have made sure that policy continued in the event he didn't live long enough to see her arrive."

"Which he did, but only just," Ashly said. "It must have been the agencies who snuffed him."

"But not Mzu," Melvyn said. "This media campaign backing her sprang up too quickly after the murder. Somebody knows she's out there. Somebody with a shitload of influence, but not in contact with her. It's going to be almost impossible for us to snatch her with public opinion being whipped up like this, Captain."

"Which is exactly the intention," Dahybi said. "Though it's more likely aimed at the intelligence agencies rather than us."

"We'll deal with that problem if we ever get to it," Joshua said. "Right now our priority is to establish a trace on Mzu."

"How?" Sarha asked.

"Ikela has a daughter; according to his public record file she's the only family he's got."

"She'll inherit," Beaulieu said bluntly.

"You got it. Her name's Voi, and she's twenty-one. She's our way in to whatever organization her daddy built up in preparation for Mzu."

"Oh, come on, Joshua," Ashly protested. "Her father's just been murdered, she's not going to make appointments with perfect strangers, let alone tell us anything about the Garissan underground, even if she has any data. Which is questionable. I wouldn't involve my daughter in anything like that. And the agencies will be wanting to question her, too."

Joshua wasn't going to argue. As soon as he reviewed Ikela's public record file he'd known Voi was the link. Ione would call it his intuition. She might even have been right. The old burn of conviction was there. "If we can just get close to her, we stand a chance," he said firmly. "Mzu can't afford to remain here now. She's going to have to make a break for it, and sooner rather than later. One way or another, Voi will be involved. It's our best shot."

"I'm not disagreeing with you," Dahybi said. "It's as good a chance as any. But how the hell are you going to get near her?"

"Weren't you listening?" asked one of the serjeants. "Voi is female and twenty-one."

Joshua grinned evilly at Dahybi.

"You have got to be joking," the stupefied node specialist insisted.

"I'll just lie back and think of the Confederation."

"Joshua . . ."

Joshua burst out laughing. "Your faces! Don't worry,

Dahybi, I'm not that conceited. But she will have friends.
There are quite a lot of rich entrepreneurs in the Dorados,
their kids will cling together in their own little social clique.
And I am a starship owner captain, after all. One of them
will get us in. All I have to do now is find her." He smiled
broadly at his crew, who were regarding him with a mixture
of umbrage and resignation. "Time to party."

Prince Lambert sealed the straps around the lanky girl's
wrists, then activated the sensenviron program. His bedroom dissolved into a circular stone-walled chamber at the
top of a castle tower, its bed at the centre of the flagstone
floor. His male slaves began to file through the iron-bound
door. Ten of them stood around the bed, looking down dispassionately at the spread-eagled figure.

He took the remote response collar from under the pillow
and fastened it around her neck.

"What is it?" the girl asked, anxiety rising into her voice.
She was very young; it was highly probable she'd never
heard of the device before.

He kissed her silent, and datavised the collar's activation
sequence. The technology was a bastardization of medical
nanonic packages, sending filaments to merge with her
spinal cord. He could use it to manipulate her body into reacting exactly how he wanted, fulfilling each of the fantasies
in turn.

"Do hope I'm not interrupting," one of the slaves said in
a sharp female voice.

Prince Lambert gave a start, jumping up from the bed.
The girl wailed in dismay as the collar began to knit
smoothly with her skin.

He cancelled the sensenviron program, retrieving the reality of his darkened bedroom, and stared at the tall skinny
figure which replaced the muscle-bound slave. "For Mary's
sake, Voi! I'm going to change this bloody apartment's door
code, I should never have let you have it." He squinted at the
figure. "Voi?"

She was pulling her chameleon suit hood off, allowing

her little crown of dreadlocks to wriggle free. A wig of unkempt gingerish hair was held carelessly in her hand. Her clothes were standard-issue biosphere agronomist overalls. "I want to talk to you."

His jaw dropped. One hand gestured ineffectually at the girl on the bed, who was tugging at the straps. "Voi!"

"Now." She went back out into the living room.

He swore, then datavised a shutdown order at the collar and started to open the strap seals.

"How old is she?" Voi asked when he emerged into the living room.

"Does it matter?"

"It might to Shea. Has she found out about your little kinks yet?"

"Why the sudden interest in my sex life? Do you miss it?"

"Like a sunbather misses birdcrap."

"That's not what you said at the time."

"Who cares?"

"I do. We were good together, Voi."

"History."

"Then why have you come running back?"

"I need something of yours."

"Mother Mary, that detox procedure was a big mistake. I preferred you as you were before."

"I'm really interested in everything you say, P.L."

"What the hell are you doing here?"

"I want you to flight prep the *Tekas*, and take me and some friends outsystem."

"Oh, sure, no problem." He collapsed into the living room's leather settee, and favoured her with a pitying gaze. "Any particular destination? New California? Norfolk? Hey, why don't we go for the big one and see if we can break through Earth's SD network?"

"It's important. It's for Garissa."

"Oh, Mary. Your poxy revolution."

"It isn't revolution, it's called honour. Access your dictionary file."

"Haven't got one. And for your information, there's a

civil starflight quarantine in operation. I couldn't fly the *Tekas* away if I wanted to."

"Do you?"

"Yes. All right, one nil. If I'd known about this quarantine in advance I would have left. The Dorados might be home, but I don't think they're the best place to live while the possessed are roaming around. You've got the right idea, Voi, you're just too late."

She held up a flek. "The Dorados governing council flight authorization: it'll be an official voyage."

"How the hell . . ."

"Daddy was on the council. I have his access codes."

Temptation haunted him like a curse. "Is it still valid?"

"Yes. Myself and three others. Deal?"

"There's a few people I'd like to bring along."

"No. You can operate that yacht by yourself, that's why I chose it. This isn't a bloody pleasure cruise, P.L. I need you to fly some complex manoeuvres for me."

"*Tekas* isn't combat-capable, you know. Who are these others?"

"Need-to-know only. And you don't. Do we have a deal?"

"Do we get to try out free-fall sex?"

"If fucking me means you'll fly the yacht for me, fuck away."

"Mother Mary, you are a complete bitch!"

"Deal?"

"All right. Give me a day to wind things up here."

"We leave in three hours."

"No way, Voi. I doubt I could even fill the cryogenic tanks by then."

"Try." She waved the flek. "If you don't; no authorization."

"Bitch."

The girl was extravagantly attractive; early twenties with lustrous ebony skin and dry chestnut hair that fell just below her bottom. Her dress was a shimmering metallic grey-blue with a skirt hem higher than the dangling ends of her hair.

Melvyn suspected she was a typical insecure rich kid. Though Joshua didn't seem to mind, the two of them were busy French-kissing on the Bar KF-T's dance floor.

"He's a devil for it," Melvyn said peevishly. He felt he should explain to Beaulieu, who was sitting at the table with him. "Never works for me. I mean, fusion specialist is a tough job. And I'm crew, that's glamorous enough, isn't it? But they just bloody stampede at him when we dock. I think he got his pheromones geneered along with everything else." He started searching through the cluster of beer bottles on the table for one that had something left inside. There were rather a lot of them.

"You don't think it's anything to do with the fact he's thirty years younger than you?" the cosmonik asked.

"Twenty-five!" Melvyn corrected indignantly.

"Twenty-five."

"Certainly not."

The cosmonik gave the Bar KF-T another automatic scan. Joshua's direction of investigation was obviously puzzling the intelligence agents who were on observation duty. Melvyn and Beaulieu had identified five of them in the club, making a game of it as they sat drinking beer and waiting for Joshua to score. It wasn't that the agents didn't mix; they drank, they danced, they chatted to people, the betraying factor was the way they maintained a rigid distance from the *Lady Mac*'s crew.

Joshua waved a sunny farewell to the girl and sat down at Melvyn's table with a satisfied sigh. "Her name's Kole, and she's invited me to a party this evening."

"I'm surprised she can hold back that long," Melvyn muttered.

"I'm meeting her and her friends at tonight's benefit gig, then they're going on to a private bash at someone's apartment."

"A benefit gig?" Beaulieu questioned.

"Some local MF bands are getting together so they can raise money for Alkad Mzu's legal costs, should she ever need to fight Confederation extradition warrants."

"She's becoming a bloody religion," Melvyn said.

"Looks that way." Joshua started counting the bottles on the table. "Come on, we need to get back to *Lady Mac*." He slipped his arm under Melvyn's shoulder and signalled Beaulieu to help. Between them, they got the drunk fusion specialist to his feet. Ashly and Sarha walked over from the bar. All four serjeants rose from their seats.

None of the agents moved. That would have been too blatant.

A pair of possessed walked into Bar KF-T. A man and woman, dressed in clothes which almost matched current fashions.

Joshua's electronic warfare block datavised an alarm.

"Get down!" the four serjeants shouted in unison.

The threat-response program which had gone primary as soon as the alarm came on sent Joshua diving for cover amid the tables and chairs. He hit the floor, rolling expertly to absorb the impact. A couple of empty chairs went flying as his legs struck them. His crew was following him down; even Melvyn, though his alcohol-polluted nerves made him slower.

Screams broke out across the club as the serjeants drew their stubby machine guns. The agents were also moving, boosted muscles turning their actions into a blur.

Both the possessed gasped at the near-instantaneous reaction to their appearance. An unnerving number of weapons were lining up on them amid the chaos of a terrified and bewildered clientele.

"Freeze," a quadriphonic voice ordered them.

They didn't have functional neural nanonics to run combat programs, but instinct was almost as fast. Both of them started to raise their arms, white fire bursting from their fingertips.

Six machine guns, three semi-automatic pistols, and a carbine opened fire.

Joshua had never heard a chemical projectile weapon before. Ten of them shooting at once was louder than a fusion rocket exhaust. He slammed his hands over his ears. The fusillade couldn't have lasted more than a couple of seconds. He risked raising his head.

Only the agents (there were actually six—Melvyn had missed one) and the serjeants were standing. Everyone else was on the floor, sprawled flat or curled up in fetal balls. Tables and chairs rolled and spun. The music and dance-floor holograms were still playing.

He heard several peculiar mechanical *snicking* sounds as fresh magazines were slammed into the guns.

Bullets had shredded the wall behind the possessed, chewing apart the composite panelling. Large splatters of blood covered the tattered splinters of composite. The two bodies—

Joshua squirmed at the sight. There wasn't much left to identify as human. A nausea suppression program switched smoothly into primary mode, though that only stopped the physical symptoms.

Moans and cries rose over the music. Several people had been hit by ricochets.

"Joshua!"

It was Sarha. She had her hand clamped around Ashly's left thigh. Blood was staining her fingers scarlet. "He's been hit."

The pilot was staring with a calm morbid interest at his wound. "Damn stupid thing." He blinked in confusion.

"Ione," Joshua shouted. "Medical nanonic."

One of the serjeants took a package from its equipment belt. Beaulieu was slitting Ashly's trouser fabric with a small metal blade that had slid out of her left wrist attachments. A dribble of grey-green fluid was leaking from a bullet hole in her brass breastplate.

"I say, do be careful," Ashly murmured.

When the wound had been fully exposed, Sarha slapped the package over it.

"Let's go," Joshua said. "Beaulieu, take Melvyn. Sarha and I will handle Ashly. Ione, cover us."

"Now wait a minute," one of the agents said. Joshua recognized him as one of the heavyweights accompanying

Pauline Webb. "You're staying right here until the police arrive."

It was a barman who had recovered fast enough to think of the financial possibilities that started recording the scene in a memory cell. Later that day and all through the night the news companies repeated it almost constantly. Six armed men in a shouting match with a young starship captain (later everyone realized it was Lagrange Calvert himself) and his crew. The captain saying that no one was going to prevent him from taking his injured friend to get proper treatment. And what authority have you got anyway? Four identical and disturbingly menacing cosmoniks stood between Calvert and the armed men. There was a short pause, then everyone's guns seemed to disappear. The starship crew left the club, carrying their wounded with them.

Anchormen speculated long and loud on the possibility that the six armed men were in fact foreign intelligence agents. Rover reporters tried desperately to hunt them down, with no success.

The police officially confirmed that the two people shot dead by the agents had been possessed (though no details about how they knew for sure were forthcoming). Ayacucho's governing council issued a statement urging everyone to remain calm. Total priority was given to search and identification procedures which were being put into operation to locate any further possessed in the asteroid. All citizens and residents were asked to cooperate fully.

There was no physical expression of panic, no angry mobs gathering in the biosphere cavern, or marches on the council chamber. People were too fearful of what might be lying in wait outside their apartment doors. Those companies and offices which had remained open started to wind down or conduct their businesses purely over the communications net; anything as long as personal contact was reduced. Parents took their children out of day clubs. Emergency services were brought up to full alert status. Company security staff were seconded to the police to help with the search.

By late afternoon several starships had been given official flight authorization by the council. Most of them were taking councillors, their families, and close aides away for conferences or defence negotiations with allies.

"And we can't stop them," Monica complained bitterly. She was sitting at the back of the office which the Edenists were using, sipping a mug of instant tea. There was little else for her to do now, which aggravated her intensely. All the ESA's assets had been activated. None of them had any idea where Mzu was; few had even heard of Voi let alone any underground group the girl was connected with.

Locating Mzu was all down to the Edenist observation operation now, and the slender hope they would get a lucky break.

"She has not embarked on any starship," Samuel said. "We are sure of that. Both axial chambers have been under constant observation, and not just by us. Nobody who comes within twenty-five per cent of Mzu's height and mass has passed into the spaceports without being positively identified."

"Yes yes," Monica said irritably.

"If we don't find her in another four hours we are going to withdraw from Ayacucho."

She'd known it was coming, but that didn't make it any easier. "That bad?"

"Yes. I'm afraid so." He had just finished watching another possession through a spider in one of the residential sections. It was the apartment of an ordinary family of five, doing as they'd been advised, staying at home and not allowing anyone else in. Until the police arrived. All three officers were possessed; and after seven minutes so were the family. "We estimate eight per cent of the population has been possessed now. With everyone isolated and sitting tight, it is becoming easier for them to spread. They have taken over the police force in its entirety."

"Bastards. They've gone for officialdom every time since Capone used the police and civil service to take over New California."

"A remarkably perceptive man, Mr Capone."

"I don't suppose it would do any good broadcasting a general warning, now?"

"We think not. There are few weapons available to the general populace; and most of those are energy weapons, which are worse than useless. We would be adding to the suffering."

"And since that bloody media campaign, nobody would trust us."

"Exactly."

"What do we do if Mzu doesn't escape?"

"That depends on what happens here. If the possessed take Ayacucho out of this universe, the problem is solved, albeit not very satisfactorily. If they remain here, then the voidhawks will enforce a permanent blockade."

She gritted her teeth, hating the mounting feeling of frustration. "We could try broadcasting a message to her, offer to take her off."

"I've considered it; and I might well use it as a last resort before we evacuate."

"Great. So now we just sit and pray she walks in front of a spider."

"You have an alternative?"

"No. I don't think any of us do."

"Perhaps not, though I remain intrigued by what Joshua Calvert and his crew were doing in that club."

"Trying to get laid by the look of it."

"No. Calvert is shrewd. If you want my guess he is attempting to approach Voi through her friends."

"He can't know who her friends are, he doesn't have the resources. We've only got three of her friends on our list, and that took five hours to acquire."

"Possibly. But he's already inserted himself in her social strata with that invitation to a party. And it's a small asteroid."

"If Voi is hiding Mzu, she's not going to reveal herself."

"True." His grin was childlike in its mischievousness.

"What?" Monica asked in annoyance.

"The irony. From being an amateur irritant, Calvert is now our only lead."

Ashly had said very little during the trip back to the spaceport. Joshua guessed the pilot's neural nanonic programs were busy suppressing the shock. But Sarha didn't seem unduly worried, and she was monitoring the medical package around his thigh.

Melvyn was doing his best to sober up fast. One of the serjeants had given him a medical nanonic package which was now wrapped around his neck to form a thick collar. It was busy filtering all traces of alcohol out of the blood entering his brain.

Joshua's only concern was the fluid which was still trickling out of the bullet hole in Beaulieu's breastplate. Medical nanonics would be of no value at all in treating the cosmonik. None of them had standardized internal systems; each was unique, and proud of it. He wasn't even sure if she was mostly mechanical or biological underneath her brass carapace.

"How are you doing?" he asked her.

"The bullet damaged some of my nutrient synthesis glands. It's not critical."

"Do you have any . . . er, spares?"

"No. That function has multiple redundancy backup. It looks worse than it is."

"Don't tell me, just a flesh wound," Ashly grunted.

"Correct."

The commuter lift's doors opened. Two serjeants slid out into the corridor first, checking for any possessed between them and the docking bay's airlock tube. "Joshua," one of them called.

His electronic warfare detector block wasn't acting up. "What?"

"Someone here for you."

He learned nothing from the tone, so he pushed off with his feet and glided out into the corridor. "Oh, Jesus wept."

Mrs Nateghi and her two fellow goons from Tayari,

Usoro and Wang were waiting outside the airlock tube. Another man was floating just behind them.

The crew followed Joshua out of the lift.

"Captain Calvert." Mrs Nateghi's voice was indecently happy.

"Can't get enough of me, can you? So what is it this time? A million-fuseodollar fine for littering? Ten years hard labour for not returning my empties to the bar? Penal colony exile for farting in public?"

"Humour is an excellent defence mechanism, Captain Calvert. But I would advise you to have something stronger in court."

"I've just saved your asteroid from being taken over by the possessed. Will that do?"

"I've accessed the NewsGalactic recording. You were lying on the floor with your hands over your head the whole time. Captain Calvert, I have a summons for you to be present at a preliminary hearing to establish proceedings which will determine the ownership of the starship *Lady Macbeth*, pursuant to the claim my client has filed upon said ship."

Joshua stared at her, too incredulous to speak.

"Ownership?" Sarha asked. "But it's Joshua's ship; it always has been."

"That is incorrect," Mrs Nateghi said. "It was Marcus Calvert's ship. I have a sensorium recording of Captain Calvert admitting that."

"He was never trying to deny it. His father is dead. *Lady Mac*'s registration is filed with the CAB. You can't challenge that."

"Yes I can." The man who had been keeping himself behind the other two lawyers slowly edged forwards.

"You!" Sarha exclaimed.

"Me."

Joshua stared at him, a very unpleasant chill sluicing into his thoughts. The angular, ebony face was . . . Jesus, I know him. But where from? "So who the hell are you?"

"My name is Liol. Liol Calvert, actually. I'm your big half brother, Joshua."

* * *

The last place Joshua wanted to bring this . . . this *fraud* was the captain's cabin. It was his father's cabin, for Christ's sake, even though most of the old fittings and personal mementos had been removed during the last refit. This was the closest Joshua had ever come to knowing a home.

But Ashly needed the deep-invasion packages in *Lady Mac*'s sickbay to remove the bullet in his thigh. That bitch queen Mrs Nateghi wasn't going to be deflected, and the summons was real enough. He also had a mission. So it was back to basics.

As soon as the cabin hatch shut behind them, Joshua asked: "Okay, shithead, how much?"

Liol didn't answer immediately, he was gazing around the cabin. His face carried an expression which was close to trepidation. "I'm finally here," he said falteringly.

"Do you know how many hours I've spent in sensevise simulations learning to fly a starship? I qualified for my C.A.B. pilot's licence when I was just nineteen." He glanced awkwardly at Joshua. "This must be very strange for you, Joshua. It is for me."

"Cut the crap, how much?"

Liol's face cleared. "How much for what?"

"To drop the claim and bugger off, of course. It's a neat scam, I'll give you that. Normally I'd just let the courts break you apart, but I'm a little pushed for time right now. I don't need complications. So name your price, but you'd better make it less than fifty grand."

"Nice one, Josh." Liol smiled and held out his Jovian Bank credit disk, silver side up. Green figures glowed on the surface.

Joshua blinked as he read out the amount of money stored inside: eight hundred thousand fuseodollars. "I don't understand."

"It's very simple, I am your brother. I'm entitled to joint ownership, at the very least."

"Not a chance. You're a con artist who knows how to use a cosmetic adaptation package, that's all. Right now, my face is as famous as Jezzibella's. You saw an opportunity to make a nuisance of yourself, and remodelled your features."

"This is my face. I've had it ever since I was born, which was before you. Access my public file if you want proof."

"I'm sure someone as smart as you has planted all the appropriate data in Ayacucho's memory cores. You've done your research, and you've shown me you have the money to buy official access codes."

"Really? And what about you?"

"Me?"

"Yes. How come you acquired this ship after my father died? In fact, how did he die? Is he even dead at all? Prove you're a Calvert. Prove you are Marcus's son."

"I didn't acquire it, I inherited it. Dad always wanted me to have it. His will is on file in Tranquillity. Anybody can access it."

"Oh, that's nice. So Tranquillity's public records are beyond reproach, while anything stored in the Dorados was put there by criminals. How convenient. I wouldn't try that one in court if I were you."

"He's my father," Joshua shouted angrily.

"Mine too. And you know it."

"I know you're a fake."

"If you were a true Calvert, you'd know."

"What the fuck are you talking about?"

"Intuition. What does your intuition tell you about me, Josh?"

For the first time in his life, Joshua knew what vertigo must feel like. To be teetering on the edge of some monstrously deep chasm.

"Ah." Liol's grin was triumphant. "Our little family quirk can be a real downer at times. After all, I knew you were real the second I accessed Kelly Tirrel's report. I also know what you're going through, Joshua. I felt exactly the same way about you. All that terrible anger, refusing to believe despite all the evidence. We're more than brothers, we're almost twins."

"Wrong. We don't even come from the same universe."

"What exactly worries you the most, Josh? That I am your brother, or I'm not?"

"I'll scuttle *Lady Mac* before I let anyone else have her. If you've got any intuition, you'll know how true that it."

"My mistake." Liol stroked the acceleration couch beside the hatch, the longing obvious in his eyes. "I can see the ship means as much to you as it does to me. No surprise there, we've both got the Calvert wanderlust. Hitting you with a big legal scene first off was bound to create some hostility. But I've been waiting for this starship to dock here for every day of my life. Dad left Ayacucho before I was even born. In my mind the *Lady Macbeth* has always been mine. She's my inheritance, too, Josh. I belong here just as much as you do."

"A starship only has one captain. And you, asteroid boy, don't know the first thing about piloting or captaining. Not that it's relevant, you'll never be in a position to fly *Lady Mac*."

"Don't fight this, Josh. You're my brother, I don't want to alienate you. Christ, just finding out you existed was a hell of a shock. Family feuds are the worst kind. Don't let's start one the moment we meet. Think how Dad would feel, his sons going at each other like this."

"You are *not* family."

"Where was *Lady Macbeth* docked in 2586, Josh? What ports?"

Joshua clenched his fists, a free-fall assault program working out possible trajectories he could leap along. He hated how smug this arrogant bastard was. Wiping that knowing superiority from his ugly flat face would be wonderful.

"The disadvantage with white skin like yours, Josh, is that I can see every blush. It's a dead giveaway. Me? I always win at poker."

Joshua seethed silently.

"So, do you want to discuss this sensibly?" Liol asked. "Personally, I'd hate to face Mrs Nateghi across a courtroom."

"I don't suppose, *Lie*, this sudden urge to acquire a starship has anything to do with your asteroid being overrun by possessed?"

"Lovely." Liol clapped his hands enthusiastically. "You're a Calvert, all right. Never see a belt without wanting to hit below it."

"That's right. So, I'll see you in court here in about a week's time. How does that sound?"

"Would you really abandon your own brother to the possessed?"

"If I had one, probably not."

"I think I'm going to like you after all, Josh. I thought you'd be soft; after all, you've had it dead easy. But you're not."

"Easy?"

"Compared to me. You knew Dad. You had the big inheritance waiting. I'd call that easy."

"I'd call that bollocks."

"If you don't believe in your own intuition, a simple DNA profile will tell you if we're related. I'm sure your sick bay could run one for you."

And Joshua was absolutely stumped at that. There was something about this complete stranger that was deeply unsettling, yet obscurely comforting at the same time. Jesus, he does look like me, and he knows about the intuition, and Dad wiped the log for 2586. It's not utterly impossible. But *Lady Mac* is mine. I could never share her.

He stared at Liol for a moment longer, then made a command decision.

The crew were all hanging around on the bridge, along with Mrs Nateghi. Nobody would make eye contact. Joshua shot out of the captain's cabin, rotated ninety degrees, and slapped his feet on a stikpad. "Sarha. Take our guest down to the sick bay. Get a blood sample, use a dagger if you want, and run a DNA profile." He jabbed a finger at Mrs Nateghi. "Not you. You're leaving. Right now."

She ignored him while managing to project her complete

disdain at the same time. "Mr Calvert, what are your instructions?"

"I just told you . . . Oh."

"Thank you so much for your help," Liol said with flawless courtesy. "I'll be in touch with your office if I decide any further legal action is required against my brother."

"Very well. Tayari, Usoro and Wang will be delighted to help. Forcing recidivists to acknowledge their responsibilities is always rewarding."

Combating her amusement, Sarha held up a warning finger as Joshua's face turned beacon red.

"Dahybi, show the lady out, please," he said.

"Aye, Captain." The node specialist gestured generously at the floor hatch and followed Mrs Nateghi through.

Liol flashed Sarha an engaging grin. "You wouldn't really use a dagger on me, would you?"

She winked. "Depends on the circumstances."

"Fancy that, Joshua," one of the serjeants said as the pair of them left the bridge. "There's two of you."

Joshua glared at the bitek construct, then executed a perfect midair somersault and zoomed back into his cabin.

Alkad's tranquillizer program wasn't nearly strong enough to keep the claustrophobia at bay. Eventually she had to admit defeat and switch a somnolence program to primary. Her only thought as she fell into oblivion was: I wonder who will be there when I wake?

The rendezvous was an elaborate one, which decreased the chances of success. But even that wasn't her main worry. Getting out of Ayacucho undetected was the big problem.

The asteroid had two counter-rotating spaceports, one at each end. The main one was used by starships and larger inter-orbit craft; while the second was mainly for heavy-duty cargo and utility tankers delivering fresh water and liquid oxygen for the biosphere. It was also the operations base for the personnel commuters and MSVs and tugs which flew between the asteroid and its necklace of industrial stations. Both were under heavy surveillance by agents. There was no chance of getting through the axial chambers and taking a commuter lift to the docking bays, so Voi had arranged for Alkad and herself to be shipped out in cargo pods.

Lodi and another youth called Eriba, who claimed to be a molecular structures student, worked on a couple of standard pods in one of T'Opingtu's storage facilities. They were converted into heavily padded coffins moulded to hold someone wearing a SII spacesuit. Both boys swore the insulation would prevent any thermal or electromagnetic leakage. The cargo pods would appear perfectly inert to any sensor sweep.

Of course, the insulation meant that Alkad couldn't datavise out for help if anything went wrong and nobody opened her pod. She believed she held her composure pretty well while she allowed them to seal her in. After that there was nothing but the tranquillizer program for the twenty minutes before she sought refuge in sleep.

A tug was scheduled to take the cargo pods out to one of T'Opingtu's foundry stations. From there they would be transferred to an inter-orbit craft that was heading for Mapire.

Alkad woke to find herself in free fall. *At least we got out of the asteroid.*

Her neural nanonics reported they were picking up a datavise.

"Stand by, Doctor, we're cracking the pod now."

She could feel vibrations through her suit, then the collar sensors were showing her slash-lines of red light cavorting around her. The top of the cargo pod came free, and someone in an SII suit and a manoeuvring pack was sliding into view in front of her.

"Hello, Doctor, it's me, Lodi. You made it, you're out."

"Where's Voi?" she datavised.

"I'm here, Doctor. Mary, but that was horrible. Are you all right?"

"Yes. Fine, thank you." As well as relief for herself, she felt strangely glad the girl had come through unscathed.

She made sure she had a secure grip on her crumpled old

backpack before she let Lodi draw her out of the pod. Held in front of him, with the manoeuvring pack puffing out fast streamers of gas, she sank into the déjà vu of Cherri Barnes towing her back to the *Udat*. Then, space had been frighteningly empty, with so little light her collar sensors had struggled to resolve anything. Now, she was deep within Tunja's disk, gliding through a redout blizzard. No stars were visible anywhere, the particles were too thick. Their size was inordinately difficult to judge, a grain of dust a centimetre from her nose, or a boulder a kilometre away, both looked exactly the same.

Ahead of her she could see the waiting starship, its fuselage shining a dim burgundy, much darker than the particles skipping across it like twisters of interference in an empty AV projection. Two thermo-dump panels were extended, resembling slow-motion propeller blades as rills of dust swirled around them. The airlock hatch was open, emitting a welcoming beam of white light.

She sank along it, relishing the return of normal colour. They entered a cylindrical chamber with grab hoops, utility sockets, harsh light tubes, environment grilles, and small instrument panels distributed at random. The sensation that reality was solidifying around her was inescapable.

The hatch closed, and she clung to a grab hoop as air flooded in. Her SII suit flowed back into a globe hanging off the collar, and she was inundated with sounds.

"We did it!" Voi was jubilant. "I told you I could get you out."

"Yes, you did." She looked around at them, Voi, Lodi, and Eriba, so dreadfully young to be sucked into this world of subterfuge, hatred, and death. Beaming faces desperate for her approval. "And I'd like to thank you; you did a magnificent job, all of you."

Their laughter and gratitude made her shake her head in wonder. Such odd times.

Five minutes later Alkad was dressed in her old ship-suit, backpack tight against her waist, following Voi into the *Tekas*'s upper deck lounge. The yacht was only large enough for one life-support capsule, with three decks. Despite the lack of volume, the fittings were compact and elegant, everything blending seamlessly together to provide the illusion of ample space.

Prince Lambert was reclining in a deep circular chair, datavising a constant stream of instructions to the flight computer. *Tekas* was under way, accelerating at a twentieth of a gee, though the gravity plane was flicking about.

"Thank you for offering us the use of your ship," Alkad said after they were introduced.

He gave Voi a sterling glance. "Not at all, Doctor, the least I could do for a national heroine."

She ignored the sarcasm, wondering what the story was with him and Voi. "So what's our current status? Did anyone follow you?"

"No. I'm fairly sure about that. I flew outside the disk for a million kilometres before I went through it. Your interorbit craft did the same thing, but on the other side. In theory no one will realize we rendezvoused. Even the voidhawks can't sense what happens inside the disk, not from a million kilometres away, it's too cluttered."

Unless they want to follow me right to the Alchemist, Alkad thought. "What about a stealthed voidhawk just outside the disk, or even inside with us?" she asked.

"Then they've got us cold," he said. "Our sensors are good, but they're not military grade."

"We'd know by now if we were being followed," Voi said. "As soon as we rendezvoused they would have moved to intercept."

"I expect so," Alkad said. "How long before we can clear the disk and jump outsystem?"

"Another forty minutes. You don't rush a manoeuvre like this; there are too many sharp rocks out there. I'm going to have to replace the hull foam as it is; dust abrasion is wearing it down to the bare silicon." He smiled unconvincingly at Alkad. "Am I going to be told what our mission is?"

"I require a combat-capable starship, that's all."

"I see. And I suppose that is connected with the work you did for the Garissan navy before the genocide?"

"Yes."

"Well, you'll excuse me if I leave the party before that."

Alkad thought of the remaining devices in her backpack, and just how tight her security margin had become. "Nobody will force you to do anything."

"Nice to hear." He gave Voi another pointed glance. "For once."

"What jump coordinate does this course give us?" Alkad asked.

"Nyvan," he said. "It's a hundred and thirty light-years away, but I can get a reasonable alignment on it without using up too much fuel. Voi told me you wanted a planet with military industrial facilities, and wouldn't ask too many questions."

The last of the starships with official flight authorization had departed ninety minutes earlier when Joshua made his way out of the spaceport. Service and maintenance staff had gone home to be with their families. Utility umbilicals supporting the remaining starships were becoming less than reliable.

Three agents were loitering in the axial chamber, talking in quiet tones. They were the only people there. Joshua gave them a blasé wave as he and his escort of three serjeants emerged from the commuter lift.

One of the agents frowned. "You're going back in there?" she asked incredulously.

"Try keeping me from a party."

He could hear the argument start behind him as the lift doors closed. Holomorph sticker cheerleaders began their chant all around him.

"If she's worried enough to question you openly, then the possessed must be gaining ground," a serjeant said.

"Look, we've been over this. I'm just going to check out the gig, and see if Kole has turned up. If she hasn't, we head straight back."

"It would have been much safer if I'd gone alone."

"I don't think so." Joshua wanted to say more, but the lift was probably overloaded with nanonic bugs. He datavised the net for a channel to *Lady Mac*.

"Yes, Joshua?" Dahybi responded.

"Certain people out here are getting twitchy about the possessed. I want you to monitor the asteroid's internal systems: transportation, power, environment, the net, everything. If any of them start downgrading I want to know right away."

"Okay."

Joshua glanced at the rigid, expressionless face of the nearest serjeant. Right now he really wanted Ione to confide in, to be able to ask her opinion, to talk things through. If anyone knew how to handle awkward family, it was her. Some deep-buried prejudice prevented him from saying anything to the serjeants. "One other thing, Dahybi. Call Liol, tell him to get himself over to the *Lady Mac* right away. Give him a passenger cabin in capsule C. Don't let him on the bridge. Don't give him any access codes for the flight computer. And make sure you check him for possession when he arrives."

"Yes, Captain. Take care."

A datavise couldn't convey emotional nuances, but he knew Dahybi well enough to guess at the amused approval.

"You accept his claim, then?" Ione asked.

"The DNA profile seems similar to mine," Joshua said grudgingly.

"Yes, I'd say ninety-seven per cent compatibility is roughly in the target area. It's not unusual for starship crews to have extended families spread over several star systems."

"Thank you for reminding me."

"If your father was ever anything like you, then it's possible Liol isn't your only sibling."

"Jesus."

"I'm just preparing you for the eventuality. Kelly Tirrel's recording has enhanced your public visibility rating by a considerable factor. Others may seek you out in the same way."

He pulled an ironic face. "Wouldn't that be something? The gathering of the Calverts. I wonder if there are more of us than there are Saldanas?"

"I very much doubt it, not if you include our illegitimates."

"And black sheep."

"Quite. What do you intend to do about Liol?"

"I haven't got a clue. He's not touching the *Lady Mac*, though. Can you imagine having board meetings every time to decide her next destination? It's the opposite of everything I am, not to mention the old girl herself."

"He'll probably come to realize this. I'm sure you can come to some arrangement. He appears to be quite smart."

"The word is smarmy."

"There's very little difference between you."

The lift dropped him off in a public hall a couple of hundred metres from the Terminal Terminus club where the benefit gig was being played. Not everyone was obeying the governing council's request to stay put at home. Kids filled the hall with laughter and shouts. Everyone was wearing a red handkerchief on their ankle.

For a moment Joshua felt disconnected from his own generation. He had formidable responsibilities (not to mention problems); they were just stimheads sliding around their perpetual circuit from one empty good time to the next. They didn't understand the universe at all.

Then a couple of them recognized Lagrange Calvert and wanted to know what it was like rescuing the children from Lalonde, and had there really been possessed in Bar KF-T? They were peppy, and the girls in the group were giving him the eye. He began to loosen up; the barriers weren't so solid after all.

The Terminal Terminus looked like some kind of chasmal junction between tunnels. Big, old mining machines were parked in arching recesses, their conical, worn-down drill mechanisms jutting out into the main chamber. Obsolete mechanoids clung to the ceiling, spider-leg waldos dangling down inertly. Drinks were served over a long section of heavy-duty caterpillar track.

A fantasy wormhole squatted in the centre, a rippling gloss-black column five metres wide stretching between floor and ceiling. Things were trapped inside, undefined creatures who clawed at the distortion effect in desperate attempts to escape; the black surface bent and distended, but never broke.

"Very tasteful, under the circumstances," Joshua muttered to a serjeant.

A stage had been set up between two of the mining machines. AV projectors powerful enough to cover a stadium stood on each side.

One of the serjeants went off to guard an emergency exit. The remaining two stuck by Joshua.

He found Kole standing with a group of her friends under one of the mining machines. Her hair had been woven through with silver and chrome-scarlet threads, which every now and then made it fan open like a peacock tail.

He paused for a moment. She was so phony; rich without Dominique's cosmopolitan verve, and absolute trash compared to Louise's simple honesty.

Louise.

Kole caught sight of him and squealed happily, kissed him, rubbed against him. "Are you all right? I accessed what happened after I left."

He grinned brashly, the legend in the flesh. "I'm fine. My . . . er, cosmoniks here are a tough bunch. We've seen worse."

"Really?" She cast a respectful eye over the two serjeants. "Are you male?"

"No."

Joshua couldn't tell if Ione was annoyed, amused, or plain didn't care. On second thought, he doubted the latter.

Kole kissed him again. "Come and meet the gang. They didn't believe I'd hooked you. Mother, I can't believe I hooked you."

He braced himself for the worst.

From her vantage point lounging casually on a coolant feed duct a third of the way up the side of a mining machine, Monica Foulkes watched Joshua greeting Kole's posse of friends. He knew exactly the attitude to take to be accepted within seconds. She took a gulp of iced mineral water as her enhanced retinas scanned the young faces below. It was hot wearing the chameleon suit, but it gave her the skin tone of Ayacucho's Kenyan-ethnic population; "foreign agents" were about as popular as the possessed right now. Except Calvert, of course, she thought sorely, he was being greeted like a bloody hero. Her characterization recognition program ran a comparison against the youngsters she was scanning, and signalled a ninety-five per cent probable match.

"Damn!"

Samuel (now black-skinned, twenty-five years old, and wearing jazzy purple sports gear) looked up from the base of the mining machine. "What?"

"You were right. Kole has just introduced him to Adok Dala."

"Ah. I knew it. He was Voi's boyfriend up until she dumped him eighteen months ago."

"Yes yes, I can access the file for myself, thank you."

"Can you hear what's being said?"

She glanced down contemptuously. "Not a chance. This place is really filling up now. My audio discrimination programs can't filter over that distance."

"Come down please, Monica."

Something in his tone halted any protest. She slithered down the pitted yellow-painted titanium bodywork of the mining machine.

"We have to decide what to do. Now."

She flinched. "Oh, God."

"Do you believe Adok Dala will know where Voi is?"

"I don't think so, but there's no guarantee. And if we snatch Dala now, it isn't going to make a whole lot of difference as far as official repercussions are concerned. He's hardly going to complain about being taken off Ayacucho, is he?"

"You're right. And it will prevent Calvert from learning anything."

Joshua's neural nanonics reported a call from Dahybi. "Two voidhawks from the defence delegation have just left the docking ledge, Captain. Our sensors can't see much from inside the bay, but we think they're keeping station five kilometres off the spaceport."

"Okay, keep monitoring them."

"No problem. But you should know that Ayacucho is suffering localized power failures. They're completely random, and the supervisor programs can't locate any physical problem in the supply system. One of the news studios has gone off-line, as well."

"Jesus. Start flight prepping *Lady Mac*; I'll wind things up here and get back to you within thirty minutes."

"Aye, Captain. Oh, and Liol has arrived. He's not possessed."

"Wonderful."

Kole was still clinging magnetically to his side. No one she'd introduced him to had mentioned Voi. His original idea had been to ask them about Ikela's murder and see what was said. But now time was running out. He looked around to find out where the serjeants were, hoping Ione wasn't going to make an issue of pulling out. Hell, we gave it our best.

The compere was striding out on the stage, holding her arms out for silence as the rowdy crowd cheered and started catcalling. She started into her spiel about the Fuckmasters.

"This is Shea," Kole told him.

It was hard for Joshua to smile; Shea was tall and skinny, almost identical to Voi's size and height. He datavised his electronic warfare block to scan her, but she was clean. What he saw was real, not a chameleon suit. It wasn't Voi.

"This is Joshua Calvert," Kole boasted, raising her voice against the rising whistle of the giant AV projectors. "He's my starship captain."

Shea's melancholia became outright distress. She started crying.

Kole gave her an astonished look. "What's the matter?"

Shea shook her head, lips sealed together.

"I'm sorry," Joshua said, earnestly sympathetic. "What did I do?"

Shea smiled bravely. "It's not you. It's just . . . my boyfriend left this afternoon. He's captaining a starship, too, and that reminded me. I don't know when I'm going to see him again. He wouldn't say."

Intuition was starting a major-league riot in Joshua's skull. The first MF band was strolling onstage. He put a protective arm around Shea's shoulders, ignoring Kole's flash of ire. "Come on, I'll buy you a drink. You can tell me about it. You never know, I might be able to help. Stranger things happen in space."

He signalled the two serjeants frantically, and turned away from the stage just as the AV projectors burst into life. A thick haze of coherent light filled the Terminal Terminus. Even though he was looking away, sensations spirited down his nerves; fragmented signals saturated with crude activant sequences. He felt good. He felt hot. He felt randy. He felt slippery.

A glance back over his shoulder had him sitting on a saddle astride a giant penis, urging it forwards.

Honestly, kids today. When he was younger MF was about the giddy pursuit, how it felt when your partner adored you in return, or spurned you without reason. Making up and breaking up. The infinite states of the heart, not the dick.

The kids around him were laughing and giggling, joyous expressions on their incredulous faces as the AV dazzle poured down their irises. They all swayed from side to side in unison.

"Joshua, four Edenists are coming this way," a serjeant warned.

Joshua could see them in the sparkling light cloud which pervaded the audience. Taller than everyone else, some kind of visor over their eyes, moving intently through the swinging throng.

He grabbed Shea's hand tightly. "This way," he hissed urgently, and veered off towards the mock wormhole in the centre of the club. One of the serjeants cleared a path, forcing people aside. Frowns and snarls lined his route.

"Dahybi," he datavised. "Get the rest of the serjeants out of zero-tau, fast. Secure a route through the spaceport from the axial chamber to *Lady Mac*. I might be needing it."

"It's being done, Captain. Parts of the asteroid's net are crashing."

"Jesus. Okay, we've got the serjeants' affinity to keep communications open if it goes completely. You'd better keep one in the bridge with you."

He reached the writhing black column and looked back. Shea was breathless and confused, but not protesting. The Edenists weren't chasing after him. "What . . . ?" Some sort of struggle had broken out over where he'd left Kole's friends. Two of the tall agents were pulling an inert body between them. It was Adok Dala, unconscious and shaking, victim of a nervejam shot. The other pair of agents and someone else were holding back some irate kids. A nervejam stick was raised and fired.

Joshua turned his head a little too far, and he was tasting nipple while he slid over dark pigmentation as if he were snowboard slaloming, leaving a huge trail of glistening saliva behind him. His neck muscles flicked back a couple of degrees, and the Edenists were retreating, completely unnoticed by the entranced euphoric audience they were shoving their way through. Behind them, Kole's friends clung together; those still standing wept uncomprehendingly over those felled by the violence which had stabbed so unexpectedly into their moment of erotic rapture.

Shea gasped at the scene and made to rush over.

"No," Joshua shouted. He pulled her back, and she recoiled, as frightened by him as the agents. "Listen to me, we have to get out of here. It's only going to get worse."

"Is it the possessed?"

"Yeah. Now come on."

Still keeping hold of her hand he slid around the wormhole. It felt like dry rubber against his side, flexing in queasy movements.

"Nearest exit," he told the serjeant in front of him. "Go." It began to plough through tightly packed bodies at an alarming speed. Blissfully unaware people were sent tumbling. Joshua followed on grimly. The Edenists must have wanted Adok Dala for the same reason he wanted Shea. Had he got the wrong friend? Oh, hell.

The cavern wall was only ten metres ahead of him now, a red circle shining above an exit. His electronic warfare block datavised an alarm.

Jesus! *"Ione."*

"I know," the lead serjeant shouted. It drew its machine gun.

"No," he cried. "You can't, not in here."

"I'm not inhuman, Joshua," the burly figure retorted.

They reached the wall and hurried along to the exit. That was when he realized Kole was still with them.

"Stay here," he told her. "You'll be safe with all these people."

"You can't leave me here," she gasped imploringly. "Joshua! I know what's happening. You can't. I don't want that to happen to me. You can't let them. Take me with you, for Mary's sake!"

And she was just a stricken young girl whose broken hair was flapping wildly.

The first serjeant slammed the door open and went through. "I'll stay here," the second said. The machine gun was held ready in one hand. It took out an automatic pistol and held it in the other. "That's a bonus, these things are ambidextrous. Don't worry, Joshua. They'll suffer if they try and get past me."

"Thanks, Ione." Then he was out in the corridor, urging the two girls along. "Dahybi," he datavised. His neural nanonics reported they couldn't acquire a net processor. "Bugger."

"The other serjeants are securing the spaceport," the serjeant told him. "And the *Lady Mac* is flight prepped. Everything is ready."

"Great." His electronic warfare block was still datavising its alarm. He took his own nine-millimetre pistol out of its holster. Its operating procedure program went primary.

They came to a crossroads in the corridor. And Joshua wasted a second querying the net on the direction he wanted. Cursing, he requested the Ayacucho layout he'd stored in a memory cell. There would be too much risk using a lift now; power supplies were dubious, transport management processors more so. His neural nanonics devised the shortest route to the axial chamber, it seemed depressingly far.

"This way." He pointed down the left hand corridor.

"Excuse me," someone said.

Joshua's electronic warfare block gave out one final warning, then shut down. He whirled around. Standing ten metres down the other corridor were a man and a woman, dressed in heavy black leather jackets and trousers with an improbable number of shiny zips and buckles.

"Run," the serjeant ordered. It stepped squarely into the middle of the corridor and levelled its compact machine gun.

Joshua didn't hesitate. Shoving at the girls, he started running. He heard a few heated words being shouted behind him. Then the machine gun fired.

He took the first turning, desperate to escape from the line of sight. His neural nanonics immediately revised his route. The corridors were all identical, three metres high, three metres wide, and apparently endless. Joshua hated that, trapped in a maze and utterly reliant on a guidance program susceptible to the possessed. He wanted to know exactly where he was, and be able to prove it. Being unaware of his exact location was an alien experience. Human doubt was superseding technological prowess.

He was looking over his shoulder as he took the next turning, making sure the girls were keeping up and there was no sign of any pursuit. His peripheral vision monitor program indexed the figure striding down the corridor towards him milliseconds before his neural nanonics crashed.

It was a man in white Arab robes. He smiled in simple gratitude as Joshua and the girls stumbled to a halt in front of him.

Joshua swung his pistol around, but the lack of any procedural program meant he misjudged its weight. The arc was too great. Before he could bring it back to line up on the target, a ball of white fire struck his hand.

Joshua howled at the flare of terrible pain as the pistol fell from his grip. No matter how vigorously he waved his arm the deadly white flame could not be dislodged from its grip around his fingers. Oily stinking smoke spouted out.

"Time to say goodbye to your life," the smiling possessed said.

"Fuck you."

He could hear the girls crying out behind him, the wails of their revulsion and horror. Shock was diminishing the pain in his hand slightly. He could feel the puke rising in his throat as more and more of his flesh charred. His whole right arm was stiffening. Somewhere behind his assailant a vast crowd of invisible people were whispering all at once. "No." It wasn't a coherent word, just a defiant grunt mangled by his contorted throat muscles. I will not submit to that. Never.

A cascade of water burst out of the corridor's ceiling to the accompanying sound of a high-pitched siren. The edge of the lighting panels turned red and started to flash.

Shea was laughing with brittle hysteria as she withdrew her fist from the fire alarm panel. Dots of blood oozed up from her grazed knuckles. Joshua punched his own hand upwards, straight underneath a nozzle. He roared triumphantly. The white flame vanished in a gust of steam, and he collapsed down onto his knees, his whole body shaking violently.

The Arab regarded the three of them with a degree of aristocratic annoyance, as if any hint of defiance was unprecedented. Water splattered on his dark headgear, turning his robe translucent as it clung to his body.

Joshua raised his head against the icy torrent to snarl at his enemy. His right hand was dead now; a supreme crush of coldness had devoured his wrist. A few spittles of vomit emerged from his mouth before he managed to growl: "Okay, shithead, my turn."

The Arab frowned as Joshua reached into a pocket with his left hand and brought out Horst Elwes's small crucifix. He thrust it forwards.

"Holy Father, Lord of Heaven and the mortal world, in humility and obedience, I do ask Your aid in this act of sanctification, through Jesus the Christ who walked among us to know our failings, grant me Your blessing in this task."

"But I am a Sunni Muslim," the bemused Arab said.

"Eh?"

"A Muslim. I have no belief in your false Jewish prophet." He raised his arms, palms upwards. The deluge of water from the nozzles turned to snow. Every flake stuck to Joshua's ship-suit, smearing him in a coat of slush. Most of his skin was numb now.

"But I believe," Joshua ground out through vibrating teeth. And did. The revelation was as shocking as the cold and the pain. But he'd come to this moment of pure clarity through reason and ordeal. All he knew, all he'd seen, all he'd done; it spoke to him that there was order in the universe. Reality was too complex for chance evolution.

Medieval prophets were a convenient lie, but something had made sense out of the chaos which existed before time began. Something started time itself flowing.

"My Lord God, look upon this servant of Yours before me, fallen to a misguided and unclean spirit."

"Misguided?" The Arab glowered, trickles of static electricity crawling up his robes. "You brain-dead infidel! Allah is the only true—oh*shit.*"

The serjeant fired, aiming for the Arab's head.

Joshua drooped limply onto the floor. "That's always how religious arguments end, isn't it?" He was only dimly conscious of the serjeant dragging him out of the downpour. His neural nanonics came back on line, and immediately started erecting axon blockades. It was a different kind of numbness than the snow had brought, less severe. The serjeant wrapped a medical nanonic package around his hand. A stimulant program coaxed Joshua's brain back to full alertness. He blinked up at the three faces peering down at him. Kole and Shea were clinging together, both of them in a shambles, drenched and stupefied. The serjeant had taken a bad pounding, deep scorch marks crisscrossed its body, all-too-human blood was bubbling out from crusted wounds.

Joshua climbed slowly to his feet. He wanted to smile reassuringly at the girls, but the will just wasn't there. "Are you okay?" he asked the serjeant.

"I'm mobile."

"Good. What about you two, any damage?"

Shea shook her head timidly, Kole was still sobbing.

"Thanks for helping," he said to Shea. "That was fast thinking. I don't know what I would have done without the water. It was all a little bit too close for comfort. But we're through the worst now."

"Joshua," the serjeant said. "Dahybi says that three of the Capone Organization's warships have just arrived."

Seven Edenists in full body armour were guarding the docking ledge departure lounge. Monica was tremendously glad to see them. Along with Samuel, she'd been covering their retreat from the Terminal Terminus, no easy duty. There had been three encounters with the possessed on the way, and the shapeshifting magicians terrified her. Nerves and neural nanonics were hyped to the maximum. Never once had she given them the opportunity to surrender or back off. Locate and shoot, that was the way to do it. And she noticed that for all his worthiness and respect for life, Samuel was wired pretty much the same.

The lighting panels were flickering and dimming as the group rushed across the lounge towards the airlock door and the waiting crew bus outside. Monica waited until the airlock hatch slid shut before taking her combat programs off line. She flicked the machine gun's safety catch on, and slowly pulled off her chameleon suit hood. The bus's cool air felt gloriously refreshing as it gusted over her sweat-soaked hair.

"Well, that was easy," she said.

The bus was rolling towards the *Hoya*, the last voidhawk left on the ledge. Nothing else moved on the shelf of smooth dark rock.

"Unfortunately, you might be right," Samuel said. He was bent over the unconscious form of Adok Dala, checking the boy with a sensor from a medical block. "Capone's ships are here."

"*What?*"

"Don't worry. The Duida Consensus has dispatched a squadron of voidhawks to support us. We are in little physical danger."

An inane impulse made Monica stare out through the bus's window in search of the Organization ships. She could barely make out the non-rotational spaceport, an eclipsed crescent with the funereal red mist of the disk swirling around its edges. "We're a long way from New California. Is this another invasion?"

"No, there are only three ships."

"Then why . . . Oh, God, you don't think he's looking for Mzu as well?"

"It is the most obvious possibility."

They reached the voidhawk, and the bus extended its airlock tube over the upper hull. Despite their situation, Monica glanced around curiously once she was on board. The crew toroid wasn't that much different from an Adamist starship's life-support capsule in terms of technology; it was a lot roomier, though. Samuel led her around the central corridor to the bridge and introduced her to Captain Niveu.

"My thanks to *Hoya*," she said, remembering her etiquette.

"Our pleasure, you have been performing a difficult job under extreme circumstances."

"Tell me about it. What's happening with the Capone ships?"

"They are accelerating down into the disk, though they have made no threatening moves. The squadron from the Duida habitats is here, we're moving out to join them now. What happens next depends on the Capone ships."

"We're under way?" Monica asked. The gravity field was rock steady.

"Yes."

"Are there any electronic sensors I can access?"

"Certainly."

Monica's neural nanonics received a datavise from the bridge's bitek processor array. *Hoya* was already sliding up through the fringes of the disk, like a bird emerging from a rain cloud. Purple and green symbols outlined the three Capone Organization ships, half a million kilometres away, and heading in towards Ayacucho at a steady third of a gravity. The squadron of voidhawks was clustered together just outside the top of the disk.

"They're not in any hurry," Monica observed.

"They probably don't wish to appear hostile," Niveu said. "If it came to a battle with us they would lose."

"Are you going to allow them to dock?"

Niveu glanced at Samuel.

"Consensus is undecided," Samuel said. "We don't have sufficient information yet. To attack them without reason is not an action we can undertake lightly."

"They can't be here on an assault mission," Niveu said. "Ayacucho has almost fallen now, attacking it would be pointless. The asteroid's new masters would probably welcome an alliance with Capone."

"Destroying them now might be the best course for us all in the long run," Monica said. "If they walk in, they'll be able to squeeze every byte of data from Voi's friends. And if Voi and Mzu didn't get off, then we really are up shit creek."

"Good point," Samuel said. "We must find out what we can. Time to talk to our guest."

Only Sarha, Beaulieu, and Dahybi were on the bridge when Joshua sailed through the floor hatch. He'd told the serjeants to take both girls to capsule C where Melvyn, Liol, and Ashly were waiting in the sick bay.

Sarha's expression was a blend of anger and worry as he drifted past her acceleration couch. "God, Joshua!"

"I'm all right, really." He showed her the medical nanonic which had enveloped his right hand. "All under control."

She scowled as he moved away trailing droplets of cold water. A neat midair twist, and he was lying on his acceleration couch with the webbing folding over him.

"The net has gone completely," Dahybi said. "We can't monitor the asteroid's systems."

"It doesn't matter," Joshua said. "I know exactly what's happening in there. That's why we're leaving."

"Did the girl help?" Beaulieu asked.

"Not yet. I just want to get us clear first. Dahybi, are any of the voidhawks screwing around with our nodes?"

"No, Captain, we can jump."

"Good." Joshua optimistically ordered the flight computer to release the cradle clamps. He was rather pleased to see them disengage, some processors were still working back in the spaceport.

The chemical verniers fired, lifting them straight up out of the bay. Sarha winced as the drab metal wall slid past the tips of the sensor clusters, there was only about five metres clearance. But Lady Mac never wavered. As soon as they emerged from the bay Joshua cut the rockets, letting the starship fly free. The sensor clusters sank down into their jump recesses. An event horizon claimed the hull. They jumped half a light year. A second after they emerged energy flashed through the patterning nodes again. This time the jump was three light-years.

Joshua let out a juddering sigh.

Sarha, Beaulieu, and Dahybi looked at him. He was completely motionless, staring at the ceiling.

"Why don't you join the others in the sick bay?" Sarha said compassionately. "Your hand should be checked properly."

"I heard them, you know."

Sarha gave Dahybi an anxious look. The node specialist gave her a curt gesture with his hand.

"Heard who?" she asked. Her webbing peeled back, allowing her to haul herself over to Joshua. A stikpad at the side of his couch captured her feet.

He didn't acknowledge her presence. "The souls in the beyond. Jesus, they're real all right, they're there waiting. One tiny act of weakness, that's all it takes, and they've got you."

Her fingers stroked his waterlogged hair. "They didn't get you."

"No. But they lie and lie about how they can help. I was angry, and stupid enough to think Horst's damn cross would save me." He held up the little crucifix and snorted at it. "Jesus, he was a Muslim."

"You're not making a lot of sense."

He looked up at her with bloodshot eyes. "Sorry. They can hurt you very badly, you know. He'd only just started with my hand, that was a warm-up. I don't know if I could have held out. I told myself I would, or at least that I wouldn't give in. I think the only way to do that is to die."

"But you didn't give in, and you're still alive, and it's only you inside your skull. You won, Joshua."

"Luck, and the tank is about empty."

"It wasn't luck you had three serjeants with you. It was healthy paranoia and good planning. You knew the possessed are extremely dangerous, and took it into account. And that's what we'll do again next time."

He gave a nervous laugh. "If I can manage a next time. It's quite something to look right down into the abyss and see what's there waiting for you, one way or the other, as possessed or possessor."

"We were up against it at Lalonde, and we're still flying."

"That was different, I was ignorant then. But now I know for sure. We're going to die, and be condemned to live in the beyond. All of us. Every sentient entity in the universe." His face screwed up in pain and anger. "Jesus, I can't believe that's all there is: life and purgatory. After tens of thousands of years, the universe finally reveals that we have souls, and then we have the glory snatched right back and replaced with terror. There has to be something more, there *has* to be. He wouldn't do that to us."

"Who?"

"God, he, she, it, whatever. This torment, it's too . . . I don't know. Personal. Why the fuck build a universe that does this to people? If you're that powerful, why not make death final, or make everyone immortal? Why *this*? We have to know, have to find out why it works the way it does. That way we can know what the answer to all this is. We have to find something that's permanent, something which will last until the end of time."

"How do you propose to do that?" she asked quietly.

"I don't know," he snapped, then just as suddenly he was thoughtful again. "Maybe the Kiint. They say they've solved all this. They won't tell us outright, but they might at least point me in the right direction."

Sarha looked down at his intense expression in astonishment. Joshua taking life so seriously was strange, Joshua mounting a crusade was frankly astonishing. For one second she thought that he had been possessed after all. "You?" she blurted.

All the suffering and angst vanished from his angular face. The old Joshua swept back. He started chuckling. "Yeah, me. I might be catching religion a little late in life, but the born-again are always the most insufferable and devout."

"It's more than your hand which needs checking out in the sick bay."

"Thank you, my loyal crew." His restraint webbing parted, allowing him up. "But we're still going to ask the Kiint." He ordered the flight computer to run a full star track search and correlate their exact position. Then he ran an almanac search for Jobis's file.

"Right now?" Dahybi asked tartly. "You're going to throw away all you achieved on Ayacucho just like that?"

"Of course not," Joshua said smoothly.

"Good. Because if we don't find Mzu and the Alchemist before the possessed do, there probably won't be any Confederation left for you to save."

Adok Dala returned to consciousness with a loud cry. He looked around fearfully at the *Hoya*'s sick bay. Not reassured by his surroundings. Not at all.

Samuel removed the medical nanonic package from the base of his neck. "Easy there. You're quite safe, Adok. Nobody is going to hurt you here. And I must apologize for the way we treated you in the club, but you are rather important to us."

"You're not the possessed?"

"No. We're Edenists. Well, apart from Monica, here; she's from the Kulu Kingdom."

Monica did her best to smile at the nervous boy.

"You're foreign agents, then?"

"Yes."

"I won't tell you anything. I'm not helping you catch Mzu."

"That's very patriotic. But we're not interested in Mzu. Frankly, we hope she got away clean. You see, the possessed are in charge of Ayacucho now."

Adok moaned in distress, clamping his hand over his mouth.

"What we'd like to know about is Voi," Samuel said.

"Voi?"

"Yes. Do you know where she is?"

"I haven't seen her for days. She put us all on standby. It was silly, we had to organize the kids in the day clubs to kill spiders. She said Lodi figured out you were using them to spy on us."

"Clever man, Lodi. Do you know where he is?"

"No. Not for a couple of days."

"Interesting. How many are there in this group of yours?"

"About twenty, twenty-five. There's no real list. We're just friends."

"Who started it?"

"Voi. She'd changed when she came out of detox. The genocide became a real cause for her. We just got sucked along by her. Everybody does when Voi gets serious about an issue."

Monica datavised a request to her processor block, retrieving a memory image from the file she'd recorded at the Terminal Terminus. It had bothered her since the snatch. The last glimpse she had of Joshua Calvert showed him tugging a girl along. She showed the enhanced image to Adok. "Do you know her?"

He blinked blearily at the little screen. Whatever drugs Samuel had administered to loosen his tongue were making him drowsy. "That's Shea. I like her, but . . ."

"Is she one of your group?"

"Not really, but she's Prince Lambert's girlfriend. He's sort of a member; and she's done a few things for us occasionally."

Monica looked at Samuel. "What have we got on this Prince Lambert character?"

"A moment." He consulted his bitek processor block. "He's registered as a pilot for the *Tekas*, an executive yacht owned by his family corporation. Monica, it was one of the starships which left Ayacucho this afternoon."

"Damn it!" She slammed her fist down on one of the cabinets beside Adok Dala's couch. "Does Voi know Prince Lambert?"

Adok smiled blithely. "Yes. They used to be lovers. He was the reason she wound up in detox."

Do you have a jump coordinate for the *Tekas*? Samuel asked Niveu.

No. It flew outside our mass perception range. None of the voidhawks registered its jump. But we do have the flight vector. It was an odd course, the ship was heading back down to the disk when it passed beyond us. If it didn't perform any drastic realignment manoeuvres there are three possible stars it could have flown to: Shikoku, Nyvan, and Torrox.

Thank you. We'll check them.

Of course. I'll inform Duida's defence command. We'll leave immediately.

Shea had changed into a grey ship-suit when Joshua floated into the sickbay. She was talking quietly to Liol, but broke off to give him a shy grin. Ashly and Melvyn were busy packing equipment away. One of the serjeants held on to a grab hoop just inside the hatch.

"How are you feeling?" Joshua asked her.

"Fine. Ashly gave me a tranquillizer. I think it helps."

"I wish he'd give me one."

Her grin brightened. "Is your hand very bad?"

He held it up. "Most of the bone is intact, but I'm going to need some clone vat tissue to build the fingers up. The package can't regenerate quite that much."

"Oh. I'm sorry."

"Tranquillity will pay for it," he said, straight-faced. "Where's Kole?"

"Zero-tau," Melvyn said.

"Good idea."

"Do you want me to go in as well?" Shea asked.

"Up to you. But I need some help before you decide."

"From me?"

"Yes. Let me explain. Contrary to everything the news studios were saying, I'm not a foreign agent."

"I know that, you're Lagrange Calvert."

Joshua smiled. "I knew it would come in useful one day. The thing is, we are looking for Alkad Mzu, but not because of any Omutan propaganda."

"Why then?"

He took her hand in his, squeezing emphatically. "There is a reason, Shea, it's a good reason, but not a very nice one. I'll tell you if you really want to know; because if you're anything like the person I think you are, you'd help us find her if you knew what's actually going on. But if you'll trust me on this, you don't want to know. It's up to you."

"Are you going to kill her?" she asked sheepishly.

"No."

"Promise?"

"I promise. We just want to take her back to Tranquillity where she's been living since the genocide. As prisons go, it isn't bad. And if we can get to her in time, it'll save an awful lot of people. Maybe an entire planet."

"She's going to drop a planet-buster on Omuta, isn't she?"

"Something like that."

"I thought so," she said in a tiny voice. "But I don't know where she is."

"I think you do. You see, we believe she's with Voi."

"Oh, *her*." Shea's face darkened.

"Yes, her. I'm sorry, this sounds painful for you. I didn't realize."

"She and Prince Lambert had a thing. He still . . . well, he'd go back to her if she'd have him."

"This Prince Lambert is your boyfriend, the starship captain?"

"Yes."

"Which ship?"

"The *Tekas*."

"And it left Ayacucho today?"

"Yes. Do you really think Alkad Mzu was on board?"

"I'm afraid so."

"Is he going to be in trouble with the authorities?"

"I couldn't care less about him. I just want to locate Mzu. Once I've done that, once she knows I'm on her tail and watching every move, the threat will be neutered. She'll have to come back with me then. Now, are you going to tell me where the *Tekas* went?"

"I'm sorry, I wish I could help, but he wouldn't tell me where they were going."

"Shit!"

"P.L. is flying the *Tekas* to Nyvan," Liol said. He looked around inquiringly at the startled faces. "Did I say something wrong?"

"How the bloody hell do you know where he was going?" Joshua demanded.

"P.L.'s a good friend of mine; we grew up together. Quantum Serendipity has the contract to service the *Tekas*. He's not the most experienced pilot, and Voi had given him a very odd manoeuvre to fly. So I helped him program the flight vector."

5

André Duchamp had half expected to be shot at by the Ethenthia asteroid's SD platforms when the *Villeneuve's Revenge* jumped into its dedicated emergence zone three thousand kilometres away. He certainly had a lot of explaining to do to the local defence command, followed up by testimony from the rover reporters. When he did finally receive docking permission he assumed the famed Duchamp forcefulness and integrity had won through again.

What actually happened was that while he was busy claiming to be a defector from the Capone Organization, Erick opened a channel to the local Confederation Navy Bureau and asked them to press the local authority for clearance. Even so, the authorities were extremely cautious. Three SD platforms were locked on to the *Villeneuve's Revenge* as it approached the spaceport.

The security teams which ransacked the life-support capsules in search of treachery were exceptionally thorough. André put on a brave face as composite panels were split open and equipment modules broken down into component parts for high-definition scanning. The cabins hadn't exactly been in optimum shape before. It would take weeks to reassemble the trashed fittings to comply with even the minimum of CAB flight-worthiness requirements.

But Kingsley Pryor was hauled away by the emotionless officers from an unnamed division of the defence forces. A big credit bonus to the intrepid crew who had outsmarted Capone.

The only possible flaw was Shane Brandes. So the *Dechal*'s fusion engineer was brought out of zero-tau while

they were still on the approach phase and given a simple ul-
timatum: cooperate or you're going to be a dead crewman
who we're in mourning over. He chose cooperation; explaining to the Ethenthia authorities why they'd abducted
him in the first place would have been a little too confusing,
he felt.

Thirteen hours after they docked, the last of Ethenthia's
security officers departed. André gazed around lugubriously
at his bridge. The consoles were little more than open grids
of processor boards; walls and decking had been stripped
down to the bare metal; environmental ducts were making
stressed whining sounds, and dirty condensation was building up on every surface.

"We did it." His clown face exhibited a genuine smile as
he looked from Erick, to Madeleine, and finally Desmond.
"We're home free."

Madeleine and Desmond began to chuckle, sharing the realization. They really had come through.

"I have a few bottles in my cabin," André said. "If those
thieving scum *anglo* police haven't stolen them. We must
celebrate. Ethenthia is as good a place as any to sit out this
war. We can keep busy with some proper maintenance. I'm
sure I can get the insurance to pay for some of this wreckage; after all, we're war heroes now. Who will argue, eh?"

"Tina might," Erick said.

The flatness in the voice dispelled André's smile. "Tina
who?"

"The girl we killed on the *Krystal Moon*. Murdered, actually."

"Oh, Erick. Dear *enfant*. You are tired. You have done
more work than most."

"Certainly more than you. But what's new there?"

"Erick," Desmond said. "Come now, it has been a terrible
time for all of us. Perhaps we should get some rest before we
decide what to do next."

"Good suggestion. I admit I haven't quite made up my
mind what to do with you yet."

"What *you* are going to do with us?" André asked indignantly. "I think your medical modules are malfunctioning; your brain is being fed the wrong chemicals. Come, we will go to bed, and in the morning none of this will be mentioned again."

"Shut up, you pompous geek," Erick said. It was the contemptuous indifference of the voice which shocked André into silence.

"My problem is that I owe Madeleine and Desmond my life," Erick went on. "But then, if you hadn't been such an arsehole, Duchamp, none of us would ever have been put in the crazy position we were. That's the kind of hazard I have to accept when I take on missions like this."

"Missions?" André didn't like the cold passion which had suddenly overtaken his crewman.

"Yes, I'm an undercover officer in the CNIS."

"Oh, fuck," Madeleine grunted helplessly. "Erick . . . Shit, I liked you."

"Yeah. That's my problem, too. I'm in a little bit deeper than I ever expected. We made a good team fighting the possessed."

"So now what?" she asked numbly. "A penal colony?"

"After everything we went through, I'm prepared to make you an offer. I owe you that, I think."

"What sort of offer?" André asked.

"An exchange. You see, I'm your case officer, I'm the one who decides if the Service prosecutes, I'm the one who provides the evidence that we attacked the *Krystal Moon* and killed a fifteen-year-old girl because you're such an incompetent captain you can't keep up the payments on a ship that isn't worth ten fuseodollars."

"Ah! Of course, money is no problem, my dear *enfant*. I can mortgage the ship, it will be done for you by tomorrow. What currency do you—"

"*Shut up!*" Madeleine bellowed. "Just shut the fuck up, Duchamp. What is it, Erick? What's he got to do? Because whatever it is, he's going to do it with a big smile on his fat stupid face."

"I want to know something, Duchamp," Erick said. "And

I think you can tell me. In fact, I'm sure you can. Because it's information which only the vilest, most deceitful pieces of shit in the galaxy are entrusted with." He drifted over until he was centimetres from the captain. Duchamp had started to tremble.

"What is the coordinate of the antimatter station, André?" he asked softly. "I know you know."

André blanched. "I . . . I cannot. Not that."

"Oh, really? Do you know why the Confederation is so unsuccessful in finding antimatter production stations, Madeleine?" Erick asked. "It's because we can't use debrief nanonics on people we suspect of knowing where they are. Nor can we use drugs, or even torture. It's their neural nanonics, you see. The price of learning a station's coordinate is a very special set of neural nanonics. The black cartel supplies them absolutely free of charge. Top-of-the-range, whatever marque you like, but always with one small modification. If they detect the owner is being subjected to any form of interrogation, such as debrief nanonics, they kamikaze. The only way the coordinate is passed on is voluntarily. So what is it, Duchamp?"

"They'll kill me," André whimpered. He made to reach out and clasp Erick's shoulder, but his hand fisted just before contact and drew back. "Did you not hear? They'll kill me!"

"Fucking tell him!" Madeleine shouted.

"Non."

"It won't be a penal colony after the trial," Erick said. "We'll take you away to a quiet little laboratory deep in Trafalgar, and try and see if this time we can beat the kamikaze mechanism."

"They'll know. They always find out. Always!"

"One of the stations is supplying Capone with antimatter. That means the cartel has already lost it to the possessed, so they're not going to care. And what about you? Do you care, do you want Capone to keep winning? And if he does beat us, what do you think he'll do with you when he finally catches up with you?"

"But suppose the station I know of isn't the one?"

"The only good antimatter station is one which has been destroyed. Now what's it going to be? The CNIS lab? The cartel? Capone? Or do I load a no further action code in your file? Make your mind up."

"I despise you, *anglo*. I want your precious Confederation to die right in front of you. I want your entire family possessed and made to fuck animals. I want your soul trapped in the beyond for all time. Only then will I have justice for what you and your kind have done to me and my life."

"The coordinate, Duchamp," Erick said impassively.

André datavised the star's almanac file over.

Lieutenant Commander Emonn Verona, the CNIS's head of station on Ethenthia, sat behind his desk and stared at Erick in what was almost a state of reverence. "You have the name of the next system Capone intends to invade, *and* an antimatter station coordinate?"

"Yes, sir. According to Pryor, Capone is going to send his fleet to the Toi-Hoi system."

"Good God. If we can ambush that fleet, we've got the bastard cold. He'll be finished."

"Yes, sir."

"Right. This bureau's only goal now is to get your information back to Trafalgar. There aren't any navy ships stationed here; I'm going to have to signal the Edenist habitats orbiting Golmo and request some voidhawks. That's fifteen light-hours away." He eyed the exhausted captain whose skin seemed to be half nanonic packages; the medical ancillary modules fastened to his belt had several orange LEDs winking on them. "We ought to have a voidhawk here within sixteen hours. That'll give you some time to have a decent rest first."

"Thanks. All of us got pretty strung out searching the ship for that nuke."

"I'll bet. Are you sure you want to drop the charges against Duchamp?"

"Not really. But I gave my word, even though that means nothing to a man like him. Besides, he knows the navy has a file on him now, he knows we'll be watching him, he'll never trust another crew member again. He'll never be able to fly another illegal flight again. And given the state of that ship, and his own abilities, he isn't going to be able to make enough from legal charters to keep going. The banks will take the *Villeneuve's Revenge* off him. For someone like him, that's worse than a penal colony or the death sentence."

"I hope I never get you at my court-martial," Emonn Verona said.

"He deserves it."

"I know. What do you want to do about Pryor?"

"Where is he now?"

"He's being remanded in custody. There are any number of charges we can bring. I can't believe a Confederation Navy officer turned like that."

"It will be interesting to find out the reason. I think there's a lot more to Kingsley Pryor than we know. The best course would be for me to take him back to Trafalgar. He can be debriefed properly there."

"Okay. I'm going to step up security around the bureau, and I don't want you to leave it until the voidhawk arrives. There's a spare office you can use to sleep in, my executive officer will show you. And I'll organize a medical team to examine you before you depart."

"Thank you, sir." Erick stood up, saluted, and walked out.

Emonn Verona had been fifteen years in the navy, and undercover officers like Erick Thakrar still unnerved him.

The office light panel dimmed for a few seconds, then flickered annoyingly up to its full brightness. Emonn Verona gave it a resigned glare: the damn thing had been getting worse for a couple of days now. He made a note in his neural nanonics general file to get an engineer in once Thakrar was safely on his way.

• • •

Right from the start, Gerald Skibbow had disliked asteroid settlements. They were worse than an arcology; the corridors were claustrophobic, while the biosphere caverns had a forced grandeur which lessened them considerably. Those initial impressions had come from Pinjarra, where the *Quadin* had left him.

It hadn't taken long, even for someone as ingenuous as himself, to find out that despite the quarantine, non-governmental cargoes were still arriving at Pinjarra from outsystem. They didn't arrive on starships, though, *Quadin* was virtually the only one docked to the asteroid's space-port, the rest were inter-orbit craft. Hours spent in the bars which their crews used gave him an outline of the operation, and a name: Koblat. An asteroid which was open to quarantine-busting flights, acting as a distribution hub for the Trojan cluster. A berth on an inter-orbit ship returning empty cost him five thousand fuseodollars.

It was the starships Gerald wanted, whose captains might conceivably accept a charter to Valisk. He had money in his Jovian Bank credit disk; so perhaps it was his manner which caused them all to shake their heads and turn their backs on him. He knew he was too anxious, too insistent, too desperate. He'd made progress in controlling the extremes of his behaviour; there were fewer tantrums when his requests were refused, and he really tried to remember to wash and shave and find clean clothes. But still the captains rejected him. Perhaps they could see the ghosts and demons dancing inside his head. They didn't understand. It was Marie they were condemning, not him.

This time he had come very close to screaming at the captain as she made a joke of his pleas. Very close to raising his fists, to punching the truth and the need into her.

Then she had looked into his eyes and realized the danger caged in there, and her smile had emptied away. Gerald knew the barman was watching closely, one hand under the bar to grip whatever it was he used to quell trouble. There was a long moment spent looking down at the captain as silence rippled out from her table to claim the Blue Fountain. He took the time to think the way Dr Dobbs said he should, to focus on goals and the proper way to achieve them, how to make himself calm when his thoughts were febrile with rage.

The possibility of violence passed. Gerald turned and made for the door. Outside, naked rock pressed in on him, creating a sense of suffocation. There were too few light panels in the corridor. Hologram signs and low-wattage AV projections tried to entice him into other clubs and bars. He shuffled past, reaching the warren of smaller corridors which served the residential section. He thought his rented room was close, the signs at every intersection were confusing, numbers and letters jumbled together; he wasn't used to them yet. Voices rumbled down the corridor, male laughs and jeers, the tone was unpleasant. They were coming from the junction ahead. Dim shadows moved on the walls. He almost stopped and turned around. Then he heard the girl's cry, angry and fearful at the same time. He wanted to run away. Violence frightened him now. The possessed seemed to be at the heart of all conflicts, all evil. It would be best to leave, to call others to help. The girl cried out again, cursing. And Gerald thought of Marie, and how lonely and afraid she must have been when the possessed claimed her. He edged forwards, and glanced around the corner.

At first, Beth had been furious with herself. She prided herself on how urban-wise she was. Koblat might be small, but that didn't mean it had much community spirit. There were only the company cops to keep order; and they didn't much bother unless they'd had their bung. The corridors could get tough. Men in their twenties, the failed rebels who now had nothing in front of them but eighty years work for the company, went together in clans. They had their own turf, and Beth knew which corridors they were, where you didn't go at any time.

She hadn't been expecting any trouble when the three young men walked down the corridor towards her. She was only twenty metres from her apartment, and they were in company overalls, some kind of maintenance crew. Not a clan, nor mates coming back from a clubbing session. Mr Regulars.

The first one whistled admiringly when they were a few metres away. So she gave them the standard blank smile and moved over to one side of the corridor. Then one of them groaned and pointed at her ankle. "Christ, she's wearing one too, a deadie."

"Are ya gay, doll? Fancy giving that Kiera one, do ya? Me too."

They all laughed harshly. Beth tried to walk past. A hand caught her arm. "Where you going, doll?"

She attempted to pull herself free, but he was too strong.

"Valisk? Going to shag Kiera? We not good enough for you here? You got something against your own kind?"

"Let go!" Beth started to struggle. More hands grabbed her. She lashed out with her free arm, but it was no good. They were bigger, older, stronger.

"Little cow."

"She's got some fight in her."

"Hold the bitch. Take that arm."

Her arms were forced behind her back, holding her still. The man in front of her grinned slowly as she twisted about. He grabbed her hair suddenly and pushed her head back. Beth flinched, very near to losing it. His face was centimetres from hers, triumphant eyes gloating.

"Gonna take you home with us," he breathed. "We'll straighten you out good and proper, doll; you won't want girls again, not after we've finished with you."

"Fuck off!" Beth screamed. She kicked out. But he caught her leg and shoved it high into the air.

"Dumb slut." He tugged at the knot which held the red handkerchief around her ankle. "Reckon this might come in useful, guys. She's got a mouth on her."

"You . . . you just bloody well leave her alone."

All four of them stared at the speaker.

Gerald stood in the corridor's junction, his grey ship-suit wrinkled and dirty, hair ruffled, three days of beard shading his face. Even more alarming than the nervejam stick he was pointing at them in a two-handed grip was the way it shook.

He was blinking as if he were having great difficulty focusing.

"Whoa there, fella," the man holding Beth's leg said. "Let's not get excited here."

"*Get away from her!*" The nervejam stick juddered violently.

Beth's leg was hurriedly dropped. The hands let go of her arms. Her three would-be rapists began to back off down the corridor. "We're going, okay? You got this all wrong, fella."

"Leave! I know what you are. You're part of it. You're part of them. You're helping them."

The three men were retreating fast. Beth looked at the unstable nervejam stick and the persecuted face behind it, and almost felt like joining them. She tried to get her breathing back under control.

"Thanks, mate," she said.

Gerald sucked on his lower lip and gradually slid down the wall until he was squatting on his heels. The nervejam stick dropped from his fingers.

"Hey, you okay?" Beth hurried forwards.

Gerald looked up at her with a pathetically placid face and started whimpering.

"Jeeze—" She looked around to make certain her assailants had gone, then hunkered down beside him. Something made her hold back from making a grab for the nervejam. She was desperately uncertain what he'd do. "Listen, they'll probably come back in a minute. Where do you live?"

Tears started streaming down from his eyes. "I thought you were Marie."

"No such luck mate, I'm Beth. Is this your corridor?"

"I don't know."

"Well, do you live near here?"

"Help me please, I have to get to her, and Loren's left me here all alone. I don't know what to do next. I really don't."

"You're not the only one," Beth grunted.

"Well who is he?" Jed asked.

Gerald was sitting at the dining-room table in Beth's

apartment, staring at the mug of tea he was holding. It was a pose he'd maintained for the last ten minutes.

"Says his name's Gerald Skibbow," Beth said. "Reckon he's telling the truth."

"Okay. How about you? You all right now?"

"Yeah. Those manky bastards got a real fright. Don't reckon we'll be seeing them again."

"Good. You know, we might be better off if we stop wearing our handkerchiefs. People are getting real uptight about it."

"What? No way! Not now. It says what I am: a Deadnight. If they can't stomach that, it ain't my problem."

"It nearly was."

"It won't happen again." She held up the nervejam and gave a brutish smirk.

"Jeeze. Is that his?"

"Yep. Said I could borrow it."

Jed regarded Gerald in dismayed confusion. "Blimey. Bloke must be pretty far gone."

"Hey." She tapped his belly with the tip of the nervejam. "Watch what you're saying. Maybe he's a little cranky, but he's my mate."

"A *little* cranky? Look at him, Beth, the guy's a walking dunny." He saw the way she tensed up. "Okay. He's your mate. What are you going to do with him?"

"He'll have a room somewhere."

"Yeah, a nice quiet one with lots of padding on the walls."

"Quit that, will you. How much you've changed, huh? We're supposed to be wanting a life where people don't jump down each other's throats the whole time. Least, that's what I thought. Am I wrong?"

"No," he grumbled. Beth these days was hard to understand. Jed had thought she'd appreciate the fact he wasn't making moves on her anymore. If anything that had made her even more intractable. "Hey, look don't worry. My head'll get straightened when we reach Valisk."

Gerald slewed around in his chair. "What did you say?"

"Hey, mate, thought you'd gone switch-off on us there," Beth said. "How you feeling?"

"What did you say about Valisk?"

"We want to go there," Jed said. "We're Deadnights, see. We believe in Kiera. We want to be part of the new universe."

Gerald stared at him, then gave a twisted giggle. "Believe her? She's not even Kiera."

"You're just like all the others. You don't want us to have a chance just because you blew yours. That stinks, man!"

"Wait wait." Gerald held up his arms in placation. "I'm sorry. I didn't know you were a Deadnight. I don't know what Deadnights are."

"It's what she said, that Kiera: *Those of us who have emerged from the dead of night can break the restrictions of this corrupt society.*"

"Oh, right, that bit."

"She's going to take us away from all this," Beth said. "Where arseholes like those three blokes don't do what they did. Not anymore. There won't be any of that in Valisk."

"I know," Gerald said solemnly.

"What? You taking the piss?"

"No. Honestly. I've been searching for a way to Valisk ever since I saw the recording. I came here all the way from Ombey on the one hope that I'd find a way. I thought one of the starships might take me."

"No way, mate," Jed said. "Not the starships. We tried. The captains have all got closed minds. I told you, they hate us."

"Yes."

Jed glanced at Beth, trying to judge what she thought, if he should risk it. "You must have quite a bit of money, you come here from Ombey," he said.

"More than enough to charter a starship," Gerald said bitterly. "But they just won't listen to me."

"You don't need a starship."

"What do you mean?"

"I'll tell you how to get to Valisk if you take us with you.

It's ten times cheaper than the way you were planning, but we still can't put that much together ourselves. As you've got to charter a whole ship for the flight anyway, it won't cost you any more for us to be on board."

"All right."

"You'll take us?"

"Yes."

"Promise?" Beth asked, her voice betraying a multitude of vulnerabilities.

"I promise, Beth. I know what it's like to be let down, to be abandoned. I wouldn't do that to anyone, least of all you."

She shifted around uncomfortably, rather pleased by what he'd said, the fatherly way he'd said it. Nobody on Koblat ever spoke to her like that.

"Okay," Jed said. "Here it is: I've got a pickup coordinate timetable for this system." He took a flek from his pocket and slotted it in the desktop block. The block's holoscreen flashed up a complex graphic. "This shows where and when a starship from Valisk will be waiting to take on anyone who wants to go there. All you have to do is charter an inter-orbit craft to get us to it."

• • •

As always, Syrinx found Athene's house relaxing. No doubt Wing-Tsit Chong and the psychological team would call it a return to the womb. And if she found that amusing, she told herself, she must be virtually recovered.

She had returned from Jobis two days earlier. After relating everything she had learned from Malva to Wing-Tsit Chong, *Oenone* had flown to Romulus and a berth in an industrial station.

I suppose I ought to be glad you're flying courier duty for our intelligence service, Athene said. The doctors must think you're recovered.

And you don't? Syrinx was walking with her mother

across the garden which seemed to grow shaggier with each passing year.

If you're not sure yourself, how can I be, my dear?

Syrinx grinned, somehow cheered by the uncanny perception. **Oh, Mother, don't fuss. Work is always a great anodyne, especially if you love your work. Voidhawk captains do nothing else.**

I want us flying missions together again, Oenone *insisted. It is good for both of us.*

For a moment, mother and daughter were aware of the gridwork surrounding *Oenone*. Technicians were busy working on the lower hull, installing combat wasp launch cradles, maser cannons, and military-grade sensor pods.

Ah well, Athene said. *Looks like I'm outvoted.*

I'll be all right, Mother, really. Going straight into the defence force would be a little too confrontational. But courier work is important. We have to act with unity against the possessed; that's vital. Voidhawks have an important role to play in that.

I'm not the one you're trying to convince.

Jesus, Mother. Everyone I know is mutating into a psychiatrist. I'm a big girl now, and my brain's back in good enough shape to make decisions.

Jesus?

Oh. Syrinx could feel the blush rising to her cheeks—only Mother could do that! **Someone I met always used it as an expletive. I just thought it was appropriate these days.**

Ah, yes. Joshua Calvert. Or Lagrange Calvert, as everyone calls him now. You had quite a thing about him, once, didn't you?

I did not! And why is he called Lagrange Calvert?

Syrinx listened with growing incredulity as Athene explained the events which had occurred in orbit around Murora. **Oh, no, fancy Edenism having to be grateful to him. And what a stupid stunt jumping inside a Lagrange point at that velocity. He could have killed everybody on board. How thoughtless.**

Dear me, it must be love.

Mother!

Athene laughed in delight at being able to needle her daughter so successfully. They'd come to the first of the big lily ponds which verged one side of the garden. It was heavily shaded now; the rank of golden yews behind it had swelled considerably in the last thirty years, their boughs reaching right across the water. She looked into the black water. Bronze-coloured fish streaked for the cover of the lily pads.

You ought to get the servitor chimps to prune the yews, Syrinx said. **They steal too much light. There are far fewer lilies than there used to be.**

Why not see what happens naturally?

It's untidy. And a habitat isn't natural.

You never did like losing arguments, did you?

Not at all. I'm always willing to listen to alternative viewpoints.

A burst of good-humoured scepticism filled the affinity band. **Is that why you're turning to religion all of a sudden? I always thought you would be the most susceptible.**

What do you mean?

Remember when Wing-Tsit Chong called you a tourist?

Yes.

It was a polite way of saying that you lack the confidence in yourself to find your own answers to life. You are always searching, Syrinx, though you never know what for. Religion was inevitably going to exert a fascination on you. The whole concept of salvation through belief offers strength to those who doubt themselves.

There's a big difference between religion and spirituality. That is something the Edenist culture is going to have to come to terms with; us, the habitats, and the voidhawks.

Yes, you're uncomfortably right there. I have to admit I was rather pleased to know that Iasius and I will be re-

united again, no matter how terrible the circumstances.
It does make life more tolerable.

That's one aspect. I was thinking more about transferring our memories into the habitat when we die. It forms
the basis of our entire society. We never feared death as
much as Adamists, which always strengthened our rationality. Now we know we're destined to the beyond, it
rather makes a mockery of the whole process. Except—

Go on.

Laton, damn him. What did he mean? Him and his
great journey, and telling us that we don't have to worry
about being trapped in the beyond. And then Malva as
good as confirmed he was telling the truth.

You think that's a bad thing?

No. If we're interpreting this properly, there is more to
the beyond than eternal purgatory. That would be wondrous.

I agree.

Then why didn't he tell us exactly what awaits? And
why would it only be us who escape the entrapment, and
not the Adamists?

Perhaps Malva was being more helpful than you realized when she told you the answer lies within us. If you
were told, you would not have found it for yourself. You
wouldn't have known it, you would simply have been
taught.

It had to be Laton, didn't it? The one person we can
never truly trust.

Even you can't trust him?

Not even I; despite the fact I owe him my life. He's
Laton, Mother.

Perhaps that's why he didn't tell us. He knew we
wouldn't trust him. He did urge us to research this thoroughly.

And so far we've failed thoroughly.

We've only just started, Syrinx. And he gave us one
clue, the kind of souls that have returned. You encoun-

tered them, darling, you have the most experience of them. What type are they?

Bastards. All of them.

Calm down, and tell me what they were like.

Syrinx smiled briefly at the reprimand, then gazed at the pink water lilies, trying to make herself remember Pernik. Something she still shied away from. I was being truthful. They really were bastards. I didn't see that many. But none of them cared about me, about how much they were hurting me. It didn't bother them, as if they were emotionally dead. I suppose being in the beyond for so long does that to them.

Not quite. Kelly Tirrel recorded a series of interviews with a possessed called Shaun Wallace. He wasn't callous, or indifferent. If anything he seemed a rather sad individual.

Sad bastards, then.

You're being too flippant. But consider this. How many Edenists are sad bastards?

No, Mother, I can't accept that. You're saying that there's some kind of selection process involved. That something is imprisoning sinners in the beyond and letting the righteous go on this final journey into the light. That cannot be right. You're saying there is a God. One that takes an overwhelming interest in every human being, that cares how we behave.

I suppose I am. It would certainly explain what's happened.

No it doesn't. Why was Laton allowed to go on the great journey?

He wasn't. Souls and memory separate at death, remember? It was Laton's personality operating within Pernik's neural strata that freed you and warned us, not his soul.

Do you really believe this?

I'm not sure. As you say, a God who takes this much interest in us as individuals would be awesome. Athene turned from the pool and slipped her arm through her daughter's. **I think I'll keep hoping for another explanation.**

Good!

Let's hope you find it for me.

Me?

You're the one gallivanting around the galaxy again. It gives you a much better chance than me.

All we're going to do is pick up routine reports from embassies and agents about possible infiltrations by the possessed, and how local governments are coping with the problem. Tactics and politics, that's all, not philosophy.

How very dull-sounding. She pulled Syrinx a little closer, allowing the worry and concern in her mind to flow freely through affinity. **Are you sure you're going to be all right?**

Yes, Mother. *Oenone* **and the crew will take good care of me. I don't want you to worry anymore.**

When Syrinx had left to supervise the last stages of *Oenone*'s refit, Athene sat in her favourite chair on the patio and attempted to involve herself in the household routine again. There were plenty of children to supervise at the moment, the adults were all away working long hours, mainly in support of the defence force. Jupiter and Saturn were both gearing up for the Mortonridge Liberation.

You shouldn't try to hold her so tight, Sinon said. **It doesn't help her confidence seeing you have so little in her.**

I have every confidence, she bridled.

Then show it. Let go.

I'm too frightened.

We all are. But we should be free to face it by ourselves.

How do you feel, then, knowing your soul has gone on?

Curious.

That's all?

Yes. I already exist in tandem with the others of the multiplicity. The beyond is not too different from that.

You hope!

One day we will know.

Let's pray it's later rather than sooner.

Like daughter, like mother.

I don't think I need a priest right now. More like a stiff drink.

Sinner. He laughed.

She watched the shadows deepen under the trees as the light tube enacted a rose-gold dusk. "There can't be a God, can there? Not really."

• • •

He doesn't look terribly happy, Tranquillity said as Prince Noton stepped into one of the ten tube stations which served the hub.

Ione pivoted her perceptual viewpoint through a complete circle, as if she were walking around the Prince. She was intrigued by his air of stubborn dignity, the kind of face and body posture that indicated he knew he was old and outdated but still insisted on interpreting the universe the way he wanted to. He wore the dress uniform of a Royal Kulu Navy admiral, with five small medal pins on his chest. When he removed his cap to climb into the tube carriage there was little hair left, and that grey; a telling sign for a Saldana.

I wonder how old he is? she mused.

A hundred and seventy. He is King David's youngest exowomb sibling. He ran the Kulu Corporation for a hundred and three years until Prince Howard took over in 2608.

How strange. Her attention flicked back to the Royal Kulu Navy battle cruiser docked in the spaceport (the first active duty ship from the Kingdom in a hundred and seventy-nine years). A diplomatic mission of the highest urgency, its captain had said when he requested permission to approach. And Prince Noton had an entourage of five Foreign Office personnel. **He's part of the old order. We're hardly likely to have anything in common. If Alastair wants something from me, surely someone younger would have been a better bet? Maybe even a Princess.**

Possibly. Though it would be hard not to respect Prince Noton. His seniority is part of the message the King is sending.

For a moment she felt a twist of worry. **I wonder. If anyone knows your true capabilities, it is my royal cousins.**

I doubt he will ask anything dishonourable.

Ione had to jog down the last twenty metres of the corridor, fumbling with the seal on the side of her skirt. She had chosen a formal business suit of green tropical weave cotton and a plain blouse; smart but not imperious. Trying to impress Prince Noton with power dressing, she suspected, would be a waste of time.

The tube carriage had already arrived at the station of De Beauvoir Palace, her official residence. Two serjeants were escorting the Prince and his entourage down the long nave. Ione raced across the audience chamber in her stockinged feet, sat behind the central desk, and jammed her shoes on.

How do I look?

Beautiful.

She growled at the lack of objectivity and combed her hair back with a hand. **I knew I should have had this cut.** She glanced around to check the arrangements. Six high-backed chairs were positioned in front of the desk. Human caterers were preparing a buffet in one of the informal reception rooms (housechimps would have been a faux pas given the Kingdom's attitude to bitek, she felt). **Change the lighting.**

Half of the floor-to-ceiling panes of glass darkened; the remainder altered their diffraction angle. Ten large planes of light converged on the desk, surrounding her in a warm astral glow. **Too much—oh, hell.**

The doors swung open. Ione rose to her feet as Prince Noton walked across the floor.

Go around the desk to greet him. Remember you are family, and technically there has never been any rift between us and the Kingdom.

Ione did as she was told, putting on a neutral smile: one she could turn to charm or ice. It was up to him.

When she put out her hand, there was only the slightest hesitation on Prince Noton's part. He gave her a politely formal handshake. His eyes did linger on her signet ring, though.

"Welcome to Tranquillity, Prince Noton. I'm very flattered that Alastair should honour me with an emissary of your seniority. I only wish we were meeting in happier times."

The staff from the Foreign Office were staring ahead rigidly. If she didn't know better she would have said they were praying.

Prince Noton took an awkwardly long time to answer. "It is a privilege to serve my King by coming here."

Ah! "Touché, cousin," she drawled.

They locked gazes while the Foreign Office staff watched nervously.

"You had to be female, didn't you?"

"Naturally, though it was completely random. Daddy never had any exowomb children. Our family tradition of primogeniture doesn't apply here."

"You hate tradition so much?"

"No, I admire a lot of tradition. I *uphold* a lot of tradition. What I will not tolerate is tradition for tradition's sake."

"Then you must be in your element. Order is falling across the Confederation."

"That, Noton, was below the belt."

He nodded gruffly. "Sorry. I don't know why the King chose me for this. Never was a bloody diplomat."

"I don't know, I think he chose rather well, actually. Sit down, please." She went back to her own chair. Tranquillity showed her the Foreign Office personnel exchanging relieved expressions behind her back. "So what exactly does Alastair want?"

"These fellers." Prince Noton clicked his finger in the direction of a serjeant. "I'm supposed to ask you if we can have their DNA sequence."

"Whatever for?"

"Ombey."

She listened with dawning unease as Prince Noton and the Foreign Office personnel related the details of the proposed Mortonridge Liberation. **Do you think this will work?**

I don't have the kind of information available to the Royal Navy, so I cannot provide an absolute. But the Royal Navy would not undertake such an action unless they were confident of the outcome.

I can't believe this is the right way to go about saving people who have been possessed. They're going to destroy Mortonridge, and a lot of people will get killed in the process.

Nobody ever claimed war is clean.

Then why do it?

For the overall objective, which is usually political. Certainly it is in this case.

So I can halt it then? If I refuse to give Alastair the sequence.

You can be the voice of sanity, certainly. Who would thank you?

The people who wouldn't get killed, for a start.

Who are the people currently possessed, and would endure any sacrifice to be freed. They do not have the luxury of your academic moral choices.

That's not fair. You can't condemn me for wanting to prevent bloodshed.

Unless you can offer an alternative, I would recommend handing over the sequence. Even if you prevaricated, you would not halt the liberation campaign. At the most you would delay it for a few weeks while the Edenists spliced together a suitable warrior servitor.

You know damn well I don't have any alternative.

This is politics, Ione; you cannot prevent the liberation from going ahead. By helping, you will form valuable alliances. Do not overlook that. You are pledged to defend all those who live within me. We may need help to do this.

No we don't. You alone of all the habitats are the final sanctuary against the possessed.

Even that is not definite. Prince Noton is correct: old orders, old certainties, are falling everywhere.

What must I do, then?

You are The Lord of Ruin. Decide.

When she looked at the old Prince, his immobile face, and his impassioned thoughts, she knew there was no choice, that there never had been. The Saldanas had sworn to defend their subjects. And in return their subjects believed in them to provide that defence. Over the Kingdom's history, hundreds of thousands had died to maintain that mutual trust.

"Of course I will provide the DNA sequence for you," Ione said. "I only wish there was more I could do."

With an irony Ione found almost painful, two days after Prince Noton departed for Kulu with the DNA sequence, Parker Higgens and Oski Katsura told her they had located a Laymil memory of the spaceholm suicide.

Almost all other research work on the Laymil project campus had stopped to allow staff from every division to assist in reviewing the decrypted sensorium memories. However, despite being the prime focus of activity, the Electronics Division was no busier than the last time she had visited. The decryption operation had been finalized, allowing all of the information within the Laymil electronics stack to be reformatted into a human access standard.

"It's only the review process itself which is causing a bottleneck now," Oski Katsura said as she ushered Ione into the hall. "We have managed to copy all of the memories in the stack, so we now have permanent access. In the end, only twelve per cent of the files were scrambled, which leaves us with eight thousand two hundred and twenty hours of recordings available. Though of course we have a team working on the lost sequences."

The Laymil electronics stack had finally been powered down. Technicians were gathered around its transparent environment sphere, checking and disconnecting it from the conditioning units.

"What are you going to do with it?" Ione asked.

"Zero-tau," Oski Katsura said. "Unfortunately, it is really too venerable to be put on exhibition. That is, unless you want it displayed to the public for a little while first?"

"No. This is your field, that's why I appointed you as division chief."

Ione saw the members of the Confederation Navy science bureau mingling with the ordinary project staff at the various research stations in the hall. It was a sign of the times that she drew no more than a few idly curious glances.

Parker Higgens, Kempster Getchell, and Lieria were standing together to watch the technicians prepare the stack for zero-tau.

"End of an era," Kempster said as Ione joined them. He appeared oblivious to any connotations in the statement. "We can't go on depending on stolen knowledge anymore. Much to the distress of the navy people, of course, no giant ray guns for them to play with. Looks like we'll have to start thinking for ourselves again. Good news, eh?"

"Unless you happen to have a possessed knocking on your door," Parker Higgens said coldly.

"My dear Parker, I do access the news studios occasionally, you know."

"How is the search for Unimeron going?" Ione asked.

"From a technical point of view, very well," Kempster said enthusiastically. "We've finished the revised design for the sensor satellite we want to use. Young Renato has taken a blackhawk down to the orbital band we intend to cover to test fly a prototype. If all goes well, the industrial stations will begin mass production next week. We can saturate the band by the end of the month. If there are any unusual energy resonances there, we ought to find them."

It wasn't going to be as quick as Ione had hoped for. "Excellent work," she told the old astronomer. "Oski tells me you have found a memory of the spaceholm suicide."

"Yes, ma'am," Parker Higgens said.

"Did they have a weapon to use against the possessed?"

"Not a physical one, I'm happy to say. They seemed inordinately complacent about the suicide."

"What do the navy people think?"

"They were disappointed, but they concur the spaceholm culture made no attempt to physically defeat the possessed Laymil approaching from Unimeron."

Ione sat at an empty research station. "Very well." **Show me.**

She never could get used to the illusive sensorium squeeze of emerging into a Laymil body. This time, her appropriated frame was one of the two male varieties, an egg producer. He was standing amid a group of Laymil, his current family and co-habitees, on the edge of their third marriage community. His clarion heads bugled softly, a keening joined by hundreds of throats around him. The melody was a slow one, rising and falling across the gentle grassy slope. Its echo sounded in his mind, gathered by the mother entity from every community in the spaceholm. Together they sang their lament, a plainsong in unison with the life spirit of the forests and meadows, the shoalminds of the animals, the mother entity. A chant taken up by every spaceholm as the cozened dead approached their constellation.

The aether was resonant with sadness, its weight impressing every organic cell within the spaceholm. Sunspires were dipping to their early and final dusk, draining away the joyful colours he had lived with all his life. Flowers relaxed into closure, their curling petals sighing for the loss of light, while their spirits wept for the greater loss which was to follow.

He linked arms with his mates and children, ready to share death as they shared life: together. The families linked arms. Drinking strength from the greater concord. They had become a single triangle on the valley floor. Component segments of three adults. Inside them, the children, protected, cherished. The whole, a symbol of strength and defiance. As with minds, so with bodies; as with thoughts, so with deeds.

"Join into rapture," he instructed his children.

Their necks wove around, heads bobbing with enchanting immaturity. *"Sorrow. Fear failure. Death essence triumphant."*

"Recall essencemaster teaching," he instructed. *"Laymil species must end. Knowledge brings birthright fulfillment. Eternal exaltation awaits strong. Recall knowledge. Believe knowledge."*

"Concur."

Beyond the rim of the spaceholm constellation, the ships from Unimeron slid out of the darkness. Stars gleaming red with the terrible power of the death essence, riding bright prongs of fusion flame.

"Know truth," the massed choir of spaceholms sang at them. *"Accept knowledge gift. Embrace freedom."*

They would not. The pernicious light grew as the ships advanced, silent and deadly.

The Laymil in the spaceholms raised their heads to the vertical and bellowed a single last triumphant note. Air rippled at the sound. The sunspires went out, allowing total darkness to seize the interior.

"Recall strength," he pleaded with his children. *"Strength achievement final amity."*

"Confirm essencemaster victory."

The spaceholm mother entity cried into the void. A pulse of love which penetrated to the core of every mind. Deep within its shell, cells ruptured and spasmed, propagating fractures clean through the polyp.

Sensation ended, but the darkness remained for a long time. Then Ione opened her eyes.

"Oh, my God. That was their only escape. They were so content about it. Every Laymil *rushed* into death. They never tried to outrun them; they never tried to fight them.

They willfully condemned themselves to the beyond to avoid being possessed."

"Not quite, ma'am," Parker Higgens said. "There are some very interesting implications in those last moments. The Laymil didn't consider they had lost. Far from it. They showed enormous resolution. We know full well how much they worship life; they would never sacrifice themselves and their children simply to inconvenience the possessed Laymil, for that is all suicide is. There are any number of options they could have explored before resorting to such an extreme measure. Yet the one whose sensorium we accessed made constant references to knowledge and truth derived from the essencemasters. That knowledge was the key to their 'eternal exaltation.' I suspect the essencemasters solved the nature of the beyond. Am I right, Lieria?"

"An astute deduction, Director Higgens," the Kiint said through her processor block. "And one which confirms the statement Ambassador Roulor made to your Assembly. For each race, the solution is unique. Surely you do not anticipate suicide as the answer for the problems facing humankind?"

Parker Higgens faced the big xenoc, his anger visible. "It was more than suicide. It was a victory. They won. Whatever the knowledge was they carried with them, it meant they were no longer afraid of the beyond."

"Yes."

"And you know what it was."

"You have our sympathy, and whatever support we can provide."

"Damn it! How dare you study us like this. We are not laboratory creatures. We are sentient entities, we have feelings, we have fears. Have you no ethics?"

Ione stood behind the trembling director and laid a cautionary hand on his shoulder.

"I am well aware of what you are, Director Higgens," Lieria said. "And I am empathic to your distress. But I must repeat, the answer to your problem lies within you, not us."

"Thank you, Parker," Ione said. "I think we're all quite clear now on where we stand."

The director gave a furious wave of his hand and walked away.

I apologize for his temper, Ione told the Kiint. **But as I'm sure you know, this terrifies us all. It is frustrating for us to know you have a solution, even though it cannot apply to us.**

Justly so, Ione Saldana. And I do understand. History records our race was in turmoil when we first discovered the beyond.

You give me hope, Lieria. Your existence is proof that satisfactory solutions can be found for a sentient race, something other than genocidal suicide. That inspires me to keep searching for our own answer.

If it is of any comfort, the Kiint are praying humans succeed.

Why, thank you.

• • •

Erick was woken by his neural nanonics. He had routinely set up programs to monitor his immediate environment, physical and electronic, alert for anything which fell outside nominal parameters.

As he sat up in the darkened office, his neural nanonics reported an outbreak of abnormal fluctuations in Ethenthia's power supply systems. When he datavised a query at the supervisor programs, it turned out that no one in the asteroid's civil engineering service was even examining the problem. A further review showed that fifteen per cent of the habitation section's lifts appeared to be inoperative. The number of datavises into the net was also reducing.

"Oh, dear God. Not here, too!" He swung his legs off the settee. A wave of nausea twisted along his spine. Medical programs sent out several caution warnings; the team Emonn Verona promised hadn't been to see him yet.

When he datavised the lieutenant commander's eddress to

the office's net processor there was no response. "Bloody hell." Erick pulled on his ship-suit, easing it over his medical packages. There were two ratings standing guard outside the office; both armed with TIP carbines. They came to attention as soon as the door opened.

"Where's the lieutenant commander?" Erick asked.

"Sir, he said he was going to the hospital, sir."

"Bugger. Right, you two come with me. We're getting off this asteroid, right away."

"Sir?"

"That was an order, mister. But in case you need an incentive, the possessed are here."

The two of them swapped a worried glance. "Aye, sir."

Erick started accessing schematics of the asteroid as they went through the Navy Bureau and out into the public hall. He followed that up by requesting a list of starships currently docked at the spaceport. There were only five; one of which was the *Villeneuve's Revenge*, which cut his options down to four.

His neural nanonics designed a route to the axial chamber which didn't use any form of powered transportation. Seven hundred metres, two hundred of which were stairs. But at least the gravity would be falling off.

They went in single file, with Erick in the centre. He ordered both ratings to put their combat programs into primary mode. People turned to stare as they marched down the middle of the public hall.

Six hundred metres to go. And the first stairwell was directly ahead. The hall's light panels started dimming.

"Run," Erick said.

Kingsley Pryor's cell measured five metres by five. It had one bunk, one toilet, and one washbasin; there was a small AV lens on the wall opposite the bed, accessing one local media company. Every surface—fittings, floor, walls—was the same blue-grey lofriction composite. It was fully screened, preventing any datavises.

For the last hour the light panel on the ceiling had been

flickering. At first, Kingsley had thought the police were doing it to irritate him. They had been almost fearful as they escorted him from the *Villeneuve's Revenge* with a Confederation Navy officer. A member of the *Capone Organization*. It was only to be expected that they would try to re-establish their superiority with such sad psychology, demonstrating who was in control. But the shifts of illumination had been too fitful for any determined effort. The AV images were also fragmenting, but not at the same time as the light. Then he found the call button produced no response.

Kingsley realized what was happening, and sat patiently on his bunk. Quarter of an hour later the humming sound from the conditioning grille fan faded away. Nothing he could do about it. Twice in the next thirty minutes the fan started up again briefly, once to blow in air which stank of sewage. Then the light panel went out permanently. Still Kingsley sat quietly.

When the door did finally open, it shone a fan of light directly across him, highlighting his almost prim posture. A werewolf crouched in the doorway, blood dripping from its fangs.

"Very original," Kingsley said.

There was a confused puppylike *yap* from the creature.

"I really must insist you don't come any closer. Both of us will wind up in the beyond if you do. And you've only just got here, haven't you?"

The werewolf outline shimmered away to reveal a man wearing a police uniform. Kingsley recognized him as one of his escorts. There was a nasty pink scar on his forehead which hadn't been there before.

"What are you talking about?" the possessed man asked.

"I am going to explain our situation to you, and I want you to observe my thoughts so that you know I'm telling the truth. And after that, you and your new friends are going to let me go. In fact, you're going to give me every assistance I require."

* * *

A hundred and fifty metres to the axial chamber. They were almost at the top of the last flight of stairs when the well's lights went out. Erick's enhanced retinas automatically switched to infrared. "They're close," he shouted in warning.

A narrow flare of white fire fountained up the centre of the stairwell, arching around to burst over the rating behind him. He grunted in pain and swung around, firing his TIP carbine at the base of the streamer. Purple sparks bounced out of the impact point.

"Help me," he cried. A smear of white fire was cloaking his entire shoulder. Terror and panic were negating all the suppression programs which his neural nanonics had doused his brain with. He stopped firing to flail at the fire with his free hand.

The other rating slithered past Erick to fire back down the stairs. A flat circle of brilliant emerald light sprang over the floor of the stairwell, then started to rise as if it were a fluid. The flare of white fire withdrew below its surface. Shadows were just visible beneath it, darting about sinuously.

The burned rating had collapsed onto the stairs. His partner was still shooting wildly down into the advancing cascade of light. The TIP pulses were turning to silver spears as they penetrated the surface, trailing bubbles of darkness.

The next door was eight metres above Erick. The ratings would never last against the possessed, he knew, a few seconds at best. That few seconds might enable him to escape. The information he had was *vital*, it had to get to Trafalgar. Millions of innocents depended on it, on him. Millions. Against two.

Erick turned and flung himself up the last few steps. In his ears he could hear a voice shouting: ". . . two of my crew are dead. Fried! Tina was fifteen years old!"

He barged through the door, ten per cent gravity projecting him in a long flat arc above the corridor floor, threatening to crack his head against the ceiling. The persecuting noises and fog of green light shut off as the door slid shut behind him. He touched down, and powered himself in another long leap forwards along the corridor. Neural nanonics outlined his route for him as if it were a starship vector plot; a tube of orange neon triangles that flashed past. Turning right. Right again. Left.

Gravity had become negligible when he heard the scream ahead of him. Fifteen metres to the axial chamber. That was all; fifteen bloody metres! And the possessed were ahead of him. Erick snatched at a grab hoop to halt his forwards flight. He didn't have any weapons. He didn't have any backup. He didn't even have Madeleine and Desmond to call on, not anymore.

More screams and pleas were trickling down the corridor from the axial chamber as the possessed chased down their victims. It wouldn't be long before one of them checked this corridor.

I have to get past. Have to!

He called up the schematic again, studying the area around the axial chamber. Twenty seconds later, and he was at the airlock hatch.

It was a big airlock, used to service the spaceport spindle. The prep room which led to it had dozens of lockers, all the equipment and support systems required to maintain space hardware, even five deactivated free-flying mechanoids.

Erick put his decryption program into primary mode and set it to work cracking the first locker's code. He stripped off his ship-suit as the lockers popped open one after the other. Physiological monitor programs confirmed everything he saw as the fabric parted. Pale fluid tinged with blood was leaking out of his medical nanonic packages where the edges were peeling from his flesh; a number of red LEDs on the ancillary modules were flashing to indicate system malfunctions. His new arm was only moving because of the reinforced impulses controlling the muscles.

But he still functioned. That was all that mattered.

It was the fifth locker which contained ten SII spacesuits. As soon as his body was sealed against the vacuum he hurried into the airlock, carrying a manoeuvring pack. He didn't bother with the normal cycle, instead he tripped the emergency vent. Air rushed out. The outer hatch irised apart as he secured himself into the manoeuvring pack. Then the punchy gas jets fired, sending him wobbling past the hatch rim and out into space.

André hated the idea of Shane Brandes even being inside the *Villeneuve's Revenge*. And as for the man actually helping repair and reassemble the starship's systems . . . *merde*. But as with most events in André's life these days, he didn't have a lot of choice. Since the showdown with Erick, Madeleine had retreated into her cabin and refused to respond to any entreaties. Desmond, at least, performed the tasks requested of him, though not with any obvious enthusiasm. And, insultingly, he would only work alone.

That just left Shane Brandes to help André with the jobs that needed more than one pair of hands. The *Dechal*'s ex-fusion engineer was anxious to please. He swore he had no allegiance to his previous captain, and harboured no grudges or ill will towards the crew of the *Villeneuve's Revenge*. He was also prepared to work for little more than beer money, and he was a grade two technician. One could not afford to overlook gift horses.

André was re-installing the main power duct in the wall of the lower deck lounge, which required Shane to feed the cable to him when instructed. Someone glided silently through the ceiling hatch, blocking the beam from the bank of temporary lights André had rigged up. André couldn't see what he was doing. "Desmond! Why must . . ." He gasped in shock. "You!"

"Hello again, Captain," Kingsley Pryor said.

"What are you doing here? How did you get out of prison?"

"They set me free."

"Who?"

"The possessed."

"Non," André whispered.

"Unfortunately so. Ethenthia has fallen."

The anti-torque tool André was holding seemed such a pitiful weapon. "Are you one of them now? You will never have my ship. I will overload the fusion generators."

"I'd really rather you didn't," Pryor datavised. "As you can see, I haven't been possessed."

"How? They take everybody, women, children."

"I am one of Capone's liaison officers. Even here, that carries enormous weight."

"And they let you go?"

"Yes."

A heavy dread settled in André's brain. "Where are they? Are they coming?" He datavised the flight computer to review the internal sensors (those remaining—curse it). As yet no systems were glitching.

"No," Pryor said. "They won't come into the *Villeneuve's Revenge*. Not unless I tell them to."

"Why are you doing this?" As if I didn't know.

"Because I want you to fly me away from here."

"And they'll let us all go, just like that?"

"As I said, Capone has a lot of influence."

"What makes you think I will take you? You blackmailed me before. It will be simple to throw you out of the airlock once we are free of Ethenthia."

Pryor smiled a dead man's smile. "You've always done exactly as I wanted, Duchamp. You were always supposed to break away from Kursk."

"Liar."

"I have been given other, more important objectives than ensuring a third-rate ship with its fifth-rate crew stay loyal to the Organization. You have never had any free will since you arrived in the New California system. You still don't. After all, you don't really think there was only one bomb planted on board, do you?"

Erick watched the *Villeneuve's Revenge* lift from its cradle. The starship's thermo-dump panels extended, ion thrusters took over from the verniers. It rose unhurriedly from the spaceport. When he switched his collar sensors to high resolution he could see the black hexagon on the fuselage where plate 8-92-K was missing.

He didn't understand it, Duchamp was making no attempt to flee. It was almost as if he was obeying traffic control, departing calmly along an assigned vector. Had the crew been possessed? Small loss to the Confederation.

His collar sensors refocused on the docking bay he was approaching, a dark circular recess in the spaceport's grid-iron exterior. It was a maintenance bay, twice as wide as an ordinary bay. The clipper-class starship, *Tigara*, which sat on the docking cradle seemed unusually small in such surroundings.

Erick fired his manoeuvring pack jets to take him down towards the *Tigara*. There were no lights on in the bay; all the gantries and multi-segment arms were folded back against the walls. Utility umbilicals were jacked in, and an airlock tube had mated with the starship's fuselage; but apart from that there was no sign of any activity.

The silicon hull showed signs of long-term vacuum exposure—faded lettering, micrometeorite impact scuffs, surface layer ablation stains—all indicating hull plates long overdue for replacement. He drifted over the blurred hexagons until he was above the EVA airlock, and datavised the hatch control processor to cycle and open. If anyone was on board, they would know about him now. But there were no datavised questions, no active sensor sweeps.

The hatch slid open, and Erick glided inside.

Clipper-class starships were designed to provide a speedy service between star systems, carrying small high-value cargoes. Consequently, as much of their internal volume as possible was given over to cargo space. There was only one life-support capsule, which accommodated an optimum crew of three. That was the principal reason Erick had chosen the *Tigara*. In theory, he would be able to fly it solo.

Most of the starship systems were powered down. He kept his SII suit on as he moved through the two darkened lower decks to the bridge. As soon as he was secured in the captain's acceleration couch he accessed the flight computer and ordered a full status review.

It could have been a lot better. *Tigara* was in the maintenance bay for a complete refit. One of the fusion generators was inoperative, two energy patterning nodes were dead, heat exchangers were operating dangerously short of required levels, innumerable failsoft components had been allowed to decay below their safety margins.

None of the maintenance work had even been started. The owners hadn't been prepared to commit that much money while the quarantine was in force.

Dear Lord, Erick thought, the *Villeneuve's Revenge* was in better condition than this.

He datavised the flight computer to disengage the bay's airlock tube, then initiated a flight prep procedure. The *Tigara* took a long time to come on-line. At every stage he had to order backup sequences to take over, or override safety programs, or re-route power supplies. He didn't even bother with the life-support functions, all he wanted was power in the energy patterning nodes and secondary drive tubes.

With a fusion generator active, he ordered some sensor clusters to deploy. An image of the bay filled his mind, overlaid with fragile status graphics. He scanned the electromagnetic spectrum for any traffic, but there was only the background hash of cosmic radiation. Nobody was saying anything to anybody. What he wanted was someone asking Ethenthia what was happening, why they'd gone off the air. A ship close by that could help.

Nothing.

Erick fired the emergency release pins which the docking cradle's load clamps were gripping. Verniers sent out a hot deluge of gas which shimmered across the bay's walls, shaking loose blankets of thermal insulation from the gantries. *Tigara* rose a metre off its cradle, straining at the nest of umbilical hoses jacked into its rear fuselage. The snapfree couplings began to break, sending the hoses writhing.

The starship was low on cryogenic fuel; he couldn't afford to waste delta-V reserve aligning himself on an ideal vector. The astrogration program produced a series of options for him.

None of them were what he'd been hoping for. So what else was new?

The last of the umbilicals broke, and the *Tigara* lurched up out of the bay. Erick ordered the flight computer to extend the communications array and align it on Golmo and the Edenist habitats orbiting there. Sensor clusters began to sink down into their recesses as energy poured into the patterning nodes.

The flight computer alerted him that an SD platform was sweeping the ship with its radar. Then it relayed a signal from traffic control into his neural nanonics.

"Is that you, Erick? We think it's you. Who else is this stupidly ballsy? This is Emonn Verona, Erick, and I'm asking you: Don't do it. That ship is completely fucked; I've got the CAB logs in front of me. It can't fly. You're only going to hurt yourself, or worse."

Erick transmitted a single message to Golmo, then retracted the communications array down into its jump configuration. The SD platform had locked on. Some of the patterning nodes were producing very strange readings in the prejump diagnostic run-through. CAB monitor programs flashed up jump proscription warnings. He switched them off.

"Game over, Erick. Either return to the docking bay or you join our comrades in the beyond. You don't want that. Where there's life, there's hope. Right? Of all people, you must believe that."

Erick ordered the flight computer to activate the jump sequence.

6

The hellhawk *Socratous* was a flat V-shaped mechanical spacecraft with a grey-white fuselage made up from hundreds of different component casings, a veritable jigsaw of mismatched equipment, not all of it astronautic. Two long engine nacelles were affixed to the stern, transparent tubes filled with a heavy opaque gas which fluoresced its way through the spectrum in a three-minute cycle.

It was an impressive sight as it slid down out of the starfield for a landing on Valisk's docking ledge. Had it been real, it would be capable of taking on an entire squadron of Confederation Navy ships with its exotic weapons.

The illusion popped as a crew bus rolled across the ledge towards it. *Socratous* reverted to a muddy-brown egg-shape with a crew toroid wrapped around its midsection. Rubra could just see two small ridges on the rear quarter which hadn't been there before. They corresponded roughly with the nacelles of the fantasy starship. He wondered if the tumours would be benign. Did the energistic ability prevent metastasis from exploding inside possessed bodies as the wished-for changes became less illusion and cells multiplied to obey the will of the dominant soul? It seemed an awfully complex requirement for such a crude power, modifying the molecular structure of DNA and taming the mitosis process. The apparent milieux of their energistic ability was blasting holes through solid walls and contorting matter into new shapes; he'd never seen any demonstrations of subtlety.

Perhaps the whole possession problem would burn itself out in an orgy of irreversible cancer. Few of the returned souls were content with the physical appearance of the bodies they had claimed.

How superbly ironic, Rubra thought, that vanity could be the undoing of entities who had acquired near-godlike powers. It was also a dangerous prospect, once they realized what was happening. Those people remaining free would become even more valuable, the attempts to possess them ever more desperate. And Edenism would be the last castle to besiege.

He decided not to mention the prospect to the Kohistan Consensus. It was another small private advantage; no one else in the Confederation had such a unique and extensive vantage point of the possessed and their behaviour as him. He wasn't sure if he could exploit the knowledge, but he wasn't going to give it away until he was certain.

A sub-routine of his principal personality was designated to observe the aberrant melanomata and carcinomas developing on the possessed inside the habitat. If the growths turned malignant the current situation would change drastically right across the Confederation.

The crew bus had left the *Socratous* to trundle back across the ledge. Kiera and about forty of her cronies were flocking into a reception lounge. When the bus docked, it disgorged about thirty-five Deadnight kids. Eager besotted youngsters with red handkerchiefs worn proudly around their ankles and wonder in their eyes that they'd reached the promised land after so much difficulty.

Damn it, you have to stop these flights, Rubra complained to the Kohistan Consensus. **That's nearly two thousand victims this week. There must be something you can do.**

We really cannot interdict every hellhawk flight. Their objective does not affect the overall balance of strategic events, and is relatively harmless.

Not to these kids it isn't!

Agreed. But we cannot be everyone's keeper. The effort and risk involved in arranging clandestine ren-

dezvous to pick up the Deadnights is disproportionate to the reward.

In other words, as long as the hellhawks are busy with this, they can't cause much trouble elsewhere.

Correct. Unfortunately.

And you used to call me a heartless bastard.

Everybody is suffering from the effects of possession. Until we discover a solution to the entire problem, all we can hope for is to reduce it to an absolute minimum wherever possible.

Right. I'd like to point out that when Kiera reaches the magic number, it's me who is going to be the one suffering.

That is some time off yet. Asteroid settlements have been alerted to these clandestine rendezvous flights. There should be less of them in future.

I bloody well knew I could never trust you lot.

We did not inflict any of this on you, Rubra. And you are quite welcome to transfer into the neural strata of one of our habitats should it look like Kiera Salter is preparing to shift Valisk out of this universe.

I'll keep it in mind. But I don't think you'll need to welcome this particular prodigal. Dariat is almost ready. Once he comes over, it'll be Kiera who is going to have to worry about where I shift Valisk.

Your attempt at subversion is a risky strategy.

That's how I built Magellanic Itg, through sheer balls. It's also why I rejected you. You don't have any.

This is not getting us anywhere.

If it works, I'll be able to start fighting back on a level you can't conceive of. Risk makes you alive, that's what you never understood. That's the difference between us. And don't try coming all over smarmy superior with me. It's me who's got an idea, me who stands a chance. Have you got any suggestions to make, an alternative?

No.

Exactly. So don't lecture me.

We would urge caution, though. Please.

Urge away.

Rubra dismissed the affinity link with his usual contempt. Circumstances might have forced him into an alliance with his old culture; but all the renewed contact had done was convince him how right he had been to reject them all those centuries ago.

He switched his primary routine's attention inward. The group of newly arrived Deadnights had been split up and taken away to be opened for possession. A temporary village had sprung up at the base of the northern endcap, extravagant tents and small cosy cottages for the possessed to dwell in. A smaller version of the camps which ringed the starscraper foyers halfway down the interior. The teams Kiera had working to make the starscrapers safe were finding progress difficult. And in any case, the possessed didn't entirely trust the areas they claimed to have secured. Rubra had never stopped his continual harassment. Nearly ten per cent of the servitor population had been killed as he deployed them on sneak attacks, but he still managed to eliminate a couple of possessed every day.

Separated from their companions, the Deadnights were easily overwhelmed. Piteous screams and pleas hung over the village like smog.

One of Rubra's newest monitor routines alerted him to a minuscule electrical discrepancy within the starscraper where Tolton was hiding. He had discovered electricity was the key to locating Bonney Lewin when she was using her energistic ability to fox his visual observation. A series of extremely sensitive routines which now monitored his own bioelectric patterns could sometimes detect a possessed from the backwash of their energistic power. In effect, the entire polyp structure had become an electronic warfare detector. It was hardly reliable, but he was constantly refining the routines.

He tracked down the wraithish presence to the twenty-seventh floor vestibule where it was moving towards the stairwell muscle membrane door. Visually, the vestibule was empty. At least, according to his local autonomic sub-routines it was. The current in one of the organic conductor cables buried behind the wall fluctuated subtly.

Rubra reduced the power to the electrophorescent cells covering the polyp ceiling. The visual image remained the same for a couple of seconds, then the ceiling darkened. It should have been instantaneous. Whatever was causing the electrical disturbance stopped moving.

He opened a channel to Tolton's processor block. "Get going, boy. They're coming for you."

Tolton rolled off the bed where he'd been dozing. He'd been staying in the apartment for five days. The original occupant's wardrobes had been ransacked for a new ensemble. He'd accessed a good number of the MF and bluesense fleks in the lounge. And he'd sampled all of the imported delicacies in the kitchen, washing them down with fine wines and a lot of Norfolk Tears. For a suffering social poet, he'd adapted to hedonism with the greatest of ease. Small wonder there was a graceless scowl on his face as he snatched up his leather trousers and wriggled his bulk into them.

"Where are they?"

"Ten floors above you," Rubra assured him. "Don't worry, you've got plenty of time. I've got your exit route ready for you."

"I've been thinking, maybe you ought to steer me toward some weapons hardware. I could start evening up the score a little."

"Let's just concentrate on the essentials, shall we? Besides, if you get close enough to a possessed to use a weapon, they're close enough to turn it against you."

Tolton addressed the ceiling. "You think I can't handle it?"

"I thank you for the offer, son, but there are just too many of them. You staying free is my victory against all of them, don't blow it for me."

Tolton clipped the processor block to his belt and fastened his straggly hair back in a ponytail. "Thanks, Rubra. We all got it way wrong about you. I know it don't mean shit to you probably, but when this is over, I'm going to tell the whole wide Confederation what you done."

"That's one MF album I'll buy. First in a long time."

Tolton stood in front of the apartment's door, breathed in like a yogamaster, flexed his shoulders like a sport pro warming up, nodded briskly, and said: "Okay, let's hustle."

Rubra felt an obdurate burst of sympathy and, strangely enough, pride as the poet stepped out into the vestibule. When Kiera started her takeover he assumed Tolton would last a couple of days. Now he was one of only eighty non-possessed left. One of the reasons he'd survived was because he followed instructions to the letter; in short, he trusted Rubra. And Rubra was damned if Bonney would get him now.

The invisible energistic swirl was on the move again, descending the stairwell. Rubra started to modify the output of the electrophorescent cells in the ceiling. HELLO, BONNEY, he printed. I HAVE A PROPOSITION FOR YOU.

The swirl stopped again.

COME ON, TALK TO ME. WHAT HAVE YOU GOT TO LOSE?

He waited. A column of air shimmered silver, as if a giant cocoon had sprung up out of the polyp. Rubra experienced it most as a slackening of pressure in the local sub-routines; a pressure he hadn't even been aware of until then. Then the silver air lost its lustre, darkening to khaki. Bonney Lewin stood on the stairs, her Enfield searching for hazards.

"What proposition?"

ABANDON YOUR CURRENT VICTIM, I WILL GIVE YOU A BETTER ONE.

"I doubt it."

DOESN'T KIERA WANT DARIAT ANYMORE?

Bonney gave the glowing letters a thoughtful stare. "You're trying to sucker me."

NO. THIS IS GENUINE.

"You're lying. Dariat hates you; he's totally bonkers about beating seven bells out of you. If we help him, he'll succeed."

SO WHY HASN'T HE COME TO YOU FOR HELP?

"Because he's . . . weird."

NO. IT IS BECAUSE USING YOU TO DEFEAT ME WOULD MEAN HAVING TO SHARE THE POWER WHICH WOULD RESULT FROM HIS DOMINATION OF THE NEURAL STRATA. HE WANTS IT ALL. HE HAS SPENT THIRTY YEARS WAITING FOR AN OPPORTUNITY LIKE THIS. DO YOU THINK HE WILL GIVE THAT AWAY? AND AFTER ME, KIERA IS GOING TO BE NEXT. THEN PROBABLY YOU.

"So you hand him over to us. That still doesn't make any sense; either way, we get to nail you."

DARIAT AND I ARE PLAYING OUR OWN GAME. I DO NOT EXPECT YOU TO UNDERSTAND. BUT I DO NOT INTEND TO LOSE TO HIM.

She worried at a fingernail. "I don't know."

EVEN WITH MY HELP, HE WILL BE DIFFICULT TO CATCH. DO YOU FEAR FAILURE?

"Don't try working that angle on me, it's pathetic."

VERY WELL. SO DO YOU ACCEPT?

"Difficult one. I really don't trust you. But it would be a superb hunt, you've got me there. I haven't had a single sniff of that tricky little boyo yet, and I've been trying for long enough." She shouldered her rifle. "All right, we've got a deal. But just remember, if you are trying to get me to walk into some ten-thousand-volt power cable, I can still come back. Kiera's recording is hauling in thousands of morons. I'll return in one of them, and then you'll wish all you had to worry about was Dariat."

UNDERSTOOD. FIND A PROCESSOR BLOCK AND SWITCH IT TO ITS BASIC ROUTINES, THAT SHOULD KEEP IT FUNCTIONING. I WILL UPDATE YOU ON HIS LOCATION.

Dariat walked along the shoreline of the circumfluous saltwater reservoir as the light tube languished to a spectacular golden-orange. The cove was backed by a decaying earth bluff which tipped an avalanche of the pink Tallok-aboriginal grass onto the sand. Curving outgrowths of the xenoc plant resembled a meandering tideline, which gave him the impression of walking along a spit between two different coloured seas. The only sounds were of the water lapping against the sand, and the birds crying out as they flew back to land for the night.

He had walked here many times as a child, an era when being alone meant happiness. Now he welcomed the solitude again; it gave him the mindspace to think, to formulate new subversion routines to insert into the neural strata; and he was free of Kiera and her greed and shallow ambitions. That second factor was becoming a dominant one. They had been looking for him ever since the Edenists destroyed the industrial stations. With both his knowledge of the habitat and energistically enhanced affinity it was absurdly easy to elude them. Few ever ventured down to the vast reservoir, preferring to cling to the camps around starscraper foyers. Without the tubes, it was a long journey across the grassland where malevolent servitor creatures lay in wait for the negligent.

Trouble, Rubra announced.

Dariat ignored him. He could hide himself from the possessed easily enough. None of them knew enough about affinity to access the neural strata properly. As a consequence he no longer bothered hiding himself from Rubra anymore, nor did he bother with the linen-suited persona. It was all too stressful. The price of release came in the form of taunts and nerve games emanating from Rubra with unimaginative regularity.

She's found you, Dariat, she's coming for you. And boy is she pissed.

Certain he'd regret it, Dariat asked: **Who?**

Bonney. There's nine of them heading right at you in a couple of trucks. I think Kiera was saying something about returning with your head. Apparently, attachment to your body was considered optional.

Dariat opened his affinity link with the neural strata just wide enough to hitch onto the observational sub-routines. Sure enough, two of the rugged trucks which the rentcops used were arrowing across the rosy grassland. "Shit." They were heading straight for the cove, with about five kilometres left to go. **How the hell did she find me?**

Beats me.

Dariat stared straight up, following the line of the coast which looped behind the light tube. **Is there someone above me with a high-rez sensor?**

If there is, I can't spot them. In any case, I doubt a sensor would work for a possessed.

Binoculars? Hell, it hardly matters.

He couldn't see the trucks with his eyes yet, the tall grass hid them. And his mind couldn't perceive their thoughts, they were too far away. So just how had they found him?

There is a tube station at the end of the cove, Rubra said. **They'll never be able to catch you in that. I can take you to anywhere in the habitat.**

Thanks. And you'll be able to run a thousand volts through me as soon as I step inside a carriage. Or had you forgotten?

I don't want you blown into the beyond. You know that. I've made my offer, and it stands. Come into the neural strata. Join your mind with me. Together we will annihilate them. Valisk can be purged. We will take them to dimensions where simply existing is an agony for them. Both of us will have revenge.

You're crazy.

Make your mind up. I can hide you for a while while you decide. Is it to be me? Or is it to be Kiera?

Dariat was still receiving the image of the trucks from the sensitive cells. They were rocking madly over the uneven ground as the drivers held them at their top speed.

I think I'll take a while longer to make up my mind. Dariat started jogging for the tube station. After a minute, the trucks swung around to intercept him. "Bloody hell." Horgan's body was reasonably fit, but he was only fifteen years old. Dariat's imagination bestowed him with athlete's legs, bulky slabs of muscle packed tight under oil-glossed skin. His speed picked up.

I wonder what that kind of overdrive does to your blood sugar levels? I mean, the power has to come from

somewhere. Surely you're not converting the energistic overspill from the beyond directly into protein?

Save the science class till later. He could see the station ahead of him, a squat circular polyp structure bordering the bluff, like some kind of storage tank half-buried in the sand. The trucks were only a kilometre away. Bonney was standing up in the passenger seat of the lead vehicle, aiming her Enfield at him over the windscreen. Motes of white fire punched into the sand around him. He ducked down for the last fifty metres, using the bluff as cover as he scuttled for the station entrance.

Inside, two broad escalators spiralled around each other, their steps moving sedately. A garishly coloured tubular hologram punctured the air up the centre of the shaft, adverts sliding along it. Dariat leapt onto the down escalator and sprinted recklessly, hands barely touching the rail.

He made it to the bottom just as the trucks braked outside; Bonney charged towards the entrance. There was a carriage waiting on the station, a shiny white aluminum bullet. Dariat stopped, panting heavily, staring at the open door.

Get in!

Rubra's mental voice contained a strong intimation of alarm, which Dariat could hardly credit. If you're fucking me, I'll come back. I'll promise myself to Anstid for that one wish to be granted.

Imagine my terror. I've told you, I need you intact and cooperative. Now get in.

Dariat closed his eyes and took a step forwards, directly into the carriage. The door slid shut behind him, and there was a faint vibration as it started accelerating along the track. He opened his eyes.

See? Rubra taunted. Not such a bogey man after all.

Dariat sat down and took some deep breaths to calm his racing heart. He used the sensitive cells to watch an apoplectic Bonney Lewin jump down from the empty platform to fire her Enfield along the dark tunnel. She was screaming obscenities. The accompanying hunters were standing well back. One of her boots was treading on the magnetic guide rail.

Fry her, Dariat said. Now!

Oh, no. This is much more fun. This way I get to find out if the dead can have heart attacks.

You are a complete bastard.

That's right. And to prove it, I'm going to show you Anastasia's secret now. The one thing she never showed you.

Dariat was instantly wary. More lies.

Not this time. Don't tell me you don't want to find out. I know you, Dariat. Fully. I've always known. I know what she means to you. I know how much she means to you. Your memory of her was strong enough to power a grudge over thirty years. That's almost inhuman, Dariat. I respect it enormously. But it leaves you wide open to me. Because you want to know, don't you? There's something I've got, or heard, or saw, that you didn't. A little segment of Anastasia Rigel you don't have. You won't be able to live with that knowledge.

I'll be able to ask her soon. Her soul is waiting for me in the beyond. When I've dealt with you, I'll go to her, and we'll be together again.

Soon will be too late.

You're unbelievable, you know that?

Good. I'll take you there.

Whatever you like. Dariat pushed his weariness behind the thought, showing just how unconcerned he was. Behind that, clutched away from the bravado and outward confidence, his teenage self huddled in worry. That same self which so idolized her. Now there was the chance, the remotest possibility that the image was flawed, less than honest. The doubt cut into him, weakening the core of resolution which had supported him for so terribly long.

Anastasia would never keep anything from him. Would she? She loved him, she said so. The last thing she ever said, ever wrote.

Rubra guided the tube carriage to a starscraper lobby station and opened the door. **It's waiting on the thirty-second floor.**

Dariat glanced cautiously out onto the little station and the wide passage which led to the lobby itself. His mind could sense the thoughts of the possessed camped outside the lobby. No one showed any interest in him. He hurried across the floor to the bank of lifts in the centre, reaching them unnoticed.

The lift deposited him at the thirty-second-floor vestibule. A completely normal residential section; twenty-four mechanical doors leading to apartments, and three muscle membranes for the stairwells. One of the mechanical doors slid open to show a darkened living room.

Dariat could sense someone inside, a dozing mind, its thought currents placid. When he tried to use the observation sub-routines for the bedroom he found he couldn't, Rubra had wiped them.

Oh, no, my boy, you go right in there and face your fate like a man.

Dariat flinched. But . . . one unaware non-possessed. How bad could it be? He walked into the apartment, ordering the electrophorescent cells to full intensity. Thankfully, they responded.

It was a woman who lay on the big bed, a duvet had worked downwards to reveal her shoulders. Her skin was very black, with the minute crinkles which spelt out the onset of middle age and the start of weight problems for anyone without much geneering in their ancestry. A tangle of finely braided jet-black hair was fanned out over the pillows, every strand tipped with a moondust-white bead.

She groaned sleepily as the light came on, and turned over. Despite a face which cellulite was busy inflating, she had a petit nose.

NO! For one moment horror claimed his senses. She was similar to Anastasia. Features, colour, even the age was almost right. If a medical team had gone out to the tepee, they might have reanimated the body, a hospital might conceivably have used extensive gene therapy to regenerate the dead brain cells. It could be done, for the President of Govcentral or Kulu's heir apparent, the effort would be made. But not a Starbridge girl regarded as vermin by the personality of the habitat in which she dwelt. The cold shock subsided.

Whoever she was, as soon as she saw him, she screamed.

"It's all right," Dariat said. He couldn't even hear his own voice above her distraught wails.

"Rubra! One of them's here. Rubra, help me."

"No," Dariat said. "I'm not. Well . . ."

"Rubra! RUBRA."

"Please," Dariat implored.

That silenced her.

"I'm not going to hurt you," he said. "I'm running from them myself."

"Uh huh?" Her gaze darted to the door.

"Really. Rubra brought me here, too."

The duvet was readjusted. Slim bronze and silver bracelets tinkled as she moved.

Dariat's chill returned. They were exactly the same kind of bracelets Anastasia wore. "Are you a Starbridge?"

She nodded, wide-eyed.

Wrong question, Rubra said. **Ask her what her name is.**

He hated himself. For giving in, for playing to Rubra's rules. "Who are you?"

"Tatiana," she gulped. "Tatiana Rigel."

Rubra's mocking, triumphant laughter shook his skull from the inside. **Got it now, boy? Meet Anastasia's little sister.**

• • •

Another day, another press conference. At least this new technology had progressed beyond flashbulbs; Al had always hated them back in Chicago. More than once he had been photographed raising a hand to ward off the brilliant bursts of light; photos which the papers always ran, because it looked as if he were trying to hide, confirming his guilt.

He had held the press conference in the Monterey Hilton's big ballroom, sitting at a long table with his back to the window. The idea was that the reporters would see the formation of victorious fleet ships which had just returned from Arnstadt, and were holding station five kilometres off the asteroid. Leroy Octavius said it should make an impressive backdrop for the dramatic news announcement.

Except the starships weren't quite in the right coordinate, so they were only just visible when rotation did bring them into view; the reporters had to look around the side of the table to see them. And everybody knew the Organization had conquered Arnstadt and Kursk, it wasn't new even though this made it sort of official.

Drama and impact, that was the sole purpose. So Al sat at the long table with its inappropriate vases of flowers; Luigi Balsmao on one side, and a couple of other ship captains on the other. He told the reporters how easy it had been to break open Arnstadt's SD network, the eagerness of the population to accept the Organization as a government after a "minimum number" of key administrative people had been possessed. How the star system's economy was turning around.

"Did you use antimatter, Al?" Gus Remar asked. A weary veteran of these affairs now, he reckoned he knew what liberties he could take. Capone did have a weird sense of honour operating; nobody got blasted for trying to work an angle, only outright opposition earned his disapprobation.

"That's a dumb kinda question, pal," Al replied, keeping the scowl from his face. "What do you want to ask that for? We got plenty of interesting dope on how the Organization is curing all sorts of medical problems which the non-possessed bring to our lieutenants. You people, you always look for the bad side. It's like a goddamn obsession with you."

"Antimatter is the biggest horror the Confederation knows, Al. People are bound to be interested in the rumours. Some of the ships' crews say they fired antimatter powered combat wasps. And the industrial stations here are producing antimatter confinement systems. Have you got a production station, Al?"

Leroy Octavius, who was standing behind Al, leaned forwards and whispered something in his ear. Some of the humour returned to Al's stony face. "I can neither confirm nor deny the Organization has access to invincible weapons."

It didn't stop them from asking again and again. He lost the press conference then. There wasn't any chance to read out the dope Leroy had prepared on the medical bonus, and how they'd prevented the kind of food shortages on Arnstadt which were being reported as affecting other possessed worlds.

Asked at the end if he was planning another invasion, Al just growled: "Wait and see," then walked out.

"Don't worry about it, we'll embargo the whole conference," Leroy said as they took a lift down to the bottom of the hotel.

"They ought to show some goddamn respect," Al grunted. "If it wasn't for me they'd be possessed and screaming inside their own heads. Those bastards never fucking change."

"You want us to lean on them a little?" Bernhard Allsop asked.

"No. That would be stupid. The only reason the Confederation news companies take our reports is because they're from non-possessed." Al hated it when Bernhard tried to be tough and demonstrate his loyalty. *I should have him wasted, he's becoming a complete pain in the ass.*

But wasting people wasn't so easy these days. They'd come back in another body, and carry a grudge the size of Mount Washington.

God*damn* the problems kept hitting on him.

The lift doors opened on the hotel's basement, a windowless level given over to environmental machinery, large pumps, and condensation-smeared tanks. A boxing ring had been set up at the centre, surrounded by the usual training paraphernalia of exercise bikes, histeps, weights, and punch bags: Malone's gym.

Whenever he wanted to loosen up, Al came down here. He'd always enjoyed sports back in Chicago; going to the game was an *event* in those days. One he missed. If he could bring back the Organization, and the music, and the dancing from that time, he reasoned, then why not the sports, too?

Avram Harwood had run a check on professions listed in the Organization's files, and found Malone, who claimed to have worked as a boxing trainer in New York during the 1970s.

Al marched into the gym area trailed by five of his senior lieutenants, Avram Harwood, and a few other hangers-on like Bernhard. It was noisy in the basement anyway, with the pumps thrumming away, and in the gym with music playing and men pounding away at leather punch bags you had to shout to be heard. This was the way it should be: the smell of leather and sweat, grunts as sparring blows hit home, Malone yelling out at his star pupils.

"How's it going?" Al asked the trainer.

Malone shrugged, his heavy face showing complete misery. "Today's people, they gone soft, Al. They don't want to hit each other, they think it's immoral or something. We ain't gonna find no Ali or Cooper on this world. But I got a few contenders, kids who've had it hard. They're working out okay." A fat finger indicated the two young men in the ring. "Joey and Gulo, here, they could have what it takes."

Al cast an eye over the two boxers dancing around in the ring. Both of them were big, fit-looking kids, wearing colourful protective gear. He knew enough about the basics to see they were holding themselves right, though they were concentrating too much on defence.

"I'll just watch awhile," Al told Malone.

"Sure thing, Al. Help yourself. Hey! Gulo, close the left, the left, asswipe."

Joey saw his opening and landed a good right on Gulo's face. Gulo went for a body lock, and both of them bounced on the ropes.

"Break, break," the ref cried.

Al pulled up a stool and gazed contentedly at the two combatants. "All right, what's the order of play for today? Speak to me, Avvy." The ex-mayor's body twitches were getting worse, Al noticed. And some of the weals still hadn't healed over despite a couple of attempts by Al's possessed lieutenants to heal them. Al didn't like having so much resentment and hostility festering close by. But the guy sure knew how to administrate; replacing him now would be a bitch.

"We now have fifteen delegations from outsystem who have arrived," Avram Harwood said. "They all want to see you."

"Outsystem, huh?" Al's flagging interest started to perk up. "What do they want?"

"Your assistance, basically," Avram said. He didn't hide his displeasure.

Al ignored it. "For what?"

"All of them are from asteroid settlements," Patricia Mangano said. "The first bunch that came here are from Toma, that's in the Kolomna system. Their problem is that the asteroid only has a population of ninety thousand. That gives them enough energistic power to shift it out of this universe easily enough. But then they realized that spending the rest of eternity inside a couple of modestly sized biosphere caverns which are totally dependent on technology wasn't exactly going to be a whole load of fun. Especially when nearly a third of the possessed come from pre-industrial eras."

"Goddamn, this is what I've been telling people all along," Al said expansively. "There ain't no point in vanishing whole planets away, not until we got the Confederation licked."

Several of the trainee boxers had drifted over to stand close by. As if aware of the growing interest, Joey and Gulo were increasing their efforts to knock each other senseless. Malone's rapid-fire monotone picked up momentum.

"So what has this got to do with me?" Al asked.

"The Toma people want to move everyone to Kolomna."

"Je-zus!"

"They want our fleet to help them. If we chose Kolomna as our next invasion target we will receive their total cooperation for as long as you want it. Every industrial station in the system will be given over to supporting the fleet, every starship captured will be converted to carry weapons or troops, they'll bring the planetary population into order along Organization lines. They say they want to sign up as your lieutenants."

Al was flattered, it turned his whole day around.

Out in the ring, both boxers were perspiring heavily. Blood was trickling out of Gulo's mouth. Joey's left eye was bruised. Cheers and whistles were swelling from the spectators.

"Risky," Luigi said. "Kolomna is First Admiral Aleksandrovich's homeworld. He probably wouldn't take too kindly to it. I wouldn't I was him. Besides, we're still getting things in order for Toi-Hoi."

Al rocked back on the stool and materialized one of his Havanas, its end was already alight. "I'm not too worried about that Admiral getting pissed with me, not with what I've got in store for him. Any chance we can split the fleet, send some ships to Kolomna?"

"Sorry, boss, that's some of the bad news I've got for you," Luigi said. "The Confederation is really hassling us bad at Arnstadt. They've got voidhawks flying above both poles dropping invisible bombs on the SD platforms in orbit. Stealth, the bastards call it. We're losing a shitload of hardware every day. And the non-possessed population are putting up some resistance—quite a lot, actually. The new lieutenants we've appointed are having to use a whole load of force to establish our authority. It gives them a sense of independence, so we have to use the SD platforms to make them see reason, too. Except the Confederation is knocking the platforms out one at a time, so instead we gotta use starships to substitute, and they're just as vulnerable."

"Well, fuck it, Luigi," Al stormed. "Are you telling me, we're gonna lose?"

"No way!" an indignant Luigi protested. "We're launching our own patrols up above the poles. We're hassling them right back, Al. But it takes five or six of our ships to block one of their goddamn voidhawks."

"They're bogging us down out there," Silvano Richmann said. "It's quite deliberate. We're also losing ships out among Arnstadt's settled asteroids. The voidhawks make lightning raids, fling off a dozen combat wasps and duck away before we can do anything about it. It's a shitty way of fighting, Al, nothing is head on anymore."

"Modern navies are built around the concept of rapid tactical assault," Leroy said. "Their purpose is to inflict damage over a wide front so that you have to overstretch your defences. They've adopted a guerilla policy to try and wear down our fleet."

"Fucking cowards' way of fighting," Silvano grumbled.

"It'll get worse," Leroy warned. "Now they've seen how effective it is against Arnstadt, they'll start doing it here. New California's SD network is just as vulnerable to stealth mines. Our advantage is that the Organization is now up and running on the planet. We don't need to enforce it the way we do on Arnstadt. I think we only used a ground strike ten times last week."

"Twelve," Emmet corrected. "But we do have a lot of industrial capacity in orbit. I'd hate to lose much of it to a stealth strike campaign. Our outer system asteroid settlements really aren't supplying us with anything like the material they should be, production simply doesn't match capacity at all."

"That's because we essentially have the same problem as the outsystem delegations," Leroy said.

"Go on," Al said glumly; he was rolling the cigar absently between his fingers, its darkened tip pointing down. But he still hadn't taken his eyes off the fight. Joey was sagging now, swaying dazedly, while the blood from Gulo's face was flowing freely down his chest to splatter the floor of the ring. No bell was going to be rung; it wouldn't finish now until one of them fell.

"Every possessed wants to live on a planet," Leroy said. "Asteroids don't have an adequate population base to sustain a civilization for eternity. We've started to see a lot of inter-orbit craft heading towards New California from the settlements. And for every possessed on their way, there are another ten waiting for the next ship."

"Goddamnit," Al shouted. "When those skid-row assholes get here, you send them right back where they came from. We need those asteroid factories working at full steam ahead. You got that?"

"I'll notify SD Command," Leroy said.

"Make sure they know I ain't fucking joking."

"Will do."

Al relit his cigar by glaring at it. "Okay, so, Luigi, when can we start to take out the Toi-Hoi system?"

Luigi shrugged. "I'll be honest with you, Al, our original timetable ain't looking too good here."

"Why not?"

"We thought we'd almost double the fleet size with Arnstadt's ships. Which we have done. But then we need a lot of them to keep order in that system, and reliable crews are getting hard to find. Then there's Kursk. We made a mistake with that one, Al, the place ain't worth a bucket of warm spit. It's those hillbilly redneck farmers. They just won't roll over."

"That's where Mickey is right now," Silvano said. "He's trying to run an offensive which will bring them to heel. It's not easy. The tricky bastards have taken to the countryside. They're hiding in trees and caves, a whole load of places the satellite sensors can't find them. And the Confederation is hitting us big-time with those stealth weapons, like Arnstadt was just a warm-up. We're losing three or four ships a day."

"I think Luigi is right when he said we made a mistake invading Kursk," Emmet said. "It's costing us a bundle, and returning zippo. I say pull the fleet out; let the possessed on the ground take care of the planet in their own time."

"That'll mean the Organization won't have any clout there," Patricia said. "Once everyone's possessed, they'll snatch it clean out of the universe."

"The only thing it ever gave to us was propaganda," Leroy said. "We can't work than angle anymore. Emmet's right. I don't think we should be aiming at any planet lower than stage four, one that can replace our losses, as a minimum requirement."

"That sounds solid to me," Al agreed. "I don't like losing Kursk, but spelt out like that I don't see that we've got one whole hell of a choice. Luigi, get Mickey back here, tell him to bring all the ships and as many of our soldiers as he can. I want to go for Toi-Hoi as soon as you can load up with supplies. People will think we've stalled otherwise; and it's important to keep the momentum going."

"You got it, boss. I'd like to send Cameron Leung as the messenger, if you ain't using him. It'll be the quickest way, cut down on any more of our losses."

"Sure, no problem. Send him pronto." Al blew a smoke ring at the distant ceiling. "Anything else?"

Leroy and Emmet gave each other a resigned look.

"There's a lot of currency cheating going on," Emmet said. "I suppose you could call it forgery."

"Je-zus, I thought you rocket scientists had that all figured out."

"Foolproof, you said," Silvano said with a demon's grin.

"It should have been," Emmet insisted. "Part of it is due to the way it's being implemented. Our soldiers aren't being entirely honest about the amount of time the possessed are devoting to redeeming their energistic debts. People are starting to complain. There's a lot of restlessness building up down there, Al. You're going to have to make it clear to the lieutenants how important it is to stick with the rules. The economy we've rigged up is shaky enough already without suffering this confidence crisis. If it fails, then we lose control and the planet goes wild, just like Kursk. You can't use the SD platforms to waste everyone who disagrees with us; we need to be subtle about how we keep the majority in line."

"All right, all right." Al waved a hand, nettled at the schoolmaster tone Emmet was using.

"Based on what we've seen so far, I'm not sure a wild possessed population could even feed themselves. Certainly the cities would have to be abandoned as soon as the supply infrastructure collapses. You do need a large area of land under cultivation to support a city like San Angeles."

"Will you cut this *crap*. I fucking understand, okay? What I want to know is, what are you going to do about it?"

"It's about time you met with the groundside lieutenants again, Al," Leroy said. "We can build on the fleet's return, show how together we are up here, how they'd be nothing without us. Make them toe the line."

"Oh, Jesus H. Christ, not another fucking tour. I just got back!"

"You're in charge of two star systems, Al," Leroy said matter-of-factly. "There are some things which have to be done."

Al winced. The fatboy manager was right, as goddamn always. This wasn't a game to be picked up when he felt like it, this was different from before. In Chicago he'd climbed on the back of the power structure to advance himself; now he was the structure. That was when he finally realized the responsibility, and enormity, of what he'd created.

If the Organization crashed, millions—living and resurrected—would fall beside him, their hopes smashed on the rocks of his selfish intransigence. Alcatraz was the result of his last brush with hubris. Alcatraz would be bliss compared to the suffering focused on him should he fail again.

The fight which was limping to its conclusion was no longer the centre of attention; most of the possessed in the gym were staring at him strangely. They could see the muddle and horror in his mind. Leroy and Avram were waiting, puzzled by the sudden, uneasy silence.

"Sure thing, Leroy," Al said meekly. "I know what I'm in charge of. And I ain't never been scared of doing what has to be done. Remember that. So set up that tour. You got that?"

"Yes, sir."

"Makes a fucking change. Right, you guys all know what you gotta do. Do it."

Gulo landed one final blow in Joey's stomach which sent him staggering backwards to collapse in a corner. Malone hopped over the ropes to examine the fallen man. Gulo stood over them, uncertain what to do next. Blood was dripping swiftly from his chin.

"Okay, kid," Malone said. "That's it for the day."

Al flicked his cigar away and stood by the ropes. He beckoned Gulo over. "You did pretty damn good out there, boy. How long you been training?"

Gulo slipped a blood-soaked gumshield from his mouth. "Nine days, Mr Capone, sir," he mumbled. Little flecks of blood splattered Al's suit jacket as he wheezed painfully.

Al took hold of the kid's head with one hand and turned it from side to side, examining the bruises and cuts inside the sparring helmet. He concentrated hard, feeling a cold tingle sweeping along his arm to infect the kid's face through his fingertips. The bleeding stopped, and the grazed bruising deflated slightly. "You'll do okay," Al decided.

Jezzibella was lounging on the circular bed. A wall-mounted holoscreen showed her an image of the gym relayed by a sensor high in the ceiling. Emmet, Luigi, and Leroy clustered together, discussing something in sober tones, their amplified murmurs filling the bedroom.

"Hard day at the office, lover?" Jezzibella asked. It was a persona of toughness wrapping a tender heart. Her face was very serious, fine features slightly flushed. A longish bob hairstyle cupped her cheeks.

"You saw it," he said.

"Yeah." She uncurled her legs and stood up, wrestling with the fabric of her long silky white robe. There was no belt, and it was open to the waist, allowing a very shapely navel to peek out. "Come here, baby. Lie down."

"Best goddamn offer I've had all day." He was bothered by his own lack of enthusiasm.

"Not that; you need to relax."

Al grunted disparagingly, but did as he was told. When he was lying on his back he stuck his hands behind his head, frowning at the ceiling. "Crazy. Me of all people; I should've known what was going to happen with the money.

Everyone skims and everyone scams. What made me think my soldiers were going to be square shooters?"

Jezzibella planted a foot on either side of his hips, then sat down. Her robe's fabric must have carried one hell of a static charge, he guessed, there was no other reason why it should cling to her skin at all the strategic zones. Her fingers dug into the base of his neck, thumbs probing deep.

"Hey, what is this?"

"I'm trying to get you to relax, remember? You're so tense." Her fingers were moving in circles now, almost strumming his hot muscle cords.

"That's good," he admitted.

"I should really have some scented oils to do this properly."

"You want I should try and dream some up?" He wasn't too certain he could imagine smells the way he could shapes.

"No. Improvising can be fun, you never know what you might discover. Turn over, and get rid of your shirt."

Al rolled over, yawning heavily. He rested his chin on his hands as Jezzibella began to move her fingertips along his spine.

"I dunno what I hate most," Al said. "Retreating from Kursk, or admitting how right that shitty slob Leroy was."

"Kursk was a strategic withdrawal."

"Running away is running away, doll. Don't matter how you dress it up."

"I think I've found something that might help you with Arnstadt."

"What's that?"

She leaned over to the bedside cabinet and picked up a small processor block, tapping the keyboard. "I only saw this recording today. Leroy should have brought it to me earlier. Apparently it's all over the Confederation. We got it from one of the outsystem delegations that arrived to plead with you."

The holoscreen switched from the gym to showing Kiera Salter lounging on her boulder.

"Yep, that certainly perks me up," Al said cheerfully.

Jezzibella slapped his rump. "Just you behave, Al Capone. Forget her tits, listen to what she's saying."

He listened to the enticing words.

"She's actually rather good," Jezzibella said. "Especially considering it's AV only, no naughty sensory activants to hammer home the message. I could have done it better, of course, but then I'm a professional. But that recording is pulling in dissatisfied kids from every asteroid settlement that ever received a copy. They call it Deadnight."

"So? Valisk is one of those frigging freaky habitat places. She's hardly gonna be a threat to us no matter how many people go there."

"It's how they get there which interests me. Kiera has managed to take over Valisk's blackhawks, they call them hellhawks."

"Yeah?"

"Yes. And all they're doing is ferrying idiot kids to the habitat. She is facing the same problem as all the possessed asteroid settlements. They're not the kinds of places you want to spend eternity in. My guess is that she's trying to beef up Valisk's population so the ones already there don't push to land on a planet. It makes sense. If they did move, Kiera wouldn't be top dog anymore."

"So? I never said she was dumb."

"Exactly. She's organized. Not on the scale you are, but she's smart, she understands politics. She'd make an excellent ally. We can supply her with people a lot faster than she can acquire them through clandestine flights. And in return, she loans us a couple of squadrons of these hellhawks, which the fleet desperately needs. They'd soon put a stop to the Confederation's stealth attacks."

"Damn!" He shuffled around inside the cage of her legs to see her poised above him, hands on her hips, content smile on her lips. "That's good, Jez. No it ain't, it's fucking brilliant. Hell, you don't need me, you could run this Organization by yourself."

"Don't be silly. I can't do what you do to me, not solitaire."

He growled hungrily and reached for the robe. Marie Skibbow's golden face smiled down on them as more and more of their clothing vanished, some into thin air, some into torn strips.

• • •

The First Admiral waited until Captain Khanna and Admiral Lalwani seated themselves in front of his desk, then datavised the desktop processor for a security level one sensenviron conference. Six people were waiting around the oval table in the featureless white bubble room which formed around him. Directly opposite Samual Aleksandrovich was the Confederation Assembly President, Olton Haaker, with his chief aide Jeeta Anwar next to him; the Kulu ambassador, Sir Maurice Hall, was on her left, accompanied by Lord Elliot, a junior minister from the Kulu Foreign Office; the Edenist ambassador, Cayeaux, and Dr Gilmore took the remaining two chairs.

"This isn't quite our usual situation briefing today, Admiral," President Haaker said. "The Kulu Kingdom has made a formal request for military aid."

Samual Aleksandrovich knew his face was showing a grimace of surprise, his sensenviron image, however, retained a more dignified composure. "I had no idea any of the Kingdom worlds were under threat."

"We are not facing any new developments, Admiral," Sir Maurice said. "The Royal Navy is proving most effective in protecting our worlds from any strikes by possessed starships. Even Valisk's hellhawks have stopped swallowing into our systems to peddle their damnable Deadnight subversion. And our planetary forces have contained all the incursions quite successfully. With the sorry exception of Mortonridge, of course. Which is why we are requesting your cooperation and assistance. We intend to mount a liberation operation, and free the citizens who have been possessed."

"Impossible," Samual said. "We have no viable method of purging a body of its possessor. Dr Gilmore."

"Unfortunately, the First Admiral is correct," the navy scientist said. "As we have found, forcing a returned soul to relinquish a body it has captured is extremely difficult."

"Not if they are placed in zero-tau," Lord Elliot said.

"But there are over two million people on Mortonridge," Samual said. "You can't put that many into zero-tau."

"Why not? It's only a question of scale."

"You'd need . . ." Samual trailed off as various tactical programs went primary in his neural nanonics.

"The help of the Confederation Navy," Lord Elliot concluded. "Exactly. We need to move a large number of ground troops and matériel to Ombey. You have transport and assault starships which aren't really involved with enforcing the civil starflight quarantine. We'd like them to be reassigned to the campaign. The combined resources of our own military forces, our allies, and the Confederation Navy ought to be sufficient to liberate Mortonridge."

"Ground troops?"

"We will initially be providing the Kingdom with half a million bitek constructs," Ambassador Cayeaux said. "They should be able to restrain individual possessed, and force them into a zero-tau pod. Their deployment will insure the loss of human life is kept to a minimum."

"*You* are going to help the Kingdom?" Samual couldn't be bothered to filter his surprise out of the question. But . . . the Edenists and the Kingdom allied! At one level he was pleased, prejudice can be abandoned if the incentive is great enough. What a pity it had to be this, though.

"Yes."

"I see."

"The Edenist constructs will have to be backed up by a considerable number of regular soldiers to hold the ground they take," Sir Maurice said. "We would also like you to assign two brigades of Confederation Marines to the campaign."

"I've no doubt your tactical evaluations have convinced you about the plausibility of this liberation," Samual said. "But I must go on record as opposing it, and certainly I do not wish to devote my forces to what will ultimately prove a futile venture. If this kind of combined effort is to be made, it should at least be directed at a worthwhile target."

"His Majesty has said he will go to any lengths to free his subjects from the suffering being inflicted on them," Lord Elliot said.

"Does his obligation only extend to the living?"

"Admiral!" Haaker warned.

"I apologize. However you must appreciate that I have a responsibility to the Confederation worlds as a whole."

"Which so far you have demonstrated perfectly."

"So far?"

"Admiral, you know the status quo within the Confederation cannot be maintained indefinitely," Jeeta Anwar said. "We cannot afford it."

"We have to consider the political objectives of this conflict," Haaker said. "I'm sorry, Samual, but logic and sound tactics aren't the only factors at play here. The Confederation must be seen to be doing something. I'm sure you appreciate that."

"And you have chosen Mortonridge as that something?"

"It is a goal which the Kingdom and the Edenists think they can achieve."

"Yes, but what would happen afterwards? Do you propose to take on every possessed planet and asteroid in a similar fashion? How long would that take? How much would it cost?"

"I sincerely hope such a process would not have to be repeated," Cayeaux said. "We must use the time it takes to liberate Mortonridge to search for another approach to the problem. However, if there is no answer, then similar campaigns may indeed have to be mounted."

"Which is why this first one must succeed," Haaker said.

"Are you ordering me to redeploy my forces?" Samual asked.

"I'm informing you of the request the Kulu Kingdom and the Edenists have made. It is a legitimate request made by two of our strongest supporters. If you have an alternative proposal, then I'll be happy to receive it."

"Of course I don't have an alternative."

"Then I don't think you have any reason to refuse them."

"I see. If I might ask, Ambassador Cayeaux, why does your Consensus agree to this?"

"We agreed to it for the sake of the hope it will provide to all the living in the Confederation. We do not necessarily approve."

"Samual, you've done a magnificent job so far," Lalwani said. "We know this liberation is only a sideshow, but it will gain us a great deal of political support. And we are going to need every scrap of support we can find in the coming weeks."

"Very well." Samual Aleksandrovich paused in distaste. What upset him most was how well he understood their argument, almost sympathising with it. Image had become the paramount motivation, the way every war was fought for politicians. But in this I am no different from military commanders down the centuries, we always have to play within the political arena in order to fight the real battle. I wonder if my illustrious predecessors felt so soiled? "Captain Khanna, please ask the general staff to draw up fleet redeployment orders based on the request from the Kulu Kingdom ambassador."

"Yes, sir."

"I wish your King every success, Ambassador."

"Thank you, Admiral. We do not wish to disrupt your current naval operations. Alastair does understand the importance of the role you are playing."

"I'm glad of that. There are going to be some difficult decisions for all of us ahead; his patronage will be essential. As I have said from the beginning, this requires an ultimate solution that can never be purely military."

"Have you considered the proposal Capone made?" Sir Maurice asked. "I know if any of the possessed can be seen in terms of a conventional enemy, it's him. But could bitek construct bodies be made to work?"

"We examined it," Maynard Khanna said. "In practical terms it is completely inviable. The numbers are impossible. A conservative estimate for the Confederation's current population is nine hundred billion, which averages out at just over one billion per star system. Even if you assume only ten dead people for everyone living, there must be approximately ten trillion souls in the beyond. If they were each given a construct body, where would they live? We would have to find between three to five thousand new terracompatible planets for them. Clearly an impossible task."

"I would contend that number," Cayeaux said. "Laton quite clearly said that not every soul remains imprisoned in the beyond."

"Even if it was only a single trillion, that would still mean locating several hundred planets for them."

"Laton's information interests me," Dr Gilmore said. "We have been assuming all along that it is incumbent on us to provide a final solution. Yet if souls can progress from the beyond to some other state of existence, then clearly it is up to them to do so."

"How would we make them?" Haaker asked.

"I'm not sure. If we could just find one of them who would cooperate we could make so much more progress; someone like that Shaun Wallace character who was interviewed by Kelly Tirrel. Those we have here in Trafalgar are all so actively hostile to our investigation."

Samual thought about making a comment concerning relevant treatment and behaviour, but Gilmore didn't deserve public rebukes. "I suppose we could try a diplomatic initiative. There are several isolated asteroid settlements which have been possessed and yet haven't moved themselves out of the universe. We could make a start with them; send a message asking them if they will talk to us."

"An excellent proposal," Haaker said. "It would cost very

little, and if we obtain a favourable response I would be prepared to give a joint research project my full support."

The sensenviron ended, leaving Dr Gilmore alone in his office. He did nothing for several minutes while the last part of the meeting ran through his mind. A man who prided himself on his methodical nature, the embodiment of the scientific method, he wasn't angry with himself, at the most he felt a slight irritation that he hadn't reasoned this out earlier. If Laton was correct about souls moving on, then the beyond was not the static environment he had assumed until now. That opened up a whole range of new options.

Dr Gilmore entered the examination room containing Jacqueline Couteur to find the staff on an extended break. Both quantum signature sensor arrays were missing from the overhead waldo arms. The electronics lab was rebuilding them once again, a near-continual process of refinement as they sought out the elusive transdimensional interface.

Jacqueline Couteur was being fed. A trolley had been wheeled in beside the surgical bed, sprouting a thick hose which hung just over her mouth. Her black head restraint had been loosened slightly, allowing her to switch between the two nipples; one for water, the other a meat paste.

Dr Gilmore walked through to stand next to the surgical bed. Her eyes followed his movement.

"Good morning, Jacqueline; how are you today?"

Her eyes narrowed contemptuously. Little wisps of steam licked up from the electrodes pressing against her skin. She opened her mouth and circled the plastic nipple with her tongue. "Fine, thank you, Dr Mengele. I'd like to speak to my lawyer, please."

"That's interesting. Why?"

"Because I'm going to sue you for every fuseodollar you own, and then have you shot down to a penal world in a one-way capsule. Torture is illegal in the Confederation. Read the Declaration of Rights."

"If you are in discomfort, you should leave. We both know you can do that."

"We're not discussing my options at the moment. It is your actions which are in question. Now may I have my one phone call?"

"I had no idea an immortal soul had civil rights. You certainly don't show your victims much in the way of autonomy."

"My rights are for the courts to decide. By denying me access to legal representation for such a test case you are compounding your crime. However, if it bothers you, then I can assure you that Kate Morley would like to see a lawyer."

"Kate Morley?"

"This body's co-host."

Dr Gilmore gave an uncertain smile. This wasn't going to plan at all. "I don't believe you."

"Again, you take the role of the court upon yourself. Do you really think Kate enjoys being strapped down and electrocuted? You are violating her basic human rights."

"I'd like to hear her ask for a lawyer."

"She has just done that. If you don't believe me, try running a voice print analysis. She said it."

"This is absurd."

"I want my lawyer!" Her voice rose in volume. "You, Marine, you are sworn to uphold the rights of Confederation citizens. I want a lawyer. Get me one."

The captain of the marine guard looked at Dr Gilmore for guidance. Everyone on the other side of the glass partition was staring in.

Dr Gilmore relaxed and smiled. "All right, Jacqueline. You cooperate with us, we'll cooperate with you. I will raise the topic with the First Admiral's legal staff to see if they consider you are entitled to legal representation. But first I want you to answer a question for me."

"The accused have a right of silence."

"I'm not accusing you of anything."

"Clever, Doctor. Ask then. But don't insult me by asking me to incriminate myself."

"When did your body die?"

"In 2036. Do I get my lawyer now?"

"And you were conscious the whole time you were in the beyond?"

"Yes, you moron."

"Thank you."

Jacqueline Couteur gave him a highly suspicious glance. "That's it?"

"Yes. For now."

"How did that help you?"

"Time passes in the beyond. That means it is subject to entropy."

"So?"

"If your continuum decays, then the entities within it can die. More pertinently, they can be killed."

"She wants a *what*?" Maynard Khanna asked.

Dr Gilmore flinched. "A lawyer."

"This is a joke, right?"

"I'm afraid not." He sighed reluctantly. "The problem is, while ordinarily I would dismiss such a request as sheer nonsense, it has opened something of a debate among the investigating staff. I know the Intelligence Service has extremely wide-ranging powers that supersede the Declaration of Rights; but personality debrief is normally conducted by another division. I'm not saying that what we're doing to Couteur and the others isn't necessary, I would just like to establish that our orders were drafted correctly, that is: legally. Naturally, I don't wish to bother the First Admiral with such trivia at this time. So if you could raise the matter with the Provost General's office I'd be grateful. Just for clarification, you understand."

● ● ●

In appearance, Golomo was no different from any of the other gas giants found among the star systems of the Confederation. A hundred and thirty-two thousand kilometres in diameter, its ring band slightly denser than usual, its storm bands a raucous mix of twirled vermillion, pale azure, splashed with coffee-cup swirls of white strands. The abnormality for which it was renowned lurked several hundred kilometres below the furrowed surface of the outer cloud layer, down where the density and temperature had risen considerably. That was where the Edenists whose habitats colonized the orbital space above located life; a narrow zone where pressure reduced the speed of the turbulence, and the strange hydrocarbon gases developed an easy viscosity. Single cells like airborne amoebas, but the size of a human fist, could survive there. They always clustered together in great colonies, resembling blankets of beluga. Why they did it, nobody could work out, none of them were specialized, all of them were independent. Yet to find singletons was unusual, at least in the areas so far observed by the probes, which admittedly was a minute percentage of the planet.

At any other time, Syrinx would dearly have loved to pay the research sites a visit. The old curiosity was still itching when *Oenone* slid out of its wormhole above the gas giant.

Other days, other priorities, the voidhawk chided.

Syrinx felt a hand patting hers; affinity was filled with if not quite sympathy, then certainly tolerance. She gave Ruben a droll glance and shrugged. **Okay, another time.** She borrowed the voidhawk's powerful affinity voice to identify them to the Golomo Consensus; SD sensors were already locking on.

The routine for each system they visited was identical: impart a summary of the Confederation's strategic disposition, then there were accounts of new developments in neighbouring systems, which asteroids and planets faced the possibility of takeovers. In exchange, the Consensus provided an intelligence update on the local system. *Oenone* could cover two, sometimes three star systems a day. So far the picture of conditions they were building up was depressing. The Edenist habitats were managing to stay on top of the situation, remaining loyal to the designated isolation and confinement policies. Adamist populations were less observant. Everywhere she went there were complaints about the hardships resulting from the quarantine, Edenist worries of local navies falling short of their designated duties, stories of illegal starship flights, a steady trickle of asteroids falling to the possessed, of political manoeuvring and advantage-trading.

We are generally more law abiding than Adamists, Oxley said. **And there are more of them than us. That's bound to produce a weighted picture.**

Don't make excuses for them, Caucus said.

Lack of education, and fear, Syrinx said. **That's what's doing it. We have to make allowances, I suppose. But at the same time, their attitude is going to be a real problem in the long term. In fact, it might mean there won't even be a long term as far as they're concerned.**

Apart from the Kulu Kingdom, and one or two other of the more disciplined societies, Ruben's suggestion was infected with irony.

She delayed her answer as she became aware of a growing unease in Golomo's Consensus. Voidhawks from the local defence force were popping in and out of wormholes, filling the affinity band with an excited buzz. **What is the problem?** she inquired.

We are confirming that the Ethenthia asteroid settlement has fallen to possession, Consensus informed *Oenone* and its crew. **We have just received a message from its Confederation Navy Bureau concerning the arrival of a CNIS captain, Erick Thakrar, from Kursk. According to the bureau chief, Thakrar had obtained information of an extremely important nature. A voidhawk was requested to carry the captain and his prisoner to Trafalgar. Unfortunately there is a fifteen-hour delay to Ethenthia. In the intervening time the possessed appear to have . . .**

Along with everyone else attuned to Consensus, Syrinx and her crew were immediately aware of the incoming message. Habitat senses perceived it as a violet star-point of microwaves, shining directly at Golomo from Ethenthia.

"This is Erick Thakrar, CNIS captain; I'm the one Emonn Verona told you about. Or at least I hope he did. God. Anyway, the possessed have taken over Ethenthia now. You probably know that by now. I managed to make it to a starship, the *Tigara*, but they're on to me. Listen, the information I've got is *vital*. I can't trust it to an open com link; if they find out what I know, it'll become useless. But right now this ship is totally fucked, and I'm not much better. I've got a partial alignment on the Ngeuni system, but there's barely anything about it in this almanac. I think it's a stage one colony. If I can't transfer to a flightworthy starship there, I'll try and slingshot back here. God, the SD platform is locking on. Okay, I'm jumping now—"

Ngeuni is a stage one colony, *Oenone* responded immediately.

Syrinx was automatically aware of its spatial location eleven light years away. When correlated with Ethenthia's current position the alignment must have been very tenuous indeed. If Thakrar's ship was as bad as he implied . . .

The colony is still in its start-up stage, *Oenone* continued. **However, there may be some starships available.**

This is something I should follow up, Syrinx told Consensus.

We concur. It will be another day before Thakrar returns here, assuming his ship remains flightworthy.

We'll check Ngeuni to see if he got there. Even as she spoke, energy was flowing through the voidhawk's patterning cells.

• • • •

Stephanie heard a loud mechanical screeching sound followed by a raucous siren blast. She grinned around at the children sitting at the kitchen table. "Looks like your uncle Moyo has found us some transport."

Her humour faded when she reached the bungalow's front porch. The bus which was parked on the road outside was spitting light in every spectrum; its bodywork a tight-packed mass of cartoon flowers growing out of paisley fields. LOVE,

PEACE, and KARMA flashed in nightclub neon on the sides. The darkest areas were its gleaming chrome hubcaps.

Moyo climbed down out of the cab, busily radiating embarrassment. The doors at the back of the bus hissed open, and another man climbed down. She'd never seen anyone with so much hair before.

The children were crowding around her, gazing out eagerly at the radiant carnival apparition.

"Is that really going to take us to the border?"

"How do you make it light up?"

"Please, Stephanie, can I get inside?"

Stephanie couldn't say no to them, so she waved them on with a casual gesture. They swarmed over the small front lawn to examine the wonderment.

"I can see how this should help us avoid any undue attention," she said to Moyo. "Have you lost your mind?"

A guilty finger indicated his new companion. "This is Cochrane, he helped me with the bus."

"So it was your idea?"

"Surely was." Cochrane bowed low. "Man, I *always* wanted a set of wheels like this."

"Good. Well now you've had it, you can say goodbye. I have to take these children out of here, and they're not going in that *thing*. We'll change it into something more suitable."

"Won't do you no good."

"Oh?"

"He's right," Moyo said. "We can't sneak about, not here. You know that. Everybody can sense everything in Mortonridge now."

"That's still no reason to use this . . . this—" She thrust an exasperated arm out towards the bus.

"It's like gonna be a mobile Zen moment for those with unpure thoughts," Cochrane said.

"Oh, spare me!"

"No really. Any cat catches sight of that bus and they're gonna have to confront like their inner being, you know. It's totally neat, a soul looking into its own soul. With this, you're broadcasting goodness at them on Radio Godhead twenty-four hours a day; it's a mercy mission that makes mothers weep for their lost children. My Karmic Crusader bus is going to shame them into letting you through. But like if you hit on people with a whole heavy military scene, like some kind of covert behind-the-lines hostility raid, you'll waste all those good vibes your karma has built up. It'll make it easy for all the cosmically uncool redneck dudes running loose out there to make it hard for us."

"Humm." He did make an odd kind of sense, she admitted grudgingly. Moyo gave her a hopeful shrug, a loyalty which lent her a cosy feeling. "Well, we could try it for a few miles I suppose." Then she gave Cochrane a suspicious look. "What do you mean, us?"

He smiled and held his arms out wide. A miniature rainbow sprang up out of his palms, arching over his head. The children laughed and clapped.

"Hey, I was at Woodstock, you know. I helped rule the world for three days. You need the kind of peaceful influence I exert over the land. I'm a friend to all living things, the unliving, too, now."

"Oh, hell."

• • •

Erick still hadn't activated the life-support capsule's internal environmental systems. He was too worried what the power drain would do to the starship's one remaining functional fusion generator. There certainly wasn't enough energy stored in the reserve electron matrix cells to power up the jump nodes.

Ngeuni's star was a severe blue-white point a quarter of a light-year away. Not quite bright enough to cast a shadow on the hull, but well above first magnitude, dominating the starfield. His sensor image was overlaid with navigation graphics, a tunnel of orange circles which seemed to be guiding the *Tigara* several degrees south of the star. After five jumps he was still matching delta-v.

Thankfully, the clipper's fusion drive was capable of a

seven-gee acceleration, and they weren't carrying any cargo. It meant he had enough fuel to align the ship properly. Getting back to Golomo was going to be a problem, though.

The flight computer warned him that the alignment manoeuvre was almost complete. *Tigara* was flashing towards the jump coordinate at nineteen kilometres per second. He started to reduce thrust and ordered the fusion generator to power up the nodes. As soon as the plasma flow increased he started receiving datavised caution warnings. The confinement field which held the ten-million-degree stream of ions away from the casing was fluctuating alarmingly.

Erick quickly loaded an emergency dump order into the flight computer, linking it to a monitor. If the confinement field fell below five per cent the generator would shut down and vent.

For some reason he was devoid of all tension. Then he realized his medical program was flashing for attention. When he accessed it, he saw the packages were filtering out a deluge of toxins and neurochemicals from his bloodstream at the same time as they were issuing chemical suppressors.

He grinned savagely around the SII suit's oxygen tube. Neutering his own reflexes at precisely the time he needed them the most. Too many factors were building up against him. And still it didn't really bother him, not snug in the heart of his semi-narcotic hibernation.

The flight computer signalled that the jump coordinate was approaching. Sensors and heat dump panels began to sink down into their recesses. The main drive reduced thrust to zero. Erick fired the ion thrusters, keeping the *Tigara* on track.

Then the energy patterning nodes were fully charged. Finally he felt a distant sense of relief, and reduced the fusion generator output. The straining confinement field surged as the plasma stream shrank by ninety per cent inside half a second. Decaying failsoft components didn't respond in time. An oscillation rippled along the tokamak chamber, tearing the plasma stream apart.

The *Tigara* jumped.

It emerged deep inside the Ngeuni system; at that instant a perfect inert sphere. The poise was shattered within an instant as the raging plasma tore through the tokamak's casing and ripped out through the hull, loosing incandescent swords of ions in all directions. A chain reaction of secondary explosions began as cryogenic tanks and electron matrices detonated.

The ship disintegrated amid a blaze of radioactive gases and ragged molten debris. Its life-support capsule came spinning out of the core of the explosion; a silvered sphere whose surface was gashed by veins of black carbon where energy bursts and tiny fragments had peppered the polished nultherm foam.

As soon as it was clear of the boiling gases, emergency rockets fired to halt the capsule's wild tumbling motion, a solid kick into stability. The beacon began to broadcast its shrill distress call.

7

Like most enterprises mounted by governments and institutions on Nyvan, the Jesup asteroid was chronically short of finance, engineering resources, and qualified personnel. The rock's major ore reserves had been mined out a long time ago. Ordinarily, the revenue would have been invested in the development of the asteroid's astroengineering industry. But the New Georgia government had diverted the initial windfall income to pay for more immediate and voter-friendly projects on the ground.

After the ore was exhausted, Jesup spent the next decades limping along both economically and industrially. Fledgling manufacturing companies shrank back to service subsidiaries and small indigenous armament corporations. Its aging infrastructure was maintained one degree from breakdown. Of the three planned biosphere caverns only one had ever been completed, leaving a vast number of huge empty cavities spaced strategically throughout the rock which would have been the kernels of fresh mining activity.

It was when Quinn was striding along one of the interminable bare-rock tunnels linking the discarded cavities that he sensed the first elusive presence. He stopped so abruptly that Lawrence almost bumped into him.

"What was that?"

"What?" Lawrence asked.

Quinn turned full circle, slowly scanning the dust-encrusted rock of the wide tunnel. Dribbles of condensation ran along the curving walls and roof, cutting small forked channels through the ebony dust as they generated fragile miniature stalactites. It was as if the tunnel were growing a fur of cactus spikes. But there was no place for anyone to hide, only the waves of shadow between the widely spaced lighting panels.

His entourage of disciples waited with nervous patience. After two days of slickly brutal initiation ceremonies the asteroid now belonged to him. However, Quinn remained disappointed with the number of true converts among the possessed. He had assumed that they of all people would despise Jesus and Allah and Buddha and the other false Gods for condemning them to an agonizing limbo. Showing them the path to the Light Bringer ought to have been easy. But they continued to demonstrate a bewildering resistance to his teachings. Some even interpreted their return to be a form of redemption.

Quinn could find nothing in the tunnel. He was sure he had caught a wisp of thought which didn't belong to any of the entourage; it had been accompanied by a tiny flicker of motion, grey on black. First reaction was that someone was sneaking along behind them.

Irritated by the distraction, he strode off again, his robe rising to glide above the filthy rock floor. It was cold in the tunnel, his breath turning to snowy vapour before his eyes. His feet began to crunch on particles of ice.

A frigid gust of air swept against him, making an audible *swoosh*. His robe flapped about.

He stopped again, angry this time. "What the fuck is going on here? There's no environmental ducts in this tunnel." He held up a hand to feel the air, which was now perfectly still.

Someone laughed.

He whirled around. But the disciples were looking at each other in confusion. None of them had dared mock his bewilderment. For a moment he thought of the unknown figure at the spaceport on Norfolk, the powerful swirl of flames he had unleashed. But that was light-years away, and no one else had escaped the planet except the Kavanagh girl.

"These tunnels are always acting erratically, Quinn," Bonham said. Bonham was one of the new converts, possessing Lucky Vin's body, which he was twisting into a ghoul-form, bleaching the skin, sharpening the teeth, and swelling the eyes. Thick animal hair was sprouting out of his silver skull. He said he had been born into a family of Venetian aristocrats in the late nineteenth century, killed before his twenty-seventh birthday in the First World War, but only after having tasted both the decadence and blind cruelty of the era. A taste which had become a voracious appetite. He had needed no persuading to embrace Quinn's doctrines.

"I asked one of the maintenance chappies, and he said it's because there aren't any ducts in the tunnels to regulate them properly. There are all sorts of weird surges."

Quinn wasn't satisfied. He was sure he'd sensed someone sneaking about. A dissatisfied grunt, and he was on his way once more.

No further oddities waylaid him before he reached the cavity where one of the teams was working. It was an almost spherical chamber, with a small flat floor, acting as a junction to seven of the large tunnels. A single fat metal tube hung downwards from the apex, rattling loudly as it blew out a wind of warm dry air. Quinn scowled up at it, then went over to the knot of five men working to secure the fusion bomb to the floor.

The device's casing was a blunt cone, seventy centimetres high. Several processor blocks had been plugged into its base with optical cables. The men stopped working and stood up respectfully as Quinn approached.

"Did anyone come through here earlier?"

They assured him no one had. One of them was non-possessed, a technician from the New Georgia defence force. He was sweating profusely, his thoughts a mixture of dread and outrage.

Quinn addressed him directly. "Is everything going okay?"

"Yes," the technician murmured meekly. He kept glancing at Twelve-T.

The gang lord was in a sorry state. Tiny jets of steam spluttered out of his mechanical body parts. Rheumy crusts were building up around the rim of bone in which his brain was resting, as though candle wax were leaking out. The membrane that clothed his brain had thickened (as Quinn wished) but was now acquiring an unhealthy green tint. He was blinking and squinting constantly as he fought the pain.

Quinn followed the man's gaze with pointed slowness. "Oh, yeah. The most feared gangster on the planet. Real hard-arsed mother who isn't gonna believe in God's Brother no matter what I do to him. Pretty dumb, really. But the thing is, he's useful to me. So I let him live. As long as he doesn't stray too far from me, he keeps on living. It's sort of like a metaphor, see? Now, you going to be a hard-arse?"

"No, sir, Mr Quinn."

"That's fucking smart." Quinn's head came forward slightly from the umbra of the hood to allow a faint light to strike his ashen skin. The technician closed his eyes to hide from the sight, lips mumbling a prayer.

"Now is this bomb going to work?"

"Yes, sir. It's a hundred megaton warhead, they all are. Once they're linked into the asteroid's net we can detonate them in sequence. As long as there are no possessed near them, they'll function properly."

"Don't worry about that. My disciples won't be here when Night dawns in the sky." He turned back to the tunnel, giving it a suspicious look. Again he had the intimation of motion, a flicker no larger than the flap of a bird's wing, and twice as fast. He was sure that someone had been watching the incident. A spoor of trepidation hung in the air like the scent of a summer flower.

When he stood at the entrance he could see the line of light panels shrink into distance before a curve took them from sight. The gentle sound of pattering water was all that emerged. He was half expecting to see that same blank human silhouette which had appeared at the hangar on Norfolk.

"If you are hiding, then you are weaker than me," he told the apparently empty shaft. "That means you will be found and brought before me for judgement. Best you come out now."

There was no response.

"Have it your way, shithead. You've seen what happens to people I don't like."

The rest of Quinn's day was spent issuing the instructions that would cause Night to fall on the innocent planet below. He commanded New Georgia's SD network now. It would be a simple matter for the platforms to interfere with Nyvan's two other functional networks, and various national sensor satellites. Under cover of this electronic warfare barrage, spaceplanes would slide down undetected to the surface. Every nation would be seeded by a group of possessed from Jesup. And Nyvan's curse of national antagonism would prevent a unified planetary response to the problem, which was the only response that could ever stand a chance of working.

The possessed would conquer here, probably with greater ease than anywhere in the Confederation. They were a single force, knowing nothing of borders and limits.

As for those who would actually be sent down, Quinn chose carefully. A couple of the devout for every spaceplane to make sure they followed their flight vectors and landed at the designated zone, but the rest were ones for whom only fear and his own proximity kept in line: unbelievers. It was quite deliberate. Free of his thrall, they would do what they always did, and seek to possess as many people as they could.

He didn't care that he would not be there to move among them and bring the word of God's Brother. Norfolk had shown him that mistake. Conversion on an individual basis was totally impractical when dealing with planetary populations.

Quinn's duty, and that of the disciples, was the same as all priests; they were simply to prepare the ground for God's Brother to walk upon, to build the temples and prepare the sacrament. It was He who would bring the final message, showing all the light.

The spaceplanes were only half of the scheme. Quinn was preparing to dispatch inter-orbit ships to the three derelict asteroids under the command of his most trusted followers. Those worthless rocks had now become a cornerstone in his plans to advance the Night.

It was after midnight when Quinn returned to the tunnel. This time he was by himself. He stood motionless under the arching entrance for a full minute, allowing whoever was there to notice him. Then he raised a hand and fired a single bolt of white fire at the electrical cable which ran along the crest of the tunnel. All the light panels went out.

"Now we will know which of us is the master of darkness," he shouted into the black air. He searched with his mind alone as he walked forwards, aware of the rock as an insubstantial pale grey tube around him. It was all that existed in a blank universe.

Feeble zephyrs of cold air rustled his robe. While out on the very cusp of perception, a tiny buzz increased; similar to the Babel of the beyond, but so much weaker.

He experienced no fright, nor even curiosity at confirming such an alien phenomenon existed. The Lords who battled for the heart of the universe and its denizens worked in ways he could never understand. All he had was his strength, and the knowledge that he knew himself. He would never quail, no matter what.

"I got you now, fuckers," Quinn whispered back at the tremulous voices.

As if in response, the air grew colder, its churning stronger. He concentrated hard, trying to focus his eldritch sight on the air currents themselves. Elusive, twisting strands; they were hard for his mind to grasp. But he persisted, seeking out the points where heat was draining out of the gas molecules.

As he delved further and further into the convoluted tides of energy a tide of light began to thicken in the air around him, sending faint streaks of colour dancing across the tunnel. It was as if the atmosphere's atoms had expanded into vast vacuous blobs, rushing around each other in frantic motion. When he slashed at one of the gliding luminescent baubles, his hand was a matt-black shape that passed clean through the hazy apparition. His fingers closed, snatching at nothing.

The misty glowing ball changed direction, ploughing through the others of its kind, rushing away from Quinn.

"Come back!" Quinn bellowed in fury, and let loose a blast of white fire in the direction it had gone. The aerial swell of colour shrank back from the bolt of energy.

Quinn saw them then, people huddled together in the darkness of the tunnel. Illuminated by the energistic discharge, they had dour, frightened faces. All of them were staring at him.

The energy bolt vanished, and with it the vision. Quinn gaped at the nebulous shoal which bobbled in agitation. They were flowing away from him steadily, picking up speed.

He thought he knew what they were, then. A whole group of possessed who had discovered how to make themselves invisible. His own energistic power began to boil through his body, mimicking the patterns inside the effervescent air. It was inordinately difficult, requiring almost his entire strength. As the energy crackled around him in the novel formation he realized what was happening. This was an effect similar to the one sought by the wild possessed on their quest to escape this universe, forcing open one of the innumerable chinks in quantum reality.

Quinn persevered, exerting himself fully, clawing at the elusive opening. After all, if they could do it, he, the chosen one, could achieve the same state. He hurried after the fleeing spectres, down the tunnel to the cavity where the bomb had been placed. The very last thing he could allow was a whole group of souls out of his control or sight.

His emergence into the new realm was gradual. The shadowy outlines of matter which his mind perceived began to take on more substance, becoming less translucent. His skin tingled, as if he were passing through a membrane of static. Then he was there. Weight was different, his body felt as if it were lighter than a drop of rain. He realized he wasn't breathing. His heart had stopped, too. Though, somehow, his body still functioned. Sheer willpower, he supposed.

He walked into the cavity to find them all, maybe a couple of hundred people; men, women and children. A large knot were gathered around the fusion bomb; if it wasn't for their blatant dismay they could have been praying to it. They were turning to face him; a collective fearful gasp went up. Children were clutched to their parents. Several held up shaking hands to ward him off.

"Peekaboo," Quinn said. "I see you, arseholes."

There was something wrong, something different between him and them. His own body glowed from the energistic power he was exerting, an image of vigour. They, by contrast, were uniformly pallid, almost monochrome. Wasted.

"Nice try," he told them. "But there's nowhere you can hide from God's Brother. Now I want you to all come back to reality with me. I won't be too hard; I've learned a useful trick tonight." He fixed his eyes on a teenage lad with flowing hair and smiled.

The lad shook his head. "We can't return," he stammered.

Quinn took five fast steps forwards and made a grab for the lad's arm. His fingers didn't exactly connect, but they did slow down as they passed through the sleeve. The lad's arm suddenly flared with brilliant colour, and he screeched in shock, stumbling backwards. "Don't," he pleaded. "Please, Quinn. It hurts."

Quinn studied his pain-furrowed face, rather enjoying the sight. "So you know my name, then."

"Yes. We saw you arrive. Please leave us alone. We can't harm you."

Quinn prowled along the front rank of the cowed group, looking at each of them as they pressed together. All of them shared the same dejection, few could meet his gaze. "You mean you were like this when I came here?"

"Yes," the lad replied.

"How? I was the first to bring the possessed here. What the fuck are you?"

"We're . . ." He glanced around at his peers for permission. "We're ghosts."

•   •   •

The hotel suite was two stories from the ground, which gave it a gravity field roughly a fifth of that which Louise was used to on Norfolk. She found it even more awkward than free fall. Every movement had to be well thought out in advance. Genevieve and Fletcher didn't much care for it either.

And then there was the air, or rather the lack of it. Both of Phobos's biosphere caverns were maintained at a low pressure. It was an intermediate stage, double that of Mars to help people en route to the planet to acclimatize themselves. Louise was glad she wasn't going down to the surface; each breath was a real effort to suck enough oxygen down into her lungs.

But the asteroid was a visual thrill—once she got used to the ground curving up over her head. The balcony gave them an excellent view across the parkland and fields. She would have loved to walk through the forests; many of the trees were centuries old. Their dignity reassured her, making the worldlet seem less artificial. From where she stood on the balcony she could see several cedars, their distinctive layered grey-green boughs standing out against the more verdant foliage. There had been no time for such leisurely activities, though. As soon as they'd left the *Far Realm*, Endron had booked them in here (though it was her money which paid for the suite). Then they'd been out shopping. She thought she would enjoy that, but unfortunately, Phobos was nothing like Norwich. There were none of the city's department stores and exclusive boutiques. Their clothes had all come from the SII general merchandise depository which was half shop, half warehouse, but of course none of them fitted her or Gen. Their bodies were a completely different shape to the asteroid's Martian and Lunar residents. Everything they chose had to be made-up. After that had come processor blocks (everyone in the Confederation used them, Endron explained, certainly travellers). Genevieve had plumped for one with a high-wattage AV projector and went on to load it with over fifty games from the depository's central memory core. Louise bought herself a block which could control the medical nanonic package around her wrist, allowing her to monitor her own physiological state.

Equipped and appearing like any normal visiting Confederation citizen, Louise had then accompanied Endron to the hostelries frequented by spaceship crews. It was a rerun of her attempts to buy passage off Norfolk, but this time she had some experience in the matter, and Endron knew his way around Phobos. Between them they took a mere two hours to find the *Jamrana*, an inter-orbit cargo ship bound for Earth, and agree on a price for Louise and the others.

That just left the passports.

Louise dressed herself in a tartan skirt (with stiffened fabric to stop it dancing up in the low gravity), black leggings, and a green polo-neck top. Clothes were the same as computers, she thought. After using the *Far Realm*'s flight computer she could never go back to the stupid keyboard-operated terminals on Norfolk, and now she had a million styles of dress available, none of them shaped by absurd concepts of what was *appropriate* . . .

She went out into the lounge. Genevieve was in her bedroom, the thin sounds of music and muffled dialogue leaking through the closed door as yet another game was run through her processor block. Louise didn't strictly approve, but objecting now would seem churlish, and it did keep her out of mischief.

Fletcher was sitting on one of the three powder-blue leather settees which made up the lounge's conversation area. He was sitting with his back to the glass window. Louise glanced at him, then the view which he was ignoring.

"I know, my lady," he said quietly. "You believe me foolish. After all, I have undertaken a voyage between the stars themselves, in a ship where I swam through the air with the grace of a fish in the ocean."

"There are stranger things in the universe than asteroid settlements," she said sympathetically.

"As ever, you are right. I wish I could understand why the ground above us doesn't fall down to bury us. It is ungodly, a defiance of the natural order."

"It's only centrifugal force. Do you want to access the educational text again?"

He gave her an ironic smile. "The one which the teachers of this age have prepared for ten-year-old children? I think I will spare myself repeated humiliation, my lady Louise."

She glanced at her gold watch, which was almost the last surviving personal item from Norfolk. "Endron should be here in a minute. We'll be able to leave Phobos in a few hours."

"I do not relish our parting, lady."

It was the one topic which she had never mentioned since the day when they had flown up to the *Far Realm*. "You are still intent on going down to Earth, then?"

"Aye, I am. Though in my heart I fear what awaits me there, I will not shirk from the task I have found for my new body. Quinn must be thwarted."

"He's probably there already. Goodness, by the time we reach the O'Neill Halo all of Earth could be possessed."

"Even if I knew that beyond all doubt, I would still not allow myself to turn back. I am truly sorry, Lady Louise, but my course is set. But do not worry yourself unduly, I will stay with you until you have found passage to Tranquillity. And I will make sure that there are no possessed on your vessel before it casts off."

"I wasn't trying to stop you, Fletcher. I think I'm a little fearful of your integrity. People in this age always seem to put themselves first. I do."

"You put your baby first, dearest Louise. Of that resolution, I am in awe. It is my one regret that by embarking on my own reckless venture that I will in all likelihood never now meet your beau, this Joshua of whom you speak. I would dearly like to see the man worthy of your love, he must be a prince among men."

"Joshua isn't a prince. I know now he is nowhere near perfect. But . . . he does have a few good points." Her hands touched her belly. "He'll be a good father."

Their eyes met. Louise didn't think she had ever seen so much loneliness before. In all the history texts they'd reviewed, he had always taken care to avoid any which might have told him what became of the family he'd left behind on Pitcairn Island.

It would have been so very easy for her to sit beside him and put her arms around him. Surely a person so alone deserved some comfort? What made her emotions worse was that she knew he could see her uncertainty.

The door processor announced that Endron was waiting. Louise made light of the moment with a chirpy smile and went to fetch Genevieve from her room.

"Do we all have to go?" a reticent Genevieve asked Endron. "I'd reached the third strata in Skycastles. The winged horses were coming to rescue the princess."

"She'll still be there when we get back," Louise said. "You can play it on the ship."

"He needs you there for a full image scan," Endron said. "No way out of it, I'm afraid."

Genevieve looked thoroughly disgusted. "All right."

Endron led them along one of the public halls. Louise was slowly mastering the art of walking in the asteroid's effete gravity field. Nothing you could do to stop yourself leaving the ground at each step; so push strongly with your toes, angling them to project you along a flat trajectory. She knew she'd never be as fluid as the Martians no matter how much practise she had.

"I wanted to ask you," Louise said as they slid into a lift. "If you're all Communists, how can the *Far Realm*'s crew sell Norfolk Tears here?"

"Why shouldn't we? It's one of the perks of being a crew

member. The only thing we don't like about bringing it in is paying import duty. And so far we haven't actually done that."

"But doesn't everybody own everything anyway? Why should they pay for it?"

"You're thinking of super-orthodox communism. People here retain their own property and money. No society could survive without that concept; you have to have something to show for your work at the end of the day. That's human nature."

"So you have landowners on Mars as well?"

Endron chuckled. "I don't mean that sort of property. We only retain personal items. Things like apartments are the property of the state; after all, the state pays for them. Farming collectives are allocated their land."

"And you accept that?"

"Yes. Because it works. The state has enormous power and wealth, but we vote on how it's used. We're dependent on it, and control it at the same time. We're also very proud of it. No other culture or ideology would ever have been able to terraform a planet. Mars has absorbed our nation's total wealth for five centuries. Offworlders have no idea of the level of commitment that requires."

"That's because I don't understand why you did it."

"We were trapped by history. Our ancestors modified their bodies to live in a Lunar gravity field before the ZTT drive was built. They could have sent their children to settle countless terracompatible worlds, but then those children would have needed geneering to adapt them back to the human 'norm.' Parent and child would have been parted at birth; they wouldn't have been descendants, just fosterlings in an alien environment. So we decided to make ourselves a world of our own."

"If I have followed this discourse correctly," Fletcher said. "You have spent five centuries turning Mars from a desert to a garden?"

"That's right."

"Are you really so powerful that you can rival Our Lord's handiwork?"

"I believe He only took seven days. We've got a long way to go yet before we equal that. Not that we'll ever do it again."

"Is the whole Lunar nation emigrating here now?" Louise asked, anxious to halt Fletcher's queries. She had caught Endron giving him puzzled glances at odd times during the voyage. It was something to watch out for; she was used to his naivete, thinking little of it. Others were not so generous.

"That was the idea. But now it's happened, the majority of those living in the Lunar cities are reluctant to leave. Those who do come here to settle are mostly the younger generation. So the shift is very gradual."

"Will you live on Mars once you've finished flying starships?"

"I was born in Phobos; I find skies unnatural. Two of my children live in Thoth city. I visit when I can, but I don't think I would fit in down there anyway. After all this time, our nation is finally beginning to change. Not very swiftly, but it's there, it's happening."

"How? How can communism change?"

"Money, of course. Now the terraforming project no longer absorbs every single fuseodollar earned by our state industries, there is more cash starting to seep into the economy. The younger generation adore their imported AV blocks and MF albums and clothes, they are placing so much value on these status symbols, ignoring our own nation's products purely for the sake of difference, which they see as originality. And they have a whole planet to range over; some of us actually worry that they might walk off into the countryside and reject us totally. Who knows? Not that I'd mind if they do discard our tenets. After all, it is their world. We built it so they could know its freedom. Trying to impose the old restrictions on them would be the purest folly. Social evolution is vital if any ethnic-nationhood is to survive; and five centuries is a long time to remain static."

"So if people did claim land for themselves, you wouldn't try to confiscate it back?"

"Confiscate? You say that with some malice. Is that what the Communists on your world say they're going to do?"

"Yes, they want to redistribute Norfolk's wealth fairly."

"Well, tell them from me, it won't work. All they'll ever do is cause more strife if they try and change things now. You cannot impose ideologies on people who do not embrace it wholeheartedly. The Lunar nation functions because it was planned that way from the moment the cities gained independence from the companies. It's the same concept as Norfolk, the difference being your founders chose to write a pastoral constitution. Communism works here because everybody supports it, and the net allowed us to eliminate most forms of corruption within the civil service and local governing councils that plagued most earlier attempts. If people don't like it, they leave rather than try and wreck it for everyone else. Isn't that what happens on Norfolk?"

Louise thought back to what Carmitha had said. "It's difficult for the Land Union people. Starflight is expensive."

"I suppose so. We're lucky here, the O'Neill Halo takes all our malcontents, some asteroids have entire low-gee levels populated by Lunar émigrés. Our government will even pay your ticket for you. Perhaps you should try that on Norfolk. The whole point of the Confederation's diversity is that it provides every kind of ethnic culture possible. There's no real need for internal conflict."

"That's a nice idea. I ought to mention it to Daddy when I get back. I'm sure a one-way starship ticket would be cheaper than keeping someone at the arctic work camps."

"Why tell your father? Why not campaign for it yourself?"

"Nobody would listen to me."

"You won't be your age forever."

"I meant, because I'm a girl."

Endron gave her a mystified frown. "I see. Perhaps that would be a better issue to campaign about. You'd have half of the population on your side from day one."

Louise managed an uncomfortable smile. She didn't like having to defend her homeworld from sarcasm, people should show more courtesy. The trouble was, she found it hard to defend some of Norfolk's customs.

Endron took them to one of the lowest habitation levels, a broad service corridor which led away from the biosphere cavern, deep into the asteroid's interior. It was bare rock, with one wall made up from stacked layers of cable and piping. The floor was slightly concave, and very smooth. Louise wondered how old it must be for people's feet to have worn it down.

They reached a wide olive-green metal door, and Endron datavised a code at its processor. Nothing happened. He had to datavise the code another two times before it opened. Louise didn't dare risk a glance at Fletcher.

Inside was a cathedral-sized hall filled with three rows of high voltage electrical transformers. Great loops of thick black cabling emerged from holes high up in the walls, stretching over the aisles in a complicated weave that linked them to the fat grey ribbed cylinders. There was a strong tang of ozone in the air.

A flight of metal stairs pinned against the rear wall led up to a small maintenance manager's office cut into the rock. Two narrow windows looked down on the central aisle as they walked towards it, the outline of a man just visible inside. Fletcher's alarm at the power humming savagely all around them was clear in the sweat on his forehead and hands, his small, precisely controlled steps.

The office had a large desk with a computer terminal nearly as primitive as the models Louise used on Norfolk. A large screen took up most of the back wall, its lucidly coloured symbols displaying the settlement's power grid.

There was a Martian waiting for them inside; a man with very long snow-white hair brushed back neatly and a bright orange silk suit worn in conjunction with a midnight-black shirt. He carried a slim, featureless grey case in his left hand.

Faurax didn't know what to make of his three new clients at all; if they hadn't been with Endron he wouldn't even have let them into the office. These were not the times to dabble in his usual sidelines. Thanks to the current Confederation crisis, the Phobos police were becoming quite unreasonable about security procedures.

"If you don't mind me asking," he said after Endron had introduced everybody. "Why haven't you got your own passports?"

"We had to leave Norfolk very quickly," Louise said. "The possessed were sweeping through the city. There was no time to apply to the Foreign Office for passports. Although there's no reason why we shouldn't have been issued with them, we don't have criminal records or anything like that."

It even sounded reasonable. And Faurax could guess the kind of financial package which the *Far Realm*'s crew would engineer concerning their passage. Nobody wanted questions at this stage.

"You must understand," he said, "I had to undertake a considerable amount of research to obtain the Norfolk government's authentication codes."

"How much?" Louise asked.

"Five thousand fuseodollars. Each."

"Very well."

She didn't even sound surprised, let alone shocked. Which tweaked Faurax's curiosity; he would have dearly liked to ask Endron who she was. The call he'd got from Tilia setting up the meeting had been very sparse on detail.

"Good," he said, and put his case on the desk, datavising a code at it. The upper surface flowed apart, revealing a couple of processor blocks and several fleks. He picked up one of the fleks, which was embossed with a gold lion: Norfolk's national symbol. "Here we are. I loaded in all the information Tilia gave me; name, where you live, age, that kind of thing. All we need now is an image and a full body bioelectric scan."

"What do we have to do?" Louise asked.

"First, I'm afraid, is the money."

She gave a hollow laugh and took a Jovian Bank credit

disk from her small shoulder bag. Once the money had been shunted over to Faurax's disk, he said: "Remember not to wear these clothes when you go through the Halo's immigration. These images were supposedly taken on Norfolk before you left, and the clothes are new. In fact, I'd advise dumping them altogether."

"We'll do that," Louise said.

"Okay." He slotted the first flek into his processor block and read the screen. "Genevieve Kavanagh?"

The little girl smiled brightly.

"Stand over there, dear, away from the door."

She did as he asked, giving the sensor lens a solemn stare. After he'd got the visual image filed, he used the second processor block to sweep her so he could record her biolectric pattern. Both files were loaded into her passport, encrypted with Norfolk's authentication code. "Don't lose it," he said and dropped the flek into her hand.

Louise was next. Faurax found himself wishing she were a Martian girl. She had a beautiful face, it was just her body which was so alien.

Fletcher's image went straight into his passport flek. Then Faurax ran the biolectric sensor over him. Frowned at the display. Ran a second scan. It took a long time for his chilly disquiet to give way into full blown consternation. He gagged, head jerking up from the block to stare at Fletcher. "You're a—" His neural nanonics crashed, preventing him from datavising any alarm. The air solidified in front of his eyes; he actually saw it flowing like a dense heat shiver, contracting into a ten centimetre sphere. It hit him full in the face. He heard the bone in his nose break before he lost consciousness.

Genevieve squealed in shock as Faurax went crashing to the floor, blood flowing swiftly from his nose.

Endron looked at Fletcher in total shock, too numb to move. His neural nanonics had shut down, and the office light panel was flickering in an epileptic rhythm. "Oh, my God. No! Not you." He glanced at the door, gauging his chances.

"Do not try to run, sir," Fletcher said sternly. "I will do whatever I must to protect these ladies."

"Oh, Fletcher," Louise groaned in dismay. "We were almost there."

"His device exposed my nature, my lady. I could do naught else."

Genevieve ran over to Fletcher and hugged him tightly around his waist. He patted her head lightly.

"Now what are we going to do?" Louise asked.

"Not you as well?" Endron bewailed.

"I'm not possessed," she said with indignant heat.

"Then what . . . ?"

"Fletcher has been *protecting* us from the possessed. You don't think I could stand against them by myself, do you?"

"But, he's one of them."

"One of whom, sir? Many men are murderers and brigands, does that make all of us so?"

"You can't apply that argument. You're a possessed. You're the enemy."

"Yet, sir, I do not consider myself to be your enemy. My only crime, so it sounds, is that I have died."

"And come back! You have stolen that man's body. Your kind want to do the same to mine and everyone else's."

"What would you have us do? I am not so valiant that I can resist this release from the torture of the beyond. Perhaps, sir, you see such weakness as my true crime. If so, I plead guilty to that ignominy. Yet, know you this, I would grasp at such an escape every time it is offered, though I know it to be the most immoral of thefts."

"He saved us," Genevieve protested hotly. "Quinn Dexter was going to do truly beastly things to me and Louise. Fletcher stopped him. No one else could. He's not a bad man; you shouldn't say he is. And I won't let you do anything horrid to him. I don't want him to have to go back there into the beyond." She hugged Fletcher tighter.

"All right," Endron said. "Maybe you're not like the Capone Organization, or the ones on Lalonde. But I can't let you walk around here. This is my home, damn it. Maybe it is unfair, and unkind that you suffered in the beyond. You're still a possessor, nothing changes that. We are opposed, it's fundamental to what we are."

"Then you, sir, have a very pressing problem. For I am sworn to see these ladies to their destination in safety."

"Wait," Louise said. She turned to Endron. "Nothing has changed. We still wish to leave Phobos, and you know Fletcher is not a danger to you or your people. You said so."

Endron gestured at the crumpled form of Faurax. "I can't," he said desperately.

"If Fletcher opens your bodies to the souls in the beyond, who knows what the people who come through will be like," Louise said. "I don't think they will be as restrained as Fletcher, not if the ones I've encountered are anything to judge by. You would be the cause of Phobos falling to the possessed. Is that what you want?"

"What the hell do you think? You've backed me into a corner."

"No we haven't, there's an easy way out of this, for all of us."

"What?"

"Help us, of course. You can finish recording Fletcher's passport for us, you can find a zero-tau pod for Faurax and keep him in it until this is all over. And you'll know for certain that we've gone and that your asteroid is safe."

"This is insane. I don't trust you, and you'd be bloody stupid to trust me."

"Not really," she said. "If you tell us you'll do it, Fletcher will know if you're telling us the truth. And once we're gone you still won't change your mind, because you could never explain away what you've done to the police."

"You can read minds?" Endron's consternation had deepened.

"I will indeed know of any treachery which blackens your heart."

"What do you intend to do once you reach Tranquillity?"

"Find my fiancé. Apart from that, we have no plans."

Endron gave Faurax another fast appraisal. "I don't think

I have a lot of choice, do I? If you stop this electronic warfare effect, I'll get a freight mechanoid to take Faurax to the *Far Realm*. I can use one of the on board zero-tau pods without anyone asking questions. Lord knows what I'll say when this is over. They'll just fling me out of an airlock, I expect."

"You're saving your world," Louise said. "You'll be a hero."

"Somehow, I doubt that."

• • • •

The cave went a long way back into the polyp cliff, which allowed Dariat to light a fire without having to worry about it being spotted. He'd chosen the beach at the foot of the endcap as today's refuge. Surely here at least he and Tatiana would be safe? There were no bridges over the circumfluous reservoir. If Bonney came for them she'd have to use either a boat or one of the tube carriages (however unlikely that was). Which meant that for once they'd have a decent warning.

The hunter's ability to get close before either he or Rubra located her was unnerving. Even Rubra seemed genuinely concerned by it. Dariat never could understand how she ever located them in the first place. But locate them she did. There hadn't been a day since he met Tatiana when Bonney hadn't come after them.

His one guess was that her perception ability was far greater than anyone else's, allowing her to see the minds of everybody in the habitat. If so, the distance was extraordinary; he couldn't feel anything beyond a kilometre at the most, and ten metres of solid polyp blocked him completely.

Tatiana finished gutting the pair of trout she'd caught, and wrapped them in foil. Both were slipped into the shallow hole below the fire. "They ought to be done in about half an hour," she said.

He smiled blankly, remembering the fires he and Anastasia had made, the meals she had prepared for him. Campfire cooking was an outlandish concept to him then. Used to regulated, heat inducted sachets, he was always impressed by the cuisine she produced from such primitive arrangements.

"Did she ever say anything about me?" he asked.

"Not much. I didn't see much of her after she set herself up as a mistress of Thoale. Besides which, I was discovering boys myself about then." She gave a raucous laugh.

Apart from the physical resemblance, it was difficult to accept any other connection between Tatiana and Anastasia. It was inconceivable that his beautiful love would have ever grown into anything resembling this cheery, easygoing woman, with an overloud voice. Anastasia would have kept her quiet dignity, her sly humour, her generous spirit.

It was hard for him to feel much sympathy for Tatiana, and harder still to tolerate her behaviour, especially given their circumstances. He persisted, though, knowing that to desert her now would make him unworthy, a betrayal of his own one love.

Damn Rubra for knowing that.

"Whatever she did say, I'd appreciate you telling me."

"Okay. I suppose I owe you that at least." She settled herself more comfortably into the thin sand, her bracelets tinkling softly. "She said her new boy—that's you—was very different. She said you'd been hurt by Anstid since the day you were born, but that she could see the real person buried underneath all the pain and loneliness. She thought she could free you from his thrall. Strange, she really believed it; as if you were some sort of injured bird she'd rescued. I don't think she realized what a mistake she'd made. Not until the end. That was why she did it."

"I am true to her. I always have been."

"So I see. Thirty years planning." She whistled a long single note.

"I'm going to kill Anstid. I have the power now."

Tatiana began to laugh, a big belly rumble that shook her loose cotton dress about. "Ho yes, I can see why she'd fall for you. All that sincerity and retention. Cupid tipped his arrows with a strong potion that day you two met."

"Don't mock."

Her laughter vanished in an instant. Then he could see the resemblance to Anastasia, the passion in her eyes. "I would never mock my sister, Dariat. I pity her for the trick Tarrug played on her. She was too young to meet you, too damn young. If she'd had a few more years to gather wisdom, she would have seen you are beyond any possible salvation. But she was young, and stupid the way we all are at that age. She couldn't refuse the challenge to do good, to bring a little light into your prison. When you get to my age, you give lost causes a wide passage."

"I am not lost, not to Chi-ri, not to Thoale. I will slay Anstid. And that is thanks to Anastasia, she broke that Lord's spell over me."

"Oh, dear, oh, dear, listen to him. Stop reading the words, Dariat, learn with your heart. Just because she told you the names of our Lords and Ladies, doesn't mean you know them. You won't kill Anstid. Rubra is not a realm Lord, he's a screwed-up old memory pattern. Sure, his bananas mind makes him bitter and vindictive, which is an aspect of Anstid, but he's not the real thing. Hatred isn't going to vanish from the universe just because you nuke a habitat. You can see that, can't you?"

Yes, go on, boy, answer the question. I'm interested.

Fuck off!

Pity you never went to university; the old school of hard knocks is never quite enough when you need to stand up for yourself in the intellectual debating arena.

Dariat made an effort to calm himself, aware of the little worms of light scurrying over his clothing. A sheepish grin unfurled on his lips. "Yes, I can see that. Besides, without hatred you could never know how sweet love is. We need hatred."

"That's more like it." She started applauding. "We'll make a Starbridge of you yet."

"Too late for that. And I'm still going to nuke Rubra."

"Not before I'm out of here, I hope."

"I'll get you out."

Yeah, and whose help are you going to need for that?

"How?" Tatiana asked.

"I'll be honest. I don't know. But I'll find a way. I owe you and Anastasia that much."

Bravo, Sir Galahad. In the meantime, three ships have arrived.

So?

So they're from New California, a frigate and two combat-capable traders. I think our current status quo might be changing.

The voidhawks on observation duty perceived the three Adamist starships emerge from their ZTT jump twelve thousand kilometres out from Valisk. As their thermo-dump panels, sensor clusters, and communications arrays deployed, the voidhawks started to pick up high-bandwidth microwave transmissions. The ships were beaming out news reports all over the Srinagar system, telling everyone who was interested how well the Organization was doing, and how New California was prospering. There were several long items on the possessed curing injuries and broken bones in the non-possessed.

The one thing the voidhawks couldn't intercept was the signal between the ships and Valisk. Whatever was said, it resulted in eight hellhawks arriving to escort the New California starships to the habitat's spaceport.

Alarmed by the implication of Capone extending his influence into the Srinagar system, Consensus requested Rubra monitor developments closely. For once, he wasn't inclined to argue.

Kiera waited for Patricia Mangano at the end of the passageway which led up to the axial chamber three kilometres above her. Without the tube carriages, every ascent and descent had to be on foot. Starting at the axial chamber, the passageway contained a ladder for the first kilometre, then gave way to a staircase for the final two as the curvature became more pronounced. It ended two kilometres above the base of the endcap, emerging from the polyp shell onto a shelflike plateau which was reached by a switchback road.

Thankfully, similar plateaus around the endcap gave them admission to the docking ledge lounges. Which meant they'd all but stopped using the counter-rotating spaceport.

If Patricia was annoyed by the time and physical effort it took her to descend, it was hidden deeper than Kiera's perception was able to discern. Instead, when Capone's envoy emerged into the light, she smiled with a simple delight as she looked around. Kiera had to admit, the little plateau was an excellent vantage point. The distinct bands of colour which comprised Valisk's interior shone lucidly in the light tube's relentless emission.

Patricia shielded her eyes with one hand as she gazed about the worldlet. "Nothing anybody says can prepare you for this."

"Didn't you have habitats in your time?" Kiera asked.

"Absolutely not. I'm strictly a twentieth-century gal. Al prefers us as his lieutenants, that way we understand each other better. Some modern types, I can only comprehend about one word in ten."

"I'm from the twenty-fourth century myself. Never set foot on Earth."

"Lucky you."

Kiera gestured at the open-top truck parked at the end of the road. Bonney was sitting in the backseat, ever vigilant.

Kiera switched on the motor and began the drive down the road. "I'll warn you from the start, anything you say in the open is overheard by Rubra. We think he tells the Edenists just about everything that goes on in here."

"What I have to say is private," Patricia said.

"I thought so. Don't worry, we have some clean rooms."

It wasn't too difficult for Rubra to infiltrate the circular tower at the base of the northern endcap. He just needed to be careful. The possessed could always detect small animals like mice and bats, which were simply blasted by a bolt of white fire. So he had to resort to more unusual servitors.

Deep in the birthing caverns of the southern endcap, incubators were used to nurture insects whose DNA templates had been stored unused since the time when Valisk was germinated. Centipedes and bees began to emerge, each one affinity-controlled by a sub-routine.

The bees flew straight out into the main cavern, where they hovered and loitered among all the temporary camps set up around the starscraper lobbies. Coverage wasn't perfect, but they provided him with a great deal of information about what went on inside the tents and cottages, where his usual perception was blocked.

The centipedes were carried aloft by birds, to be deposited on the roof of the tower and other substantial buildings. Like the spiders which the Edenist intelligence agency used to infiltrate their observation targets, they scuttled along conditioning ducts and cable conduits, hiding just behind grilles and sockets where they could scrutinize the interior.

Their deployment allowed Rubra and the Kohistan Consensus to watch as Kiera led Patricia Mangano into Magellanic Itg's boardroom. Patricia had one assistant with her, while Kiera was accompanied by Bonney and Stanyon. No one else from Valisk's new ruling council had been invited.

"What happened?" Patricia asked after she had claimed a chair at the big table.

"In what respect?" Kiera replied cautiously.

"Come on. You've got your hellhawks flitting about the Confederation with impunity to bring back warm bodies. And when they get here, the habitat looks like it's a Third World refugee camp left over from my own century. You're living in the iron age, here. It doesn't make any sense. Bitek is the one technology that keeps working around us. You should be lording it up in the starscraper apartments."

"Rubra happened," Kiera said bitterly. "He's still in the neural strata. The one expert we had on affinity who could possibly remove him has . . . failed. It means we've got to go through the starscrapers a centimetre at a time to make them safe. We're getting there. It'll take time, but we've got eternity, after all."

"You could leave."

"I don't think so."

Patricia lounged back, grinning. "Ah, right. That would mean evacuating to a planet. How would you keep your position and authority there?"

"The same way Capone does. People need governments, they need organizing. We're a very socially oriented race."

"So why didn't you?"

"We're doing all right here. Have you really come all this way just to take cheap shots?"

"Not at all. I'm here to offer you a deal."

"Yes?"

"Antimatter in return for your hellhawks."

Kiera glanced at Bonney and Stanyon; the latter's face was alive with interest. "What exactly do you think we can do with antimatter?"

"The same as us," Patricia said. "Blow Srinagar's SD network clean to hell. *Then* you'll be able to get off this dump. The planet will be wide open to you. And as you'll be running the invasion, you'll be able to shape whatever society springs up among the possessed down there. That's the way it works for the Organization. We begin it, we rule it. Whether it works here, depends on how good you are. Capone is the best."

"But not perfect."

"You have your problems, we have ours. The Edenist voidhawks are causing a lot of disruption to our fleet activities. We need the hellhawks to deal with them. Their distortion fields can locate the stealth bombs being flung at us."

"Interesting proposition."

"Don't try and bargain, please. That would be insulting. We have an irritant; you have a potential disaster looming."

"If you don't take too much offence at the question, I'd like to know how much antimatter you'll deliver."

"As much as it takes, and the ships to deploy them, providing you can keep your end. How many hellhawks can you offer?"

"We have several out collecting Deadnight kids. But I can probably let you have seventy."

"And you can keep them under control, make them follow orders?"

"Oh, yes."

"How?"

Kiera gloated. "It's not something you'll ever be able to duplicate. We can return the souls possessing the hellhawks directly into human bodies. That's what they all want eventually, and that's what we'll give them, providing they obey."

"Smart. So do we have a deal?"

"Not with you. I'll travel to New California myself and talk to Capone. That way we'll both know how much we can trust the other."

Kiera hung back after Patricia left the boardroom. "This changes everything," she said to Bonney. "Even if we don't get enough antimatter to knock over Srinagar, it'll give us the deterrence to prevent another voidhawk attack."

"It looks like it. Do you think Capone is on the level?"

"I'm not sure. He must need the hellhawks pretty badly, or he wouldn't have offered us the antimatter. Even if he's got a production station, it won't exactly be plentiful."

"You want me to come with you?"

"No." The tip of her tongue licked over her lips, a fast movement by a lash of forked flesh. "We're either going to be leaving here for Srinagar, or I'll deal with Capone to provide us with enough bodies to fill the habitat. Either way, we won't be needing that shit Dariat anymore. See to it."

"You bet."

Can you stop the hellhawks from leaving? Rubra asked.

No, the Kohistan Consensus said. **Not seventy of them. They are still armed with a considerable number of conventional combat wasps.**

Bugger.

If Kiera does acquire antimatter combat wasps from Capone, we don't think we will be able to provide an adequate level of reinforcement to Srinagar's Strategic Defence network. The planet may fall to her.

Then call in the Confederation Navy. Srinagar's been paying its taxes, hasn't it?

Yes. But there is no guarantee the navy will respond. Its resources are being deployed over a wide area.

Then call Jupiter. They're bound to have spare squadrons.

We will see what can be done.

Do that. In the meantime, there are some important decisions to be taken. By me and Dariat both. And I don't think Bonney Lewin is going to give us much more time.

⚫ ⚫

Erick was sure that the explosion, followed by the capsule's equally violent stabilization manoeuvre, had torn loose some of his medical nanonic packages. He could feel peculiar lines of pressure building up under the SII suit, and convinced himself it was fluid leakage. Blood or artificial tissue nutrient from the packages and their supplements, he wasn't sure which. Over half of them no longer responded to his datavises.

At least it meant they couldn't contribute to the medical program's dire pronouncements of his current physiological state. His right arm wouldn't respond to any nerve impulses at all, nor was he receiving any sensation from it. The only positive factor was a confirmation that blood was still circulating inside the new muscles and artificial tissue.

There wasn't much he could do to rectify the situation. The capsule's reserve electron matrices didn't have enough power to activate the internal life-support system. The thin atmosphere was already ten degrees below zero, and falling rapidly. Which meant he was unable to take the suit off and replace the nanonic packages. And just to twist the knife, an emergency survival gear locker containing fresh medical nanonic packages had popped open in the ceiling above him.

Backup lighting had come on, casting a weak pale blue glow across the compartment. Frost was forming on most of the surfaces, gradually obscuring the few remaining active holoscreen displays. Various pieces of refuse had been jolted loose from their nesting places to twirl whimsically through the air, throwing avian-style shadows across the acceleration couches.

Potentially the most troubling problem was the intermittent dropouts from which the flight computer's datavises were suffering. Erick wasn't entirely sure he could trust its status display. It still responded to simple commands, though.

With his personal situation stable for a moment, he instructed the capsule's sensors to deploy. Three of the five responded, pistonlike tubes sliding up out of the nultherm foam coating. They began to scan around.

Astrogration programs slowly correlated the surrounding starfield. If they were working correctly, then the *Tigara* had emerged approximately fifty million kilometres from the coordinate he was aiming for. Ngeuni was only an unremarkable blue-green star to one side of the glaring A2 primary.

He wasn't sure if they would pick up the capsule's distress beacon. Stage one colonies did not have the most sophisticated communications satellites. When he instructed the capsule's phased array antenna to focus on the distant planet, it didn't acknowledge. He repeated the instruction, and there was still no activity.

The flight computer ran a diagnostic, which gave him a System Inviable code. Without actually going outside to examine it, there was no way of telling what was wrong.

Alone.

Cut off.

Fifty million kilometres from possible rescue.

Light-years from where he desperately needed to be.

All that was left for him now was to wait. He began switching off every piece of equipment apart from the attitude rockets, the guidance system which drove them, and the computer itself. Judging by the frequency of the thruster firings, the capsule was venting something. The last diagnostic sweep before he shut down the internal sensors couldn't pinpoint what it was.

After he'd reduced the power drain to a minimum, he pressed the deactivation switch for his restraint webbing. Even that seemed reluctant to work, taking a long time to fold back below the side of the cushioning. At this movement, levering himself up from the couch, fluid stirred across his abdomen. He found that by moving very slowly, the effect (and perhaps the harm) was moderated.

Training took over, and he began to index the emergency gear which had deployed from the ceiling. That was when the emotional shock hammered him. He suddenly found himself shaking badly as he clung to a four person programmable silicon dinghy.

Indexing his position! Like a good little first-year cadet.

A broken laugh bubbled around the SII suit's respirator tube. The glossy black silicon covering his eyes turned permeable to vent the salty fluid burning his squeezed up eyelids.

Never in his life had he felt so utterly helpless. Even when the possessed were boarding the *Villeneuve's Revenge* he'd been able to do something. Fight back, hit them. Orbiting above New California with the Organization poised to obliterate them at the first false move, he'd been able to store most of the sensor images. There had always been something, some way of being positive.

Now he was humiliatingly aware of his mind crumbling away in mimicry of his tattered old body. Fear had risen to consume him, flowing swiftly out of the dark corners of the bridge. It produced a pain in his head far worse than any physical injury ever could.

Those muscles which still functioned disobeyed any lingering wishes he might have, leaving him ignominiously barnacled to the dinghy. Every last reserve of determination and resolve had been exhausted. Not even the ubiquitous programs could shore up his mentality anymore.

Too weak to continue living, too frightened to die: Erick Thakrar had come to the end of the line.

• • •

Eight kilometres west of Stonygate, Cochrane tooted the horn on the Karmic Crusader bus and turned off the road. The other three vehicles in the convoy jounced over the grass verge and came to a halt behind it.

"Yo, dudettes," Cochrane yelled back to the juvenile rioters clambering over the seats. "Time out for like the big darkness." He pressed the red button on the dash, and the doors hissed open. Kids poured out like a dam burst.

Cochrane put his purple glasses back on and climbed down out of the cab. Stephanie and Moyo walked over to him, arm in arm. "Good place," she said. The convoy had halted at the head of a gentle valley which was completely roofed over by the rumbling blanket of crimson cloud, rendering the mountain peaks invisible.

"This whole righteous road trip is one major groove."

"Right."

He materialized a fat reefer. "Hit?"

"No thanks. I'd better see about cooking them some supper."

"That's cool. I can't psyche out any hostile vibes in this locale. I'll like keep watch, make sure the nazgul aren't circling overhead."

"You do that." Stephanie smiled fondly at him and went to the back of the bus, where the big luggage hold was. Moyo started pulling out the cooking gear.

"We should manage to reach Chainbridge by tomorrow evening," he said.

"Yes. This isn't quite what I expected when we started out, you know."

"Predictability is boring." He put a big electric camping

grille on the ground, adjusting the aluminum legs to make it level. "Besides, I think it's worked out for the best."

Stephanie glanced around the improvised campsite, nodding approval; nearly sixty children were scampering around the parked vehicles. What had started off as a private mission to help a handful of lost children had rapidly snowballed.

Four times during the first day they had been stopped by residents who had told them where non-possessed children were lurking. On the second day there were over twenty children packed on board; that was when Tina Sudol had volunteered to come with them. Rana and McPhee joined up on the third day, adding another bus.

Now there were four vehicles, and eight possessed adults. They were no longer making a straight dash for the border at the top of Mortonridge. It was more of a zigzag route, visiting as many towns as they could to pick up children. Ekelund's people, who had evolved into the closest thing to a government on Mortonridge, maintained the communications net between the larger towns, albeit with a considerably reduced bit capacity than previously. News of Stephanie's progress had spread widely. Children were already waiting for the buses when they reached some towns; on a couple of occasions dressed smartly and given packed lunches by the possessed who had taken care of them. They had borne witness to some very tearful partings.

After the children had eaten and washed and been settled in their tents, Cochrane and Franklin Quigley sliced branches off a tree and piled them up to form a proper campfire. The adults came to sit around it, enjoying the yellow light flaring out to repel the clouds' incessant claret illumination.

"I think we should forget going back to a town when we're done with the kids," McPhee said. "All of us get along okay, we should try a farm. The towns are starting to run out of food, now. We could grow some and sell it to them. That would give us something to do."

"He's been back a whole week, and he's already bored," Franklin Quigley grunted.

"Bore-*ing*," Cochrane said. He blew twin streams of smoke out of his nostrils. They spiralled through the air to jab at McPhee's nose like a cobra.

The giant Scot made a pass of his hand, and the smoke wilted, turning to tar and splattering on the ground. "I'm not bored, but we have to do something. It makes sense to think ahead."

"You might be right," Stephanie said. "I don't think I'd like to live in any of the towns we've passed through so far."

"The way I see it," said Moyo, "is that the possessed are developing into two groups."

"*Please* don't use that word," Rana said. Sitting cross-legged next to the flamboyantly feminine Tina Sudol, Rana appeared fastidiously androgynous with her short hair and baggy blue sweater.

"What word?" Moyo asked.

"Possession. I find it offensive and prejudicial."

"That's right, babe," Cochrane chortled. "We're not possessors, we're just like dimensionally disadvantaged."

"Call our cross-continuum placement situation whatever you wish," she snapped back. "You cannot alter the fact that the term is wholly derogatory. The Confederation's military-industrial complex is using it to demonize us so they can justify increased spending on their armaments programs."

Stephanie pressed her face into Moyo's arm to smother her giggles.

"Come on, we're not exactly on the side of the saints," Franklin observed.

"The perception of common morality is enforced entirely by the circumstances of male-dominated society. Our new and unique circumstances require us to re-evaluate that original morality. As there are clearly not enough living bodies to go around the human race, sensory ownership should be distributed on an equitable basis. It's no good the living protesting about us. We have as much right to sensory input as they do."

Cochrane took the reefer from his mouth and gave it a sad stare. "Man, I wish I could manifest your trips."

"You ignore him, darling," Tina Sudol said to Rana. "He's a perfect example of male brutality."

"I suppose a fuck is out of the question tonight, then?"

Tina sucked in her cheeks theatrically as she glowered at the unrepentant hippie. "I'm only interested in men."

"And always have been," McPhee said, in an unsubtle whisper.

Tina flounced her glossy, highlighted hair back with a manicured hand. "You men are animals, all of you, simply *rancid* with hormones. No wonder I wanted to escape that *prison* of flesh I was in."

"*The two groups*," Moyo said, "seem to be divided into those that stay put, like the café proprietors, and the restless ones—like us I suppose, though we're an exception. They complement each other perfectly. The wanderers go around playing tourist, drinking down the sights and experiences. And wherever they go, they meet the stayers and tell them about their journeys. That way both types get what they want. Both of us exist to relish experience; some like to go out and find it, others like it brought to them."

"You think that's what it's going to be like from now on?" McPhee asked.

"Yes. That's what we'll settle down into."

"But for how long? Wanting to see and feel is just a reaction from the beyond. Once we've had our fill, human nature will come back. People want to settle down, have a family. Procreation is our biological imperative. And that's one thing we never can do. We will always be frustrated."

"I'll like give it a try," Cochrane said. "Me and Tina can make babies in my tepee anytime."

Tina gave him a single disgusted look, and shuddered.

"But they wouldn't be yours," McPhee said. "That isn't your body, and it certainly isn't your DNA. You will never have a child again, not one of your own. That phase of our lives is over, it cannot be regained no matter how much of our energistic ability we expend."

"You're also forgetting the third type walking among us," Franklin said. "The Ekelund type. And I do know her. I signed up with her for the first couple of days. She seemed to know what she was doing. We had 'objectives' and 'target assignments,' and 'command structures'—and God help anyone who disobeyed those fascists. She's a straight power nut with a Napoleonic complex. She's got her little army of wannabe toughs running around in combat fatigues thinking they're reborn special forces brigades. And they're going to keep sniping away at the Royal Marines over the border until the Princess gets so pissed with us she nukes Mortonridge down to the bedrock."

"That situation won't last," McPhee said. "Give it a month, or a year, and the Confederation will fall. Don't you listen to the whispers in the beyond? Capone is getting his act together out there. It won't be long before the Organization fleet jumps to Ombey. Then there will be nobody left for Ekelund to fight, and her command structure will simply fade away. Nobody is going to do what she tells them for the rest of time."

"I don't want to live for the rest of time," Stephanie said. "I really don't. That's almost as frightening as being trapped in the beyond. We're not made to live forever, we can't handle it."

"Lighten up, babe," Cochrane said. "I don't mind giving eternity a try; it's the flipside which is the real bummer."

"We've been back a week, and Mortonridge is already falling apart. There's hardly any food left, nothing works properly."

"Give it a chance," Moyo said. "We're all badly shocked, we don't know how to control this new power we've got, and the non-possessed want to hunt us down and fling us back. You can hardly expect instant civilization under those circumstances. We'll find a way to adjust. As soon as the rest of Ombey is possessed we'll take it out of this universe altogether. Once that happens, things will be different. You'll see; this is just an interim stage." His put his arm around her as she leaned into him. She kissed him lightly, mind shining with appreciation.

"Yo, love machines," Cochrane said. "So while you two screw like hot bunnies for the rest of the night, who's going into town to track down some food?"

*   *   *

Got a beacon, Edwin announced. His mind was hot with triumph.

Around *Oenone*'s bridge, the communal tension level reduced with a strong mental sigh. They had arrived above Ngeuni twenty minutes ago. Every sensor extended. The crew in alert status one. Weapons powered up. Ready for anything. To retrieve Thakrar. To fight possessed starships that had captured Thakrar.

And there had been nothing. No ships in orbit. No response from the small development company advance camp on the planet.

Oenone accelerated into a high polar orbit, and Edwin activated every sensor they had.

It's very weak, some kind of capsule emergency signal. Definitely the *Tigara*'s identification code, though. The ship must have broken up.

Lock on to it, please, Syrinx said. She was aware of the astrogration data from the sensors flooding into the bitek processor array. From that, she and *Oenone* understood exactly where the signal was in relation to themselves.

Go.

The voidhawk swallowed through a wormhole that barely had any internal length at all. Starlight blue-shifted slightly as it twisted into a tight rosette, kissing the hull, then expanding. A life-support capsule was spinning idly ten kilometres in front of the terminus as *Oenone* shot out. Local space was smeared with scraps of debris from the *Tigara*'s violent end. Syrinx could feel the capsule's mass in her mind as it hung in *Oenone*'s distortion field. Sensors and communications dishes in the lower hull pods swung around to point at the dingy sphere.

There's no response from the capsule, Edwin said. **I'm registering some power circuits active in there, but they're very weak. And it's been venting its atmosphere.**

Oxley, Serina, take the MSV over there, Syrinx ordered. **Bring him back.**

Oenone's crew watched through Serina's armour suit sensors as she crept through the decks of the life-support capsule, searching for Captain Thakrar. It was a shambles inside, with equipment torn off bulkheads, hatches jammed, lockers broken open to send junk and old clothes floating free. The air had gone, allowing several pipes to burst and release globules of fluid, which had subsequently frozen solid. She had to use a high-powered fission cutter on the latches around the final hatch before she could worm her way into the bridge. At first she didn't even recognize the SII-suited figure clutching at one of the emergency supply cases on the ceiling. Granules of frost had solidified on him as they had on every surface, glinting a dusty grey in the beams thrown out by her helmet lights. In his fetal position he looked like some kind of giant mummified larva.

At least he got into a suit, Oxley said. **Is there any infrared emission?**

Check the electronic warfare block first, Syrinx said.

Negative electronic warfare emission. He's not possessed. But he is alive. The suit's a couple of degrees above ambient.

Are you sure it's not just natural body heat residue? Those suits are a good insulator. If he's alive, then he hasn't moved since the frost formed on him. That must have been hours ago.

Serina's bitek processor block converted her affinity voice into a straight datavise. "Captain Thakrar? Are you receiving this, sir? We're Edenists from Golomo; we received your message." The ice-encrusted figure didn't move. She waited a moment, then made her way towards him. **I've just** datavised his suit processor for a status update. **He's still breathing. Oh, damn.**

They all saw it at the same time: ancillary medical modules anchored to Thakrar by small plastic tubes which burrowed through the SII suit material. Two of the modules had red LEDs shining under their coating of frost, the others were completely dark. The tubes had all frozen solid.

Get him back here, Syrinx instructed. **Fast as you can, Serina.**

Caucus was waiting with a stretcher right outside the MSV's airlock. *Oenone* had stopped generating a gravity field in the crew torus so that Serina and Oxley could tow Thakrar's inert form through the cramped little tube without too much difficulty. He was shedding droplets as they went, the layer of frost melting in the warm air. They got him onto the stretcher, and *Oenone* immediately reinstated gravity in the torus, tugging the crew down to the decking again. Oxley held on to the dead medical modules as they raced around the central corridor to the sick bay.

Deactivate the suit, please, Caucus told Serina as the stretcher was wheeled under the diagnostic scanner. She issued the order to the suit's control processor, which examined the external environment before obeying. The black silicon retreated from Thakrar's skin, sliding from his extremities to glide smoothly toward his throat. Dark fluids began to stain the stretcher. Syrinx wrinkled her nose up at the smell, putting a hand over her nose.

Is he all right? *Oenone* asked.

I don't know yet.

Please, Syrinx, it is him who is hurt, not you. Please don't remember like this.

I'm sorry. I didn't know I was being so obvious.

To the others, perhaps not.

It does make me remember, I won't deny that. But his injuries are very different.

Pain is pain.

My pain is only a memory, she recited; in her mind it was

Wing-Tsit Chong's voice which spoke the phrase. **Memories do not hurt, they only influence.**

Caucus winced at the sight which was unveiled. Thakrar's lower right arm was new, that much was obvious. The medical packages wrapped around it had shifted, opening large gashes in the translucent immature skin. AT muscles lay exposed, their drying membranes acquiring a nasty septic tint. Scars and skin grafts on the legs and torso were a livid red against the snowy skin. The remainder of his packages appeared to have withered, green surfaces crinkling up like aging rubber, pulling the edges back from the flesh they were supposed to heal. Sour nutrient fluids dripped out of torn inlet plugs.

For a moment, all Caucus could do was stare in a kind of revolted dismay. He simply didn't know where to start.

Erick Thakrar's bruised eyelids slowly opened. What alarmed Syrinx the most was the lack of confusion they showed.

"Can you hear me, Erick?" Caucus said in an overloud voice. "You're perfectly safe now. We're Edenists, we rescued you. Now please don't try and move."

Erick opened his mouth, lips quivering.

"We're going to treat you in just a moment. Are your axon blocks functional?"

"No!" It was very clear, very determined.

Caucus picked up an anaesthetic spray from the bench. "Is the program faulty, or have your neural nanonics been damaged?"

Erick brought his good arm around and pressed his knuckles into Caucus's back. "No, you will not touch me," he datavised. "I have a nerve burst implant. I will kill him."

The spray fell from Caucus's hand to clatter on the deck.

Syrinx could barely credit what was happening. Her mind instinctively opened to Caucus, offering support to his own frightened thoughts. All the crew were doing the same.

"Captain Thakrar, I am Captain Syrinx, this is my voidhawk *Oenone*. Please deactivate your implant. Caucus was not going to harm you."

Erick laughed, an unsteady gulp which shook his whole body. "I know that. I don't want to be treated. I'm not going back, not out there. Not again."

"Nobody is going to send you anywhere."

"They will. They always do. You do, you navy people. Always one final mission, one little bit of vital information to collect, then it will all be over. It never is, though. Never."

"I understand."

"Liar."

She gestured to the outlines of the medical packages visible through her ship-tunic. "I do have some knowledge of what you have been through. The possessed had me for a brief time."

Erick gave her a scared glance. "They'll win. If you saw what they can do, you'll know that. There's nothing we can do."

"I think there is. I think there must be a solution."

"We'll die. We'll become them. They're us, all of us."

Captain? I've got a clean shot at him.

Syrinx was aware of Edwin, out in the central corridor, a maser carbine raised. The blank muzzle was pointing at Erick Thakrar's back. A feed from the weapon's targeting processor showed it was aimed precisely on Thakrar's spinal column. The coherent microwaves would sever his nerves before he could use the implant.

No, she said. **Not yet. He deserves our efforts to talk him out of this.** For the first time in a long time, she was angry at an Adamist for being just that, an Adamist. Closed mind, locked up tight in its skull. No way of knowing what others were thinking, never really knowing love, kindness, or sympathy. She couldn't take the simple truth to him directly. Not the easy way.

"What do you want us to do?" she asked.

"I have information," Erick datavised. "Strategic information."

"We know. Your message to Golomo said it was important."

"I will sell it to you."

There was a collective burst of surprise from the crew.

"Okay," Syrinx said. "If I have the price on board, you will have it."

"Zero-tau." Erick's face became pleading. "Tell me you have a pod on board. For God's sake."

"We have several."

"Good. I want to be put inside. They can't get to you in there."

"All right, Erick. We'll put you in zero-tau."

"Forever."

"What?"

"Forever. I want to stay in zero-tau forever."

"Erick . . ."

"I thought about this; I thought about it a lot, it can work. Really it can. Your habitats can resist the possessed. Adamist starships don't work for them, not properly. Capone is the only one who has any military ships, and he won't be able to keep them going for long. They'll need maintenance, spares. He'll run out eventually. Then there won't be any more invasions, only infiltrations. And you won't let your guard down. We will, Adamists will. But not you. In a hundred years from now there will be nothing left of our race, except for you. Your culture will live forever. You can keep me in zero-tau forever."

"There's no need for this, Erick. We can beat them."

"No," he brayed. "Can't can't can't." The effort of speaking made him cough painfully. His breathing was very heavy now. "I'm not going to die," he datavised. "I'm not going to be one of them; not like little Tina. Dear little Tina. God, she was only fifteen. Now she's dead. But you don't die in zero-tau. You're safe. It's the only way. No life, but no beyond, either. That's the answer." Very slowly, he took his hand away from Caucus. "I'm sorry. I wouldn't have hurt you. Please, you have to do this for me. I can tell you where Capone is going to invade next. I can give you the coordinate of an antimatter station. Just give me your word, as an Edenist, as a voidhawk captain; your word that you will take my pod to a habitat, and that your culture will always keep me in zero-tau. Your word, please, it's so little to ask."

What do I do? she asked her crew.

Their minds merged, awash with compassion and distress. The answer, she felt, was inevitable.

Syrinx walked over and took Erick's cold, damp hand in hers. "All right, Erick," she said softly. Wishing once more for a single second of genuine communication. "We'll put you in zero-tau. But I want you to promise me something in return."

Erick's eyes had closed. His breathing was very shallow now as he datavised several files into the toroid's net. Caucus was exuding concern at the read-out from the diagnostic scanner. **Hurry**, he urged.

"What?" Erick asked.

"I want your permission to take you out of zero-tau if we find a proper solution to all this."

"You won't."

"But if we do!"

"This is stupid."

"No it isn't. Edenism was founded on hope, hope for the future, the belief that life can get better. If you have faith in our culture to preserve you for eternity, you must believe in that. Jesus, Erick, you have to believe in something."

"You are a very strange Edenist."

"I am a very typical Edenist. The rest just don't know it yet."

"Very well, deal."

"I'll talk to you soon, Erick. I'll be the one who wakes you up and tells you."

"At the end of the universe, perhaps. Until then . . ."

8

Alkad Mzu hadn't seen snow since she left Garissa. Back in those days she'd never bothered indexing a memory of winter in her neural nanonics. Why waste capacity? The season came every year, much to Peter's delight and her grudging acceptance.

The oldest human story of all: I never knew what I had until I lost it.

Now, from her penthouse in the Mercedes Hotel, she watched it falling over Harrisburg, a silent cascade as inexorable as it was gentle. The sight made her want to go outside and join the children she could see capering about in the park opposite.

The snow had begun during the night, just after they landed at the spaceport, and hadn't let up in the seven hours since. Down on the streets tempers were getting shorter as the traffic slowed and the pavements turned slippery with the slush. Ancient municipal mechanoids, backed up by teams of men with shovels, struggled to clear the deep drifts which blockaded the main avenues.

The sight didn't exactly bode well. If the Tonala nation's economy was so desperate that they used human labour to clean the streets of their capital . . .

So far Alkad had managed to keep her objective in focus. She was proud of that; after every obstacle thrown in her way she had proved herself resourceful enough to keep the hope alive. Even back on the *Tekas* she'd thought she would soon be retrieving the Alchemist.

Nyvan had done much to wreck her mood and her confidence. There were starships docked at the orbiting asteroids, and the local astroengineering companies could probably provide her with the equipment she wanted; yet the decay and suspicion native to this world made her doubt. The task was slipping from her grasp once more. Difficulties were piling up against her, and now she had no more fallback positions. They were on their own now: she, Voi, Lodi, and Eriba, with money as their only resource. True to his word, Prince Lambert had taken the *Tekas* out of orbit as soon as they'd disembarked. He said he was flying to Mondul, it had a strong navy, and he knew people there.

Alkad resisted accessing her time function. Prince Lambert must have made his third ZTT jump by now, and another potential security hazard was no more.

"That's a new one," Eriba announced. He was stretched out along the settee, bare feet dangling over the armrest. It meant he could just see the holoscreen on the far wall. A local news show was playing.

"What is?" Alkad asked him. He had been consuming news ever since they arrived, switching between the holoscreen and the communications net's information cores.

"Tonala has just ordered every border to be closed and sealed. The cabinet claims that New Georgia's actions are overtly hostile, and other nations can't be trusted. Apparently, the SD networks are still blasting each other with electronic warfare pulses."

Alkad grimaced. That clash had been going on when the *Tekas* arrived. "I wonder how that affects us? Are those the land borders, or are they going to prohibit spaceflight as well?"

"They haven't said."

The door chimed as it admitted Voi. She strode into the big living room shrugging out of her thick navy-blue coat and shaking grubby droplets of melted snow on the white carpet. "We've got an appointment for two o'clock this afternoon. I told the Industry Ministry we were here to buy defence equipment for the Dorados, and they recommended the Opia company. Lodi ran a check through the local data cores, and they own two asteroid industrial stations along with a starship service subsidiary."

"That sounds promising," Alkad said guardedly. She had left all the organization to Voi. The agencies would be looking for her; zipping around town would be asking for trouble. As it was, using the Daphine Kigano passport when they arrived was a risk, but she didn't have any others prepared.

"Promising? Mary, it's spot on. What do you want, the Kulu Corporation?"

"I wasn't criticising."

"Well it sounded like it."

Voi had slowly reverted to her original temper during the voyage. Alkad wasn't sure if the waspy girl was recovering from her father's death or reacting to it.

"Has Lodi found out if there are any suitable starships for hire?"

"He's still checking," Voi said. "So far he's located over fifty commercial vehicles stranded insystem due to the quarantine. Most of them are docked in low orbit stations and the asteroid ports. He's running performance comparisons against the requirements you gave us. I just hope he can find us one at a Tonala facility. Did you hear about the border restrictions? They're even closing down net interface points with the other nations."

"That's a minor problem compared to the one we'll have crewing the ship."

"What do you mean?"

"Our flight is not the kind of job you normally give mercenaries. I'm not sure money will guarantee loyalty for this mission."

"Why didn't you say so, then? Mary, Alkad, how can I help if you keep complaining after the fact? Be more cooperative."

"I'll bear it in mind," Alkad said mildly.

"Is there anything else we should know?"

"I can't think of anything, but you'll be the first to be told if I do."

"All right. Now, I've arranged for a car to take us to

Opia's offices. The security company which supplied it is also providing bodyguards. They will be here in an hour."

"Good thinking," Eriba said.

"Elementary thinking," Voi shot back. "We're foreigners who have arrived in the middle of an Assembly-imposed quarantine. That's hardly an optimum low-visibility scenario. I want to downgrade our risk to a minimum."

"Bodyguards ought to help, then," Alkad said prosaically. "You should go and take a rest before we visit Opia. You haven't slept since we landed. I'll need you to be fresh for the negotiations."

Voi gave a distrustful nod, and went into her bedroom.

Alkad and Eriba exchanged a glance and smiled simultaneously.

"Did she really say *low-visibility scenario*?" he asked.

"Sounded like it to me."

"Mary, that detox therapy was a bad idea."

"What was she like before?"

"About the same," he admitted.

Alkad turned back to the window and the snow softening the city skyline.

The door chimed again.

"Did you order something from room service?" she asked Eriba.

"No." He gave the door a worried look. "Do you think it's the bodyguards Voi hired?"

"They're very early, then; and if they're professional they would datavise us first." She picked up her shoulder bag and selected one of the devices inside. When she datavised the penthouse's net processor to access the camera in the corridor outside there was no response. The cut crystal wall lights began to flicker. "Stop!" she told Eriba, who had drawn his laser pistol. "That won't work against the possessed."

"Do you think . . ."

He trailed off just as Voi burst back into the lounge. She was gripping a maser carbine tight in her hand.

The penthouse's entrance door swung open. Three people

were standing behind it, their features lost in the darkened corridor.

"Do not come in," Alkad said loudly. "My weapons will work, even against you."

"Are you quite sure, Doctor?"

Sections of Alkad's neural nanonics were dropping out. She datavised a primer code at the small sphere she held in her hand before she lost even that ability. "Fairly sure. Do you want to be the first experimental subject?"

"You haven't changed; you were always so confident you were right."

Alkad frowned. It was a female voice, but she couldn't place it. She didn't have the processing power left in her neural nanonics to run an audio comparison program. "Do I know you?"

"You used to. May we come in, please? We really aren't here to harm you."

Since when did the possessed start saying please? Alkad thought the circumstances out and said: "It only needs one of you to speak. And if you're not a threat, stop glitching our electronics."

"That last request is difficult, but we will try."

Alkad's neural nanonics started to come back on-line. She quickly re-established full control over the device.

"I'll call the police," Voi datavised. "They can send a Tac Squad. The possessed won't know until it's too late."

"No. If they wanted to hurt us, they would have done it by now. I think we'll hear what she has to say."

"You shouldn't expose yourself to a negative personal safety context. You are the only link we have to the Alchemist."

"Oh, shut up," Alkad said aloud. "All right, come in."

The young woman who walked into the penthouse was in her early twenties. Her skin was several shades lighter than Alkad's, though her hair was jet black, and her face was rounded by a little too much cellulite for her to be pretty; it fixed her expression to one of continual shy resentment. She wore a long tartan-print summer dress, with a kilt-style skirt that had been the fashion on Garissa the year of the genocide.

Alkad ran a visual comparison program search through her memory cells. "Gelai? Gelai, is that really you?"

"My soul, yes," she said. "Not my body. This is just an illusion, of course." For a moment the solid mirage vanished, revealing a teenaged Oriental girl with fresh jagged scars on her legs.

"Mother Mary!" Alkad croaked. She'd hoped the tales of torture and atrocity were just Confederation propaganda.

Gelai's usual profile returned. The flicker of exposure was so fast, it made Alkad's mind want to believe Gelai's was the true shape; the abused girl was something decency rejected.

"What happened?" Alkad asked.

"You know her?" Voi demanded indignantly.

"Oh, yes. Gelai was one of my students."

"Not one of your best, I'm sorry to say."

"You were doing all right, as I recall."

"This enhances stress relief nicely," Voi said. "But you haven't told us why you're here."

"I was killed in the planet-buster attack," Gelai said. "The university campus was only five hundred kilometres from one of the strikes. The earthquake levelled it. I was in my residence hall when it hit. The thermal flash set half of the building alight. Then the quake arrived; Mary alone knows how powerful it was. I was lucky, I suppose. I died in the first hour. That was reasonably quick. Compared to a lot of them, anyway."

"I'm so sorry," Alkad said. She had rarely felt so worthless; confronted by the pitiful evidence of the greatest failure it was possible to have. "I failed you. I failed everybody."

"At least you were trying," Gelai said. "I didn't approve at the time. I took part in all the peace demonstrations. We held vigils outside the continental parliament, sang hymns. But the media said we were cowards and traitors. People actually spat on us in the streets. I kept going, though, kept protesting. I thought if we could just get our government to talk to the Omutans, then the military would stop attacking each other. Mary, how naive."

"No, Gelai, you weren't naive, you were brave. If enough of us had stood for that principle, then maybe the government would have tried harder to find a peaceful solution."

"But they didn't, did they?"

Alkad traced Gelai's cheeks with her finger, touching the past she'd thought was so far behind her, the cause of the present. Feeling the ersatz skin was all she needed to know she had been right to do what she'd done thirty years ago. "I was going to protect you. I thought I'd sold my very soul so that you would all be safe. I didn't care about that. I thought you were worth the sacrifice; all you bright young minds so full of the silliest hopes and proudest ideals. I would have done it, too, for you. Slain Omuta's star, the biggest crime in the galaxy. And now all that's left of us are the ones like these." She waved a hand limply at Voi and Eriba. "Just a few thousand kids living in rocks that mess with their heads. I don't know which of you suffered the worst fate. At least you had a taste of what our people might have achieved if we'd lived. This new generation are just poor remnants of what they could've been."

Gelai puffed up her lips and stared firmly at the floor. "I wasn't sure what I was going to do when I came here. Warn you or kill you."

"And now?"

"I didn't realize why you were doing it, why you went off to help the military. You were this aloof professor that we were all a bit in awe of, you were so smart. We respected you so much, I never gave you human motives, I thought you were a lump of chilled bitek on legs. I see I was wrong, though I still think you are wrong to have built anything as evil as the Alchemist."

Alkad stiffened. "How do you know about the Alchemist?"

"We can see this universe from the beyond, you know. It's very faint, but it's there. I watched the Confederation Navy trying to get people off Garissa before the radiation killed them. I've seen the Dorados, too. I even saw you a few times in Tranquillity. Then there are the memories that we tear from each other. Some soul I encountered knew about you. Perhaps it was more than one, I don't know. I never kept count; you don't, not when you do that hundreds of times a day. So that's how I know what you built, although no one knows what it is. And I'm not the only one, Doctor; Capone knows about it too, and quite a few other possessed."

"Oh, Mother Mary," Alkad groaned.

"They've shouted into the beyond, you see. Promised every soul bodies if they cooperated in finding you."

"You mean the souls are watching us now?" Voi asked.

Gelai smiled dreamily. "Yes."

"Fuck!"

Mzu glanced at the penthouse's door, which was closed on Gelai's two companions. "How many possessed are on Nyvan?"

"Several thousand. It will belong to us within a week."

"That doesn't leave us much time," Alkad said.

Voi and Eriba were starting to look panic-stricken.

"Forget the Alchemist," Voi said heatedly. "We must get ourselves outsystem."

"Yes. But we have a few days grace. That gives us time to be certain about our escape, we can't afford a mistake now. We'll charter a ship as we always intended; Opia's service subsidiary can do that for us. But I don't think there will be enough time to have the carrier built. Ah well, if it comes to it, we can always load the Alchemist onto a combat wasp."

"You can fit it on a combat wasp?" Voi was suddenly intrigued. "Just how big is it?"

"You don't need to know."

The tall girl scowled.

"Gelai, will you warn us if any of the possessed come close?"

"Yes, Doctor, we'll do that much. For a couple of days anyway, just while you find a ship. Are you really going to use the Alchemist after all this time?"

"Yes, I am. I've never been as sure about it as I am now."

"I don't know if I want you to, or not. I can never accept that revenge wrought on such a scale is right. What can it ever achieve except make a few bitter old refugees feel better? But if you don't use it against Omuta, then someone else will take it from you and fire it at another star. So if it must be fired, then I suppose I'd rather it was Omuta." Naked distress swarmed over her face. "Funny how we all lose our principles at the end, isn't it?"

"You haven't," Alkad told her. "Killed by the Omutans, thirty years in the beyond, and you would still spare them. The society that can produce you is a miracle. Its destruction was a sin beyond anything our race had committed before."

"Except perhaps possession."

Alkad slipped her arms around the distraught girl and hugged her. "It will be all right. Somehow, this dreadful conflict will finish up without us destroying ourselves. Mother Mary wouldn't condemn us to the beyond forever, you'll see."

Gelai broke away to study Mzu's face. "You think so?"

"Strange as it seems for a semi-atheist, yes. But I know the structure of the universe better than most, I've glimpsed order in there, Gelai. There has always been a solution to the problems we've posed. Always. This won't be any different."

"I'll help you," Gelai said. "I really will. We'll make sure all three of you get off the planet unharmed."

Mzu kissed her forehead. "Thank you. Now what about the two who came with you, are they Garissans as well?"

"Ngong and Omain? Yes. But not from the same time as me."

"I'd like to meet them. Ask them to come in, then we can all decide what to do next."

"What bloody high life?" Joshua challenged. "Listen, I risked everything—balls included—to earn the money to refit *Lady Mac*. You wouldn't catch me crawling to the banks and finance companies like you did. True Calverts are independent. I'm independent."

"How we established ourselves was due entirely to circumstances," Liol retorted. "My only prospect came from the Dorados Development Agency grants. And by God did I take it. Quantum Serendipity was built up from nothing. I'm self-made and proud of it, I wasn't born with your kind of privileges."

"Privileges? All Dad left me was a broken down starship and eighteen years unpaid docking fees. Hardly a plus factor."

"Crap. Just living in Tranquillity is a privilege which half of the Confederation aspires to. A plutocrat's paradise floating in the middle of a xenoc gold mine. You were never not going to make money. All you had to do was stick your hand out to grab a nugget or two."

"They tried to kill me in that fucking Ruin Ring."

"Then you shouldn't have been so sloppy, should you? Earning your wealth is always only half of the problem. Hanging on to it, now that's tough. You should have taken precautions."

"Absolutely," Joshua purred. "Well I've certainly learned that lesson. I'm hanging on to what I've got now."

"I'm not going to stop you from captaining *Lady Mac*. But . . ."

"*If it's of any interest*," Sarha announced loudly. "We've emerged in the middle of a hostile electronic environment. I've got two of Nyvan's SD networks asking for our flight authorization at the same time they're saturating our sensors with overload impulses."

Joshua grunted disparagingly, and returned his attention to the datavised displays from the flight computer. He chided himself for the lapse, it wasn't like him not to pay attention to the jump emergence sequence. But when you've got a so-called brother with a lofriction conscience . . .

Sarha was right. Space between Nyvan and its orbiting asteroids was being subjected to a variety of powerful electronic disruption effects. *Lady Mac*'s sensors and discrimination programs were sophisticated enough to pierce most of the clutter; Nyvan's SD networks were using archaic techniques, it was the sheer wattage behind them that was causing the trouble.

With Sarha's help, Joshua managed to locate the network command centres and transmit *Lady Mac*'s standard identification code, followed by their official Tranquillity flight authorization. Only Tonala and Nangkok responded, giving him permission to approach the planet. New Georgia's SD network, based at Jesup, remained silent.

"Keep trying them," Joshua told Sarha. "We'll head in anyway. Beaulieu, how are you doing tracing the *Tekas*?"

"Give me a minute more, Captain, please. This planet has a very strange communications architecture, and their usual interfaces seem to be down today. I expect that is a result of the network barrage. I am having to access several different national nets to find out if the ship arrived."

On the other side of the bridge from the cosmonik, Ashly snorted bitterly. "Boneheads, nothing on this damned world ever changes. They always brag about how different they are to each other; I never noticed myself."

"When were you here last?" Dahybi asked.

"About 2400, I think."

Joshua watched Liol slowly turn his head to look at the pilot; his eyebrow was raised in quizzical dissension.

"When?" Liol asked.

"Twenty-four hundred. I remember it quite well. King Aaron was still on Kulu's throne. There was some kind of dispute between Nyvan's countries because the Kingdom had sold one of them some old warships."

"Right," Liol said. He was waiting for the punch line.

Lady Mac's crew propagated dispassionate expressions right across the bridge.

"I've found a reference," Beaulieu said. "The *Tekas* arrived yesterday. According to Tonala's public information core it had an official flight authorization issued by the Dorados council. It docked at one of their national low orbit stations, the *Spirit of Freedom*, then departed an hour later;

with a flight plan filed for Mondul. Four people disembarked, Lodi, Voi, Eriba, and Daphine Kigano."

"Jackpot," Joshua said. He datavised traffic control for an approach vector to the *Spirit of Freedom*. After the eighth attempt, traffic control confirmed contact through the jamming and gave him a vector.

Spirit of Freedom was Tonala's main low-orbit civil spaceport, orbiting seven hundred and fifty kilometres above the equator. A free-floating hexagonal grid two kilometres in diameter and a hundred metres thick. Tanks, lounges, corridor tubes, thermal-dump panels, and docking bays were sandwiched between the framework of grey-white alloy struts, tapering spires extended out from each corner, tipped with a cluster of fusion drive tubes to hold the structure's attitude stable.

As well as a port for commercial starships and cargo spaceplanes, it was also the flight hub for the huge tugs which brought down the metal mined from Floreso asteroid. Several of the heavy-duty craft were keeping station alongside the *Spirit of Freedom* as *Lady Mac* approached; open lattice pyramids with a clump of ten big fusion drive tubes at the tip, and load attachment points at each corner.

They were designed to ferry down four ironbergs apiece. Seventy-five thousand tonnes of spongesteel: incredibly pure metal foamed with nitrogen while it was still in its molten state. Floreso's industrial teams solidified it into a squat pear shape, with a base that was scalloped by twenty-five gently rounded ridges. After that, the ironbergs were attached to the tugs for a three-week flight, spiralling down into a slightly elliptical two-hundred-kilometre orbit. For the last two days of the voyage, electric motors in the load attachment points would spin them up to one rotation per minute. In effect, they became the biggest gyroscopes in the galaxy, their precession keeping them perfectly aligned as they flew free along the final stretch of their trajectory.

Injecting the ironbergs into the atmosphere was an inordinately difficult operation for the tugs, requiring extreme precision. Each ironberg had to be at the correct attitude, and following its designated flight path exactly, so that its blunt base could strike the upper atmosphere at an angle which would create the maximum aerobrake force. Once its velocity started to drop off, gravity would pull it down in a steepening curve, which created yet more drag, accelerating the whole process. Hypersonic airflow around the scalloped base would also perpetuate the spin, maintaining stability, keeping it on track.

If everything went well—if the asteroid crews had got the internal mass distribution balanced right, if the injection point was correct—the ironberg would be aerobraked to subsonic velocity about five kilometres above the ocean. After that, nothing else mattered, no force in the universe could affect that much mass hanging in the sky in a standard gravity field. It fell straight down at terminal velocity to splash into the water amid an explosion of steam that resembled the mushroom cloud of a small nuclear bomb. And there it bobbed among the waves, its foamed interior making it buoyant enough to float without any aids.

When all four ironbergs from one tug had splashed down, the recovery fleet would sail in. The ironbergs would be towed into a foundry port ready to be broken up and fed to Tonala's eager mills. An abundant supply of cheap metal, obtained without any ecological disturbance, was a healthy asset to the nation's economy.

So not even the chaotic electronic war being fought between the SD networks was allowed to interrupt the operation. The tugs around the *Spirit of Freedom* continued to receive their regular maintenance schedule. SII-suited engineering crews crawled over the long struts, while MSVs and tankers drifted in close attendance. The service craft were the only other vehicles flying apart from *Lady Mac*. Joshua had a trouble-free approach, making excellent time. As they flew over the station, sensors showed him eleven other starships nestled snugly in the docking bays.

The inspection from port officers was one he was expecting; checking everyone on board for possession, then going through the life-support capsules and the two ancillary craft with electronic warfare blocks to make sure there were no unexplained glitches. Once they'd been cleared, Joshua received an official datavised welcome from Tonala's Industry Ministry, with an invitation to discuss his requirements and how local firms could help. They were also authorized to fly *Lady Mac*'s spaceplane down to Harrisburg.

"I'll take a pair of serjeants, Dahybi, and Melvyn," Joshua announced. "You too, Ashly, but you stay in the spaceplane in case we need evacuating. Sarha, Beaulieu, I want *Lady Mac* maintained at flight-ready status. Same procedure as before, we may have to leave in a hurry, so keep monitoring groundside, I want to be told if and when the crap hits the fan."

"I can come with you," Liol said. "I know how to handle myself if it gets noisy down there."

"Do you trust my command judgement?"

"Of course I do, Josh."

"Good. Then you stay up here. Because my judgement is that you won't follow my orders."

It was dark in Jesup's biosphere cavern now, a permanent joyless twilight, and cold. Quinn had ordered it so. The solartubes strung out along the axial gantry were producing an enfeebled opalescent glow, whose sole purpose was to show people where they were going.

As a result, an impossible autumn had visited the lush tropical vegetation. After a futile search twisting around on their stems in search of light, the leaves were yellowing. In many places they had begun to fall, their edges crisping black from the bitter air. Already the neat filigree of pretty streams was clogging with soggy mush, overspill channels were blocked, pools were flooding the surrounding ground.

The experience of accelerated decay was one which Quinn savoured. It demonstrated his power over his surroundings. No reality dysfunction this, making things different as long as you didn't blink. This was solid change, irreversible. Potent.

He stood before the stone altar which had been built in the park, studying the figure bound to the inverted cross on top. It was an old man, which in some ways was good. This way Quinn confirmed his zero-rated compassion; only children held equal status.

His loyal disciples stood in a circle around him, seven of them clad in blood-red robes. Faces shone as bright as their minds, fuelled by greed and ominous desire.

Twelve-T was also in attendance, sagging with the formidable burden of merely staying alive. His maltreated head was permanently bowed now. No possessed was imposing change upon him, but he was becoming almost Neanderthal in his posture.

Outside the elite coterie the acolytes formed a broad semicircle. All of them were wearing grey robes with the hoods thrown back. Their faces illuminated by the unnaturally hot bonfires flanking the altar, a flickering topaz light caressing their skin with fake expressions.

Quinn could sense several ghosts standing among them. They were frightened and demoralized as always and, as he had discovered, utterly harmless. They were completely unable to affect any aspect of the physical world. Trivial creatures with less substance than the shadows they craved.

In a way he was glad they were attending. Spying. This ceremony would show them what they were dealing with. They could be tyrannized, he was sure, in that they were no different from any other human. He wanted them to realize that he would never hesitate to inflict what pain he could upon them if they chose not to obey.

Satisfied, Quinn sang: "We are the princes of the Night."

"We are the princes of the Night," the acolytes chorused, it was a sound similar to the threat of thunder beyond the horizon.

"When the false lord leads his legions away into oblivion, we will be here."

"We will be here."

The old man was shaking now, moving his lips in prayer. He was a Christian priest, which was why Quinn had selected him. A double victory. Victory over the false lord. And victory for the serpent beast. Taking a life for no reason other than you wished it, for the pain it would cause others.

Such sacrifices had always focused on authority and its enforcement. A spectacle to coerce the weak. In pre-industrial times, this rite might have been about the summoning of dark witchcraft; but in an age of nanonic technology man had long surpassed magic, black or white. The sect arcology had known and encouraged the value of image, the psychology of precise brutality. And it worked.

Who now among this gathering would stand to challenge him? It was more ordination than anything else, confirming his right to reign.

He held out a hand, and Lawrence placed the dagger in his palm. Its handle was an elaborate ebony carving, but the blade was plain carbotanium and very sharp.

The priest cried out as Quinn slid the tip into his paunchy abdomen. It deepened to a whimper as Quinn recited: "Accept this life as a token of our love and devotion."

"We love you, and devote ourselves to you, Lord," growled the acolytes.

"God grant you deliverance, son," the priest choked.

Blood was running down Quinn's arm, splattering the altar. "Go fuck yourself."

Lawrence laughed delightedly at the priest's anguish. Quinn was immensely proud of the boy; he'd never known anyone to offer himself up to God's Brother so unreservedly.

The priest was dying to the harsh cheers of the acolytes. Quinn could sense the old man's soul rising from the body, twining like smoke in a listless sky to vanish through a chink in reality. He pressed himself forwards to lick ravenously at the ephemeral stream with a narrow black tongue, enraptured.

Then another soul was pushing back down the trickle of energy, surging into the body.

"Shithead!" Quinn spat. "This body is not for you. It is our sacrament. Get the fuck out of it."

The skin on the priest's upside-down face began to flow

like treacle. The features twisted themselves through a hundred and eighty degrees so that the mouth was superimposed on the forehead. Then the skin hardened again and the eyes snapped open.

Quinn took a pace back in surprise. It was his own face staring at him.

"Welcome to the beyond, you little prick," it told him. Then it smiled wickedly. "Remember this part?"

A streamer of white fire lashed out of the knife which was plunged deep into the priest's chest. It struck Twelve-T's right arm, puncturing his chrome and steel wrist. The smoking mechanical hand dropped to the floor, fingers waggling as if they were playing piano keys. His wrist joint was reduced to a jagged bracelet of metal with green hydraulic fluid spraying out, and the frayed end of a power cable fluttering about.

"Do it!" the forged face yelled.

Twelve-T lunged towards Quinn, shoving his broken arm forwards. A mad smile cracked his face.

Lawrence wailed: *"No,"* and flung himself into Twelve-T's path.

The broken wrist joint rammed into Lawrence's throat. A bright spark of electricity twinkled at the end of the ragged power cable as it touched the boy's skin.

Lawrence shrieked as his whole body silently detonated into sunlight brilliance. He froze with his arms still outstretched, a frantic expression etched on his face. The light was so fierce he became translucent—a naked angel bathing in the heart of a star. Then his extremities began to shrivel, turning black. He had time to shriek once more before the internecine fire ate him away.

The dreadful light shrank, revealing a patch of baked earth and droppings of fine white ash. Twelve-T lay next to it where he had stumbled, the fall jolting his brain out of his half skull like wine from a goblet. It was rolling over the grass.

"Ah well," said the forged face. "I guess we both lost this time around. Be seeing you, Quinn." It began to untwist, reverting to the priest's startled death rictus. The incursive soul flowed away, retreating into the beyond.

"COME BACK!" Quinn roared.

There was a last ironic laugh, and his tormenter was gone. For all his power and strength, there was nothing Quinn could do. Absolutely nothing. His impotence was an agonizing humiliation. He screamed, and the altar shattered, sending the priest's battered body tumbling. The acolytes began to run. Quinn kicked Twelve-T's brain, and the grisly organ burst apart, sending a splat of gore across his terrified disciples. He turned back and discharged a bolt of searing white fire into the priest's remnants. The body ignited instantly, but the flames were only an effete mockery of the incendiary heat which had consumed Lawrence.

The disciples shrank away as Quinn sent blast after blast of white fire into the pyre, reducing the body and the crumbling stones to radiant magma. When they reached the boundary of light given off from the bonfires, they too turned and fled after the acolytes.

Only the ghosts remained, safe from the fury of the black-robed figure in their secluded lifeless realm. After a while they saw him sink to his knees and make the sign of the inverted cross on his chest.

"I will not fail you, my Lord," he said quietly. "I will quicken the Night as I promised. All I ask as the price of my soul is that when it has fallen you bring me the fucker who did this."

He rose and made his way out of the park. This time he was truly alone. Even ghosts quailed before the terrifying thoughts alight inside his head.

Hoya was the first of the four voidhawks to emerge above Nyvan. Niveu and his crew immediately began scanning the local environment for threats.

"No ships within twenty thousand kilometres," he said, "but the SD networks are shooting off electronic warfare blitzes at each other. Looks like the nations are in their usual confrontational state."

Monica accessed the sensor suite in the voidhawk's lower hull, and the starfield projected into her mind came alive with vivid coloured icons. Two more voidhawks were holding formation a hundred kilometres away. As she watched, another wormhole terminus opened to disgorge the fourth. "Are we being targeted by the platforms?" she asked. She appreciated the way the Edenists unfailingly spoke out loud in her presence, keeping her informed. But their display symbology was very different to that used by the Royal Navy, she hadn't quite mastered the program yet.

"There are very few specific targets," Samuel said. "The networks appear intent on jamming and disrupting every processor out to geosync orbit."

"Is it safe for us to approach?"

Niveu shrugged. "Yes. For now. We'll monitor the local news to find out what's going on. If there's any indication of them advancing the hostilities to an active stage, I'll review the situation again."

"Does your service have any stations down there?" she asked Samuel.

"There are some assets, but we don't have any active operatives. We don't even have an embassy. There's no gas giant in this system, it was colonized long before their presence was deemed necessary to develop an industrialized economy. Frankly, the price of having to import all their He$_3$ is partly responsible for Nyvan's current state."

"It also means we have no backup," Niveu said.

"Okay, let me have a communications circuit. We have a couple of embassies and several consuls. They should be monitoring starship traffic."

It took a long time to establish contact. After hours subjected to the output from the SD platforms, the national civil communications satellites were now almost completely inoperative. She eventually got around the problem by aligning one of *Hoya*'s antennae directly on the cities she wanted, which limited her to those on the half of the planet ahead of the voidhawks.

"Mzu's here," she said at last. "I got through to Adrian

Redway, our station chief in the Harrisburg embassy. The *Tekas* arrived yesterday. It docked at Tonala's principal low orbit station, and four people took a spaceplane down to Harrisburg. Voi was one of them, and so was Daphine Kigano."

"Excellent," Samuel said. "Is the *Tekas* still here?"

"No. It departed an hour later. And no other starship has left since. She's still down there. We've got her."

"We have to go in," Samuel told Niveu.

"I understand. But you should know that several governments are claiming New Georgia has fallen to the possessed. New Georgia is denying it of course, though it does seem as though they have lost their asteroid, Jesup. Apparently Jesup dispatched some inter-orbit ships to the three abandoned asteroids. It is being heralded as a breach of sovereignty, which of course is taken extremely seriously here."

"Could the ships be carrying escapees?" Monica asked.

"It is possible, I suppose. Although I can't think of any reason why anyone should consider those asteroids to be a refuge; they were badly damaged in the '32 conflict. No one even bothered to salvage them. But we ought to know what the Jesup ships are doing before too long; the governments which own the abandoned asteroids have dispatched their own ships to investigate."

"If it turns out those ships from Jesup are crewed by possessed, then the situation will deteriorate rapidly," Samuel said. "The other governments are unlikely to come to New Georgia's aid."

"True enough," Monica said pensively. "They're more likely to nuke the whole country."

"I don't imagine we will be staying long," Samuel said. "And we will have the flyers with us, we can evacuate within minutes."

"Yeah sure. There's one other thing."

"Oh?"

"Redway said one other starship has arrived since the *Tekas* left. The *Lady Macbeth*, she's docked at Tonala's main low-orbit station."

"How intriguing. The Lord of Ruin obviously knew what she was doing when she chose this Lagrange Calvert."

Monica was sure there was a note of admiration in his voice.

The four voidhawks accelerated in towards Nyvan. After receiving permission from traffic control, they slotted into a six-hundred-kilometre orbit, adopting a diamond formation. Four ion field flyers left their hangars and curved down towards the planet, heading into the huge swirl of angry cloud that covered most of Tonala.

Jesup's Strategic Defence control centre had been hollowed out of the rock deep behind the habitation section. It was New Georgia's ultimate citadel: safe from any external attack which didn't actually crack Jesup open, equipped with enough security systems to fend off an open mutiny by the asteroid's population, and fitted with a completely independent environmental circuit. No matter what happened to Jesup and New Georgia's government, the SD officers could continue to fight on for weeks.

Quinn waited for the monolithic innermost door to slide open, displaying a serenity that was harrowing in its depth. Only Bonham accompanied him now as he strode around the asteroid, the other disciples were too afraid.

There had been a few modifications to the control centre. Console technology had devolved considerably; in most cases processors and AV projectors had abated to a simple telephone. A whole rank of the black and silver machines were lined up along a wall, where they were jangling incessantly. A group of officers in stiff grey uniforms were snatching up the handsets as fast as they could. In front of them was a big square table with a picture of Nyvan and its orbiting asteroids covering its surface. Five young women were busy moving wooden markers across it with long poles.

The adrenaline-powered clamour faltered as Quinn walked in. There was no sign of any face inside his robe's hood; light fell into the oval opening never to return. Only the pearl-white hands emerging from his sleeves suggested a human was in residence.

"Keep going," he told them.

The voices sprang back, far louder than before so as to demonstrate their loyalty and commitment.

Quinn went over to the commander's post, a pulpitlike podium which overlooked the table. "What is the problem?"

Shemilt, who was running the control centre, saluted sharply. He was wearing a heavily decorated Luftwaffe uniform from the Second World War, every inch the Teutonic warrior aristocrat. "I regret to inform you, sir, that ships have been sent to intercept our teams working in the other asteroids. The first will make contact in forty minutes."

Quinn studied the table; it was becoming cluttered. Four vultures were grouped together just above the planet. New Georgia's SD platforms were diamond-studded pyramids. Ruby pentagons showed opposing platforms. Three red-flagged markers were being shoved slowly over the starmap. "Are they warships?"

"Our observation stations are having a lot of trouble in this foul weather, but we don't think so. Not frigates, anyway. I expect they will be carrying troops, though; they're definitely big enough for that."

"Don't get too carried away, Shemilt."

Shemilt stood to attention. "Yes, *sir.*"

Quinn pointed at one of the red flags. "Can our SD platforms hit these ships?"

"Yes, sir." Shemilt pulled a clipboard off a hook inside his command post and flicked through the typewritten sheets. "Two of them are in range of our X-ray lasers, and the third can be destroyed with combat wasps."

"Good. Kill the little shits."

"Yes, sir." Shemilt hesitated. "If we do that, the other networks will probably shoot at us."

"Then shoot back, engage every target you can reach. I want an all-out confrontation."

Activity around the table slowed as operators glanced at

Quinn. Resentment was building in their thoughts, capped, as always, by fear.

"How do we get out, Quinn?" Shemilt asked.

"We wait. Space warfare is very fast, and very destructive. By the end of today, there won't be a working laser cannon or a combat wasp left orbiting Nyvan. We'll get hit a few times, but fuck, these walls are two kilometres thick. This is the mother of all fallout shelters." He gestured at the table, and every marker ignited, yellow candlelike flames squirting out black smoke. "Then when it's over, we can fly away in perfect safety."

Shemilt nodded hurriedly, using speed to prove he'd never doubted. "I'm sorry, Quinn, it's obvious really."

"Thank you. Now kill those ships."

"Yes, sir."

Quinn left the control centre with Bonham scurrying after him, always trailing by a few paces. The giant door slid shut behind them, its bass grumbles echoing along the broad corridor.

"Are there really enough ships here to take everyone off?" Bonham asked.

"I doubt it. And even if there were, the spaceport will be a prime target."

"So . . . some of us should leave early, then?"

"Fast, Bonham, very fast. That's probably why you got where you did."

"Thank you, Quinn." He quickened his steps; Quinn's voice was slightly fainter.

"Of course, if they see me leaving now, they'd know I'd abandoned them. Discipline would go straight to shit."

"Quinn?" He could hardly hear the dark figure at all now.

"After all, it's not as if you could bind them . . ."

Bonham squinted at the figure he was now almost running to catch up with. Quinn seemed to be gliding smoothly over the rock floor without moving his legs. His black robe had faded to grey. In fact it was almost translucent. "Quinn?" This latest performance was frightening him more than anything to date. The anger and wrath which Quinn radiated so easily were simple to understand, almost reassuring in comparison. This though, Bonham didn't know if it was something being done to Quinn, or something he was doing to himself. "What is this? Quinn?"

Quinn had become completely transparent now, only the slightest rippling outline of rock betrayed his position; even his thoughts were evaporating from Bonham's perception. He stumbled to a halt. Panic set in. Quinn was no longer present anywhere in the corridor.

"Holy Christ, now what?"

He felt a breath of cold air strike his face. He frowned.

A bolt of white fire smashed into the back of his skull. Two souls were cast out of the corpse as it collapsed onto the floor, both of them keening in dread at the fate which awaited.

"Wrong God." A chuckle drifted down the empty corridor.

When Joshua landed just after midday local time, rumour was blanketing Harrisburg as thickly as the snow. It seemed to be the one weapon in the armoury of the possessed which was the same the Confederation over. The more people heard, the less they knew, the more fearful they became. One freak outbreak of urban mythology and entire populations would become paralysed, either that or regress straight into survivalist siege mode.

On most worlds, government assurances and rover reporters on the scene managed to restart the engines of ordinary existence. People would creep sheepishly back to work and wait for the next canard of Genghis Khan riding a Panzer tank into the suburbs.

Not on Nyvan. Here governments were the ones gleefully shooting out savage accusations at their old antagonists. A coordinated global response to the prospect of the possessed landing was never even considered, a realpolitik impossibility.

As soon as they landed Joshua loaded a search request into the city's commercial data core. The number of armed guards and lack of flights at the spaceport made his intuition rebel. He knew they didn't have much time; the quiet approach—questions, contacts, money—would never work here.

They hired a car and set off down hotel row, a potholed six-lane motorway which linked the spaceport to the city ten kilometres away. Only two lanes were cleared of snow, and there was hardly any other traffic.

Dahybi used his electronic warfare detector block to sweep the eight-seater cabin for bugs. "Seems clean," he told the others.

"Okay," Joshua said. "Our processor technology is probably more advanced than the locals, but don't count on it for a permanent advantage. I need to find her as fast as we can, which is going to mean sacrificing subtlety."

As they approached the hotel they'd booked, Joshua datavised an update into the car's control processor. The car swept past the hotel's entrance, heading for the city.

"There goes our deposit," Melvyn complained.

"It bothers me," Joshua said. "Ione, are we being followed?"

One of the serjeants was sitting at the back of the cab, pointing a small circular sensor pad through the rear window. "One car, possibly two. I think there are three people in the first one."

"Probably some kind of local security police," Joshua decided. "I'd be surprised if they weren't keeping tabs on foreigners right now."

"So what do we do about them?" Dahybi asked.

"Not a damn thing. I don't want to give them an excuse to interfere." He accessed the car's net processor and established an encrypted link to the spaceplane. "What's your situation, Ashly?"

"So far so good. I'll have the electron matrices completely recharged in another three minutes. That'll expand your options."

"Good. We'll keep a channel open to you from now on. If

the city's net starts to crash, come get us. That's our cut-off point."

"Aye, Captain. *Lady Macbeth* just fell below the horizon, so I've lost contact. Every civil communications satellite is out now."

"If their situation alters, they'll change orbit and re-establish a link. Sarha knows what to do."

"I certainly hope so. Before I lost contact, Beaulieu told me four voidhawks have arrived. They're heading for low orbit."

"They must have come from the Dorados," Joshua decided. "Ashly, when *Lady Mac* comes back on-line, tell Sarha to monitor them as best she can. And let me know if any of their spaceplanes land."

The snowfall had thickened considerably by the time Joshua's car reached the address his search program had identified for him. It reduced Harrisburg to a sequence of shabby granite streets that were hard to tell apart. Nothing was alive apart from people, wrapped in their insulated coats as they kicked their way through the pavement slush. Hologram billboards and neon signs were all that remained unaffected by the weather, flashing and morphing as always.

"I should have brought Liol down," Joshua muttered, half to himself. "He said he wanted a taste of exotic worlds."

"You're going to have to come to terms with him eventually, Joshua," Melvyn said.

"Maybe. Jesus, if he just wasn't such a pushy bastard. Can't you tell him to lighten up, Ione? You spend a lot of time talking to him."

"It didn't work before," one of the serjeants said.

"You've already told him?"

"Let's say I've been through the procedure earlier. He's not the only one who needs to relax, Joshua. Neither of you are going to make any progress the way you both carry on."

He wanted to explain. How it was. How he didn't feel quite so alone anymore, and how that left him troubled. How he wanted to welcome his brother, but at the same time knew him so well he didn't trust him. To be honest with him would be seen as a weakness. Liol was the interloper. Let him make the first gesture. I saved his arse from the Dorados, I was the honourable one, and what thanks do I get?

When he glanced around the car, he knew that anything he said which verged on truth would make him sound petulant. A year ago I would've told the lot of them to bugger off. Jesus, life was simpler then, when there was just me. "I'll do what I can," he conceded.

Their car turned off the street and dipped down into an underground garage. The building it served was a ten-storey block with small shops at street level (half of them empty), and the upper floors given over to offices and design bureaus.

"Going to tell us why we're here now?" Dahybi asked as they climbed out of the car.

"Simple," Joshua said. "When you need a job doing fast and effectively, go to a professional."

The office of Kilmartin and Elgant, Data Security Specialists, was on the seventh floor. There was nobody behind the desk in the reception room. Joshua paused for a second, expecting a secretarial program to query them, but the desktop processor wasn't switched on. The inner door slid open when he approached it.

In a rash of optimistic bravado accompanying their firm's launch, Kilmartin and Elgant had taken a fifty-year lease on sufficient floor space to house fifteen operatives. There were still enough desks for fifteen in the open-plan office; seven of them had dust covers thrown over processors which were fairly dubious even by Nyvan's technological standards; four desks had niches where processors used to be; one patch of carpet showed imprints where a desk used to stand.

Only one desk had a decent cluster of modern blocks, which shared the surface with a thoroughly dead potted plant. Two men were sitting behind it, staring intently into the hazy aura of an AV pillar. The first was tall, young, and broad-shouldered, sporting a long blond ponytail tied with a colourful leather lace. He wore an expensive black suit, tailored to provide maximum freedom of movement. He was not openly belligerent, but had a presence that would make people think twice before tackling him. The second was well into middle age, dressed in a faded grey-brown jacket, tufty chestnut hair askew. He looked as if he belonged behind the complaints desk in a tax office.

They regarded Joshua and his odd delegation with mild surprise.

Joshua looked from one to the other, slightly uncertain as intuition tickled his skull. Then he clicked his fingers decisively and pointed at the younger of the two. "I bet you're the data expert and your friend handles the combat routines. Good disguise, right?"

The aura from the AV pillar faded as the younger man tilted his chair back and put his hands behind his head. "Clever. Are we expecting you, Mr . . . ?"

Joshua gave a faint smile. "You tell me."

"All right, Captain Calvert, what do you want?"

"I need to access some information, and fast. Can you manage that for me?"

"Sure. Nationwide net access, no problem, whatever file you want. Hey listen, I know what this place looks like. Forget that. Talent isn't something you can eyeball. And I'm so far on top of things I'm getting oxygen starvation. Someone's search program locates my public file, I know about it before they do. You came down from the *Lady Macbeth* an hour ago. One of your crew is still with your spaceplane. Want to know how much the service company is ripping you off for your electron matrix recharge? You're in the right place."

"I don't care. Money doesn't concern me."

"Okay, I think we've reached interface here." He turned to his colleague and muttered something. The older man gave him a disgruntled look, then shrugged. He walked out of the office, giving the two serjeants a curious glance as he passed.

"Richard Keaton." The athletic young man leaned over

the desk, holding his hand out and smiling broadly. "Call me Dick."

"I certainly will." They shook hands.

"Sorry about Matty, there. He's got enough implants to chop up a squad of marines. But he gets overprotective, and I don't need him hovering right now. Smart of you to see which of us was which. I don't think anyone's ever done that before."

"Your secret's safe with me."

"So what can I do for you, Captain Calvert?"

"I need to find someone."

Keaton raised a forefinger. "If I could just interrupt. First, there is my fee."

"I'm not going to quibble. I might even pay a bonus."

One of the serjeants tapped a foot pointedly on the worn carpet.

"Nice to hear, Captain. Okay then; my fee is one flight off this planet on the *Lady Macbeth*, just as soon as you leave. Destination: who cares."

"That's an . . . unusual fee. Any particular reason?"

"Like I said, Captain, you came to the right place. This might not be the biggest firm in town, but I fish the data streams. There are possessed on Nyvan. They've already taken over Jesup, that wasn't just propaganda by our upstanding government. The electronic warfare barrage in orbit? That was cover to help them get down here. There aren't too many in Tonala yet—not according to the Special Investigation Bureau, anyway. But they're spreading through the other countries."

"So you want to be gone?"

"I sure do. And I figure you won't be here when they reach Harrisburg, either. Look, I won't be any trouble on board. Hell, shove me into zero-tau, I don't mind."

Joshua didn't have the time to argue. Besides, taking Keaton with them actually reduced the risk of exposure. A flight off Nyvan wasn't such a high price. "You bring only what you've got with you; I'm not waiting while you go home to pack. We don't have any slack built into our mission profile."

"We have a deal, Captain."

"Very well, welcome aboard, Dick. Now, the person I want is called Dr Alkad Mzu, alias Daphine Kigano. She arrived on the starship *Tekas* last night with three companions. I don't know where she is or who she might attempt to contact; however, she will be trying to stay hidden." He datavised over a visual file. "Find her."

Twenty thousand kilometres above Nyvan, the Organization frigate *Urschel* emerged from its ZTT jump. It was swiftly followed by the *Raimo* and the *Pinzola*. They were nowhere near a designated emergence zone, but only the four void-hawks were aware of their arrival. None of Nyvan's gravitonic-distortion detector satellites were functioning; the waves of electronic warfare assaults had crashed them beyond repair.

After five minutes assessing the local situation, their fusion drives came on, pushing them towards a low-orbit injection point. Once they were on their way, Oscar Kearn, the small flotilla's commander, concentrated on the eternal, beseeching voices crying into his head.

Where is Mzu? he asked them.

The possessed among the crew, including Cherri Barnes, joined his silky cajoling, adding to the tricksy promises he made. Theirs was a multiple chant which hummed through the beyond, a harmonic passed between every desperate soul. It agitated them, its very existence a taunt; plots and scheming were an exquisitely tortuous reminder of what lay on the other side of their dreadful continuum, what they could partake of once again if they just helped.

Where is Mzu?

What is she doing?

Who is with her?

There are bodies waiting for worthy hosts. Millions of bodies, out here among the light and air and *experience*, held ready for Capone's friends. One could be yours. If—

Where is Mzu? Exactly?

Ah.

When they reached a five hundred kilometre orbit, each of the frigates dispatched a spaceplane. The three black delta-shapes sliced down through Nyvan's atmosphere, their tapering noses lining up on Tonala, hidden behind the planet's curvature seven thousand kilometres ahead.

Oscar Kearn ordered the frigates to manoeuvre again, and they began to raise their orbit.

"This really doesn't look good," Sarha said. "The sensors are showing three of them. I don't think their transponders are responding to the station."

"You don't think?" Beaulieu queried.

"Who knows? Those bloody SD platforms are still at it. I doubt we could pick up an em pulse through all this jamming."

"What are their drive exhausts like?" Liol asked.

Sarha ignored the datavised displays inside her skull long enough to fire a disgusted glance at him. The three of them were alone on *Lady Mac*'s bridge. All the remaining serjeants were down in B capsule, guarding the airlock tube. "What?" There were times when he was a little bit too much like Joshua, that is: quite infuriating.

"If there are possessed on board, they'll be affecting the ship's systems," Liol recited. "Their drives will fluctuate. The recordings from Lalonde taught us that. Remember?"

Sarha didn't trust herself to answer directly. Yes he was like Joshua, gallingly right the whole time. "I'm not sure our discrimination programs will be much use at this distance. I can't get a radar lock to determine their velocity."

"Want me to try?"

"No thank you."

"When Josh said don't give me access to the flight computer, I don't think he meant I wasn't supposed to help you survive an assault by the possessed," Liol said peevishly.

"You will be able to ask him directly soon," Beaulieu

said. "We should be over Ashly's horizon in another ninety seconds."

"Those ships are definitely heading for a rendezvous with the *Spirit of Freedom*," Sarha said. "The optical image is good enough for a rough vector analysis."

"I'd like to point out that the three highly similar ships which appeared at the Dorados before we left were all from New California," Liol said.

"I am aware of that," Sarha snarled back.

"Jolly good. I'd hate to be possessed by anyone I didn't know."

"What are the voidhawks doing?" Beaulieu asked.

"I don't know. They're on the other side of the planet." Sarha was uncomfortably aware of the perspiration permeating her shipsuit. She datavised the conditioning grille above her for some cool, dry air—cooler, dryer air. And to think, I'd always been slightly envious about Joshua having command of a starship. "I'm disengaging the airlock," she told the other two. "Station staff might try to come on board once they realize those starships are heading here." It was a logical action. And actually doing something made her feel a whole lot better.

"I've got the spaceplane beacon," Beaulieu announced.

"You're still intact, then?" Ashly datavised.

"Yeah, still here," Sarha replied gamely. "What's your situation?"

"Stable. Nothing much is moving at the spaceport. The four Edenist flyers arrived half an hour ago. They're parked about two hundred metres away from me right now. I tried datavising them, but they're not answering. A whole group of people set off into town as soon as they landed. There were cars here waiting for them."

The flight computer signalled that Joshua was coming on line. "Any signs of possession on the planet yet?" he asked.

"I'd have to say yes, Captain," Beaulieu told him. "The national nets are suffering considerable degrees of dropout. But there's no real pattern to it. Several countries don't have a single glitch."

"They will," Joshua datavised.

"Joshua, three Adamist starships appeared an hour ago," Sarha datavised. "We believe they sent some spaceplanes or flyers down to the planet; they were in the right orbit for it. Liol thinks they're the same Organization ships that were at the Dorados."

"Oh, well, if the starflight expert says so . . ."

"Josh, those frigates are heading for this station," Liol datavised.

"Oh, Jesus. Okay, get clear of the station. And, Sarha, try to get a positive ident."

"Will do. How are things your end?"

"Promising, I think. Expect us . . . today, what . . . outcome."

"I'm losing the link," Beaulieu warned. "Heavy interference, and it's focused directly at us."

"Josh, let me have access authority for the flight computer. Sarha and Beaulieu are being overloaded up here, for Christ's sake. I can help."

". . . think . . . mummy's boy . . . on my ship . . . fucking . . . because I'll . . . first . . . trust . . ."

"Lost them," Beaulieu said.

"The frigates have started jamming us directly," Sarha said. "They know we're here."

"They're softening up the station for an assault," Liol said. "Give me the access codes, I can fly *Lady Mac* away."

"No, you heard Joshua."

"He said he trusted me."

"I don't think so."

"Look, you two have to operate the on-board systems, monitor the electronic warfare battle, and now you've got to watch the frigates as well. If we launch now they might think we're going to defend the station. Can you fly *Lady Mac* and fight at the same time as everything else?"

"Beaulieu?" Sarha asked.

"Not my decision, but he does have a point. We need to leave, now."

"Sarha, Josh is all emotionally tangled up when it comes

to me. Fair enough, I didn't handle him well. But you can't endanger his life and ours on a single bad decision made from ignorance. I'll do my best here. Trust me. Please."

"All right! Damn it. But fusion drive authority only. You're not jumping us anywhere."

"Fine." And the dream finally happened, just as he'd always known it would. *Lady Mac*'s flight computer opened to him, and all the systems were on-line, filling his mind with glorious wing-sweeps of colour. They fitted just perfectly.

He designated the procedure menus he needed, bringing the thrusters and drive tubes up to active flight status. Beaulieu and Sarha were working smoothly together, activating the remaining on board systems. Umbilicals retracted from the fuselage, and the cradle started to elevate them out of the shallow docking bay. The viewfield which the flight computer was datavising at him expanded as more of *Lady Mac*'s sensor clusters lifted above the rim. Three bright, expanding stars were ringed in antagonistic red as they crept up over the curvature of the brilliant blue horizon.

Liol fired the verniers to take them off the cradle, not caring if the other two could see the stupid smile on his face. For a moment, all the envy and bitterness returned, the irrational pique he'd felt when he first learned that Joshua existed, a usurper brother who was captaining the ship which was rightfully his. This was the rush that belonged to him. The power to traverse the galaxy.

One day, he and Joshua were going to have to settle this. But not today. Today was when he proved himself to his brother and the crew. Today was when he started living the life he knew belonged to him.

When they were a hundred metres above the docking bay, Liol fired the secondary drive, selecting a third of a gee acceleration. *Lady Mac* immediately veered off the vector he'd plotted. He pumped a fast correction order into the flight computer, deflecting the exhaust angle. Overcompensating. "Wowshit!" The acceleration couch webbing gripped him tighter.

"The spaceplane hangar is empty," Sarha said witheringly. "That means our mass distribution is off centre. Perhaps you'd care to bring the level seven balance calibration programs on-line?"

"Sorry." He searched desperately around the flight control menus and found the right program. *Lady Mac* juddered back onto her original vector.

"Joshua is going to throw me out of the airlock," Sarha decided.

It had taken some time for Lodi to get used to having Omain sitting in the hotel suite with him. A possessed for Mary's sake! But Omain turned out to be quiet and polite (a little sad, to be honest), keeping out of the way. Lodi slowly managed to relax, though this must surely be the strangest episode in his life. Nothing was ever going to out-weird this.

At first he had jumped every time Omain even spoke. Now, he was relatively cool about the whole scene. His processor blocks were spread out over one of the tables, enabling him to cast trawl programs into the net streams, fishing out relevant information. It was what he did best, so Voi had left him to it while she, Mzu, and Eriba went to the Opia company. His main concern at the moment was monitoring the civil situation now the government had closed the borders. Voi wanted to make sure they would be allowed to get back into orbit. So far, it looked as if they could. There had even been one piece of good luck, the first since they arrived at Nyvan. A starship called *Lady Macbeth* had docked at the *Spirit of Freedom*, and it was exactly the type of ship Mzu wanted.

"They are asking for her," Omain said.

"Huh?" Lodi cancelled the datavised displays, blinking away the afterimage the graphics left in his mind.

"Capone's people are in orbit," Omain said. "They know Mzu is here. They are asking for her."

"You mean you can tell what's going on in orbit? Mary! I can't, not with all the interference from the SD platforms."

"Not tell, exactly. This is whispered gossip, distorted by

the many souls it has passed through. I have only the vaguest notion of the facts."

Lodi was fascinated. Once he began talking, Omain knew some seriously interesting facts. He'd lived on Garissa, and was quite willing to share his impressions. (Lodi had never summoned the courage to ask Mzu what their old world was like.) From Omain's melancholic descriptions it sounded like a good place to live. The Garissans, Lodi was sure, had lost more than their world by the sound of it; their whole culture was different now, too tight-arsed and Western-ethnic orientated.

One of the processor blocks datavised a warning into Lodi's neural nanonics. "Oh, bollocks!"

"What is it?"

They had to speak in raised voices, almost shouting at each other. Omain was sitting in the corner of the living room furthest from Lodi, it was the only way the blocks would remain functional.

"Someone has accessed the hotel's central processor. They've loaded a search program for the three of us, and it's got a visual reference for Mzu, too."

"It cannot be the possessed, surely?" Omain said. "Neural nanonics don't function for us."

"Might be the Organization ships. No. They'd never be able to access Tonala's net from orbit, not with the platforms still going at it. Hang on, I'll see what I can find out." He felt almost happy as he started retrieving tracker programs from the memory fleks he'd brought. The net dons in this city probably had ten times the experience he'd got from snooping around Ayacucho's communications circuits, but his programs were still able to flash back through the junctions, tracing the origin of the searchers.

The answer sprang into his mind just as the hotel's central processor crashed. "Wow, that was some guardian program. But I got them. You know anything about a local firm called Kilmartin and Elgant?"

"No. But I haven't been here long, not in this incarnation."

"Right." Lodi twitched a smile. "I'll see what . . . that's odd."

Omain had risen from his chair. He was frowning at the suite's double door. "What is?"

"The suite's net processor is down."

The door chimed.

"Did you . . ." Lodi began.

Something very heavy smashed into the door. Its panels bulged inwards. Splintering sounds were spitting out of the frame.

"Run!" Omain shouted. He stood before the door, both arms held towards it, palms outwards. His face was clenched with effort. The air twisted frantically in front of him, whipping up a small gale.

Another blow hammered the door, and Omain was sent staggering backwards. Lodi turned to run for the bedroom. He was just in time to see a fat three-metre-long serpent slither vertically up the outside of the window. Its huge head reared back, levelling out to stare straight at him. The jaws parted to display fangs as big as fingers. Then it lunged forwards, shattering the glass.

From his elevated position in the command post, Shemilt studied the ops table below him. One of the girls leaned over and pushed a red-flagged marker closer to the deserted asteroid.

"In range, sir," she reported.

Shemilt nodded, trying not to show too much dismay. All three of the inter-orbit ships were in range of New Georgia's SD network now. And Quinn had not returned to change his orders. His very specific orders.

If only we weren't so bloody terrified of him, Shemilt thought. He still felt sick every time he remembered the zero-tau pod containing Captain Gurtan Mauer. Quinn had opened it up during two of the black mass ceremonies.

If we all grouped together—But of course, death was no longer the end. Throwing the dark messiah into the beyond would solve nothing.

There was a single red telephone in his command post. He picked up the handset. "Fire," he ordered.

Two of the three inter-orbit ships on their way to find out what the teams from Jesup were doing in the deserted asteroids were struck by X-ray lasers. The beams shone clean through the life support capsules and the fusion drive casings. Both crews died instantly. Electronics flash evaporated. Drive systems ruptured. Two wrecks tumbled through space, their hulls glowing a dull orange, vapour squirting from split tanks.

The third was targeted by a pair of combat wasps.

The officers of the other two national SD networks saw them streaking away from New Georgia's platform, heading towards the helpless inter-orbit ship. They requested and received fire authority codes. By then the attacking combat wasps had begun dispensing their submunitions drones. Infrared decoys shone like micro-novas amid the shoal of drive exhausts; electronic warfare pulses screamed at the sensors of any SD platform within five thousand kilometres. The offensive was a valid tactic; combat wasps launched to try to protect the remaining ship were confused for several seconds. A time period which in space warfare was critical.

A flock of one-shot pulsers finally got close enough to discharge into the remaining inter-orbit ship, killing it immediately. That didn't prevent the kinetic missiles from arrowing in on it at thirty-five gees. Nor submunitions with nuclear warheads from detonating when they were within range.

Lady Mac's sensors picked up most of the brief battle, though the overspill from the electronic warfare submunitions overlapping the general assault waged by the SD platforms caused several overload dropouts.

"This is becoming a seriously hazardous location," Sarha mumbled. The external sensor image was quivering badly as if something was shaking the starship about. Artificial circles of green, blue, and yellow were splashing open against the starfield like raindrop graffiti. Intense blue-white flares started to appear among them.

"It just went nuclear," Beaulieu said. "I don't think I've seen overkill on that scale before."

"What the hell is going on up there?" Sarha asked.

"Nothing good," Liol said. "A possessed would have to be very determined to make a trip to one of those abandoned asteroids; there are no biospheres left, that'll leave them heavily dependent on technology."

"How are the Organization ships reacting?" Sarha asked. Twenty minutes after *Lady Mac* had left the *Spirit of Freedom*, the three frigates had docked. Quarter of an hour after that all communication with the station had ceased. They were now holding orbit eight hundred kilometres ahead of *Spirit of Freedom*, which gave their sensors a reasonable resolution.

"I'm way ahead of you," Liol said. "Two of them are launching—wait, they all are. They're going down into a lower orbit. Damn, I wish we could see what the voidhawks are doing."

"I'm registering activity within the station's defence sensor suite," Beaulieu said. "They're sweeping us."

"Liol, take us another five hundred kilometres away."

"No problem."

Sarha consulted the orbital display. "We'll be over Tonala in another thirty minutes. I'm going to recommend Joshua pulls out."

"There's a lot of ship movements beginning down here," Beaulieu said. "Two more low-orbit stations are launching ships; and those are the ones we can see."

"Bugger it," Sarha grunted. "Okay, go to defence-ready status."

Lady Mac's standard sensor clusters retreated down into their recesses; the smaller, bulbous combat sensors slid smoothly upwards to replace them, gold-chrome lenses reflecting the last twinkling explosions in high orbit. Her combat wasp launch tubes opened.

All around her, Nyvan's national navies and SD platforms were switching to the same status.

Since arriving at Jesup, Dwyer had spent almost every hour helping to modify the bridge systems of the cargo clipper *Mount's Delta*. Given his minimal technical background, his time was spent supervising the non-possessed technicians who did most of the installation.

The bridge compartment was badly cramped, which meant only a couple of people could work in it at any one time. Dwyer had become highly proficient at dodging flying circuit boards and loose console covers. But he was satisfied with the result, which was far less crude than the changes they'd made to the *Tantu*. With the huge stock of component spares available in the spaceport, the consoles looked as if they'd slipped off the factory production line mere hours earlier. Their processors were now all military grade, capable of functioning while they were subjected to the energistic effect of the possessed. And the flight computer had been augmented until it was capable of flying the ship following the simplest of verbal orders.

This time there was none of the black sculpture effect, every surface was standard. Quinn had insisted the clipper's life support capsule must stand up to inspection when they arrived at Earth. Dwyer was confident he had reached that objective.

Now he was hovering just outside the small galley alcove on the mid-deck watching a female technician replacing the old hydration nozzles with the latest model. A portable sanitation sucker hovered over her shoulder, its fan humming eagerly as it ingested the occasional stale globule which burped out of the tubes she'd unscrewed.

The unit's hum rose sharply, becoming strident. A draught of cold air brushed Dwyer's face.

"How's it going?" Quinn asked.

Dwyer and the technician both yelped in surprise. The clipper's airlock was in the lower deck, and the floor hatch was closed.

Dwyer spun around, grabbing at support struts to wrestle

his inertia back under control. Sure enough, Quinn was sliding down through the ceiling hatch from the bridge. His robe's hood was folded back, sticking to his shoulders as if he were in his own private gravity field. For the first time in days his flesh tone was almost normal. He grinned cheerfully at Dwyer.

"God's Brother, Quinn. How did you do that?" Dwyer glanced over his shoulder to check the floor hatch again.

"It's like style," Quinn said. "Some of us have it . . ." He winked at the female technician and flung a bolt of white fire straight into her temple.

"Fuck!" Dwyer gasped.

The corpse banged back into the galley alcove. Tools fluttered out of her hands like iron butterflies.

"We'll dump her out of the airlock when we're under way," Quinn said.

"We're leaving?"

"Yes. Right now. And I don't want anyone to know."

"But . . . what about the engineering crew in the bay's control centre? They have to direct the umbilical retraction."

"There is no more crew. We can relay the launch instructions to the management computer through the bay's datanet."

"Whatever you say, Quinn."

"Come on, you'll enjoy Earth. I know I will." He performed a somersault in midair, and slow-dived back up through the hatch.

Dwyer took a moment to compose himself, clenching his hands so the way his fingers trembled didn't show, then followed Quinn up into the bridge.

Anger and worry isolated Alkad from the mundanities of the drive back to the hotel. She hadn't thought this fast and hard since the days she was working on the Alchemist theory. Options were closing all around her, like the sound of prison doors slamming shut.

The meeting with two of Opia's vice presidents had been a typical sounding-you-out session. All very cordial, and achieving very little. They had agreed on the principle of the company finding her a starship and crew, which at some yet-to-be-specified time would be equipped with specialist defence systems for duties in the Dorados' defence force.

The one hold she had over them was the prospect that this would be the first order by the Dorados council; and if all went smoothly, more would follow. Possibly a great deal more.

Greed had taken root. She had seen it so many times before in the industrialists who had been supplying Garissa's navy.

They would have followed her requests, ignoring the oddities of the situation. She was convinced of it. Then just as the meeting was winding down the Tonala government announced a state of emergency. New Georgia's SD platforms had opened fire on three ships, one of which belonged to Tonala. Such an action, the Defence Ministry insisted, proved beyond any doubt that the possessed had captured Jesup, that the New Georgia government was lying, and possibly even possessed itself.

Once again Nyvan's national factions were at war with each other.

The Opia executives loaded a program for a crestfallen expression into their neural nanonics. Sorry, but the contract would have to go into suspension. Temporarily. Just until Tonalan might has reigned triumphant.

The car drew up underneath the sweeping portico of the Mercedes Hotel. Ngong was first out, scouring the broad street for threats. Now they had him and Gelai protecting them, Alkad had dispensed with the security firm Voi had hired; although they'd kept the company's car with its armoured bodywork and secure circuitry.

There wasn't much traffic on the street. The team of men shovelling snow had vanished, leaving the dilapidated mechanoids to struggle on by themselves. Ngong nodded and beckoned. Alkad eased herself off the seat and scurried over to the lobby's rotating door, Gelai a pace behind her the whole time. They had told her of the Organization's ships during the trip back. It baffled Alkad how Capone had ever heard of her. But there was no disguising Gelai's rising concern.

The five of them bundled into the penthouse lift, which rose smoothly. Only the annoying flicker of the light panel betrayed Gelai and Ngong for what they were.

Alkad ignored the lighting. The state of emergency was dangerous. It wouldn't be long before Tonala retaliated against New Georgia's SD network. Those starships docked above Nyvan would be pressed into service, if the captains didn't simply ignore the quarantine and leave. She would soon be trapped here without any transport and the Capone Organization closing in. Unless she did something fast, she would belong to the possessed one way or the other, and with her came the Alchemist.

The spectre of what the device could do to the Confederation if it was used on a target other than Omuta's star was now preying on her mind. What if it was used against Jupiter? The Edenist habitats would die, Earth would be deprived of the He_3 without which it could never survive. Or what if it was used against Sol itself? What if it was switched to the nova function?

There had never been any conceivable prospect of this before. I was always in control. Mother Mary forgive my arrogance.

She cast a sideways glance at Voi, who was looking as irritable as always with the lift's progress. Voi would never entertain any change in their mission priorities. The concept of failure was not allowed for.

Like me at that age.

I have to get off this planet, she realized abruptly. I have to reopen the options again. I can't let it end like this.

The lift's floor indicator said they were three floors below the penthouse when Gelai and Ngong exchanged a questioning glance.

"What's the matter?" Voi asked.

"We can't sense Omain, or Lodi," Gelai said.

Alkad immediately tried to datavise Lodi. There was no

response. She ordered the lift to stop. "Is there anyone up there?"

"No," Gelai said.

"Are you sure?"

"Yes."

Of all the facets of possession, the perception ability fascinated Alkad the most. She'd only just started considering the mechanism of possession. The whole concept would ultimately mean quantum cosmology having to be completely restructured again. So far, she'd made very little theoretical progress.

"I told him to stay put," Voi said indignantly.

"If his neural nanonics aren't responding, then this is rather more serious than him simply wandering off," Alkad told her.

Voi pulled a face, unconvinced.

Alkad ordered the lift to restart.

Gelai and Ngong were standing in front of the doors when they opened on the penthouse vestibule. Trickles of static skipped over their clothes as they readied themselves for trouble.

"Oh, Mary," Eriba said. The double doors to the penthouse had been smashed apart.

Gelai waved the others back as she edged cautiously into the living room. Alkad heard an intake of breath.

The body Omain had been possessing was lying across one of the big settees, covered with deep scorch marks. Snow was blowing in through a gaping hole in the window.

Ngong hurriedly checked the other rooms. "No body. He's not here," he told them.

"Oh, Mother Mary, now what?" Alkad exclaimed. "Gelai, have you got any idea who did this?"

"None. Aside from the obvious that it was some possessed."

"They know about us," Voi said. "And now Lodi's been possessed, they know too much about us. We must leave immediately."

"Yes," Alkad said reluctantly. "I suppose so. We'd better

go directly to the spaceport, see if we can hook up with a starship there."

"Won't they know we're going to do that?" Eriba said.

"What else can we do? This planet can't help us anymore."

One of the processor blocks on the table let out a bleep. Its AV projector sparkled.

Alkad looked straight into it. And she was looking out through a set of eyes at a man dressed in a traditional Cossack costume.

"Can you hear me, Dr Mzu?" he asked.

"Yes. Who are you?"

"My name is Baranovich, not that it particularly matters. The important fact here is that I have agreed to work for Mr Capone's Organization."

"Oh, shit," Eriba groaned.

Baranovich smiled and held a small circular mirror up. Alkad could see Lodi's frightened face reflected in the surface.

"So," Baranovich said. "As you can see, we have not harmed your comrade. This is his datavise you are receiving. If he was possessed, he would be unable to do this. No? Say something, Lodi."

"Voi? Dr Mzu? I'm sorry. I couldn't—Look there are only seven of them. Omain tried . . ." Something hissed loudly behind him. The image blurred. Then he blinked.

"A brave boy." Baranovich clapped Lodi on the shoulder. "The Organization has a place for those with such integrity. I would hate to see another come to use this body."

"You might have to," Alkad said. "I cannot consider swapping a lone man for the device, no matter how well I know him. There have been far bigger sacrifices made to get me to this point. I would be betraying those who made them, and that I can never do. I'm sorry, Lodi, really I am."

"My dear doctor," Baranovich said. "I was not offering you Lodi in exchange for the Alchemist. I am simply using him as a convenient instrument through which I can deal with you, and perhaps demonstrate our intent."

"I don't need to deal with you."

"Your pardon, Doctor, I believe you do. You will not get off this planet unless the Organization takes you off. I think you know that now. After all, you weren't going to try and run to the spaceport, now were you?"

"I'm not about to discuss my departure arrangements with you."

"Bravo, Doctor. Resistance to the very end. I respect that. But please understand, the circumstances in which you find yourself have changed radically since you began your quest for vengeance. There will be no revenge against Omuta anymore. What would be the point? In a few short months Omuta as it is today will not exist. Whatever you can do to it will not exceed the coming of possession. Will it, Doctor?"

"No."

"So you see, you have only yourself to consider now, and what will happen in your personal future. The Organization can offer you a decent future. You know that with us millions of valuable people remain unpossessed, and secure in their jobs. You can be one of them, Doctor. I have the authority to offer you a place with us."

"In return for the Alchemist."

Baranovich shrugged magnanimously. "That is the deal. We will take you—and your friends too if you want them— off this planet today, before the orbital battle becomes any worse. Nobody else will do that. You either stay here and become possessed, an eternity spent in the humiliation of physical and mental bondage; or you come with us and live out the rest of your life as fruitfully as possible."

"As destructively as possible, you mean."

"I doubt the Alchemist would have to be used many times, not if it's as good as rumour says. Yes?"

"It wouldn't need many demonstrations," Alkad agreed slowly.

"Alkad!" Voi protested.

Baranovich beamed happily. "Excellent, Doctor, I see you are acknowledging the truth. Your future *is* with us."

"There's something you should know," Alkad said. "The activation code is stored in my neural nanonics. If I am killed and moved into another body in a bid to make me more compliant, I will not be able to access them. If I am possessed, the possessor will not be able to access them. And, Baranovich, there are no copies of the code."

"You are a prudent woman."

"If I come with you, then my companions are to be given passage to a world of their choice."

"No!" Voi shouted.

Alkad turned from the projection and told Gelai: "Keep her quiet."

Voi squirmed helplessly as the possessed woman pinned her arms behind her back. A gag solidified out of thin air to cover her mouth.

"Those are my terms," Alkad told Baranovich. "I have spent most of my life in pursuit of my goal. If you do not agree to my terms, then I will not hesitate to defy you in the only way I have left. I have that determination, it is the one real weapon I have always had. You have pushed me into this position, do not doubt that I will use it."

"Please, Doctor, there is no need for such vehemence. We will be happy to carry your young friends to a safe place."

"All right. We have a deal."

"Excellent. Our spaceplanes will pick you and your friends up at the ironberg foundry yard outside the city. We'll be waiting at Disassembly Shed Four with Lodi. Be there in ninety minutes."

9

Admiral Motela Kolhammer and Syrinx arrived at the First Admiral's office just as the Provost General was coming out. He almost bumped into them, head down and scowling. Kolhammer was given a brief grunt of apology before he strode off, chased by three aides in an equally flustered mood. The admiral gave them a curious look before stepping into the office.

Captain Maynard Khanna and Admiral Lalwani were sitting in front of the First Admiral's desk. Two more blue-steel chairs were distending up out of the circular pools of silver on the floor.

"What was all that about?" Kolhammer asked.

"We have a small legal problem with one of our guests," Lalwani said dryly. "It's just a question of procedures, that's all."

"Bloody lawyers," Samual Aleksandrovich muttered. He gestured Kolhammer and the voidhawk captain to sit.

"Is it relevant to Thakrar's information?" Kolhammer asked.

"No, fortunately." Samual smiled a fast welcome at Syrinx. "My thanks to *Oenone* for such a swift flight."

"I'm happy to be contributing, sir," Syrinx said. "Our journey time from Ngeuni was eighteen hours."

"That's very good."

"Good enough?" Kolhammer asked.

"We believe so," Lalwani said. "According to our New California surveillance operation, Capone is only just starting to refuel and rearm his fleet again."

"How up-to-date is that information?" Kolhammer asked.

"There's a voidhawk flight each day from the Yosemite Consensus, so at the most we're only thirty hours behind. According to the Consensus, it will be another week at the most before they're ready to launch."

"At Toi-Hoi, allegedly," Kolhammer mused. "Sorry to play the heretic, but how reliable is this Captain Thakrar?"

Syrinx could only give an empty gesture. *If only I had some way of imparting Erick's intensity, his devotion, to them.* "I have no doubt Captain Thakrar's data is genuine, Admiral. Apart from his unfortunate collapse at the finish of his mission he's proved an absolute credit to the CNIS. Capone does intend to invade Toi-Hoi next."

"I accept the information as essentially accurate," Lalwani affirmed. "We really are going to be able to intercept the Organization fleet."

"Which is going to eliminate the Capone problem completely," Maynard Khanna said. "With him gone, all we have to concern ourselves with is the quarantine."

"And that damnfool Mortonridge Liberation which the Kingdom's foisted on to us," Kolhammer complained.

"Psychologically, the elimination of Capone's fleet will be considerably more important," Lalwani said. "Capone is interpreted as a far more active threat by Confederation citizens—"

"Yeah, thanks to the damn media," Kolhammer said.

"—so when they see there is no further chance of his fleet appearing in their skies, and the navy has achieved that for them, we will have a great deal more leverage with the Assembly when it comes to implementing our policy."

"Which is?" Samual Aleksandrovich asked sardonically. "Yes, yes, Lalwani. I know. I simply don't welcome the notion of holding things together while we pray that Gilmore and all the others like him can find a solution for us; it smacks of inactivity."

"The more we thwart them, the more we can expect them to cooperate in finding a solution," she said.

"Very optimistic," Kolhammer said.

Samual datavised a request into his desktop processor and

the fat AV cylinder hanging from the middle of the ceiling began to sparkle. "This is our current strategic disposition," he said as the chairs swivelled their occupants around to face the projection. They were looking down on the Confederation stars from galactic south, where tactical situation icons orbited around the suns of inhabited worlds like technicolour moons. At the centre, Earth's forces were portrayed by enough symbols to form a ring of gas giant proportions. "You're going to get your chance, Motela," the First Admiral said quietly. "That 1st Fleet squadron you assembled to deal with Laton is the only possible force we can engage Capone with. We don't have time to put anything else together."

Kolhammer studied the projection. "What does the Yosemite Consensus estimate Capone's fleet size to be this time?"

"Approximately seven hundred," Lalwani said. "Numerically, that's slightly down on last time. Arnstadt is tying up a lot of his mid-capacity ships. However, he has acquired a disturbing number of Arnstadt's navy ships. Consensus believes the fleet will contain at least three hundred and twenty front-line warships. The rest are made up from combat-capable traders and civil craft modified to carry combat wasps."

"And they're armed with antimatter," Kolhammer said. "My squadron has a maximum of two hundred ships. We both went to the same academy, Lalwani, you need a two to one advantage to guarantee success. And that's just theoretically."

"The Organization crews are not highly motivated or efficient," she replied. "Nor do their ships function at a hundred per cent capacity with possessed on board screwing up the systems."

"Neither of which will matter a damn to their damn forty-gee combat wasps once they're launched. They function just fine."

"I will assign you half of the 1st Fleet vessels here at Avon," the First Admiral said. "That will bring your strength up to four hundred and thirty, including eighty voidhawks. In addition, Lalwani has suggested that we request support from every Edenist Consensus within a seventy-light-year radius of Toi-Hoi."

"Even if they only release ten per cent of their voidhawks, that should give you nearly three hundred and fifty voidhawks," she said.

"Seven hundred and eighty front-line warships," Kolhammer said. "A force that big is very cumbersome."

Lalwani turned from the projection to give him a reproachful stare. She found him grinning straight at her.

"But I think I can cope."

"Our tactical staff want to use Tranquillity as the rendezvous point," Khanna said. "It's only eighteen light-years from Toi-Hoi; which means you can be there in five hours once you know the Organization fleet is on its way."

"One ship takes five hours, yes, but we're dealing with nearly eight hundred. I wasn't joking about such a force being cumbersome. Why don't the tactical staff want us to use Toi-Hoi itself?"

"Capone must have it under observation. If he sees that kind of task force arrive he'll simply abort and choose another target. We'd be back at square one. Tranquillity is close, and it's not an obvious military base. Once our observation operation confirms the Organization fleet is leaving for Toi-Hoi a voidhawk will fly directly to Tranquillity and alert you. You can be at Toi-Hoi before Capone's ships arrive. You can destroy them as they jump in."

"Perfect tactics," Kolhammer said, almost to himself. "How long before the rest of the 1st Fleet ships can join the squadron?"

"I've already issued recall orders," the First Admiral said. "The bulk will be at Trafalgar within fifteen hours. The remainder can fly directly to Tranquillity."

Kolhammer consulted the AV projection again, then datavised a series of requests into the desktop processor. The scale changed, expanding while the viewpoint slipped around to put Toi-Hoi at the centre. "The critical factor here is that Tranquillity is secure. We need to prevent any ship from leaving, and also make sure it's not under any kind of stealth observation before we arrive."

"Suggestion?" Samual asked.

"It'll be four and a half days before the task force gets to Tranquillity. But Meredith Saldana's squadron is still at Cadiz, correct?"

"Yes, sir," Khanna said. "The ships were docked at a 7th Fleet supply base. The Cadiz government requested they remain and support local forces."

"So, a voidhawk could reach Cadiz within . . ." He gave Syrinx an inquiring glance.

"From Trafalgar? Seven to eight hours."

"And Meredith could get to Tranquillity in a further twenty hours. Which would give him almost three days to check local space for any kind of clandestine surveillance activity, as well as preventing any locals from leaving."

"Get the orders drafted," the First Admiral told Khanna. "Captain Syrinx, my compliments to the *Oenone*, I'd be obliged if you can convey them to Cadiz for me."

Now this is real flying, *Oenone* said excitedly.

Syrinx concealed her own delight at the voidhawk's enthusiasm. "Of course, Admiral."

Samual Aleksandrovich cancelled the AV projection. He felt the same kind of anxiety that had beset him the day he turned his back on his family and his world for a life in the navy. It came from standing up and taking responsibility. Big decisions were always made solo; and this was the biggest in his career. He couldn't remember anyone sending close-on eight hundred starships on a single combat assignment before. It was a frightening number, the firepower to wreck several worlds. And by the look of him, Motela was beginning to acknowledge the same reality. They swapped a nervous grin.

Samual stood up and put out his hand. "We need this. Very badly."

"I know," Kolhammer said. "We won't let you down."

• • • •

Nobody in Koblat's spaceport noticed the steady procession
of kids slipping quietly down the airlock tube in bay WJR-
99 where the Leonora Cephei was docked. Not the port of-
ficials, not the other crews (who would have taken a dim
view of Captain Knox's charter), and certainly not the company cops. For the first time in Jed's life, the company's
policy meant that things were swinging his way.

The spaceport's internal security surveillance systems
were turned off, the CAB docking bay logs had been disabled, customs staff were on extended leave. No inconvenient memory file would ever exist of the starships that had
come and gone since the start of the quarantine; nor would
there be a tax record of the bonuses everyone was earning.

Even so, Jed was taking no chances. His small chosen
tribe convened in the day club where he and Beth checked
them over, making them take off their red handkerchiefs before dispatching them up to the spaceport at irregular intervals.

There were eighteen Deadnights he and Beth reckoned
they could trust to keep quiet; and that was stretching the
Leonora Cephei's life-support capacity to its legal capacity.
Counting himself and Beth, there were four left when Gari
finally arrived. That part was pre-arranged; if both of them
had been gone from the apartment for the whole day, their
mother might have wondered what they were up to. What
had definitely not been arranged was Gari having Navar in
tow.

"I'm coming, too," Navar said defiantly as she saw Jed's
face darken. "You can't stop me."

Her voice was that same priggish bark he had come to
loathe over the last months, not just the tone but the way it
always got what it wanted. "Gari!" he protested. "What are
you doing, doll?"

His sister's lips squeezed up as a prelude to crying. "She
saw me packing. She said she'd tell Digger."

"I will, I swear," Navar said. "I'm not staying here, not when I can go and live in Valisk. I'm going, all right."

"Okay." Jed put his arm around Gari's quivering shoulders. "Don't worry about it. You did the right thing."

"No she bloody didn't," Beth exclaimed. "There's no room on board for anyone else."

Gari started crying. Navar folded her arms, putting on her most stubborn expression.

"Thanks," Jed said over his sister's head.

"Don't leave me here with Digger," Gari wailed. "Please, Jed, don't."

"No one's leaving you behind," Jed promised.

"What then?" Beth asked.

"I don't know. Knox is just going to have to find room for one more, I suppose." He glared at Gari's erstwhile antagonizer. How bloody typical that even now she was messing things up, right when he thought he was going to escape the curse of Digger forever. By rights he should deck her one and lock her up until they'd gone. But in the world Kiera promised them, all animosities would be forgiven and forgotten. Even a mobile pain-in-the-arse like Navar. It was an ideal he was desperate to achieve. Would dumping her here make him unworthy of Kiera?

Seeing his indecision, Beth stormed: "Christ, you're so useless." She rounded on Navar, the nervejam suddenly in her hand. Navar's smirk faded as she found herself confronting someone who for once wasn't going to be wheedled or threatened. "One word out of you, one complaint, one show of your usual malice, and I use this on your bum before I shove you out of the airlock. Got that?" The nervejam was pressed against the end of Navar's nose for emphasis.

"Yes," the girl squeaked. She looked as miserable and frightened as Gari. Jed couldn't remember seeing her so disconcerted before.

"Good," Beth said. The nervejam vanished into a pocket. She flashed Jed a puzzled frown. "I don't know why you let her give you so much grief the whole time. She's only a girly brat."

Jed realized he must be blushing as red as Gari. Explanations now would be pointless, not to mention difficult.

He pulled his shoulder bag out from under the table. It was disappointingly light to be carrying everything he considered essential to his life.

Captain Knox was waiting for them in the lounge at the end of the airlock tube: a short man with the flat features of his Pacific-island ancestry, but the pale skin and ash-blond hair which one of those same ancestors had bought as he geneered his family for free-fall endurance. His light complexion made his anger highly conspicuous.

"I only agreed to fifteen," he said as Beth and Jed drifted through the hatch. "You'll have to send some back; three at least."

Jed tried to push his shoes onto a stikpad. He didn't like free fall, which made his stomach wobble, his face swell, and clogged his sinuses. Nor was he much good at manoeuvring himself by hanging on to a grab hoop and using his wrists to angle his body. Inertia fought every move, making his tendons burn. When he did manage to touch his sole to the pad there was little adhesion. Like everything else in the inter-orbit ship, it was worn down and out-of-date.

"Nobody is going back," he said. Gari was clinging to his side, the mass of her floating body trying hard to twist him away from the stikpad. He didn't let go of the grab hoop.

"Then we don't leave," Knox said simply.

Jed saw Gerald Skibbow at the back of the lounge; as usual he was in switch-off, staring at the bulkhead with glazed eyes. Jed was beginning to wonder if he had a serious habit. "Gerald." He waved urgently. "Gerald!"

Knox muttered under his breath as Gerald came awake in slow stages, his body twitching.

"How many passengers are you licensed for?" Beth asked.

Knox ignored her.

"What is it?" Gerald asked. He was blinking as if the light were too bright.

"Too many people," Knox said. "You've gotta chuck some off."

"I have to go," Gerald said quietly.

"No one is saying you don't, Gerald," Beth said. "It's your money."

"But my ship," Knox said. "And I'm not carrying this many."

"Fine," Beth said. "We'll just ask the CAB office how many people you're licensed to carry."

"Don't be stupid."

"If you won't carry us, then return the fee and we'll find another ship."

Knox gave Gerald a desperate glance, but he looked equally bewildered.

"Just three, did you say?" Beth asked.

Sensing things were finally flowing in his favour, Knox smiled. "Yes, just three. I'll be happy to fly a second charter for your friends later."

Which was rubbish, Beth knew. He was only worried about his own precious skin. A ship operating this close to the margin really would be hard put to sustain nineteen Deadnights plus the crew. It was the first time Knox had shown the slightest concern about the flight. The only interest he'd shown in them before was their ability to pay. Which Gerald had done, and well over the odds, too. They didn't deserve to be pushed around like this.

But Gerald was totally out of the argument, back in one of his semi-comatose depressions again. And Jed . . . Jed these days was focused on one thing only. Beth still hadn't made up her mind if she was annoyed about that or not.

"Put three of us in the lifeboat, then," she said.

"What?" Knox asked.

"You do have a lifeboat?"

"Of course."

Which is where he and his precious family would shelter

if anything did go wrong, she knew. "We'll put the three youngest in there. They'd be the first in anyway, wouldn't they?"

Knox glared at her. Ultimately, though, money won the argument. Skibbow had paid double the price of an ordinary charter, even at the inflated rates flights to and from Koblat were currently worth.

"Very well," Knox said gracelessly. He datavised the flight computer to close the airlock hatch. Koblat's flight control was already signalling him to leave the docking bay. His filed flight plan gave a departure time of five minutes ago, and another ship was waiting.

"Give him the coordinate," Beth told Jed. She took Gerald by the arm and gently began to tug him to his couch.

Jed handed the flek over to Knox, wondering how come Beth was suddenly in charge.

The *Leonora Cephei* rose quickly out of the docking bay; a standard drum-shaped life-support capsule separated from her fusion drive by a thirty-metre spine. Four thermo dump panels unfolded from her rear equipment bay, looking like the cruciform fins of some atmospheric plane. Ion thrusters flared around her base and nose. Without any cargo to carry, manoeuvring was a lot faster and easier than normal. She rotated through ninety degrees, then the secondary drive came on, pushing her out past the rim of the spaceport.

Before *Leonora Cephei* had travelled five kilometres, the *Villeneuve's Revenge* settled onto the waiting cradle of bay WJR-99. Captain Duchamp datavised a request to the spaceport service company for a full load of deuterium and He$_3$. His fuel levels were down to twenty per cent, he said, and he had a long voyage ahead.

•   •   •   •

The clouds over Chainbridge formed a tight stationary knot of dark carmine amid the ruby streamers which ebbed and swirled across the rest of the sky. Standing behind Moyo as he drove the bus towards the town, Stephanie could sense the equally darkened minds clustered among the buildings. There were far more than there should have been; Chainbridge was barely more than an ambitious village.

Moyo's concern matched hers. His foot eased off the accelerator. "What do you want to do?"

"We don't have a lot of choice. That's where the bridge is. And the vehicles need recharging."

"Go through?"

"Go through. I can't believe anyone will hurt the children now."

Chainbridge's streets were clogged with parked vehicles. They were either military jeeps and scout rangers or lightly armoured infantry carriers. Possessed lounged indolently among them. They reminded Moyo of ancient revolutionary guerillas, with their bold-print camouflage fatigues, heavy lace-up boots, and shoulder-slung rifles.

"Uh oh," Moyo said. They had reached the town square, a pleasant cobbled district bounded by tall aboriginal leghorn trees. Two light-tracked tanks were drawn up across the road. The machines were impossibly archaic with their iron slab bodywork and chuntering engines coughing up diesel smoke. But that same primitive solidity gave them a unique and unarguable menace.

The Karmic Crusader had already stopped, its cheap effervescent colours quite absurd against the tank's stolid armour. Moyo braked behind it.

"You stay in here," Stephanie said, squeezing his shoulder. "The children need someone. This is frightening for them."

"This is frightening for me," he groused.

Stephanie stepped down onto the cobbles. Sunglasses spread out from her nose in the same fashion as a butterfly opening its wings.

Cochrane was already arguing with a couple of soldiers who were standing in front of the tanks. Stephanie came up behind him and smiled pleasantly at them. "I'd like to talk to Annette Ekelund, please. Would you tell her we're here."

One of them glanced at the Karmic Crusader and the inquisitive children pressed against its windscreen. He nodded, and slipped away past the tanks.

Annette Ekelund emerged from the town hall a couple of minutes later. She was wearing a smart grey uniform, its leather jacket lined in scarlet silk.

"Oh, wow," Cochrane said as she approached. "It's Mrs Hitler herself."

Stephanie growled at him.

"We heard you were coming," Annette Ekelund said in a tired voice.

"So why have you blocked the road?" Stephanie asked.

"Because I can, of course. Don't you understand anything?"

"All right, you've demonstrated you're in charge. I accept that. None of us has the slightest intention of challenging you. Can we go past now, please?"

Annette Ekelund shook her head in bemused wonder. "I just had to see you for myself. What do you think you're doing with these kids? Do you think you're saving them?"

"Frankly, yes. I'm sorry if that's too simple for you, but they're really all I'm interested in."

"If you genuinely cared, you would have left them alone. It would have been kinder in the long run."

"They're children. They're alone now, and they're frightened now. Abstract issues don't mean very much compared to that. And you're scaring them."

"Not intentionally."

"So what is all this martial jingoism for? Keeping us under control?"

"You don't show a lot of gratitude, do you? I risked everything to bring lost souls back to this world, including yours."

"And so you think that gives you a shot at being our empress. You didn't risk anything, you were compelled, just like all of us. You were simply the first, nothing more."

"I was the first to see what needed to be done. The first to organize. The first to fight. The first to claim victory. The first to stake out our land." She swept an arm out towards a squad of troops who had taken over a pavement café on the other side of the square. "That's why they follow me. Because I'm right, because I know what needs to be done."

"What these people need is some kind of purpose. Mortonridge is falling apart. There's no food left, no electricity, nobody knows what to do. With authority comes responsibility. Unless you're just a bandit queen, of course. If you're a real leader, you should apply your leadership skills where they'll do the most good. You made a start, you kept the communications net working, you gave most towns a council of sorts. You should have built on that."

Annette Ekelund grinned. "What exactly were you before? They told me you were just a housewife."

"It doesn't matter," Stephanie said, impatient with the whole charade. "Will you let us through?"

"If I didn't, you'd only find another way. Of course you can go through. We even have a few children scooting around the town that you can take with you. See? I'm not a complete monster."

"The buses need recharging first."

"Naturally." Ekelund sighed. She beckoned to one of the tank guards. "Dane will show you where a working power point is. Please don't ask us for any food, I haven't got enough to spare. I'm having trouble supplying my own troops as it is."

Stephanie looked at the tanks; if she concentrated hard she could make out the fantasm shapes of the farm tractor mechanoids behind the armour. "What are you and your army doing here?"

"I would have thought that was obvious. I've taken that responsibility you prize so highly. I'm protecting Mortonridge for you. We're only thirty kilometres from the firebreak they slashed across the top of the ridge; and on the other side, the Saldana Princess is preparing. They're not going to leave us alone, Stephanie Ash. They hate us and they fear us. It's a nasty combination. So while you go gallivanting around doing your good deeds, just remember who's holding back the barbarians." She started back for the tanks, then paused. "You know, one day you're really going to have to decide where your loyalties lie. You said you'd fight to stop them throwing you back; well if you do, it'll be at my side."

"Ho wow, one iron-assed lady," Cochrane muttered.

"Definitely," Stephanie agreed.

Dane climbed into the Karmic Crusader with Cochrane and showed them the way to a line of warehouses which served the wharf. Their long roofs were all made from solar collector panels. When the buses were plugged in, Stephanie called her people together and told them what Ekelund had said.

"If any of you want to wait here while the buses go to the firebreak, I'll understand," she said. "The Kingdom military might get nervous about four large vehicles heading towards them."

"They won't shoot us out of hand," McPhee said. "Not as long as we don't cross the line. They'll be curious."

"Do you think so?" Tina said anxiously. A large lace hankie was pressed to her lips.

"I've been there," Dane said. "It was a scout mission. I watched them watching me. They won't start any trouble. Like your friend said, they'll be curious."

"We're almost there." Stephanie's fixed smile betrayed her nerves. "Just a few more hours, that's all." She glanced back at the buses, putting on a cheerful expression as she waved at the children pressed up against the windows. They had all picked up on the gloomy aura of the darkened clouds overhead. "McPhee, Franklin; give me a hand with them will you. We'll let them stretch their legs here and use a toilet."

"Sure."

Stephanie let Moyo hold her for a moment. He planted a kiss on her forehead. "Don't give up now."

She smiled shyly. "I won't. Can you take a look in the warehouses for me, see if you can find some working toilets. If not, we'll have to make do with tissues and the river."

"I'll go check."

The big sliding doors of the closest warehouse were open. It was used to store tubing, row after row of floor-to-ceiling stacks. All its lights were off, but there was enough pink-tinged sunlight coming through the doors for him to see by. He started checking around for an office.

Silent forklift mechanoids were standing in the aisles, holding up bundles of tubing that had been destined for urgent delivery. It wouldn't take much effort to start them up again, he thought. But what would be the point? Did a society of possessed need factories and farms? Some infrastructure was necessary, yes, but how much and of what kind? Something simple and efficient, and extremely long-lasting. He was quietly glad that kind of decision wasn't his.

A pyramid of tubing shielded the man from Moyo's perception. So he convinced himself later. Whatever the reason, he didn't notice him until he had rounded a corner and was barely five metres away. And he wasn't a possessed. Moyo knew his own kind, the internal glimmer of cells excited by the energistic overspill. This man's bioelectric currents were almost black, while his thoughts were fast and quiet. He was excessively ordinary in appearance; wearing pale green trousers, a check shirt, and a sleeveless jacket with DataAxis printed on its left breast pocket.

Moyo was chilled by a rush of panic. Any non-possessed creeping around here had to be a spy, which meant he'd be armed, most likely with something potent enough to terminate a possessed with minimum fuss.

White fire punched out of Moyo's palm, an instinctive response.

The seething streamer splashed against the man's face and flowed around him to strike the tubing behind him. Moyo grunted in disbelief. The man simply stood there as if it were water pouring over him.

The white fire dimmed, its remnants retreating into Moyo's hand. He whimpered, expecting the worst. I'm going to be blown back into the beyond. They've found a way of neutralizing our energistic power. We've lost. There's only the beyond now. For always.

He closed his eyes. Thinking with fond longing: Stephanie.

Nothing happened. He opened his eyes again. The man was looking at him with a mildly embarrassed expression. Behind him, molten metal was dribbling down the side of the stacked tubing.

"Who are you?" Moyo asked hoarsely.

"My name's Hugh Rosler. I used to live in Exnall."

"Did you follow us here?"

"No. Although I did watch your bus leave Exnall. It's just coincidence I'm here now."

"Right," Moyo said carefully. "You're not a spy then?"

The question was one which Rosler apparently found quite amusing. "Not for the Kulu Kingdom, no."

"So how come the white fire didn't affect you?"

"I have a built in resistance. It was thought we should have some protection when this time came around. And the reality dysfunction ability has proved inordinately useful over the years. I've been in a few tight corners in my time; completely inadvertently I might add. I'm not supposed to be obtrusive."

"Then you are an agent. Who do you work for?"

"Agent implies an active role. I only observe, I'm not part of any faction."

"Faction?"

"The Kingdom. The Confederation. Adamists. Edenists. The possessed. Factions."

"Uh huh. Are you going to shoot me, then, or something?"

"Good heavens no. I told you, I'm here purely on observation duty."

What was being said, apparently in all sincerity, wasn't helping to calm Moyo at all. "For which faction?"

"Ah. That's classified, I'm afraid. Technically, I shouldn't even be telling you this much. But circumstances have changed since my mission began. These things aren't quite so important today. I'm just trying to put you at ease."

"It's not working."

"You really do have nothing to fear from me."

"You're not human, are you?"

"I'm ninety-nine per cent human. That's good enough to qualify, surely?"

Moyo thought he would have preferred it if Hugh Rosler had launched into an indignant denial. "What's the one per cent?"

"Sorry. Classified."

"Xenoc? Is that it? Some unknown race? We always had rumours of pre-technology contact, men being taken away to breed."

Hugh Rosler chuckled. "Oh, yes, good old Roswell. You know I'd almost forgotten about that; the papers were full of it for decades afterwards. But I don't think it ever really happened. At least, I never detected any UFOs when I was on Earth, and I was there quite a while."

"You were . . . ? But . . ."

"I'd better be going. Your friends are starting to wonder where you've got to. There's a toilet in the next warehouse which the children can use. The tank is gravity fed, so it's still working."

"Wait! What are you observing us for?"

"To see what happens, of course."

"Happens? You mean when the Kingdom attacks?"

"No, that's not really important. I want to see what the outcome is for your entire race now that the beyond has been revealed to you. I must say, I'm becoming quite excited by the prospect. After all, I have been waiting for this for a very long time. It's my designated goal function."

Moyo simply stared at him, astonishment and indignation taking the place of fear. "How long?" was all he managed to whisper.

"Eighteen centuries." Rosler raised an arm in a cheery wave and walked away into the shadows at the back of the warehouse. They seemed to lap him up.

"What's the matter with you?" Stephanie asked when Moyo shambled slowly out into the gloomy light of the rumbling clouds.

"Don't laugh, but I think I've just met Methuselah's younger brother."

•   •   •

Louise heard the lounge hatch slide open, and guessed who it was. His duty watch had finished fifteen minutes ago. Just long enough to show he wasn't in any sort of rush to see her.

The trouble with the *Jamrana*, Louise thought, was its layout. Its cabin fittings were just as good as those in the *Far Realm*, but instead of the pyramid of four life-support capsules, the inter-orbit cargo craft had a single cylindrical life-support section riding above the cargo truss. The decks were stacked one on top of the other like the layers of a wedding cake. To find someone, all you had to do was start at the top, and climb down the central ladder. There was no escape.

"Hello, Louise."

She reached for a polite smile. "Hello, Pieri."

Pieri Bushay had just reached twenty, the second oldest of three brothers. Like most inter-orbit ships, *Jamrana* was run as a family concern; all seven crew members were Bushays. The strangeness of the extended family, the looseness of its internal relationships, was one which Louise found troubling; it was more company than any family she understood. Pieri's elder brother was away serving a commission in the Govcentral navy, which left his father, twin mothers, brother, and two cousins to run the ship.

Small wonder that a young female passenger would be such an attraction to him. He was shy, and uncertain, which was endearing; nothing like the misplaced assurance of William Elphinstone.

"How are you feeling?"

His usual opening line.

"Fine." Louise tapped the little nanonic package behind her ear. "The wonders of Confederation technology."

"We'll be flipping over in another twenty hours. Halfway there. Then we'll be flying ass . . . er, I mean, bottom backwards to Earth."

She was impatient with the fact it was going to take longer to fly seventy million kilometres between planets than it had to fly between stars. But at least the fusion drive was scheduled to be on for a third of the trip. The medical packages didn't have to work quite so hard to negate her sickness. "That's good."

"Are you sure you don't want me to datavise the O'Neill Halo to see if there's a ship heading for Tranquillity?"

"No." That had been too sharp. "Thank you, Pieri, but if a ship is going, then it's going, if not, there's nothing I can do. Fate, you see."

"Oh, sure. I understand." He smiled tentatively. "Louise, if you have to stay in the Halo till you find a starship, I'd like to show you around. I've visited hundreds of the rocks. I know what's hot out there, what to see, what to miss. It would be fun."

"Hundreds?"

"Fifty, at least. And all the major ones, including Nova Kong."

"I'm sorry, Pieri, that doesn't mean much to me. I've never heard of Nova Kong."

"Really? Not even on Norfolk?"

"No. The only one I know is High York, and that's only because we're heading to it."

"But Nova Kong is famous; one of the first to be flown into Earth orbit and be made habitable. Nova Kong physicists invented the ZTT drive. And Richard Saldana was the asteroid's chairman once; he used it as his headquarters to plan the Kulu colonization."

"How fabulous. I can't really imagine a time when the Kingdom didn't exist, it seems so . . . substantial. In fact all of Earth's prestarflight history reads like a fable to me. So, have you ever visited High York before?"

"Yes, it's where the *Jamrana* is registered."

"That's your home, then?"

"We mostly dock there, but the ship's my real home. I wouldn't swap it for anything."

"Just like Joshua. You space types are all the same. You've got wild blood."

"I suppose so." His face tightened at the mention of Joshua; the guardian angel fiancé Louise managed to mention in every conversation.

"Is High York very well organized?"

He seemed puzzled by the question. "Yes. Of course. It has to be. Asteroids are nothing like planets, Louise. If the environment isn't maintained properly you'd have a catastrophe on your hands. They can't afford not to be well organized."

"I know that. What I meant was, the government. Does it have very strong law enforcement policies? Phobos seemed fairly easygoing."

"That's the devout Communists for you; they're very trusting, Dad says they always give people the benefit of the doubt."

It confirmed her worries. When the four of them had arrived at the *Jamrana* a couple of hours before its departure, Endron had handed over their passport fleks to the single Immigration Officer on duty. He had known the woman, and they'd spoken cheerfully. She'd been laughing when she slotted the fleks into her processor block, barely glancing at the images they stored. Three transient offworlders with official documentation, who were friends of Endron . . . She even allowed Endron to accompany them on board.

That was when he'd taken Louise aside. "You won't make it, you know that, don't you?" he asked.

"We've got this far," she said shakily. Though she'd had her doubts. There had been so many people as they made their tortuous way to the spaceport with the cargo mechanoid concealing Faurax's unconscious body. But they'd got the forger on board the *Far Realm* and into a zero-tau pod without incident.

"So far you've had a lot of luck, and no genuine obstacle. That's going to end as soon as the *Jamrana* enters Govcentral-controlled space. You don't understand what it's going to be like, Louise. There's no way you'll ever get inside High York. Look, the only reason you ever got inside Phobos was because we smuggled you in, and no one bothered to inspect the *Far Realm*. You got out, because no one is bothered about departing ships. And now you're heading straight at Earth, which has the largest single population in the Confederation, and runs the greatest military force ever assembled—a military force which along with the leadership is very paranoid right now. Three forged passports are not going to get you in. They are going to run every test they can think of, Louise, and believe me, Fletcher is not going to get through High York's spaceport." He was almost pleading with her. "Come with me, tell our government what's happened. They won't hurt him, I'll testify that he's not a danger. Then after that we can find you a ship to Tranquillity, all above board."

"No. You don't understand, they'll send him back to the beyond. I saw it on the news; if you put a possessed in zerotau it compels them out of the body they're using. I can't turn Fletcher in, not if they're going to force him back there. He's suffered for seven centuries. Isn't that enough?"

"And what about the person whose body he's possessing?"

"I don't know!" she cried. "I didn't want any of this. My whole planet's been possessed."

"All right. I'm sorry. But I had to say it. You're doing a damn sight worse than playing with fire, Louise."

"Yes." She held on to his shoulder with one hand to steady herself and brushed her lips to his cheek. "Thank you. I'm sure you could have blown the whistle on us if you really wanted to."

His reddening cheeks were confirmation enough. "Yeah,

well. Maybe I learned from you that nothing is quite black
and white. Besides, that Fletcher, he's so . . ."

"Decent."

Louise gave Pieri the kind of look that told him she was
immensely interested in every word he spoke. "So what
will happen when we arrive at High York, then? I want to
know everything."

Pieri started to access all his neural nanonic-filed memories of High York spaceport. With luck, and a surfeit of details, he could make this last for a good hour.

• • •

The Magistrature Council was the Confederation's ultimate
court. Twenty-five judges sat on the Council, appointed by
the Assembly to deal with the most serious violations of
Confederation law. The majority of cases were the ones
brought against starship crews captured by navy ships,
those accused of piracy or owning antimatter. Less common
were the war crimes trials, inevitably resulting from asteroid independence struggles. There were only two possible
sentences for anyone found guilty by the Magistrature:
death, or deportation to a penal colony.

The full Magistrature Council also had the power to sit in
judgement of sovereign governments. The last such sitting
had determined, in absentia, Omuta to be guilty of genocide, and ordered the execution of its cabinet and military
high command.

The Council's final mandate was the authority to declare
a person, government, or entire people to be an Enemy of
Humanity. Laton had been awarded such a condemnation,
as had members of the black syndicates producing antimatter, and various terrorists and defeated warlords. Such a
proclamation was essentially a death warrant which em-
powered a Confederation official to pursue the renegade
across all national boundaries and required all local governments to cooperate.

That was the pronouncement the Provost General was

now aiming to have applied against the possessed. With that in the bag, the CNIS would be free to do whatever they wanted to Jacqueline Couteur and the other prisoners in the demon trap. But first her current status had to be legally established, if she was a hostile prisoner under the terms of the state of emergency, or a hapless victim. In either case, she was still entitled to a legal representative.

The courtroom in Trafalgar chosen for the preliminary hearing was maximum security court three. It had none of the trimmings of the public courts, retaining only the very basic layout of docks, desks for the prosecution and defence counsels, the judge's bench, and a small observer gallery. There was no permitted or designated place for the media or the public.

Maynard Khanna arrived five minutes before the hearing was scheduled to begin, and sat at the front of the small gallery. As someone used to the order of military life, he had an intense distrust and dislike of the legal profession. Lawyers had abolished the simple concept of right and wrong, turning it into degrees of guilt. And in doing so they cut themselves in for fees which came only in large multiples of a navy captain's salary.

The accused were entitled to a defence, Maynard conceded, but he still never understood how their lawyers avoided feeling equally guilty when they got them off.

Lieutenant Murphy Hewlett sat down behind Maynard, pulling unhappily at the jacket of his dress uniform. He leaned forward and murmured: "I can't believe this is happening."

"Me neither," Maynard grumbled back. "But the Provost General says it should be a formality. No court in the galaxy is going to let Jacqueline Couteur walk out of the door."

"For God's sake, Maynard, she shouldn't even be let out of the demon trap. You know that."

"This is a secure court; and we can't give her defence lawyer an opportunity to mount an appeal on procedural grounds."

"Bloody lawyers!"

"Too right. What are you doing here, anyway?"

"Provost General's witness. I'm supposed to tell the judge how we were in a war situation on Lalonde, which makes Couteur's capture legitimate under the Assembly's rules of engagement. It's in case her lawyer goes for a wrongful jurisdiction plea."

"You know, this is the first time I've ever disagreed with the First Admiral. I said we should just keep her in the demon trap, and screw all this legal crap. Gilmore is losing days of research time over this."

Murphy hissed in disgust and sat back. For the eighth time that morning, his hand ran over his holster. It contained a nine-millimetre semi-automatic pistol, loaded with dumdum bullets. He loosened the cover, allowing his fingers to rest on the grip. Yesterday evening he had spent two hours at the range in the officers' mess, shooting the weapon without any aid from neural nanonics programs. Just in case.

An eight-strong marine squad and their sergeant, each of them armed with a machine gun, marched the four prisoners into the court. Jacqueline Couteur was the first in line, dressed in a neat grey suit. If it hadn't been for the carbotanium manacles she would have been a picture of middle-class respectability. A slim sensor bracelet had been placed around her right wrist, monitoring the flow of energy through her body. She looked around, noting the marine guards at each of the three doors. Then she saw Murphy Hewlett scowling, and grinned generously at him.

"Bitch," he grunted under his breath.

The marine squad sat Jacqueline in the dock and fastened her manacles to a loop of chain. The other three possessed—Randall, Lennart, and Nena—were made to sit on the bench beside her. Once their manacles were secured, the marines took up position behind them. The sergeant datavised his processor block to check that the sensor bracelets were working, then gave the clerk of the court a brief nod.

The four defence lawyers were ushered in. Jacqueline

manoeuvred a polite welcoming smile into place. This was the third time she'd seen Udo DiMarco. The lawyer wasn't entirely happy to be appointed her counsel, he'd admitted that much to her, but then went on to say he'd do his best.

"Good morning, Jacqueline," he said, doing his nervous best to ignore the marines behind her.

"Hello, Udo. Did you manage to obtain the recordings?"

"I filed a release request with the court, yes. It may take some time; the navy claims their Intelligence Service research is classified and exempt from the access act of 2503. I'll challenge that, of course, but as I said this is all going to take some time."

"They tortured me, Udo. The judge has to see those recordings. I'll walk free in seconds if the truth is ever known."

"Jacqueline, this is only a preliminary hearing to establish that all the required arrest procedures were followed, and clarify your legal custody status."

"I wasn't arrested, I was abducted."

Udo DiMarco sighed and plunged on. "The Provost General's team is going to argue that as a possessor you have committed a kidnap, and are therefore a felon. That will give them a basis for holding you in custody. They're also arguing that your energistic power constitutes a new and dangerous weapons technology, which will validate the Intelligence Service's investigation. Please don't expect to walk out of court this morning."

"Well I'm sure you'll do your best." She gave him an encouraging smile.

Udo DiMarco flexed his shoulders uncomfortably and withdrew to the defence counsel's bench. His sole comfort was the fact that the media weren't allowed in; no one would know he was defending a possessed. He datavised his processor block, reviewing the files he'd assembled. Ironically, he could put up quite a good case for Couteur's release, but he'd made the decision five minutes after having the case dumped on him that he was only going to make a show of defending her. Jacqueline could never know, but Udo DiMarco had a lot of family on New California.

The clerk of the court rose to his feet and announced: "Please stand for Judge Roxanne Taynor. This Magistrature Council court is now in session."

Judge Taynor appeared at the door behind the bench. Everyone stood, including the four possessed. Their movement meant the marine guards had to alter the angle they were pointing their machine guns. For a moment their concentration was less than absolute. Everybody's neural nanonics crashed. The lighting panels became incandescent. Four balls of white fire exploded around the machine guns, smashing them into a shower of molten fragments.

Murphy Hewlett bellowed a wordless curse, yanking his pistol up, thumb flicking at the safety catch. Like most people he was caught halfway to his feet, an awkward position. A brutally white light was making him squeeze his eyelids closed; retinal implants were taking a long time to filter out the excess photons. The sound of the detonating machine guns was audible above the startled cries. He swung the pistol around to line up on Couteur. Marines were screaming as their hands and lower arms were shredded along with their weapons. The lights went out.

From dazzling brilliance to total blackness was too much for his eyes. He couldn't see a thing. A machine gun fired. Muzzle blasts sent out a flickering orange light.

The possessed were all moving. Fast. The gunfire turned their motions into speedy flickers. They'd run straight through the dock, smashing the tough composite apart. Fragments tumbled through the air.

Two lightning streaks of white fire lashed out, striking a couple of marines. The lawyers were scrambling for the closest door. Roxanne Taynor was already through the door to her chambers. One of the marines was standing in front of it, sweeping her machine gun in a fast arc as she tried to line it up on a possessed.

"Close the doors!" Murphy yelled. "Seal this place."

A machine gun was firing again as the light from the

white fire shrank away. People screamed as they dived and stumbled for cover. Ricochets hummed lethally through the blackness.

Murphy caught sight of Couteur in the segments of illumination thrown out by another burst of gunfire. He twisted his pistol around and fired five shots, anticipating her direction for the last two. Dumdum bullets impacted with penetrating booms. Murphy dropped to his knees and rolled quickly. A pulse of white fire ripped through the air where he'd been standing. "Shit!" Missed her.

He could hear a siren wailing outside. Sensor modules on the walls were starting to burn, jetting out long tongues of turquoise flame which dissolved into a fountain of sparks. Three more bolts of white fire zipped over the gallery seats. There were heavy thuds of bodies hitting the floor.

When he risked a quick glance above the seat backs he could see Nena and Randall crouched low and zigzagging towards the door behind him. Eyeblink image of the door to one side of the smashed dock: three marines standing in defensive formation around it, almost flinging a lawyer out into the corridor beyond. But the door behind him was still open. It was trying to slide shut, but the body of a dead marine was preventing it from closing.

Murphy didn't have an option. They couldn't be allowed out into Trafalgar, it was inconceivable. He vaulted over the seats just as an odd rosette of white fire spun upwards from behind the judge's bench. It hit the ceiling and bounced, expanding rapidly into a crown made up from writhing flames which coiled around and around each other. The three marines guarding the door fired at it as it swooped down at them, bullets tearing out violet bubbles which erupted into twinkling starbursts. Murphy started firing his pistol at Randall as he sprinted for the door, trigger finger pumping frantically. Seeing the dumdum rounds rip ragged chunks out of the possessed's chest. Shifting his aim slightly. Half of Randall's neck blew away in a twister of blood and bone chippings. A screaming Nena cartwheeled backwards in panic, limbs thrashing out of control.

The crown of agitated white fire dropped around one of the marines like an incendiary lasso. It contracted with vicious snapping sounds, slicing clean through his pelvis. His machine gun was still firing as his torso tumbled down, spraying the whole courtroom with bullets. He tried to say something as he fell, but shock had jammed his entire nervous system. All that came out was a coughed grunt as his head hit the ground. Dulled eyes stared at his legs which were still standing above him, twitching spastically as they slowly buckled.

The other two marines froze in terror. Then one vomited. *"Close it!"* Murphy gagged. "For Christ's sake, get out and close it." His eyes were hot and sticky with fluid, some of it red. His foot hit something, and he half tripped flinging himself at the gap. He landed flat on the dead marine and rolled forwards. Figures were running around at the far end of the corridor, confused movements blurring together. White fire enveloped his ankle.

"Does it hurt? We can help."

"No, fuck you!" He flopped onto an elbow and aimed the pistol back through the door, firing wildly. Pain from his ankle was making his hand shake violently. Noxious smoke sizzled up in front of him.

Then hands were gripping his shoulders, pulling him back along the floor. Bullish shouts all around him. The distinctive thud of a Bradfield slammed against his ears, louder than thunder in the close confines of the corridor. A marine in full combat armour was standing above him, firing the heavy-calibre weapon into the courtroom. Another suited marine was pulling the corpse clear of the door.

Murphy's neural nanonics started to come back on-line. Medical programs established axon blocks. The courtroom door slid shut, locks engaging with a *clunk*. A fire extinguisher squirted thick white gas against Murphy's smouldering dress uniform trousers. He flopped down onto the corridor floor, too stunned to say anything for a while. When he looked around he could see three people he recognized from the court, all of them ashen-faced and stupefied, slumped against the walls. The marines were tending to two of them. That was when Murphy realized the corridor floor was smeared with blood. Spent cartridge cases from his pistol rolled around.

He was dragged further away from the courtroom door, allowing the marine squad to set up two tripod-mounted Bradfields, pointing right at the grey reinforced silicon.

"Hold still," a woman in a doctor's field uniform told him. She began to cut his trousers away; a male nurse was holding a medical nanonic package ready.

"Did any of them get out?" Murphy asked weakly. People were tramping up and down the corridor, paying no attention to him.

"I don't know," the doctor said.

"Fuck it, find out!"

She gave him a calculating look.

"Please?"

One of the marines was called over. "The other doors are all closed," he told Murphy. "We got a few people out, but the possessed are safely locked up in there. Every exit is sealed tight. The captain is waiting for a CNIS team to advise him what to do next."

"A few people?" Murphy asked. "A few people got out?"

"Yeah. Some of the lawyers, the judge, court staff, five marines. We're proud of the fight you put up, sir, you and the others. It could have been a lot worse."

"And the rest?"

The marine turned his blank shell helmet towards the door. "Sorry, sir."

The roar of the machine gun ended, leaving only the screams and whimpers to fester through the darkened courtroom. Maynard Khanna could hear his own feeble groans contributing to the morass of distress. There was little he could do to prevent it, the tiniest movement sent sickening spires of pain leaping into his skull. A gout of white fire had struck him seconds into the conflict, wrapping around his leg like a blazing serpent, felling him immediately. His temple had struck one of the seats, dazing him badly. After that, all the noise and flaring light swarmed around him, somehow managing to leave him isolated from the fray.

Now the white fire had gone, leaving him alone with its terrible legacy. The flesh from his leg had melted off. But his bones had remained intact, perfectly white. He could see his skeletal foot twitching next to his real one, its tiny bones fitting together like a medical text.

The splintered remnants of the dock were burning with unnatural brightness, throwing capering shadows on the wall. Maynard turned his head, crying out as red stars gave way to an ominous darkness. When he flushed the involuntary tears from his eyes he could see the heavy door at the back of the court was shut.

They hadn't got out!

He took a few breaths, momentarily puzzled by what he was doing in the dark, the waves of pain seemed to prevent his thoughts from flowing. The screams had died, along with every other sound except for the sharp crackling of the flames. Footsteps crunched through the debris. Three dark figures loomed above him; humanoid perhaps, but any lingering facet of humanity had been bred out generations ago.

The whispers began, slithering up from a bottomless pit to comfort him with the sincerity of a two-timing lover. Then came the real pain.

Dr Gilmore studied the datavised image he was receiving direct from Marine Captain Rhodri Peyton's eyes. He was standing in the middle of a marine squad which was strung out along one of the corridors leading to maximum security court three. Their machine guns and Bradfields were deployed to cover the engineering officers who were gingerly applying sensor pads to the door.

When Dr Gilmore attempted to access the officers' processor blocks there was no response. The units were too close to the possessed inside the courtroom. "Have they made any attempt to break out?" he asked.

"No, sir," Rhodri Peyton datavised. His eyes flicked to

brown scorch lines on the walls just outside the door. "Those marks were caused when Lieutenant Hewlett was engaging them. There's been nothing since then. We've got them trapped, all right."

Gilmore accessed Trafalgar's central computer and requested a blueprint of the courtroom. There were no service tunnels nearby, and the air-ducts weren't large enough for anyone to crawl down. It was a maximum security court after all. Unfortunately it wasn't the kind of security designed with the possessed in mind. He knew it would only be a matter of time before they got out. Then there really would be hell to pay.

"Have you confirmed the number of people in the courtroom?"

"We're missing twelve people, sir. But we know at least four of those are dead, and the others sustained some injuries. And Hewlett claims he terminated one of the possessed, Randall."

"I see. That means we now have a minimum of eleven possessed to contend with. That much energistic potential is extremely dangerous."

"This whole area is sealed, sir, and I've got a squad covering each door."

"I'm sure you have, Captain. One moment." He datavised the First Admiral and gave him a brief summary. "I have to advise we don't send the marines in. Given the size of the courtroom and the number of possessed, I'd estimate marine casualties of at least fifty per cent."

"Agreed," the First Admiral datavised back. "The marines don't go in. But are you certain everyone in there is now possessed?"

"I think it's an inevitable conclusion, sir. This whole legal business was quite obviously just a ploy by Couteur to gain a foothold here. That many possessed represent a significant threat. My guess is that they may simply try to tunnel their way out; I expect they'll be able to dissolve the rock around them. They must be neutralized as swiftly as possible. We can always acquire further individuals to continue my team's research."

"Dr Gilmore, I'd remind you that my staff captain is in there, along with a number of civilians. We must make at least one attempt to subdue them. You've had weeks to research this energistic ability, you must be able to suggest something."

"There is one possibility, sir. I accessed Thakrar's report; he used decompression against the possessed when they tried to storm the *Villeneuve's Revenge*."

"To kill them."

"Yes. But it does indicate a weakness. I was going to recommend that we vent the courtroom's atmosphere. That way we wouldn't have to risk opening one of the doors to fire any sort of weapon in there. However, we could try gas against them first. They can force matter into new shapes, but I think altering a molecular structure would probably be beyond them. It needn't even be a chemical weapon, we could simply increase the nitrogen ratio until they black out. Once they've been immobilized, they could be placed into zero-tau."

"How would you know if a gas assault worked? They destroyed the sensors, we can't see in."

"There are a number of electronic systems remaining in the courtroom; if the possessed do succumb to the gas those systems should come back on line. But whatever we do, Admiral, we will have to open the door at some stage to confirm their condition."

"Very well, try the gas first. We owe Maynard and the others that much."

"We're not going to have much time to get out," Jacqueline Couteur said.

Perez, who had come into Maynard Khanna's body a few minutes earlier, was struggling to keep his thoughts flowing lucidly under a torrent of pain firing in from every part of his new frame. He managed to focus on some of the most badly damaged zones, seeing the blood dry up and torn discoloured flesh return to a more healthy aspect. "*Mama*, what did you do to this guy?"

"Taught him not to be so stubborn," Jacqueline said emotionlessly.

He winced as he raised himself up onto his elbows. Despite his most ardent wishes, his damaged leg felt as if fireworms were burrowing through it. He could *imagine* it whole and perfect, and even see the image forming around reality, but that wasn't quite enough to make it so. "Okay, so now what?" He glanced around. It was not the most auspicious of environments to welcome him back. Bodies were straddling the court's wrecked fittings, small orange fires gnawed hungrily at various jagged chunks of composite, and hatred was beaming through each of the doors like an emotive X ray.

"Not much," she admitted. "But we have to look for some kind of advantage. We're at the very centre of the Confederation's resistance to us. There must be something we can do to help Capone and the others. I had hoped we could locate their nuclear weapons. The destruction of this base would be a significant blow to the Confederation."

"Forget that; those marines were good," Lennart said grudgingly. He was standing in front of the judge's bench, one hand pulling on his chin as he gazed intently at the floor. "You know, there's some kind of room or corridor about twenty metres straight down." The tiling started to flow away from his feet in fast ripples, exposing the naked rock below. "It won't take long if we break this rock together."

"Maybe," Jacqueline said. "But they'll know we're doing it. Gilmore will have surrounded us with sensors by now."

"What then?" asked one of the others they'd brought back. "For Christ's sake, we can't stay in here and wait for the Confederation Marines to bust down the door. I've only just returned. I'm not giving this body up after only ten minutes. I couldn't stand that."

"Christ?" Jacqueline queried bitingly.

"You might have to anyway," Perez said. "We all might wind up back there in the beyond."

"Oh, why?" Jacqueline asked.

"This Khanna knows of an ambush the Confederation Navy is planning against Capone. He is confident they will destroy the Organization fleet. Without Capone to crack new star systems open, we're going to be stalled. Khanna is convinced the quarantine will prevent possession from spreading to any new worlds."

"Then we must tell Capone," Jacqueline said. "All of us together must shout this news into the beyond."

"Fine," Nena said. "Do that. But what about us? How are we going to get out of here?"

"That is a secondary concern for us now."

"Not for me it bloody well isn't."

When Jacqueline scowled at her, she saw beads of sweat pricking the woman's brow. Nena was swaying slightly, too. Some of the others looked as if they were exhausted, their eyes glazing over. Even Jacqueline was aware her body had grown heavier than before. She sniffed the air suspiciously, finding it contaminated with the slightly clammy ozone taint of air-conditioning.

"What exactly is the navy planning to do to Capone?" she asked.

"They know he's going to attack Toi-Hoi. They're going to hide a fleet at Tranquillity, and intercept him when they know he's on the way."

"We must remember that," Jacqueline said firmly, fixing each of them in turn with a compelling stare. "Capone must be told. Get through to him." She ignored everything else but the wish that the air in the courtroom was pure and fresh, blown down straight from some virgin mountain range. She could smell a weak scent of pine.

One of the possessed sat down heavily. The others were all panting.

"What's happening?" someone asked.

"Radiation, I expect," Jacqueline said. "They're probably bombarding us with gamma rays so they don't have to come in to deal with us."

"Blast a door open," Lennart said. "Charge them. A few of us might get through."

"Good idea," Jacqueline said.

He pointed a finger at the door behind the judge's bench, its tip wavering about drunkenly. A weak crackle of white fire licked out. It managed to stain the door with a splatter of soot, but nothing more. "Help me. Come on, together!"

Jacqueline closed her eyes, imagining all the clean air in the courtroom gathering around her and her alone. A light breeze ruffled her suit.

"I don't want to go back," Perez wailed. "Not there!"

"You must," Jacqueline said. Her breathing was easier now. "Capone will find you a body. He'll welcome you. I envy you for that."

Two more of the possessed toppled over. Lennart sagged to his knees, hands clutching at his throat.

"The navy must never know what we discovered," Jacqueline said thickly.

Perez looked up at her, too weak to plead. It wouldn't have been any use, he realized, not against that mind tone.

The shaped electron explosive charge sliced clean through the courtroom door with a lightning-bolt flash. There was very little blowback against the marine squad crouched fifteen metres away down the corridor. Captain Peyton yelled "Go!" at the same time as the charge was triggered. His armour suit's communications block was switched to audio, just in case the possessed were still active.

Ten sense-overload ordnance rounds were fired through the opening as the wrecked door spun around like a dropped coin. A ferocious blast of light and sound surged back along the corridor. The squad rushed forward into the deluge.

It was a synchronized assault. All three doors into the courtroom were blown at the same time. Three sets of sense-overload ordnance punched in. Three marine squads.

Dr Gilmore was still hooked into Peyton's neural nanonics, receiving the image direct from the captain's shell helmet sensors. The scene which greeted him took a while to interpret. Dimming flares were sinking slowly through the air as tight beams of light from each suit formed a crazy jumping crisscross pattern above the wrecked fittings. Bodies lay everywhere. Some were victims of the earlier fight. Ten of them had been executed. There was no other explanation. Each of the ten had been killed by a bolt of white fire through the brain.

Peyton was pushing his way through a ring of nearly twenty marines that had formed in the middle of the courtroom. Jacqueline Couteur stood at the centre, her shape blurred by a grey twister that had formed around her. It looked as if she'd been cocooned by solid strands of air. The twister was making a high-pitched whining sound as it undulated gently from side to side.

Jacqueline Couteur's hands were in the air. She gazed at the guns levelled against her with an almost sublime composure. "Okay," she said. "You win. And I think I may need my lawyer again."

10

There were nearly three thousand people in the crowd which assembled outside the starscraper lobby. Most of them looked fairly pissed at being summoned, but nobody actually argued with Bonney's deputies when they came calling. They wanted a quiet life. On a planet they could have just walked away into the wilderness; here that option did not exist.

Part of the lobby's gently arching roof had crumpled, a remnant of an early battle during their takeover of the habitat. Bonney started to walk up the pile of rubble. She held a processor block in one hand, turning it so she could see the screen.

"Last chance, Rubra," she said. "Tell me where the boyo is, or I start getting serious." The block's screen remained blank. "You overheard what Patricia said. I know you did, because you're a sneaky little shit. You've been manipulating me for a while now. I'm always told where he is, and he's always gone when I get there. You're helping him as much as you're helping me, aren't you? Probably trying to frighten him into cooperating with you. Was that it? Well, not anymore, Rubra, because Patricia has changed everything; we're playing big boys' rules now. I don't have to be careful, I don't have to respect your precious, delicate structure. It was fun going one on one against all those little bastards you stashed around the place. I enjoyed myself. But you were cheating the whole time. Funny, that's what Dariat warned us about right from the start." She reached the roof, and walked to the edge above the crowd. "You going to tell me?"

The screen printed: THOSE LITTLE DEADNIGHT GIRLS THAT COME HERE, YOU REALLY ENJOY WHAT YOU DO WITH THEM, DON'T YOU, DYKE?

Bonney dropped the processor block as if it were a piece of used toilet paper. "Game over, Rubra. You lose; I'm going to use nukes to crack you in half."

Dariat, I think you'd better listen to this.

What now?

Bonney, as usual. But things have just acquired an unpleasant edge. I don't think Kiera should have left her unsupervised.

Dariat hooked into the observation routines in time to see Bonney raise her hands for silence. The crowd gazed up at her expectantly.

"We've got the power of genies," she said. "You can grant yourself every wish you want. And we still have to live like dogs out in these shantytowns, grabbing what food we can, whipped into line, told where we can and can't go. Rubra's done that to us. We have starships for fuck's sake. We can travel to another star system in less time than it takes your heart to beat once. But if you want to go from here to the endcap, you have to walk. Why? Because that shit Rubra won't let us use the tubes. And up until now, we've let him get away with it. Well, not anymore."

Passionate lady, Dariat said uncomfortably.

Psycho lady, more like. They're not going to disobey her, they wouldn't dare. She's going to marshal them together and send them after you. I can't keep you ahead of an entire habitat of possessed hunting you. For once, boy, I'm not lying.

Yeah. I can see that. Dariat went over to the fire at the back of the cave. It had almost burnt out, leaving a pyramid of coals cloaked in a powder of fine grey ash. He stood looking at it, feeling the slumbering heat contained within the pink fragments.

I have to decide. I can't beat Rubra. And Rubra will be destroyed by Kiera when she returns. For thirty years I

would have welcomed that. Thirty fucking years. My entire life.

But he's willing to sacrifice his mental integrity, to join my thoughts to his. He's going to abandon two centuries of his belief that he can go it alone.

Tatiana stirred on the blanket and sat up, bracelets chinking noisily. Sleepy confusion drained from her face. "That was a strange dream." She gave him a shrewd glance. "But then this is a strange time, isn't it?"

"What was your dream?"

"I was in a universe which was half light, half darkness. And I was falling out of the light. Then Anastasia caught me, and we started to fly back up again."

"Sounds like your salvation."

"What's the matter?"

"Things are changing. That means I have to decide what to do. And I don't want to, Tatiana. I've spent thirty years not deciding. Thirty years telling myself this was the time I was waiting for. I've been a kid for thirty years."

Tatiana rose and stood beside him. He refused to meet her gaze, so she put an arm lightly on his shoulder. "What do you have to decide?"

"If I should help Rubra; if I should join him in the neural strata and turn this into a possessed habitat."

"He wants that?"

"I don't think so. But he's like me, there's not much else either of us can do. The game's over, and we're running out of extra time."

She stroked him absently. "Whatever you decide, I don't want you to take me into account. There are too many issues at stake, big issues. Individuals don't matter so much; and I had a good run against that Bonney. We annoyed her a lot, eh? That felt nice."

"But individuals do matter. Especially you. It's odd, I feel like I've come full circle. Anastasia always told me how precious a single life was. Now I have to decide your fate. And I can't let you suffer, which is what's going to happen if Rubra and I take on the possessed together. I'm responsible for her death, I can't have yours on my hands as well. How could I ever face her with that weighing on my heart? I have to be true to her. You know I do." He tilted his head back, his voice raised in anger. "Do you think you've won?"

I never even knew we were fighting until this possession happened, Rubra said sadly. You know what hopes I had for you in the old days, even though you never shared them. You know I never wanted anything to spoil my dreams for you. You were the golden prince, the chosen one. Fate stopped you from achieving your inheritance. That's what Anastasia was, for you and for me. Fate. You would call it an act of Thoale.

You believe all this was destined to be?

I don't know. All I know is that our union is the last chance either of us has to salvage something from all this shit. So now you have to ask yourself, do the living have a right to live, or do the dead rule the universe?

That's so like you, a loaded question.

I am what I am.

Not for very much longer.

You'll do it?

Yes.

Come in then, I'll accept you into the neural strata.

Not yet. I want to get Tatiana out first.

Why?

We may be virtually omnipotent after I come into the neural strata, but Bonney and the hellhawks still have the potential to damage the habitat shell very badly. I doubt we can quell them instantaneously, yet they will know the second I come into the neural strata. We are going to have a fight on our hands, I don't want Tatiana hurt.

Very well, I will ask the Kohistan Consensus for a voidhawk to take her off.

You have a method?

I have a possible method. I make no promises. You'd

better get yourselves along to the counter-rotating spaceport before Bonney starts her hunt.

It wasn't merely a hunting party Bonney was organizing. She was keenly aware that Dariat could always flee her in the tube carriages, while she was reduced to chasing after him in one of the rentcop force's open-top trucks. If Dariat was to be caught, then she would first have to cripple his mobility.

The crowd she had assembled was split into teams, given specific instructions, and dispatched to carry them out. Each major team had one of her deputies to ensure they didn't waver.

Every powered vehicle in the habitat set out from the starscraper lobby, driving along the tracks through the overgrown grass. Most of them travelled directly to the other camps ringing starscraper lobbies, coercing their occupants into Bonney's scheme. It was a domino effect, spreading rapidly around Valisk's midsection.

Kiera had wanted the tubes left alone so that when they moved Valisk out of the universe the transport system could be brought back on-line to serve them. Bonney had no such inhibitions. The possessed made their reluctant way into the starscraper lobbies, and down into the first-floor stations. There they combined their energistic power and started to systematically smash the tube tunnels. Huge chunks of polyp were torn out of the walls and roof to crash down on the magnetic guide rail. Power cables were ripped up and shorted out. Carriages were fired, adding to the blockages and sending thick plumes of black smoke billowing deep into the tunnels. Management processor blocks were blasted to cinders, exposing their interface with Valisk's nerve fibres. Wave after wave of static discharges were pumped at the raw ends, sending what they hoped were pulses of pure pain down into the neural strata.

Bolstered by their successful vandalism, and Rubra's apparent inability to retaliate, the possessed began to move en mass down into the starscrapers. They sent waves of energistic power surging ahead of them, annihilating any mechanical or electrical system, wrecking artefacts and fittings. Every room, every corridor, every stairwell, were searched for non-possessed. Floor by floor they descended, recapturing the heady excitement and spirit of the original takeover. Unity infected them with strength. Individuals began to shapeshift into fantastic monsters and Earthly heroes. They weren't just going to flush out the traitor enemy, they were going to do it with malevolent finesse.

Hellhawks fluttered up from the docking ledges and began to spiral around the tubular starscrapers: an infernal flock peering into the bright oval windows with their potent senses, assisting their comrades inside.

Together they would flush him out. It was only a matter of time now.

Dariat sat opposite Tatiana in the tube carriage they took from the southern endcap. "We're going to put you in one of the spaceport's emergency escape pods," he told her. "It's going to be tough to start with, they launch at about twelve gees to get away fast. But it only lasts for eight seconds. You can take that. There's a voidhawk squadron from Kohistan standing by to pick you up as soon as you're clear."

"What about the possessed?" she asked. "Won't they try and stop me, shoot at me or something?"

"They won't know what the hell's going on. Rubra is going to fire all two hundred pods at once. The voidhawks will swallow in and snatch your pod before the hellhawks even know you're out there."

A smirk of good-humoured dubiety stroked Tatiana's face. "If you say so. I'm proud of you, Dariat. You've come through when it really counts, shown your true self. And it's a good self. Anastasia would be proud of you, too."

"Why, thank you."

"You should enjoy your victory, take heart from it. Lady Chi-ri will be smiling on you tonight. Bask in that warmth."

"We haven't won yet."

"You have. Don't you see? After all those years of struggle you've finally beaten Anstid. He hasn't dictated what you're doing now. This act is not motivated by hatred and revenge."

Dariat grinned. "Not hatred. But I'm certainly enjoying putting one over on that witch queen Bonney."

Tatiana laughed. "Me too!"

Dariat had to grab at his seat as the carriage braked sharply. Tatiana gasped as she clung to one of the vertical poles, hanging on frantically as the lights began to dim.

"What's happening?" she asked.

The carriage juddered to a halt. The lights went out, then slowly returned as the vehicle's backup electron matrix came on line.

Rubra?

Little bastards are smashing up the station you were heading for. They've cut the power to the magnetic rail, I haven't even got the reserve circuits.

Dariat hooked into the neural strata's observation routines to survey the damage. The starscraper station was a scene of violent devastation. Smouldering lumps of polyp were chiselled out of the tunnel by invisible surges of energy; the guidance rail writhed and flexed, screaming shrilly as its movements yanked its own fixing pins out of the floor; severed electrical cables swung from broken conduits overhead, spitting sparks. Laughter and catcalls rang out over the noise of the violence.

A rapid flick through other stations showed him how widespread the destruction was.

Bloody hell.

Damn right, Rubra said. **She's overdosing on the fury routine, but she's playing smart with it.**

A schematic of the tube network appeared in Dariat's mind. **Look, there are plenty of alternative routes left up to the spindle.**

Yes, right now there are. But you'll have to go back two stations before I can switch you to another tunnel. I can't restore power to the rail in your tunnel, they've

fucked the relays. The carriage will have to make it there on its own power reserve. You'd almost be quicker walking. And by the time you get there, the possessed will have wrecked a whole lot more stations. Bonney's thought this out well; the way she's isolating each stretch of tunnel will break up the entire network in another forty minutes.

So how the hell do we get to the spindle now?

Forwards. Go up to the station and walk though it. I can bring another carriage to the tunnel on the other side; that'll get you directly up to the endcap.

Walk through? You're kidding.

There's only a couple of possessed left to guard each station after they've had their rampage. Two won't be a problem.

All right, do it.

The lights dipped again as the carriage slid forwards slowly.

"Well?" Tatiana asked.

Dariat began to explain.

Starscrapers formed the major nodes in the habitat's tube network; each of them had seven stations ringing the lobby, enabling the carriages to reach any part of the interior. Individual stations were identical; chambers with a double-arch ceiling and a central platform twenty metres long which served two tubes. The polyp walls were a light powder-blue, with strips of electrophorescent cells running the entire length above the rails. There were stairs at each end of the platform, one set leading up to the starscraper lobby, the other an emergency exit to the parkland.

In the station ahead of Dariat, the possessed finished their wrecking spree and went off up the stairs to start searching the starscraper. As Rubra predicted, they left two of their number behind to watch over the four tunnel entrances. Smoke from the attack was layering the air. Flames were still licking around the big piles of ragged polyp slabs blocking the end of each tunnel. Several hologram adverts flashed on and off overhead; an already damaged projector suffering from the proximity of the possessed turned the images to a nonsense splash of colours.

Given that the fire was dying away naturally, the two possessed were somewhat bemused when, seven minutes after everyone else left, the station's sprinklers suddenly came on.

Dariat was three hundred metres down the tube tunnel, helping Tatiana out of the carriage's front emergency hatch. The tunnel had only the faintest illumination, a weak blue glow coming from a couple of narrow electrophorescent strips on the walls. It curved away gently ahead of him, putting enough solid polyp between him and the station to prevent the two possessed from perceiving him.

Tatiana jumped down the last half metre and steadied herself.

"Ready?" Dariat asked. He was already using the habitat's sensitive cells to study the pile of polyp they would have to climb over to get into the station. It didn't look too difficult, there was an easy metre and a half gap at the top.

"Ready."

Let's go, Dariat said.

The two possessed guards had given up any attempt to shield themselves from the torrent of water falling from the sprinklers. They were retreating back to the shelter of the stairs. Their clothes had turned to sturdy anoraks, streaked with glistening runnels. Every surface was slick with water now: walls, platform, floor, the piles of polyp.

Rubra overrode the circuit breakers governing the cables which powered the tube, then shunted thirteen thousand volts back into the induction rail. It was the absolute limit for the habitat's integral organic conductors, and three times the amount the carriages used. The broken guide rail jumped about as it had while it was being tormented by the possessed. Blinding white light leapt out of the magnetic couplings as it split open. It was as though someone had fired a fusion drive into the station. Water droplets spraying out of the overhead nozzles fluoresced violet, and vaporized. Metal surfaces erupted into wailing jets of sparks.

At the heart of the glaring bedlam, two bodies ignited, flaring even brighter than the seething air.

It wasn't just the one station, that would have drawn Bonney's attention like a combat wasp's targeting sensor. Rubra launched dozens of attacks simultaneously. Most of them were electrical, but there were also mass charges of servitor animals, as well as mechanoids switched back on, slashing around indiscriminately with laser welders and fission blades as energistic interference crashed their processors.

Reports of the tumult poured into the starscraper lobby where Bonney had set up her field headquarters. Her deputies shouted warnings into the powerful walkie-talkies they used to keep in contact with each other.

As soon as the blaze of white light shone down the tunnel, Dariat started to run towards it. He kept hold of Tatiana's hand, pulling her onwards. A loud caterwaul reverberated along the tunnel.

"What's Rubra doing to them?" she shouted above the din.

"What he had to."

The abusive light died and the sound faded away. Dariat could see the pile of polyp now, eighty metres ahead. A crescent-shaped sliver of light straddled it, seeping in from the station beyond.

Their feet began to splash through rivulets of water flowing down the tunnel. Tatiana grimaced as they reached the foot of the blockage, and hitched her skirt up.

Bonney listened to the frantic shouting all around her, counting up the incidents, the number of casualties. They'd got off lightly. And she knew that was wrong.

"Quiet," she bellowed. "How many stations attacked? Total?"

"Thirty-two," one of the deputies said.

"And over fifty attacks altogether. But we've only lost about seventy to eighty people in the stations. Rubra's just getting rid of the sentries we posted. If he wanted to seriously harm us he'd do it when the wrecking crews were down there."

"A diversion? Dariat's somewhere else?"

"No," she said. "Not quite. We know he uses the tubes to get around. I'll bet the little shit's in one right now. He must be. Only we've already blocked him. Rubra is clearing the sentries out of the way so Dariat can sneak through. That's why he spread the attacks around, so we'd think it was a blanket assault." She whirled around to face a naked polyp pillar and grinned with malicious triumph. "That's it, isn't it, boyo? That's what you're doing. But which way is he going, huh? The starscrapers are dead centre." She shook her head in annoyance. "All right you people, get sharp. I want someone down in each and every station Rubra attacked. And I want them down there now. Tell them to make sure they don't step in the water, and be on the lookout for servitors. But get them down there."

The image of her yelling orders at her deputies boiled into Dariat's mind like a particularly vigorous hangover. He had just reached the top of the polyp pile and squeezed under the ceiling. The station was filled with thick white mist, reducing visibility to less than five metres. Condensation had penetrated everywhere, making this side of the polyp mound dangerously unstable.

Smart bitch, Rubra said. **I didn't expect that.**

Can you delay them?

Not in this station, I can't. I haven't got any servitors nearby, and the cables have all burnt out. You'll have to run.

Image relay of a deputy with a walkie-talkie pressed to his ear hurrying across the lobby above. "I'm on it, I'm on it," he was yelling into the mike.

"Tatiana, move it!" Dariat shouted.

Tatiana was still wriggling along on her belly as she slithered over the top of the pile. "What's the matter?"

"Someone's coming."

She gave one final squirm and freed her legs. Together

they scooted down the side of the pile, bringing a minor avalanche of slushy gravel with them.

"This way." Dariat pointed into the mist. His perception filled in glass-grey outlines of the station walls through the swirls of cold vapour, enabling him to see the tunnel entrance. Valisk's sensitive cells showed him the carriage waiting a hundred and fifty metres further on. They also showed him the deputy reaching the top of the stairs.

"Wait here," he told Tatiana, and vaulted up onto the platform. His appearance changed drastically, the simple one-piece thickening to an elaborate purple uniform, complete with gold braid. The most imposing figure to dominate his youth: Colonel Chaucer. A weekly AV show of a renegade Confederation officer, a super vigilante.

Rubra was laughing softly in his head.

The deputy was halfway down the stairs when he started to slow up. He raised the walkie-talkie. "Somebody's down here."

Dariat reached the bottom of the stairs. "Only me," he called up cheerfully.

"Who the hell are you?"

"You first. This is my station."

The deputy's mind revealed his confusion as Dariat started up towards him with powerful, confident strides. This was not the action of someone trying to hide.

Dariat opened his mouth wide and spat a ball of white fire directly at the deputy's head. Two souls bawled in terror as they vanished into the beyond. The body tumbled past Dariat.

"What's happening?" The walkie-talkie was reverting back to a standard communications block as it clattered down the stairs. "What's happening? Report. Report."

There's four more on their way up from the first floor, Rubra said. Bonney ordered them to the station as soon as the deputy said he sensed someone.

Shit! We'll never make it to the carriage. They can outrun Tatiana no problem.

Call her up. I'll hide you in the starscraper.

What?

Just move!

"Tatiana! Up here, now!" He was aware of all the lift doors in the lobby sliding open. The four possessed had reached the bottom of the first-floor stairs. Tatiana jogged along the platform. She gave the corpse a quick, appalled glance.

"Come on." Dariat caught her hand and tugged hard. Her expression was resentful, but the rising anxiety in his voice spurred her. They raced up the stairs together.

Daylight shone through the circular lobby's glass walls. It had suffered very little damage; scorch marks on the polyp pillars and cracked glass were the only evidence that the possessed had arrived to search the tower.

Dariat could hear multiple footsteps pounding up one of the stairwells on the other side of the lobby, hidden by the central bank of lifts. His perception was just starting to register their minds emerging from behind the shield of polyp. Which meant they'd also be able to sense him.

He scooped Tatiana up, ignoring her startled holler, and sprinted for the lifts. Huge muscles pumped his legs in an effortless rhythm. She weighed nothing at all.

The phenomenal speed he was travelling at meant there was no chance at all of slowing once he passed the lift doors; he would have needed ten metres to come to a halt. They slammed straight into the rear wall. Tatiana shrieked as her shoulder, ribs, and leg hit flat on, with Dariat's prodigious inertia driving into her. Then his face smacked into silvery metal, and there was no energistic solution to the blast of pain jabbing into his brain. Blood squirted out of his nose, smearing the wall. As he fell he was dimly aware of the lift doors sliding shut. The light outside was growing inordinately bright.

Dariat reeled around feebly, clutching at his head as if the pressure from his fingers alone could squeeze the bruises back down out of existence. Slowly the pain subsided, which allowed him to concentrate on vanquishing the remainder. "Ho fuck." He slumped back against a wall and let his breathing calm. Tatiana was lying on the lift floor in front of him, hands pressed against her side, cold sweat on her brow.

"Anything broken?" he asked.

"I don't think so. It just hurts."

He went onto his hands and knees and crawled over to her. "Show me where."

She pointed, and he laid his hand on. With his mind he could see the smooth glowing pattern of living flesh distorted and broken below his fingers, the fissures extending deep inside her. He willed the pattern to return to its unblemished state.

Tatiana hissed in relief. "I don't know what you did, but it's better than a medical nanonic."

The lift stopped at the fiftieth floor.

Now what? Dariat asked.

Rubra showed him.

You are one evil bastard.

Why, thank you, boy.

Stanyon was leading the possessed down through the starscraper in pursuit of Dariat. He'd started off with thirty-five under his command, and that number was rapidly swelling as Bonney directed more and more from neighbouring starscrapers to assist him. She'd announced she was on her way herself. Stanyon was going balls-out to find Dariat before she arrived. He got hot just thinking about the praise (and other things) Kiera would direct at the champion who erased her bête noire from the habitat.

Eight different teams of possessed were searching, assigned a floor each. They were working their way steadily downwards, demolishing every mechanical and electrical device as they went.

He strode out of the stairwell onto the thirty-eighth-floor vestibule. For whatever reason, Rubra was no longer putting up any resistance. Muscle-membrane doors opened obediently, the lighting remained on, there wasn't a servitor in sight. He looked around, happy with what he found. The floor's mechanical utilities office had been broken open, and the machinery inside reduced to slag, preventing the sprinklers from being used. Doors into the apartments and bars and commercial offices were smashed apart, furniture and fittings inside were blazing with unnatural ferocity. Big circles of polyp flooring were cracking under the intense heat, grainy white marble surface blackening. Wisps of dirty steam fizzed up from the crannies.

"Die," Stanyon snarled. "Die a little bit at a time. Die hurting big."

He was walking towards the stairwell door when his walkie-talkie squawked: "We got him! He's down here."

Stanyon snatched the unit from his belt. "Where? Who is this? Which floor are you on?"

"This is Talthorn the Greenfoot; I'm on floor forty-nine. He's just below us. We can all sense him."

"Everybody hear that?" Stanyon yelled gleefully. "Fiftieth floor. Get your arses down there." He sprinted for the stairwell.

"They're coming," Dariat said.

Tatiana flashed him a worried-but-brave grin, and finished tying the last cord around her pillow. They were in a long-disused residential apartment; its polyp furniture of horseshoe tables and oversized scoop armchairs dominating the living room. The chairs had been turned into cushion nests to add a dash of comfort. The foam used to fill the cushions was a lightweight plastic that was ninety-five per cent nitrogen bubbles.

They were, Rubra swore, perfect buoyancy aids.

Dariat tried on his harness one last time. The cords which he'd torn from the gaudy cushion fabric held a pillow to his chest and another against his back. Seldom had he felt so ridiculous.

His doubt must have leaked onto his face.

If it works, don't try to fix it, Rubra said.

Ripe, from someone who's devoted his existence to meddling.

Game set and match, I won't even appeal. Would you like to get ready?

Dariat used the starscraper's observation routines to check on the possessed. There were twelve of them on the floor above. A rock-skinned troll was leading the pack; followed by a pair of cyber-ninjas in black flak jackets; a xenoc humanoid that was all shiny amber exoskeleton and looked like it could rip metal apart with its talons; a faerie prince wearing his forest hunting tunic and carrying a long-bow in one hand, a walkie-talkie in the other; three or four excessively hairy Neanderthals; and regular soldiers in the uniforms of assorted eras.

"The loonies are on the warpath tonight," Dariat muttered under his breath. "Finished?" he asked Tatiana.

She shifted her front pillow around and tightened the last strap to hold it in place. "I'm ready."

The bathroom's muscle-membrane door parted silently. Inside was an emerald-green suite: a circular bath, vaguely Egyptian in design, matched by the basin, bidet, and toilet. They were still all in perfect condition. It was the plumbing which had degraded. Water was dripping from the brass shower head above the bath; over the years it had produced a big orange stain on the bottom. Slimy blue-green algae was growing out of the plug. The sink was piled high with bars of soap; so old and dry now that they'd started to crumble, snowing flecks over the rim.

Dariat stood in the doorway, with Tatiana pressed against him, looking eagerly over his shoulder. "What's supposed to be happening?" she asked.

"Watch."

A bass crunching sound was coming from the toilet. Cracks appeared around its base, expanding rapidly outwards. Then the whole bowl lurched upwards, spinning around precariously before toppling over. A two-metre circle of floor around it was rising up like a miniature volcanic eruption. Polyp splintered with a continual brassy crackling. A fine jet of water sprayed out of the fractured flush pipe.

"Lord Tarrug, what are you doing?" Tatiana asked.

"That's not Tarrug, that's Rubra," Dariat told her. "No dark arts involved."

Affinity with the local sub-routines allowed him to feel the toilet's sphincter muscle straining as it contorted in directions it was never intended, rupturing the thin shell of polyp floor. It halted, fully expended. The cone which it had produced quivered slightly, then stilled. Dariat hurried over. There was a crater at the centre, leading down to an impenetrable darkness. The muscle tissue which made up the sides was a tough dark red flesh, now badly lacerated. Pale yellow fluid was oozing out of the splits, running down to disappear in the unseen space below.

"Our escape route," Dariat said, echoing Rubra's pride.

"A toilet?" she asked incredulously.

"Sure. Don't go squeamish on me now, please." He sat on the edge of the sphincter and swung his legs over the crater. It was a three-metre slither down into the sewer tubule below. When his feet touched the bottom he knelt down and held a hand out. His skin began to glow with a strong pink light. It revealed the tubule stretching on ahead of him, a circular shaft just over a metre in diameter, and angled slightly downwards.

"Throw the pillows down," he said.

Tatiana dropped them, peering over the edge of the crater with a highly dubious expression. Dariat shoved the two harnesses into the tubule, and started to worm his way in after them. "When I'm in, you follow me, okay?" He didn't give her the chance to answer. It was awkward going, pushing the pillows ahead of him as he crawled along. The grey polyp was slippery with water and fecal sludge. Dariat could hear Tatiana grunting and muttering behind him as she discovered the residue smearing the sides.

There were ridges encircling the tubule every four metres, peristaltic muscle bands that assisted the usual water flow. Despite Rubra expanding them wide, they formed awkward constrictions which Dariat had to pull himself through. He had just squeezed past the third when Rubra said: **They've reached the fiftieth floor. Can you sense them?**

Not a chance. So in theory they won't be able to find me.

They know the general direction, and they're heading towards the apartment.

Dariat was too intent on inching himself along to review the images. **What about the rest?**

On their way down. The stairwells are absolutely packed. It's like a freak-show stampede out there.

He elbowed his way through another muscle band. The light from his hand showed the tubule walls ending two metres ahead. A thick ring of muscle membrane surrounded the rim. Beyond that was a clear empty space. He could hear a steady patter of rain in the darkness.

"We made it," he shouted.

His only answer was another outbreak of grunted curses.

Dariat pushed the filthy pillows and their tangled cords over the edge, hearing them splash into the water. Then he was sliding himself over.

The main ingestion tract into which the sewer tubule emptied ran vertically up the entire height of the starscraper. It collected the human waste, discarded organic matter, and dirty water from every floor and carried it down to the large purification organs at the base of the starscraper. They filtered out organic compounds which were pumped back to the principal nutrient organs inside the southern endcap via their own web of specialist tubules. Poisons and toxins were disposed of directly into space. Fresh water was recirculated up to the habitat's storage reservoirs and parkland rivers.

Normally the main ingestion tract was a continual waterfall. Now, though, Rubra had closed the inlet channels and reversed the flow from the purification organs, allowing the water level to rise up the tract until it was level with the fiftieth floor.

The cold surface closed over Dariat's head, and he felt his feet clear the tubule. A couple of swift kicks and he surfaced, puffing a spray of droplets from his mouth. Thankfully this water was clean—relatively.

He held an arm up in the air, a sharp blue flame flickering up from his fingertips. Its light showed the true extent of the tract: twenty metres in diameter, with walls of neutral grey polyp that had the same crinkly surface texture as granite. Sewer tubule outlets formed black portals all around, their muscle-membrane rims flexing like fish mouths. The pillows were bobbing about a few metres away.

Tatiana had pushed her shoulders past the tubule's muscle membrane, and was craning her head back to look around. The tract's height defeated the illumination thrown out by Dariat's small flame, revealing barely fifteen metres of the walls above the water level. A heavy shower was falling out of the darkness which roofed them, chopping up the water's surface with small ripples.

"Come on, out you come," Dariat said. He swam back to her and helped ease her through the opening. She gasped at the water's chilly grip, arms thrashing about for a moment.

Dariat retrieved the two sets of pillows and strapped himself into the harness. He had to tie Tatiana's cords for her, the cold had numbed her fingers. When he was finished, the sewer tubules all started to close silently.

"Where are we going now?" Tatiana asked nervously.

"Straight up." He grinned. "Rubra will pump fresh water back into the base of the tract. It should take about twenty minutes to reach the top. But expect an interruption."

"Yeah?"

"Oh, yeah."

Stanyon arrived at the fiftieth floor to find it in turmoil. The vestibule was packed with excitable possessed. None of them seemed to know what was going on.

"Anybody seen him?" Stanyon shouted. Nobody had.

"Search around, there must be some trace. I want the teams that were searching floors thirty-eight and thirty-nine to go down to fifty-one and check it out."

"What's happening?" Bonney's voice asked from the walkie-talkie; there was a lot of crackling interference.

Stanyon held the unit to his face, pulling out more aerial. "He's dodged us again. But we know he's here. We'll have him any minute now."

"Make sure you stick with procedure. Remember it's not just Dariat we're up against."

"You're not the only council member left. I know what I'm doing."

"I'm a minute away from the lobby. I'll join you as fast as I can."

He gave the walkie-talkie a disgusted look and switched it off. "Terrific."

"Stanyon," someone called from the other end of the vestibule. "Stanyon, we've found something."

It was the troll, the faerie prince, and both of the cyber-ninjas who had broken into the apartment. They were hanging around the bathroom door when Stanyon arrived. He pushed his way past them impatiently.

The sides of the ruptured toilet sphincter had sagged, squeezing more of the yellow fluid out. It was running down the outside of the cone to smear the surrounding dune of polyp chippings. Water from the fractured pipe was sloshing over the floor.

Stanyon edged forwards, and peered cautiously over the crater's lip. There was nothing to see, nothing to sense. He pointed at the smaller of the two cyber-ninjas. "You, go see where it leads to."

The cyber-ninja looked at him. Red LEDs on his visor flashed slowly, an indolent blinking to mirror the thoughts they fronted.

"Go on," Stanyon said impatiently.

After a brief rebellious moment, the cyber-ninja demate-rialized his flak jacket and lowered himself down into the sewer tubule.

Dariat had been worried about the undercurrents. Need-lessly, as it turned out. They were rising fast up the giant tract with only the occasional swirl of bubbles twisting around them. It was still raining heavily, but the whole process was eerily silent.

He maintained the small flame burning coldly from his fingers, mainly for Tatiana's benefit. There was nothing to see above them, only the empty blackness. They slid smoothly past the intermittent circlets of closed tubules with monotonous regularity, their only real measure of progress.

Dariat was warm enough, circulating heat through his skin to hold the water's numbing encroachment at bay. But he did worry about Tatiana. She'd stopped talking, and her chittering teeth were clearly audible. That left him alone with his own thoughts of what was to come. And the whispers of the damned, they were always there.

Rubra, have you ever heard of someone called Alkad Mzu? he asked.

No. Why?

Capone is very interested in finding her. I think she's some kind of weapons expert.

How the hell do you know what Capone wants?

I can hear it. The souls in the beyond are calling for her. They're quite desperate to find her for the Organization.

Affinity suddenly gave him a sense of space opening around him. Then an astonishingly resolute presence emerged from the new distance. Dariat was at once fearful and amazed by its belief in itself, a contentment which was almost the opposite of hubris; it knew and accepted itself too well for arrogance. There was a nobility about it which he had never experienced, certainly not during the life he had led. Yet he knew exactly what it was.

Hello, Dariat, it said.

The Kohistan Consensus. I'm flattered.

It is intriguing for us to communicate with you. It is a rare opportunity to talk to any non-Edenist, and you are a possessor as well.

**Make the most of it, I won't be around for much
longer.**

**The action you and Rubra are undertaking is an hon-
ourable one, we applaud your courage. It cannot have
been easy for either of you.**

It was realistic.

His answer was accompanied by Rubra's emission of
irony.

We would like to ask a question, Consensus said. **Several, in fact.**

On the nature of possession, I assume. Fair enough.

**Your current viewpoint is unique, and extremely valu-
able to us.**

It's going to have to wait a minute, Rubra said. **They've
found the toilet.**

The cyber-ninja had squeezed down into the sewer tubule
and was squirming along on his belly. His mind tone was
one of complete disgust. Pale violet light illuminated the
lenses on his low-light enhancement goggles, casting a
faint glow across the polyp directly in front of him. "They
were in here," he yelled back over his shoulder. "This shit's
all been smeared around."

"Yes!" Stanyon banged a fist against the muscle-membrane
door. "Get down there," he told the second cyber-ninja.
"Help him."

The cyber-ninja did as he was told, sitting on the edge of
the crater and slinging his legs over.

"Anyone know where these pipes lead?" Stanyon asked.

"I've never been in one myself," the faerie prince said
airily. "But it'll empty into the lower floor eventually. You
could try searching down there. Unless, of course, he's simply popped up inside someone else's john and walked out."

Stanyon gave the slack cone an irritated look. The
prospect of Dariat simply walking through the habitat's
pipes to escape in the throng was intolerable. But with
everyone wearing their illusionary form it would be ap-

pallingly easy. Why can we never *organize* ourselves properly?

With extreme reluctance he switched the walkie-talkie back on. "Bonney, come in please."

Rubra opened the sphincter muscle below every single toilet on the forty-ninth, fiftieth, and fifty-first floor. It was an action which nobody noticed. There were over a hundred and eighty possessed milling around on those three levels, with more still arriving. Some were obediently searching through the rooms; most were now there simply for a piece of the action. As there was no organized plan, none of them were suspicious when all the remaining apartment doors slid open. At the same time, emergency fire-control doors quietly closed off the lift shafts.

Dariat pulled Tatiana to his chest and held her tight, locking his fingers together behind her back. "Stay with it," he said. The surface of the water was just rising over the sewer tubules of the twenty-first floor.

Bonney reached the twelfth floor well ahead of the five deputies accompanying her. She could hear them clumping down the stairwell above her. They competed against her heart hammering away inside her ribs. So far she didn't feel any fatigue, but she knew she'd have to slow down soon. It was going to take a good twenty minutes to reach the fiftieth floor.

"Bonney," her walkie-talkie said. "Come in please."

She started down the stairs to the thirteenth floor and raised the walkie-talkie to her face. "Yes, Stanyon."

"He's vanished into the pipes. I've sent some of my people after him; but I don't know where they all lead to. It's possible he might have doubled back on us. It might be an idea to leave some guards in the lobby."

"Fuckhead." Bonney slowed to a halt as mystification overshadowed her initial anger. "What pipes?"

"The waste pipes. There's kilometres of them under the floors. We found one of the toilets all smashed up. That's how he got in there."

"You mean sewer pipes?"

"Yeah."

Bonney stared at the wall. She could sense the thought routines gliding through the neural strata a metre or so behind the naked polyp. In his own fashion, Rubra was staring right back at her. He was content.

She didn't know anything about the sewer pipes, except how obvious they were in hindsight. And Rubra had absolute control over every single environmental aspect of the habitat. Dariat had been spotted for a few brief seconds, which had sent everyone chasing after him. Then he'd vanished. If the sewers could hide him so thoroughly, he should never have been found in the first place.

"Out!" she yelled at the walkie-talkie. "Get out of there! Stanyon, for fuck's sake, move!"

Rubra opened the muscle-membrane rims of the sewer tubules which served the forty-ninth, fiftieth, and fifty-first floors. The pressure exerted by a thirty-storey-high column of water filling the ingestion tract was a genuinely irresistible force.

Stanyon saw the cyber-ninja bullet out of the cone of ruined muscle to smash against the ceiling. The gust of air which blew him there gave way to a massive fist of water which howled upwards to strike the spread-eagled man full on. Its roar was pitched at roughly the level of a sense-overload sonic. Stanyon's skin blistered scarlet as his capillaries ruptured. Before he could even scream the bathroom was filled with high-velocity rain which knocked him to his feet as if he were being hammered by a fusillade of rubber bullets. He crashed back into the bath where a slim laser-straight pillar of water had burst out of the plug hole. It might just as well have been a chain saw.

Throughout the three condemned floors, every bathroom, every kitchen, and every public toilet were host to the same lethal eruption of water. The lights had gone out, and into this tormented night came the water itself, icy foaming waves that rushed through rooms and vestibules like a horizontal guillotine.

Tatiana cried out fearfully as the water began to drop.

The two of them began to circulate around the edge of the ingestion tract; slowly to start with, then picking up speed. Small waves rippled back and forth, slapping against each other to produce wobbling spires. A loud gurgling sound rose as the water fell faster.

Dariat watched in dismay as the surface tilted. At the centre of the tract it was discernibly lower than it was at the walls. They began to spiral in towards it. The gurgling grew louder still.

Rubra!

Don't worry. Another thirty seconds, that's all.

Bonney was helpless against the torrent of anguish rushing around her; the flock of souls arising from those trapped below to depart the universe, their sobs of bitterness and fright striking her harder than any physical blow. They were too near, too strong, to avoid; raw emotion amplified to insufferable levels.

She fell to her knees, muscles knotted. Tears dripped steadily from her eyes. Her own soul was in danger of being pulled along with them, a migration which commanded attendance. She fisted her hands and punched the polyp step. The pain was no more than a gentle tweak against the compulsion to join the damned once more. So she punched again, harder. Again.

Finally the carnage was over, the three floors filled to capacity with water. Narrow fan-sprays of water squirted out from the rim seals on several of the lift fire-control doors, filling the empty shafts with a fine drizzle, but the doors themselves held against the pressure. As did the stairwell muscle-membrane doors on the fifty-second floor, preventing the lower half of the starscraper from flooding. Pulverised bodies that had pressed against the ceiling were sinking slowly as pockets of air leaked out of their wounds, trailing ribbons of blood as they went.

The starscraper's ingestion tract did strange things to the gurgling sound produced by the frothing water, channelling it into an organlike harmonic that rattled Tatiana's bones.

She was inordinately glad when it began to subside. Dariat was moaning feebly in her embrace as if he were in great pain. The flame he'd produced had snuffed out, leaving them in absolute blackness. Although she couldn't see anything, she knew the water was slowing, its surface levelling out. The cold was giving her a pounding headache.

Dariat started coughing. "Bloody hell."

"Are you okay?" she asked.

"I'll survive."

"What happened?"

"We're not being chased anymore," he said flatly.

"So what's next?"

"Rubra is going to start pumping water back into the tract. We should reach the top in about fifteen minutes." He held up his hand and rekindled the little blue flame. "Think you can last that long?"

"I can last."

Bonney walked slowly out of the starscraper lobby, still shivering despite the balmy parkland air ruffling her khaki jacket. Nearly a dozen possessed were loitering outside on the grass. They were gathered together in small clusters, talking quietly in worried tones. When she appeared, all conversation ended. They stared at her, thoughts dominated by resentment, their expressions hard, unforgiving. It was the germ of the revolution.

She gazed back at them, coldly defiant. But she knew they would never take orders from her again. The authority of Kiera's council had drowned back there in the starscraper. If she wanted to go up against Dariat and Rubra now, it would be on her own. One on one, the best kind of hunt there was. She brought a hand up to her face, licking the bloody grazes which scarred each knuckle. Her smile made those possessed closest to her back away.

There were several trucks parked beside the lobby. She chose the nearest and twisted the accelerator hard. Spinning tyres tore up long scars of grass as she tugged the steering wheel around. Then the truck was speeding away from the lobby, heading for the northern endcap.

Her walkie-talkie gave a bleep. "Now what?" Rubra asked. "Come on, it was a grand hunt, but you lost. Drive over to a decent bar, have a drink. My treat."

"I haven't lost yet," she said. "He's still out there. That means I can win."

"You've lost everything. Your so-called colleagues are evacuating the starscrapers. Your council is busted. There's going to be nothing left of Kiera's little empire with this lot running around out of control."

"That's right, there's nothing left. Nothing except me and the boyo. I'm going to catch him before he can escape. I worked that one out already. You're helping him reach the spaceport. Lord knows why, but I can still spoil your game, just as you did mine. That's justice. It's also fun."

One wacko lady, Dariat commented.

She's genuine trouble, though. Always has been, Rubra said.

And continues to be so by the look of it. Especially if she gets to the spindle before me. Which is a good possibility. The water was now up to the second floor. Dariat could see the top of the ingestion tract now, the black tube puncturing a bubble of hazy pink light.

Another ninety seconds brought him level with the floor of the cistern chamber. He had emerged into the centre of a big hemispherical cavern whose walls were pierced by six huge water pipe outlets. Ribbons of water were still trickling across the sloping floor to the lip of the tract.

He struck out for the edge with a strong sidestroke, towing Tatiana along. She was almost unconscious; the cold had penetrated her body to the core. Even with his energistic strength, hauling her out of the water was tough going. Once she was clear he flopped down beside her, wishing himself warm and dry. Steam began to pour out of their clothes.

Tatiana tossed her head about, moaning as if she were

caught in a nightmare. She sat up with a spasm of muscle, her few remaining bangles chiming loudly. Vapour was still effervescing out of her dress and dreadlocks. She blinked at it in amazement. "I'm warm," she said in astonishment. "I didn't think I would ever be warm again."

"The least I could do."

"Is it over now?"

The wishful childlike tone made him press his lips together in regret. "Not quite. We still have to get up to the spaceport; there's a route through these water pipes which will eventually take us to a tube tunnel, we don't have to go up to the surface. But Bonney survived. She'll try to stop us."

Tatiana rested her chin in her hands. "Lord Thoale is testing us more than most. I'm sure he has his reasons."

"I'm not." Dariat lumbered to his feet and untied the pillow harness. "I'm sorry, but we have to get going."

She nodded miserably. "I'm coming."

The search teams which Bonney and her deputies had organized were wending their way out of Valisk's starscrapers. Shock from the flooding was evident in their shuffling footsteps and tragic eyes. They emerged from the lobbies, consoling each other as best they could.

It shouldn't have happened, was the thought which rang among them like an Edenist Consensus. They'd made it back to the salvation of reality. They were the chosen ones, the lucky ones, the blessed. Eternal life, and the precious congruent gift of sensation, had been within their grasp. Now Rubra had shown them how tenuous that claim was.

He was able to do that because they remained in a universe where his power was a match to theirs. It shouldn't be like that. Whole planets had escaped from open skies and Confederation retribution, while they stayed to entrap new bodies. Kiera's idea—and it had been a good one, bold and vigorous. Eternity spent within the confines of a single habitat would be a difficult prospect, and she had seen a way forwards.

That was why they'd acquiesced to her rule and that of the council, because she'd been right. At the start. Now though, they had increased their numbers, Kiera had flown off to negotiate their admission to a dangerous war, and Bonney committed them against Rubra to satisfy her personal vendettas.

No more. No more risks. No more foolhardy adventures. No more sick savagery of hunting. The time had come to leave it all behind.

The truck raced along the hardened track which countless wheels had compacted across the semi-arid plain surrounding Valisk's northern endcap. Bonney had the throttle at maximum, the axial motors complemented by her energistic power. Small flattened stones and cracked ridges which lay along the track sent the vehicle flying through the air in long shallow hops.

Bonney didn't even notice the jouncing, which would have caused whiplash injuries to any non-possessed riding beside her. Her mind was focused entirely on the endcap whose base was five kilometres in front of her. She imagined her beefy old vehicle beating the sleek tube capsule slicing along its magnetic rail in the tunnel below her. The one she knew he would be riding.

Up ahead she could just make out the dark line of the switchback road which wound up to the small plateau two kilometres above the plain. If she could only reach the passageway entrance before Dariat got out of the sewer tunnels and into a tube carriage she might conceivably reach the axis chamber before him.

A feeling of contentment began to seep into her mind. An insidious infiltration which called on her to respond, to generate her own dreamy satisfaction, to pledge it to the whole.

"Bastards!" She slapped furiously at the steering wheel, anger insulating her from the loving embrace which was rising up all around her. They had begun it, the gathering of power, the sharing, linking their wills. They'd submitted, *capitulated*, to their craven fear. Valisk would soon sail calmly out of this universe, sheltering them from any conceivable threat, committing them to a life of eternal boredom.

Well not for her. One of the hellhawks could take her off, away where there was struggle and excitement. Only after she'd dealt with Dariat, though. There would be time. There *had* to be.

The truck's speed began to pick up. Her stubborn insistence was diverting a fraction of the prodigious reality dysfunction which was coalescing around the habitat. The utterly implausible was becoming hard fact.

Bonney laughed gleefully as the truck shot along the track, ripping up a churning cloud of thick ochre dust behind it. While all around her, the tiny clumps of scrub grass, cacti, and lichen sprawls were sprouting big adventitious flower buds. The bland desert was quietly and miraculously transforming itself into a rich colour-riot garden as Valisk's new masters prepared to enact their vision of paradise.

The Kohistan Consensus had a thousand and one questions on the nature of possession and the beyond. Dariat sat quietly in the tube carriage taking him to the axis chamber and tried to supply answers for as many as he could. He even let them hear the terrible cries of the lost souls that infested his every thought. So that they'd know, so they'd understand the dreadful compulsion driving each possessor.

I feel strange, Rubra announced. It's like being drunk, or light headed. I think they're starting to penetrate my thought routines.

No, Dariat said. He was aware of it himself now, the reality dysfunction starting to pervade the polyp of the shell. In the distance, a chorus of minds were singing a joyous hymn of ascension. They're getting ready to leave the universe. We don't have much time.

We can confirm that, the Consensus said. Our void-hawks on observation duty are reporting large squalls of red light appearing on your shell, Rubra. The hell-

hawks appear most agitated. They are leaving their docking pedestals.

Don't let it happen, boy, Rubra said. **Come into me, please, transfer over now. We can win, we can stop them taking Valisk to their bloody haven. We can screw them yet.**

Not with Tatiana here. I won't condemn her to that. We've still got time.

Bonney's almost at the plateau.

And we're almost at the base of the endcap. This carriage can go straight up to the axis chamber. She's got to climb three kilometres of stairs. We'll make it easily.

Blue smoke spouted out of the truck's tyres as Bonney skid-braked the vehicle outside the passageway's dark entrance. When she jumped down from the driver's seat her sharp upper teeth were protruding over her lower lip, producing a permanent feral grin. Her painfully red-rimmed eyes narrowed to lethargic slits as she gazed up at the steepening cliff of grey polyp in front of her, as if puzzled by its appearance. Every movement took on a dullard's slowness. Breath wheezed heavily out of her nostrils.

She ignored the passageway and stood perfectly still, bringing her arms to rest in front of her so her hands crossed above her crotch. Her head drooped, bowing deeply, the eyes closing completely.

What the hell is she doing now? Dariat asked. **She was frantic to get up there.**

It looks like she's praying.

Somehow, I really doubt that.

The tube carriage reached the base of the endcap and started to sweep up the slope towards the hub. An urgent whining sound permeated the inside. Dariat could feel it slowing, then it accelerated again.

Damn it, I'm getting power dropouts right across the habitat. That's in the sections of myself I can still per-

ceive. I'm shrinking, boy, there are places where my
thoughts have ceased. Help me!

The reality dysfunction is strengthening. Five minutes. Hang on for five more minutes.

Bonney's khaki suit was darkening, at the same time its texture changed to a glossier aspect. She was starting to hunch
up, her legs bowing out and becoming spindly. Pointed ears
emerged from a shortening crop of hair. There was no suit
anymore, only a black pelt.

She suddenly raised her rodent head and emitted an ear-
piercing screech through a circular mouth caged by fangs.
Eyes glittered a devilish red. She opened what had been her
arms to spread her new wings wide. The leathery membrane was thin enough to be translucent, revealing a lace-
work of minute black veins beneath the dark amber surface.

Oh, fuck, Rubra exclaimed. No bloody way! I don't
care what she looks like, she weighs too much to fly.

That won't matter anymore, Dariat said. The reality
dysfunction is powerful enough to sustain her; we're in
the universe of fables, now. If she wants to fly, she will.

Bonney ran a couple of paces across the plateau, then her
wings gave a fast downwards sweep, and she was airborne.
She beat her wings steadily, rising quickly, her triumphant
screeching echoing over the blank polyp. Her flight curved
around sharply as she gained altitude, evolving into a spiral
as the beats became smoother, more insistent.

She'll catch me, a stricken Dariat said. She's going to
reach the axis chamber before me. I'll never get Tatiana
out. "Anastasia!" he cried. "My love, it can't end like this.
Not again. I can't fail you again."

Tatiana stared at him in fright, not understanding.

Do something, he begged.

Like what? Rubra's mental voice was faint, lacking interest.

Remember your classics, the Kohistan Consensus said.
Before today, Icarus and Daedalus were the only people

ever to fly with their own wings. Only one survived.
Think what happened to Icarus.

Bonney was already three hundred metres above the
plateau, swooping upwards on a tempestuous thermal,
when she noticed the change. The light was altering, which
it could never do in a habitat. She shifted her balance, twisting on a wingtip, howling at the sheer exhilaration of the
wind buffeting her face. The cylindrical landscape stretched
out in front of her, dabbed with curving smears of flushed
red cloud. For the first time, the lively sparkle coming off
the circumfluous reservoir was absent. The entire band of
water seemed to be darkened; she could barely see a single
feature on the southern endcap. Yet around her the light was
growing. That should never be. Both endcaps were always
maintained in a dappled shade. The effect was due entirely
to the nature of the light tube, a slender cylindrical mesh of
organic conductors which mimicked the shape of the habitat itself. At each end the mesh narrowed to a near solid
bundle of cable which suspended the main segment between the two hubs. The plasma it contained dwindled to a
mild violet haze eight hundred metres from the hub itself.

She could now see that horn of ions retreating from the
southern hub as Rubra increased the power flowing through
the cables at that end. The magnetic field was expanding to
squeeze the plasma along the tube. At the northern end, he
cut the power completely to one specific section of the
mesh. Plasma rushed out of the gap, inflating flamboyantly
as it liberated itself from the constricting flux lines.

From Bonney's position it was as if a small fusion bomb
had detonated above her, sending its billowing mushroom
cloud hurtling downwards.

"All this," she cried disbelievingly, "for me?"

The air caught in the cup of the endcap was torn asunder
by the racing plasma, sending her spinning madly, broken
wings wrapping her body like a velvet cloak. Then the
wave front of inflamed atoms swept across her like the
breath of an enraged sungod. It had none of the fury and
strength of a genuine fusion explosion; by the time it

reached her the plasma was nothing more than a tenuous electrically charged fog that was rapidly losing cohesion. But nevertheless, it was moving five times faster than any natural tornado, and with a temperature of tens of thousands of degrees. Her body disintegrated into splinters of vivid copper light which trailed contrails of black smoke all the way down to the resplendent desert far below.

A siren started to whistle as soon as Dariat broke the hatch seal; half of the corridor lighting panels turned red, flashing urgently. He ignored the clamour and floated through the small metallic airlock chamber.

The escape pod was a simple one-deck sphere, four metres in diameter, with twelve thickly padded acceleration couches laid out petal fashion. Dariat emerged from a hatch set at their centre. There was only one instrument panel, barely more than a series of power-up switches. He flicked them all on, watching the status schematics turn green.

Tatiana hauled herself gingerly through the airlock, looking dangerously queasy. Her dreadlocks swarmed around her head, their beads making tiny *clacking* sounds as they knocked against each other.

"Take any couch," Dariat instructed. "We're coming on line."

She rotated herself carefully into one of the couches. Webbing unfurled from its sides to creep over her.

Dariat took the couch opposite to her, so that they were feet to feet. **Are the other pods armed?**

Yes. Most of them. Dariat, I don't exist on the other side of the starscrapers anymore; I see nothing, I feel nothing, I don't even think down there.

A minute more, that's all. He reached up and pressed the launch sequencer. The airlock hatch hinged down. "I'm going to leave soon, Tatiana. Horgan will be back in charge of his own body again. Take care of him, he's only fifteen. He's going to be suffering."

"Of course I will."

"I . . . I know Rubra only forced us together to put pressure on me. But I'm still glad I met you."

"Me too. It laid a lot of old demons to rest. You showed me I was wrong."

"How?"

"I thought she'd made a mistake with you. She hadn't. The cure just took a very long time. She's going to be proud of you when you finally catch up with her."

Two-thirds of Valisk's shell was now fluorescing a lambent crimson; dazzling dawn-red light shone out of the starscraper windows. Inside, the possessed were united, they could perceive the entire habitat now. The flow of its fluids and gases through the plexus of tubules and pipes and ducts was as intimate to them as the blood pumping around their own veins and arteries. Rubra's flashing thought routines, too, were apparent, snapping through the neural strata like volleys of sheet lightning. Under their auspices his thoughts were slowing and dimming, retreating down the length of the cylinder as their will to banish the curse of him from their lives grew dominant.

They knew now of all the remaining non-possessed Rubra had hidden throughout the interior. Twenty-eight had survived Bonney's pursuit, cowering in obscure niches and alcoves dotted about the shell structure, frightened and uncertain at the ruby glimmer that was emerging within the polyp. The possessed didn't care about them, not anymore. That struggle was over. They even perceived Dariat and Tatiana lying prone on the escape pod's acceleration couches as the computer counted down the seconds. Nobody objected if they wanted to leave.

Profound changes were propagating outside the habitat. Nanonic-sized interstices flicked open, only to decay within milliseconds. The incessant foam of fluctuations was creating distortion waves similar to those generated by voidhawks. But these lacked any sort of order or focus. Chaos had visited local space-time, weakening the fabric around the shell.

Furious hellhawks swarmed above the northern endcap.

Harpies and hyperspace starships spun and swooped around each other at hazardous velocities, their flights dangerously unstable as the massive distortion effects buffeted them as a tempest treated leaves.

The bodies! they clamoured to these possessed snug inside who were capable of affinity. **Kiera promised us the bodies in zero-tau. If you leave now we will never have them. You are condemning us to a life in these constructs.**

Sorry, was the only, sheepishly embarrassed reply.

Combat sensors deployed as the hunger for retribution reverberated across the affinity band. Activation codes were loaded into combat wasps.

If we are denied eternity in human form, then you will join us in the same abyss.

The only functional thought routines Rubra had left were those in the northern endcap. Everything else was blank to him, his senses amputated. A few mysterious images were still reaching him from those bitek processors which interfaced him with the electronic architecture of the counter-rotating spaceport. Wavering sepia pictures of empty corridors, stationary transit capsules, and barren external grid sections. With them came the data streams from the spaceport's communications network.

And he'd almost lost interest in it. Dariat, he thought, had left the transfer too late; the boy was too caught up in his obsession and guilt. The end is here, night is finally eclipsing me after all these centuries. A shame. A crying shame. But at least they'll remember my name with a curse as they vegetate their way through eternity.

He jettisoned every escape pod in the spaceport.

Now, Dariat sighed.

Twelve gees rammed him down into the acceleration couch. His vision disappeared into a purple sparkle. And after thirty years the neural strata no longer resisted him.

Two entities—two egos—collided. Memories and personality patterns merged at a fundamental level. Hostility, antipathy, anger, regret, shame, an abundance of it all pouring out from both sides, and there could be no hiding from it anymore. The neural strata thrummed from collective moments of outraged pique as secrets long hidden were exposed to searing scrutiny. But the indignation cooled as the two differing strands of thought began the process of twining and integrating into a functional whole.

One half brought size to the mating, the huge neural strata, alive yet quiescent under the spell of the reality dysfunction; from the other half came the energistic effect, small in a single human, but with unlimited potential. For the first five seconds of the transfer, Dariat's essence was operating within a section of the neural strata only a few cubic metres in volume. At that level it was sufficient to halt the reality dysfunction of the possessed from paralysing any more of the neural strata. As the integration progressed and the thought routines amalgamated and multiplied it began to expand. More and more of the neural strata awoke to accommodate it.

The horrified possessed, quite literally, watched their dreams shatter around them.

Okay, you fuckers, bespoke Valisk's new personality. **PARTY'S OVER.**

As soon as the escape pods launched, a hundred voidhawks from the Kohistan Consensus swallowed in. Their appearance ten kilometres from Valisk's counter-rotating spaceport startled the already frantic hellhawks. The gulf between the two antagonistic swarms of bitek starships was slashed by targeting lasers and radar pulses.

Do not engage any targets, the voidhawks ordered. **The habitat is to be left intact, the escape pods must not be harmed.**

Two hellhawks immediately launched a salvo of combat wasps. Solid rockets had barely propelled them clear of their launch cradles before they were struck by X-ray lasers from the voidhawks. It was a perfect demonstration of the disadvantage the hellhawks suffered in any short-range combat situation. The energistic effect downgraded their electronic systems to a woefully inferior state.

Wormhole interstices sprang open, and the hellhawks dived down them, eluding any further conflict, abandoning their erstwhile abode with nothing more dangerous than a backwash of obscenities and threats.

Over two hundred escape pods were plunging away from Valisk's spaceport. Solid fuel rockets burned a glaring topaz, gifting the drab grey gridiron of the spaceport with an unrivalled dawn. As the distended skirts of flame and smoke died away, a cluster of five voidhawks surged forwards to intercept a single pod.

Tatiana knew Dariat had gone; his body had shrunk somehow, not in size, but certainly in presence. It was as if the terrible crush of acceleration had left him behind, diminishing the teenage boy lying on the couch. Horgan began to wail. She released her webbing and floated over to him. Her own free-fall nausea forgotten in the face of someone whose suffering was far worse.

"It's all right," Tatiana whispered as she hugged him. "It's all over now. He's left you for good." She even managed to surprise herself at the note of regret which had crept into her voice.

The voidhawks rendezvoused with Tatiana's pod, claimed its occupants, then swooped away from the habitat at seven gees. Valisk was now host to a war of light. The original red fluorescence was besieged by a vigorous purple shimmer sweeping down the shell from the northern endcap. As the purple area grew in size, so it grew in intensity.

Ten minutes after the escape pods were launched, the last glimmer of red was extinguished. The voidhawks were seven hundred kilometres away when it happened, and still retreating at two gees. Nobody quite knew what constituted a safe separation distance. Then their distortion fields detected Valisk's mass starting to reduce. The last image of the habitat which their sensor blisters received was of a purple-white micro-star blazing coldly. At the core of the photonic rupture, space itself broke down as bizarre energy patterns exerted a catastrophic stress.

When the glare faded and space regained its equipoise there was no evidence of the habitat's existence. However hard the voidhawks probed, they could find no residue of energy, no particles larger than a mote of dust. Valisk had neither vaporized nor shattered, it had simply and cleanly departed the universe.

11

The Kulu embassy was situated just outside Harrisburg's central governmental district; a five-storey building in the civic tradition, granite block walls and elaborately carved windows. Slender turrets and retro-modernist sculptures lined the roof in an attempt to grant the stark facade some degree of interest. To no avail; Harrisburg's ubiquitous granite reduced the most ornate architecture to the level of a neo-Gothic fortress. Even the setting, in one of the wealthier districts laid out with parks, wide streets, and century-old trees, didn't help. An office cube was an office cube, no matter what cosmetics it dabbed on.

Its neighbours comprised rich legal practices, capital-city headquarters of large companies, and expensive apartment blocks. Directly opposite, in an office which claimed to be an aircraft charter broker, Tonala's security police kept a twenty-four hour watch on everyone who went in or out. Forty minutes ago they had gone up to alert condition amber three (foreign covert action imminent) when five large, screened cars from the diplomatic fleet slid down into the embassy's underground car park. None of the officers on duty were sure if that particular alert status applied in this case; according to their colleagues at the city spaceport, the cars were full of Edenists.

The arrival of Samuel and his team had drawn considerable interest from staff inside the embassy, too. Curious, slightly apprehensive faces peered out of almost every doorway as Adrian Redway led Monica Foulkes and her new allies through the building. They took a lift eight stories below ground, to a floor which didn't exist on any blueprints logged on the city council's civil engineering computer.

Adrian Redway stopped at the door to the ESA station's operational centre and gave Samuel an awkward look. His eyes slid over the tall Edenist's shoulders to the other six Edenists waiting patiently in the corridor.

"Listen," he said heavily. "I don't mean to be an oaf about this. But we do run and correlate our entire Tonala asset network from here. Surely, you don't all need to come in?" His eyebrows quivered hopefully.

"Of course not," Samuel said graciously.

Monica gave a disgruntled sigh. She knew Samuel well enough now not to need affinity to hear the thought in his head: strange concept. If one Edenist went inside, then technically all of them did. Her hand fluttered towards him in a modestly embarrassed gesture. He winked back.

The operations centre could have been the office of any medium-sized commercial enterprise. Air-conditioned yet strangely airless, it had the standard desks with (more sophisticated than usual) processor blocks, big wall screens, ceiling-mounted AV pillars, and side offices with heavily tinted glass walls. Eleven ESA staffers were sitting in big leather chairs, monitoring what they could of the planet's current military and politico-strategic situation. Information was becoming a precious resource as Tonala's communications net started to suffer glitches; the only certainty gained from the overall picture was how close the orbital situation was getting to all-out confrontation.

Tonala's state of emergency had been matched by that of the other nations. Then in the last twenty minutes Tonala's high command had confirmed it had lost the *Spirit of Freedom* station to unknown foreign elements. In response, five warships had been dispatched to intercept the *Urschel*, *Raimo*, and the *Pinzola* to try to find out what had happened. Every other government was complaining that their deployment at this time constituted a deliberately provocative act.

Adrian led Monica and Samuel through into a conference room on the far side of the operations centre. "My chief analyst gives us two hours tops before the shooting starts for real," he said glumly as he sat at the head of the table.

"I hate to say this, but that really is secondary to our mission," Monica said. "We must secure Mzu. She cannot be killed or captured. It would be a disaster for the Confederation."

"Yeah, I accessed the report," Adrian said glumly. "The Alchemist by itself is bad enough, but in the hands of the possessed . . ."

"A fact you may not have yet," Samuel said. "The frigates *Urschel*, *Raimo*, and *Pinzola* are all Organization starships. Capone must know Dr Mzu is here; his representatives will not demonstrate any restraint or subtlety at all. Their actions could well trigger the war."

"Jeeze, they sent some spaceplanes down after they arrived. Nobody knows where the hell to, the planetary sensor coverage is wiped."

"What about local air defence coverage for the city?" Monica asked.

"Reasonably intact. Kulu supplied the hardware about eleven years ago; hardly top grade but it's still functioning. The embassy has an over-the-shoulder feed from the Tonala defence force headquarters."

"So if the Organization spaceplanes approach Harrisburg you'll be able to warn us."

"No problem."

"Good, that ought to give us a couple of minutes breathing space. Next question, did you find her?"

Adrian pretended offence. "Of course we found her," he said, grinning. "We're the ESA, remember?"

"Right; truth is always worse than rumour. Where is she?"

Adrian datavised the officer running the surveillance mission on Mzu. "She booked in at the Mercedes Hotel, or rather Voi did, as soon as they arrived. They made very little effort to cover their tracks; Voi used a credit disk registered under an alias, but it's still got her biolectric pattern. I mean, how amateur can you get?"

"They're not even amateurs, they're just kids," Samuel

said. "They eluded us on their home ground because we were rushed. Out here they're completely defenceless against any professional agency."

"Voi did approach a local security firm," Adrian said. "But she hasn't followed it up. Her request for bodyguards was cancelled. They seem to have linked up with some locals instead. We're not sure who they are. There certainly aren't any Garissa partizan cadres on Nyvan."

"How many locals?" Monica asked.

"Three or four, we think. As we don't know who they are, it's hard to be sure."

"Any interest from other agencies?"

"There have been three probes launched into the hotel's computer system. We couldn't get an origin on any of them. Whoever it was, their blocker programs are first rate."

"Is Mzu still at the Mercedes?" Monica asked.

"Not at this exact moment; but she is on her way back there from a meeting with the Opia company. Her group is passing themselves off as representatives from the Dorados defence force, which gives them a valid reason to buy armaments. I should be receiving a report on the meeting from our asset in the company any minute."

"Fine," Monica said. "We'll intercept her at the hotel."

"Very well." Adrian gave her an edgy glance. "The local police won't appreciate that."

"Sad, but irrelevant. Can you load a priority flight clearance authorization into the city's air defence network?"

"Sure, we supplied it, we have the ultimate authority codes."

"Fine, stand by to do it for the Edenist flyers. We'll use them to evac as soon as we've acquired her."

"The Kingdom will probably get expelled from this entire system if you pull a stunt like that," Adrian said. "If there's one thing Nyvan's nations hate more than each other, it's outsystem foreigners."

"Mzu wanted somewhere that was dishonest and greedy enough to supply her with weapons on a no-questions-asked basis. If this planet had built themselves a decent civilization in the first place, she wouldn't even be here. They've only themselves to blame. I mean, they've had five centuries for God's sake."

Samuel groaned chidingly.

Adrian paused, not meeting Monica's stare. "Um, my second surveillance team leader is reporting in. I've had them following that Calvert character, as you asked."

"Yes?" There was a sense of grudging inevitability in this moment, Monica thought.

"The captain contacted a data security expert as soon as he landed, a Richard Keaton. It would seem Keaton has done a good job for him. In fact, he probably origined one of the probes into the hotel computer. They're currently in a car which is heading in the general direction of the Mercedes Hotel. He'll get there before you can."

"Shit! That bloody Calvert."

"Do you want him eliminated?"

"No," Samuel said. He stopped Monica's outburst with a firm stare. "Any action at the hotel now will draw the police to it before we can get there. Our interception will be difficult enough as it is."

"All right," she grumbled.

"My team could intercept Mzu for you," Adrian said.

Monica was tempted—anything to get this *resolved.* "How many have you got on her?"

"Three cars, seven personnel."

"Mzu has at least four people with her," Samuel said.

"Agreed," Monica said regretfully. "That's too many, and God knows what they're carrying, especially these unknown locals. We have to guarantee first attempt success. Tell your team to continue their observation, Adrian, we'll join them as soon as we can."

"Do you think she'll resist?" Adrian asked.

"I would hope not," Samuel said. "After all, she is not stupid; she must know Nyvan's situation is decaying by the minute. That may well make this easier for us. We should start with an open approach to fly her outsystem. Once she realizes she has to leave with us, either willingly or by force, it would be logical for her to capitulate."

"Easier?" Monica gave him a pitying look. "This mission?"

"Mother Mary, *why*?" Voi demanded as soon as the five of them crowded back into the penthouse lift. "You can't sell out now. Think of what you've been through—Mary, what we've done for you. You can't hand it over to Capone!"

Her impassioned outburst stopped dead as Alkad turned to stare at her. "Do not argue with one of my decisions ever again."

Even Gelai and Ngong were daunted by the tone, but then they could sense the thoughts powering her.

"As Baranovich made quite clear, the Omuta option is now closed to me," Alkad said. "Worthless piece of trash though he is, he happens to be right. You cannot begin to imagine how much I resent that, because it means the one thing I never allowed myself to think in thirty years has become real. Our vengeance has become irrelevant."

"Nonsense," Voi said. "You can still hit the Omutans before the possessed do."

"Please don't display your ignorance in public, it's offensive."

"Ignorance, you bitch. Mary, you're giving the Alchemist to Capone. Giving it! You think I'm going to keep quiet about that?"

Alkad squared her shoulders; with an immense effort she spoke in a level voice to the ireful girl. "You are a simple immature child, with an equally childish fixation. You have never once thought through the consequences should your wish be granted, the suffering it will cause. For thirty years I have thought of nothing else. I created the Alchemist, Mary have mercy on me. I understand the full reality of what it can do. The responsibility for that machine is mine alone. I have never, nor will ever, shirk that. To do so would be to divorce myself from what remains of my humanity. And the consequences of the possessed obtaining it are very bad indeed. Therefore I will accept Baranovich's offer to leave this doomed planet. I will lead Capone's forces to the Alchemist. And I will then activate it. It will never be available for anyone to study and duplicate."

"But—" Voi looked around the others for support. "If you activate it, surely . . ."

"I will die. Oh, yes. And with me will die the one man I ever loved. We've been separated for thirty years, and I still love him. That purely human entanglement doesn't matter. I will even sacrifice him for this. Now do you understand my commitment and responsibility? Maybe I will come back as a possessor, or maybe I will stay in the beyond. Whatever my fate, it will be no different to any other human being. I am afraid of that, but I don't reject it. I'm not arrogant enough to think I can cheat our ultimate destination.

"Gelai and Ngong have shown me that we do retain our basic personality. That's good, because if I do come back in someone else's body, my resolve will remain intact. I *will* not build another Alchemist. Its reason for being is gone, it must go too."

Voi bent her knees slightly so her eyes were closer to Alkad's face, as if that would give her a deeper insight into the physicist's mind. "You really will, won't you? You'll kill yourself."

"I think kamikaze is a more appropriate term. But don't worry, I'm not going to dragoon you two along. I don't even consider this to be your fight, I never did. You're not Garissans, not really; you have no reason to dip your hands into blood this deep. Now be quiet and pray to Mother Mary that we can save something from this pile of shit, and get the pair of you as well as Lodi out of here. But be assured, I still consider you expendable to my goal." She turned to Gelai. "If either of you have any objection to this, then speak now, please."

"No, Doctor," Gelai said. There was the faintest smile on her lips. "I don't object. In fact, I'm rather glad it won't be used against a planet by you or Capone. But believe me, you don't want to kill yourself; once you've known the beyond, the pressure Capone can exert by promising you a body is going to be extraordinary."

"I know," Alkad said. "But choice has never played a large part in my life."

Tonala's state of emergency had drastically reduced the volume of road traffic in the capital. Normally, the churning wheels of the afternoon gridlock would turn the snow to mush and spray it over the pedestrians. Now, however, the big flakes were beginning to accumulate on the roads. Harrisburg's civic mechanoids were losing their battle to clear it away.

The transport department considered the effects such an icy blanket would have on brake response time, and ordered a general speed reduction to avoid accidents. The proscription was datavised into the control processor of individual vehicles.

"You want me to neutralize the order for this car?" Dick Keaton asked. Joshua gave the data security expert an edgy glance as he tried to decide. The answer was yes, but he said, "No," anyway, because speeding when you're a suspect foreigner in a nation on the brink of war and being followed by two local police cars is an essentially dumb thing to do.

Thanks to the general lack of cars, their tail was a prominent one, keeping a precise fifty metres behind. Its presence didn't have much effect on Joshua and his companions. The two serjeants were as vigilant as mechanoids, while Melvyn stared out at the city covered in its crisp grey mantle, the opposite of Dahybi who sat hunched up in his seat, hands clasped and paying no attention to their surroundings, almost as if he were at prayer. Dick Keaton was enjoying the ride, a pre-teen excitement which Joshua found annoying. He was trying to balance mission priorities at the same time as he reviewed what he was going to say to Mzu. A sincere but insistent invitation to return to Tranquillity, point out the shit she was in, how he had a starship waiting. It wasn't that he was bad with words, but these were just so damn important. Exactly how do you tell the semi-psychotic owner of a doomsday device to come along quietly and not make any fuss?

His communications block accepted Ashly's secure datavise and relayed it straight into his neural nanonics.

"New development," Ashly reported. "The Edenist flyers just activated their ion fields."

"Are they leaving?"

"No sign of that yet. They're still on the ground, but they're in a rapid response condition. Their agents must be close to Mzu."

"Bugger. Any news from orbit?"

"Not a thing. *Lady Macbeth* isn't due above the horizon for another eight minutes, but the spaceplane sensors haven't detected any low-orbit weapons activity yet."

"Okay. Stand by, we're approaching the hotel now. I might need you in a hurry."

"Do my best. But if these flyers don't want me to lift off, it could get tricky."

"*Lady Mac* is your last resort. She can take them out. Use her if you have to."

"Understood."

Dahybi was leaning forward in his seat to catch a glimpse of the Mercedes Hotel as the car swept along the last two hundred metres of road.

"That park would make a handy landing spot for Ashly," Melvyn commented.

"Acknowledged," Joshua said. He squinted through the windscreen as the car turned onto the loop of road which led to the hotel's broad portico. There was a car already parked in front of the doors.

Joshua datavised a halt order into their car's control processor, then directed it to one of the parking slots outside the portico. Tyres crunched on the virgin snow as they pulled in.

The two police cars stopped on the road outside.

"What is it?" Dick Keaton asked, he was almost whispering.

Joshua pointed a forefinger at the car under the portico. Several people were climbing in.

"That's Mzu," one of the serjeants said.

After so long on the trail, so much endured, Joshua felt something akin to awe now he could finally see her. Mzu hadn't changed much from the visual file stored in his neural nanonics during their one brief encounter. Features and hair the same, and she was wrapped up well in a thick navy-blue coat, but the flaky professor act had been dumped. This woman carried a deadly confidence.

If he'd ever doubted the Alchemist and Mzu's connection to it, that ended now.

"What do you want to do?" Dahybi asked. "We can stop her car. Make our pitch now."

Joshua held up a hand for silence. He'd just noticed the last two people getting into the car with Mzu. It wasn't a premonition he got from them, more like fear hot-wired direct into his brain. "Oh, Jesus."

Melvyn's electronic warfare blocks datavised a warning. He accessed the display. "What the hell?"

"I don't want to alarm you guys," Dick Keaton said. "But the people in the next car are giving us a real unfriendly look."

"Huh?" Joshua glanced over.

"And they're aiming a multiband sensor at us, too," Melvyn said.

Joshua returned the hostile stare from the two ESA agents in the car parked beside them. "Oh, fucking wonderful."

"She's leaving," one of the serjeants called.

"Jesus," Joshua grumbled. "Melvyn, are you blocking that sensor?"

"Absolutely." He gave the agents a broad toothy smile.

"Okay, we follow her. Let's just hope she's going somewhere I can have a civilized chat."

The five embassy cars carrying Monica, Samuel, and a mixed crew of ESA and Edenist operatives disregarded the city's new speed limit altogether as they raced for the hotel.

All the security police did was follow and observe; they were anxious to see where this was all leading.

They were still a kilometre from the Mercedes Hotel when Adrian Redway datavised Monica to advise her that Mzu was on the move again. "There's definitely only four people with her this time. The observation team launched a skyspy outside the hotel. It looks like there's been some sort of fight in the penthouse. Do you want access?"

"Please."

The image from the small synthetic bird hovering above the park filled her brain. Its artificial tissue wings were flapping constantly to hold it steady in the middle of the snowstorm, producing an awkward juddering. A visual-wavelength optical sensor was scanning across the penthouse's broad windows. One of them had a large jagged hole in the middle.

"I can see a lot of glass on the carpet," Monica datavised. "Something came in through that window, not out."

"But what?" Adrian asked. "That's the twenty-fifth floor."

Monica continued her review. The living-room doors had been smashed open. Long black scorch marks were chiselled deep into the one lying on the floor.

Then she switched focus to a settee. There was a foot dangling over the armrest.

"No wonder Mzu was in a hurry to leave again," she said out loud. "The possessed have tracked her down."

"Her car isn't heading for the spaceport," Samuel said. "Could the two locals with her be possessed?"

"Possible," Monica agreed hesitantly. "But the observation team said she seemed to be leading the others. They didn't think she was being coerced."

"Calvert has started following her," Adrian datavised.

"Okay. Let's see where they're all so eager to get to." She datavised the car's control processor to catch up with the observation team's vehicles.

"Someone else has now joined us," Ngong said. His voice was split between amusement and surprise. "That makes over a dozen cars now."

"And poor old Baranovich said to come alone," Alkad said. "Is he in one of them?"

"I don't know. One car certainly has some possessed in it."

"Doesn't that bother you?" Voi asked.

Alkad sank down deeper into her seat, getting herself comfortable. "Not really. This is like old times for me."

"What if they stop us?"

"Gelai, what are the police thinking?"

"They're curious, Doctor. Make that very curious."

"That's okay then; as long as they aren't going to stop us we're all right. I know the agencies, they will want to know where we're going first before they make their move."

"But Baranovich—"

"They're his problem, not ours. If he doesn't want me followed then it's up to him to do something about it."

Alkad's car navigated itself along Harrisburg's abandoned streets at a doggedly legal speed. Despite that, they made good progress, leaving the closely packed buildings of the city centre behind to venture out into the more industrial suburbs. Thirty minutes into the journey, the last of the urban clutter was discarded behind them. The slightly elevated roadway cut straight across a flat alluvial plain that was open all the way to the sea eighty kilometres away. It was a vast expanse of huge fallow fields from which tractor mechanoids and tailored bugs had eradicated any unauthorized vegetation. Trees were stunted and bent by the wind that blew in from the shore, standing hunched along the line of the drainage canals which had been dug to tame the rich black soil.

Nothing moved off the road, no animals or vehicles. They were driving across a snow desert. Large, stiff flakes were hurled horizontally against the car by the wind, taxing the guarantee of the lofriction windshield to stay clear. Even so, that didn't prevent them from seeing the fifteen cars which were now following them, a convoy that made no attempt to hide itself.

*   *   *

Adrian Redway had settled himself into one of the chairs in the ESA's operation centre and datavised his desktop processor for a filter program to access the station's incoming information streams. Even with the filter he was almost overwhelmed by the quantity of data available. Neural nanonics assigned priority gradings. Sub-routines took over from his mind's natural cross-indexing ability, leaving his consciousness free to absorb relevant details.

He focused on Mzu, principally through the observation team, then defined a peripheral activity key to alert him of any incoming factors which would affect her situation. The rate at which external events were developing on Nyvan made it unlikely he would be able to secure Monica much advance warning, but as a veteran of twenty-eight years ESA service he knew even seconds could change the entire outcome of a field operation.

"It has to be the ironberg foundry yard," he datavised to Monica after they had been driving over the farmland for twenty uneventful minutes.

"We think so, too," Monica replied. "Are the foundry's landing pads equipped with beacon guidance? If she's looking for a spaceplane pickup, they'll need a controlled approach in this weather."

"Unless they have military-grade sensors. But yes, the foundry's pads have beacons. I wouldn't like to vouch for their reliability, mind. I doubt they've been serviced since the day they were installed."

"Okay, can you run a data sweep of the foundry? And if you can access it, a security sensor review would be helpful. I'd like to know if there's anyone there waiting for her."

"I don't think you quite understand what you're asking for, that foundry is big. But I'll put a couple of my analysts on it. Just don't expect too much."

"Thanks." She gave Samuel a forlorn look. "Something wrong?"

The Edenist had been accessing their exchange via his bitek processor block. "I am reminded of the time she left

Tranquillity. We were all following after her rather like this, and look what happened that time. Possibly we should be the ones taking the initiative. If the foundry is her intended destination, she may well have a method of eluding us already in place."

"Could be. But the only way of stopping her now is to shoot the car. That would bring the police storming in."

Samuel accessed the ESA operations centre computer and reviewed the security police deployment status. "We are a long way from their designated reinforcements; and we can have the flyers here in minutes. Hurting the feelings of the Tonala government is an irrelevance compared to securing the Alchemist. Mzu has done us a favour by coming to such a remote place."

"Yeah. Well, if you're willing to bring your flyers in to evac us, I'm certainly prepared to commit our people. We've got enough firepower to stomp on the police if—" She broke off as Adrian datavised again.

"The city air defence network has just located those missing Organization spaceplanes," he told her. "They're heading right at you, Monica; three of them coming in over the sea at Mach five. Looks like you were right about the foundry being a pickup zone."

"My God, she is selling out to Capone. What a bitch."

"Looks that way."

"Can you direct the city network to shoot the spaceplanes?"

"Yes, if they get closer, but at the moment they're out of range."

"Will they be in range at the foundry?" Samuel asked.

"No. The network doesn't have any missiles, it's all beam weapons. Tonala relies on its SD platforms to kill any threat approaching from outside its boundaries."

"The flyers," Monica asked Samuel. "Can they intercept?"

"Yes." **Launch please**, he instructed the pilots.

Monica datavised her armour suit management processor to run a readiness diagnostic, then pulled her shell helmet on and sealed it. The other agents began checking their own weapons.

"Joshua, the flyers are all leaving," Ashly datavised.

"I was wondering about that," Joshua replied. "We're only about ten kilometres from the ironberg foundry now. Mzu must have arranged some kind of rendezvous there. Dick's been running some checks for us; he says that sections of the foundry electronics are glitched. There could be some possessed up ahead."

"Do you need an evac?"

Joshua glanced around the car. Melvyn and Dahybi weren't giving anything away, while Dick Keaton was merely curious. "We're not in any danger yet," one of the serjeants said.

"No. But if it happens, it's going to happen fast; and we're not in the strongest position."

"You can't pull out now. We're too close."

"You're telling me," he muttered. "All right, we'll keep on her for now. If we can get close enough to make our offer, well and good. But if the agencies start getting aggressive, then we back off. Understood, Ione?"

"Understood."

"I may be able to offer some assistance," Dick Keaton said.

"Oh?"

"The cars in this convoy are all local models. I have some program commands which could cause trouble in their control processors. It might help us get closer to your target."

"If we start doing that to the agencies, they'll use their own electronic warfare capability on us," Melvyn said. "That's if they don't just use a TIP carbine. Everybody knows what's at stake."

"They won't know it's us," Dick Keaton said.

"You hope," Melvyn said. "They're good, Joshua. No offence to Dick, but the agencies have entire departments of computer science professors writing black software for them."

Joshua enjoyed the idea of screwing up the other cars, but the way they were driving further and further into isolation was a big mitigating factor. Normal agency rules of minimum visibility wouldn't apply out here. If he upset the status quo, Melvyn was probably right about the reaction he'd get. What he really wanted was *Lady Mac* above the horizon to give them some fire support, although even her sensors would struggle to resolve anything through this snowstorm, and she wasn't due up for another forty minutes. "Dick, see what you can do to strengthen our car processors against agency software. I'll use your idea if it looks like she's getting away from us."

"Sure thing."

"Ashly, can you launch without causing undue attention?"

"I think so. There has to be someone observing me, but I'm not picking up any active sensor activity."

"Okay, launch and fly a low-visibility holding pattern ten kilometres from the yard. We'll shout for you."

The four Edenist flyers picked up velocity as they curved around the outskirts of Harrisburg, hitting Mach two thirty kilometres from the coast. Their smoothly rounded noses lined up on the ironberg foundry. Snowflakes flowing through their coherent magnetic fields sparkled a vivid blue around the forward fuselages, then vaporised to fluorescent purple streamers. To anyone under their path, it appeared as though four sunburst comets were rumbling through the atmosphere.

It was the one failing of Kulu's ion field technology that it could never be successfully hidden from sensors. The three Organization spaceplanes streaking in from the sea spotted them as soon as they lifted from the spaceport. Electronic warfare arrays were activated, seeking to blind the flyers with a full-spectrum barrage. Air-to-air missiles dropped out of their wing recesses and shot ahead at Mach ten.

The Edenist flyers saw them coming through the electronic hash. They peeled away from each other, arcing through the sky in complex evasion manoeuvres. Chaff and signature decoys spewed out of the flyers. Masers locked on and fired continuous pulses at the incoming drones.

Explosions thundered unseen above the farmland. Some of the missiles succumbed to the masers, while others followed their programs to detonate in preloaded patterns. Clouds of kinetic shrapnel threw up lethal blockades along the trajectories they predicted the flyers would use. But there were too few missiles left to create an effective kill zone.

The flyers stormed through.

It should have ended then, a duel between energy beam weapons and fuselage shielding, the two opponents so far away that in all probability they would never even see each other. But the snow forbade that; absorbing maser and thermal induction energy, cutting the effective strike range of both sides to less than five hundred metres. Flyers and spaceplanes had to get close to each other, spiralling around and around, looping, twisting, diving, climbing. Aggressors desperate to keep their beams on one point of their target's fuselage; targets frantic to keep moving, spinning to disperse the energy input. A genuine dogfight developed. Pilots blinded by the snow and clouds, dependent on sensors harassed by unremitting electronic warfare impulses. Given that both the flyers and the spaceplanes were multi-role craft, the manoeuvres lacked any real acrobatic innovation. Predication programs were the true knights of the sky, allowing pilots to keep a steady lock on their opponents. The flyers' superior agility began to pay dividends. The spaceplanes were limited by the ancient laws of aerodynamic lift and stability, restricting their tactics to classical aerial manoeuvres. While the flyers could move in any direction they wanted to providing their fusion generators had enough power.

The Organization was always going to lose.

One by one, the crippled spaceplanes tumbled out of the sky. Two of them smashed into the frozen soil outside the foundry yard, the third into the sea.

Overhead, the flyers closed formation and began to circle the vast foundry yard in anticipation of claiming their prize.

Urschel and *Pinzola* slid up over the horizon. Warned by the screams of souls torn back into the beyond, they knew what to look for. X-ray lasers stabbed down four times, their power unchecked by gravid clouds or swirling ice crystals.

The docking cradle rose out of the spaceport bay, exposing the fuselage of the *Mount's Delta* to a blaze of sunlight. At this juncture of a normal departure, a starship would spread its thermo-dump panels before it disengaged. Quinn told Dwyer to switch their heat exchange circuits to an internal store. Umbilical feeds withdrew from their couplings in the lower hull, then the hold-down latches retracted.

"Fly us fifty kilometres along Jesup's spin axis," Quinn said. "Then hold us there."

Dwyer flicked a throat mike down from his headset and muttered instructions to the flight computer. Ion thrusters lifted the clipper-class ship clear of the bay, then the secondary drive came on. *Mount's Delta* accelerated away at a fifteenth of a gee, following a clean arc above the surface of the counter-rotating spaceport.

Quinn used the holoscreens surrounding his acceleration couch to display images from the external sensor suite. Nothing else moved around the gigantic asteroid. The surrounding industrial stations had been shut down for days and were now drifting out of alignment. An inert fleet of personnel commuters, MSVs, inter-orbit cargo craft, and tankers were all docked to Jesup's counter-rotating spaceport, filling nearly every bay.

As soon as the starship rose away from the apex of the spaceport, Quinn switched the optical sensors to track the other asteroids. Dwyer watched the screens in silence as the three deserted asteroids appeared. This time there was movement visible, tiny stars were closing on the dark rocks at high velocity.

"Looks like we're just in time," Quinn said. "The nations

are getting upset about losing their ships." He spoke briefly into his mike, instructing the flight computer.

Four secure military-grade laser communicators deployed from the starship's fuselage. One pointed back at Jesup, while the other three acquired a lock on the abandoned asteroids. Each one fired an ultraviolet beam at their target, its encrypted code requesting a response. In answer, four similar ultraviolet beams transfixed the *Mount's Delta*. Impossible to intercept or interfere, they linked Quinn into the equipment his teams had been setting up.

Diagrams flashed up on the bridge screens as modulated information flooded back along the beams. Quinn entered a series of codes and watched in satisfaction as the equipment acknowledged his command authority.

"Ninety-seven nukes on-line," he said. "By the look of it, they're rigging another five as we speak. Dumb arseholes."

"Is that enough?" Dwyer asked anxiously. Loyalty would probably not be any defence if things weren't going precisely to plan. He just wished he knew what that plan was.

Quinn's grin was playful. "Let's find out, shall we?"

"No survivors," Samuel said. "None." His dignified face betrayed a profound sorrow, one hardened by the grey light of the snow-veiled landscape.

For Monica the loss was heightened by the terrible remoteness of the event. A few swift diffuse flashes of light lost among the occluded sky above the convoy, as if sheet lightning were flaring amid the snowstorm. They had seen and heard nothing of the decimated flyers crashing on the eastern edge of the foundry yard.

We have the pilots safe, the *Hoya* told Samuel and the other Edenists. Fortunately the flyers' shielding held out long enough for the transfer to complete.

Thank you, that's excellent news, Samuel said. "But not their souls," he whispered under his breath.

Monica heard him, and met his gaze. Their minds were a unison of grief, less than affinity but certainly sharing awareness.

"Practicalities," he said forlornly.

"Yes."

The car gave a fast unexpected lurch as the brakes suddenly engaged, then cut out. Everyone inside was flung forwards against their seat straps.

"Electronic warfare," shouted the ESA electronics expert who was riding with them. "They're glitching our processor."

"Is it the possessed?" Monica asked.

"No. Definitely coming through the net."

The car braked again. This time the wheels locked for several seconds, starting to skid across the slushy road before an emergency program released them.

"Go to manual," Monica instructed. She could see other cars in the convoy twisting and slithering across the dual roadway. One of the police vehicles hit the safety barrier and shot down the embankment into a frozen ditch, spraying snow as it went. Another of the big embassy cars thumped into the rear of Monica's car, crunching some of the bodywork. The impact spun them around. Monica's armour suit stiffened as she was shaken from side to side.

"It's not affecting Mzu," Samuel said. "She's pulling away from us."

"Disable the police cars," Monica told the electronics expert. "And that bloody Calvert, too." She felt a sincerely unprofessional glee as she ordered that, but it was perfectly legitimate. By separating herself and Mzu from the police and Calvert she was reducing the opportunity for interference in the mission goal.

Their driver finally seemed to master the intricacies of the car's manual controls, and they shot forwards, weaving around the other disorientated cars. "Adrian?" Monica datavised.

"With you. Nobody here can origin that electronic warfare outbreak."

"Doesn't matter, we're on top of it."

"Calvert's in front of us," the driver said. "He's right on Mzu's tail, this hasn't affected him at all."

"Shit!" Monica directed her shell helmet sensors to switch to infrared, and just caught the pink blob of Calvert's car hidden by snow a hundred and twenty metres ahead of them. Behind her, two embassy cars were already pulling away from the stalled police vehicles, while another one was creeping along the verge, trying to get around.

"Adrian, we're going to need an evac. Fast."

"Not easy."

"What do you fucking mean? Where are the embassy's Royal Marine utility planes? They should be on backup, for God's sake!"

"They're both liaising with the local defence force. It would have been suspicious if I'd called them back."

"Do it now!"

"I'm on it. You should have one there in about twenty minutes."

Monica thumped an armoured fist into the seat, splitting some of the fabric. The car was racing on through the snow, surprisingly stable for one under manual control. Four sets of headlights were visible behind them. A fast datavised review informed Monica they were all embassy cars, which gave her some satisfaction.

She put her machine gun down and picked up a maser carbine, then undid her seat belt.

"Now what?" Samuel asked as she leaned forward to get a better view through the windscreen.

"Joshua Calvert, your time is up."

"Uh oh," said the electronics expert. He looked up in reflex.

Ashly approached the ironberg foundry yard from the west, following five minutes behind the Edenist flyers. The spaceplane's forward passive sensor suite revealed the basics of the missile launch and dogfight. Then the X-ray lasers had fired from orbit. He held his breath as the sensors reported a microwave radar beam sweep across the fuselage. It came from the starships seven hundred kilometres above.

Now is not a good time to die. Especially as I know

what's in store if I do. Kelly was right: screw fate and destiny, just spend the rest of time in zero-tau. I think I might try that if I get out of this.

Nothing happened.

Ashly let out a shudder of breath, finding his palms sweating. "Thank you whoever thought up low-visibility profiling," he said out loud. With its top-grade stealth systems active, the spaceplane was probably invisible to any sensor on, or orbiting, Nyvan. His only worry had been an infrared signature, but the thick snow eradicated that.

He ordered the spaceplane's computer to open a secure channel to Tonala's net, hoping no one with heavy weaponry would detect the tiny signal. "Joshua?" he datavised.

"Jesus, Ashly, we thought you'd been hit."

"Not in this machine."

"Where are you?"

"Thirty kilometres from the foundry yard. I'm about to go into a holding pattern. What's happening down there?"

"Some idiot used electronic warfare on the cars. We're okay; Dick hardened our programs. But the police are out of it for the moment. We're still on Mzu's tail. I think a couple of embassy cars are behind us, maybe more."

"Is Mzu still heading for the foundry yard?"

"Looks like it."

"Well unless the cavalry comes up over the hill, we're the only pickup she's got left. There's nothing flying within my sensor range."

"Unless they're stealthed, too."

"You've always got to look on the bleak side, haven't you?"

"Just being cautious."

"Well if they're stealthed, I . . ." Ashly broke off as the flight computer warned him of another radar sweep emanating from the starships. The beam was configured differently this time, a ground scan profile. "Joshua, they're hunting you. Get out! Get out of the car!"

Every electronic warfare block in the embassy car was datavising frantic alerts.

We are being targeted by the Organization frigates, Samuel told *Hoya* and Niveu. There was little he could do to conceal his rising panic. Once, the knowledge that his memories would be held safely in the *Hoya* would have been enough for him. Now he wasn't so sure that was all that mattered. **You must stop them. If they kill Mzu, it's all over.**

The snow-lashed sky behind the car flashed purple.

After tens of kilometres of entirely passive pursuit across the tundralike farmland, the Tonala security police had been caught out badly by the sudden electronic warfare attack. Of all the cars, theirs came off worst, leaving them scattered across both roadways as their surveillance suspects, quite infuriatingly, dodged around them as if they were nothing more than inconvenient roadcones. It took time for them to rally; processors had to be disengaged to allow the manual controls to be activated, officers from cars that had gone over the embankment or smashed into the barrier sprinted for cars that were still functional, swiping huge gobs of crash cushion foam from their suits. Once they had reorganized they began to drive fast after their quarry.

It meant that their cars were still bunched together, supplying the Organization starships with the biggest target. Oscar Kearn, uncertain which one contained Mzu, decided to start there and eliminate the other cars one at a time until her soul was claimed by the beyond. With that, they would have won. Bringing her back, one way or another, was all that mattered. Now the spaceplanes had been destroyed, she would have to die. Fortunately, as an ex-military man himself, he had prepared his fallback options. So far Mzu had proved amazingly elusive, or just plain lucky. He was determined to put an end to that.

The ironberg foundry yard pickup had been planned in some detail with Baranovich, its location and timing quite critical. Although Oscar Kearn hadn't actually mentioned *how* critical to the newly allied Cossack, nor why. But he was satisfied that if things went bad for the Organization on the ground, Mzu would never survive.

Firstly, the frigates would be overhead, able to initiate a ground strike. And if she somehow escaped that . . .

While the Organization starships were docked with the *Spirit of Freedom* they had gained command access to the tugs delivering Tonala's ironbergs for splashdown. A small alteration had been made to the trajectory of one tug.

Far above Nyvan's ocean, to the west of Tonala, an ironberg was already slipping through the ionosphere. This time, no recovery fleet would be needed. No ships would be employed to tow it on a week-long voyage to the foundry yard.

It was taking the direct route.

The first X-ray laser blast struck the police car which was lying down the embankment, hood embedded in the ditch. It vaporized in a violent shock wave, sending droplets of molten metal, roasted earth, and superheated steam churning into the air. All the snow within a two-hundred-metre radius was ripped from the ground before the heat turned it back into water. The other car abandoned on the road was somersaulted over and over, smashing its windows and sending wheels spinning through the air.

The first explosion made Alkad wince. She glanced out of the rear window, seeing an orange corona slowly shrinking back down into the road.

"What the hell did that?" Voi asked.

"Not us," Gelai said. "Not one of the possessed, not even a dozen. We don't have that much power."

A second explosion sounded, rattling the car badly.

"It's me," Alkad said. "They want me."

Another explosion lit up the sky. This time the pressure wave pushed at their car, sending it skidding sideways before the control processor could compensate.

"They're getting closer," Eriba cried. "Mother Mary, help us."

"There's not much She can do for us now," Alkad said. "It's up to the agencies."

The four voidhawks were in a standard five-hundred-kilometre equatorial parking orbit above Nyvan when *Hoya* received Samuel's frantic call. Their position allowed them to shadow the Organization frigates which were strung out along a high-inclination orbit. At the time, only the *Urschel* and the *Pinzola* were above the ironberg foundry yard's horizon. *Raimo* was trailing them by two thousand kilometres.

Although it was four thousand kilometres from the *Urschel* and *Pinzola*, *Hoya*'s sensors could just detect the brilliant purple discharge in the clouds below the Organization frigates as they fired on a fourth car. The voidhawk began to accelerate at seven gees, followed by its three cousins. All four went to full combat alert status. A salvo of fifteen combat wasps slid out of *Hoya*'s lower hull cradles, each one charging away in a different direction at thirty gees, leaving the voidhawk at the centre of an expanding and dimming nimbus of exhaust plasma. After five seconds, the drones curved around to align themselves on the Organization frigates.

Urschel and *Pinzola* had no choice but to defend themselves. Their reaction time was hardly optimum, but twenty-five combat wasps flew out of each frigate to counter the attackers, antimatter propulsion quickly pushing them up to forty gees. The frigates broke off their attack on the cars, realigning their X-ray lasers ready for the inevitable swarm of submunitions.

Raimo launched its own salvo of combat wasps in support of its confederates, opening up a new angle of attack against the voidhawks. Two of them responded with defensive salvos.

Over a hundred combat wasps launched in less than twenty seconds. The glare from their drives shimmered off the nighttime clouds below, a radiance far exceeding any natural moonlight.

Despite the continuing electronic warfare emission from the SD platforms, none of the orbiting network sensors could miss such a deadly spectacle. Threat analysis programs controlling each network initiated what they estimated was an appropriate level of response.

Officially, Tonala's ironberg foundry yard sprawled for over eighteen kilometres along the coast, extending back inland between eight and ten kilometres according to the lie of the land. That, anyway, was the area which the government had originally set aside for the project in 2407, with an optimism which matched the one prevalent during Floreso's arrival into Nyvan orbit three years earlier. Apart from the asteroid's biosphere cavern, the foundry became Tonala's largest ever civil engineering development.

It started off in a promising enough fashion. First came a small coastal port to berth the tugs which recovered the ironbergs from their mid-ocean splashdown. With that construction under way, the engineers started excavating a huge seawater canal running parallel to the coastline. A hundred and twenty metres wide and thirty deep, it was designed to accommodate the ironbergs, allowing them to be towed into the Disassembly Sheds which were to be the centrepiece of the yard. The main canal branched twenty times, sprouting kilometre-long channels which would each end at a shed.

After the first seven Disassembly Sheds were completed, an audit by the Tonalan Treasury revealed the nation didn't require the metal production capacity already built. Funds for the remaining Disassembly Sheds were suspended until the economy expanded to warrant them. That was in 2458. Since then, the thirteen unused branch canals gradually choked up with weeds and silt until they eventually became nothing more than large, perfectly rectangular saltwater marshes. In 2580, Harrisburg University's biology department successfully had them declared part of the national nature park reserve.

Those Disassembly Sheds which did get built were massive cuboid structures, two hundred metres a side, and very basic. An immense skeletal framework was thrown up, bridging the end of the branch canal, then cloaked in flat composite panels. A vertical petal door above the canal allowed the ironberg egress. Inside, powerful fission blades on the end of gantry arms performed a preprogrammed dissection, slicing the ironberg into thousand-tonne segments like some gigantic metal fruit.

A second network of smaller canals connected the Disassembly Sheds with the actual foundry buildings, allowing the bulky, awkwardly shaped segments of spongesteel to be floated directly to the smelter intakes. The desolate land between the Disassembly Sheds, foundry buildings, and canals was crisscrossed by a maze of roads, some no more than dirt tracks, while others were broad decaying roadways built to carry heavy plant during the heady early days of construction. None of them had modern guidance tracking cables; foundry crews didn't care, they knew the layout and drove manually. It meant that any visitors venturing deep into the yard invariably took wrong turnings. Not that they could ever get lost, the gargantuan Disassembly Sheds were visible for tens of kilometres, rising up out of the featureless alluvial plain like the blocks some local god had forgotten to sculpt mountains out of during Nyvan's creation. They made perfect navigational reference aides. Under normal conditions.

The road was over eighty years old; coastal winters had washed soil away from under it and frozen the surface, flexing it up and down until it snapped. There wasn't a single flat stretch anywhere, a fact disguised by fancifully wind-sculpted drifts of snow. Alkad's car lumbered along at barely more than walking pace as the suspension rocked the body from side to side.

They'd driven into the yard at a dangerously high speed along the roadway. A fifth car had been wiped out behind them, then the blasts of energy from space seemed to stop. Alkad datavised the car's control processor to turn off at the first junction. According to the map she had loaded into her neural nanonics memory cell, the Disassembly Sheds were strung out across the yard's northern quadrant.

But as she was rapidly discovering: the map is not the territory.

"I can't see a bloody thing," Voi said. "I don't even know if we're on a road anymore."

Eriba peered forwards, his nose almost touching the windshield. "The Sheds have to be out there somewhere. They're huge."

"The guidance processor says we're heading north," Alkad said. "Keep looking." She glanced out of the back window to see the car following her bouncing about heavily, its headlight beams slashing about through the snow. "Can you sense Baranovich?" she asked Gelai.

"Faintly, yes." Her hand waved ahead and slightly to the left. "He's out there; and he's got a lot of friends with him."

"How many?"

"About twenty, maybe more. It's difficult at this distance, and they're moving about."

Voi sucked her breath in fiercely. "Too many."

"Is Lodi with them?"

"Possibly."

A massive chunk of machinery lay along the side of the road, some metallic fossil from the age of greater ambitions. Once they'd passed it, a strong red-gold radiance flooded over the car. A faint roar made the windows tremble.

"One of the smelters," Ngong said.

"Which means the Disassembly Sheds are on this side." Voi pointed confidently.

The road became smoother, and the car picked up speed. Its tyres began to squelch through slush that had melted in the radiance of the smelter. They could see the silhouette of the furnace building now, a long black rectangle with hangarlike doors fully open to show eight streams of radiant molten metal pouring out of the hulking smelter into narrow channels which wound away deeper into the building. Thick jets of steam were shooting out of vents in the roof. Snowflakes reverted to sour rain as they fell through them.

Alkad yelled in fright, and datavised an emergency stop order to the car's control processor. They juddered to a halt two metres short of the canal. A segment of ironberg was sliding along sedately just in front of them, a tarnished silver banana shape with its skin pocked by millions of tiny black craters.

The sky above turned a brilliant silver, stamping a black and white image of the canal and the ironberg segment on the back of Alkad's retina. "Holy Mother Mary," she breathed.

The awesome light faded.

"My processor block's crashed," Eriba said. He was twisting his head around, trying to find the source of the light. "What was that?"

"They're shooting at the cars again," Voi said.

Alkad datavised the car's control processor, not surprised when she couldn't get a response. It confirmed the cause: emp. "I wish it was only that," she told them, marvelling sadly at their innocence. Even now they didn't grasp the enormity of what was involved, the length to which others would go. She reached under the dashboard and twisted the release for the manual steering column. Thankfully, it swung up in front of a startled Eriba. "Drive," she instructed. "There'll be a bridge or something in a minute. But just drive."

"Oh, bloody hell," Sarha grumbled. "Here we go again."

Lady Mac's combat sensor clusters were relaying an all-too-clear image of space above Nyvan into her neural nanonics. Ten seconds ago all had been clear and calm. The various SD platforms were still conducting their pointless electronic war unabated. Ships were moving towards the three abandoned asteroids, two squadrons of frigates from different nations were closing on Jesup; while Tonala's low-orbit squadron was moving to intercept the Organization ships. This orbital chess game between the nations could have gone on for hours yet, allowing Joshua and the others plenty of time to get back up to the ship, and for all of them to jump the hell away from this deranged planet.

Then the Organization frigates had started shooting. The voidhawks accelerated out of parking orbit. And space was full of combat wasps.

"Velocity confirmed," Beaulieu barked. "Forty gees, plus. Antimatter propulsion."

"Christ," Liol said. "Now what do we do?"

"Nothing," Sarha snapped. So far, the conflict was ahead of them and at a slightly higher altitude. "Standby for emp." She datavised a procedural stand-by order into the flight computer. "Damn, I wish Joshua were here, he could fly us out of this in his sleep."

Liol gave her a hurt look.

Four swarms of combat wasps were in flight, etching dazzling strands of light across the darkened continents and oceans. They began to jettison their submunitions, and everything became far too complicated for the human mind to follow. Symbols erupted across the display Sarha's neural nanonics provided as she asked the tactical analysis program for simplified interpretations.

Nyvan's nightside had ceased to become dark, enlivened by hundreds of incandescent exhausts blurring together as they engaged each other. It was the fusion bombs which went off first, then an antimatter charge detonated.

Space ahead of *Lady Mac* went into blazeout. No sensor was capable of penetrating that stupendous energy release.

Tactically, it wasn't the best action. The blast destroyed every combat wasp submunitions friend or foe within a hundred kilometres, while its emp disabled an even larger number.

"Damage report?" Sarha asked.

"Some sensor damage," Beaulieu said. "Backups coming on-line. No fuselage energy penetration."

"Liol!"

"Uh? Oh. Yeah. Flight systems intact, generators on-line. Attitude stable."

"The SD platforms are launching," Beaulieu warned. "They're really letting loose. Saturation assault!"

"I can get us out of here," Liol said. "Two minutes to jump altitude."

"No," Sarha said. "If we move, they'll target us. Right now we stay low and inert. We don't launch, we don't emit. If anything does lock on, we kill it with the masers and countermeasure its launch origin. Then you shift our inclination three degrees either way, not our altitude. Got that?"

"Got it." His voice was hot and high.

"Relax, Liol, everyone's forgotten about us. We just stay intact to pick Joshua up, that's our mission, that's all we do. I want you cool for a smooth response when it comes. And it will. Use a stim program if you have to."

"No. I'm all right now."

Another antimatter explosion obliterated a vast section of the universe. Broken submunitions came spinning out of the epicentre.

"Lock on," Beaulieu reported. "Three submunitions. One kinetic, two nukes. I think; catalogue match is sixty per cent. Twenty gees only, real geriatrics."

"Okay," Sarha said, proud to find how calm she was. "Kick-ass time."

A deluge of light from the second antimatter explosion revealed the Disassembly Sheds to all the cars speeding across the foundry yard. A row of blank two-dimensional squares receding to the horizon.

"Go for it!" Alkad urged.

Eriba thumbed the throttle forwards. The snow was abating now, revealing more of the ground ahead, giving him confidence. Furnaces glowed in the distance, coronas of slumbering dragons smeared by flurries of grey flakes. The battered road took them past long-forsaken fields of carbon concrete where ranks of sun-bleached gantries stood as memorials to machinery and buildings aborted by financial reality. Pipes wide enough to swallow the car angled up out of the stony soil like metallized worms; their ends capped by rusting grilles which issued strange heavy vapours. Lonely wolf-analogues prowled among the destitute technological carcasses, skulking in the shadows whenever the car's headlights ventured close.

Seeing the other cars falling behind, Eriba aimed for a swing bridge over the next small canal. The car wheels left the floor as it charged over the apex of the two segments. Alkad was flung forwards as it banged down on the other side.

"That's Shed Six," Voi said, eagerly looking out of a side window. "One more canal to go."

"We're going to make it," Eriba shouted back. He was completely absorbed by the race, adrenaline rush giving his world a provocative edge.

"That's good," Alkad said. Anything else would have sounded churlish.

The snow clouds above the yard were slowly tearing open, showing ragged tracts of evening sky. It was alight with plasma fire; drive exhausts and explosions merging and expanding into a single blanket of iridescence that was alive with choppy internal tides.

Joshua kinked his neck back at a difficult angle to watch it. The car jounced about, determined to deny him an uninterrupted view. Since the first antimatter bomb's emp had wrecked their car's electronics Dahybi had been driving them manually. It was a bumpy ride.

Another antimatter explosion turned the remaining clouds transparent. Joshua's retinal implants prevented any lasting damage to his eyes, but he still had to blink furiously to clear the brilliant purple afterimage away.

"Jesus, I hope they're all right up there."

"Sarha knows what she's doing," Melvyn said. "Besides, we've got another twenty minutes before they're above the horizon, and that blast was almost directly overhead."

"Sure, right."

"Hang on," Dahybi called.

The car shot over a swing bridge, taking flight at the top. They thumped down, skittling sideways until the rear bumper smacked into the road's side barrier. A wicked grinding sound told them they'd lost more bodywork until Dahybi managed to straighten out again.

"She's pulling ahead," Melvyn pointed out calmly.

"Can you do any fucking better?" Dahybi yelled back.

Joshua couldn't remember the composed node specialist ever getting so aggrieved before. He heard another *crunch* behind them as the first embassy car cleared the bridge.

"Just keep on her," Joshua said. "You're doing fine."

"Where the hell is she going?" Melvyn wondered out loud.

"More to the point, why doesn't she care that this circus procession is following her?" Joshua replied. "She has to be pretty confident about whoever she's meeting."

"Who or what." Melvyn sucked in a breath. "You don't think the Alchemist is hidden around here, do you? I mean, look at this place, you could lose a squadron of starships out here."

"Don't let's imagine things worse than they are," Joshua said. "My main concern is those two possessed with her."

"I should be able to deal with them," a serjeant said. It touched one of the weapons clipped to its belt.

Joshua managed a twitched smile. It was becoming harder for him to associate these increasingly combat-adept serjeants with the old sweet, sexy Ione.

"What's the Alchemist?" Dick Keaton asked.

When Joshua turned back to their passenger, he was startled by the flood of curiosity emanating from the man. It was what he imagined Edenist affinity must be like. The emotion *dominated.* "Need to know only, sorry."

Dick Keaton seemed to have some trouble returning to his usual blasé cockiness.

It bothered Joshua quite badly for some reason. The first glimpse of something hidden behind the mask. Something very wrong, and very deeply hidden.

"They're changing direction," Dahybi warned.

Mzu's car had left the narrow road which ran between the swing bridges, turning onto a more substantial road which led towards Disassembly Shed Four. Dahybi tugged the steering column over as far as it would go, almost missing the junction as they careered around after her.

After standing up against two centuries of saltwater corrosion, cheap slipshod maintenance, bird excrement, algae, and in one memorable instance a small aircraft crash, the walls and roof of Disassembly Shed Four were in a sorry state. Despite that, the structure's scale was still impressive to the point of intimidating. Joshua had seen far bigger buildings, but not in isolation like this.

"Joshua, look at the last car," a serjeant said.

Five other cars were still part of the chase. Four of them were big towncars from the Kulu embassy; all smooth dark bodies with opaque windows and powerful fanbeam headlights. The fifth had started out an ordinary car with dark green bodywork; now it was some primitive monstrosity with bright scarlet paint that was covered in brash stickers. Six round headlights were affixed to a lattice of metal struts which covered the front grille. Primitive it might have been, but it was closing up fast on the last embassy car, its broad tyres giving it excellent traction on the slush.

"Jesus, they're in front and behind."

"This might be a good time for us to retire gracefully," Melvyn said.

Joshua glanced ahead. They were already in the shadow thrown by Disassembly Shed Four. Mzu's car was almost at the base of the colossal wall, and braking to a halt.

It was very tempting. And he was in an agony of denial not knowing what had happened to *Lady Mac*.

"Trouble," Dick Keaton said. He was holding up a processor block, swinging it around to try to locate something. "Some kind of electronic distortion is focusing on us. Don't know what kind, it's more powerful than the emp though."

Joshua ordered his neural nanonics to run a diagnostic. The program never completed. "Possessed!" intuition was screaming at him. "Out, everybody out. Go for cover."

Dahybi slammed the brakes on. The doors were opening

before they stopped. Mzu's car was fifteen metres in front of them, stationary and empty.

Joshua threw himself out of the car, taking a couple of fast steps before flinging himself flat onto the slush. One of the serjeants hit the road beside him.

A tremendous jet of white fire squirted down from the shed. It swamped the top of the car, sending ravenous tentacles curling down through the open doors. Glass blew out, and the interior combusted instantly, burning with eerie fury.

Ione knew exactly what she had to do, one consciousness puppeting two bodies. As soon as the first wave of heat swelled overhead she was rising, adopting a crouch position. Four hands were bringing four different guns to bear. As there was one serjeant on either side of the car, she could triangulate the source of the energistic attack perfectly: a line of dirt-greyed windows thirty metres up the shed wall. Two of them had swung open.

She opened fire. First priority was to suppress the possessed, give them so much to worry about they'd be unable to continue their own assault. Two of the guns she held were rapid-fire machine pistols, capable of firing over a hundred bullets a second. She used them in half-second bursts, swinging them in fast arcs. The windows, surrounding panels, stress rods, and secondary structural girders disintegrated into an avalanche of scything chips as the bullets savaged them. The heavy-calibre rifles followed, explosive-tipped shells chewing ferociously at the edges of the initial devastation. Then she began slamming rounds into the panelling where she estimated the walkway the possessed were using was situated.

"Go!" she bellowed from both throats. "Get inside, there's cover there."

Joshua rolled over fast and started sprinting. Melvyn was right behind him. There was nothing to hear above the bone-jarring vibration of the rifles, no pounding footsteps or shouts of alarm. He just kept running.

A streamer of white fire churned through the air above

him. It was hard to distinguish in the light fluxing down from the orbital battle. The foundry yard was soaked in a brightness twice as great as the noonday sun, a glare made all the worse by the snow.

Ione saw the fire coming right at her down one half of her vision and pointed the rifle and machine gun along the angle of approach. She held the triggers down on both of them, bullets flaring indigo as if they were tracer rounds. The white fire struck, and she cancelled the serjeant's tactile nerves, banishing pain. Her machine-gun magazine was exhausted, but she kept on firing the rifle, holding it steady even though the fire burned away her eyes along with her leathery skin.

Then her consciousness was in only one of the bitek constructs; she could see the flaming outline of the other fall to the ground. And shadows were flittering in the dusk behind the yawning hole she'd blasted in the wall. She slapped a new magazine in the machine gun and raised both barrels.

Joshua had just passed Mzu's car when the explosive round went crack mere centimetres from his skull. He flinched, throwing his arms up defensively. A small door in the shed wall just in front of him disintegrated. It took a tremendous act of trust, but he kept on going. Ione had opened the way. There had to be some kind of sanctuary in there.

Alkad Mzu didn't regard the interior of Disassembly Shed Four as sanctuary, exactly, but she was grateful to reach it nonetheless. The cars were still pursuing her, berserk high-speed skids and swerves across the road showing just how intent their occupants were. At least inside the shed she could choose her opponents.

Just as Ngong closed the small door she caught a glimpse of the surviving police cars leaping the swing bridge, their blue and red strobes flashing. The snow was hot with irradiated light from the battle above, and growing ever brighter. Ngong clanged the door shut and slammed the bolts across.

Alkad stood waiting for her retinal implants to adjust to

the sombre darkness. It took them longer than it should; and her neural nanonics were totally off-line. Baranovich was close.

They made their way forwards through a forest of metal pillars. The shed's framework structure extended some distance from the panel wall it was supporting, uncountable trusses and struts melding together in asymmetric junctions. Looking straight up, it was impossible to see the roof, only the labyrinthine intertexture of black metal forming an impenetrable barrier. Each tube and I-beam was slick with water, beads of condensation tickled by gravity until they dropped. With the shed's conditioning turned off, the inside was a permanent drizzle.

Alkad led the others forwards, out from under the artless pillars. There was no ironberg in the huge basin at the middle of the shed, so the water was slopping quietly against the rim. The cranes, the gantry arms with their huge fission blades, the mobile inspection platforms, all of them hung still and silent around the sides of the central high bay. Sounds didn't echo here, they were absorbed by the prickly fur of metal inside the walls. Scraps of light escaped through lacunas in the roof buttresses, producing a crisscross of white beams that always seemed to fade away before they reached the ground. Big seabirds scurried about through the air, endlessly swapping perches as if they were searching for the perfect vantage point.

"Up here, Dr Mzu," a voice called out.

She turned around, head tilted back, hand held in a salute to shield her face from the gentle rain. Baranovich was standing on a walkway forty metres above the ground, leaning casually against the safety railing. His colourful Cossack costume shone splendidly amid the gloom. Several people stood in the shadows behind him.

"All right," she said. "I'm here. Where's my transport off-planet? From what I can see, there's some difficulty in orbit right now."

"Don't get smart with me, Doctor. The Organization isn't

going to be wiped out by one small war between SD platforms."

"Lodi is up there," Gelai said quietly. "The other possessed are becoming agitated by the approaching cars."

"I don't suppose it will," Alkad shouted back. "So our arrangement still stands. You let Lodi go, and I'll come with you."

"The arrangement, Doctor, was that you come alone. But I'm a reasonable man. I'll see to it that you reach the Organization. Oh, and here's Lodi."

He was flung over the safety barrier just as Ione's guns started to demolish the windows and panelling. His screams were lost amid the roar of the explosive arounds. Arms windmilled in pathetic desperation, their motion caught by the strobe effect of the explosions. He hit the carbon concrete with a dreadful wet thud.

"See, Doctor? I let him go."

Alkad stared at the lad's body, desperate to reject what she'd seen. It was, she realized in some shock, the first time she'd actually witnessed somebody being killed. Murdered.

"Mother Mary, he was just a boy."

Voi whimpered behind her.

Baranovich was laughing. Those on the walkway with him joined hands. A plume of white fire speared down towards Alkad.

Both Gelai and Ngong grabbed hold of her arms. When the white fire hit, it was like a sluice of dazzling warm water. She swayed backwards under the impact, crying out from surprise rather than pain. The strike abated, leaving her itching all over.

"Step aside," Baranovich shouted angrily. "She belongs to us."

Gelai grinned evilly and raised a hand as if to wave. The walkway under Baranovich's feet split with a loud brassy creak. He gave a dismayed yell and made a grab for the safety rail.

"Run!" Gelai urged.

Alkad hesitated for an instant, looking back at Lodi's

body for any conceivable sign of life. There was too much blood for that. Together with the others, she pelted back to the relative safety of the metal support pillars.

"I can't die yet," she said frantically. "I have to get to the Alchemist first. I have to, it's the only way."

A figure stepped out in front of her. "Dr Mzu, I presume," said Joshua. "Remember me?"

She gaped at him, too incredulous to speak. Three other men were standing behind him; two of them were nervously pointing machine guns at Gelai and Ngong.

"Who is *this*?" a very confused Voi asked.

Alkad gave a little laugh that was close to hysteria. "Captain Calvert, from Tranquillity."

Joshua clicked his heels and did a little bow. "On the button, Doc. I'm flattered. And *Lady Mac*'s in orbit here ready to take you back home. The Lord of Ruin is pretty pissed at you for disappearing, but she says she'll forgive you providing your nasty little secret stays secret forever."

"You work for Ione Saldana?"

"Yeah. She'll be here in the sort-of flesh in a minute to confirm the offer. But right now, my priority is to get you and your friends out of here." He gave Gelai and Ngong the eye. "Some of your friends. I don't know what the story with these two is, but I'm not having—" The cold, unmistakable shape of a pistol muzzle was pressed firmly into the back of his neck.

"Thank you, Captain Calvert," Monica's voice purred with triumph. "But us professionals will take it from here."

The air on board the *Urschel* was clotted by rank gases and far too much humidity. Those conditioning filters still functioning emitted an alarmingly loud buzzing as fan motors spun towards overload. Innumerable light panels had failed, hatch actuators were unreliable at best, discarded food wrappers fluttered about everywhere.

Cherri Barnes hated the sloppiness and disorder. Efficiency on a starship was more than just habit, it was an essential survival requirement. A crew was utterly dependent on its equipment.

But two of the possessed (her fellow possessed, she tried to tell herself) were from the late nineteenth–early twentieth century. Arrogant oafs who didn't or wouldn't understand the basic preconditions of shipboard routine. And their so-called commander, Oscar Kearn, didn't seem too bothered, either. He just assumed that the non-possessed crew would go around scooping up the shit. They didn't.

Cherri had given up advising and demanding. She was actually quite surprised that they'd survived the orbital battle for so long—although antimatter-powered combat wasps did load the odds in their favour. And for once the non-possessed were understandably performing their duties with a high level of proficiency. There was little for the possessed to do except wait. Oscar Kearn occupied himself by studying the hologram screen displays, and muttering the odd comment to his non-possessed subordinate. In reality he was contributing little, other than continually urging their combat wasps be directed at the voidhawks. The concept of keeping a reserve for their own defence seemed elusive.

When the explosions and energy cascades outside the hull were reaching an appalling crescendo, Cherri slipped quietly out of the bridge. Under ordinary combat conditions the companionways linking the frigate's four life-support capsules should have been sealed tight. Now, she glided past open hatches as she made her way along to B capsule's maintenance engineering deck. As soon as she was inside she closed the ceiling hatch and engaged the manual lock.

She pulled herself over to one of the three processor consoles and tapped the power stud. Not being able to datavise the frigate's flight computer was a big hindrance; she wasn't used to voice response programs. Eventually, though, she established an auxiliary command circuit, cutting the bridge officers out of the loop. The systems and displays she wanted slowly came on-line.

Combat wasps and their submunitions still flocked through space above Nyvan, though not quite as many as before. And the blanket electronic warfare interference had ended; quite simply, there were no SD platforms left intact to wage that aspect of the conflict.

One of the ten phased array antennae positioned around the *Urschel*'s hull focused on the *Lady Macbeth*. Cherri pulled herself closer to the console's mike.

"Is anyone receiving this? Sarha, Warlow, can you hear me? If you can, use a five-millimetre aperture signal maser for a direct com return. Do not, repeat not lock on to *Urschel*'s main antenna."

"Signal acknowledged," a synthesised voice replied. "Who the hell is this?"

"Warlow, is that you?"

"No, Warlow isn't with us anymore. This is Sarha Mitcham, acting first officer. Who am I speaking with?"

"Sarha, I'm sorry, I didn't know about Warlow. It's Cherri Barnes, Sarha."

"God, Cherri, what the hell are you doing on an Organization frigate?"

Cherri stared at the console, trying to get a grip on her raging emotions. "I . . . I belong here, Sarha. I think. I don't know anymore. You just don't know what it's like in the beyond."

"Oh, fuck, you're a possessor."

"Guess so. Not by choice."

"Yeah. I know. What happened to *Udat*, Cherri? What happened to you?"

"It was Mzu. She killed us. We were a complication to her. And Meyer . . . she had a grudge. Be careful of her, Sarha, be very careful."

"Christ, Cherri, is this on the level?"

"Oh, yes, I'm on the level."

"Acknowledged. And . . . thanks."

"I haven't finished. Joshua's down on Nyvan chasing after Mzu, we know that much."

"Okay, he's down there. Cherri, please don't ask me why. I can't discuss it."

"That's okay. I understand. It doesn't matter; we know

about the Alchemist, and you know we know. But you have to tell Joshua to back off, he must get away from Mzu. Right away. We know we can't get her offplanet now our space-planes are gone. That means the Organization has only one option. If she's dead, she'll have to join us."

"Is that why *Urschel* and *Pinzola* were shooting at the ground?"

"Yes. But that's not all—"

The timid, halting voice echoed around *Lady Macbeth*'s bridge. It sent something like cold electricity racing down Liol's nerves. He turned his head to look at Sarha, who seemed equally stupefied.

"Is she for real?" he asked, praying the answer would be no. Events seemed to be pushing them towards an inevitable active response. Despite his outward bravado back on the station, he had distinctly mixed feelings about piloting *Lady Mac* under conditions any more adverse than their current ones—though a rogue part of his mind was determined that Sarha would never know that. Egotism was obviously the opposite trait of his intuition, the Calvert family's Achilles heel.

"I knew her," was all Sarha would say, and that reluctantly. "Beaulieu, can you confirm that ironberg's trajectory?"

"I will have to use active sensor analysis to obtain its precise flight path."

"Do it."

"We're thirty minutes from Joshua's horizon," Liol said. Alternative orbital trajectories were flashing through his mind as he datavised the flight computer for possible vectors.

"Nothing I can do about that," Sarha said. "We can try calling him through the Tonala communications net."

"The net: bollocks. You know there isn't a working processor left on that planet after all this emp activity. I can drop us down; if we skim the atmosphere we can be above his horizon in eight minutes."

"No! If we start changing our orbit we'll be targeted."

"There's nothing left out there *to* target us. Access the sensors, damn you. The combat wasps are all spent."

"They've deployed all their submunitions, you mean."

"He's my brother!"

"He's my captain, and we can't risk it."

"*Lady Mac* can beat any poxy submunitions. Take fire control, I can pilot this manoeuvre."

"Ironberg trajectory confirmed," Beaulieu said. "Barnes was telling the truth. It's heading straight at them."

"Altitude?" Sarha asked. "Can we nuke it?"

"Ninety kilometres. That's too deep into the ionosphere for the combat wasps. They can't operate in that kind of pressure."

"Shit!" Sarha groaned.

"Get positive, Sarha," Liol demanded. "We have to get over Joshua's horizon."

"I've got lock-on," Beaulieu said calmly. "Two nukes, active seeker heads. They acquired our radar emission."

Sarha initiated the maser cannon targeting program without conscious thought. Her brain was churning with too much worry and indecision to actually think. Bright violet triangles zeroed the approaching submunitions.

"Would Josh leave one of us down there?" Liol asked.

"You piece of shit!" The masers fired, triggered by the heatlash in her mind. Both submunitions broke apart, their fusion drives dying.

"We can beat them," Beaulieu said.

The imperturbability of the cosmonik's synthetic voice chided Sarha. "Okay. I'll handle fire control. Beaulieu, switch to active sensors, full suite; I want long-range warning of any incoming hostiles. Liol, take us down."

They were hammering on the maintenance engineering deck's hatch. Its edges had started to shine cherry-red, paint was blistering.

Cherri gave the circle of metal a jaded look. "All right, all right," she mumbled. "I'll make it easy all around. Besides, what would you lot ever know about fraternity?"

After the hatch's locking mechanism melted away, an equally hot Oscar Kearn dived through the smouldering rim. Any hope of retribution died instantly as he saw the figure curled up and sobbing dejectedly in front of the console. The soul of Cherri Barnes had already vacated the flesh, retreating to the one place where he was never going to chase after her.

Monica finally felt as though she was regaining control of the mission. There were twelve operatives with her in the Disassembly Shed providing overwhelming firepower, and their evac craft was on the way. None of their processor blocks were working, nor their neural nanonics. Everyone had taken off their shell helmets so they could see; the sensors were glitched, too. The lack of protection made her nervous, but she could live with that. *I've got Mzu!*

She applied some pressure to the pistol barrel at the side of Calvert's neck, and he moved aside obediently. One of the Edenists claimed his machine gun. He didn't protest when he was made to stand with his three compatriots, all of them with their hands in the air and covered by a couple of operatives.

"Doctor, please take your hand away from that backpack," Monica said. "And don't try to datavise any activation codes."

Alkad shrugged and held her hands up. "I can't datavise anything anyway," she said. "There are too many possessed in here."

Monica signalled one of the operatives to retrieve Mzu's backpack.

"You were in Tranquillity," Alkad said. "And the Dorados too, if I'm not mistaken. Which agency?"

"ESA."

"Ah. Yet some of your friends are obviously Edenists. How odd."

"We both consider your removal from this planet to be of

paramount importance, Doctor," Samuel said. "However, you have my assurance you will not be harmed."

"Of course," Alkad told them equitably. "If I am, we all know who I'll end up with."

"Exactly."

Gelai looked up. "They're coming, Doctor."

Monica frowned. "Who?"

"The possessed from the Organization," Alkad told her. "They're up in the shed's framework somewhere."

The operatives responded smoothly, scanning the metal lattice above them for any sign of movement. Monica stepped smartly over to Alkad's side and grabbed her arm. "Okay, Doctor, we'll take care of them, now let's move."

"Damn," Samuel said. "The police are here."

Monica glanced back to the hole blown into the wall where they'd entered. Two Edenists had been left to cover their retreat back to the cars. "We can deal with them."

Samuel gave a resigned grimace. The operatives formed a protective cordon around Monica and Mzu and started to walk back towards the wall.

Monica realized that Joshua and the others were hurrying after them. "Not you," she said.

"I'm not staying in here," Joshua said indignantly.

"We can't——" Samuel began.

A portcullis slammed down out of the tangle of girders above. It struck two of the operatives, punching them to the ground. The valency generators in their armour suits were glitched, preventing the fabric from stiffening into protective exoskeletons as they should have done. Long iron spikes along the bottom of the portcullis punctured the suit fabric, skewering their bodies to the wet carbon concrete.

Four of the operatives opened fire with their machine guns, shooting straight up. Bullets ricocheted madly, grazing sprays of sparks off the metal.

Training compelled Monica to look around and locate the follow up. It was coming at her from the left, a huge pendulum blade swinging straight at Mzu. If her neural nanonics had been on line and running threat response programs she might have made it. As it was, boosted muscles slewed her weight around to pirouette Mzu out of the blade's arc. They went tumbling onto the floor together. The blade caught Monica's left leg a glancing blow. Her armoured boot saved her foot from being severed, but her ankle and lower shinbone were shattered by the impact. Shock dulled the initial pain. She sat up, groaning in dismay, and clutched at the ruined bones. Bile was rising in her throat, and it was very difficult to breathe.

Something extraordinarily heavy hit her shoulder, sending her sprawling. Joshua landed on the ground right beside her, rolling neatly to absorb the impact. A burst of hatred banished Monica's pain. Then the blade sliced through the air where she had been a second before, a tiny whisper the only sound of its passing. Pendulum, she thought dazedly, it comes back.

One of the embassy operatives raced over to Monica. He was holding a square medical nanonic package and cursing heavily. "It's glitched, too, I can't get a response."

Joshua glanced at the package glove covering his hand. Ever since he'd come into the shed, it had been stinging like crazy. "Tell me about it," he grumbled.

Gelai joined them, squatting down, her face full of concern. She put her hand over Monica's ankle.

The original intensity of the pain had frightened Monica, but this was plain horrifying. She could feel the fragments of bone shifting around inside her skin, she could even see the suit's trouser fabric ripple around Gelai's hand—her *glowing* hand. Yet it didn't hurt.

"I think that's it," the bashful girl said. "Try standing."

"Oh, my God. You're a . . ."

"Didn't you professionals know?" Joshua said evilly.

Samuel dodged around the pendulum and crouched beside them, alert, his machine gun pointing high. "I thought you'd been hit," he said as Monica gingerly applied some weight to her left foot.

"I was. She cured me."

He gave Gelai a fast appraisal. "Oh."

"We'd better get going," Monica said.

"They'll hit us again if we move."

"They'll hit us if we stay."

"I wish I could see them," he moaned, blinking away the drizzle. "There's no target for us. Shooting wild is pointless, there's too much metal."

"They're up there," Gelai said. "Three of them are just above the pendulum hinge. They're the ones giving it substance."

Samuel jerked his head about. "Where?"

"Above it."

"Damn it." If he could have just switched his retinal implants to infrared there might have been something other than mangled blackness. He fired his machine gun anyway, sluicing the bullets over the area he imagined Gelai was talking about. The magazine was spent in less than a second. He ejected it and slapped in a fresh one—mindful of how many were left clipped to his belt. When he looked up again, the pendulum had vanished. Instead, a length of thick black cabling was swaying to and fro. "That's it? Did I get them?"

"You hurt two," Gelai told him. "They're backing off."

"Hurt? Great."

"Come on," Monica said. "We can get to the cars." She raised her voice. "Random suppression fire, vertical. I want those bastards fleeing us. Okay, *move*."

Eight machine guns opened fire into the overhead lattice as everyone rushed towards the hole in the wall.

High above them, and safe in his web of metal cables, Baranovich looked out of a filthy window at the three Tonalan police cars drawn up outside. There were long skid marks in the snow behind each of them, evidence of their hard braking. One other surviving police car was chasing after the twenty-first-century rally car, siren blaring and lights flashing as they both tore along the bottom of the shed wall. Dark-clad officers were advancing towards the embassy cars.

"Let's liven things up a little," he said above the fractious roar of the machine guns and whining ricochets. He joined hands with the three possessed beside him. Together they launched a huge fireball and sent it curving down on one of the stationary police cars.

The response was immediate and overwhelming. After having their car processors glitched, then crashing, being shot at by starship X-ray lasers, losing their suspects, and now having to verify whether the embassy cars were occupied by armed ESA operatives, the Tonalan security police were by now understandably a little tense. Every weapon they had was abruptly trained on Disassembly Shed Four.

Monica was twenty metres from the smashed door when the ancient, brittle panels were bombarded by hollow-case bullets, TI pulses, maser beams, and small EE rounds. Blinding light ruptured the gloom ahead of her. She hit the floor hard as white-hot fragments slashed through the air. Smoking particles rained down around her, sizzling on the moist concrete. Several landed on her head, singeing through her hair to sting her scalp.

"THIS IS THE POLICE. ABANDON YOUR WEAPONS. COME OUT ONE AT A TIME WITH YOUR BLOCKS AND IMPLANTS DEACTIVATED. YOU WILL NOT BE TOLD AGAIN."

"Holy fuck," Monica grunted. She raised her head. A huge strip of the wall had vanished; maleficent shifting light from the orbital battle shone in. It illuminated a multitude of broken girders whose fractured ends dripped glowing droplets. The framework structure emitted a distressed groan; weakened junctions were snapping under the stress of the new loading, starting a chain reaction. She could see whole levels of metal bending then dropping in juddery motions.

"Move!" she shouted. "It's going to land on us."

A flare of white fire billowed down out of the darkness, pummelling an operative to her knees. Her screams vanished beneath the plangent crackling of her armour suit and skin igniting.

Four machine guns opened up in response.

"No," Monica said. That was exactly what they wanted. It

was a near-perfect snare manoeuvre, she admitted angrily as she flung her arms over her head again. *And we blundered right into it.*

The security police heard the machine guns and opened fire once more.

Baranovich hadn't been expecting quite such an emphatic rejoinder from the forces of law and order—these modern weapons were so fearsomely powerful. Twice now the weakened framework had shifted around him, forcing him to snatch at the girders and reinforce their solidity with his energistic power. That was dangerous. The metal was grounding out the EE rounds, and while he was some distance away from their impact zone, those kind of voltages were lethal to a possessed and it only took one wild shot.

When the second around of shooting started he jumped down onto the nearest walkway and sprinted away. His impressive costume's shiny leather boots changed to yankee-style trainers with inch-thick soles; a fervent hope in his mind that imagined rubber would be as effective an insulator as the real stuff. He could sense others of his group on the move, shaken by the ferocity of the attack.

Joshua looked up to see the last frayed streamers of electrons writhing down the metal pillars. The whole of the smashed-up framework above and around him was grinding loudly. It was going to collapse any second. Self-preservation kicked in strong—*fuck Mzu, I'm going to die if I stay here.* He scrambled to his feet and slapped Melvyn, who still had his hands over his head, face jammed against the floor.

"Shift it, both of you, now!" He started running, out from under the framework, and angling away from the gigantic hole the police had blown in the wall. There were a lot of footsteps splashing through the puddles behind him. He scanned around quickly. It wasn't just Melvyn, Dahybi, and Keaton who were following him; all the agency operatives and Mzu's wacko entourage were coming too. Everybody racing across the Disassembly Shed's high bay floor in pursuit as if he were showing them the way to salvation. "Jesus wept!" He didn't want this! Just having Melvyn and Dahybi coming with him across an open space would have proved tempting for the possessed, but Mzu too . . .

Unlike the Baranovich group who had set up the meeting, the ESA and the Edenists who had unlimited access to the Kulu embassy's memory files, and the security police who knew their home territory, Joshua didn't quite appreciate the layout of the Disassembly Sheds. Even their madcap drive through the foundry yard hadn't conclusively demonstrated to him that the canals ran straight through the centre of every shed. So he certainly didn't know that the only way over the water was a bridge which ran along the door above the smaller canal.

What he did know was that there was a perilously dark and wide gulf in the floor ahead of him, and getting closer very fast. Only now did he hear the gentle slopping of the water, and realize what it was. He nearly went sprawling headlong as he came to a confounded halt a metre from the edge, arms flapping eccentrically for balance. He turned to see everyone rushing en masse towards him, because they'd thought he knew what he was doing, and there hadn't been time to ask questions. Behind them, Baranovich's possessed were mustering on the walkway, garish costumes agleam in the rainy dusk.

Alkad was running with her head ducked down, forcing her game leg along. Gelai and Ngong were on either side of her, holding her tight. A bubble of air around the three of them swirled with tiny glimmers of silver light.

Baranovich's laughter poured out into the vast enclosed space of the central high bay. He pointed, and Joshua could do nothing but stare dumbly as the bolt of white fire streaked across the intervening space straight at him.

Dick Keaton was leading the pack of desperadoes on the floor of the high bay, running hard. He was less than four metres from an aghast Joshua when Baranovich's fire bolt hit the data security expert clean between his shoulder blades. It burst open in a spectacular cloud of dancing twisters that drained away into the drizzle. And Dick Keaton was completely unharmed.

"Close one," he jeered happily. His arms wrapped around Joshua, momentum carrying the pair of them over the edge of the central basin just as the mutilated framework collapsed. Fractured girders were tossed out of the crumpling wreckage in all directions, clanging loudly as they hit the floor. A huge split tore up the wall like a lightning bolt in reverse. It was a hundred and seventy metres high when it finally stopped. The framework structure settled into an uneasy silence.

The black water in the ironberg basin was freezing. Joshua yelled out as it closed around him, seeing bubbles bumble past his face. The cold shock was intense enough to make his heart jump—frightening him badly. Salt water rushed into his open mouth. And—Jesus, *thank you*—his neural nanonics came back on-line.

Nerve impulse overrides squeezed his throat muscles tight, preventing any water flooding his lungs. Analysis of his spinning inner ears revealed his exact orientation. His thrashing became purposeful, shunting him straight up.

He broke surface to draw down a huge desperate gulp of air. People in flexible armour suits were flying through the air above him; human lemmings landing in the basin with a tremendous splash. He saw Mzu, her small figure unmistakable in its prim business suit.

Keaton shook his head dog-fashion, blowing his cheeks out. "Hell, it's cold."

"Who the fuck are you?" Joshua demanded. "They hit you dead on, and it never even blistered you."

"Right question, sir, but unfortunately the wrong pronoun. As I once said to Oscar Wilde. Stumped him completely; he wasn't quite as hot on the riposte as legend says."

All Joshua could do was cough. The cold was crippling. His neural nanonics were battling hard to prevent his muscles from cramping. And they were going to lose.

White fire smashed against the basin rim five metres above him. Radiant dribbles of magma ran down the basin wall.

"What in God's name did you bring us here for?" Monica shouted.

"I didn't fucking bring you!"

Her hand grabbed the front of his ship-suit. "How do we get out?"

"Jesus, I don't know."

She let go, her arm shaking badly. Another strike of white fire lashed above them. The rim was outlined like a dawn horizon from orbit.

"They can't hit us here," Samuel said, his long face was dreadfully strained.

"God, so what," Monica answered. "They've only got to walk over here and we'll be dead."

"We won't last that long. Hypothermia will get us before then."

Monica glared at Joshua. "Can anyone see some steps?"

"Dick," Joshua said. "Are your neural nanonics working?"

"Yes."

"Access the shed's management computer. Find us a way out. Now!"

This is a last-ditch madness, I know, Samuel called to the *Hoya*. But is there anything you can do?

Nothing. I am so sorry. You're too far away, we cannot provide fire support.

We're retreating, Niveu told him, his tone full of savage regret. It's this diabolical antimatter. We've fired every combat wasp in defence, and they're still coming through. The nations have gone insane, every SD platform went offensive. *Ferrea* was damaged by a gamma ray pulser, and *Sinensis* had to swallow out to avoid a direct impact. There's only the two of us left now. We can't last much longer. Do you wish to transfer? We can delay a few seconds more.

No. Go, warn the Consensus.

But your situation—

Doesn't matter. Go!

"Half the shed's processors are glitched," Dick Keaton said. "The rest are in standby mode. It's been mothballed."

"What?" Joshua had to shout to make his mouth work. His kicks to tread water were difficult now.

"Mothballed. That's why there's no ironberg in here. The small canal leaks. They drained it for repairs."

"Drained it? Let me have the file."

Keaton datavised it over, and Joshua assigned it to a memory cell. Analysis programs went primary, tearing into the information. What he wanted was a way to drain the basin, or at the very least a ladder. Which wasn't quite what he found when the schematics display rose into his mind. "Ione!" he shouted. "Ione." His voice was pathetically weak. He worked his elbows, swivelling around to face Samuel. "Call her."

"Who?" the bewildered Edenist asked.

"Ione Saldana, the Lord of Ruin. Call her with affinity."

"But—"

"Do it or we're going to die in here."

The gee force on *Lady Macbeth*'s bridge began to abate, sliding down from a tyrannical eight to an unpleasant three.

He certainly flies the same way as Joshua, Sarha thought. The few seconds she'd spared from fire control to monitor their vector had shown her a starship which was keeping pretty close to the course which the navigation program had produced. Not bad for a daydreamer novice.

"The *Urschel* is accelerating," Beaulieu said. "Seven gees, they're going for altitude. Must be a jump."

"Good," Sarha said firmly. "That means no more of those bloody antimatter combat wasps."

All three of them had cheered when the *Pinzola* was struck by a fusion blast. The resulting explosion as all the frigate's antimatter confinement chambers were destroyed had blown half of *Lady Mac*'s sensors, and *Pinzola* had been eleven thousand kilometres away, almost below the horizon.

The orbital conflict had been played out hard and fast over the last eleven minutes. Several starships had been hit, but over fifteen had risen to a jump altitude and escaped. There were no more SD platforms left in low orbit, although plenty of combat wasps were still prowling. But they were all a long way from *Lady Mac*. That was Sarha's prime concern. As Beaulieu had said, the old girl could cope with Nyvan's geriatric weapons. They had a couple of new scars on the hull from kinetic debris, and three radioactive hot spots from pulser shots. But the worst of it was over now.

"Gravitonic distortion," Beaulieu said. "Another void-hawk has left."

"Sensible ship," Sarha muttered. "Liol, how long until we're over Joshua's horizon?"

"Ninety seconds—mark."

She datavised an order into the starship's communications system. The main dish slid out of its recess and swung around, pointing at the horizon ahead.

Ione eased herself around the metal pillar to take another look into the shed's high bay. The possessed up on the walk-way were squirting a continual stream of white fire at the rim of the basin. That must mean Joshua and the others were still alive.

Now appeared to be the optimum time to enter the fray. She had hung back ever since she'd sprinted into the shed ahead of the agency operatives. This whole situation was so fluid, the outcome could well be decided by who had the greatest tactical reserve. She wasn't quite sure where that decision had come from; some tactics file her 'original' self and Tranquillity had loaded into the serjeant, or internal logic. How much inventiveness she owned in this aspect she wasn't sure of. But wherever it had come from, it had been proved right.

She had watched the events play out from the cover of the framework, hovering on the brink of intervention. Then the police had arrived and fouled up everything. And Joshua had fled across the high bay to the basin.

She couldn't work that one out. It was seawater in the

basin, which must be close to the freezing point. Now he was pinned down.

If she could get a clear shot at the walkway the possessed were using, she might be able to bring them all crashing down. But she wasn't sure how effective even the heavy-calibre rifle would be against such a concentration of energistic power.

Ione. Ione Saldana?

Cold accompanied the affinity call, she knew exactly what it was like to be immersed in the basin. **Agent Samuel,** she acknowledged.

I have a message.

He widened his mind still further. She looked out at anguished heads bobbing in the water. Joshua was right in front of her, hair plastered down over his forehead. His throat laboured hard to force the words out. "Ione—shoot—out—the—small—canal—lock—gate—blow—that—fucker—away—good—and—be—quick—we—can't—last—long."

She was already running towards the end of the shed. There was a rectangular gap in the framework structure over the small canal. It framed the door which slid up to allow the ironberg segments through. The bottom of the door closed to within a metre of the water itself. Below that, she could see the two lock gates which held back the water while the canal outside was being repaired. They were solid metal, tarnished by age, and thick with fronds of sapphire-coloured seaweed.

She squatted down beside the edge of the canal and fired the heavy-calibre rifle. Trying to puncture the gates themselves would be hopeless, they weren't made from any modern laced-molecule alloy, but their thickness made them completely impenetrable. Instead, the explosive-tipped shells pounded into the canal's old carbon-concrete walls, demolishing the hinges and their mountings.

The gates moved slightly as water squirted around the crumbling concrete. Their top hinges were almost wrecked, making them gradually pivot downwards, a motion which prised them further apart. A V-shaped gap appeared between them, with water gushing out horizontally. Ione fired again and again, concentrating on one wall now, mauling it to smithereens. One of the hinges gave way.

Look out, Samuel warned. **They have stopped attacking us. That must mean—**

Ione saw the shadows shifting behind her, knowing what it meant. Then the shadows were fading away as the light grew brighter. She switched her aim to the stubborn gate itself, using the explosions to punch it down, adding their weight to that of the water.

White fire engulfed her.

The gates were wrenched apart, and the water plummeted into the empty canal beyond.

"Go with it," Joshua datavised as the first stirrings of a current stroked his faltering legs. "Stay afloat."

A waterfall roar reverberated around the shed's high bay, and he was pulled along the basin wall. The others were twirling around him. Quiet, unseen currents sucked them towards the end of the basin where it narrowed like a funnel into the small canal. They started to pick up speed as they drew closer to the mouth. Then the basin was behind them. Water was surging along the canal.

"Joshua, please acknowledge. This is Sarha, acknowledge please, Joshua." His neural nanonics told him the signal was being routed to his communication block via the spaceplane. Everyone, it seemed, had survived the orbital battle.

"I'm here, Sarha," he datavised. The canal water was boiling tempestuously as it flowed under the door, dipping down sharply; and he was racing towards it at a hazardous rate. It was becoming very hard to keep afloat, even here where the level was sinking. He tried a few feeble side-strokes to get away from the wall where the churning was at its worst.

"Joshua, you're entering into an emergency situation."

Two curling vortex waves recoiled off the canal walls to converge above him as he passed under the shed door. "No shit!" The waves closed over his head. Neural nanonics triggered a massive adrenaline secretion, enabling him to fight his way back to the surface with recalcitrant limbs. Distorted daylight and iron-hard foam crashed around him as he floundered back into the air.

"I'm serious, Joshua. The Organization has tampered with one of the ironbergs. They altered its aerobrake trajectory so that it will land on the foundry yard. If they can't get Mzu offplanet with them, they want her dead so she'll have to join the Organization that way. It's timed to crash after the spaceplane pickup was scheduled, so that if anything went wrong they'd still win."

The canal opened up ahead of Joshua, a rigid gully stretching away to the foundry building three kilometres distant. Water rampaged along it, a thundering white-water torrent which propelled him along helplessly. He wasn't alone. Voi came close enough for him to touch if the pounding water hadn't been so strong, snatching her away again immediately.

"Jesus, Sarha, this *is* after the spaceplanes were scheduled."

"I know. We're tracking the ironberg, it's going to hit you in seven minutes."

"What? Nuke the bastard, now, Sarha."

The leading edge of the water reached the first section of scaffolding, a lattice of heavy walkways, cage lifts, and machinery platforms. It swept the lower members away, toppling the rest of the structure. The stronger segments held together for a few seconds as the spume rolled them along, then after a few revolutions they began to break apart, metal poles sinking to the bottom.

"We can't, Joshua. It's already in the lower atmosphere. The combat wasps can't reach it."

The water reached the second stretch of scaffolding. This was larger than the first, supporting big construction mechanoids and concrete hoppers. Their weight lent a degree of stability to the edifice as the water seethed around it; several members broke free, but it managed to remain relatively intact against the initial onrush.

"Don't worry, Joshua," Ashly datavised. "I'm on my way.

Fifty seconds and I'll be there. We'll be airborne long before the ironberg crashes. I can see the sheds already."

"No, Ashly, stay back, there are possessed here; a lot of them. They'll hit the spaceplane if they see you."

"Target them for me; I've got the masers."

"Impossible." He saw the scaffolding up ahead and knew this was his one chance. The physiological monitor program had been issuing cautions for some time: the cold was killing him. His muscles were already badly debilitated, slow to respond. He had to get out of the water while he had some strength left. "Everybody," he datavised, "grab the scaffolding or just crash into it if that's all you can manage. But make sure you don't go past. We have to get out."

The first rusty poles were coming up very fast. He reached out a hand. None of his fingers worked inside the medical package glove, not even when his neural nanonics commanded them. "Mzu?" he datavised. "Get to the scaffolding."

"Acknowledged."

It wasn't much practical use to him, but the relief that she was still alive kept that small core flame of hope flickering. The mission wasn't an utter disaster, he still had purpose. Surprisingly important right now.

Dahybi had already reached the scaffolding, hugging a post as the water stormed past. Then Joshua was there, trying to hook his arm around a V-junction and shift his head out of the way at the same time to avoid a crack on the temple. The metal banged against his chest, and he never even felt it.

"You okay?" Dahybi datavised.

"Fucking wonderful."

Voi was flashing past, just succeeding in jamming an arm on a pole.

Joshua inched himself further into the shaking structure. There was a ladder two metres away, and he flopped against it. The water wasn't quite so strong now, but it was rising fast.

Mzu came thumping into the end of the scaffolding.

"Mother Mary, my ribs," she datavised. Samuel landed beside her, and wrapped a protective arm around her.

Joshua clambered up the ladder, thankful it was at a low angle. Dahybi followed him. Two more operatives caught the scaffolding, then Monica snagged herself. Gelai and Ngong swam quite normally across the canal, the cold having no effect on them at all. They grabbed the scaffolding and started shoving the numb survivors up out of the water.

"Melvyn?" Joshua datavised. "Where are you, Melvyn?" He'd been one of the first to reach the canal after Ione blew the lock gate. "Melvyn?" There wasn't even a carrier band from the fusion specialist's neural nanonics.

"What's happening?" Ashly datavised. "I can't acquire any of you on the sensors."

"Stay back, that's an order," Joshua replied. "Melvyn?"

One of the ESA operatives floated past, facedown.

"Melvyn?"

"I'm sorry, Captain Calvert," Dick Keaton datavised. "He went under."

"Where are you?"

"End of the scaffolding."

Joshua looked over his shoulder, seeing the limp figure suspended in the crisscross of poles thirty metres away. He was alone.

Jesus no. Another friend condemned to the beyond. Looking back at reality and begging to return.

"That's all of us, now," Monica datavised.

Altogether six of the operatives from the combined Edenist/ESA team had survived along with her and Samuel. Eriba's corpse was swirling past amid a scum of brown foam. Fifteen people, out of the twenty-three who had entered Disassembly Shed Four, more if you counted the two serjeants.

"What now?" Dahybi asked.

"Climb," Joshua told him. "We've got to get up to the top of the scaffolding. Our spaceplane is on its way."

"So is a bloody ironberg."

"Gelai, where are the possessed?" Joshua croaked.

"Coming," she said. "Baranovich is already out of the shed. He won't let the spaceplane land."

"I don't have a weapon," Monica said. "There's only two machine guns left between all of us. We can't hold them back." Her body was trembling violently as she crawled along a narrow conveyer belt connected to one of the concrete hoppers.

Joshua went up another three rungs on the ladder, then sagged from the effort.

"Captain Calvert," Mzu datavised. "I won't give anybody the Alchemist no matter what. I want you to know that. And thank you for your efforts."

She'd given up, sitting huddled limply in a junction. Ngong was holding her, concentrating hard. Steam began to spout out of her suit. Joshua looked around at the rest of them, defeated and tortured by the cold. If he was going to do anything to salvage this, it would have to be extreme.

"Sarha, give me fire support," he datavised.

"Our sensor returns are being corrupted," she replied. "I can't resolve the foundry yard properly. It's the same effect we encountered on Lalonde."

"Jesus. Okay, target me."

"Joshua!"

"Don't argue. Activate the designator laser and target my communications block. Do it. Ashly, stand by. The rest of you: come on, move, we have to be ready." He took another couple of steps up the ladder.

Lady Macbeth's designator laser pierced the wispy residue of snow clouds. A slim shaft of emerald light congested with hazy sparkles as gusting snowflakes evaporated inside it. It was aligned on a road three hundred metres away.

"Is that on you?" Sarha asked.

"No, track north-east, two-fifty metres."

The beam shifted fast enough to produce a blurred sheet of green light across the sky.

"East eighty metres," Joshua instructed. "North twenty-five."

His retinal implants had to bring their strongest filters on line as the scaffolding was swamped by brilliant green light.

"Lock coordinate—mark. Preclude one-five-zero metres. Switch to ground-strike cannon. Spiral one kilometre. Scorch it, Sarha."

The beam moved away, its colour blooming through the spectrum until it was a deep ruby-red. Then its intensity grew; snowflakes drifting into it no longer evaporated, they burst apart. Thick brown fumes and smoking pumice gravel jetted up from the disintegrating carbon concrete at its base. It changed direction, curving around to gouge a half-metre groove in the ground. A perfect circle three hundred metres in diameter was etched out in polluted flame, with the canal scaffolding at the centre. Then the beam began to speed up, creating a hollow cylinder of vivid red light which expanded inexorably. The ground underneath it ignited, vaporizing the cloak of snow into a rolling cloud which broiled the land ahead of the beam.

It slashed across the corner of Disassembly Shed Four. Cherry-red embers flew out of the panels up the entire height of the wall. A thin sliver of composite and metal began to peel away from the bulk of the shed. Then the laser struck it again. It cut a deeper chunk this time, which started to pitch over in pursuit of the first. Both of them were surrounded by a cascade of embers. The beam continued around on its spiral.

Disassembly Shed Four died badly, chopped into thin curving slices by the relentless laser. The individual wedges collapsed and crumpled against each other, softened and sagging from the immense thermal input to descend in slippery serpentine riots. When almost a fifth of it had gone, the remaining framework could no longer sustain itself. The walls and roof buckled groggily, twisting and imploding. Its final convulsions were illuminated by the laser, which continued to chop the falling wreckage into ribbons of slag. Steam geysers roared upwards as pyrexic debris slithered into the basin, flattening out to obscure the bubbling ruin in a virgin-white funeral shroud.

Nothing could survive the ground strike. The security police raced for their cars as soon as it began, only to be overtaken by the outwards spiral. Baranovich and his fellow possessed took refuge back in the Disassembly Shed under the assumption that anything that massive was bound to be safe. When that folly was revealed, some of them dived into the canal, only to be parboiled. A couple of hapless foundry yard staff on their way to investigate the noises and light coming from the mothballed shed were caught and reduced to a fog of granular ash.

The laser beam vanished.

Secure at the vestal centre of the remorseless sterilization he had unleashed, Joshua datavised the all-clear to Ashly. The spaceplane streaked out of the roiling sky to land beside the canal. Joshua and the others waited at the top of the scaffolding, hunched up as the warm wind created by the laser's passage blew against them.

"Hanson evac service," Ashly datavised as the airstairs slid out from the airlock. "Close shaves a speciality. Shift your arses, we've only got two minutes till it hits."

Alkad Mzu was first up the airstairs, followed by Voi.

"I won't take you as you are," Joshua told Gelai and Ngong. "I can't, you know that." Monica and Samuel were standing behind the two ex-Garissans, machine guns cradled ready.

"We know," Gelai said. "But do you know you will be in our position one day?"

"Please," Joshua said. "We don't have time for this. None of us are going to jeopardize Mzu now, not after what we've been through to get her. Not even me. They'll shoot you, and I won't try to stop them."

Gelai nodded morosely. Her black skin faded to a pasty white as the possessing soul relinquished control, ruffled ginger hair tumbled down over her shoulders. The girl sank to her knees, jaw open to wail silently.

Joshua put his arms under her shoulders to carry her into the spaceplane. Samuel was doing the same for the old man who had been possessed by Ngong.

"Dick, give me a hand," Joshua grunted as he reached the bottom of the airstairs.

"Sorry, Captain," Dick Keaton said. "But this is where necessity dictates we part company. I have to say, though, it's been quite an experience. Wouldn't have missed it for anything."

"Jesus, there's an ironberg falling on us!"

"Don't worry. I'll be perfectly safe. And I can hardly come with you now my cover's been blown, now can I?"

"What the fuck are you?"

"Closer, Captain." He grinned. "Much closer, this time. Goodbye, and good luck."

Joshua glared at the man—if that's what he really was—and hauled the semi-conscious girl up the airstairs.

Keaton stood back as the spaceplane took off, its compressor efflux whipping his ice-speckled hair about. He waved solemnly as it pitched up and accelerated away over the ruined smoking land.

High in the western sky, a red dot glimmered malevolently, growing larger by the second.

The spaceplane cabin canted up sharply, slinging Joshua back into a chair. Acceleration was two gees and rising fast. "What's our status, Ashly?"

"Good. We've got an easy twenty seconds left. Not even a real race against the clock. Did I tell you about the time when I was flying covert landings for the Marseilles Militia?"

"You told me. Pump the cabin temperature up, please, we're freezing back here." He accessed the spaceplane's sensor suite. They were already two kilometres high, well out over the lacklustre grey sea. The ironberg was level with them, and sinking rapidly.

Joshua, who had grown up in a bitek habitat and captained a faster-than-light starship for a living, regarded it in dismayed awe. Something that big simply did not belong in the air. It was falling at barely subsonic velocity, spinning with slow elegance to maintain its trajectory. A thick braided vapour trail streaked away from its rounded tip, creating a perfectly straight line through the sky before rupturing two hundred metres higher up when the massive horizontal shock waves created by its turbulence crashed back together. Aerobrake friction made its scalloped base shine a baleful topaz at the centre, grading down to bright coral pink at the rim.

For the doomed staff left in the yard the strangest aspect of its drop was the silence. It was unreal, looking up at the devil's fist as it descended upon you, and hearing nothing but the lazy squawking of seabirds.

The energy burst from seventy-five thousand tonnes of steel striking the ground at three hundred metres per second was cataclysmic. The blast wave razed the remaining Disassembly Sheds, sending hundreds of thousands of shattered composite panels ripping through the air. They were instantly ignited by the accompanying thermal release, crowning the maelstrom with a raging halo of flame. Last came the ground shock, a mini-quake which rippled out for several kilometres through the boggy soil, plucking the huge smelters from the skeletal remains of their furnace buildings and flinging them across the marshy wasteland at the rear of the yard. The sea retreated hastily from the catastrophe, deserting the shoreline in a series of huge breakers which fought against the incoming tide for several minutes. But in the end, the tremors ceased, and the water came rushing back to obliterate any last sign that the yard had ever existed.

"Ho, man, that is just orgasmic," Quinn said. The bridge's holoscreens were pumping out a blaze of white light as the first of the antimatter explosions blossomed above Nyvan. So much destruction excited him; he could see hundreds of combat wasps in flight above the nightside continents. "God's Brother is helping us, Dwyer. This is His signal to start. Just look at those mothers go at it. There won't be a single nuke left on the planet to fight off the fall of Night."

"Quinn, the other nations are firing combat wasps at Jesup. We're naked out here, we've got to jump."

"How long till they arrive?"

"Three, four minutes."

"Plenty of time," Quinn said smoothly. He checked the communications displays to ensure the starship's secure lasers were still linked with Jesup and the three abandoned asteroids. "An occasion like this, I ought to say something, but fuck it, I'm not in the dignity business." He typed in the arming code and watched as the display symbology turned a beautiful dangerous red. His finger went straight to the execute command key and tapped it eagerly.

Ninety-seven fusion bombs detonated; the majority of them one-hundred-megaton blasts.

The sensors which were protruding above the fuselage of *Mount's Delta* observed Jesup wobble. Quinn had ordered his trusted disciples to place the bombs in a line below the biosphere cavern where the rock was thinnest. Huge flakes of rock fell away from the asteroid's crinkled outer surface, allowing jets of raw plasma to stab out. It was a precision application of force, splitting the rock clean open. The biosphere cavern was ruined instantly as nuclear volcanoes erupted out of the floor to exterminate all the life it sustained. Shock waves hurtled through the rock, opening up immense fracture patterns and shattering vast sections already weakened from centuries of mining.

Centrifugal force took over from the bombs to complete the destruction, applying intolerable torque stresses on the remaining sections of rock. Hill-sized chunks of regolith crumbled away, rotation flinging them clear. Tornadoes of hot, radioactive air poured into space, forming a thin cyclone around the fragmenting asteroid.

Quinn slammed a fist into his console. "Fucked!" he yelled victoriously. "Totally fucking fucked. I did it. Now they'll know His might is for real. The Night is going to fall, Dwyer, sure as shit floats to the top."

Sensors aligned on the three abandoned asteroids revealed similar scenes of devastation.

"But—Why? Why, Quinn?"

Quinn laughed joyfully. "Back on Earth we learned

everything there was to know about climate, all those doomsdays waiting to bite our arses if we aren't good obedient little Govcentral mechanoids. Don't violate the environmental laws else you'll wind up drowning in your own crap. Garbage like that. Everybody knows the entire flekload, the whole arcology from the tower nerds to the subtown kids. I heard about nuclear winters and dinosaur killers before I could walk." He banged a finger on the holoscreen's surface. "And this is it. Earth's nightmare out of the box. Those rocks are going to pulverize Nyvan. Doesn't matter if they smash down on land or water; they're going to blast gigatonnes of shit up into the atmosphere. I'm not talking some crappy little smog layer up in the sky, it's going to *be* the fucking sky. Wet black soot stretching from the ground to the stratosphere, so thick it'll give you cancer just breathing it for five minutes. They'll never see sunlight again, never. And when the possessed take over the whole fucking ball game down there, it still ain't going to help them. They can shunt Nyvan out of the universe, but they haven't got the power to clean the air. Only He can do that. God's Brother will bring them light." Quinn hugged Dwyer energetically. "They'll pray to Him to come and liberate them. They can't do anything else. He is their only salvation now. And I did it for Him. Me! I've brought Him a whole fucking planet to join His legions. Now I know it works, I'm going to do it to every planet in the Confederation. Every single one, that's my crusade now. Starting with Earth."

Secure communications lasers slid back down inside the fuselage, along with the sensors; and the *Mount's Delta* vanished inside an event horizon. Behind it, the low-orbit battle ran its course, the protagonists unaware of the true holocaust growing above them. The four tremendous clouds of rocky detritus were expanding at a constant rate, watched by the horrified surviving asteroids. Seventy per cent of the mass would miss the planet. But that still left thousands of fragments which would rain down through the atmosphere over the next two days. Each one would have a destructive potential hundreds of times greater than the ironberg. And with their planet's electronics reduced to trash, its spaceships smashed, its SD platforms vaporized, and its astroengineering stations in ruins, there was absolutely nothing Nyvan's population could do to prevent the onrush. Only pray.

Just as Quinn prophesied.

12

The *Leonora Cephei*'s radar was switched to long-range scanning mode, searching for any sign of another ship. After five hours gliding inertly along its orbital path, there hadn't been a single contact.

"How much longer do you expect me to muck in with this charade of yours?" Captain Knox asked scathingly. He indicated the holoscreen which was displaying the ship's radar return. "I've seen Pommy cricket teams with more life in them than this bugger."

Jed looked at the console; its symbology meant nothing to him, for all he knew the flight computer could be displaying schematics for *Leonora Cephei*'s waste cycling equipment. He felt shamed by his own technological ignorance. He only ever came into the compartment when he was summoned by Knox; and the only summonses he got was when the captain found something new to complain about. He now made damn sure he brought Beth and Skibbow with him each time; it made the whole experience a little less like being humiliated by Digger.

"If this is the coordinate, they'll be here," Jed insisted. This was the right time for the rendezvous. So where was the starship? He didn't want to look at Beth again. She didn't appear entirely sympathetic to his plight.

"Another hour," Knox said. "That's what I'll give you, then we head for Tanami. There are some cargoes for me there. Real ones."

"We'll wait a damn sight more than one hour, matey," Beth said.

"You get what you paid for."

"In that case we'll be here for six months; that's how much cash we bloody well shelled out."

"One hour." Knox's pale skin was reddening again; he wasn't used to his command decisions being questioned on his own bridge.

"Balls. We're here for as long as it takes, pal. Right, Jed?"

"Er. Yes. We should wait a bit longer." Beth's silent contempt made him want to cringe.

Knox gestured broadly in mock-reasonableness. "Long enough for the oxygen to run out, or can we head for port before that?"

"You regenerate the atmosphere," Beth said. "Stop being such a pain. We wait until our transport turns up. That's final."

"You flaming kids, you're all crazy. You don't see my children becoming Deadnights. Deadheads more like. What do you think is going to happen to you if you ever reach Valisk? That Kiera is bullshitting you."

"No she's not!" Jed said heatedly.

Knox was surprised at his resentment. "Okay, kid. I understand, I used to let my balls think for me when I was your age." He winked at Beth.

She glowered back at him.

"We wait as long at it takes," Gerald said quietly. "We are going to Valisk. All of us. That's what I paid you for, Captain." It was hard for him to be silent when people talked about Marie, especially the way they talked about her, as if she were some kind of communal girlfriend. Since the voyage started he had managed to hold his tongue. He found life a lot easier on board the small ship; the simple daily routine in which everything was laid out for him in advance was quite a comfort. So what they said about Marie, their idolization of the demon who controlled her, didn't snarl him up with anguish. They spoke from ignorance. He was wise to that. Loren would be proud of him for exercising such control.

"All right, we'll wait awhile," Knox said. "It's your charter." It always embarrassed him when Skibbow spoke. The man had *episodes*, you never knew how he was going to behave. So far there had been no anger or violence. So far.

Fifteen minutes later, Captain Knox's little quandaries and problems were banished as the radar detected a small object three kilometres away which hadn't been there a millisecond before. There was the usual weird peripheral fuzz indicating a wormhole terminus, and the object was expanding rapidly. He accessed the *Leonora Cephei*'s sensors to watch the bitek starship emerging.

"Oh, sweet Christ Almighty," he groaned. "You crazy bastards. We're dead meat now. Bloody dead!"

Mindor slipped out of the wormhole terminus and stretched its wings wide. Its head swung around so that one eye could fix the *Leonora Cephei* with a daunting stare.

Jed looked into one of the bridge's AV pillars, seeing the huge hellhawk flap its wings in slow sweeps, closing the distance with deceptive speed. Disquiet gave way to a kind of reverence. He whooped enthusiastically and hugged Beth. She grinned indulgently back at him.

"That's something, huh?"

"Sure is."

"We did it, we bloody did it."

A terrified Captain Knox ignored the babbling, insane kids and ordered the main communications dish to point at Pinjarra so he could call the Trojan cluster capital for help. Not, he guessed, that it would do the slightest good.

Rocio Condra was ready for it. After several dozen clandestine pickups he knew exactly how the captains reacted to his appearance. Out of the eight short-range defence lasers secured to his hull, only three were still functioning, and that was only because they utilized bitek processor control circuitry. The rest had succumbed to the vagaries of his energistic power, which he could never quite contain. He targeted the dish as it started to track around, and sent a half-second pulse into its central transmission module.

"Do not attempt to contact anyone," he broadcast.

"I understand," a shaken Knox datavised.

"Good. Are you carrying Deadnights for transfer?"

"Yes."

"Stand by for rendezvous and docking. Tell them to be ready."

The monster bird folded its wings as it manoeuvred closer to the spindly inter-orbit craft. Its outline began to waver as it rolled around its long axis; feathers giving way to dull green polyp, avian shape reverting to the earlier compressed-cone hull. There were changes, though: the scattered purple rings were now long ovals, mimicking its feather pattern. Of the three rear fins, the central one had shrunk, while the two outer ones had elongated and flattened back.

With the roll manoeuvre complete, *Mindor*'s life-support module lay parallel to the *Leonora Cephei*. Rocio Condra extended the airlock tube. Now, he could sense the minds inside the inter-orbit ship's life-support capsule. It contained the usual split between trepidatious crew and ridiculously exuberant Deadnights. This time there was an addition, a strange mind, dulled yet happy, with thoughts moving in erratic rhythms.

He watched with idle curiosity through the internal optical sensors as the Deadnights came aboard. The interior of the life-support module had come to resemble a nineteenth-century steamship, with a profusion of polished rosewood surfaces and brass fittings. According to the pair of possessed, Choi-Ho and Maxim Payne, who served as maintenance crew, there was also a fairly realistic smell of salt water. Rocio was pleased with the realism, which was far more detailed and solid than the possessed usually achieved. That was due to the nature of the hellhawk's neuron cell structure which contained hundreds of subnodes arranged in processorlike lattices. They were intended to act as semi-autonomous regulators for his technological modules. Once he had conjured up the image he wanted and loaded it into a subnode it was maintained without conscious thought, and with an energistic strength unavailable to an ordinary human brain.

The last few weeks had been a revelation to Rocio Condra. After the initial bitter resentment, he had discovered that life as a hellhawk was about as rich as it was possible to have, although he did miss sex. And he'd been talking to some of the others about that; theoretically they could simply grow the appropriate genitalia (those that didn't insist on imagining themselves as techno starships). If they accomplished that, there was no real reason to go back into human bodies. Which of course would make them independent of Kiera. For an entity that lived forever, the variety which would come from trying out a new creature's body and life cycle every few millennia might just be the final answer to terminal ennui.

Accompanying the revelation was a growing resentment at the way Kiera was using them—to which the prospect of fighting for Capone was a worrying development. Even if he was offered a human body now, Rocio was doubtful he wanted to go with the habitat. He wasn't frightened of space like the rest of the returned souls, not anymore, not possessing this magnificent creature. Space and all its emptiness was to be loved for its freedom.

Gravity returned slowly as Gerald drifted through the airlock tube, his shoulder bag in tow. The airlock compartment he landed in was almost identical to the one he had left behind. But it was larger, its technology more discreet, and outside the hatch Choi-Ho and Maxim Payne greeted him with smiles and comforting words where behind Knox and his eldest son had stood guard over their hatch with TIP carbines and scowls.

"There are several cabins available," Choi-Ho said. "Not enough for everyone, so you'll probably have to double up."

Gerald smiled blankly, which came over more as a frightened grimace.

"Pick any one," she told him kindly.

"When will we get there?" Gerald asked.

"We have a rendezvous in the Kabwe system in eight hours, after that we'll be going back to Valisk. It should be about twenty hours."

"Twenty? Is that all?"

"Yes."

"Twenty." It was said with deference. "Are you sure?"

"Yes, quite sure." People were starting to bunch up in the airlock behind him; all of them curiously reluctant to push past. "A cabin," she suggested hopefully.

"Come on, Gerald, mate," Beth said breezily. She took his arm and pulled gently. He walked obediently down the corridor with her. He only stopped once, and that was to look over his shoulder and say an earnest, "Thank you," to an oddly intrigued Choi-Ho.

Beth kept going right to the end of the U-shaped corridor. She thought it would be best to get Gerald a cabin away from the rest of the Deadnights. "Can you believe this place?" she said. She was walking on a deep red carpet past portholes that shone brilliant beams of sunlight into the corridor (although she couldn't see out through them). The doors were all golden wood. In her usual sweatshirt, two jackets, and baggy jeans she felt uncomfortably out of place.

She peered around a door and found an empty cabin. There were two bunk beds clipped to a wall, and a small sliding door to the bathroom. The plumbing was similar to the toilet in the *Leonora Cephei*, except this was all heavy brass with small white glazed ceramic buttons.

"This ought to do you," she said confidently. A quiet pule made her turn around. Gerald was standing just inside the door, his knuckles pressed into his mouth.

"What's the matter, Gerald?"

"Twenty hours."

"I know. But that's good, isn't it?"

"I'm not sure. I want to be there, to see her again. But she's not her anymore, not my Marie."

He was quaking. Beth put an arm around his shoulders and eased him down onto the bottom bunk. "Easy there, Gerald. Once we're at Valisk, all this is going to seem like a bad dream; honestly, mate."

"It doesn't end there, it starts there. And I don't know what to do, I don't know how to save her. I can't put her in zero-tau by myself. They're so strong, and evil."

"Who, Gerald? Who are you talking about? Who's Marie?"

"My baby."

He was crying now, his head pressed into her shoulder. She patted the back of his neck instinctively.

"I don't know what to do," he gasped out. "She's not here to help me."

"Marie's not here?"

"No. Loren. She's the only one that can help me. She's the only one who can help any of us."

"It's all right, Gerald, really, you'll see."

The reaction wasn't what she expected at all. Gerald started a hysterical laugh which was half screams. Beth wanted to let go and get out of the cabin fast. He'd flipped, totally flipped now. The only reason she kept hold of him was because she didn't know what would happen if she didn't. He might get worse.

"Please, Gerald," she begged. "You're frightening me."

He grabbed both of her shoulders, squeezing hard enough to make her flinch. "Good!" His face had reddened with anger. "You should be frightened, you stupid, stupid little girl. Don't you understand where we're going?"

"We're going to Valisk," Beth whispered.

"Yes, Valisk. That doesn't frighten me, I'm bloody terrified. They're going to torture us, hurt you so bad you'll beg a soul to possess you and stop them. I know they will. That's all they ever do. They did it to me before, and then Dr Dobbs made me go through it again, and again and again just so he could know what it was like." The anger drained out of him, and he sagged forwards into her awkward embrace. "I'll kill myself. Yes. Maybe that's it. I can help Marie that way. I'm sure I can. Anything's better than possession again."

Beth started rocking him as best she could, soothing him as she would any five-year-old who'd woken from a nightmare. The things he was saying plagued her badly. After all, they only had Kiera's word that she was building a fresh society for them. One recording that promised she was differ-

ent from the rest. "Gerald?" she asked after a while. "Who's
this Marie you want to help?"

"My daughter."

"Oh. I see. Well how do you know she's at Valisk?"

"Because she's the one Kiera's possessing."

Rocio Condra parted his beak in what passed for a smile.
The sensor in Skibbow's cabin wasn't the best, and his affin-
ity link with its bitek processor suffered annoying dropouts.
But what had been said was plain enough.

He wasn't entirely sure how he could use the knowledge,
but it was the first sign of any possible chink in Kiera's armour. That was a start.

*   *   *

Stephanie could finally see the end of the red cloud cover.
The heavy ceiling had been dropping closer to the ground
for some time now as the convoy drove unimpeded along
the M6. Individual clumps and streamers churned against
each other in a motion reminiscent of waves crashing on
rocks, bright slivers of pink and gold rippled among the distorted underbelly. They acted like a conductor for a current
of pure agitation. The will of the possessed was being
thwarted, their shield against the sky arrested by the Kingdom's firebreak.

The cliff of white light sleeting down along the boisterous
edge appeared almost solid. Certainly it took her eyes a
while to acclimatize, slowly resolving the grainy shadows
which crouched at the end of the road.

"I think it might be a good idea to slow down now," Moyo
said in her ear.

She applied the brakes, reducing their speed to a crawl.
The other three buses behind matched her caution. Two hundred metres from the flexing curtain of sunlight she stopped
altogether. The cloud base was only four or five hundred
metres high here, hammering on the invisible boundary in
perpetual ferment.

Two sets of bright orange barriers had been erected across

the road. The first was under the edge of the cloud, sometimes bathed in red light, sometimes in white; the second was three hundred metres north, guarded by a squad of Royal Marines. Behind them, several dozen military vehicles were drawn up on the hard shoulder, armoured troop transports, ground tanks, general communications vehicles, lorries, a canteen, and several field headquarters caravans.

Stephanie opened the bus doors and stepped down onto the road. The thunder was an aggressive growl here, warning outsiders to keep back.

"What did they do to the grass?" Moyo shouted. Just inside the line of sunlight, the grass was dead, its blades blackened and desiccated. Already it was crumbling into dust. The dead zone lay parallel to the border of the red cloud as far as the eye could see, forming a rigid stripe that cut cleanly across every contour.

Stephanie looked along the broad swath of destruction, trees and bushes had been burned to charcoal stumps. "Some kind of no-man's-land, I suppose."

"That's a bit extreme, isn't it?"

She laughed, and pointed up at the glowing cloud.

"Okay, you got a point. What do you want to do next?"

"I'm not sure." She resented her indecision immediately. This was the culmination of enormous emotional investment. For all that, the practicalities of the moment had been ignored. *I almost wish we were still travelling, it gave me such a sense of satisfaction. What have we got after this?*

Cochrane, McPhee, and Rana joined them.

"Some terminally unfriendly looking dudes we have here," Cochrane yelled above the thunder. The marines lining the barrier were motionless, while more were hurrying from the cluster of vehicles to reinforce them.

"I'd better go and talk to them," Stephanie said.

"Not alone?" Moyo protested.

"I'll look a lot less threatening than a delegation." A white handkerchief sprouted from Stephanie's hand; she held it up high and clambered over the first set of barriers.

Lieutenant Anver watched her coming and gave his squad

their deployment assignments, sending half of them out to flank the road and watch for any other possessed trying to sneak over, not that they'd ever get past the satellites. His helmet sensors zoomed in for a close-up on the woman's face. She was squinting uncomfortably at the light as she emerged from under the dappled shadow of the red cloud. A pair of sunglasses materialized on her face.

"Definitely possessed, sir," he datavised to Colonel Palmer.

"We see that, thank you, Anver," the colonel replied. "Be advised, the security committee is accessing your datavise now."

"Sir."

"There's no other activity along the firebreak," Admiral Farquar datavised. "We don't think she's a diversion."

"Go see what she wants, Anver," Colonel Palmer ordered. "And be very careful."

"Yes, sir."

Two of his squad slid a section of the barrier aside, and he stepped forwards. For all that it was only a hundred-metre walk, it lasted half of his life. He spent the time trying to think what to say to her, but when they stopped a few paces from each other, all he said was: "What do you want?"

She lowered her hand with the handkerchief and gave him a cautious smile. "We brought some children out. They're in the buses back there. I, um . . . wanted to tell you so you wouldn't . . . you know." The smile became one of embarrassment. "We weren't sure how you'd react."

"Children?"

"Yes. About seventy. I don't know the exact number, I never actually counted."

"Does she mean non-possessed?" Admiral Farquar datavised.

"Are these children possessed?"

"Of course not," Stephanie said indignantly. "What do you think we are?"

"Lieutenant Anver, this is Princess Kirsten."

Anver stiffened noticeably. "Yes, ma'am."

"Ask her what she wants, what the deal is."

"What do you want for them?"

Stephanie's lips tightened in anger. "I don't *want* anything. Not in return, they're just children. What I'd like is an assurance that you military types aren't going to shoot them when we send them over."

"Oh, dear," Princess Kirsten datavised. "Apologize to her, Lieutenant, on my behalf, please. And tell her that we're very grateful to her and those with her for bringing the children back to us."

Anver cleared his throat, this wasn't quite what he expected when he started his lonely walk out here. "I'm very sorry, ma'am. The Princess sends her apologies for assuming the worst. We're very grateful to you for what you've done."

"I understand. This isn't easy for me, either. Now, how do you want to handle this?"

Twelve Royal Marines came back to the buses with her; volunteers, without their armour suits and weapons. The bus doors were opened, and the children came down. There were a lot of tears and running around in confusion. Most of them wanted a last kiss and a hug from the adults who had rescued them (Cochrane was especially popular), much to the amazement of the marines.

Stephanie found herself almost in tears as the last batch started off down the broad road, clustering around the big marine; one of them was even being given a piggyback. Moyo's arm was around her shoulders to hold her tight.

Lieutenant Anver came over to stand in front of her and saluted perfectly (to which Cochrane managed a quite obscene parody). He looked badly troubled. "Thank you again, all of you," he said. "That's me saying it, I can't datavise under the cloud."

"Oh, do take care of the little darlings," Tina said, sniffing hard. "Poor Analeese has the most dreadful cold, none of us could cure her. And Ryder hates nuts; I think he's got an allergy, and—" She fell silent as Rana squeezed her forearm.

"We'll take care of them," Lieutenant Anver said gravely.

"And you, you take care of yourselves." He glanced point-edly out to the firebreak where a procession of vehicles was massing around the barrier to greet the children. "You might want to do that away from here." A crisp nod at Stephanie, and he was walking back towards the barrier.

"What did he mean?" Tina asked querulously.

"Wowee." Cochrane let out a long breath. "We like *did it*, man, we showed the forces of bad vibes not to mess with us."

Moyo kissed Stephanie. "I'm very proud of you."

"Ugh," Cochrane exclaimed. "Don't you two cats ever stop?"

A smiling Stephanie leaned forwards and kissed him on his forehead, getting hair caught on her lips. "Thank you, too."

"Will somebody tell me what he meant," Tina said. "Please."

"Nothing good," McPhee said. "That's a fact."

"So now what do we do?" Rana asked. "Go round up an-other group of kids? Or split up? Or settle that farm we talked about? What?"

"Oh, stay together, definitely," Tina said. "After every-thing we've done I couldn't bear losing any of you, you're my family now."

"Family. That's cosmic, sister. So like what's your posi-tion on incest?"

"I don't know what we'll decide," Stephanie said. "But I think we should take the lieutenant's advice, and do it a long way away from here."

* * *

The spaceplane rose out of Nyvan's stratosphere on twin plumes of plasma flame, arching up towards its orbital in-jection coordinate a thousand kilometres ahead. Submuni-tions were still peppering space with explosions and decoy flares, while electronic warfare drones blasted gigawatt pulses at any emission they could detect. Now its reaction drive rockets were on, the spaceplane was no longer invisible to the residuals of the combat wasp battle.

Lady Macbeth flew cover a hundred kilometres above it, sensors and maser cannon deployed to strike any missile which acquired lock-on. The starship had to make continual adjustments to its flight vector to keep the spaceplane within its protective radius. Joshua watched its drive flaring, reducing velocity, accelerating, switching altitude. Five times its masers fired to destroy incoming submunitions.

By the time the spaceplane had reached orbit and was manoeuvring to dock, the sky above Nyvan had calmed considerably. Only three other starships were visible to *Lady Mac*'s sensors, all of them were frigates belonging to local defence forces. None of them seemed interested in *Lady Mac*, or even each other. Beaulieu began a thorough sensor sweep, alert for the inevitable chaotic showers of post-explosion debris which would make low orbit hazardous for some time to come. Some of the returns were odd, making her redefine the sweep's parameters. *Lady Mac*'s sensors shifted their focus away from the planet itself.

Joshua slid cleanly through the hatchway into the bridge. His clothes had dried out in the hot air of the spaceplane's cabin, but the dirt and stains remained. Dahybi's ship-suit was in a similar state.

Sarha gave him an apprehensive glance. "Melvyn?" she asked quietly.

"Not a chance. Sorry."

"Bugger."

"You two did a good job up here," Joshua said. "Well done, that was some fine piloting to stay above the spaceplane."

"Thanks, Josh."

Joshua looked from Liol, who was anchored to a stikpad by the captain's acceleration couch, to Sarha, whose expression was utterly unrepentant.

"Oh, Jesus, you gave him the access codes."

"Yes, I did. My command decision. There was a war up here, Joshua."

It wasn't, he decided, worth making an issue out of, not in view of everything else that was happening. "That's why I left you in charge," he said. "I had confidence in you, Sarha."

She frowned suspiciously. He *sounded* sincere. "So you got Mzu, then. I hope it was worth it."

"For the Confederation I suppose it is. For individuals . . . you'd have to ask them. But then individuals have been dying because of her for some time now."

"Captain, please access our sensor suite," Beaulieu said.

"Right." He rolled in midair, and landed on his acceleration couch. The images from the external sensor clusters expanded into his mind. Wrong. They had to be wrong. "Jesus wept!" His brain was already acting in conjunction with the flight computer's astrogration program to plot a vector before he'd fully admitted the reality of the tide of rock descending on the planet. "Prepare for acceleration, thirty seconds—mark. We have to leave." A fast internal sensor check showed him his new passengers hurrying towards couches; images superimposed with purple and yellow trajectory plots that wriggled frantically as he refined their projected trajectory.

"Who did that?" he asked.

"No idea," Sarha said. "It happened during the battle, we didn't even know until afterwards. But it sure as hell wasn't random combat wasp strikes."

"I'll monitor the drive tubes," Joshua said. "Sarha, take systems coverage, please. Liol, you've got fire control."

"Aye, Captain," Liol said.

It was a strictly neutral tone. Joshua was satisfied with that. He triggered *Lady Mac*'s fusion drives, bringing them up to a three-gee acceleration.

"Where are we going?" Liol asked.

"Bloody good question," Joshua said. "For now I just want us out of here. After that, it rather depends on what Ione and the agents decide, I expect."

There must be someone who knows. One of you.

We know it is real. We know it is hidden.

Two bodies await. A male and a female. Youthful, splendid. Do you hear them? Do you taste them? Pleading for one of you to enter them. You can. All the riches and pleasures of reality can be yours again. If you have the admission price, one tiny piece of information. That's all.

She didn't hide it by herself. She had help from somebody. Probably many. Were you one?

Ah. Yes. You. You are being truthful. You know.

Come then. Come forwards, come through. We reward you with—

He cried out in wonder and misery as he struggled his way into the victim's agonized nervous system. There was pain, and shame, and humiliation to cope with; tragic, terrible pleas from the body's true soul. One by one, he faced them down, mending the broken flesh, suppressing and ignoring the protest, until there was only his own shame left. Not so easily abandoned.

"Welcome to the Organization," said Oscar Kearn. "So, you were part of Mzu's mission?"

"Yes. I was with her."

"Good. She's a clever woman, that Mzu. I'm afraid she's eluded us once again, thanks to that traitor bitch Barnes. Even so, only the amazingly resourceful can duck an ironberg when it's falling on their heads. I didn't realize what I was dealing with before. I don't suppose she would have helped us even if we had caught her. She's like that, tough and determined. But now her luck's run out. You can tell me, can't you? You know where the Alchemist is."

"Yes," Ikela said. "I know where it is."

Alkad Mzu floated into the bridge, accompanied by Monica and Samuel. She acknowledged Joshua with a small twitch of her lips, then blinked when she saw Liol. "I didn't know there were two of you."

Liol grinned broadly.

"Before we all start arguing over what to do with you, Doctor," a serjeant said. "I'd like you to confirm the Alchemist does or did exist."

Alkad tapped her toe on a stikpad beside the captain's couch, preventing herself from drifting about. "Yes, it exists. And I built it. I wish to Mary I hadn't, now, but the past is past. My only concern now is that it doesn't fall into anybody's hands, not yours, and certainly not the possessed."

"Very noble," Sarha said, "from someone who was going to use it to kill an entire planet."

"They wouldn't have been killed," Alkad said wearily. "It was intended to extinguish Omuta's star, not turn it nova. I'm not an Omutan barbarian; they're the ones who kill entire worlds."

"Extinguish a star?" Samuel mused in puzzlement.

"Please don't ask for details."

"I propose Dr Mzu is taken back to Tranquillity," the serjeant said. "We can formalize the observation to insure she doesn't pass the information on. I don't think you will anyway, Doctor, but intelligence agencies are highly suspicious entities."

Monica consulted Samuel. "I can live with that," she said. "Tranquillity is neutral territory. It isn't all that different to our original agreement."

"It isn't," Samuel agreed. "But, Doctor, you do realize you cannot be allowed to die. Certainly not until the problem of possession has been resolved."

"Fine by me," Alkad said.

"What I mean, Doctor, is that when you are very old, you must be placed in zero-tau to prevent your soul from entering the beyond."

"I will not give anyone the Alchemist technology, no matter what the circumstances."

"I'm sure that is your intention at the moment. But how will you feel after a hundred years trapped in the beyond? A thousand? And to be indelicate, the choice is not yours to make. It is ours. You lost the right to self-determination when you built the Alchemist. If you give yourself enough power to make a galaxy fear you and what you can achieve, you abrogate that right to those whom your actions affect."

"I agree," the serjeant said. "You will be placed in zero-tau before you die."

"Why not just put me in now?" Alkad said crustily.

"Don't tempt me," Monica said. "I know the kind of contempt you moron intellectuals hold the government services in. Well listen good, Doctor, we exist to protect the majority so they can run around living their lives as decently and as best they can. We protect them from *shits* like you, who never fucking stop to think what you're doing."

"You didn't protect my bloody planet, did you!" Alkad yelled back. "And don't you dare lecture me on responsibility. I'm prepared to die to stop the Alchemist being used by anybody else, especially your imperialist Kingdom. I know my responsibilities."

"You do now. *Now* you realize what a mistake you made, now people are dying just to keep your precious arse safe."

"Okay, that's it," Joshua said loudly. "We're all agreed where the doc is going, end of discussion. Nobody is going to start shouting about moral philosophy on my bridge. We're all tired, we're all emotional. Pack it in, the pair of you. I'm going to plot a course to Tranquillity, you go to your cabins and cool off. We'll be home inside of two days."

"Understood," Monica said through clenched teeth. "And . . . thank you for getting us off. It was—"

"Professional?"

She almost snapped back at him, but that grin . . . "Professional."

Alkad cleared her throat. "I'm sorry," she said apologetically. "But there is a problem. We can't go straight back to Tranquillity."

Joshua massaged his temple and asked: "Why not?" if only to stop Monica from flying at Mzu's throat.

"The Alchemist itself."

"What about it?" Samuel asked.

"We have to collect it."

"All right," Joshua said in a far-from-reasonable tone. "Why?"

"Because it isn't secure where it is."

"It's managed to stay secure for thirty years. Jesus, just take the secret of its location to zero-tau with you. If the agencies haven't found it by now, they never will."

"They won't have to look anymore, nor will the possessed, especially if our current situation continues for more than a few years."

"Go on, we may as well hear it all."

"There were three ships on our strike mission against Omuta," Alkad said. "The *Beezling*, the *Chengho*, and the *Gombari*. *Beezling* was the Alchemist's deployment vessel, I was on board; the other two were our escort frigates. We were intercepted by blackhawks before we could deploy the Alchemist. They destroyed the *Gombari*, and hit us and the *Chengho* pretty badly. We were left for dead in interstellar space. Neither of us could jump, and the nearest inhabited star was seven light-years away.

"After the attack, we spent a couple of days repairing our internal systems, then we rendezvoused. It was Ikela and Captain Prager who came up with the eventual solution. *Chengho* was smaller than *Beezling*, it didn't need as many energy patterning nodes to perform a ZTT jump. So the crew removed some of the *Beezling*'s intact nodes and installed them in the *Chengho*. We didn't have the proper tools for that kind of job; and then the nodes had different power ratings and performance factors, they had to be completely reprogrammed. It took us three and a half weeks, but we did it. We rebuilt ourselves a ship that could make a ZTT jump—not very well, and not very far, but it was functional. That was when things started to get difficult. The *Chengho* was too small to take both crews, even for just a small jump. There was only one life-support capsule, and it could hold eight of us at a push. We knew we couldn't risk a flight back to Garissa, the nodes would never last that long, and we guessed that Omuta would have launched some kind of big attack by then. After all, that's why we'd been dispatched in the first place, to stop them. So we jumped to the nearest inhabited star system, Crotone. The idea was that we'd charter a ship and get back to Garissa that way. Of course, when we arrived at Crotone, we heard about the genocide.

"Ikela and Prager had even formulated a worst case option. Just in case, they said. We'd brought some antimatter with us on the *Chengho*; if we sold that together with the frigate it would fetch millions. Assuming the Garissan government no longer existed, we would have all the money we needed to operate independently for decades."

"The Stromboli Separatist Council," Samuel said suddenly.

"Right," Alkad acknowledged. "That's who we sold it to."

"Ah, we never did find out how they got their antimatter. They blew up two of Crotone's low-orbit port stations with the stuff."

"After we left, yes," Alkad said.

"So Ikela took the money and founded T'Opingtu."

"Correct; once we found out that the Confederation Assembly granted the Dorados to the survivors of the genocide, all seven navy officers were given an equal share. The plan was for them to invest the money in various companies, the profits from which would be used to help fund the partizans. We needed committed nationalists to crew the ship that they were supposed to prepare for me. After that, they would buy or charter a combat-capable starship to complete the Alchemist mission. As you know, Ikela didn't fulfill the last part of the plan. I don't know about the others."

"Why wait thirty years?" Joshua asked. "Why didn't you just hire a combat-capable starship as soon as you had the money from the sale of the frigate, and go straight back to the *Beezling*?"

"Because we couldn't be sure exactly where it was. You see, we didn't just repair the *Chengho*. There were thirty people and the Alchemist left behind on the *Beezling*. Suppose the *Chengho* didn't make it, or suppose we were caught and interrogated by the CNIS or some other agency? There was even the possibility the blackhawks might return. We had to plan for all those factors as well, the remaining crew had to be given their chance, too."

"They went into zero-tau," Joshua said. "How does that prevent you from knowing the exact coordinate?"

"Yes, obviously they went into zero-tau, but that's not all. We also repaired their reaction drive. They flew a vector to an uninhabited star which was only two and a half light-years away."

"Jesus, a sub-lightspeed journey through interstellar space? You've got to be kidding. That's impossible, it would take—"

"Twenty-eight years, we estimated."

"Ah!" Realization came to Joshua like the silent detonation of Norfolk Tears after it hit the stomach. He felt a surge of admiration for those lost desperate crews of thirty years ago. Not caring what the odds were, just going for it. "They used antimatter propulsion."

"Yes. We transferred every gram from our remaining combat wasps into the *Beezling*'s confinement chambers. It was enough to accelerate them up to about nine per cent lightspeed. So now tell me, Captain, how difficult would it be to locate a ship that is moving away from its last known coordinate at eight or nine per cent lightspeed? And if you did find it, how would you rendezvous?"

"Not possible. Okay, you have to wait until the *Beezling* decelerated and arrived at that uninhabited star. How come you didn't make a dash for them two years ago?"

"Because we weren't sure just how efficient the drive would be over such a long period of use. Two years gave us an adequate safety margin; and of course as it turned out, the sanctions would be over. There was always a remote chance the Confederation Navy blockade squadron would detect us, after all it's their job to be looking for sanction-buster starships emerging in odd places around Omuta. So after we sold the *Chengho* we decided on thirty years."

"You mean the *Beezling* is just orbiting that star waiting for you to make contact?" Liol asked.

"Yes. Providing everything worked as it was supposed to. They are supposed to wait for another five years; the time is irrelevant in zero-tau, but the support systems cannot last indefinitely. If they hadn't been contacted by then, either by myself and the *Chengho* crew, or the Garissan government, they were to destroy the Alchemist and start signalling for help. Uninhabited star systems within the Confederation boundaries are inspected on a regular basis by navy patrol ships to make sure they aren't being used by antimatter production stations. They would have been rescued eventually."

Joshua glanced around to the serjeant, wishing the construct had some way of displaying emotion; he'd like to know what Ione made of the story. "Makes sense," he said. "What do you want to do?"

"We have to see if the *Beezling* completed its journey," the serjeant said.

"And if it has?" Samuel asked.

"Then the Alchemist must be destroyed. After that, any surviving crew will be taken back to Tranquillity."

"Question, Doc," Joshua said. "If anybody sees the Alchemist, will that give them a clue to its nature?"

"No. You have no worries on that score, Captain. There is however someone among the crew who could tell you how to build another. His name is Peter Adul, he will have to remain in Tranquillity with me. After that, you will be safe again."

"Okay, what's the star's coordinate?"

It was a long time before Alkad said: "Mother Mary, this is not what was meant to be."

"Nothing ever is, Doc. I learned that long ago."

"Ha! You're too young."

"Depends how you fill the years, doesn't it?"

Alkad Mzu datavised the coordinate over.

• • •

A wormhole terminus is opening, Tranquillity announced.

At the time, Ione was standing knee deep in the warm water of the cove, rubbing Haile's flank with a big yellow bath sponge. She straightened her back and began wringing out the sponge. Her real attention was focused on a point in space a hundred and twenty thousand kilometres away from the habitat where the vacuum's gravity density was building rapidly. Three SD platforms orbiting the emergence zone locked their X-ray lasers on to the terminus as it expanded. Five patrol blackhawks accelerated in at four gees.

A large voidhawk slipped out of the two-dimensional rent. *Oenone*, **Confederation Navy ship SLV-66150, requesting approach and docking permission,** it said. **Our official flight authentication code follows.**

Granted, Tranquillity replied after it verified the code. The SD platforms were switched back to alert status. Three of the blackhawks resumed their patrol, while the remaining two curved around to form an escort as *Oenone* accelerated in towards the habitat.

"I'm going to have to leave you," Ione said.

Jay Hilton's vexed face peeped over the top of Haile's gleaming white back. "What is it this time?" she asked petulantly.

"Affairs of state." Ione started wading towards the shore. She scooped some water up and tried to flush the sand out of her bikini top.

"You always say that."

Ione gave the disgruntled girl a forlorn smile. "Because it always is, these days." **Sorry,** she added.

Haile formshifted the tip of an arm into a human hand and waved. **Goodbye, Ione Saldana. I have much sorrow you are leaving, my endlegs itch like hell.**

Haile!

I form a communication wrongness? I have shame.

Not wrong, exactly.

Gladness. That was a Joshua Calvert expression. Much favoured.

Ione snapped her teeth together. That bloody Calvert! Anger gave way to something more confusing, a sort of resentment . . . possibly. Hundreds of light-years away, and he still intrudes. **It would be. Please don't use it around Jay.**

Understanding is me. I have a great many human emphasis phrases conveyed by Joshua Calvert.

I'll bet you have.

I want properness in my communication. I ask your assistance in reviewing my word collection. You may edit me.

Yes, all right.

Much gladness!

Ione took another pace, then laughed. Reviewing everything Joshua had said to the young Kiint would take hours. Hours she hadn't been spending on the beach of late. Haile was becoming very crafty.

Jay leaned against her friend, watching Ione put her sandals on and start back up the path to the tube station. There was a slightly distracted expression on the woman's face, that Jay knew meant she was busy talking to the habitat personality. She didn't like to dwell on the topic. More than likely, it would be the possessed again. That was all the adults talked about these days, and it was never reassuring talk.

Haile's arm twined around Jay's, the tip stroking her gently.

You taste of sadness.

"I don't think these horrible possessed will ever go away."

They will. Humans are clever. You will find a way.

"I hope so. I do want Mummy back."

Shall we build the castles of sand now?

"Yes!" Jay grinned enthusiastically and started splashing her way back up to the beach. They'd made the discovery together that Haile with her tractamorphic arms was the universe's best ever builder of sand castles. With Jay directing, they had made some astonishing towers along the shoreline.

Haile emerged from the water in a small explosion of spray. **Betterness. You have happiness again.**

"So do you. Ione promised to come back for the words."

It is the best niceness when the three of us play together. She knows this really.

Jay giggled. "She turned purple when you said that. Good job you didn't say fuck to her."

* * *

The *Oenone*, Ione reflected. **Why do I know that name?**

Atlantis.

Oh, yes.

And a certain interception in the Puerto de Santa Maria star system. We received an intelligence update from the Confederation Navy last year.

Oh, bloody hell, *yes*.

Captain Syrinx wishes to talk to you.

Ione sat down in the tube carriage and began towelling her hair. **Of course.** The affinity contact broadened, allowing Syrinx to proffer her identity trait.

Captain, Ione acknowledged.

I apologize for the haste, but please be advised a Confederation Navy squadron will start arriving in another nine minutes and thirty seconds—mark.

I see. Is Tranquillity in danger?

No.

What then?

I am carrying the squadron's commander, Admiral Meredith Saldana. He requests an interview at which he can explain our full strategic situation to you.

Granted. Welcome to Tranquillity. The captain faded from the affinity band.

She was curious about you, Tranquillity said. **It was quite plain from her emotional content.**

Everybody's always curious about me. She borrowed the habitat's external senses to observe local space. They were in Mirchusko's umbra, with Choisya and Falsia hovering just above the gas giant's crescent horizon. Apart from the flotilla of blackhawks on patrol around the habitat's shell, there was little spaceship activity. The *Oenone* was the first starship to arrive in seventy-six hours. Some MSVs and personnel commuters continued to glide between the counter-rotating spaceport and Tranquillity's bracelet of industrial stations, but they were running a much reduced flight schedule. A lone dazzle-point of fusion flame was rising up past the drab grey loop of the Ruin Ring, an He_3

tanker en route from the habitat's cloudscoop to the space-port. **Program the squadron's arrival into the SD plat-forms,** she said. **And warn the blackhawks, we don't want any mistakes.**

Naturally.

Meredith Saldana. That's two family visits in less than a month.

I don't think this is a family visit.

You're probably right.

It was a suspicion which was proved unpleasantly correct soon after Syrinx and the admiral were shown into the audi-ence chamber of De Beauvoir Palace. As she listened to Meredith Saldana explain the proposed ambush of Capone's fleet at Toi-Hoi a swarm of ambiguous feelings lay siege to her mind.

I don't want to involve us in front line campaigns, she confided to Tranquillity.

To be pedantic, we're in the campaign, not the front line itself. And the eradication of the Organization fleet is not a strategic opportunity which can be overlooked.

No choice?

No choice.

I still think we're too important for this.

But safe. The safest place in the Confederation, re-member that.

We hope. I'd hate to put that to the test, right now.

I don't see how it will. Not from this action. We will es-sentially be a supply and rendezvous base.

"Very well," she told the admiral. "You have my permis-sion to use Tranquillity for your task force's port station. I'll see that you get all the He_3 you need."

"Thank you, ma'am," Meredith said.

"I'm slightly concerned by this flight restriction you wish to place on starships until the ambush, although I do appre-ciate the logic behind it. I currently have over twenty black-hawks deploying sensor satellites around the orbit where the

Laymil home planet used to be. It's extremely important research work. I'd hate to see it jeopardized."

"They would only have to be recalled for three or four days at the most," Syrinx said. "Our scheduling is very tight, here. Surely a small delay wouldn't effect the research too much?"

"I'll recall them for now. But if you're still here after a week, I'll have to review the policy. As I said, this is part of the effort to find an overall solution. That is not to be regarded lightly."

"Believe me, we don't, ma'am," Meredith said.

She stared at him, trying to work out what was going on behind his blue eyes. But his answering stare offered no clue. "I have to say, I find it ironic that Tranquillity has become so important to the Confederation and the Kingdom after all this time," she said.

"Ironic or pleasing? Chance has finally brought you the chance to vindicate your grandfather's actions."

There was no humour in his tone, which surprised her. She'd assumed he would be more sympathetic than Prince Noton. "You think Grandfather Michael was wrong?"

"I think he was wrong to pursue such an unorthodox course."

"Unorthodox to the family, perhaps. But I assure you it's not chance which has brought us together. This whole situation will prove how right he was to act on his foresight."

"I wish you every success."

"Thank you. And who knows, one day I might earn your approval, too."

For the first time, he produced a grudging smile. "You don't like losing arguments, do you, Cousin Ione?"

"I am a Saldana."

"That much is painfully obvious."

"As are you. I don't think every Confederation admiral would have coped as well as you at Lalonde."

"I did not cope well. I ensured my squadron survived; most of it, anyway."

"A Confederation officer's first duty is to follow orders.

Second duty is to the crew. So I believe," she said. "As your original orders didn't cover what you encountered, I'd say you did all right."

"Lalonde was . . . difficult," he said heavily.

"Yes. I know all about Lalonde from Joshua Calvert."

Syrinx, who had been looking considerably ill at ease while the two Saldanas conducted their verbal fencing, glanced sharply at Ione, her eyebrows raised in interest.

"Oh, yes," Meredith reflected. "Lagrange Calvert. Who could forget him?"

"Is he here?" Syrinx asked. "This is his registered port."

"He's away at the moment, I'm afraid," Ione told her. "But I'm expecting him back any day now."

"Good."

Ione couldn't quite fathom the Edenist's attitude. **Why do you think she's interested in Joshua?**

I have no idea. Unless she wants to punch him on the nose for Puerto de Santa Maria.

I doubt it. She's an Edenist, they don't do things like that. You don't suppose she and Joshua . . . ?

I doubt it. She's an Edenist, they have more taste.

● ● ●

Athene didn't want him to come to the house. It would be too upsetting for the children, she explained. Though they both knew it was she who was discomforted by the whole idea; keeping him away was a way of establishing a psychological barrier.

Instead, she chose one of the spaceport reception lounges in the habitat's endcap. There was nobody else in the spacious room when she arrived, not that there could be any mistake. The hulking figure was sitting on a deep settee in front of the long window, watching service crews bustling around the voidhawks on their pedestals outside. It was a squadron assigned to assist the Kulu Kingdom in the Mortonridge Liberation campaign, one of them would soon be transporting him to Ombey.

I missed this, he said, not turning around, **I watched the voidhawks through the sensitive cells, of course, but I still miss this. The habitat perception doesn't provide any sense of urgency. And my emotions were not suppressed exactly, but less colourful, not so keenly felt. Do you know, I think I'm actually becoming excited.**

She walked over to the settee, an extraordinary sense of trepidation simmering in her mind. The figure stood, revealing its true height, several centimetres taller than she. As with all Tranquillity serjeants, its exoskeleton was a faint ruddy colour, although a good forty per cent of its body was covered in bright green medical nanonic packages. It held up both hands, and turned them around, studying them intently, its eyes just visible at the back of their protective slits.

I must be quite a sight. They force-cloned all the organs separately, then stitched them together. Serjeants take fifteen months to grow to full size usually; that would be far too long. So here we are, Frankenstein's army, patched together and rushed off the assembly line. The packages should have done their work before we reach Ombey.

Athene's shoulders drooped, mirroring the dismay in her mind. Oh, Sinon, what *have* you done?

What I had to. The serjeants must have some controlling consciousness. And seeing as how there were all us individual personalities already available . . .

Yes, but not you!

Somebody has to volunteer.

I didn't want you to be one.

I'm just a copy, my darling, and an edited down one at that. My real personality is still in the neural strata, suspended for now. When I get back, or if this serjeant is destroyed, I'll return to the multiplicity.

This is so wrong. You've had your life. It was a wonderful life, rich and exciting, and full of love. Transferring into the multiplicity is our reward for living true to our culture, it should be like being a grandparent forever, a grandparent with the largest family of relatives in the universe. You carry on loving, and you become part of something precious to all of us. She looked up at the hard mask that was its face, her own frail cheeks trembling. You don't come back. You just don't. It's not right, Sinon, it isn't. Not for us, not for Edenists.

If we don't help the Kingdom to liberate Mortonridge, there may not be any Edenists for very much longer.

No! I won't accept that. I never have. I believe Laton if no one else does. I refuse to fear the beyond like some inadequate Adamist.

It's not the beyond we have to worry about, it's those that have returned from it.

I was one of those who opposed this Mortonridge absurdity.

I know.

By committing ourselves to it, we're no better than animals. Beasts lashing out; it's filthy. Humans can be so much more.

But rarely are.

That's what Edenism was supposed to be about, to lift us above this primitivism. All of us.

The serjeant put its arm out towards her, then withdrew it hurriedly. Shame leaked out into the affinity band. I'm sorry. I shouldn't have asked you to come. I see how much this hurts you. I just wanted to see you with my own eyes one last time.

They're not your own eyes; and you're not even Sinon, not really. I think that's what I hate most about this. It's not just Adamist religions the beyond undermines, it's ruined the whole concept of transference. What's the point? You are your soul, if you are anything. The Kiint are right, simulacrum personalities are nothing more than a sophisticated library of memories.

In our case, the Kiint are wrong. The habitat personality has a soul. Our individual memories are the seeds of its consciousness. The more there are of us in the multiplicity, the richer its existence and heritage becomes. Knowledge of the beyond hasn't ruined our culture.

Edenism can adapt, it can learn and grow. Surmounting
this time intact will be our triumph. And that's what I'm
fighting for, to give us that physical chance. I know the
Mortonridge Liberation is a fraud, we all do. But that
doesn't stop it from being valid.

You're going to kill people. However careful you are,
however well intentioned you are, they will die.

Yes. I didn't start this, and I won't be the one who
stops it. But I must play my part. To do nothing would be
to sin by omission. What I and the others do on Mortonridge might buy you enough time.

Me?

You, Consensus, the Adamist researchers, maybe
even priests. All of you have to keep looking. The Kiint
found a way to face the beyond and survive. It's here
somewhere.

I'll do what I can, which at my age is very limited.

Don't underestimate yourself.

Thank you. You haven't been edited down that much,
you know.

Some parts of me can't be edited, not if I want to
keep being me. Bearing that in mind, I have one last
favour to ask of you.

Go on.

I'd like you to explain this to Syrinx for me. I know
my little Sly-minx, she'll go nova when she hears I volunteered for this.

I'll tell her. I don't know if I can explain, but . . .

The serjeant bowed as best the medical packages would
allow. **Thank you, Athene.**

I can't give you my blessing. But do please take care.

• • •

There was no lavish farewell party this time. Monterey had
a more serious, less triumphant air these days. But Al
chose the Hilton's ballroom anyway to watch the fleet
coming together, and to hell with any bad feelings and re-

sentiment it stirred up in his head. He stood in front of the window, gazing out at the starships clustered around Monterey. There were over a hundred and fifty of them, dwindling away until the more distant ones were nothing more than big stars. Ion thrusters fired microsecond jets of gauzy blue neon to keep their attitude locked. MSVs and personnel commuters swam among them, delivering new crew and combat wasps.

The stealthed mines which the voidhawks from Yosemite had scattered were no more, returning space around New California to a more peaceful state. Even the voidhawks sent to observe the Organization were finding it increasingly difficult to maintain their inspection high above New California's poles.

As if to emphasise the change in local strategic fortunes, a hellhawk hurtled past the Hilton tower, twisting about in complex curves to dodge the stationary Adamist starships. It was one of the harpies, a red-eyed beast with a hundred-and-eighty-metre wingspan and a vicious-looking beak.

Al pressed himself up against the window to watch as it skirred around the asteroid. "Go you beaut," he yelled after it. "Go get 'em. Go!"

A small puff of pink dust erupted from nowhere as a stealthed spyglobe was masered. The hellhawk performed a victory roll, wingtip feathers standing proud to twist the solar wind.

"Wow!" Al pulled back from the window, smiling magnanimously. "Ain't that something else?"

"Glad I can live up to my part of the bargain," Kiera said with cool objectivity.

"Lady, after this, you got as many fresh bodies as you want for Valisk. Al Capone knows how to reward his friends. And believe me, this is what I call friendly."

A serene smile ghosted her beautiful young face. "Thank you, Al."

The cluster of Organization lieutenants at the rear of the ballroom kept their expressions stoic, while their minds palpitated with jealousy. Al liked that; introduce a new favourite in court, and see how the old-timers bid to prove themselves. He sneaked a look at Kiera's profile; she was wearing a loose-fitting purple blouse and second-skin-tightness trousers, hair tied back with fussy decorum. Her face was beguiling, with its prim features kept firmly under control. But smouldering deep behind it was the old familiar illness of powerlust. She had more class than most, but she wasn't so different.

"How we doing, Luigi?" Al bellowed.

"Pretty good, Al. The hellhawk crews say they should have cleared away every mine and spyglobe in another thirty-two hours. We're pushing those asshole voidhawks back further and further, which means they can't launch any more crap at us. They don't know what we're doing anymore, and they can't hurt us so bad. It makes one hell of a difference. The fleet's shaping up great now. The guys, they're getting their morale back, you know."

"Glad to hear it." Which was an understatement. It had been looking bad for a while, what with the voidhawks launching their unseen weapons and the lieutenants down on the planet abusing their authority to carve themselves out some territory. Funny how all problems locked together. Now the hellhawks had arrived the situation in space was improving by the hour. The crews were no longer living in constant fear of a strike by a stealthed mine, which improved their efficiency and confidence by orders of magnitude. People on the ground sensed the fresh tide above them and wanted to play ball again. The number of beefs was dropping; and the guys Leroy had working the Treasury electric adding machines said fraud was levelling out—not falling yet, but shit you couldn't expect miracles.

"How do you keep the hellhawks in line?" Al asked.

"I can guarantee them human bodies when their work's finished," Kiera said. "Bodies which they can go straight into without having to return to the beyond first. They're very special bodies, and you don't have any."

"Hey." Al spread his arms wide, puffing out a huge

cloud of cigar smoke. "I wasn't trying to muscle in on you, sister. No way. You got a neat operation. I respect that."

"Good."

"We need to talk terms about another squadron. I mean, between you and me, I'm in deep shit over Arnstadt—pardon my French. The goddamn voidhawks there are wasting a couple of my ships each day. Something's gotta be done."

Kiera gave a noncommittal moue. "And what about this fleet? Won't you need a squadron to protect it from voidhawks at Toi-Hoi?"

Al didn't need to consult Luigi over that one, he could sense the hunger in the fleet commander's mind. "Now you come to mention it, it might not be a bad idea."

"I'll see to it," Kiera said. "There should be another group of hellhawks returning to Valisk today. If I dispatch a messenger now, they should be back here within twenty-four hours."

"Sounds pretty damn good to me, lady."

Kiera raised her walkie-talkie, and pulled a long length of chrome aerial out of it. "Magahi, would you return to Monterey's docking ledge, please."

"Roger," a crackling voice said from the walkie-talkie. "Give me twenty minutes."

Al was aware of an uncomfortable amount of satisfaction in Kiera's mind. She was pretty sure she'd just won something. "Couldn't you just tell Magahi to go straight back to the habitat?" he inquired lightly.

Kiera's smile widened gracefully. It was the same welcoming promise which had ended the Deadnight recording. "I don't think so. There's a big security factor if we radio the order; after all there are still some spyglobes out there. I don't want the Edenists to know Magahi is flying escort on a frigate convoy."

"Escort? What frigates?"

"The frigates carrying the first batch of my antimatter combat wasps to Valisk. That was your part of the bargain, Al, wasn't it?"

Damn the bitch! Al's cigar had gone out. Emmet said their stocks of antimatter were nearly exhausted, and the fleet needed every gram to insure success at Toi-Hoi. He looked at Leroy, then Luigi. Neither of them could offer him a way out. "Sure thing, Kiera. We'll get it organized."

"Thank you, Al."

Tough little ironass. Al couldn't decide if he respected that or not. He didn't need any more complications right now. But he was awful glad that she was lining up on his side.

He took another sidelong look at her figure. Who knows? We could get to be real close allies. Except Jez would kill me for real . . .

The ballroom's huge double doors swung open to admit Patricia and someone Al had never seen before. A possessed man, who managed to cringe away from Patricia at the same time as he scampered along beside her. Judging by the perilously fragile state of his thoughts he had only just come into his new body.

He saw Al, and made an effort to compose himself. Then his eyes darted to the huge window. His discipline crumpled. "Holy cow," he whispered. "It is true. You are going to invade Toi-Hoi."

"Who the fuck is this goofball?" Al shouted at Patricia.

"His name's Perez," she said calmly. "And you need to listen to him."

If it had been anyone else who spoke to him like that, they would've been kiboshed. But Patricia was one he really trusted. "You're shitting me, right?"

"Think what he just said, Al."

Al did. "How did you know about Toi-Hoi?" he asked.

"Khanna! I got it from Khanna. She told me to tell you. She said one of us must get through. Then she killed me. She killed all of us. No, not killed, executed, that's what she did, executed us. Smash smash smash with the white fire. Straight through my brain. That bitch! I'd only been back for five minutes. Five goddamn minutes!"

"Who told you, fella? Who's this she you got the beef with?"

"Jacqueline Couteur. Back in Trafalgar. The Confederation Navy got her banged up in the demon trap. I hope she rots there. Bitch."

Patricia smiled a superior I-told-you-so, which Al acknowledged frugally. He put his arm around Perez's shaking shoulders, and proffered the man a Havana. "Okay, Perez. You got my word, the word of Al Capone, which is the toughest currency of all, that nobody here is gonna send you back into the beyond again. Now, you wanna start at the beginning for me?"

13

Earth.

A planet whose ecology was ruined beyond repair: the price it paid for elevating itself to be the Confederation's supreme industrial and economic superpower. Overpopulated, ancient, decadent, and utterly formidable. This was the undeniable imperial heart of the human dominion.

It was also home.

Quinn Dexter admired the images building up on the bridge's holoscreens. This time he could savour them with unhurried joy. Their official Nyvan flight authority code had been accepted by Govcentral Strategic Defence Command. As far as anyone was concerned, they were a harmless ship sent by a tiny government to buy defence components.

"Traffic control has given us a vector," Dwyer said. "We have permission to dock at the Supra-Brazil tower station."

"That's good. Can you fly it?"

"I think so. It's tough, we have to go around the Halo, and they've given us a narrow flight path, but I can handle that."

Quinn nodded his permission without saying anything. Dwyer had been a perfect pain in the arse for the whole voyage, making out how difficult everything was before the flight computer performed whatever was required with faultless efficiency. An extraordinarily transparent attempt to show how indispensable he was. But then Quinn knew the effect he had on people, it was part of the fun.

Dwyer was immediately busy talking to the flight computer. Icons flurried over the console displays. Eight minutes later they were under power, accelerating at a third of a gee to curve southwards around the O'Neill Halo.

"Are we going down to the planet first?" Dwyer asked. He was growing progressively twitchier in contrast to Quinn's deadly calm. "I didn't know if you wanted to take over an asteroid."

"Take over?" Quinn asked faintly.

"Yeah. You know, bring them the gospel of God's Brother. Like we did for Jesup and the other three."

"No, I don't think so. Earth isn't so arse backwards as Nyvan, it would never be that simple to convene the Night here. It must be corrupted from within. The sects will help me do that. Once I show them what I've become they'll welcome me back. And of course, my friend Banneth is down there. God's Brother understands."

"Sure, Quinn, that's good. Whatever you say." The communications console bleeped for attention, which Dwyer happily gave it. Script flowed down one of the screens, which only amplified his distress as he read it. "Hell, Quinn, have you seen this?"

"God's Brother gave me a great many gifts, but being psychic isn't one of them."

"It's the clearance procedures we have to comply with after we dock. Govcentral security wants to ensure no possessed are on board."

"Fuck that."

"Quinn!"

"I do hope, I really fucking do hope that you're not questioning me, Dwyer."

"Shit, no way, Quinn. You're the man, you know that." His voice was verging on hysteria.

"Glad to hear it."

The Brazilian orbital tower sprouted from the very heart of the South American continent, extending fifty-five thousand kilometres out into space. When it was in Earth's penumbra, as it was when the *Mount's Delta* approached, it was invisible to every visual sensor. However, in other electromagnetic wavelengths, and particularly the magnetic spectrum, it *gleamed*. A slim golden strand of impossible length, with minute scarlet particles skimming along it at tremendous speed.

There were two asteroids attached to the tower. Supra-Brazil, the anchor, was in geostationary orbit thirty-six thousand kilometres above the ground, where it had been mined to extract the carbon and silicon used in the tower's construction. The second asteroid sat right at the tip, acting as a mass counterbalance to ensure the anchor remained stable, and damp down any dangerous harmonic oscillations in the tower which built up from running the lift capsules.

Because Supra-Brazil was the only section of the tower that was actually in orbit, it was the one place where ships could dock. Unlike every settled asteroid it didn't rotate, nor were there any internal biosphere caverns. The three-hundred-metre-diameter tower ran cleanly through the rock's centre; its principal structure perfectly black and perfectly circular. Positioned around the lower segment that stretched down to Earth were twenty-five magnetic rails along which the lift capsules rode, delivering tens of thousands of passengers and up to a hundred thousand tonnes of cargo a day. The other segment, reaching up to the counterbalance, supported a single rail, which was used barely once a month to ferry inspection and maintenance mechanoids to the individual section platforms.

The surface of the asteroid was covered with docking bays and all the usual spaceport support equipment. After three hundred and eighty-six years of continual operation, and the tower's steady capacity expansion, there wasn't a square metre of rock left visible.

Even with the Confederation quarantine operating, over six thousand ships a day were still using it, the majority of them from the Halo. They approached by positioning themselves ahead of the port, a long ribbon of diverse craft dropping down from a higher orbit. Navigation strobes and secondary drives produced twinkling cataracts of light as they split into a complex braid of traffic lanes a kilometre above the surface to reach their allocated bays. Departing ships formed an equally intricate helical pattern as they rose away into a higher orbit.

Mount's Delta slotted into its designated traffic lane, gliding around the vast stem of the tower to dock in the floor of a valley formed by pyramids of heat exchangers, tanks, and thermo-dump panels, three times the size of the Egyptian originals. When the docking cradle had drawn it down into the bottom of the bay, a necklace of lights around the rim came on, illuminating every centimetre of the hull. Figures in black space armour were secured around the bay walls, ready to deal with anyone trying to leave the ship by irregular means.

"Now what?" Quinn asked.

"We have to give the security service total access to our flight computer. They're going to run a complete diagnostic to make sure there aren't any unexplained glitches anywhere in the ship. They'll also monitor us through the internal sensors at the same time. Once they're satisfied there's no glitch we're allowed out into the bay. We have to undergo a whole series of tests, including datavises from our neural nanonics. *Quinn*, we haven't got any bloody neural nanonics, and a starship's crew always have them fitted. Always!"

"I told you," Quinn's hollow voice said from deep within his hood, "I will deal with it. What else?"

Dwyer gave the display a wretched stare. "Once we've been cleared, we're put in a secure holding area while the ship is searched by an armed security team. After it's cleared, we will be allowed out."

"I'm impressed."

Dwyer's communications console was showing a demand from the port's security service to access the flight computer. "What do we do?" he shrieked. "We can't fly away, we can't comply. We're trapped. They'll storm us. They'll have projectile weapons we can't beat. Or they'll rip the capsule bulkhead open and decompress us. Or electrocute us with—"

"You're trapped." It was only a tiny whisper, but it stopped Dwyer's rant dead.

"You can't! Quinn, I did everything you asked. Everything! I'm loyal. I've always been fucking loyal to you."

Quinn extended an arm, a single white finger emerging from the end of his black sleeve.

Dwyer threw out both hands. White fire screamed out of his palms to lash at the black-robed incarnation of Death. Bridge consoles flickered madly as corkscrews of pale flame bounced off Quinn, flashing through the air to bury themselves in bulkheads and equipment.

"Finished?" Quinn asked.

Dwyer was sobbing.

"You're weak. I like that. It means you'll serve me well. I will find you again, and use you."

Dwyer evacuated his stolen body just before the first burn of pain smashed along his spinal cord.

The security team assigned to the *Mount's Delta* knew something was wrong as soon as the starship docked. Its routine datavises began to drop out for seconds at a time. When the bay's management officer tried to contact the captain there was no reply. A level one alert was declared.

The docking bay and its immediate surroundings were sealed up and isolated from the rest of Supra-Brazil. One squad of combat officers and another of technical experts were rushed to the docking bay to complement the original team. Communications lines were opened to an advisory panel made up from senior commanders in the Govcentral Internal Security Directorate and the Strategic Defence force.

Four minutes after it docked, the clipper-class starship's datavises had returned to normal, but there was still no response from the captain nor any other member of the crew. The security advisory panel authorized the team to go to the next stage.

A datalink umbilical jacked into a socket on the starship's hull. The GISD's most powerful decryption computers were brought on line to crack the flight computer's access codes; it took less than thirty seconds. The nature of the bridge's modified processors and programs were obvious: customized to be run by possessed. Almost simultaneously, the sensors began relaying their images from the interior of the small life-support capsule. There was nobody inside. However, there was one anomaly whose cause wasn't immediately apparent. A thick red paste was splashed across almost every surface in the bridge. Then an eyeball drifted past one of the sensors, and that mystery was solved—leaving a bigger paradox. The blood hadn't yet congealed. Some one or thing on board had slaughtered the crew member only minutes ago. GISD could not permit an unknown threat to remain at large; if the possessed had developed a fresh method of attack it had to be investigated.

An airlock tube extended out from the side of the bay. After arming themselves with chemical explosive fragmentation grenades and submachine guns, five GISD combat officers advanced through it to the life-support capsule. Each of them encountered a small squall of cold air in the tube as they pulled themselves along, barely noticeable through their armour.

Once inside, they opened every storage locker and cabinet to try to locate the missing crew members. There was nobody to be found. Even the flight computer confirmed no atmosphere was being consumed.

An engineering crew from the port was sent in to strip down the life-support capsule. It took them six hours to remove every single fitting, including the decking. The advisory council was left with an empty sphere seven metres in diameter with severed cables and hoses poking through sealed inlets. A meticulous examination of the flight computer records, evaluating power consumption, command interfaces, fuel expenditure, and utilities usage showed that there must have been two people on board when the *Mount's Delta* docked. But DNA analysis on the blood and tissue smearing the bridge showed it had all come from one body.

The *Mount's Delta* was powered down, and its cryogenic tanks emptied. Then the entire ship was slowly and methodically cut up into sections, from the support framework to the fusion generators, even the energy patterning nodes. No unit or module bigger than a cubic metre was left intact.

The media, of course, soon discovered the "ghost flight" from Nyvan; and rover reporters swarmed around the bay, demanding and bribing information from anyone they could find connected to the security operation. It wasn't long before they managed to gain legal access to a sensor in the bay itself thanks to two judges whose motives were somewhat financially inclined. Several tens of millions of people in Earth's arcologies started accessing the investigation directly, watching the starship being cut up by mechanoids, and waiting eagerly for a possessed to be captured.

Quinn saw no reason to stay inside the dry deprivation of the ghost realm once he had passed unseen through all the security checks; he rematerialized and sat in a luxurious active contour leather seat in the lift capsule's Royale Class lounge. He was near one of the panoramic windows, which would allow him to watch the dawn rise over South America as he descended vertically towards it at three thousand kilometres an hour. With his hawkish, stressed face and expensively conservative blue silk suit he slotted perfectly into the character of an aristocratic businessman.

For the last quarter of the journey down the tower he sipped his complimentary Norfolk Tears, which was continually topped up by a stewardess, and gave the AV projector above the cocktail bar an occasional glance. Earth's media companies competed enthusiastically to update him on the progress of the search through the dissected components of the *Mount's Delta*. If the rest of the lounge wondered at his intermittent guffaws of contempt, Earth's obsessive cult of personal privacy forbade them from enquiring as to the reason.

• • •

Jed spent most of the voyage sitting on the pine floorboards in the *Mindo*r's lounge, gazing out at the starfield. There had never been a time in his life when he felt more content. The stars themselves were beautiful seen like this, and every now and then the hellhawk would swallow through a wormhole. That was exciting, even though there wasn't much to see then, just a kind of dark grey fog swirling around outside that was never quite in focus. Coupled with the sense of invulnerability generated by riding in the hellhawk was the anticipation of Valisk, never stronger than now.

I did it. For the first time in my life I set myself a solid goal and saw it through. Against some pretty nasty odds, too. Me and all the other kids from nowhere, we made it to Valisk. And Kiera.

He had brought his modified recording of her, although he no longer needed it. Every time he closed his eyes he could see that smile, thick soft hair falling over her bare shoulders, perfectly rounded cheeks. She would congratulate him personally when they arrived. She must, because he was the leader. So they would probably get to talk, because she'd want to know how difficult it was for them, how they had struggled. She would be sympathetic, because that was her nature. Then perhaps—

Gari and Navar bounded into the lounge, laughing happily together. Some kind of truce had been declared since they came on board. A minor omen, Jed thought; things were steadily getting better.

"What are you doing?" Gari asked.

He grinned up at her and gestured to the window with its thick rim of brass. "Just looking. So what are you two doing?"

"We came to tell you. We just talked to Choi-Ho. She says this is the last swallow before we get to Valisk. Another hour, Jed!" Her face rose with elation.

"Yeah, another hour." He snatched another glance at the alien greyness outside. Any minute now they'd be back in real space. Then he realized Beth wasn't here to witness their triumph. "Back in a minute," he told the two girls.

The *Mindor* was quite crowded now. The rendezvous in the Kabwe system had brought another twenty-five Deadnights on board. Everyone was doubling up in the cabins. He walked right to the end of the main corridor, where the light was slightly darker. "Beth?" He gave her cabin door a fast knock and turned the handle. "Come on, girl, we're almost there. You'll miss the—"

Both of Beth's jackets and her lace-up boots were lying on the floor, looking like they'd just been flung there. Beth herself was stirring on the bed, a skinny hand clawing lank strands of hair away from her face as she peered around blearily. Gerald Skibbow was next to her, sound asleep.

Indignation and pure anger made it impossible for Jed to move.

"What is it?" Beth grunted.

Jed couldn't believe it; she didn't display the slightest hint of shame. Skibbow was old enough to be her bloody great-grandfather! He glared at her, then stomped out, slamming the door loudly behind him.

Beth stared after him, her puzzled thoughts slowly slotting together. "Oh, Jeeze, you've got to be bloody joking," she groaned. Not even Jed was that stupid. Surely? She swung her legs out from under the duvet, taking care not to pull it off Gerald. It had taken her hours to get him to sleep. Holding him, reassuring him.

Despite her best efforts, she did dislodge the cover. The fabric seemed to stick to her jeans, and her sweatshirt was all twisted around, making every movement difficult.

Gerald Skibbow woke with a cry, looking around fearfully. "Where are we?"

"I don't know, Gerald," she said as calmly as she could. "I'll go find out, then I'll bring you back some breakfast. Okay, mate?"

"Yes. Um, I think so."

"You go slip into the shower. Leave everything else to me." Beth laced her boots up, then retrieved one of her jackets from the floor. She gave the inside pocket a determined pat to make sure the nervejam was there before she left the cabin.

* * *

Rocio Condra sensed the voidhawks waiting before he even started to emerge from the wormhole terminus. Seven of them, spiralling slowly around the point where he expected Valisk to be.

The terminus closed behind him, and he spread his wings wide, letting the thin streamers of solar ions gust against the feathers. All he did was glide along his orbital path while he tried to understand. Confusion was almost total. At first he thought he might even have emerged above the wrong gas giant, however unlikely that was. But no, this was Opuntia, its system of moons easily distinguishable. He could even feel the mass of Valisk's wrecked industrial stations in their proper coordinate. The only thing missing was the habitat itself.

What has happened to Valisk? he asked his erstwhile enemies. **Did you destroy it?**

Obviously not, one of the voidhawks replied. **There is no debris. Surely you can sense that?**

I can sense that. But I don't understand.

Rubra and Dariat finally settled their differences, and merged. The entire neural strata became possessed, creating an enormously powerful reality dysfunction. Valisk left the universe, taking everyone inside with it.

No!

I am not lying to you.

My body is inside. Even as he protested, he knew he wasn't really bothered. The decision he had been nerving himself up to make had been taken for him. He allowed energy to flow through his patterning cells, exerting pressure on a particular point in space.

Wait, the voidhawk called. **You have nowhere to go. We can help, we want to help.**

Me, join your culture? I don't think so.

You have to ingest nutrients to sustain yourself. You know that, even the possessed have to eat. Only habitats can provide you with the correct fluids.

So can most asteroid settlements.

But how long will the production machinery function when the settlement becomes possessed? You know they have no interest in such matters.

One of them does.

Capone? He will send you to fight to earn your food. How long will you last? Two battles? Three? With us you will be safe.

There are other tasks I can perform.

For what purpose? Now Valisk has gone, you have no human body into which you can return. They cannot reward you, only threaten.

How do you know that was promised to us?

From Dariat; he told us everything. Join us. Your assistance would be invaluable.

Assistance for what?

Finding a solution to this whole crisis.

I have solved it for myself. Energy flashed through the cells, forcing an interstice open. The wormhole's non-length deepened to accept his bulk.

The offer remains, the voidhawk proclaimed. Consider it. Come back to us at any time.

Rocio Condra closed the interstice behind his tail. His mind instinctively retrieved the coordinate for New California from the *Mindor*'s infallible memory. He would see what Capone had to offer before making any hasty decisions. And the other hellhawks would be there; whatever final choice they made, they would make it together.

After he explained what had happened to Choi-Ho and Maxim Payne, they agreed not to burden the Deadnights with the knowledge that their false dream had ceased to be.

•   •   •

Jay peeled the gold insulating wrapper off her chocolate and almond ice cream; it was her fifth that morning. She lay back happily on her towel and started licking the nuts off the ice cream's surface. The beach was such a lovely place, and her new friend made it just about perfect.

"Sure you don't want one?" she asked. There were several more sweets scattered over the warm sand; she had stuffed her bag full of them when she left the pediatric ward that morning.

No, with many thanks, Haile said. **Coldness makes me sneeze. The chocolate tastes like raw sugar with much additional acid.**

Jay giggled. "That's mad. Everyone likes chocolate."

Not I.

She bit off a huge chunk and let it slither around her tongue. "What do you like?"

Lemon is acceptable. But I am still milking from my parent.

"Oh, right. I keep forgetting how young you are. Do you eat solid stuff when you're older?"

Yes. In many months away.

Jay smiled at the wistfulness carried by the mental voice. She had often felt the same at her mother's rules, restrictions designed purely to stop her enjoying herself. "Do your parents all go out for fancy meals and things in the evening like we do? Are there Kiint restaurants?"

Not here in the all around. I know not exactly about our home.

"I'd love to see your home planet. It must be super, like the arcologies but clean and silver, with huge towers built right up into the sky. You're so advanced."

Some of our worlds have that form, Haile said with cautious uncertainty. **I believe. Racial history cosmology educationals have not fully begun yet.**

"That's okay." Jay finished the treat. "Gosh, that's lovely," she mumbled around the freezing mouthful. "I didn't have any ice cream the whole time I was on Lalonde. Can you imagine that!"

You should ingest properly balanced dietary substances. Ione Saldana says too much niceness is bad for you. Query correctness?

"Completely wrong." Jay sat up and tossed the ice cream stick into her bag. "Oh, Haile, that's wonderful!" She scrambled to her feet and ran over to the baby Kiint. Haile's tractamorphic arms were withdrawing from the sand castle like a nest of snakes that had been routed. She'd built a central tapering tower two and a half metres tall, surrounded by five smaller matching pinnacles; elaborate arching fairy bridges linked them all together. There were turrets leaning out of the sides at cockeyed angles, rings of pink shell windows, and a solid fortress wall with a deep moat around the outside.

"Best yet." Jay stroked the Kiint's facial ridge just above the breathing vents. Haile shivered in gratitude, big violet eyes looked directly into Jay.

I like, muchness.

"We should build something from your history," Jay said generously.

I have no intricacy to contribute, only home domes, the Kiint said sadly. **Our full past has not been made available. I must do much growth before I am ready for acceptance.**

Jay put her arms around the Kiint's neck, pressing up against her supple white hide. "That's all right. There are lots of things Mummy and Father Horst wouldn't tell me, either."

Much regret. Little patience.

"That's a shame. But the castle looks great now it's finished. I wish we had some flags to stick on top. I'll see what I can find to use for tomorrow."

Tomorrow the sand will be dry. The top will crumble in air, and we must start again.

Jay looked along the row of shapeless mounds that now ran along the shoreline. Each one carried its own particular memory of joy and satisfaction. "Honestly, Haile, that's the whole point. It's even better when there's a tide, then you can see how strong you've built."

So much human activity is intentionally wasteful. I doubt my ever knowing you.

"We're simple, really. We always learn more from our

mistakes, that's what Mummy says. It's because they're more painful."

Much oddness.

"I've got an idea; we'll try and build a Tyrathca tower tomorrow. That's nice and different. I know what they look like, Kelly showed me." She put her hands on her hips and considered the castle warmly. "Pity we can't build their Sleeping God altar, or whatever it was, but I don't think it would balance, not if you make it out of sand."

Query Sleeping God altar or whatever?

"It was sort of like a temple that you couldn't get inside. The Tyrathca on Lalonde all sat around it and worshipped with chanting and stuff. It was this shape, really elaborate." Her hands swept through the air in front of the Kiint, tracing broad curves. "See?"

Lacking perception, I. This is worship like your ritual to support Jesus the Christ?

"Um, sort of, I suppose. Except their God isn't our God. Theirs is sleeping somewhere far away in space; ours is everywhere. That's what Father Horst says."

There are two Gods, query?

"I don't know," Jay said, desperately wishing she hadn't got on to this topic. "Humans have more than two Gods, anyway. Religion is funny, especially if you start thinking about it. You're just sort of supposed to believe. Until you get old, that is, then it all becomes theology."

Query theology?

"Grown-up religion. Look here, don't you have a God?"

I will query my parents.

"Good; they'll explain everything much better than me. Come on, let's go and wash this horrid sand off, then we can go riding together."

Much welcome.

•   •   •   •

The Royal Kulu Navy ion field flyer swept in over Mortonridge's western seaboard, its glowing nose pointed directly at the early morning sun. Ten kilometres to the south, the red cloud formed a solid massif right across the horizon. It was thicker than Ralph Hiltch remembered. None of the peninsula's central ridge of mountains had managed to rise above it; they'd been swallowed whole.

The upper surface was as calm as a lake during a breathless dawn. Only when it started to dip earthwards along the firebreak border were the first uneasy stirrings visible—while right on the edge there appeared to be a full-scale storm whipping up individual streamers. Ralph had the uncomfortable impression that the cloud was aching to be let free. Perhaps he was picking up the emotional timbre of the possessed who created it? In this situation he could never be quite sure that any feeling was the genuine article.

He thought he could see a loose knot swirling along the side of the cloud, a twist of vermillion shadow amid the scarlet, keeping pace with his flyer. But when he ordered the sensor suite to focus on it, all he could see were random patterns. A trick of the eye, then, but a strong one.

The pilot began to expand the ion field, reducing the flyer's velocity and altitude. Up ahead, the grey line of the M6 was visible, slicing clean across the virgin countryside. Colonel Palmer's advance camp was situated a couple of kilometres outside the black firebreak line. Several dozen military vehicles were drawn up along the side of the motorway, while a couple were speeding along the carbon concrete towards the unnervingly precise band of incinerated vegetation.

Any possessed marching up to the end of the red cloud would see a predictably standard garrison operation being mounted with the Kingdom's usual healthy efficiency. What they couldn't see was the new camp coming together twenty-five kilometres further to the north; a city of programmable silicon laid out in strict formation which was erupting across the endless green undulations of the peninsula's landscape. With typical military literalism it had been named Fort Forward. Over five hundred programmable silicon buildings had already been activated, two-storey barracks, warehouses, mess halls, maintenance shops, and various ancillary structures; though as yet its only residents were the three battalions of Royal Kulu Marine Engineers whose job it was to assemble the camp. Their mechanoids had ploughed the ground up around each building, installing water and sewage pipes, power lines, and datalinks. Huge drums of micro-mesh composite were being unrolled over the fresh soil to provide roads which wouldn't turn to instant quagmires. Five large filter pump houses had been established on the banks of a river eight kilometres away to feed the expanding districts.

Mechanoids were already busy digging out vast new utility grids ready for more buildings, giving an indication of just how big Fort Forward would be when it was completed. Long convoys of lorries were using the M6 to deliver matériel from the nearest city spaceport, fifty kilometres away. Though that arrangement would soon be cancelled as Fort Forward's own spaceport became operational. Marine engineers were levelling long strips of land in preparation for three prefabricated runways. The spaceport's hangars and control tower had been activated two days ago so that technical crews could fit and integrate their systems.

When Ralph's battleship emerged above Ombey he had seen nine Royal Navy Aquilae-class bulk transport starships in parking formation around a low-orbit port station along with their escort of fifteen front-line frigates. There were only twenty-five of the huge transporters left on active service; capable of carrying seventeen thousand tonnes of cargo they were the largest starships ever built, and hugely expensive to fly and maintain. Kulu was gradually phasing them out in favour of smaller models based on commercial designs.

They were being supported by big old delta-wing CK500-090 Thunderbird spaceplanes, the only atmospheric craft capable of handling the four-hundred-tonne cargo pods carried by the Aquilae transporters. Again, a fleet on the verge of retirement; they had been the first consignment ferried to Ombey by the transports. Most of the Thunderbirds had spent the last fifteen years in mothball status at the Royal Navy's desert storage facility on Kulu. Now they were being reactivated as fast as the maintenance crews could fit new components from badly depleted war stocks.

Even more portentous than the buildup of navy ships were the voidhawks. Nearly eighty had arrived so far, with new ones swallowing in every hour, their lower hull cargo cradles full of pods (which could be handled by conventional civil flyers). Never before had so many of the bitek starships been seen orbiting a Kingdom world.

Ralph had experienced the same kind of uncomfortable awe he'd known at Azara as he observed them flitting around the docking stations. He was the one who had started this, creating a momentum which had engulfed entire star systems. It was unstoppable now. All he could do was ride it to a conclusion.

The ion field flyer landed at Colonel Palmer's camp. The colonel herself was waiting for him at the base of the airstairs, Dean Folan and Will Danza prominent in the small reception committee behind her, both grinning broadly.

Colonel Palmer shook his hand, giving his new uniform a more than casual inspection. "Welcome back, Ralph, or should I say sir?"

He wasn't completely used to the uniform himself yet, a smart dark blue tunic with three ruby pips glinting on his shoulder. "I don't know, exactly. I'm a general in the official Liberation campaign army now, its very first officer. Apart from the King, of course. The formation was made official three days ago, announced in the court of the Apollo Palace. I've been appointed chief strategic coordination officer."

"You mean you're the Liberation's numero uno?"

"Yeah," he said with quiet surprise. "I guess I am at this end."

"Rather you than me." She gestured northwards. "Talk about coming back with reinforcements."

"It's going to get wonderfully worse. One million bitek serjeants are on their way, and God alone knows how many human troops to back them up. We've even had mercenaries volunteering."

"You accepted them?"

"I've no idea. But I'll use whatever I'm given."

"All right, so what are your orders, sir?"

He laughed. "Just keep up the good work. Have any of them tried to break out?"

She turned her head to face the wall of angry cloud, her expression stern. "No. They stick to their side of the firebreak. There have been plenty of sightings. We think they're keeping an eye on us. But it's only my patrols who are visible to them." A thumb jabbed back over her shoulder. "They don't know anything about all this."

"Good. We can't keep it secret forever, of course; but the longer the better."

"Some kids came out last week. It was the first interesting thing to happen since you left."

"Kids?"

"A woman called Stephanie Ash bused seventy-three nonpossessed children right up to the firebreak. Gave the roadblock guard a hell of a fright, I can tell you. Apparently she'd collected them from all over the peninsula. We evacuated them to a holding camp. I think your friend Jannike Dermot has got her experts debriefing them on conditions over there."

"Now that's a report I'd like to access." He squinted at the red cloud. That elusive knot of shadow seemed to have returned. It was elliptical this time, hanging over the M6. It didn't take much imagination to suspect it of staring at him. "I think I'll take a closer look before I set up my command at Fort Forward," he announced.

Will and Dean rode shotgun on the Marine Corps runabout which took him up to the orange roadblock. It was good to talk with them again. They'd been attached to Palmer's brigade as combat liaison for the agency, supporting the various technical teams Roche Skark had dispatched to the firebreak. Both of them wanted to know every detail of his meetings with the King. They were annoyed he wouldn't datavise his visual files of Prince Edward playing at the Apollo Palace, but they were confidential. And so grows the mystique, Ralph thought, amused that he should be contributing to it.

The marines at the roadblock saluted smartly as Ralph and the Colonel arrived. Ralph chatted to them as cordially as he could manage. They didn't seem to mind the red cloud; he found it intimidating in the extreme. It loomed barely three hundred metres above him, vigorous thrashing streamers packed so close together there was no gap between them, layer upon layer stacked up to what seemed like the edge of space. The sonorous reverberations from its internal brawling was diabolically attuned to the harmonic of human bones. Millions of tonnes of contaminated water hanging suspended in the air by witchcraft, ready to crash down like the waterfall at the end of the world. He wondered how little effort on behalf of the possessed it would take to do just that. Could it be he really had underestimated their power? It wasn't the scale of the cloud which perturbed him so much as the *intent*.

"Sir," one of the barrier guards shouted in alarm. "Visible hostile, on foot, three hundred metres."

Dean and Will were abruptly standing in front of Ralph, their gaussguns pointing across the firebreak.

"I think this is enough front-line inspection for today," Colonel Palmer said. "Let's get you back to the runabout, please, Ralph."

"Wait." Ralph looked between the two G66 troopers to see a single figure walking up the M6. A woman dressed in a neatly cut leather uniform, her face stained warrior-scarlet by the nimbus of the seething clouds. He knew exactly who it was, in fact he would almost have been disappointed if she hadn't appeared. "She's not a threat. Not yet, anyway."

He slipped between Will and Dean to stand full square in the middle of the road, facing her down.

Annette Ekelund stopped at the forwards barrier on her side of the firebreak. She took a slim mobile phone from her pocket, extended its ten-centimetre aerial, then tapped in a number.

Ralph's communications block announced a channel opening. He switched it to audio function.

"Hello, Ralph. I thought you would come back, you're the kind that does. And I see you've brought some friends with you."

"That's right."

"Why don't you bring them on over and join the party?"

"We'll pick our own time."

"I have to say I'm disappointed; that's not quite what we agreed to back in Exnall, now is it? And with a Saldana Princess, too. Dear me, you can't trust anyone these days."

"A promise made under duress is not legally binding. I'm sure you'll have enough lawyers on your side to confirm that."

"I thought I explained all this to you, Ralph. We can't lose, not against the living."

"I don't believe you. No matter what the cost, we must defeat you. The human race will end if you are allowed to win. I believe we deserve to keep on going."

"You and your ideals, the original Mr Focused. No wonder you found a profession which allowed you to give loyal service. It suits you perfectly. Congratulations, Ralph, you have found yourself, not everyone can say that. In another universe, one that isn't so warped as this, I'd envy you."

"Thank you."

"There was a nasty little phrase coined in my era, Ralph; but it's still appropriate today, because it too came from a dogmatic soldier in a pointless war. *We had to destroy the village in order to save it.* What do you think you're going to do to Mortonridge and its people with this crusade of yours?"

"Whatever I have to."

"But we'll still be here afterwards, Ralph, we'll always be here. The finest minds in the galaxy have been working on this problem. Scientists and priests scurrying for hard answers and bland philosophies. Millions—billions of man-hours have already been spent on the quandary of what to do with us poor returned souls. And they've come up with nothing. Nothing! All you can do is mount this pathetic, vindictive campaign of violence in the hope that some of us will be caught and thrown into zero-tau."

"There isn't an overall solution yet. But there will be."

"There can't be. We outnumber you. It's simple arithmetic, Ralph."

"Laton said it can be done."

She chuckled. "And you believe him?"

"The Edenists think he was telling the truth."

"Oh, yes, the newest and most interesting of all your friends. You realize, don't you, that they could well survive this while you Adamists fall. It's in their interest for this monstrous diversion to work. Adamist planets will topple one by one while your Confederation is engrossed here."

"And what about the Kiint?"

There was a slight pause. "What about them?"

"They survived their encounter with the beyond. They say there is a solution."

"Which is?"

He gripped the communications block tighter. "It doesn't apply to us. Each race must find its own way. Ours exists, somewhere. It will be found. I have a lot of faith in human ingenuity."

"I don't, Ralph. I have faith in our sick nature to hate and envy, to be greedy and selfish, to lie. You forget, for six centuries I couldn't hide from the naked emotions which drive all of us. I was condemned to them, Ralph. I know exactly what we are in our true hearts, and it's not nice, not nice at all."

"Tell that to Stephanie Ash. You don't speak for all the possessed, not even a majority."

Her stance changed. She no longer leaned casually on the barrier but stood up straight, her head thrust forwards challengingly. "You'll lose, Ralph, one way or the other. You, personally, will lose. You cannot fight entropy."

"I wish your faith wasn't so misdirected. Think what you could achieve if you tried to help us instead."

"Stay away from us, Ralph. That's what I really came here to tell you. One simple message: Stay away."

"You know I can't."

Annette Ekelund nodded sharply. She pushed the phone's aerial back in and closed the little unit up.

Ralph watched her walk back down the M6 with a degree of sorrow he hadn't expected. Shadows cavorted around her, hoaxing with her silhouette before swallowing her altogether.

"Ye gods," Colonel Palmer muttered.

"That's what we're up against," Ralph said.

"Are you sure a million serjeants is going to be enough?"

Ralph didn't get to answer. The discordant bellows of thunder merged together into a continuous roar.

Everyone looked up to see the edge of the red cloud descending. It was as if the strength of the possessed had finally waned, allowing the colossal weight of water to crash down. Torrents of gaudy vapour plunged out of the main bank, hurtling earthwards faster than mere gravity could account for.

Along with the others, Ralph sprinted away from the roadblock, neural nanonics compelled a huge energy release from his muscle tissue, increasing his speed. Animal fear was pounding on his consciousness to turn and fire his TIP pistol at the virulent cascade.

His neural nanonics received a plethora of datavises from SD Command on Guyana. Low-orbit observation satellites were tracking them. Reports from patrols and sensors positioned along the firebreak: the whole front of cloud was moving.

"SD platforms are now at Ready One status," Admiral Farquar datavised. "Do you want us to counterstrike? We can slice that bastard apart."

"It's stopping," Will yelled.

Ralph risked a glance over his shoulder. "Wait," he datavised to the admiral. A hundred and fifty metres behind him, the base of the cloud had reached the ground, waves rebounding in all directions to furrow the surface. But the bulk of it was holding steady, not advancing. Even the thunder was muffled.

"They are not aggressing, repeat, not aggressing," Ralph datavised. "It looks like . . . hell, it looks as though they've slammed the door shut. Can you confirm the situation along the rest of the firebreak?"

When he looked from side to side, the cloud was clinging to the scorched soil as far as his enhanced retinas could see. A single, simple barrier that curved back gently until it reached an apex at about three kilometres high. In a way it was worse than before; without the gap this was so uncompromisingly final.

"Confirm that," Admiral Farquar datavised. "It's closed up all the way along the firebreak. The coastline edges are lowering, too."

"Great," Colonel Palmer swore. "Now what?"

"It's a psychological barrier, that's all," Ralph said quietly. "After all, it's only water. This changes nothing."

Colonel Palmer slowly tilted her head back, scanning the height of the quivering fluorescent precipice. She shivered. "Some psychology."

•   •   •

Ione.

A chaotic moan fluttered out between her lips. She was sprawled on her bed, sliding quietly into sleep. In her drowsy state, the pillow she was cuddling could so easily have been Joshua. **Oh, now what, for Heaven's sake? Can't I even dream my fantasies anymore?**

I am sorry to disturb you, but there is an interesting situation developing concerning the Kiint.

She sat up slowly, feeling stubbornly grumpy despite Tranquillity's best efforts to emphasise its tender concern. It had been a long day, with Meredith's squadron to deal with on top of all her normal duties. And the loneliness was starting to get to her, too. It's all right. She scratched irritably at her hair. Being pregnant is making me feel dreadfully randy. You're just going to have to put up with me being like this for another eight months. Then you'll have postnatal depression to cope with.

You have many lovers to choose from. Go to one. I want you to feel better. I do not like it when you are so troubled.

That's a very cold solution. If getting physical was all it took, I'd just swallow an antidote pill instead.

From what I observe, most human sex is a cold activity. There is an awful lot of selfishness involved.

Ninety per cent of it is. But we put up with that because we're always looking for the other ten per cent.

And you believe Joshua is your ten per cent?

Joshua is floating somewhere between the ninety and the ten. I just want him right now because my hormones are completely out of control.

Hormonal production does not usually peak until the later months of a pregnancy.

I always was an early developer. A swift thought directed at the opaqued window allowed a dappled aquamarine light into the bedroom. She reached lethargically for her robe. All right, self-pity hour over. Let's see what our mysterious Kiint are up to. And God help you if it isn't important.

Lieria has taken a tube carriage to the StClément starscraper.

So bloody what?

It is not an action which any Kiint has performed before. I have to consider it significant, especially at this time.

Kelly Tirrel hated being interrupted while she was running her Present Time Reality programs. It was an activity she was indulging more often these days.

Some of the black programs she had bought were selective memory blockers, modified from medical trauma erasure programs, slithering deep into her natural brain tissue to cauterize her subconscious. They should have been used under supervision, and it certainly wasn't healthy to suppress the amount of memory she was targeting, nor for as long. Others amplified her emotional response to perceptual stimuli, making the real world slow and mundane in comparison.

One of the pushers she'd met while she was making a documentary last year had shown her how to interface black programs with standard commercial sensenvirons to produce PTRs. Such integrations were supposedly the most addictive stim you could run. Compulsive because they were the zenith of denial. Escape to an alternative personality living in an alternative reality, where your past with all its inhibitions had been completely divorced, allowing only the present to prevail. Living for the now, yet stretching that now out for hours.

In the realms through which Kelly moved, possession and the beyond were concepts which did not nor could ever exist. When she did emerge, to eat, or pee, or sleep, the real world was the one which seemed unreal; terribly harsh by comparison to the hedonistic existence she had on the other side of the electronic divide.

This time when she exited the PTR she couldn't even recognize the signal her neural nanonics was receiving. Memories of such things were submerged deep in her brain, rising to conscious levels with the greatest of reluctance (and taking longer each time). It was a few moments before she even understood where she was, that this wasn't Hell but simply her apartment. The lights off, the window opaqued, the sheet on which she was lying disgustingly damp, and stinking of urine, the floor littered with disposable bowls.

Kelly wanted to plunge straight back into her electronic refuge. She was losing her grip on her old personality, and didn't give a fuck. The only thing she did monitor was her own decay; overriding fear saw to that.

I will *not* allow myself to die.

No matter how badly the black stimulant programs

screwed up her neurones, she wouldn't permit herself to go completely over the edge, not physically. Before that would be zero-tau. The wonderful simplicity of eternal oblivion.

And until then, her brain would live a charmed life, providing pleasure and excitement, and not even knowing it was artificial. Life was to be enjoyed, was it not? Now she knew the truth about death, how did it matter how that enjoyment was achieved?

Her brain finally identified the signal from the apartment's net processor. Someone was at the door, requesting admission. Confusion replaced her dazed resentful stupor. Collins hadn't called on her to present a show for a week (or possibly longer); not since her interview with Tranquillity's bishop when she shouted at him, angry about how cruel his God was to inflict the beyond upon unsuspecting souls.

The signal repeated. Kelly sat up, and promptly vomited down the side of the bed. Nausea swirled inside her brain, shaking her thoughts and memories into a collage which was the exact opposite of the PTR: Lalonde in all its infernal glory. She coughed as her pale limbs trembled and the scar along her ribs flamed. There was a glass on the bedside table, half full of a clear liquid which she fervently hoped was water. Her shaking hand grabbed at it, spilling a quantity before she managed to jam it to her lips and swallow. At least she didn't throw it all back up.

Almost suffocating in misery she struggled off the bed and pulled a blanket around her shoulders. Her neural nanonics medical program cautioned her that her blood sugar level was badly depleted and she was on the verge of dehydration. She cancelled it. The admission request was repeated again.

"Piss off," she mumbled. Light seemed to be shining straight through her eye sockets to scorch her fragile brain. Sucking down air, she tried to work out why her neural nanonics had stopped running the PTR program. It shouldn't happen just because someone datavised her apartment's net processor. Perhaps the slender filaments meshed with her synaptic clefts were getting screwed by her disturbed body chemistry?

"Who is it?" she datavised as she tottered unsteadily through into the main living room.

"Lieria."

Kelly didn't know any Lieria; at least not without running a memory cell check. She slumped down into one of her deep recliners, pulled the blanket over her legs, and datavised the door processor to unlock.

An adult Kiint was standing in the vestibule. Kelly blinked against the light which poured in around its snow-white body, gawped, then started laughing. She'd done it, she'd totally fucked her brain with the PTR.

Lieria lowered herself slightly and moved into the living room, taking care not to knock any of the furniture. She had to wriggle to fit the major section of her body through the door, but she managed it. An intensely curious group of residents peered in behind her.

The door slid shut. Kelly hadn't ordered it to do that. Her laughter had stopped, and her shakes were threatening to return. This was actually happening. She wanted to go back into the PTR real bad now.

Lieria took up nearly a fifth of the living room, both tractamorphic arms were withdrawn into large bulbs of flesh, her triangular head was swinging slightly from side to side as her huge eyes examined the room. No housechimp had been in for weeks to clean up; dust was accumulating; the door to the kitchen was open, showing worktops overflowing with empty food sachets; a loose pile of underwear decorated one corner; her desk was scattered with fleks and processor blocks. The Kiint returned her gaze to Kelly, who curled her limbs up tighter in the recliner.

"H-how did you get down here?" was all Kelly could ask.

"I took the service elevator," Lieria datavised back. "It was very cramped."

Kelly started. "I didn't know you could do that."

"Use an elevator?"

"Datavise."

"We have some command of technology."

"Oh. Yes. It's just . . . skip it." Her reporter's training began to assert itself. A private visit from a Kiint was unheard of. "Is this confidential?"

Lieria's breathing vents whistled heavily. "You decide, Kelly Tirrel. Do you wish your public to know what has become of you?"

Kelly stiffened her facial muscles, whether to combat tears or shame she wasn't sure. "No."

"I understand. Knowledge of the beyond can be disturbing."

"How did you beat it? Tell me, please. For pity's sake. I can't be trapped there. I couldn't stand it!"

"I am sorry. I cannot discuss this with you."

Kelly's cough had come back. She used the back of her hand to wipe her eyes dry. "What do you want, then?"

"I wish to purchase information. Your sensevises of Lalonde."

"My . . . why?"

"They are of interest to us."

"Sure. I'll sell them. The price is knowing how to avoid the beyond."

"Kelly Tirrel, you cannot buy that, the answer is inside you."

"Stop being so fucking obtuse!" she shouted, fury surmounting her consternation of the big xenoc.

"It is the profound wish of my race that one day you will understand. I had intended that by purchasing the data directly from you the money would bring or buy you some peace of mind. If I go directly to the Collins corporation, it will become lost in their accounts. You see, we do not mean you harm. It is not our way."

Kelly stared at the xenoc, depressed by her own incomprehension. Okay, girl, she thought, let's try and work this one out logically. She put her medical monitor program into primary mode, and used the results to bring appropriate suppressor and stimulant programs on-line to try to stabilize body and brain. There wasn't a great deal they could do, but at least she felt calmer and her breathing steadied. "Why do you want to buy them?"

"We have little data on humans who are possessed by returned souls. We are interested. Your visit to Lalonde is an excellent firsthand account."

Kelly felt the first stirrings of excitement; reporter's instinct inciting her interest. "Bullshit. That's not what I meant. If all you wanted was information on possessed humans, you could have recorded my reports directly from Collins as soon as they were released. God knows, they've been repeated often enough."

"They are not complete. Collins has edited them to provide a series of highlights. We understand their commercial reasons for doing so, but this is of no use to us. I require access to the entire recording."

"Right," she said with apparent gravity, as if she was giving the proposition appropriately weighty thought. An analysis program had gone primary, refining possible questions in an attempt to narrow the focus. "I can give you full access to the times I came up against the possessed, and my observations of Shaun Wallace. That's no problem at all."

"We require a full record from the time you arrived in the Lalonde star system until you departed. All details are of interest to us."

"All details? I mean, this is a human sensevise, I kept the flek recording the whole time. Standard company procedure. Unfortunately, that includes time when I was visiting the little girls' room, if you catch on."

"Human excretion functions do not embarrass us."

"Shall I cut the time in *Lady Macbeth* for you?"

"Observations and crew impressions of the reality dysfunction from orbit are an integral part of the record."

"So, how much were you thinking of offering me for this?"

"Please name your price, Kelly Tirrel."

"One million fuseodollars."

"That is expensive."

"It's a lot of hours you're asking for. But the offer to edit it down still stands."

"I will pay you the required amount for a complete recording only."

Kelly pressed her teeth together in annoyance; it wasn't going to work, the Kiint was far too smart for verbal traps. Don't push, she told herself, get what you can and work out the why later on. "Fair enough. Agreed."

Lieria's tractamorphic flesh extended out into an arm, a Jovian Bank credit disk held between white pincers.

Kelly gave it an interested glance, and rose stiffly from the recliner. Her own credit disk was somewhere on her desk. She walked over to it, all three paces, then plonked herself down in the grey office chair a little too quickly.

"I would suggest you eat something and rest properly before you return to your sensenviron," Lieria datavised.

"Good idea. I was going to." She froze in the act of shoving the fleks and their empty storage cases around. How the hell had the Kiint known what she'd been running? *We have some command of technology.* She gripped the blanket harder with one hand as the other fished her disk from under a recorder block. "Found it," she said with forced lightness.

Lieria shunted the full amount across. The soft flesh of the pincers engulfed the Jovian Bank disk, then parted again to reveal a small dark blue processor block. It was like a conjuring trick which Kelly was in no state to unravel.

"Please insert your fleks in the block," Lieria datavised. "It will copy the recordings."

Kelly did as she was told.

"I thank you, Kelly Tirrel. You have contributed valuable information to our race's store of knowledge."

"Make the most of it," she said grumpily. "The way you're treating us we probably won't be around to contribute for much longer."

The living-room door slid open, scattering a startled crowd of StClément residents. Lieria backed out with surprising ease. When the door closed again Kelly was left by herself with the disconcerting impression that it could all very easily have been a dream. She picked up her credit disk, looking at it in wonder. One million fuseodollars.

It was the key to permanent zero-tau. Her lawyer had been negotiating with Collins to transfer her pension fund into an Edenist trust account, just like Ashly Hanson. Except she wouldn't be coming out to take a look around every few centuries. Collins's accountants had been reluctant.

Another problem which had sent her into the sham escape of PTR. Now all she needed to do was get to an Edenist habitat. Only their culture had a chance of holding her safe through eternity.

Although . . . that stubborn old part of her mind was asking a thousand questions. What the hell did the Kiint really want?

"Think," she ordered herself fiercely. "Come on, damn it. Think!" Something happened on Lalonde. Something so important that a Kiint walks into my apartment and pays me a million fuseodollars for a record of it. Something we didn't think was important or interesting, because it wasn't released by Collins. So if it wasn't released, how the hell did the Kiint know about it?

Logically, someone must have told them—presumably today or very recently. Someone who has reviewed the whole recording themselves, or at least more of it than Collins released.

Kelly smiled happily, an unfamiliar expression of late. And someone who must have a lot of contact with the Kiint.

Review every single conversation which the Kiint were involved in over the last week, Ione said. **Anything that anyone mentioned about Lalonde, anything at all, however trivial. And if you can't find it, start going through your earlier memories.**

I am already reviewing the relevant scenes. There may be a problem with going back further than four days. My short-term memory capacity is only a hundred hours; after that the details are discarded so I may retain salient information. Without this procedure even my memory would be unable to cope with events inside me.

I know that! But it has to be recent for Lieria to go visiting in the middle of the night. I don't suppose the Kiint said anything among themselves? Grandfather's non-intrusion agreement can hardly apply in this case.

I concur that it cannot be considered. However, I have never been able to intercept detailed affinity conversations between the adult Kiint. At best I can sometimes distinguish what I would define as a murmur.

Damn! If you can't remember, we'll have to haul all the Laymil project staff in and question them individually.

Not necessary. I have found it.

"Brilliant!" Show me.

The memory burst open around her. Bright light was shining down on the beach while glassy ripples lapped quietly against the shoreline. A huge sand castle stood directly in front of her. Oh, bloody hell.

Jay was woken by a hand shaking her shoulder with gentle insistence. "Mummy," she cried fearfully. Wherever she was, it was dark, and even darker shadows loomed over her.

"Sorry, poppet," Kelly stage-whispered. "It's not your mum, it's only me."

Horror fled from the little girl's face, and she hitched herself up in the bed, wrapping her arms around her legs. "Kelly?"

"Yep. And I am really sorry, I didn't mean to frighten you like that."

Jay sniffed the air, highly curious now. "What's that smell? And what time is it?"

"It's very late. Nurse Andrews is going to kill me if I stay for more than a couple of minutes. She only let me in because she knows you and I spent all that time together on *Lady Mac*."

"You haven't visited for ages."

"I know." Kelly was almost crushed by the surge of emotion the girl triggered, the accusation in her tone. "I haven't been terribly well lately. I didn't want you to see me the way I was."

"Are you all right now?"

"Sure. I'm on the way back."

"Good. You promised you'd show me around the studios you work in."

"And I'll keep it, too. Listen, Jay, I've got some really important questions. They're about you and Haile."

"What?" she asked suspiciously.

"I need to know if you told Haile anything about Lalonde, especially in the last couple of days. It's vital, Jay, honest. I wouldn't ask if it wasn't."

"I know." She screwed up her lips, thinking hard. "There was some stuff about religion this morning. Haile doesn't understand it very well, and I'm not very good at explaining it."

"What about religion, exactly?"

"It was how many gods there are. I'd told her about the Tyrathca's Sleeping God temple, you know, the one you showed me, and she wanted to know if that was the same thing as Jesus."

"Of course," Kelly hissed. "It wasn't human possession, it was the Tyrathca section, we never released any of that." She leaned over and kissed Jay. "Thank you, poppet. You've just performed a miracle."

"Was that *all*?"

"Yeah. That was all."

"Oh."

"You snuggle down and get some sleep now. I'll come visit tomorrow." She helped pull Jay's duvet back up and gave the girl another kiss. Jay sniffed inquisitively again, but didn't comment.

"So?" Kelly asked softly as she walked away from the bed. "You've been watching, you know this must be serious. I want to talk to the Lord of Ruin."

The pediatric ward's net processor opened a channel to Kelly's neural nanonics. "Ione Saldana will see you now," Tranquillity datavised. "Please bring the relevant recordings."

* * *

Despite being on what he considered excellent terms with the Lord of Ruin, Parker Higgens could still be chilled to the marrow when she gave him one of her expectant looks.

"But I don't know anything about the Tyrathca, ma'am," he complained. Being dragged out of bed straight into a highly irregular crisis conference was playing havoc with his thought processes. Accessing the sensevise recording of Coastuc-RT and seeing the strange silvery structure which the builder-caste Tyrathca had constructed in the middle of the village didn't contribute much to his composure, either.

When he glanced at Kempster Getchell for support he saw the astronomer's eyes were closed as he accessed the recording a second time.

"You're the only xenoc specialists I've got, Parker."

"Laymil specialists."

"Don't quibble. I need advice, and I need it fast. How important is this?"

"Well . . . I don't think we knew the Tyrathca had a religion before this," he ventured.

"We didn't," Kelly said. "I ran a full search program through the Collins office encyclopedia. It's as good as any university library. There's no reference to this Sleeping God at all."

"And neither did the Kiint, so it would seem," Parker said. "They actually came and woke you to ask for the recording?"

"That's right."

Parker was somewhat put out by the reporter's dishevelled appearance. She sat wedged into one corner of the sofa in Ione's private study, a thick cardigan tugged around her shoulders as if it were midwinter. For the last five minutes she had been snatching up salmon sandwiches from a large plate balanced on the sofa's arm, pushing them forcefully into her mouth.

"Well I have to say, ma'am, that it's a relief to find out they don't know everything." A housechimp silently handed him a cup of coffee.

"But is it relevant?" Ione asked. "Were they just so surprised they didn't know about the Sleeping God myth that Lieria simply rushed over to Kelly to confirm it? Or does it have some bearing on our current situation?"

"It's not a myth," Kelly said around another sandwich. "That's exactly what I said to Waboto-YAU; and it nearly set the soldiers on me for that remark. The Tyrathca believe absolutely in their Sleeping God. Crazy race."

Parker stirred his coffee mechanically. "I've never known the Kiint to be excited about anything. But then I've never known them to be in a rush either, which they obviously were tonight. I think we should examine this Sleeping God in context. You are aware, ma'am, that the Tyrathca do not have fiction? They simply do not lie, and they have a great deal of trouble understanding human falsehoods. The nearest they ever come to lying is withholding information."

"You mean there really is a Sleeping God?" Kelly asked.

"There has to be a core of truth behind the story," Parker said. "They are a highly formalized clan species. Individual families maintain professions and responsibilities for generations. Sireth-AFL's family was obviously entrusted with the knowledge of the Sleeping God. At a guess, I'd say that Sireth-AFL is a descendant of the family which used to deal with electronics while they were on their arkship."

"Then why not just store the memory electronically?" Kelly asked.

"It probably is stored, somewhere. But Coastuc-RT is a very primitive settlement, and the Tyrathca only ever use appropriate technology. There will be Tyrathca families in that village who know exactly how to build fusion generators and computers, but they don't actually need them yet, therefore the information isn't used. They employ water wheels and mental arithmetic instead."

"Weird," Kelly said.

"No," Parker corrected. "Merely logical. The product of a mind that is intelligent without being particularly imaginative."

"Yet they were praying," Ione said. "They believe in a God. That requires a leap of imagination, or at least faith."

"I don't think so," Kempster Getchell said. He grinned around, clearly enjoying himself. "We're messing about with semantics here, and an electronic translator, which is never terribly helpful, it's too literal. Consider when this God appeared in their history. Human gods are derived from our pre-science era. There are no new religions, there haven't been for thousands of years. Modern society is far too sceptical to allow for prophets who have personal conversations with God. We have the answer for everything these days, and if it isn't recorded on a flek it's a lie.

"Yet here we have the Tyrathca, who not only don't lie, but encounter a God while they're in a starship. They have the same intellectual analytical tools as we do, and they still call it a God. And they *found* it. That's what excites me, that's what is so important to this story. It isn't indegenous to their planet, it isn't ancient. One of their arkships encountered something so fearfully powerful that a race with the technology to travel between the stars calls it a God."

"That would also mean it isn't exclusive to them," Parker said.

"Yes. Although, whatever it is, it was benign, or even helpful to the arkship in question. They wouldn't consider it to be *their* Sleeping God otherwise."

"Powerful enough to defend the Tyrathca from possessed humans," Ione said. "That's what they claimed."

"Yes indeed. A defence mounted from several hundred light-years distant, at least."

"What the fuck could do that?" Kelly asked.

"Kempster?" Ione prompted as the old astronomer stared away at the ceiling.

"I have absolutely no idea. Although 'sleeping' does imply an inert status, which can be reversed."

"By prayer?" Parker said sceptically.

"They thought it would be able to hear them," Kempster said. "Stronger than all living things was what that breeder said. Interesting. And that mirror-spire shape was supposed to be what it looked like. I'd like to say some kind of celestial event or object, that would fit in finding it in deep space.

Unfortunately, there is no natural astronomical object which resembles that."

"Take a guess," Ione said icily.

"Powerful, and in space." The astronomer's face wrinkled up with effort. "Humm. Trouble is, we have no idea of the scale. Some kind of small nebula around a binary neutron star; or a white hole emission jet—which might account for the shape. But none of those are exactly inert."

"Nor would they be much use against the possessed," Parker said.

"But its existence is enough to fluster the Kiint," Ione said. "And they can manufacture moons, plural."

"Do you think it could help us?" Kelly asked the astronomer.

"Good point," Kempster said. "A highly literal race thinks it can help them against the possessed. QED, it would be able to do the same thing for us. Although the actual encounter must have taken place thousands of years ago. Who knows how much the account had been distorted in that time, even by the Tyrathca? And if it was an event rather than an object, it would presumably be finished by now. After all, Confederation astronomers have catalogued our galaxy pretty thoroughly; and certainly anything odd within ten thousand light-years would be listed. Which is why I'm inclined to go for the inert object hypothesis. I must say, this is a delightful puzzle you've brought to us, young lady; I'd love to know what they did actually find."

Kelly made an impatiently dismissive gesture and leaned forward. "See?" she said to Ione. "This is critical, just like I said. I've provided you with enough to go on. Haven't I?"

"Yes," Ione said with considerable asperity.

"Do I get my flight authorization?"

"What is this? What flight?" Parker asked.

"Kelly wishes to visit Jupiter," Ione said. "To do that she needs my official authorization."

"Do I get it?" Kelly was almost shouting.

Ione's nose crinkled with distaste. "Yes. Now please be silent unless you have a cogent point to make."

Kelly flung herself back into the sofa, a fearsome grin on her face.

Parker studied her for a moment, not at all liking what he found, but forwent any comment. "The evidence we have so far is depressingly small, but to my mind it does seem to indicate that the Sleeping God is something other than a natural object. Perhaps it is a functional Von Neumann machine, that would certainly have godlike abilities ascribed to it by any culture with inferior technology. Or, I regret to say, some kind of ancient weapon."

"A manufactured artefact which can attack the possessed over interstellar space. Now that really is an unpleasant thought," Kempster said. "Although the sleeping qualifier would admittedly be more pertinent in such a case."

"As you say," Ione said. "We don't have nearly enough information to make anything other than wild guesses at this time. That must be rectified. Our real problem is that the Tyrathca have severed all contact with us. And I really don't think we have any alternative but to ask them."

"I would certainly advise we pursue that avenue, ma'am. The very possibility that the Sleeping God is real, and may even be able to defeat the possessed on some level, warrants further investigation. If we could . . ." His voice died away as Ione gripped the arms of her chair, blue eyes widening to express something Parker had never thought he would see there: horror.

Meredith Saldana drifted into the *Arikara*'s bridge; every one of the acceleration couches in the C&C section of the bridge was occupied as his staff officers dedicated themselves to scanning and securing space around Mirchusko.

He slid onto his own acceleration couch and accessed the tactical situation computer. The flagship was hanging a thousand kilometres off Tranquillity's counter-rotating spaceport, with every sensor cluster and communications system extended. Some spacecraft moved around the habitat's spaceport and outlying industrial stations, a couple of blackhawks were curving around the spindle to land on the outermost docking ledge, and three He$_3$ cryogenic tankers were rising over the gas giant's natural rings en route for the habitat. Apart from that, the only ships flying were squadron members. The frigates were moving smoothly into their englobing positions, forming a protective eight thousand kilometre sphere around Tranquillity, complementing the habitat's own formidable SD platforms. His squadron's nine voidhawks were currently deployed right around the gas giant in an attempt to probe the rings for any observation system or hidden ship. An unlikely event, but Meredith was aware of just how much was riding on the Toi-Hoi ambush. When it came to this duty, he was a firm believer in the motto: I'm paranoid, but am I paranoid enough?

"Lieutenant Grese, our current situation, please?" he asked.

"One hundred per cent on-line, sir," the squadron intelligence officer reported. "All starship traffic is shut down. Those blackhawks you can see docking are the last of the flight deploying sensor satellites looking for an energy displacement signature from the Laymil home planet. All of them have obeyed the recall order. We're allowing personnel commuters and tugs to fly out to the industrial stations providing we're informed of their movements in advance. Tranquillity is supplying us with a direct feed from its SD sensor network, which is extremely comprehensive out to one million kilometres. Our only problem with that is that it doesn't appear to have any gravitonic distortion detectors."

Meredith frowned. "That's ridiculous, how does it detect emerging starships?"

"I'm not sure, sir. We did ask, but it just said we're receiving the full datavise from each sensor satellite. My only explanation is that the Lord of Ruin doesn't want us to know the habitat's full detection capability."

Which wasn't something Meredith believed. Somewhat to his surprise, he'd been quite impressed by his young cousin; especially as he'd gone in to meet her with a lot of firmly held preconceptions. He'd been forced to revise most of them under her unyielding dignity and astute political grasp. One thing he was sure of, if she was deliberately imposing limits on her cooperation she wouldn't be duplicitous about it.

"Can our own sensors compensate?" he asked.

"Yes, sir. At the moment, the voidhawks will provide us with an immediate warning of any emergence. But we've launched a full complement of gravitonic distortion detector satellites. They'll provide coverage out to quarter of a million kilometres when they're in position; that's in about another twenty minutes, which will free the voidhawks for their next duty."

"Good, in that case we won't make an issue of this."

"Sir."

"Lieutenant Rhoecus, voidhawk status, please."

"Yes, Admiral," the Edenist replied. "There are definitely no ships inside any of Mirchusko's rings. However, we cannot give any guarantees about smaller stealthed spy satellites. Two hundred and fifty ELINT satellites have been deployed so far, which gives us a high probability of detecting any transmission should there be a spy system observing the habitat. The *Myoho* and the *Oenone* are launching further ELINTs into orbit around each of Mirchusko's moons in case there's anything hiding on or under the surface."

"Excellent. What about covering the rest of the system?"

"We've already worked out a swallow flight plan for each voidhawk which will allow them to conduct a preliminary survey in fifteen hours. It will be somewhat cursory, but if there is another ship within two AUs of Mirchusko they should find it. Clear space provides much fewer problems than a gas giant environment."

"Several blackhawk captains offered to assist us, Admiral," Commander Kroeber said. "I declined for now, but told them that Admiral Kolhammer may want them for the next stage."

Meredith resisted a glance in the flagship captain's direction. "I see. Have you ever served with Admiral Kolhammer, Mircea?"

"No, sir, I haven't had that pleasure."

"Well, for your information, I consider it unlikely he'd want the blackhawks along."

"Yes, sir."

Meredith raised his voice to address the bridge officers in general. "Well done, ladies and gentlemen. You seem to have organized this securement most efficiently. My compliments. Commander, please take the *Arikara* out to our englobement coordinate, in your own time."

"Aye, aye, sir."

Acceleration returned to the bridge, building to a third of a gee. Meredith studied the tactical situation display, familiarising himself with the squadron's formation. He was quietly content with the way his ships and crews were performing, especially after the trauma of Lalonde. Unlike some navy officers, Meredith didn't regard the blackhawks as universally villainous, he liked to consider himself a more sophisticated realist than that. If they were going to be betrayed, it was likely to be by an outside agency such as a stealthed spy satellite. But even then, a starship would have to collect the information.

"Lieutenant Lowie, would it be possible to eliminate any spy system hiding in the rings by emp-ing them?"

"Sir, it would require complete saturation," the weapons officer said. "If the Organization has hidden a satellite out there its circuitry will be hardened. The fusion explosion would have to be inside twenty kilometres to guarantee elimination. We don't have that many bombs."

"I see. Just an idea. Rhoecus, I'd like to keep a couple of voidhawks in orbit around Mirchusko so they can monitor starships emerging outside our own sensor range. What effect will that have on the survey?"

"Approximate increase of six hours, Admiral."

"Damn, that's pushing our time envelope." He consulted the tactical situation display again, running analysis programs to calculate the most effective option.

A red dot flared into existence barely ten thousand kilometres away, surrounded by symbols: a wormhole terminus disgorging a ship. And it was nowhere near any of Tranquillity's designated emergence zones. Another red dot appeared less than a second later. A third. A fourth. Three more.

"What the hell?"

"Not voidhawks, sir," Lieutenant Rhoecus said. "No affinity broadcasts at all. They're not responding to Tranquillity or squadron voidhawks, either."

"Commander Kroeber, squadron to combat status. Rhoecus, recall the voidhawks. Can someone get me a visual identification?"

"Coming, sir," Lieutenant Grese datavised. "Two of the intruders are close to an SD sensor satellite."

More wormhole termini were opening. *Arikara*'s thermo-dump panels and long-range sensor clusters sank back into their fuselage recesses. The warship's acceleration increased as it sped out to its englobement coordinate.

"Got it, Admiral. Oh, Lord, definitely hostile."

The image relayed into Meredith's neural nanonics showed him a charcoal-grey eagle with a wingspan of nearly two hundred metres; its eyes gleamed yellow above a long chrome-silver beak. His body tensed in reflex, pushing him deeper into the acceleration couch. That was one massively evil-looking creature.

"Hellhawk, sir. Must be from Valisk."

"Thank you, Grese. Confirm the other intruder identities, please."

The tactical situation display showed him twenty-seven bitek starships had now emerged from their wormholes. Another fifteen termini were opening. It was only seven seconds since the first had appeared.

"All of them are hellhawks, sir; eight bird types, four bogus starships, the rest conform to standard blackhawk profile."

"Admiral, the voidhawks have all swallowed back to Tranquillity," Rhoecus said. "Moving out to reinforce the englobement formation."

Meredith watched their purple vector lines slice across the tactical situation display, twisting around to reach the other squadron ships. No use, Meredith thought, no use at all. Fifty-eight hellhawks were ranged against them now, forming a loose ring around the habitat. Tactical analysis programs were giving him an extremely small probability of a successful defensive engagement, even with the squadron backed up by Tranquillity's SD platforms. And that was reducing still further as more hellhawks continued to swallow in.

"Commander Kroeber, get those blackhawks Tranquillity was using as patrol ships out here as fast as possible."

"Aye, sir."

"Sir!" Grese shouted. "We're registering more gravitonic distortions. Adamist ships, this time. Multiple emergence patterns."

The tactical situation display showed Meredith two small constellations of red dots lighting up. The first was fifteen thousand kilometres ahead of Tranquillity, while the second trailed it by roughly the same amount. Dear God, and I thought Lalonde was bad. "Lieutenant Rhoecus."

"Yes, Admiral?"

"The *Ilex* and the *Myoho* are to disengage. They are ordered to fly to Avon immediately and warn Trafalgar what has happened here. Under no circumstances is Admiral Kolhammer to bring his task force to Mirchusko."

"But, sir . . ."

"That was an order, Lieutenant."

"Aye, sir."

"Grese, can you identify the new intruders?"

"I think so, sir. I think it's the Organisation fleet. Visual sensors show front-line warships; I've got frigates, some battle cruisers, several destroyers, and plenty of combat-capable commercial vehicles."

Large sections of the tactical situation display dissolved into yellow and purple hash as electronic warfare pods spun away from the hellhawks, coming on line as soon as they were clear of the energistic effect. The voidhawks continued to supply information on emerging starships. There were now seventy hellhawks ringing Tranquillity; with a hundred and thirty Adamist ships holding station on either side of it.

Arikara's bridge had fallen completely silent.

"Sir," Rhoecus said. "*Ilex* and *Myoho* have swallowed out."

Meredith nodded. "Good." There wasn't a hell of a lot more he could say. "Commander Kroeber, please signal the enemy fleet. Ask them . . . Ask them what they want."

"Aye, sir."

The tactical situation computer datavised an alarm.

"Combat wasp launch!" Lowie shouted. "The hellhawks have fired."

At such close range, there was nothing the electronic warfare barrage could do to hide the burst of yellow solid rocket exhausts from Meredith's squadron. Each of the hellhawks had launched fifteen combat wasps. Spent solid rocket casings separated as the dazzling plumes of fusion fire sprang out, and they began to accelerate in towards the habitat at twenty-five gees. Over a thousand drones forming an immense noose of light which was swiftly contracting.

Tactical programs went primary in Meredith's neural nanonics. In theory, they had the capacity to fight off this assault, which would leave them with practically zero reserves. And he had to decide now.

It was a hopeless situation, one where instinct fought against duty. But Confederation citizens were being attacked; and to a Saldana duty was instinct.

"Full defensive salvo," Meredith ordered. "Fire."

Combat wasps leapt out of their launch tubes in every squadron ship. Tranquillity's SD platforms launched simultaneously. For a short while, space around the habitat's shell ceased to be an absolute vacuum. Hot streams of energized vapour from the exhausts of four thousand combats wasps sprayed in towards Tranquillity, creating a faint iridescent nebula beset with giddy squalls of turquoise and amber ions. Jagged petals of lightning flared out from the tip of every starscraper, ripping away into the chaotically unstable vortex.

Blackhawks were rising from Tranquillity's docking ledges, over fifty of them sliding out under heavy acceleration to join the fight. Meredith's tactical analysis program began revising the odds. Then he saw several swallow away. In his heart he didn't blame them.

"Message coming in, Admiral," the communications officer reported. "Someone called Luigi Balsmao, he claims he's the Organization fleet's commander. He says: Surrender and join us, or die and join us."

"What a melodramatic arsehole," Meredith grunted. "Please advise the Lord of Ruin, it's as much her decision as it is mine. After all, it's her people who will suffer."

"Oh, fuck! *Sir!* Another combat wasp launch. It's the Adamist ships this time."

Under Luigi's command, all one hundred and eighty Organization starships fired a salvo of twenty-five combat wasps apiece. Their antimatter drives accelerated them in towards Tranquillity at forty gees.

14

The star wasn't important enough to have a name. The Confederation Navy's almanac office simply listed it as DRL0755-09-BG. It was an average K-type, with a gloomy emission in the lower end of the orange spectrum. The first scoutship to explore its planets, back in 2396, took less than a fortnight to complete a survey. There were only three unremarkable inner, solid planets for it to investigate, none of which were terracompatible. Of the two outer gas giants, the one furthest from the star had an equatorial diameter of forty-three thousand kilometres, its outer cloud layer a pale green with none of the usual blustery atmospheric conditions. As worthless as the solid planets. The innermost gas giant did raise the interest of the scoutship's crew for a short while. Its equatorial diameter was a hundred and fifty-three thousand kilometres, making it larger than Jupiter, and coloured by a multitude of ferocious storm bands. Eighteen moons orbited around it, two of which had high-pressure atmospheres of nitrogen and methane. The complex interaction of their gravity fields prohibited any major ring system from forming, but all of the larger moons shepherded substantial quantities of asteroidal rubble.

The scoutship crew thought that such abundant resources of easily accessible minerals and ores would make it an ideal location for Edenist habitats. Their line company even managed to sell the survey's preliminary results to Jupiter. But once again, DRL0755-09-BG's mediocrity acted against it. The gas giant was a good location for habitats, but not exceptional; without a terracompatible planet the Edenists weren't interested. DRL0755-09-BG was ignored

for the next two hundred and fifteen years, apart from intermittent visits from Confederation Navy patrol ships to check
that it wasn't being used by an antimatter production station.

As the *Lady Mac*'s sensor clusters gave him a visual
sweep of the penurious star system, Joshua wondered why
the navy wasted its time.

He cancelled the image and looked around the bridge.
Alkad Mzu was lying prone on one of the spare acceleration
couches, her eyes tight shut as she absorbed the external
panorama. Monica and Samuel were hovering in the background, as always. Joshua really didn't want them on the
bridge, but the agencies weren't prepared to allow Mzu out
of their sight now.

"Okay, Doc, now what?" he asked. He'd followed Mzu's
directions so that *Lady Mac* emerged half a million kilometres above the inner gas giant's southern pole, near the undu-
lating boundaries of the planet's enormous magnetosphere. It
gave them an excellent viewpoint across the entire moon system.

Alkad stirred on her couch, not opening her eyes. "Please
configure the ship's antenna to broadcast the strongest signal it can at the one-hundred-and-twenty-five-thousand-
kilometre equatorial orbital band. I will give you the code to
transmit when you're ready."

"That was the *Beezling*'s parking orbit?"

"Yes."

"Okay. Sarha, get the dish ready for that, please. I think
you'd better allow for a twenty-thousand-kilometre error
when you designate the beam. No telling what state they
were in when they got here. If they don't respond, we'll
have to widen the sweep pattern out to the furthest moon."

"Aye, Captain."

"How many people left on this old warship of yours,
Doc?" Joshua asked.

Alkad broke away from the image feeding into her neural
nanonics. She didn't want to. This was it, the star represented by that stupid little alphanumeric she had carried
with her like a talisman for thirty years. Always expecting

him to be waiting here for her; there had been a million first lines rehearsed in those decades, a million loving looks. But now she'd arrived, seen that pale amber star with her own eyes, doubt was gripping her like frostbite. Every other aspect of their desperate plan had fallen to dust thanks to fate and human fallibility. Would this part of it really be any different? A sublight voyage of two and a half light-years. What had the young captain called it? Impossible. "Nine," she said faintly. "There should be nine of them. Is that a problem?"

"No. *Lady Mac* can take that many."

"Good."

"Have you thought what you're going to tell them?"

"I'm sorry?"

"Jesus, Doc; their home planet has been wiped out, you can't use the Alchemist for revenge, the dead are busy conquering the universe, and they are going to have to spend the rest of their lives locked up in Tranquillity. You've had thirty years to get used to the genocide, and a couple of weeks to square up to the possessed. To them it's still good old 2581, and they're on a navy combat mission. You think they're going to take all this calmly?"

"Oh, Mother Mary." Another problem, before she even knew if they'd survived.

"The dish is ready," Sarha said.

"Thanks," Joshua said. "Right, Doc, datavise the code into the flight computer. Then start thinking what you're going to say. And think good, because I'm not taking *Lady Mac* anywhere near a ship armed with antimatter that isn't extremely pleased to see me."

Mzu's code was beamed out by the *Lady Macbeth* in a slim fan of microwave radiation. Sarha monitored the operation as it tracked slowly around the designated orbital path. There was no immediate response—she hadn't been expecting one. She allowed the beam another two sweeps, then shifted the focus to cover a new circle just outside the first.

It took five hours to get a response. The tension and expectation which had so dominated the bridge for the first thirty minutes had expired long ago. Ashly, Monica, and Voi were all in the galley preparing food sachets when a small artificial green star appeared in the display which the flight computer was feeding Sarha's neural nanonics. Analysis and discrimination programs came on-line, filtering out the gas giant's constant radio screech to concentrate on the signal. Two ancillary booms slid up out of *Lady Macbeth*'s hull, unfolding wide broad-spectrum multi-element receiver meshes to complement the main communications dish.

"Somebody's there, all right," Sarha said. "Weak signal, but steady. Standard CAB transponder response code, but no ship registration number. They're in an elliptical orbit, ninety-one thousand kilometres by one hundred and seventy thousand four-degree inclination. Right now they're ninety-five thousand kilometres out from the upper atmosphere." A strangely muffled gulp made her abandon the flight computer's display to check the bridge.

Alkad Mzu was lying flat on her acceleration couch, with every muscle unnaturally stiff. Neural nanonics were busy censoring her body language with nerve overrides. But Sarha could see a film of liquid over her red-rimmed eyes which was growing progressively thicker. When she blinked, tiny droplets spun away across the compartment.

Joshua whistled. "Impressive, Doc. Your old crewmates have got balls, I'll say that for them."

"They're alive," Alkad cried. "Oh, Mother Mary, they're really alive."

"The *Beezling* made it here, Doc," Joshua said, deliberately curt. "Let's not jump to conclusions without facts. All we've got so far is a transponder beacon. What is supposed to happen next, does the captain come out of zero-tau?"

"Yes."

"Okay. Sarha, keep monitoring the *Beezling*. Beaulieu, Liol, let's get back to flight status, please. Dahybi, charge up the nodes, I want to be ready to jump clear if things turn out bad." He started plotting a vector which would take them over to the *Beezling*.

Lady Mac's triple fusion drive came on, quickly building

up to three gees. She followed a shallow arc above the gas giant, sinking towards the penumbra.

"Signal change," Sarha announced. "Much stronger now, but it's still an omnidirectional broadcast, they're not focusing on us. Message coming in, AV only."

"Okay, Doc," Joshua said. "You're on. Be convincing."

They were still four hundred and fifty thousand kilometres away from the *Beezling*, which produced an awkward time delay. Pressed back into her couch, Alkad could only move her eyes to one side, glancing up at a holoscreen which angled out of the ceiling above her. A magenta haze slowly cleared to show her the *Beezling*'s bridge compartment. It looked as though some kind of salvage team had ransacked the place, consoles had been broken open to show electronic stacks with their circuit cards missing, wall panels had been removed exposing chunks of machinery which were half dismantled. To add to the disorder, every surface was dusted with grubby frost. Over the years, chunks of packaging, latch pins, small tools, items of clothing, and other shipboard debris had all stuck where they'd drifted to rest, giving the impression of inorganic chrysalides frozen in the act of metamorphosis. Awkward, angular shadows overlapped right around the compartment, completing the image of gothic anarchy. There was only one source of illumination, a slender emergency light tube carried by someone in an SII spacesuit.

"This is Captain Kyle Prager here. The flight computer reports we've picked up our activation trigger code. Alkad, I want this to be you. Are you receiving this? I've got very little left in the way of working sensors. Hell, I've got little in the way of anything that works anymore."

"I'm receiving you, Kyle," Alkad said. "And it is me, it's Alkad. I came back for you. I promised I would."

"Mother Mary, is that really you, Alkad? I'm getting a poor image here, you look . . . different."

"I'm old, Kyle. Very very old now."

"Only thirty years, unless relativity is weirder than we thought."

"Kyle, please, is Peter there? Did he make it?"

"He's here, he's fine."

"Almighty Mary. You're sure?"

"Yes. I just checked his zero-tau pod. Six of us made it."

"Only six? What happened?"

"We lost Tane Ogilie a couple of years ago after he went outside to work on the drive tube. It had to be repaired before we could decelerate into this orbit; there was a lot of systems decay over twenty-eight years. Trouble is, the whole antimatter unit is badly radioactive now. Not even armour could save him from receiving a lethal dose."

"Oh, Mother Mary, I'm sorry. What about the other two?"

"Like I said, we've had a lot of systems decay. Zero-tau can keep you in perfect stasis, but its own components wear out. They went sometime during the voyage, we only found out when we came out to start the deceleration. Both of them suicided."

"I see," she said shakily.

"What happened, Alkad? You're not in any Garissan navy uniform I remember."

"The Omutans did it, Kyle. Just like we thought they would. The bastards went ahead and did it."

"How bad?"

"The worst. Six planet-busters."

Joshua cancelled his link to the communications circuit, turning to the more mundane details of the flight. Some things he just didn't want to hear: the reaction of a man being told his home planet has died.

Lady Mac's sensors were slowly gathering more information on the *Beezling*, allowing the flight computer to refine the warship's location beyond Sarha's initial rough estimate. The gas giant's violent magnetic and electromagnetic emissions were making it difficult. Even this far above the outer atmosphere space was a thick ionic soup, congested with severe energy currents which degraded sensor efficiency.

Joshua altered their flight vector several times as the new figures came in. *Lady Mac* was well over the nightside now, the swirl of particles around her forward fuselage glowing a faint pink as they were buffeted through the planetary magnetosphere. It played havoc with the support circuitry.

Beaulieu and Liol would datavise flurries of instructions to contain the dropouts, returning the systems to operational status. Joshua monitored Liol's performance, unable to find fault. *He'd make a good crewman. Maybe I could offer him Melvyn's slot, except his ego would never allow him to accept. There has to be a way we can settle this.*

He turned his attention back to the communications link. After the shocks he'd received, Kyle Prager was reacting badly to Mzu's news of her deal with the agencies and Ione.

"You know I cannot hand it over to anybody else," Prager said. "You should never have brought them here, no matter what you agreed with them."

"What, and leave you to rot?" Alkad replied. "I couldn't do that. Not with Peter here."

"Why not? We planned for it. We would have destroyed the Alchemist and signalled the Confederation Navy for help. You know that. And as for this fable about the dead being alive . . ."

"Mother Mary. We can barely pick up your signal now, and I knew where to look. What sort of condition would you be in five years from now? Besides, there might not be any Confederation left in another five months, let alone five years."

"Better that than risk others learning how to build an Alchemist."

"Nobody is going to learn from me."

"Of course not, but there are so many temptations for governments now the knowledge of its existence has leaked."

"It leaked thirty years ago, and the technology is still safe. This rescue mission is designed to clear up the last loose end."

"Alkad, you're asking too much. I'm sorry my answer has to be no. If you try to rendezvous I will switch off the confinement chambers. We still have a quantity of antimatter left."

"No!" Alkad yelled. "Peter's on board."

"Then stay away."

"Captain Prager, this is Captain Calvert. I'd like to offer a simple solution."

"Please do," Prager answered.

"Shoot the Alchemist down into the gas giant. We'll pick you up after it's gone. Because I can assure you, I'm not going to come anywhere near the *Beezling* with that kind of threat hanging over me."

"I'd like to, Captain, but it will take some time to check over the Alchemist's carrier vehicle. Then the antimatter would have to be reloaded. And even if it still works, you might be able to intercept it."

"That's a very unhealthy case of paranoia you've got there, Captain."

"One that has kept me alive for thirty years."

"All right, try this. If we were possessed or simply wanted to acquire Alchemist technology we wouldn't even have come here. We already have the doc. You're military, you know there are a great many ways information can be extracted from unwilling donors. And we certainly wouldn't have thrown in a crazy story like the possessed to confuse the issue. But we're not possessed, or even hostile to you, so we told you the truth. So I'll tell you what. If you're still not convinced that we want to end the Alchemist threat, then go right ahead and kamikaze."

"No!" Alkad yelled.

"Quiet, Doc. First though, Captain, you put this Peter Adul character in a spacesuit, boot him out the airlock, and let us pick him up. He cannot be allowed to die, not if he knows how to build an Alchemist. The possessed would have him then. Guarding against that technology leakage is part of your duty, too, now. Once we have him, I'll blow you to shit myself if that's what it takes."

"You would, too, wouldn't you?" Prager asked.

"Jesus, yes. After what I've been through chasing the doc, it'll be a pleasure to finish this properly."

"It may be just the lousy reception I'm getting, but you look very young, Captain Calvert."

"Compared to most starship captains, I probably am. But I'm also the only option you have. You either die, or you come with me."

"Kyle," Alkad pleaded. "For Mary's sake!"

"Very well. Captain Calvert, you can rendezvous with the *Beezling* and take my crew off. After that the *Beezling* will be scuttled with the Alchemist on board."

Joshua heard someone on the bridge let out a heavy breath. "Thank you, Captain."

"Christ, what an ungrateful bastard," Liol complained. "Just make sure you invoice him a huge rescue bill, Josh."

"Well that finally settles that question," Ashly chuckled. "You're definitely a Calvert, Liol."

The *Beezling* was in a sorry state. That became increasingly apparent on *Lady Mac*'s final approach phase, when they were rising up behind it from a slightly lower orbit. Both ships were deep inside the penumbra now, although the gigantic orange and white crescent they were fleeing from still cast a glorious coronal glow across them. It was enough for *Lady Mac*'s visual sensors to provide a detailed image while they were still ten kilometres away.

Almost the entire lower quarter of the warship's fuselage plates were missing, with only a simple silver petal pattern left surrounding the drive tubes. The hexagonal stress structure was clearly visible, fencing in black and tarnished chrome segments of machinery. Some units were obviously foreign, jutting up through the centre of the hexagons where they'd been hurriedly inserted to complement or enhance original components. From the midsection forward, the fuselage was relatively intact. There was very little protective foam remaining, just a few dabs of blackened cinderlike flakes. Long silvery scars etched across the dark mono-bonded silicon told the story of multiple particle impacts. There were hundreds of small craters where the fuselage's molecular-binding generators had suffered localized overloads. Punctures whose vapour and shrapnel had been absorbed by whatever module or tank was directly underneath. None of the delicate sensor clusters had survived. Only two thermo-dump panels were extended, and they were badly battered; one had a large chunk missing, as if something had taken a bite out of it.

"I'm registering a strong magnetic emission," Beaulieu said as they closed the last kilometre. "But the ship's thermal and electrical activity is minimal. Apart from an auxiliary fusion generator and three confinement chambers the *Beezling* is basically inert."

"No thruster activity, either," said Liol. "They've picked up a tumble. One rotation every eight minutes nineteen seconds."

Joshua checked the radar return, computing a vector around the crippled old ship so he could reach its airlock. "I can dock and stabilize you," he datavised to Captain Prager.

"Not much point," Prager replied. "Our airlock chamber was breached by particle impact; and I doubt the latches will work anyway. If you just hold station we'll transfer across in suits."

"Acknowledged."

"Captain," Beaulieu said. "Two fusion drives. They're on an approach vector."

"Jesus!" He accessed the sensors. Half of the image was a ghostly apricot-coloured ocean illuminated by the planetary-sized aurora borealis storms which floated serenely above it. The nighttime sky which vaulted it was a perfect orrery dome of stars where the only movement came from tiny moons racing along their ordained pathways. Red icons were bracketing two of the brighter stars just outside the ecliptic. When Joshua keyed in the infrared they became brilliant. Purple vector lines sprouted out of them, projecting their trajectory in towards him.

"Approximately two hundred thousand kilometres away," Beaulieu said, her synthesized voice sounding completely uncaring. "I think I can confirm the drive signatures; it appears to be our old friends the *Urschel* and the *Raimo*. Both plasma exhausts have very similar instabilities. If not them, then there are certainly possessed on board."

"Who else?" Ashly grunted morosely.

Alkad looked around frantically, trying to make eye contact with the crew. They were all looking at Joshua as he lay on his couch, eyes closed, his flat brow producing neat parallel furrows as he frowned in concentration. "What are you waiting for?" she asked. "Take the survivors on board and run. Those ships are too far away to threaten us."

Sarha waved her hand in annoyance. "They are now," she said in a low voice. "They won't be for long. And we're too close to the gas giant to jump out. We need to be another hundred and thirty thousand kilometres away. In other words, up where they are. That means we can't boost straight up; we'd fly straight into them."

"So . . . what then?"

Sarha pointed a finger at Joshua. "He'll tell us. If there's a vector out of here, Joshua will find it."

Alkad was surprised by the amount of respect in the normally volatile crew woman. But then all of the crew were regarding their captain with the kind of hushed expectancy that was usually the province of holy gurus. It made Alkad very uneasy.

Joshua's eyes flipped open. "We have a problem," he announced grimly. "Their altitude gives them too much tactical advantage. I can't find us a vector." A small regretful dip at the corner of his mouth. "There isn't even a convenient Lagrange point this time. And I wouldn't like to risk it anyway, not while we're so close to a gas giant as big as this one."

"Fly a slingshot," Liol said. "Dive straight at the gas giant and go for a jump on the other side."

"That's over three hundred thousand kilometres away. *Lady Mac* can probably accelerate harder than the Organization ships, but they've got antimatter combat wasps, remember. Forty-five-gee acceleration; we'd never make it."

"Christ."

"Beaulieu, put a com beam on them," Joshua said. "If

they respond, ask them what they want. I'm sure we know, but if nothing else I'd like confirmation."

"Yes, Captain."

"Doc, how do we go about firing the Alchemist at them?"

"You can't," she said simply.

"Jesus, Doc, this is no time for principles. Don't you understand? We have no other way out. None. That weapon is the only advantage we've got left. If we don't kill them, they'll get you, and Peter."

"This is not a question of principle, Captain. It's not physically possible to deploy the Alchemist against starships."

"Jesus." He couldn't believe it. But the doc looked frightened enough. Intuition convinced him she was telling the truth. The navigation program was still producing flight vectors. Dumb forced-calculation, trying out every conceivable probability to find one which would let them escape. The plots flickered in and out of existence at a subliminal speed, miniature purple lightning bolts crackling around the inside of his head. Throw in wild card manoeuvres, lunar slingshots, Lagrange points. Pray! It didn't make the slightest difference. The Organization frigates had thoroughly outmanoeuvred him. His one hope had been the Alchemist, a super-doomsday machine, a nuke to kill a couple of ants.

I have come so far I can actually see the ship it's stored in. I can't lose now, not with these stakes.

"Okay, Doc, I want to know exactly what your Alchemist does, and how it does it." He clicked his fingers at Monica and Samuel. "You two, I'll stay in Tranquillity if we survive this, but I have to know."

"God, Calvert, I'll stay there with you if that's what it takes," Monica told him. "Just get us out of this."

"Joshua," Sarha said. "You can't."

"Give me an alternative. It gets Liol's vote. He'll be captain then."

"I'm crew, Josh. This is your ship."

"Now he tells me. Datavise the file, Doc. Now, please." Information leapt into his mind as the files came over. Theory, application, construction, deployment, operational parameters. All neatly indexed with helpful cross-referencing. The blueprints of how to slay a star; in fact, build enough and you could slay an entire galaxy; or even just . . . Joshua flicked instantaneously back to the operational aspects. Pumped a few figures of his own into Mzu's coldly simple equations.

"Jesus, Doc, it wasn't a rumour. You really are dangerous, aren't you?"

"Can you do it?" Monica asked. She wanted to shout the question at him, jolt him out of that infuriating complacency.

Joshua winked at her. "Absolutely. Look, we came off badly down in that ironberg yard because that's not my territory. This is. In space, we win."

"Is he serious?" Monica appealed to the rest of the bridge.

"Oh, yes," Sarha said. "If anyone gets hostile with *Lady Mac*, they just crash straight into his ego."

• • •

High York posed a difficult problem of interpretation for Louise. The AV pillar in the *Jamrana*'s lounge shone its image down her optic nerve throughout the entire approach phase. There was no colour, space was so black she couldn't even see the stars. The asteroid was different to Phobos's chiselled cylinder, a grizzled irregular lump which the ship's sensors seemed incapable of bringing into proper focus. Mechanical artefacts were shunting out of its puckered surface at all angles, though she wasn't quite sure if she had the scale right. If she had, then they were bigger than the largest ship ever to ply Norfolk's seas.

Fletcher was in the lounge with her. From the few comments he made he understood even less of the image than she did.

Genevieve, of course, was in her tiny cabin playing games on her processor block. She'd found a soul mate in one of Pieri's younger cousins; the pair of them had taken to locking themselves away for hours at a time to tackle battalions of Trafalgar Greenjackets or skate through puzzles of five-dimensional topology. Louise wasn't entirely happy with her sister's new hobby, but on the other hand she was grateful she didn't have the duty of keeping her amused during the flight.

High York's disk-shaped spaceport traversed the AV image, eclipsing the asteroid itself. A high-pitched whine vibrated out of the lounge walls, and the *Jamrana* drifted forwards. And still there was no glimpse of Earth. Louise had really been looking forwards to that. Pieri would align a sensor on the planet for her if she asked, she was sure; but right now the whole Bushay family was involved in the docking procedure.

Louise asked her processor block for an update on their approach, and studied the display which appeared on its screen while it accessed the ship's flight computer. "Four minutes until we dock," she said. Assuming she was reading the tables of figures and coloured lines correctly.

She'd spent a large portion of the flight working through the block's tutorial programs until she could manage the unit's more basic display and operation modes. She didn't need to ask anyone's help to manage her medical nanonic packages, and she could monitor the baby's health continually. It gave her a good feeling. So much of Confederation life was centred around the casual use of electronics.

"Why so nervous, my lady?" Fletcher asked. "Our voyage ends. With Our Lord's mercy we have prevailed once more against the most inopportune circumstances. We have returned to the good Earth, the cradle of humanity. Though I fear that which has befallen me, I can do naught but rejoice at our homecoming."

"I'm not nervous," she protested unconvincingly.

"Come now, lady."

"All right. Look, it's not getting here; I'm really delighted we've made it. I suppose it's silly of me, but something about being on Earth is very reassuring. It's old and it's very strong, and if people are going to be safe anywhere, then it'll be here. That's the problem. Something Endron said about it keeps bothering me."

"You know that if I can assist you, I will."

"No. It's nothing you can help with. That's the point. Endron told me we wouldn't get through High York's spaceport; that there would be inspections and examinations, awfully strict ones. It'll be nothing like arriving at Phobos. And everything I've heard from Pieri just confirms that. I'm sorry, Fletcher, I don't think we're going to make it, I really don't."

"And yet we must," he said softly. "That fiend Dexter cannot prevail. Should the necessity become apparent, I will surrender myself and warn Earth's rulers."

"Oh, no, Fletcher, you can't do that. I don't want you to be hurt."

"Yet still you doubt me, Lady Louise. I see your heart crying in pain. That is a source of grief for me."

"I don't doubt you, Fletcher. It's just that . . . If we can't get through, then Quinn Dexter won't manage it either. That would mean your whole journey is for nothing. I hate that."

"Dexter is stronger than I, lady. I hold that bitter memory quite plainly. He is also more cunning and ruthless. If there is but a single chink in the armour of Earth's valiant harbourmasters he will find it."

"Heavens, I hope not. Quinn Dexter loose on Earth is too horrible to think about."

"Aye, my lady." His fingers clasped hers to emphasise his determination. Something he rarely did, shying away from physical contact with people. It was almost as if he feared contamination.

"That is why you must swear faithfully to me that should I stumble in my task you must pick up the torch and carry on. The world must be warned of Quinn Dexter's devilish intent. And if possible you must also seek out this Banneth of whom he spoke with such animosity. Alert her to his presence, emphasise the danger she will face."

"I'll try, Fletcher, really I will. I promise." Fletcher was prepared to sacrifice his new life and eternal sanity to save

others. Her own goal of reaching Joshua seemed so petty
and selfish in comparison. "Be careful when we disembark,"
she urged.

"I place my trust in God, my lady. And if they catch me—"

"They won't!"

"Ah, now who has adopted a frail bravado? As I recall,
'twas you who warned me of what lies crouched beside the
road ahead."

"I know."

"Forgive me, lady. I see that once again my tact is left
wanting."

"Don't worry about me, Fletcher. I'm not the one they'll
put into zero-tau."

"Aye, lady, I confess that prospect is one I shrink from. I
know in my heart I will not last long in such black confinement."

"I'll get you out," she vowed. "If they put you in zero-tau
I'll get it switched off, or something. There will be lawyers
I can hire." She patted her ship-suit's breast pocket, feeling
the outline of the Jovian Bank credit disk. "I have money."

"Let us hope it proves sufficient, my lady."

She gave him what she hoped was a bright smile, making
out that everything was settled. So that's that.

The *Jamrana* trembled, shaking loose small flocks of
jumble. Clangs rumbled down the central ladder shaft as the
spaceport docking latches engaged.

"That's funny," Louise said. The display on the block's
screen was undergoing a drastic change.

"Is something the matter, lady?"

"I don't think so. It's just odd, that's all. If I'm reading
this right, the captain has given the spaceport total access to
the flight computer. They're running some really comprehensive diagnostic programs, checking everything on
board."

"Is that bad?"

"I'm not sure." Louise stiffened, glancing around self-
consciously. She cleared her throat. "They're also accessing
the internal cameras. Watching us."

"Ah."

"Come along, Fletcher. We must get ready to leave."

"Yes, ma'am, of course."

He had dropped right back into the estate servant role without a blink. Louise hoped the cameras wouldn't pick up her furtive smile as she pushed off from the deck.

Genevieve's cabin was full of four inch light cubes, each of them a different colour. Little creatures were imprisoned inside them, as if they were cages made of tinted glass. The projection froze as Louise activated the door, an orchestral rock track faded away.

"Gen! You're supposed to be packed. We're here, you know, we've arrived."

Her little sister peered at her through the transparent lattice, red-eyed and frazzled. "I've just disarmed eight of the counter-program's Trogolois warriors, you know. I've never got that far before."

"Bully for you. Now get packed, you can play it again later. We're leaving."

Genevieve's face darkened in petulant rebellion. "It's not fair! We're always having to leave places the moment we arrive."

"Because we're travelling, silly. We'll get to Tranquillity in another couple of weeks, then you can put down roots and sprout leaves out of your ears for all I care."

"Why can't we just stay in the ship? The possessed can't get inside if we're flying about."

"Because we can't fly about forever."

"I don't see—"

"*Gen*, do as you're told. Turn this off and get packed. Now!"

"You're not Mother."

Louise glared at her. Genevieve's stubborn mask collapsed, and she started to sob.

"Oh, Gen." Louise skimmed across the narrow space and caught hold of the small girl. She ordered the processor block off, and the glowing bricks flickered into dewy sparkles before vanishing altogether.

"I want to go home," Genevieve blurted. "Home to Cricklade, not Tranquillity."

"I'm sorry," Louise cooed. "I haven't being paying you much attention on this flight, have I?"

"You've got things to worry about."

"When did you go to sleep last?"

"Last night."

"Humm." Louise put a finger under her sister's chin and lifted her face, studying the dark lines under her eyes.

"I can't sleep much in zero-gee," Genevieve confessed. "I keep thinking I'm falling, and my throat all clogs up. It's awful."

"We'll book into a High York hotel, one that's on the biosphere's ground level. Both of us can have a real sleep in a proper bed then. How does that sound?"

"All right, I suppose."

"That's the way. Just imagine, if Mrs Charlsworth could see us now. Two unmarried landowner girls, travelling without chaperones, and about to visit Earth with all its decadent arcologies."

Genevieve attempted a grin. "She'd go loopy."

"Certainly would."

"Louise, how am I going to take this block back home? I really don't want to give it up now."

Louise turned the slim innocuous unit around in front of her. "We escaped the possessed, and we've flown halfway across the galaxy. You don't really think smuggling this back to Cricklade is going to be a problem for the likes of us, do you?"

"No." Genevieve perked up. "Everyone's going to be dead jealous when we get back. I can't wait to see Jane Walker's face when I tell her we've been to Earth. She's always going on about how exotic her family holidays on Melton island are."

Louise kissed her sister's forehead and gave her a warm hug. "Get packed. I'll see you up at the airlock in five minutes."

There was only one awkward moment left. All of the

Bushay family had gathered by the airlock at the top of the life-support section to say goodbye. Pieri was torn between desperation and having to contain himself in front of his parents and his cluster of extended siblings. He managed a platonic peck on Louise's cheek, pressing against her for longer than required. "Can I still show you around?" he mumbled.

"I hope so." She smiled back. "Let's see how long I'm there for, shall we?"

He nodded, blushing heavily.

Louise led the way along the airlock tube, her flight bag riding on her back like a haversack. A man was floating just beyond the hatch at the far end, dressed in a pale emerald tunic with white lettering on the top of the sleeve. He smiled politely.

"You must be the Kavanagh party?"

"Yes," Louise said.

"Excellent. I'm Brent Roi, High York customs. There are a few formalities we have to go through, I'm afraid. We haven't had any outsystem visitors since the quarantine started. That means my staff are all sitting around kicking their heels with nothing to do. A month ago you could have shot straight through here and we wouldn't even have noticed you." He grinned at Genevieve. "That's a huge bag you've got there. You're not smuggling anything in are you?"

"No!"

He winked at her. "Good show. This way please." He started off down the corridor, flipping at the grab hoops to propel himself along.

Louise followed with Genevieve at her heels. She heard a whirring sound behind. The hatch back to the *Jamrana* was closing.

No way back now, she thought. Not that there ever had been.

At least the customs man appeared friendly. Perhaps she had been fretting too much about this.

The compartment Brent Roi led her into was just like a broader section of the corridor, cylindrical, ten metres long

and eight wide. There were no fittings apart from five lines
of grab hoops radiating out from the entrance.

Brent Roi bent his legs and kicked off hard as soon as he
was through the hatch. When Louise went in he had already
joined the others lining the walls. She looked around, her
heart fluttering apprehensively. A dozen people were anchored to stikpads all around her, she couldn't see their
faces, they all wore helmets with silver visors. Each of them
was holding some sort of boxy gun. The stub muzzles were
pointed at Fletcher the instant he popped out of the hatchway.

"Is this customs?" she asked in a failing voice.

Genevieve's small hand curled around her ankle.
"Louise!" She clambered up her big sister's body like mobile ivy. The two girls clung to each other fearfully.

"The ladies are not possessed," Fletcher said calmly. "I
ask you not to endanger them. I shall not resist."

"Too fucking right you won't, you son of a bitch," Brent
Roi snarled.

•   •   •   •

Ashly fired the MSV's thrusters: too hard, too long. He
cursed. The drift had been reversed, not halted. Pressure was
wiring him close to overload. Mistakes like this could cost
them a lot more than their lives. He datavised another set of
directives into the craft's computer, and the thrusters fired
again, a shorter, milder burst this time.

The MSV came to rest three metres above the launch
tube's hatch. Like the rest of the *Beezling*'s fuselage it was
badly scarred and mauled. But intact.

"No particle penetration," he datavised. "It seems to be
undamaged."

"Good, get it open," Joshua answered.

Ashly was already extending three of the MSV's waldo
arms. He shoved a clamp hand straight into the mounting
hole left by a broken sensor cluster and expanded the segments, securing the MSV in place. A fission blade came on,

burning a lambent saffron at the tip of the second arm. Ashly used it to slice into the fuselage at the rim of the hatch, then began to saw around.

Both the *Beezling* and the MSV trembled energetically. The computer datavised a series of clamp stress cautions, their grip on the mounting had shifted slightly. "Joshua, another one of those and you're going to shake me loose."

"Sorry. Won't happen again, we're docked now."

Ashly accessed the MSV's small sensor suite. The *Lady Mac* had attached herself to the rear of the *Beezling*, her aft hold-down latches engaging with the warship's corresponding locks. A slim silver piston slid out of her ring of umbilical couplings, weaving around slowly as it sought out a socket on the *Beezling* to mate with.

Spacesuited figures wearing manoeuvring packs were flitting towards the bright circle of light which was *Lady Macbeth*'s open airlock. A third of the way around her fuselage one of her combat wasp launch tubes had opened. The front section of a combat wasp had risen up out of it, a dark tapering cylinder bristling with sensors and antennae. Beaulieu was working on it, her glossy body alive with reflected streaks of salmon-pink light that rippled fluidly with every movement. She had anchored her feet in the midsection grid which contained the drone's tanks and generators. One of the submunitions chamber covers had already been removed; now she was busy extracting the cluster of electronic warfare pods from inside.

The MSV's waldo arm finished cutting around the *Beezling*'s hatch. Ashly grabbed it with the heavy-load arm and pulled it free. A strew of dust motes and composite shavings popped out, quickly dwindling away. The MSV's external lights swung around, and he was looking straight down into a smooth white cylinder which nested a sleek conical missile whose silver surface was polished brighter than any mirror.

"Is this the right one?" he asked, including his retinal image into the datavise.

"That is the Alchemist carrier, yes," Mzu replied.

"There's no response from any processors in there. Temperature is a hundred and twenty absolute."

"It won't have affected the Alchemist."

Ashly said nothing, hoping her self-confidence was as justified as Joshua's. He extended one of the MSV's manipulator waldos into the launch tube and fastened it around the apex of the carrier vehicle's nose cone. Triangular keys found the locking pins, and turned them. He retracted the arm carefully, bringing the nose cone with it. The base was studded with junctions for the thermal shunt circuits, which were reluctant to separate; after thirty years the vacuum and the cold had melded them together. Ashly increased the tension on the waldo, and they tore free with a judder which the arm's inertia absorber could barely cope with.

"That's it?" Ashly datavised when the nose cone was lifted clear.

"That's it," Mzu confirmed.

The Alchemist was a single globe one and a half metres in diameter, its seamless surface a neutral grey colour. It was held in place by five carbotanium spider-leg struts which encased it neatly, their inner surfaces lined with adjustable pads to maintain a perfect grip.

"You should be able to detach the entire restraint mechanism," Mzu datavised. "Sever the data and power cables if necessary; they're not necessary anymore."

"Okay." He moved the manipulator waldo down the side of the Alchemist and used its small sensors to inspect the machinery he found below it. "This shouldn't take long, the rivets are standard. I can cut them."

"Fast, please, Ashly," Joshua datavised. "The Organization ships are only twenty-four minutes away."

"Gotcha. I'll have this with Beaulieu in three minutes." He moved the first of the manipulator's tools forwards. "Doctor?"

"Yes."

"Why bother with a specialist carrier vehicle if it can be deployed in an ordinary combat wasp?"

"That carrier vehicle is designed to shoot the Alchemist

into a star. Admittedly that's a large target, but we can't take starships very close to one. The carrier has to be fully insulated from the star's heat and radiation, and it also has to be fast enough to avoid interception from combat wasps in the event we were detected. We built it to accelerate up to sixty-five gees."

Ashly would have liked to have called her bluff. But given their current situation, ignorance and blind faith made life altogether less stressful.

Monica didn't leave Alkad alone in the EVA preparation compartment, but she did permit her a discreet distance. Two other operatives were with her, ready to inspect the *Beezling*'s crew to make sure they brought nothing threatening with them into the *Lady Macbeth*.

Alkad didn't really notice the agent's presence, every aspect of her life had been under continual observation for so long now that intrusion meant nothing. Not even for this most precious occasion.

She anchored herself to a stikpad in front of the airlock hatch, waiting with outwards patience. When she sorted through her feelings she found the rightful edgy anticipation, but perhaps not so much of it as there should have been. Thirty years. Can you really stay in love with someone for that long? Or did I just keep the ideal of love alive? One small illusion of humanity in a personality which deliberately and methodically set about excluding any other form of emotional weakness.

Well enough, there were memories of the good times. Memories of shared ideals. And of course memories of affection, adoration, and intimacy. But shouldn't real love require the continuing presence of the loved one in order to sustain itself and constantly renew? Has Peter really become nothing more than a concept suborned, just another excuse to retain my commitment?

The doubts tempted her to turn and flee from the moment. In any case, I'm over sixty and he's still thirty-five. A hand started up towards her face, wanting to fork her hair back or tidy it. Silly. If she was so concerned about her appearance she should have done something about it long ago. Cosmetic packages, hormone gland implants, gene therapy. Except Peter would have hated her resorting to such untruthful indignities.

Alkad forced the delinquent hand down. The LEDs on the airlock's control processor changed from red to green, and the circular hatch swung back.

Peter Adul was first out, the others had allowed him that civility. His SII suit's silicon film had withdrawn from his head so she could see all the features she remembered so well. He stared back at her, a frightened smile on his lips. "White hair," he said gently. "I never imagined that. Lots of things, but never that."

"It's not so bad. I imagined much worse happening to you."

"But it didn't. And we're here. And you came to rescue us. After thirty years, you really came back here for us."

"Of course I did," she said, abruptly indignant.

Peter grinned wickedly. She laughed back, and launched herself into his arms.

Joshua was accessing the MSV's external sensors to monitor Ashly's and Beaulieu's efforts to integrate the Alchemist with their combat wasp. Ashly was using a waldo arm to edge the device down into the submunitions chamber which the cosmonik had cleared. The Alchemist would fit, but the restraint arms folded around it were causing problems. Beaulieu had already sliced a couple of chunks off the carbotanium struts when they scraped against the chamber walls. This was one incredibly crude kludge-up from start to finish. But it didn't need excessive sophistication to work, just a secure mounting.

Superimposed across the sensor image were the *Lady Mac*'s systems schematics, enabling him to keep a slightly more than cursory eye on their performance. Liol and Sarha were prepping the ship for high acceleration, shutting down all redundant ancillary equipment, cycling fluids back out of weight-vulnerable pipes and into their tanks, bringing the tokamaks up to full capacity so their power would be available for the molecular-binding force generators. Dahybi was running diagnostics through all the zero-tau facilities on board.

By rights the expectancy should have reduced his brain to a small knot of psychoses by now. Instead he had the oldest excuse of being too busy to worry. That and a wonderful burn of pure arrogance. It *can* work. After all, it was only marginally more crazy than the Lagrange point stunt.

Too bad I'll never be able to brag about this one in Harkey's Bar.

Which was actually more of a concern than the manoeuvre itself. I can't stay in Tranquillity for the rest of my life. I should never have mentioned it to the agents.

He saw Ashly extract the waldo from the combat wasp, leaving the Alchemist behind. Beaulieu reached forwards to hold a hose over the top of the submunitions chamber. A frayed jet of treacly topaz-coloured foam shot out of the nozzle, surging all around the Alchemist. It was a duopoxy scalant, used by the astronautics industry for quick, temporary repairs. The cosmonik moved the nozzle in smooth assured motions, making sure the foam completely encapsulated the Alchemist, cementing it into the combat wasp.

"Ashly, take the MSV around to the main airlock and transfer over in your suit," Joshua datavised.

"What about the MSV?"

"I'm dumping it here. It was never designed to withstand the kind of acceleration we'll be undergoing. That makes it a hazard, especially with all the reaction thruster volatiles it has in its tanks."

"You're the captain. But what about the spaceplane?"

"I know. You just get back in; we've only got sixteen minutes left before the Organization ships get here."

"Acknowledged, Captain."

"Liol."

"Yes, Captain?"

"Jettison the spaceplane, please. Beaulieu, how's it going?"

"Fine, Captain. I've got it covered. The sealant is bonding, should be set in another fifty seconds."

"Excellent work. Get back inside." Joshua datavised the flight computer for a secure channel to the combat wasp. The drone came on-line, and he started its launch sequence program. Once its internal processors were operative he loaded in the flight vector he'd formatted. "Doc, it's time to find out how good you are."

"I understand, Captain."

She accessed the processor governing the combat wasp's chamber which the Alchemist was riding in and used it to datavise a long activation code at the device. It datavised an acknowledgement back to her. The display in Joshua's mind opened out rapidly to accommodate the new iconic representation: parallel sheets of dark information stacked as high as Heaven. They came alive with interlocking grids of purple and yellow that shone like channelled starfire. Perspective switch, and the sheets were concentric spherical shells, coming alight from the core outwards. Information and energy arranging themselves in a precise, and very specific, pattern.

"It's working," Alkad datavised.

"Jesus Christ." The neurovirtual jewel glimmered at the centre of his brain, complex beyond human comprehension. It was an outrageous irony that something so deliciously intricate and beautiful should be the harbinger of so much destruction. "Okay, Doc, set it for neutronium. I'm launching in twenty seconds—mark."

Lady Mac's spaceplane had risen up out of her hangar as thermo-dump panels and sensor cluster booms shrank back the other way. Ashly caught one last glimpse of it as he swept down into the airlock. The circular docking ring clamped around its nose cone had just disengaged, allowing it to drift free, then Beaulieu's shiny brass silhouette occluded the airlock hatch behind him, and that was the end of it.

Pity, he thought, it was a lovely little machine.

As soon as the airlock's outer hatch closed the cylindrical chamber was fast-flooded with air. The flight computer's datavised display revealed their status. Joshua was already firing the thrusters to align them on their new flight vector. Combat wasp launch tubes were opening.

Ashly and Beaulieu dived out of the airlock, racing for the bridge. There was nobody in any of the decks they passed through. Several open cabin doors showed them active zero-tau pods.

The combat wasp carrying the Alchemist completed its fusion drive ignition sequence and launched. A quick cheer from the bridge echoed through *Lady Mac*'s empty compartments. Then ten more combat wasps were firing out of their tubes and chasing after the first. The whole salvo headed down towards the gas giant at twenty-five gees.

Ashly flew through the bridge's floor hatch just behind Beaulieu.

"Stations, please," Joshua said. He triggered *Lady Mac*'s three fusion tubes, giving Ashly barely enough time to roll onto his acceleration couch before gravity pushed down. Restraint webbing closed over him.

"Signal from the Organization ships," Sarha said. "They know who we are, they're asking for you by name, Joshua."

Joshua accessed the communications circuit. The image which his neural nanonics provided was shaky and stormed with static. It showed him a frigate's bridge, with figures lying flat on acceleration couches. One of them was dressed in a double-breasted suit of chocolate-brown worsted with slim silver-grey pinstripes, a wide-brimmed black fedora was resting on the console beside him. Joshua puzzled that one for a moment, the frigate was decelerating at seven gees. The fedora should have been squashed flat.

"Captain Calvert?"

"You got me."

"I'm Oscar Kearn, and Al put me in charge around here."

"Joshua," Liol datavised. "The frigates are flipping over again. They're starting to chase us."

"Acknowledged." He increased the *Lady Mac*'s acceleration, taking her up to seven gees.

Ashly groaned in chagrin before activating his acceleration couch's zero-tau field. Black stasis closed around him, ending the punishing force. Alkad Mzu and Peter Adul joined him.

"Glad to meet you, Oscar," Joshua had to datavise, his jaw was far too heavy to move.

"My people, they tell me you just fired something down at the big planet. I hope you ain't been stupid, pal, I really do. Was it what I think it was?"

"Absolutely. No more Alchemist for anybody."

"You dumb asshole. That's a third of your options gone. Now you listen good, sonny boy, you switch off your ship's engines and you hand over Mzu to me and there ain't nobody gonna get hurt. That's your second option."

"No shit? Let me guess what the third is."

"Don't be a pumpkinhead, sonny. Remember, after we waste you and your rinky-dink ship, we're only interested in giving the Mzu dame a new body. It's the beyond for you, pal, for the rest of time. And take a tip from someone who's been there, it ain't worth it. Nothing is. So you just hand her over nice and smooth, and I don't say nothing to the boss about you deep-sixing the Alchemist."

"Mr Kearn, go screw yourself."

"You call that Alchemist back, sonny. I know you got a radio control on the combat wasp. You call it back or I tell my crews to open fire."

"If you blow up the *Lady Mac* you'll definitely never get it, will you? Think about it, I'll give you as much time as you need." Joshua closed the communications link.

"How much more of this bloody acceleration?" Monica datavised.

"Seven gees?" Joshua replied. "None at all." He increased the thrust up to a full ten gees.

Monica couldn't even groan; her throat was sagging

under its own weight. It was ridiculous, her lungs couldn't inhale properly, her artificial tissue muscle implants were all in her limbs, not her chest. If she tried to hang on she'd end up asphyxiating. Keeping Mzu under observation was no longer an option. She would simply have to trust Calvert and the other crew members. "Good luck," she datavised. "See you on the other side."

The flight computer informed Joshua she'd activated her acceleration couch's zero-tau field. That left him with only three people who hadn't sought refuge in stasis: Beaulieu, Dahybi, and of course Liol.

"Status report, please," he datavised to them.

Lady Mac's systems and structure were both holding up well. But then Joshua knew she was capable of withstanding this acceleration, her real test was going to come later.

Seventy thousand kilometres behind her, the two Organization frigates were accelerating at eight gees, which was the limit of their afflicted drives. Their crews were hurriedly assembling situation outlines and summaries for Oscar Kearn, detailing how long it would be before the *Lady Macbeth* was outside the interception range of their combat wasps.

Ahead of all three ships, the salvo of eleven combat wasps were rushing towards the gas giant. There was no way any sensor could determine which was carrying the Alchemist, making any interdiction virtually impossible.

The status quo was held for over fifteen minutes before Oscar Kearn reluctantly admitted to himself that Calvert and Mzu weren't going to hand over the device, nor surrender themselves. He ordered the *Urschel* and the *Raimo* to launch their combat wasps at *Lady Macbeth*.

"No good," Joshua grunted savagely as *Lady Mac*'s sensors showed him the sudden upsurge in the frigates' infrared emission signature. "You can't dysfunction this chunk of reality, pal."

The Alchemist was ninety seconds away from the gas giant's upper atmosphere. Its management programs began to orchestrate the complex energy patterns racing through its nodes into the sequence Mzu had selected. Once it was primed, activation occurred within two picoseconds. Visually it could hardly be less spectacular; the Alchemist's surface turned infinitely black. The physics behind the change was somewhat more involved.

"What I did," Alkad had datavised to Joshua when he asked her how it functioned, "was to work out how to combine a zero-tau field and the energy compression technique which a starship jump node utilizes. In this case, just as the energy density approaches infinite the effect is frozen. Instead of expelling the patterning node out of the universe, you get a massive and permanent space-time curvature forming around it."

"Space-time curvature?"

"Gravity."

Gravity at its strongest is capable of bending light itself, pulling at individual photons with the same tenacity as it once did Newton's apple. In nature, the only mass dense enough to produce this kind of gravity is formed at the heart of a stellar implosion. A singularity whose gravity permits nothing to escape: no matter, no energy.

At its highest setting the Alchemist would become such a cosmological entity; its surface concealed by an event horizon into which everything can fall and nothing return. Once inside the event horizon, electromagnetic energy and atoms alike would be drawn to the core's surface and compress to phenomenal densities. The effect is cumulative and exponential. The more mass which the black hole swallows, the heavier and stronger it becomes, increasing its surface area and allowing its consumption rate to rise accordingly.

If the Alchemist was fired into a star, every gram of matter would eventually plunge below the invincible barrier which gravity erected. That was Alkad Mzu's humane solution. Omuta's sun would not flare and rupture, would never endanger life on the planet with waves of heat and radiation. Instead the sun would shrink and collapse into a small black sphere, with every erg of its fusing nuclei lost to the universe for ever. Omuta would be left circling a non-radiative husk, its warmth slowly leaking away into the now permanent night. Ultimately, the air itself would become cold enough to condense and fall as snow.

But there was the second setting, the aggressive one. Paradoxically, it actually produced a weaker gravity field.

The Alchemist turned black as zero-tau claimed it. However, the gravity it generated wasn't strong enough to produce a singularity with an event horizon. However, it was easily capable of overcoming the internal forces which designate an atom's structure. The combat wasp immediately flashed into plasma and enfolded it. All electrons and protons within the envelope were crushed together, producing a massive pulse of gamma radiation. The emission faded rapidly, leaving the Alchemist cloaked in a uniform angstrom-deep ocean of superfluid neutrons.

When it struck the outer fringes of the atmosphere a searing white light flooded out to soak hundreds of square kilometres of the upper cloud bands. Seconds later the deeper cloud layers were fluorescing rosy pink while internal shadows surged through torn cyclones like mountain-sized fish. Then the light vanished altogether.

The Alchemist had reached the semisolid layers of the gas giant's interior, and was punching through with almost no resistance. Matter under tremendous pressure was crushed against the device, which absorbed it greedily. Every impacting atom was squeezed directly into a cluster of neutrons that plated themselves around the core. The Alchemist was swiftly buried under a mantle of pure neutronium, which boasted a density that exceeded that of atomic nuclei.

As the particles were compressed by the device's extraordinary gravity field, they liberated colossal quantities of energy, a reaction far more potent than mere fusion. The surrounding semisolid material was heated to temperatures which destroyed every atomic bond. A vast cavity of nuclear instability inflated around the Alchemist as it soared ever deeper into the gas giant. Ordinary convection currents were wholly inadequate to syphon off the heat at the same rate it was being produced, so the energy abscess simply had to keep on expanding. Something had to give.

Lady Mac's sensors detected the first upwelling while the ship was still seven minutes from perigee. A smooth-domed tumour of cloud, three thousand kilometres in diameter, glowing like gaseous magma as it swelled up through the storm bands. Unlike the ordinary great spots infesting gas giants it didn't spiral, its sole purpose was to elevate planetary masses of tortuously heated hydrogen up from the interior. Hurricanes and cyclones which had blasted their way through the upper atmosphere for centuries were thrust aside to allow the thermal monster its bid for freedom. Its apex distended over a thousand kilometres above the tropopause, casting a pernicious copper light over a third of the nightside.

Right at the centre, the glow had become unbearably bright. A spire of solid white light punctured the top of the cloud dome, streaking out into space.

"Holy Christ," Liol datavised. "Was that it? Did it just detonate?"

"Nothing like," Joshua replied. "This is only the start. Things are going to get a little nasty from now on."

Lady Mac was already far ahead of the fountaining plasma stream, racing around the gas giant's curvature for the dawn terminator. Even so, thermal circuits issued a grade three alarm as the plasma's radiance washed over the hull. Emergency cryogenic exchangers vented hundreds of litres of inflamed fluid to shunt the heat out. Processors were failing at a worrying rate in the immense emp backlash of the wavering plasma stream; even the military-grade electronics were suffering. On top of that, electric currents started to eddy through the fuselage stress structure as the planetary flux lines trembled.

Dahybi had withdrawn into zero-tau, leaving Joshua and Liol to datavise instructions into the flight computer, bringing backups on-line, isolating leakages, stabilizing power surges. They worked perfectly together, keeping the flight systems on-line; each intuitively knowing what was required to support the other.

"Something very odd is happening to the planetary magnetosphere," Beaulieu reported. "Sensors are registering extraordinary oscillations within the flux lines."

"Irrelevant," Joshua replied. "Concentrate on keeping our primary systems stable. Four minutes more, that's all, we'll be on the other side of the planet then."

On board the *Urschel*, Ikela watched the lightstorm eruption on one of the bridge screens. "Holy Mary, it works," he whispered. "It actually bloody works." A perverse sense of pride mingled with fatalistic dismay. *If only* . . . But then, fruitless wishes were ever the province of the damned.

He ignored Oscar Kearn's semi-hysterical (and totally impossible) orders to turn the ship around and get them the hell away from this badass planet. Twentieth-century man simply didn't understand orbital mechanics. They had been accelerating along their present course for twenty-two minutes now, their trajectory effectively committed them to a slingshot flyby. Their best hope was to stay on track, and pray they got past perigee before another upwell exploded out of the atmosphere. That was what the *Lady Macbeth* was attempting. Good tactic, Ikela acknowledged grudgingly.

Somehow, he didn't think the *Urschel* would make it. He didn't know exactly how the Alchemist worked, but he doubted one eruption was the end of it.

With a sense of inevitability that curiously neutralized any regret or gloom, he settled back passively in his acceleration couch and watched the screens. The original spout of plasma was dying away, the cloud dome flattening out to dissipate into a thousand new hypervelocity storms. But underneath the frothing upper atmosphere a fresh stain of light was spreading, and it was an order of magnitude larger than the first.

He smiled contentedly at his god's-eye view of what promised to be a truly dazzling Armageddon.

The Alchemist was slowing, it had passed through the

semisolid layers into the true core of the planet. Now the density of surrounding matter was intense enough to affect its flight. That meant matter was being pressed against it in ever-greater quantities, and with it the rate of neutronium conversion was accelerating fast. The energy abscess which it generated stretched out back along its course through the planet's interior like a comet's tail. Sections of it were breaking apart; ten-thousand-kilometre lengths pinching into elongated bubbles which rose up through the disrupted tiers of the planet's internal structure. Each one greater than the last.

The second upwelling rampaged out of the upper atmosphere; its tremendous scale making it appear absurdly ponderous. Vast fonts of ions cascaded from its edges as the centre broke open, twisting into scarlet arches which fell gracefully back towards the boiling cloudscape. A coronal fireball spat out of the central funnel, bigger than a moon, its surface slippery with webs of magnetic energy which condensed the plasma into deeper purple curlicues. Ghost gases flowered around it, translucent gold petal wings unfurling to beat with the harmonic of the planetary flux lines.

Lost somewhere among the rising glory of light were two tiny sparkles produced by antimatter detonating inside both Organization frigates.

Lady Mac swept triumphantly across the terminator and into daylight, surfing at a hundred and fifty kilometres per second over the hurricane rivers of phosphorescence which flowed through the troposphere. An arrogant saffron dawn waxed behind her, far outshining the natural one ahead.

"Time to leave," Joshua datavised. "You ready?"

"All yours, Josh."

Joshua datavised his order into the flight computer. Zerotau claimed the last three acceleration couches on the bridge. *Lady Mac*'s antimatter drive ignited.

The starship accelerated away from the gas giant at forty-two gees.

Finally, the Alchemist had come to rest at the centre of the gas giant. Here was a universe of pressure unglimpsed except through speculative mathematical models. The heart of the gas giant was only slightly less dense than the neutronium itself. Yet the difference was there, permitting the inflow of matter to continue. The conversion reaction burned unabated. Pure alchemy.

Energy blazed outwards from the Alchemist, unable to escape. The abscess was spherical now, nature's preferred geometry. A sphere at the heart of a sphere; dangerously tormented matter confined by the perfectly symmetrical pressure exerted by the mass of seventy-five thousand kilometres of hydrogen piled on top of it. This time there was no escape valve up through the weak, nonsymmetrical, semisolid layers. This time, all it could do was grow.

For six hundred seconds *Lady Macbeth* accelerated away from the mortally wounded gas giant. Behind her, the Alchemist's trail of fragmented energy abscesses pumped up out of the darkside clouds, transient volcanoes of feculent gas rising higher than worlds. The planet began to develop its own billowing photosphere; a dark burgundy orb enclosed by a glowing azure halo. Its ebony moons sailed on indomitably through their new sea of lightning.

The starship's multiple drive tubes cut out. Joshua's zero-tau switched off, depositing him abruptly into free fall. Sensor images and flight data flashed straight into his brain. The planet's death convulsions were as fascinating as they were deadly. It didn't matter, they were over a hundred and eighty thousand kilometres from the disintegrating storm bands. Far enough to jump.

Deep beneath the benighted clouds, the central energy abscess had swollen to an intolerable size. The pressure it was exerting against the confining mass of the planet had almost reached equilibrium. Titanic fissures began to tear open.

An event horizon engulfed *Lady Macbeth*'s fuselage.

With a timing that was the ultimate tribute to the precision of Mzu's decades-old equations, the gas giant went nova.

•   •   •   •   •

The singularity surged into existence five hundred and eighty thousand kilometres above Mirchusko's pale jade blizzards of ammonia-sulphur cirrus. Its event horizon blinked off to reveal the *Lady Macbeth*'s dull silicon fuselage. Omnidirectional antennae were already broadcasting her CAB identification code. Given the reception they got on returning from Lalonde, Joshua wasn't going to take any chances this time.

Sensor clusters telescoped outwards, passive elements scanning around, radars pulsing. The flight computer datavised a class three proximity alert.

"Charge the nodes," Joshua ordered automatically. His mistake, he never expected to jump into trouble here. Now that might cost them badly.

The bridge lights dimmed fractionally as Dahybi initiated an emergency power up sequence. "Eight seconds," he said.

The external sensor image flashed up in Joshua's mind. At first he thought they were being targeted by electronic warfare pods. Space was flecked with small white motes. But the electronic sensors were the only ones not being taxed, the whole electromagnetic environment was eerily silent. The flight computer reported its radar track-while-scan function was approaching capacity overload as it designated multiple targets. Each of the white motes was being tagged by purple icons to indicate position and trajectory. Three were flashing red, approaching fast.

It wasn't interference. *Lady Mac* had emerged just outside a massive particle storm unlike anything Joshua had ever seen before. The motes weren't ice, nor rock.

"Jesus, what is this stuff?" He datavised a set of instructions into the flight computer. The standard sensor booms began to retreat, replaced by the smaller, tougher combat sensors. Discrimination and analysis programs went primary.

The debris was mostly metallic, melted and fused scraps no bigger than snowflakes. They were all radioactive.

"There's been one brute of a fight here," Sarha said. "This is all combat wasp wreckage. And there's a lot of it. I think the swarm is about forty thousand kilometres in diameter. It's dissipating, clearing from the centre."

"No response to our identification signal," Beaulieu said. "Tranquillity's beacons are off air, I cannot locate a single artificial electromagnetic transmission. There isn't even a ship's beacon active."

The centre of the debris storm had a coordinate Joshua didn't even have to run a memory check on. Tranquillity's orbital vector. *Lady Mac*'s sensor suite revealed it to be a large empty zone. "It's gone," he said numbly. "They blew it up. Oh, Jesus, no. Ione. My kid. My kid was in there!"

"No, Joshua," Sarha said firmly. "It hasn't been destroyed. There isn't nearly enough mass in the swarm to account for that."

"Then where is it? Where the hell did it go?"

"I don't know. There's no trace of it, none at all."

TIMELINE

2020 . . . Cavius base established. Mining of Lunar sub-crustal resources starts.

2037 . . . Beginning of large-scale geneering on humans; improvement to immunology system, eradication of appendix, organ efficiency increased.

2041 . . . First deuterium-fuelled fusion stations built; inefficient and expensive.

2044 . . . Christian reunification.

2047 . . . First asteroid capture mission. Beginning of Earth's O'Neill Halo.

2049 . . . Quasi-sentient bitek animals employed as servitors.

2055 . . . Jupiter mission.

2055 . . . Lunar cities granted independence from founding companies.

2057 . . . Ceres asteroid settlement founded.

2058 . . . Affinity symbiont neurons developed by Wing-Tsit Chong, providing control over animals and bitek constructs.

2064 . . . Multinational industrial consortium (Jovian Sky Power Corporation) begins mining Jupiter's atmosphere for He_3 using aerostat factories.

2064 . . . Islamic secular unification.

2067 . . . Fusion stations begin to use He_3 as fuel.

2069 . . . Affinity bond gene spliced into human DNA.

2075 . . . JSKP germinates Eden, a bitek habitat in orbit around Jupiter, with UN Protectorate status.

2077 . . . New Kong asteroid begins FTL stardrive research project.

2085 . . . Eden opened for habitation.

2086 . . . Habitat Pallas germinated in Jupiter orbit.

2090 . . . Wing-Tsit Chong dies, and transfers memories to Eden's neural strata. Start of Edenist culture. Eden and Pallas declare independence from UN. Launch buyout of JSKP shares. Pope Eleanor excommunicates all Christians with affinity gene. Exodus of affinity capable humans to Eden. Effective end of bitek industry on Earth.

2091 . . . Lunar referendum to terraform Mars.

2094 . . . Edenists begin exowomb breeding programme coupled with extensive geneering improvement to embryos, tripling their population over a decade.

2103 . . . Earth's national governments consolidate into Govcentral.

2103 . . . Thoth base established on Mars.

2107 . . . Govcentral jurisdiction extended to cover O'Neill Halo.

2115 . . . First instantaneous translation by New Kong spaceship, Earth to Mars.

2118 . . . Mission to Proxima Centauri.

2123 . . . Terracompatible plant found at Ross 154.

2125 . . . Ross 154 planet named Felicity, first multiethnic colonists arrive.

2125–2130 . . . Four new terracompatible planets discovered. Multiethnic colonies founded.

2131 . . . Edenists germinate Perseus in orbit around Ross 154 gas giant, begin He$_3$ mining.

2131–2205 . . . One hundred and thirty terracompatible planets discovered. Massive starship building programme initiated in O'Neill Halo. Govcentral begins large-scale enforced outshipment of surplus population, rising to 2 million a week in 2160: Great Dispersal. Civil conflict on some early multiethnic colonies. Individual Govcentral states sponsor ethnic-streaming colonies. Edenists expand their He_3 mining enterprise to every inhabited star system with a gas giant.

2139 . . . Asteroid Braun impacts on Mars.

2180 . . . First orbital tower built on Earth.

2205 . . . Antimatter production station built in orbit around sun by Govcentral in an attempt to break the Edenist energy monopoly.

2208 . . . First antimatter-drive starships operational.

2210 . . . Richard Saldana transports all of New Kong's industrial facilities from the O'Neill Halo to an asteroid orbiting Kulu. He claims independence for the Kulu star system, founds Christian-only colony, and begins to mine He_3 from the system's gas giant.

2218 . . . First voidhawk gestated, a bitek starship designed by Edenists.

2225 . . . Establishment of a hundred voidhawk families. Habitats Romulus and Remus germinated in Saturn orbit to serve as voidhawk bases.

2232 . . . Conflict at Jupiter's trailing Trojan asteroid cluster between belt alliance ships and an O'Neill Halo company hydrocarbon refinery. Antimatter used as a weapon; twenty-seven thousand people killed.

2238 . . . Treaty of Deimos; outlaws production and use of antimatter in the Sol system; signed by Govcentral, Lunar nation, asteroid alliance, and Edenists. Antimatter stations abandoned and dismantled.

2240 . . . Coronation of Gerrald Saldana as King of Kulu. Foundation of Saldana dynasty.

2267–2270 . . . Eight separate skirmishes involving use of antimatter among colony worlds. Thirteen million killed.

2271 . . . Avon summit between all planetary leaders. Treaty of Avon, banning the manufacture and use of antimatter throughout inhabited space. Formation of Human

Confederation to police agreement. Construction of Confederation Navy begins.

2300 . . . Confederation expanded to include Edenists.

2301 . . . First Contact. Jiciro race discovered, a pre-technology civilization. System quarantined by Confederation to avoid cultural contamination.

2310 . . . First ice asteroid impact on Mars.

2330 . . . First blackhawks gestated at Valisk, independent habitat.

2350 . . . War between Novska and Hilversum. Novska bombed with antimatter. Confederation Navy prevents retaliatory strike against Hilversum.

2356 . . . Kiint homeworld discovered.

2357 . . . Kiint join Confederation as "observers."

2360 . . . A voidhawk scout discovers Atlantis.

2371 . . . Edenists colonize Atlantis.

2395 . . . Tyrathca colony world discovered.

2402 . . . Tyrathca join Confederation.

2420 . . . Kulu scoutship discovers Ruin Ring.

2428 . . . Bitek habitat Tranquillity germinated by Crown Prince Michael Saldana, orbiting above Ruin Ring.

2432 . . . Prince Michael's son, Maurice, geneered with affinity. Kulu abdication crisis. Coronation of Lukas Saldana. Prince Michael exiled.

2550 . . . Mars declared habitable by Terraforming office.

2580 . . . Dorado asteroids discovered around Tunja, claimed by both Garissa and Omuta.

2581 . . . Omuta mercenary fleet drops twelve antimatter planet-busters on Garissa, planet rendered uninhabitable. Confederation imposes thirty-year sanction against Omuta, prohibiting any interstellar trade or transport. Blockade enforced by Confederation Navy.

2582 . . . Colony established on Lalonde.